A View From A Height

J. E. Murphy

Containing:
Book 1 ~~The Dakini and
Book 2 ~~The Bodhisattva
In one volume

A View from a Height

Copyright 2011 by J. E. Murphy

U.S. First Edition 2005
U.S. Second Edition 2008
U.S. Third Edition 2011

Published by Portraits of Earth Press
www.portraitsofearthpress.com
Direct inquiries to

jemurphy@portraitsofearthpress.com

or to

Portraits of Earth Press
16900 Lone Pine Road
North Little Rock, Arkansas 72118
U.S.A.

Library of Congress Control Number: 2008920106

ISBN 978-0-6151-4792-5

Special Thanks

I would like to thank everyone who gave me encouragement through the many years that it took to put this story down on paper. I would like to offer my special thanks to my wife, Pam, for her constructive criticisms and patience, and for the original idea; to Anne Avant and Stuart Mathews for reading and critiquing my first effort many years ago, and to Beth Powell and Doug Haynes, who were my cheerleading section for the last couple of years and whom I consider to be the godparents of this present book. Much appreciation also goes to Robin Harper, Jaime Thrasher and Paul Barnett who made final edits and last minute suggestions that made this story better than it otherwise would have been. And last, but certainly not least, my special thanks to Teresa Tidwell for her dedicated efforts in finding and correcting my uncountable grammatical errors.

J. E. Murphy
August, 2011

Photo Courtesy of NASA

A — Chomolungma   B — Lho-la and Khumbu Glacier
C — Rongbuk Glacier   D — Rongbuk Valley
E — Chinese army   F — Rongbuk Monastery
G — Cho Oyu   H — Nangpa-la

Table of Contents

Book 1 ~~ The Dakini

Notes from the Translator

[Here is a love story. It is not the usual kind of love story. It is about the kind of love that few of us experience in this life. It is about the kind of love that can turn a hopeless young girl into an angel of deliverance. It is about the kind of love that can redeem a saint that has fallen from grace. It is about a love for the world that is not worldly - a love that does all and asks nothing. This is about the kind of love that saves souls, changes the course of history, and sends the world spinning in new directions; and does it without the world even knowing that it was done.

This is the autobiography of Xiao Chen Bang, a person who, depending on where you stand, had perhaps the most significant impact on the world that it has ever known, or had no impact at all.

I have stopped telling people how I came to possess the following document. I think you will come to understand why this is so. I would be very surprised if you told me you had ever heard of Xiao Chen Bang, or of the astonishing destruction of government buildings in Beijing. But I would not find it totally unbelievable. I no longer totally disbelieve anything.

~~ Tomas ~~
End of translator's notes.]

[Editor's note: 'Xiao' is pronounced 'tsheeow' (rhymes with 'meow', the sound a cat makes). There is a falling and then rising inflection as if asking a question. 'Chen' is pronounced with a vowel like the 'e' in 'the', almost like 'Chun'. There is a rising inflection. 'Bang', is pronounced 'Bahng' with a high, flat inflection, and a vowel sound similar to 'father'.]

Chapter 1 – Of Death and Rebirth.

I have always gotten everything I have ever wanted out of life, including my own death. When you look upon my wrecked body and at my empty eyes, how can you believe this? When I was young, once, and beautiful, how can I now say I have everything I have ever wanted? How could I want what I have become? It is because when I look at my life now, it is as if I am viewing it from a height. Many things that happened to me in my life do not look the same from this high place at the end of life.

When you see me here, many of you think you know who I am. This is natural because of the things you have heard, but you cannot truly know me because you do not even truly know yourselves.

Many people have called me many things, and by naming me, they thought they understood me and thought they knew me. I have come to know that names mean nothing; they are worse than nothing; they are a trap. They seem to carry a great deal of meaning, but the only meaning they have is that which is found in illusion. The only knowledge that is real is the knowledge that surpasses the ability to speak it. At their very best words can only put a frame around the truth. So you who listen to me here, empty your minds and I will put a frame around my story and around my life so that you will know who I am, so that you will know who you are.

I did not wish for death, but we often do not know our own desires enough to wish for them. Death is something that we seldom think to ask for, and so it usually comes as an unexpected gift. In my case, I think it was an answer to a prayer.

Even as a small child, I knew there was something wrong with the world. I knew that somehow I did not fit—did not belong here, as if I were not from here but from another place where things were better. Many times, I have read that my home, the islands of Hawaii, is like paradise on Earth. What those writers mean, of course, is that the islands are so beautiful that they must resemble in some way what paradise must be like – a paradise that is separate from this world. What I saw, even as a child, was that there was no separation except what we had made. The whole world was an island in the middle of paradise, and all we had to do was just to see that.

In the Honolulu of my childhood, my days and nights were beautiful. In the daytime, there was the sunshine, the ocean, the fragrance of flowers always on the breeze. At night, there was the indigo sky, the moon, the stars, the glowing clouds, the sparkle of the sea, and when I lay down on the cool sheets of my bed at night, the dream.

In my dream, I was high in the sky, higher than the clouds, higher than the mountains. Sometimes I was so high that I floated beneath the stars and saw the curvature of the earth. Sometimes the world seemed covered in clouds that glowed silver in the moonlight, and there was only one mountain peak that rose above them. I knew this mountain was special to me, but I did not know how. Sometimes it seemed to tell me its name, but in the morning, I could not remember what it had said. The mountain seemed to be at least as much asleep as I was and I often had the impression that we were sharing the same dream. I knew the clouds below the mountain peak hid something mysterious — something that waited for me — something that I was not ready to see. I could not make myself go into the clouds, but knew that someday I would.

As I grew older, the dream came less often and gradually became nothing but a memory — a memory of a dream. I would sometimes remember the dream and wonder why I no longer had it, but eventually, I even forgot to remember.

Every night of my childhood, I was always ready for bed. In the evenings, the parents always called in the girls before the boys, but I never resented going inside earlier. Tired from playing under the streetlights and star lights, I would slip shivering between the sheets, ready for the dreams of flying between the stars like a flickering beam of unfettered light. A soaring ray of ever-changing colors, I would fly through limitless space, flash across the heavens and play between the stars. And sometimes I would come back to earth at the mountain and wonder what waited below the clouds. In the morning, I was always ready to get up, ready to see what the day would bring—another day in paradise—as I often heard my father say, as he got ready to go to work.

And it almost was paradise, even if my father did joke about it. As I grew older, I wanted to tell people that they could just reach out and touch paradise—that what kept it from being paradise was themselves—people. I tried to tell a few of my friends, but it was as if I was suddenly speaking a different language. I told them that all they had to do to find paradise was to open their eyes—to reach out and touch it. They would just call me a crazy Ching-chong and walk away.

Ching-chong was what the younger kids called us Chinese. Later, they called me a Banana because I didn't act like other Chinese. They said I was yellow on the outside but white on the inside, although there seemed to be no whites that understood me anymore than the Hawaiians, Thais, Philippinos, or Japanese did. Later, when I started dating Japanese boys, I would hear the kids calling me Banan-anime in the hallways at school. It was as if people were constantly looking for ways to isolate and alienate me from them, but I knew it was not just me—everyone did it to everyone else. That was what kept paradise from being paradise.

But I knew they were right—about me, at least. I was different. Not because of the color of my skin or the shape of my eyes, but because I knew that if you peeled back the sky, you would see the hidden reality behind this one—the real truth of existence that very few, if anyone else, knew about. And because I knew if you could somehow get a pinch of that delicate fabric of reality between your thumb and finger and manage to peel some back, that behind it you would find angels and demons and all sorts of other beings watching us—waiting to see how things were going to turn out for us. And I also knew I was different because I had much keener hearing than anyone I knew. I not only heard the name-calling and squabbling that went on every day at school, but I heard it all over Honolulu, and even all over the world. It was a constant background noise to me like the fussing of birds in the trees at dusk, and usually meant little more to me than that.

The sounds that did have an effect on me were the cries of pain, of anguish, of remorse, of fear, of desire, of sorrow, of longing, and sometimes, of joy and of hope that constantly washed over me until I felt I was drowning in a sea of human emotion. There was some of the nobility of humanity in it, but most of it was negative, and it was a negativity born of the same ignorance—the same blindness—that was at the heart of the squabbling, bickering, and constant power struggles that seemed to be always a part of another day in paradise. This negativity was what led to my decline.

Being human, I was frustrated with my inability to change things. I could not make people see paradise all around them; I could not make them open their eyes; I could not make them realize they were all one and should cease their spitefulness—that what they did to the least of each other, they also did to themselves.

Being human, I fought on until they won. I am sure every kid in America has used the sticks-and-stones reply to name-calling: "Sticks and stones can break my bones, but words will never hurt me." It isn't true—negativity can wear you down. Even though I felt I was carrying the weight of everyone else's negativity, which seemed to be my burden in life, still I struggled on. It was the name-calling that became the final little extra weight that broke me.

In Hawaii, when I was growing up, the Americans, ran everything, the Japanese owned everything and the Hawaiians thought nobody ought to be there but them. The Chinese were nothing in that place. It seemed everyone had their own ethnic slurs for the Chinese. The Japanese called us Chankoro, a derogatory word passed down from World War II; and everyone called us such names as Slant-eye, Pan-face, Chink, Forty-fiver, Kung-fu, Lizard, Mook, and Baby-muncher. Even the older generation of Chinese called the younger generation ABCs (American-born Chinese), meaning someone born in America who did not understand Chinese culture.

The Hawaiian Chinese were rejects even from their own country. Most of them left China because to stay meant prison or worse. Their own government didn't even want them, although it didn't want them to leave either, because that meant loss of face.

As I grew older, I changed under this negative pressure. Before I went to grade school I lived in paradise. When I went to school I learned to live in the world, but I still dragged paradise along with me everywhere that I went. As I went up through the grades, paradise began to slip away from me and I also began to wonder if I had made a bad choice being born Chinese, or even to have been born at all, and perhaps my parents should not have done their part to bring me into the world.

Being called a baby muncher was what first sent me to the library. It was such a hideously cruel thing to be called. It was a reference to the ethnic slur that Chinese ate their own babies. Of course, I knew in my heart that this was not true. My parents were just as loving and doting as any parents that I knew. Nevertheless, I went to the library to find proof that this name was a lie. I could find no proof, but instead found ignorant and self-serving references to just such acts, which, being a gullible child, I believed. I also discovered that Chinese couples sometimes drowned girl children because they were considered worthless to the family. I also read about the Communist Revolution and then the Cultural Revolution, in which times, judging from the horrors about which I read, the entire country must have gone insane and had nearly self-destructed. I spent days in the library, and afterwards I could not find paradise again.

I no longer dreamed. I lost my grip on the true reality and began to be wholly in the world. Unable to change the world, I entered fully into it and its beliefs became my beliefs. The world became a sad, lonely, and futile place. I lost my true sanity and became like everyone else—dazedly trying to sleepwalk through life. But more sadly, I thought, my hearing remained acute, and for this malady, I could find no relief except in alcohol and drugs. Even in sleep, there was no relief. I dreamed of people dying and calling out to me for help, but I could not help them. I no longer looked forward to going to bed at night. In the morning, I would wake up in a sweat and begin looking for my next fix.

By the time I reached high school, I was already stealing from the tourists, or the 'Nikons', as we called the rich Japanese because they always had expensive cameras with them. I became an expert at breaking into rental cars.

Sometimes when we were high, we would take a video camera that we had stolen from some car and go down where the tourists came out of the Arizona Memorial. We would pretend that we were a news crew and ask the Japanese visitors what they thought of the monument they had made. We usually got the expected horrified expressions in response before they hurried away. One old man, however, stopped and examined us through squinted eyes. "What is it that asks this question?" he inquired solemnly. We never went back after that because we never came up with an answer and the question was disquieting.

In high school I found another use for the Japanese; I began dating rich Japanese boys; it was an easier way to get money and drugs than stealing. Japanese and Chinese do not, as a rule, like each other very much, but the Japanese boys gave me the same non-respect that I had come to think that I deserved. They nearly always had fast cars, lots of cash, and a steady supply of drugs. I was pretty then with no scars or wrinkles upon my face. My eyes were dark and my hair fell on my shoulders like a cascade of thick black silk. I knew how to smile demurely and bat my eyelashes in the way that the Japanese boys liked. I could almost read their minds to know what they wanted, and this made it easy for me to get whatever I needed to make the cries in my head go away. I came to resent the world for being no better than it was, and I resented myself for the same reason. Gradually the voices faded.

I knew that my behavior was killing my parents. I heard my mother crying at night, but I didn't care; I hardened my heart, as well as my resolve to self-destruct. After all, they were just Chankoro, Mooks, and Baby-munchers, themselves. A part of me even blamed them for the fact that I was Chinese—a worthless Chinese girl, to be exact. By what method could I have known then just how my life would become intertwined with the life of a country that I had learned to despise – China – Chung-kuo – The Middle Kingdom.

My parents were Buddhists, and had converted a storage room in our house into a shrine to the Buddha. My mother would drag me in there almost daily to pray for my salvation. This only caused me to lose even more respect for them. I had read enough of Buddhism when I was younger to be able to argue with them about it. "The Buddha never asked anyone to pray to him. This is stupid," I would say.

"The Buddha and other buddhas hear our prayers," they would tell me. "Prayers are answered."

"You are like dogs that look at the master's hand instead of where he is pointing for them to look," I would retort. "You don't even understand your own religion."

"Then help us to understand, darling daughter. At what was the Buddha pointing?"

"At nothing, probably," I would say, before turning and walking off as if I had won an argument.

One day, my parents made me go with them to the Kwan Yin Temple on Vineyard Boulevard. I would not have gone except that my mother said that Kwan Yin would surely hear our prayers, as she was one who heard the cries of the world. I was intrigued, as I too often felt that I heard the cries of the world, although I wished that I didn't. I went to learn more about Kwan Yin, and perhaps in that temple Kwan Yin did listen, and perhaps that is really why I died—it was in answer to my parents' prayers.

I know now that there are as many ways to die as there are people. For my parents and my few friends, the really surprising thing about my death, was that I did not die in any of the ways that they would have thought. I wasn't shot in a robbery; I didn't die of hepatitis or a drug overdose; I wasn't stabbed to death by a drunken boyfriend (my parents' number one prediction); I didn't drown in my own vomit. Instead, I was electrocuted in a muddy ditch because I tried to save a goose on the highway.

My current Japanese boyfriend, whose name was Natsuo, had a very fast sports car, and I loved going fast. The faster he drove, the higher grew the probability of my death. I may not have admitted it, even to myself, but death was where I was headed, and I was in a hurry.

One thing that you will learn if you ever live in Hawaii is that you quickly run out of highway. It isn't long before you have seen all the pavement there is many times over. If you are easily bored, you may turn to other forms of excitement besides just driving around. My current boyfriend had taken to running down birds and the occasional small animals in kamikaze fashion, and keeping a tally. He told me about his new game when he picked me up. You may think that it is difficult to hit birds with a car. I suppose that was part of the challenge, but when I say that he had a fast car, I mean really fast. He could be going sixty, and if he floored the accelerator, it would still throw your head back. When he picked me up, he showed me a few feathered trophies on the grill of his car to prove that he could do it.

I had grown up, grown out of paradise, and into the world, and had left my dreams behind; I had learned to manipulate others to get what I wanted and had gradually become the very kind of person that I would never ever have wanted to be. That is who I was when I died, but I think that I was redeemed, in the end, by the fact that I loved animals—loved the incorruptibility of them—loved their innocence. I, who had not been shocked by anything in the last five years of my life, was horror-struck by his description of this new game. However, I was not quite ready to believe that his game wasn't just with me and that he had only showed me the results of an accidental encounter with a small flock of birds to get a reaction from me. I began to believe him, however, when he reached into the back seat and grabbed a loaf of bread and began throwing pieces out onto the highway as we sped along. This was to bait the birds, he said, to improve his chances on the return trip. Realizing how sickened I was at this, Natsuo laughed, became quite excited, and began feverishly looking for something to run down. Telling him that I would not put up with his murderous behavior only made him laugh harder. I told him I wanted out of the car but he only grinned and said no one was stopping me — but he would not slow down. I told him that if he tried to kill any birds or animals while I was around that I would kill him instead with my bare hands.

The Nene goose is endangered because it has little fear of man. They are not normally found on the island of Oahu because the eggs and young are eaten by mongooses and the adults tend to become highway fatalities. The few remaining ones are found mainly on Kauai and the Big Island. Even having lived here in Hawaii all my life, I had never seen one alive before, as I had never left Oahu. I do not know what brought this lone bird to this junction of highway and murderous intent, but my boyfriend saw a rare opportunity to hurry a species along toward extinction.

It was innocence that he was going to kill—the innocence of an animal, a pure spirit, living in paradise—the innocence that I had once had in my childhood—the innocence that would finally die forever within me if I let him kill this bird. Deep inside of me, I harbored a last wisp of this innocence and I suddenly became terrified that Natsuo was going to rob me of that tiny precious thing if I let him. Abruptly, I found myself striking Natsuo and pulling his arm, and just as quickly, we were off the road. The car slid down an embankment and crashed into a power pole. There were no airbags to provide a cushion for us; he had not replaced them from his last accident.

The next thing I remembered was looking at the palm of my hand and wondering how I had gotten blood on it. I looked at Natsuo and thought that his blood must have splashed on me because there was quite a bit of it on his head and face. He appeared to be looking at his blood on the steering wheel, but he wasn't moving — just staring. Nothing was making sense to me. I opened the door, stepped out, and slid down into a ditch filled with muddy water. To pull myself up, I reached for what I thought was a broken vine dangling in front of me.

Suddenly, I was lifted right up into the air over the ditch. It was as if I had been swinging on the vine and had let go at the highest point, the point of weightlessness that occurs just before beginning to fall back. But I didn't fall. I hung suspended in mid air and there was no explanation for it — there was nothing holding me up. As I waited to fall, confused and beginning to doubt my experience, I looked down to see where I might land once gravity did kick in, and realized that when I fell, I was going to fall on someone else. There was a girl lying face up in the shallow muddy water, directly below me, her dark hair spreading delicately like a halo around her head. She appeared to be dead or near to it. She seemed so vulnerable, innocent, and helpless that I desperately began to think of how I could help her — possibly the first time in years that I had thought of someone else's needs instead of my own.

While I tried to think what to do, help began to arrive. A couple of burly men in flowered shirts came sliding down the muddy bank. They eyed the "vine" warily and I followed their eyes up to the power lines above. With dismay, I slowly began to realize that the girl in the ditch was me! I was gazing down upon my own dead body. I had climbed partway out of the water and had grabbed the live power-line, which had been broken loose by the car's impact with the pole. So this was death? I seemed perfectly fine. In fact, I felt better than fine; I had never felt better.

The men quickly dragged my body up to the highway and frantically began checking for a pulse, a breath, any sign of life. They tried breathing into my mouth. They tried beating on my chest. One of them sat astraddle of me and shoved violently on my chest with both hands while the other tilted my head back and breathed deep breaths into my open mouth.

I tried to stop them. "I'm OK! She's OK," I shouted into their deaf ears. "Leave her alone!" I spoke as if my body were a separate entity now. I tried to make them stop, but nothing I did had the slightest effect on them. I tried to stop them because I was distressed by the roughness and violence of their methods on my body, and because I felt I had nearly left violence behind me forever, and if this final violence could be stopped, I would never have to confront it again. And I tried to stop them because I did not want to go back to the way I was. I did not want to wake up to the taste of mud and vomit in my mouth and the stench of the world in my nostrils. And I tried to stop them because I no longer wanted to be that girl that they were trying to revive.

I saw Natsuo's body where they had laid it out on the pavement. He was obviously dead, his eyes still staring at nothing. I never saw Natsuo himself again or knew what happened to him after that; if he was a ghost like I was, he was not still hanging around, or if he was, I could not see him.

As I looked around for Natsuo's ghost, I noticed a slender girl who was standing nearby, watching me. She caught my eye for a couple of reasons, one being that no one else seemed to be able to see me at all, and another being that she had an unearthly glow, a shining aura, around her. As she held out her hand to me, I realized, too, that I could see right through her body as if it was made of shimmering golden glass. Feelings of comfort and assurance seemed to pass from her to me, and I reached out to her and took her offered hand.

I heard a siren and saw an ambulance cresting a distant hill. The sound of the siren changed into a buzzing sound, almost more of a feeling than a sound, as if I myself were vibrating faster and faster. And then the world changed. It was as if I were being swept up into a whirlwind. The buzzing grew louder and more powerful as I hurtled along through a spinning tube of darkness. At the far end I could see a bright light and suddenly I was in the light. The buzzing had stopped and I was filled with such a feeling of peace and love that I knew I was home.

There are no words to describe what I saw and what I heard and what I felt. Words are for the world I had left behind. Words are the poorest approximation of communication, and will likely give the entirely wrong impression of what I am trying to say, but they are all that you and I currently have. "Saw" and "heard" and "felt" do not even apply to the sensations of this other world — the world I have come to think of as the borderland.

I was in light! I was light! Everything glowed with the most beautiful and indescribable inner luminance. This light seemed to be love itself, for everything was bathed in and seemed to glow with the very light of love. I was loved. I was "in" love. Love was in me; love was above me; love was below me; love was behind me; love was before me. For me to remember what it was like to be loved so unreservedly is enough to make tears run even now from these empty eyes.

What did this borderland look like? For me it looked like forests and rolling hills, but I have since come to understand that, by its infinite nature, heaven can present itself as all things to all souls. I was in an ancient forest whose trees formed an arching canopy overhead. There was not a tree visible whose gnarled trunks any three people could hope to encircle. Although it seemed shady, it was also bright. The trunks and leaves glowed with their own light. Grass and small scented flowers grew beneath the trees and they too had their own inner light. There were paths meandering among the flowering under-story shrubs and trees. Between the giant shaggy trunks, I could see meadows and glades and low hills rolling off into the distance under the radiant sky. The scent of sweet flowers, of incense, and of moss filled the air. I wanted to lie down on that moss, shut my eyes, and never rise again.

Glowing human figures approached me, and I was engulfed in a new wave of unconditional love. This overwhelming love was not at all what I expected as my reward for the life I had lived, which made it all the more beautiful; nothing in my life warranted such love, acceptance, and understanding.

These beings gave the impression of wearing white robes from their necks down to the ground. I say impression, because everything about this place, except for the palpable vividness of it, was like a dream in which a thing can be a thing, and another thing, and still yet another thing, all at the same time, and the mind just accepts it the way the mind of a child accepts the world. These beings radiated the light of love so brilliantly and fully and unreservedly that other features were indistinct, and paled to relative unimportance.

We communicated — I will say "talked", these beings and I, although it seemed to be a direct and instantaneous transfer of thoughts, concepts, ideas, and images. To compare this to talking would be like comparing the Internet to Morse code.

I was told many things and shown many things. I was told I was a hero. Not just me, but all of us who go into the world are seen as heroes in this place. We go into the world, they informed me, to put ourselves in peril in order to grow, and few of us return unscathed. Yet most of us go back into the world again and again until we have suffered everything, and experienced everything, and conquered the greatest danger. And if you think climbing glaciers and jumping out of aircraft is dangerous, then you do not know what real danger is. The real danger is not bodily death—it is not physical at all.

You have probably heard it said that when near to death a person's life flashes before his eyes. I was the greatest skeptic of this statement before I, myself, died. Yet here in this place, the beings of light reviewed my life with me, and I did indeed see my life flashing before me. This was the least pleasant experience of my death; in my case, it was extremely unpleasant. I saw every bad thing I had ever done. I saw every good thing as well, but, in my case, the good things were scarce and widely scattered.

The beings that showed me my life did so with sympathy and understanding and without diminishing the love they had for me, yet still, they made me aware that I was totally responsible for my own actions; everything that I had done, I had done of my own volition. I could not blame my parents or my school, or God, or fate, or any of the other things I had sometimes blamed in the past.

The worst part of the life review was that I not only re-experienced my actions, but I got to experience what it was like for the people I had wronged. I felt what I had done to them as if I were them, and not only them but all the people who were in turn affected by the people whose lives I had affected. I saw how my actions, whether good or bad, rippled out through the fabric of space and time and affected everything that now existed or that ever would. And the anguish my parents felt, I felt. The pain my real friends felt, and that my teachers felt, I felt.

As I have said, it is impossible to put into words exactly what the experience was like in this borderland. There is a danger of a too literal interpretation of my words into a supposed understanding of what really transpired there. But to risk it, let me say that there was a boundary here of which I became more aware after my life review. It was on the other side of the boundary that true paradise lay — unbounded bliss — whatever I imagined paradise to be. The boundary between the borderland and paradise presented itself to me as a beautiful flowing river of steep mossy banks and unfathomable bottom. Lustrous flowers nodded over the water as if studying their reflections, and creeping vines lazily dangled their tendrils in the ripples. There was a bridge of sturdy timbers across it, and I knew that to cross that bridge was to go on and not look back. This was the way I saw the boundary, but I know that some have described it as a wall with a gate, others as a lake with a boat, and others as a thin veil that separates one world from the next. These various interpretations, I have since decided, are attempts by the brain to bring into the context of the world the mind's experience of things that do not exist in the physical plane.

I wanted very much to cross over to the other side, but the beings of light prevented me. They said I had much more to accomplish — more work to do — more to learn. They said I would not be happy with myself if I left undone all the things I had planned for myself in the life I would be leaving. They showed me a hint of my future but it did not make much sense to me, as it contained elements that did not currently exist in the world and were not part of my experience. The only way I could relate was to interpret what I was shown in some way. One of the mysteries they showed me was a giant whale, flying high over cities and countryside. I would see this whale someday in my future, they said, and it would be a trigger for me — a pivot around which my life would turn. It would be a time of decision. They said that more would be revealed to me at the time I saw the whale, but that now I should return at once to my life, as time was becoming a critical factor for me and for my body.

As much as I wanted to stay, there was no arguing, for with a whoosh, I found myself jerked back into my body. Even though I could not see anything right away, I knew I was in my body, because all of the pain of my accident had returned to me.

I moaned and struggled to sit up. The sheet with which I had been covered fell away from my eyes and I saw a woman in a white lab coat staring wide-eyed at me while a young man in similar garb was collapsing to the floor.

My life changed after that. I told my parents that things were going to be different, but it took months for them to accept that fact. I didn't tell my parents what had happened while I was dead because I knew they would not believe me and would only be frightened. I knew this because I had tried to tell the doctors in the hospital during my time of being under observation, and I was treated at first as if I was a child describing a dream. The more I persisted in insisting that I had really experienced what I had described, the more concerned the doctors became, the more tests they ran, and the stronger the drugs became that they prescribed for me. When I finally gave up and quit talking about it, the doctors seemed to sigh with relief and I was soon allowed to go home. I learned from that experience to keep my mouth shut while I waited for the flying whale.

My death was difficult for my parents. They were heartbroken with grief at the death of the daughter they had loved so much despite her cruelty to them. The grief was quickly followed by unexpected joy at her miraculous resurrection and recovery. This then was followed in the next days and weeks by bewildered astonishment at how their daughter had changed. They were doubtful at first, as if I had learned some new cruel trick they had not yet fathomed, or perhaps as if they thought I had suffered some reversible brain damage. Then, gradually, they became glad for this change that had been wrought in me. Yet sometimes they looked at me as if they wondered if some other spirit besides that of their daughter now inhabited my body.

During the years that followed, I strove to be the best person I could be. I found only good things to say about people, the world, and my life. I looked for the good in people and for ways to do good things for them. I never wanted to experience another life review such as the one I had. I had learned a lesson that never left me. I tried in every way to always put other people first. I strove to be non-judgmental, like the beings I had met, and every day I actively looked for some way, no matter how small or how great the effort, to give something back to life. I listened with an open mind to people, and tried to let them know that they had value, and because of that, many people began to bring their problems for me to help them solve. This listening and helping brought me to the soup kitchens and the homeless shelters and I became more involved with programs to ease hunger, first locally, and then world-wide, finally concentrating my focus in China.

*

When I was in my twenties, I became involved with the international food programs and traveled often to China. My father had originally come from northern China and spoke Mandarin, but my mother had come from southern China and spoke Cantonese. Therefore, in my early childhood, before I became ashamed of being Chinese, I had learned to speak both languages. Because of this, I found myself much in demand to travel to China to help with agricultural programs there.

I saw what a marvelous and wonderful country China was and how strong and brave the people were in the face of their great national adversity. I studied history to learn what had happened to this "Middle Kingdom" to bring it so low and nearly destroy it to the point that now so many of its people lived in poverty and oppression. All of these things that happened to me were a natural growth of my desire to help others. I no longer thought much about myself at all, except that I continued to wait for the flying whale.

Another natural progression of my life was in my dreams. My dreams began to change. I dreamed of being in classrooms where new and wonderful things were being taught. Although, when I awoke, I could not remember any of the subject matter, still, I remembered the concept of being taught. And I dreamed of helping people. In my dreams, though, I helped dead people, not live ones.

One of the earliest dreams of this kind that I remember was this: I was riding in a convertible with three other people whom I did not recognize from this life, but who seemed to be on very familiar terms with me and with each other. As we traveled down the highway at a great rate of speed, we joked and talked, but we knew we were on a very important mission and that when we arrived at our destination, we would do our best to accomplish the task that had been given to us.

As we drove, we suddenly veered off and turned up a wide dry creek bed, strewn with boulders and overhung with huge trees. I realized then that the car had no wheels but was flying just above the ground. As we flew along above the boulders, with the newly leafed trees of spring arching overhead, the creek began to look less and less like a natural water course, and more like a road that had existed years ago, but was now washed out and eroded down to the bedrock.

At the end of this road, there was a clearing, and in the clearing was a magnificent stone mansion—or it had been in its day. Now the roof was gone; the doors hung rotten on their hinges; the windows had only shards of glass in their frames, and vines grew in and out of them with abandon. We went in through the double front door and saw that the main floor had collapsed into the basement, which was full of water, decayed furniture, and large stones, fallen in from various parts of the house. We descended easily into the water and stood looking around. I felt that we were searching for the original inhabitants — and with that thought, we began to see the floor above us, now back in its original position as it had once been. But the floor was transparent to us and we could see the original furniture arranged about the floor, looking as it had once looked. Sitting in the chairs were a man and a woman. They seemed to me to be husband and wife. As we became aware of them, they also became aware of us. The man stood up, looked down at us, his face twisted in rage, and yelled at us to leave them alone and to get out of his house at once. So intense was his anger, that I felt the vibrations of it throughout my being, and we scattered like a flock of sparrows. Something told me he could not hurt us (my training perhaps), but still, that expedition was now over. We accomplished little except for gaining the experience, yet no harm was done either. Perhaps I learned that one should not try to force awakenings. If people do not want to be awakened, they can become quite angry about it.

Another early dream mission that I remember was when I found myself standing on a narrow beach in a deep fog. In the darkness, I could barely see the waves lapping near my feet or the black steep cliffs just behind me. While I stood there on the sand, wondering why I was there, the fog began to lift a little until I could see that out in the ocean a ship was sinking. I was struck by the magnificence of this tragedy unfolding under the now clear and beautiful sky, black and full of stars, the yellow lights from the ship flickering and flashing in the darkness. While I watched, dumbfounded, not knowing what I was supposed to do, I saw something coming rapidly toward me in the water, and in just a matter of moments, a young girl pulled herself up on the beach. She did not appear tired as she sat up and looked at me. "That was pretty scary at first," she said, holding herself tightly. "Were you on the ship too, or are you a rescuer?" she asked me.

"I guess I am a rescuer of sorts," I replied, smiling at her. "I have been waiting here for you."

She looked puzzled. "You must live around here; you saw the ship sinking didn't you? Are you the first one here?" She stood up.

She seemed to be about twelve or thirteen years old. "Funny, I thought the water would be cold, but I am not cold at all. That is a good thing, because I don't see any blankets here. But, I guess you can't expect real life to be just like the movies, can you?" She looked around her and noticed, as I was now noticing, that the cliff came right down to the sea on both sides of us. The beach was only a couple of yards wide and deep and looked like it was normally submerged at high tide. "How did you get here? I don't see a boat or even a rope ladder. And where are the rest of the survivors? Why aren't they here?"

"There were no survivors."

"You mean I am the only one? Oh my God!"

"No. I mean there were no survivors — not one." I held out my hand to her but she did not take it. She stared at me as if she were trying to decide if I was playing a bad joke or if I were truly insane. "This is not easy for anyone to accept at first," I said.

"I don't see how I can possibly listen to another word that you say. I thought you had come to help me. Where are the other people with the blankets and flashlights? I want to talk to someone else."

"I'm afraid I'm all you've got," I said gently. "Please don't be scared; being dead is perfectly safe."

"I am not dead! I swam here; didn't you see me?"

"Didn't it seem to you that you were swimming amazingly fast?"

"I am a good swimmer! Quit lying to me, because I remember what happened. There was an explosion. There was a fire and lots of smoke. I couldn't breathe the smoke, and I remember getting down on the floor like they had taught us. Then there was water. I was under water, but I swam through some doors and then up to the air, and then I swam here."

"You lost consciousness from the smoke, and then, when the water rushed in, you drowned. You swam here because that is what you would have done in your physical body. Your physical body is gone now, and you no longer need it. You could have just as easily walked here. Take my hand and I will show you."

"Well, if I am dead, and everyone else is dead, then where are they? Why can't I see them?"

"I don't know the answers to everything, but I do know that not everyone makes the transition easily or in the same way as others. You are one of those who needs help to cross over." I was still holding out my hand. I pointed out to sea where the ship had been. Large bubbles were still boiling up from the deep. "Can you see where the ship was?" She nodded. "That must be at least two miles. Have you ever swum two miles?" She shook her head to say no. "When you left the ship the bow was still above water. Do you think you could possibly swim that distance before the ship finished sinking?" She simply stared at me. "You said you thought the water would be cold, and the water *is* cold, but you didn't feel it. Look at your pajamas; they are not even wet."

"Well, if I am dead," she challenged, "then why am I even wearing pajamas?"

"Because when we die, we continue to see things the way we are accustomed to seeing them. Look at my hand." I held it up to the sky. "Look through it. Do you see the stars through my hand?" She nodded. I reached out for her to take it. She did. "How can you explain the fact that my hand, which was just now transparent to the stars, now feels solid to you?" I didn't wait for her to answer. "It is because you and I are made of the same substance. Look down." When she had taken my hand, I had begun lifting us both above the beach, and now her feet were several inches above the damp sand. "Look down. Do you see any footprints down there?" She floated there, looking down at the beach and the waves, her blond hair hiding her face and glowing in the starlight. She turned her face to me and gave me a huge beautiful smile. I smiled back. "Let's go," I said, and we flew away as fast as thought across the field of night.

Unlike when I was younger, now when I dreamed of people dying, I was able to help them, and I did not try to escape it. As the years passed and I waited for my flying whale, I have been on countless dream missions. I have been to every part of the world — anywhere that I am needed—from the depths of the ocean of water to the heights of the ocean of air. I have been to earthquakes, train wrecks, car wrecks, plane wrecks, burning buildings, executions, exploding factories and natural disasters. I have been to emergency rooms, nursing homes, hospices, and nurseries. I have seen every way to die. I have seen people drown, and I have seen them die of thirst; I have seen them freeze and I have seen them burn. I have seen them die of poison, and of starvation, of disease and of the treatment. I have seen them torn asunder, and I have seen them crushed. I have seen them die of old age and I have seen them still-born. I have been present at murders and at suicides and battlefield after battlefield. I have seen the dead continue to struggle for survival, and even to fight each other in the field of battle while their bodies lie at their feet.

I have heard the cries of fear and the wailing of sorrow — the moaning of pain and the sobs of longing. I have seen the heart-rending deaths, the tender deaths, the agonizing deaths. I have seen shame, horror, pathos, beauty and ecstasy in death, and I have seen the mercy of Heaven fall upon everyone the same. I have seen hate lock people into this world so that they could go neither forward nor backward, and I have seen love bring back the dead.

I have seen the dead and the dead have seen me. They see in me what they expect or want to see. They see Moses or Siddhartha or Jesus or Shiva or an angel or their dead mother or grandfather. It is not my job to disillusion them—it is only my job to make their transitions from this world to the borderland easy ones. The others take over there.

There are many of us who do this work in our dreams, although few of us remember. I may have even seen you there, stepping over the bodies, trying to convince the dead to stop fighting—debating with the dead that they are dead. I have come to know the name by which we who do this work are called. We are called the Dakini, and there are those who needlessly fear us. Sometimes the dead need us to help them understand what is happening to them, and sometimes they do not and may not even notice our presence as they rush to paradise.

The ranks of the Dakini are made of spirits who may or may not have bodies of their own. Some Dakini awaken in the morning with vague memories of their night's work, or, more often, with no memory at all of what they have been doing while their bodies slept. They get out of bed, have their tea or coffee, and go off to their labors like everyone else. Other Dakini have no physical presence in the world, but work tirelessly to help the dead and dying.

In every case, I was there to help others make the transition from life to death. This can be difficult when people are convinced the world is all there is, and that if they are still thinking and observing, then they must still be alive. In almost every case this was my mission — except for one. My most remarkable mission was not one in which I was trying to help someone die, but one in which I was instead trying to help him stay alive.

Although, most of my dream time was spent helping the dying, things did not always happen in any sort of systematic way. Outcomes were not always happy. I often witnessed things I did not wish to see or really understand. I witnessed some events repeatedly for reasons I could not explain. Sometimes I dreamed of a man being beaten in the middle of a crowded street and sometimes I had a vision of a particular hand in my dream. It was a strangely mutilated hand with abbreviated, fingers. I could not see the owner of the hand, but there was a knife through the center of the palm. The owner of the hand appeared to be struggling with two other men, whom I also could not see clearly. Over and over through the years I saw a man fall from a height and smash into the sea as hard as if he were hitting concrete. Most difficult was the repeated vision of bodies scattered across a frozen landscape accompanied by the feeling of anguish from an immense intelligence. These things I saw as infrequent, yet recurring, dreams throughout my life as a Dakini. I was not able to help these people and I neither knew why I could not help nor why I was witness to these events.

The dream in which I helped someone live instead of die was not a recurring dream, but it shared some similarities in that I did not know why I was seeing this or what I was expected to do about it.

I often did not know why I found myself where I did, but this was something I had come to accept. I would go to sleep, and the next thing I knew, I would be where I needed to be. I would wait then, to see what was happening and who I should be helping. However, there in that place where I found myself at that time there was nothing happening.

I looked around me at the blackness of space and the icy harshness of the stars. The moon was painfully bright and it shown silvery on an endless sea of clouds far below. I waited. Being there seemed familiar; I felt I had been there before but could not remember the occasion. I watched the Milky Way. I watched the faint glow of dawn on the distant curvature of the earth. I watched the clouds roiling like waves on the vast ocean. What a storm that must be, I thought as I watched. Only one landmark was visible. It was an ice-covered mountain peak that extended like an island above the clouds. The clouds broke against it, rolled around it, and washed over it, obscuring it from view over and over, and more and more each time. I decided that if anything was happening that I should be concerned about, that peak was my beacon, and I had better locate myself next to it while I could still find it.

By thinking it, I was there beside the peak. The clouds reached up for me as if to pull me down and I recoiled. Suddenly, I remembered — this was the dream — the dream of a single mountain peak like an island in an ocean of clouds. This was the time of which I had once dreamed and waited. Tonight was the night that I would go into the clouds and solve their mystery. I hesitated, but I knew I had to go in — I had to see what had been hidden from me. There was no other choice.

Slipping down the side of the mountain, I found myself awash in a terrible storm, ice blowing like slivers of glass into crevices of scoured rock, or falling abruptly into the darkness below. I dropped further and further into this icy hell and found a man dangling, his hand entangled in a rope, blowing back and forth and crashing over and over into the side of the precipice. He was dressed in heavy mountain-climbing gear, parka, goggles, heavy gloves, and this was probably what was keeping him from being beaten to death against the rocks.

I was surprised to find nothing more than this beneath the clouds. Yet I could sense that this was not exactly "nothing". Here was a man dangling halfway down a nightmare abyss, yet struggling to live. Demons from the cold depths of hell beat and lashed him, and if heaven's angels had arrived then, they could have done nothing more than to make sure his hand was securely tied. I had no explanation for the resemblance of this place to my childhood dream. However, it was clear the man would be dead soon, and I could do little more than wait, hoping the end would be quick, for his sake.

However, the drama did not end that night. I awoke on my cot to the sound of roosters crowing in the little Chinese village where my work had recently brought me. I worried all through breakfast about the man I had left hanging from the mountainside. I hoped, and supposed it would be, that I had been replaced at the end of my watch, and that the man, whose death was surely eminent, would find a guide, a Dakini, waiting for him after his terrible final night. I wondered, however, why I had dreamed of that place so many years before. There was nothing significantly different about this man's death than any other. We all found our own ways to die, and he had found his on a mountain top.

After breakfast, I began to feel feverish, as if I was coming down with something, and I went back to bed. As soon as I fell asleep I was once more back at the gigantic mountain. It was daylight now, and the sky was a deep blue, so deep that it seemed unnatural and stark against the white snow and ice. The sun lit up the ice on the mountains, and the glaciers below reflected the light back like a million suns. I felt a presence in this mountain. I think I might have had an inkling of it the night before. It was neither good nor evil, but just there, not quite watching — a sleeping intelligence, ancient and immense — and distant.

I saw the man. He was a tiny speck against the side of the mountain. There were thousands of feet of mountain above him and thousands more below. He appeared to be dead, but as I drew closer, I realized the soul was still with the body. He still hung by one hand from a rope tied to a piton not far above him. The rope appeared to be part of a series of ropes, which might have been left in place for re-use by climbers. The ropes followed a narrow ledge, now piled high with new snow.

"If you are not going to die," I said to the man, "then you should try to get up to that ledge and get off this mountain." I seldom spoke to the living when I was on these missions. They couldn't hear me, and so when I did speak it was more in the nature of a commentary or observation to myself than that I expected a response. The man moved his head as if he had heard me. He tried to see how far above him the ledge was. He studied his twisted hand. "If you don't try it, then you surely won't make it." He tried to pull himself up with the tied hand but fell back. I took a great pity on him and tried something I had never even thought of before, much less attempted. The very thought of it terrified me, yet it seemed to be something I must do. I moved closer and closer to him until I was occupying the same space as he in an attempt to give him my strength. "You must do it now," I said, and heard the sound of my words come through his gritted teeth, gruff and hoarse.

We swung our right arm and grabbed our left arm as high up as we could reach and began to pull our body up, using our entangled left arm like an extension of the rope. When we had pulled the body up far enough, we grabbed the left hand glove in our teeth just long enough to let go with our right hand and grab the rope. The pain in the left hand was almost unbearable as the bouncing of the rope ground the bones of the hand together, and I felt him almost black out several times. We swung our right leg over the rope, grimacing with the pain, and were then able to grab a second rope, secured independently above us. This allowed us to disentangle our crushed hand and pull ourselves up so that we were standing on the lower rope from which we had once hung, while holding on to an upper rope which ran parallel to it. We then scrambled up to the narrow ledge, and, still holding the upper rope, began to inch our way along it.

Without warning, I was back on my cot. There was a wet rag on my forehead and someone was trying to feed me soup. "Please, no food," I said weakly. "I need to sleep." The person insisted that I would have to eat something so I gave in, knowing that I was only prolonging my waking state. I gulped the hot soup, not waiting for it to cool, and tried to lie back. The person, one of my co-workers, I realized, remarked that I was ravenous and said she would go and get another bowl. "No!" I wept. "Please just let me sleep."

Soon, I was once again back beside the man on the mountain. He had actually made some progress along the rope and had come to a large gradual slope where, if not for the altitude, the accumulated snow might have given one the expectation of seeing skiers at any moment. He stood in the snow without assistance and I noticed that the unfortunate man had no boots but only thick wool socks. I did not recall whether he had boots on before, as it had not seemed important when I thought he was going to die. Of course, he could still die, but if he did not, now he would be without feet, for at this altitude, his feet would inevitably freeze solid, with or without socks.

What was worse, however, was that he had taken his gloves and snow goggles off and thrown them away. There was nothing I could do about the goggles; the feet would die no matter what happened; but I had to try to save his hands. He was waving his broken hand at the mountain peak and raving. "Chomolungma!" he shouted, "I am alive! I know you hear me, Chomolungma. I died and now I live. Was it you, Chomolungma? Why? Why did you take Jia Li and spare me?"

I understood Chomolungma to be the name of the mountain, and I once more got an uneasy feeling that there was something more here than just rock and ice. I tried talking to the man. "You should put your socks on your hands."

"Jia Li! Is that you?" He spun around, looking through me. "My eyes . . . ." He waved his hands drunkenly before his face. I did not answer him. I did not know who Jia Li was or how Jia Li might answer him. In addition, I had never had any other living person hear me while I was in this non-corporeal state, and did not know what to say next.

"Jia Li!" He fell to his knees on the snow and held his arms wide. "I have seen the gates of heaven and lived!" That set me back again. Had he been where I had been and seen what I had seen? "Chomolungma killed me to bring me back! Chomolungma killed me but did not crush me!" He shouted at the mountain peak, "What does a mountain care about a man?" Then, "Jia Li, where are you? I thought you had died. Did Chomolungma bring you back as well?" His speech was slurred and getting worse as he talked. His head lolled around like it would fall off his shoulders.

The man was suffering from cerebral edema caused by lack of oxygen. His brain was swelling inside his skull. This had caused his confusion, resulting in the loss of his gloves, his goggles, his boots, and perhaps his sanity. He would soon lose his consciousness and his life if I could not get him down to a lower altitude in a hurry. But first I had to try to save his hands. "Look at your poor hands," I said. He held them up to his eyes and squinted. His fingertips were black, as if they had been thrust into a fire; other parts of his hands were pale and bloodless. On his crushed left hand he wore a pale yellow ring, like ivory or bone, carved with ornate designs and Chinese characters.

"I can't see them very well," the man replied.

"They look bad. You need to protect them. Your feet are already dead. Take your socks and put them on your hands."

"Are you Jia Li?"

"Perhaps. Do what I say or you will lose your hands."

"Say something in Chinese."

I realized I was communicating to him telepathically and it didn't matter what language I thought I was using, it would still sound the same to him. I thought instead of the Chinese pictograms for Jia Li —

"good and beautiful": 嘉丽 . This seemed to satisfy him. He fell back in the snow and began to pull his socks off. He had two pair on, a thick outer pair for warmth, and a thin inner pair to wick moisture away from his skin. I had him put both pairs on his hands. His feet were already beginning to turn black with necrotic tissue from their close proximity to the heat draining cold of the ice and snow.

"OK, Jia Li. Now what? Do you want me to walk on my hands?" He laughed at his joke. "Look at my feet. My socks must have faded on them." They were black with dead tissue.

"You need to get down the mountain quickly. I will be with you and help you."

"How do I do that?"

I sent him an image of himself sliding down the mountain slope on his pants. He crawled over to the slope, sat down on the ledge, and pushed himself off. He went down as fast as a bob-sled. He did not have all of the necessary equipment for glissading down a mountain, such as an ice-ax to steer with, but he was attempting to use his elbows in an instinctive attempt at steering.

He went down thousands of feet at a rapid rate of descent with me at his side. After a few minutes of this, I could see that at the bottom of the slope there was a level area to one side, which contained a couple of tents. "Aim for those tents," I instructed him. He did a good job of steering, but did not — or simply could not — slow his travel sufficiently to avoid slamming into one of the tents. The tent collapsed under the blow, and the man bounced right over it and crashed into a jagged pile of rocks. He lay still for a while, and I thought I was finally going to do the job I had originally come here for — although I thought it was a shame after all of his effort. He really wanted to live.

After a few minutes, he began to stir. He sat up and looked around stupidly. He squinted at his feet, which were now broken and torn and would have been bleeding profusely if they were not frozen. He began to crawl around in the snow as if looking for something he had lost. "Go get in the tent while you still can," I insisted.

"Not 'till I find my missing toes," he replied.

"They will keep perfectly in the snow," I said. "You can find them later if you want them."

He nodded and crawled clumsily to the tent. Inside the tent there were sleeping bags, oxygen bottles and a camp stove and a pot set up for the melting of snow into drinking water. He crawled into one of the sleeping bags, zipped it up, and suddenly, after all of this, began to shake. "Oxygen," I said. He put the mask of one of the bottles over his mouth and nose and turned the valve on the bottle. He took several deep breaths and without warning I was back in the little Chinese village. I could smell supper cooking. My fever had broken, and I was hungry.

*

As a result of my work in China, I found I had garnered a certain reputation so that when villages heard I was coming, all the people turned out in celebration. I was received joyously, and feasts were provided with whatever food the peasants could scrape together. I also found this did not sit well with the Chinese government whose own attempts at forcing the Chinese people to love it at gunpoint had resulted in the same sentimentality one could expect from any rape victim. My early dislike of things Chinese had, over the years, turned to a dislike of the current Chinese government. This dislike was augmented by my natural rebellion against authority.

The primary goal of a government, I had discovered, was to remain in power. For some governments, that was the only goal. The Chinese government, like all governments before it, knew, but did not acknowledge, that it remained in power because the people allowed it. Motivated by this realization, this fear, and recognizing the power of fear, the government used fear as its primary tool in convincing the populace to abdicate its power to those who claimed to be the country's rightful leaders. Anything that alleviated that fear or caused the people to realize that their lives could be vastly improved without the status quo, caused great agitation in Beijing. I did not do anything to enhance that agitation, as I knew that increased fear in the government would result in, at best, my inability to work in China, and, at worst, violence, bloodshed, and death. So far, I had worked with the government's approval and support—the only way I could work. Fortunately, I did not work in the large cities very much and so was able to keep a low profile. However, to make matters worse, I had become out of necessity over the years, a fairly good planner and organizer. I had eventually created my own foundation, *The China Food Foundation,* of which I was the president. I sought out volunteers from all fields of endeavor, evaluated their talents, and found ways for each to make a contribution. I organized villages the same way. The Party was doubly suspicious of organizers who were not directly accountable to it, but they could not find any reason to expel me from the country. As far as they could tell, I was practicing what they were preaching and everybody was prospering from it.

My dream missions continued, but I felt I had hit a plateau in my spiritual development. Like all people, I continued to make mistakes in my life; I continued to have fears and doubts and questions. I did things in my life that hurt people. I might be rude, insensitive, and even gruff or arrogant. I still sometimes found myself concerned about what I wanted and how I felt rather than the needs of other people. I felt conflicted as I was pulled in so many different directions. I wanted children, but did not see that happening. I had no romance or even opportunity for a one-on-one relationship.

My parents wanted me to move back to Hawaii to take care of them in their old age, but I felt that if I left my work now, it would collapse back in on itself, and everything I had done would be undone. I often felt alone and deserving of pity. I sometimes questioned my motives in doing what I did to help people. Was I only doing good deeds to get into heaven? Even my dream missions began to sometimes seem like a salaried job for which I had only so far received promises of future payment. Yet, I did not have any proof the dream missions were even real. I never spoke of them to anyone, and I never encountered anything in my waking life to prove to me that they were anything more than fantastic dreams.

All of that was changed one night by a different sort of dream, and I began to feel again that I had come into the world in order to do exactly what I was doing. I was not doing this to get into heaven — I was simply living my life as I had wanted it to be.

In my dream that night I went to a strange place where I had never been before. I was in a cloud of luminous fog. I could see nothing — not even myself. I heard a voice in my head, very much as if I were speaking with the beings of light again, except that this time I felt I was understanding actual words. "Xiao Chen, my time of learning is almost at an end. Someday we will meet. You learn too."

"Who are you? How do you know my name?" I asked. In answer, the mist began to clear a little and I could dimly begin to see a dark figure, lit by moonlight, sitting cross-legged on the ground under some tall pines on a rocky cliff. That was all, but when I awoke, I felt recharged, as if I had been waiting for this moment. I wondered though what was meant by "you learn too". Was the person paying me a compliment by saying that I was learning as well? I didn't think so. Surely that effort in communication wasn't spent on a compliment. I was being instructed to continue my learning so I would be ready when we met in person. But how was I to do this?

The person had called me "Xiao Chen", which, roughly translated, meant "early light" and would pass for a fairly literal translation of my American name, Dawn, into Chinese. My parents had wanted me to have an American name, but struggled to find one suitable. In China, girls are traditionally given pretty, graceful names, such as Little Flower or Flowing River. In America, a name like that would be a heavy burden for a child. Given my early disposition, if I had been named Flowing River, I would probably be on death row by now. Fortunately, they settled on "Dawn", a pretty name, yet a bearable one, and one that, in its way, was both Chinese and American. In China, the villagers, having misheard my name, had begun calling me "Dong", meaning "to supervise", and later "Dong Shi", "The Director". No one called me "Xiao Chen", so I wondered if that name was a clue.

As for the learning: I knew I was supposed to be learning things. I had brought that back with me from the borderland. Learn everything, never quit learning, is a directive that nearly all survivors of death can tell you about. But what are we to learn? It is not easy to know where to focus. Is one thing more important than another? Is it even possible to learn some things until you are ready? A child cannot learn to write until his hands have developed. Perhaps there were things to learn that we could not even imagine. I couldn't tell you if I had learned anything important over the years. I had learned thousands of ways to die, and I had learned that dying was not to be feared; life was more to be feared than death. I had learned that existence was not dependent on this world. I had learned that there were other beings who were concerned about us. But I knew nothing of why. Like you, I had only curiosity about what lay beyond the borderland, who the beings of light were, and why they cared about us. Many nights I had laid awake trying to plumb the depths of my life and finding nothing solid. In fact, I could not say for certain that I knew anything of any real significance.

But perhaps I was learning the most important thing without realizing it. Like the little girl who had drowned on the ocean liner, as I gradually learned that there was nothing solid beneath my feet, I was also learning I could fly! However, in those days, I was still probing for that solid ground — some foundation.

How was I to begin the next phase of my learning? I felt as if I must hurry, but did not know in what direction. Should I go east, toward the "dawn" or "early light" as the mysterious dream visitor had perhaps indicated? I needed a teacher, but in China, spiritual teachers were scarce, and the few who might still be around did not advertise. The government felt that spiritual teachers might alienate it from the affection of its people. Tens of thousands of religious leaders had died ("had been purged" was the politically correct term) under this government because of its jealous fear. Hundreds of thousands more had been imprisoned until they recanted their faith. Many never saw freedom again. To even ask about a teacher was to put yourself and everyone around you at risk.

The answer to my quest came several weeks later at the next village where my foundation was preparing to begin a new agricultural teaching program. I would usually begin an operation by visiting the village leaders along with some of the foundation members who would be working directly with them, and letting them know, if they didn't already know, who we were, and what we wanted to do. We would usually make the first visit brief after driving in from the nearest town large enough to have lodgings. We would spend the day meeting everyone, generally begin our efforts on a positive note and then, at the end of the day drive back the way we had come.

On this particular day, a heavy rain came up and washed out a wooden bridge we had crossed that morning. We were stranded in the village with no place to stay. The villagers told us there was an abandoned house that had plenty of room for all of us if we had our own bedding. This we did have, as we had learned our lessons about preparedness long ago. I asked who had lived in the house and was told "xiao chen", meaning, in this context and inflection, not "early light", but "a minor official". He had fallen out of favor with the Party and had been "criticized", as the Chinese put it. The unfortunate man and his family were in prison somewhere for whatever they had done to slight the government. I said we would be grateful for the use of the house, and we were shown the way. I noted the coincidence of the words used to describe the resident of the house being somewhat the same words that had been used to address me in my dream. To the Chinese ear, they were completely different words, but to an English-speaking person, they were barely distinguishable.

Except for dust and cobwebs, the house was just as the official and his family had left it when they had been marched off. For a couple of reasons, the villagers had not touched it. The official had been one of the rare Party members who had not been corrupted by politics, and had tried to improve the lives of the villagers under his jurisdiction, and they were still hoping he might return. But in addition, the villagers would not have dared touch property that belonged to a party member, no matter how many families could have lived in it. It would decay into rubble before anyone would risk a criticism from the government.

Unlike other local dwellings, this house had several bedrooms, and each of us picked one for ourselves. The beds still had mattresses, but they had been slashed open and the stuffing pulled out. Drawers had been pulled from desks and emptied on the floor. Clothes from wardrobe cabinets were piled in the middle of each room and the cabinets tipped on top of the piles. In the kitchen there was a small amount of blood on the floor as well as a splattering of blood on the wall.

My surprise came as we were each straightening out our own rooms. We had decided to try to put some order back to the rooms so that we could at least walk around. Also it was depressing to imagine what had happened at the end of this family's last hour in their home; the piles of personal belongings, family photographs, broken pottery, and so forth, kept the thought in the front of our minds. So we put clothes back, refilled drawers, straightened photographs, swept, and even dusted a little.

While I was sweeping up a broken mirror in my room, one of my staff called us to come to her room and see what she had found. She had been moving her bed away from a drip in the ceiling and had stepped on a loose board that had been under the bed. Pulling up the board had revealed a stash of books wrapped in clear plastic. Most of the books were western books that had been translated into Chinese, but there were purely Chinese books as well. It was difficult to imagine why the books should have been hidden, but I am sure the official knew the danger of keeping them. There was a textbook on local government, another textbook on American Literature, a book about Buddhism, some comic books (for the kids, I supposed), and some cheap novels by authors of whom I had never heard. The book that caught my attention, however, was a worn and ragged one with a title that roughly translated as "Secret..." or "Hidden..." The rest of the title was missing from the torn cover. The author's name evidently had also been on the cover, but now there was only the designation "Teacher". Taken as a whole, the cover of the book read "Hidden Teacher".

As the last thing this official needed in his life now, wherever he was, was to have these books found on his property, we divided them among ourselves and took them with us when the bridge was repaired. I later heard that the mother, a teen-age daughter, and a young son had returned to live in the house, but the father was never heard from again. I was glad we had cleaned the house up a little.

*

Once I had established a relationship with a village, I never voluntarily let that relationship die. My foundation maintained contact with virtually every village we had ever taught or organized. The foundation even held annual seminars and paid the way for all village leaders who wished to attend. At the seminars, villagers learned from each other, villagers learned from us, and we learned from the villagers.

You may wonder how the foundation could afford this. The answer is easy; money poured in to us from overseas. Millions of Chinese had fled their homeland within the last century, not because they did not love it, but because to stay was to perish. These Chinese and their descendants had, as a rule, become very successful in their new homes where opportunities were available. They had become doctors, business owners, lawyers, politicians, inventors, engineers, and, in a word, wealthy. They had wanted for years to do something to help the people they had left behind, the aunts, uncles, cousins, nephews, nieces, and even parents, who still tilled the earth for a living. The foundation had produced demonstrable and documented results, and so the money came.

As a secondary benefit, the villages had established regular communications with each other and had become, as a result, not just separate villages but a community of villages that spanned China.

What I didn't realize, but was perfectly clear to the Party, was that I had stumbled onto the formula for taking over a country. I am sure they were in a quandary about this. Over the past decade, the foundation had increased the overall agricultural productivity of China by at least twelve percent, twenty in some areas. The government even gave token contributions to the foundation to show its support. How they must have puzzled and argued and discussed in Beijing about what my true intentions were and what to do about me. They must have examined plan after plan in a search for a way to surgically remove me and the threat of my supposed designs without damaging the foundation. If they could put one of their own in place of me, then the foundation would be safely in the Party fold and they could go back to robbing the citizens and sleeping soundly at night.

What may have frightened them the most was the title I had acquired in the rural areas of China; the villagers had begun to call me Dong Shi, The Director. To the government, this indicated an inordinate level of influence.

The thing that had saved me so far was the genuine naiveté I demonstrated whenever I met with Party officials. My books were open; I answered every question about my operations without pause, and never acted as if I was trying to hide anything, because, in truth, I wasn't. At that time I had no clue whatsoever that I posed any danger to the government, but only thought I was dealing with a huge bureaucracy with endless questions. However, the government privately recognized that I had created a huge reservoir of fuel for a fiery revolution and all that was required was the appropriate spark. The spark came from an unlikely direction: Tibet.

*

I laughed the first time I heard the tale. "They say he is Chamba, the sixth Buddha," the child was saying. "Have you seen him?" He was the son of a villager and had been following us around the dirt streets pestering us with questions while we tried to survey the local situation.

"No, I haven't seen a Buddha around lately, and you had better be careful about who hears you talking about Buddhas, sixth or any number."

"They say he escaped our whole army in Tibet. He sleeps in caves with snow leopards."

"I suppose he is ten feet tall and eats little children."

"No Buddha would eat meat!" He was aghast. "But they say that he can step right across a wide river and can walk through walls."

"How do you know so much about Buddhas?" I asked him teasingly. He looked startled at the question. His mother, hovering nearby, grabbed his little hand and trotted him off.

I gave the story no credence, but over the next year or so, I heard little bits about this Buddha, here and there, now and again.

Between visits to villages, long meetings with foundation board members, and endless paperwork, I somehow found time to read the book "Hidden Teacher". This was not a translation of a Western text. It may have been translated from another language — I couldn't tell — but it was definitely Eastern in origin. I quickly realized that it was a book about techniques of meditation. There is a completely different view of meditation in Eastern countries than the prevailing view in America. In America, meditation is often used to help one relax — to alleviate stress, but in the East, it is considered a tool for personal spiritual development. It puts the soul in touch with the source of its being; it allows release of attachments; and it unleashes the innate power of the spirit. At least that is the claim. As for me, it just made me fidgety. In this way I was just like China's government.

Fortunately, the book said to expect these sorts of difficulties while learning to meditate. It also said that perseverance was the key to learning the techniques. I continued to make the effort for a number of reasons. One: the book had belonged to a man who had died protecting it. And two: I believed in signs. I had seen enough in my life to know that there are forces about which we know next to nothing but that control our destinies in unimagined ways. In this case there were obvious clues. There was the play-on-words with my Chinese name and the Chinese ideograms for minor official, whose house was vacant. And there was my desire to find a teacher along with the Chinese ideogram for "teacher" on the cover of the meditation book. All of this together was as obvious a sign to me as if someone had drawn an arrow in the dirt with the words, "Go this way."

So I continued trying to meditate, and I gradually got better at it. At first, as I said, I could hardly sit still long enough to have a good session. Thoughts kept jumping into my head. I thought of things I had to do, and I would jump up and start out of the room. After about a week of jumping up and down like I was at a kangaroo convention, I developed enough self-control to stay seated during a complete session. Things didn't get much easier, though, because then the emotions began rising. A thought would come into my head from nowhere; it might have been a childhood memory, or something I had said or done or heard just last week. I would get angry and the adrenaline would flow, or I would get sad and begin to weep, or sometimes a feeling of overwhelming joy would wash over me until I felt like I was lifting right off of the chair. It took a lot of discipline to return my focus back to my meditation.

After several months of attempting to meditate twice a day, I gradually fell into a routine I thought was acceptable. I would sit quietly and begin to feel a sense of peace envelop my body. I always knew when I was doing this correctly because I would sneeze one or more times at the beginning of the session. This told me physiological changes were taking place in my body, just as the book said would happen.

I had been reading the book and following its instructions a chapter at a time, as it had suggested, and was surprised at what the next chapter suggested. The book was now recommending that the meditations be extended for longer and longer periods of time — up to a day at this point. I did not know where I would find the time for this, and decided to read even further ahead to see what else was in store for me.

It got worse. The next chapters contained techniques for really extended meditations for weeks at a time. This required isolation and assistants who would bring you food and water, as well as techniques for eating and drinking the minimum amount for survival without breaking the meditative trance. The chapters after that dealt with techniques for such esoteric procedures as projecting one's self out of one's body, generating heat from the body so that one could survive extreme cold, and focusing power from an unknown source into the body in order to perform super-human feats. "I really have my work cut out for me," I laughed at the time.

*

The foundation was never allowed to go into Tibet. It was because of the political unrest, the Chinese government had said. We were in danger of being harmed by underground counterrevolutionary forces, they claimed, or even by counter-counter-revolutionaries. The Party members liked to think of themselves as the glorious revolutionaries, even though they had been in power for the better part of a century. Dissident parties were labeled as counter-revolutionaries and squashed as quickly as possible. The real danger of going into Tibet was not to us but to the Party, in that we might learn what was really going on in an occupied country and report it back to the rest of the world.

Mongolia, however, was open to us. That country had won its independence from China in 1921 and had attempted to chart its own course since then. This was difficult because of its involvement with both China and the USSR. China was its main trading partner at this time, buying up to sixty percent of all of Mongolia's exports. We typically did not go into Mongolia because the Chinese Ministry of Agriculture considered Mongolia to be its private domain and had not asked for our help. Also much of the population was nomadic and did very little farming on its own. The Chinese, however, did a significant amount of farming on a large commercial scale, but this was not the size of farm for which the foundation was set up to work.

We went to Mongolia because a large group of nomads had reported a strange epidemic that was hobbling their horses. The Mongols were very dependent on their horses and were in a panic about the disease. The Mongolian government asked the foundation to evaluate the situation because we were close, mobile, and had veterinarians in our animal husbandry division. I went because I had never seen Mongolia.

Mongolia was endless golden grassland under an inverted bowl of blue sky. These particular nomads whom we had come to help had the appearance of having been in this area for a while. The grass had been closely grazed by their horses, goats and sheep. They had given up traveling and had been staying close to a local town so that they could trade hides and meat for wheat, vegetables, and factory-made goods. The land here was eroded from industrialization and high impact farming.

The veterinarians quickly determined that the horses had laminitis, a painful separation of the layers of a horse's hooves, often resulting in the inability of the horse to walk. The laminitis was caused by allowing the horses to graze on piles of discarded beet tops from one of the commercial canneries. The prognosis was that if the horses were removed to their normal pasturage in the open grasslands, they would soon recover. At this news, the Mongols called for a great feast in our honor.

They slaughtered a goat, and we had boiled goat meat, dumplings with innards and onions, cabbage salad, and salted tea with mutton fat. We drank fermented mare's milk long into the night as we sat around a bonfire that threw streams of sparks into the vaulted sky. We were entertained by an inimitable form of singing from the Mongolian women, and by tales of adventure, heroism and slapstick from the Mongolian men. Among these tales were stories of Chenresig.

The Mongolians are cousins to the Tibetans, have a shared religious belief, and do a limited amount of trading with them. Whether the Chinese intentionally allowed this, I did not know. Under Chinese rule, Mongolia had been officially atheistic. Now, technically under their own rule, there was a resurgence of Tibetan Buddhism in Mongolia, and it was not unusual to find an occasional Mongol who had made one or more trips into Tibet.

The stories of Chenresig came primarily from Tibet; the Mongols had never actually seen him. One man said he had heard that Chenresig had been sighted in Mongolia near Dalandzadagad. Someone else named another town.

After listening for a while about this being who could take the form of animals, heal the sick, and disappear at will, I began to wonder if this was the same being that I had heard called Chamba. I asked if Chenresig was the same person who the Chinese thought to be the sixth Buddha. Almost in unison, all the men frowned, crossed their arms and looked thoughtfully into the fire. Then one of them said something that sounded like a question. A loud response followed, and then they all began to argue in Mongolian. These men had been speaking primarily in Mandarin until now so that we visitors could join in. Their Chinese was broken, spotty, and highly accented, and the men would fall back on Mongolian when excited. I was having trouble following the discussion and I asked one of the women if she could help me understand. "Did I say something wrong?" I asked.

"They are discussing whether it is possible that it is a Buddha, rather than a Bodhisattva that walks the land," She explained. "Some are arguing that there is no difference because Chenresig can operate in the realm of Hell just as the sixth Buddha does."

"The realm of Hell?"

"Yes, there are six realms, and six Buddhas who work in those realms. Surely you know the six-syllable mantra?"

"No. I'm sorry."

One of the men had been listening to us and started to explain, "It is Chenresig's mantra, 'auhm mahnay pehmay hoong'."

"Oh, 'om mani padme hum!" I exclaimed, "Kwan Yin!" They looked puzzled. "That is Kwan Yin's mantra. Surely you have heard the Chinese speak of Kwan Yin."

"The Han are soulless animals," another man interjected. "They have no religion."

This started another round of drunken arguing about whether animals had souls. The consensus was yes, and the man who made the remark apologized for his insensitivity to animals but not for his insult to the Han Chinese. The argument took off on the tack of whether humanity's insensitivity toward animals might be the reason why Chenresig and/or the sixth Buddha had come.

One argument led to another until nearly dawn. My translator friends tried to keep me abreast of the debates, but there were too many at once, and the mare's milk was having an effect on me. I left the fire for a while and walked off into the darkness. Looking back at the men sitting around the fire, dressed in skins and carrying gigantic knives in their belts, it was hard to imagine them having such serious discussions about religion, compassion, and whether animals were sentient beings. I had heard more about religion in one evening in Mongolia than I had heard in the whole length of my stay in China. Kwan Yin was the Chinese goddess of compassion, but all that I knew about her came from my childhood in Hawaii, not from living in China. Kwan Yin — the one who hears the cries of the world — came into the world time after time to fulfill a vow to save all sentient beings. I took a vow myself to learn more about Kwan Yin the next time I went back to Hawaii, and that is how I began thinking about going home.

*

I did not go back to Hawaii right away. One thing after another kept me in China. There had been a massive crop failure at one of "our" villages, and the M of A (Ministry of Agriculture), angry about our trip into Mongolia, was hoping to prove that the techniques we had taught the villagers were the cause of the failure. We spent months researching the disaster, and eventually were able to prove that it was caused by fertilizer that had been trucked in by the M of A in order to show that they could help the villagers more than outsiders could. Unfortunately, the fertilizer was transported in containers that had previously held broad-band herbicides, and this tainted fertilizer had stunted the crops, to the great embarrassment of the M of A.

This turned out to be a no-win situation for us, as the M of A, having lost face, called its Party friends in Beijing and made some very harsh accusations against us. I had to go to Beijing, taking the foundation's books, and spend additional wasted months proving we were not selling village produce on the black market and keeping the money for ourselves.

Much of this time was spent waiting in my hotel room for soldiers to be sent to summon me to appear at the hearings. I used this free time to practice my meditation techniques, and began to feel as if I was making some progress.

On weekends I went out into the city, almost as much to get away from the phone as to see the sights. I had made the mistakes of first telling my parents that I was thinking of coming home, and second, that I was under investigation by the Chinese government. Now I got a phone call every day from them. They wanted to remind me to be careful. They wanted to know how the investigation was going. When was I coming home? They even asked if I had met any nice Chinese boys in Beijing, as if I could smuggle one out of the country in my luggage.

Out in the city, there was tension and expectation in the air. In the restaurants, people whispered excitedly to each other and glanced furtively over their shoulders to make sure they were not heard. But they were heard. I, who had no one to whisper with, could only listen. Everywhere I went in Beijing I heard the low voices speaking of Chang Da Wai. Without seeing the words written down, it is impossible to know what they meant exactly. However, I guessed from the pronunciation that the meaning was Mature Foreigner—of course I had guessed wrong. As you know, Chinese dialects are difficult even for the Chinese, and it is not unusual to see people conversing entirely by pencil and paper, as the pictographs, or ideograms, are much easier to understand than the spoken word. Therefore, not having seen anything written, I could do no more than guess at what I was hearing.

Even though the entire city seemed to be talking of nothing else, I never saw the ideograms of this name so that I could make a more accurate translation, because there was nothing in the newspapers and nothing on the television about Chang Da Wai. This was impressive in itself, because the government, by refusing to openly acknowledge this phenomenon, had disclosed their own quaking fear of it. After my outings, I would return to my room, followed by my ever-present guard, and there I would ponder the stories about Chang Da Wai.

That night I had a dream, and later, a personally meaningful dream mission. I make a distinction between dreams and dream missions because they have a different feel to them. Outside of the fact that I never knew why or how I found myself where I did in dream missions, they seemed to be purposeful, and there seemed to be free will on my part. Dreams have a feel like I am being blown about in an irresistible psychic wind. In my dream I went back to the cliff where I saw the seated figure in the moonlight. The pine trees were there, looming in the darkness, but the person of my dream was gone. I floated over the cliffs and saw the shadowy valley below and more cliffs across the way. Back at the edge of the forest, there was a cave, and in the cave was a small wooden table accompanied by two crude chairs. On the table was a bowl made from a human skull, and a flute made from a thigh bone. Water dripped from the cave ceiling into the bowl and overflowed onto the table. "Xiao Chen",

曉 晨

had been painted on the cave wall. The wind blew through the pines and across the cave entrance, making the sound "HOOONNG".

Then, as if called back to work, I was on a mission. I found myself in a hospital room. The sun was streaming in a window. On the bed, his arms just beginning to reach out to me, and staring at me as if he could surely see me, was my father. He was working his mouth, but no sound was coming out. Two nurses rushed over and laid him back on his pillow, but he continued to stare and to hold one hand up as if pointing at me.

Suddenly, there was a pounding on my hotel room door. I got out of bed, slipped on a gown, and opened the door to find a Chinese soldier who had been sent to take me to that morning's hearing. I told him I had to make a phone call first — that my father might be dying — but he was insistent that I call no one. I was to get dressed and go directly to the hearing.

At the hearing, I answered the questions as best I could, but I was distracted, worrying about my father, and probably looked guilty as charged. I was not worried that my father would die. I no longer had any fear of death for me or anyone close to me. But my father looked to be in pain and afraid; and suffering is still suffering.

I had been patient through these proceedings up until today, but I was becoming irritated at the injustice of the whole thing. I had done nothing but help this government. I had been falsely accused and I was sure they knew that already. And now I had been refused a phone call to check on a dying parent.

As the hearing seemed to be drawing to a close that morning, I asked to be allowed to address the judges. I told them I had reason to believe my father was near death and that I would like for them to wrap up these hearings as I had every intention of leaving the country very soon. They looked alarmed and said the hearings were not close to being finished and that I would be placed under house arrest to make sure I did not leave the country or make any further phone calls.

To my surprise, one of the judges then held up the book on meditation that I had found in the empty farm house. I realized with dismay that the police had gone through my personal belongings and had found what they considered to be contraband.

"Does this belong to you?" the judge asked me.

"Yes." There was no point in lying about this.

"Did you bring this into China?"

The implications of the question were enormous. I quickly tried to analyze the potential results of any answer I gave. If I said I had brought the book into the country, then I would be guilty of breaking Chinese law that forbade the import of articles that could be used to incite the populous against the government. If I said I had found the book in the farm house, then the poor family that had lived there would be in even more trouble than they were now. "No," I answered truthfully.

"Then where did you get it?"

"I bought it at a bookstore."

"Where is this bookstore?"

"I do not remember."

"There is no bookstore in China that would openly sell such a book. I think you are lying."

"I do not see what difference it makes where I got it."

"This book was written by a Chinese person for Chinese people to read. Its purpose is to weaken the government. It is full of lies that delude the citizens. It creates wrong thinking and wrong action that is counter to the goals of the republic. Now that we know you are lying about this book, all of your actions are suspect."

"I think I need to call the U.S. Embassy."

"Enemies of the state are not allowed to have communications."

"I am not an enemy of the state!" I exclaimed.

"It is a constant battle for this government to maintain right thinking in the minds of our citizens. Many of them are in prison already for distributing literature and propaganda such as this. If our own citizens are imprisoned for such crimes, how should we look upon you who are not even from this country, and whose parents abandoned it for another?"

"I need to speak to a lawyer."

"There will be no lawyers. This is a crime against the state. There is no legal defense."

"But what about my father? I think he is dying! I need to call him."

"No phone calls."

I had never completely conquered the bad temper of my youth, and it picked this unlucky time to boil over. I told them that the trial was a sham, and that they knew it. They angrily ordered me to be quiet. I demanded that they take me to the American consulate, which they denied again with increasing agitation. They ordered the guards to take me to jail immediately. I then said that they were the real criminals, and that if there was any justice in China, they would be the ones behind bars. One of the guards grabbed my arm. I swore at the judges in Mandarin and called them embezzlers, bullies, liars, and thieves. Then I tore myself away from the guard, turned over the table where I had been sitting, breaking the water pitcher, and making a big mess of wet papers on the floor. "You are the traitors!" I yelled. "You are the enemies of the state."

I promptly found myself pinned on the floor by two guards, handcuffed, gagged and under arrest. I was then quickly dragged off to a Chinese jail cell as I yelled muffled insults after me in Mandarin.

Chapter 2 – Of Imprisonment and the Source of Power.

I remember saying, as they dragged me from the courtroom, that the whole glorious Communist Party was nothing but a fraud and a front for thugs and gangsters. This is probably why they did not keep me in jail and continue with the hearings, but instead transferred me to a prison after a couple of days. I was lucky that they did not execute me; they regularly executed their own citizens for making such statements. I was a U.S. citizen, however, and would have normally been put on the next plane out of the country for saying what I had said, except that in my case, they thought that I actually was up to something seditious, and they did not trust me out of their sight. My statements had only revealed, they thought, my truly treacherous nature that I had tried to hide until then.

I never heard any charges, not even of breaking a government owned water pitcher. I was never told what their intentions were. I never received any communication from the outside. Instead, I was shackled and taken off on a two-day ride in the back of a panel truck with wooden seats, and soon deposited into a cesspool of a prison. The prison was downwind from a swamp, but the smell of rotted vegetation and soured water, was like a zephyr from a spring meadow compared to the smell of the prison itself. The prison literally, and without exaggeration, smelled like an open sewer.

I did not feel remorse for my actions; I felt hatred and fury, and everything about the prison seemed designed to infuriate me more. The beds were wooden planks with thin straw mattresses, which were heavily infested with fleas and bed-bugs. The toilets were holes in the floor, and they frequently overflowed, covering the whole cell floor with fecal matter. For clothing, I was given a gray shift with an old brown stain around the collar. I hated to think what had happened to the previous owner. I was also given boots that were made entirely of felt, which soaked up the sewage on the floor and kept it constantly on one's feet until they began to rot and stink on their own.

The inmates were a cross section of China and Tibet. There were peasants, students, working-class women, teachers, prostitutes and nuns. The prisoners were all women, but the guards were all brutal and sadistic men. They bullied the women and talked openly about how the women looked. They would say that this one looked like a pig and that one looked like a cow; this one had only a few more good times left in her, but that one with the black eye was especially pleasing last night. The prostitutes among the prisoners probably would have gladly traded sex for cigarettes, but they were only beaten. The nuns, however, were raped regularly.

It was autumn when I was sent to the prison. As the year advanced, it became colder and colder until the swamp froze over and quit stinking. We were given quilted, feather-stuffed coats to wear, but they had seen so much usage that we continually had to stuff the feathers back into the rips and tears. The gashes in the fabric served the useful purpose of giving the fleas a warm place to breed.

The prison was heated by steam pipes, which banged and whined all through the night. However, the noise helped to drown out the sound of sobbing and weeping, some of which was mine. But when the steam pipes quit working was when we learned to appreciate them. This happened about once a week. Then it would become so cold that I would often have doubts that I would see morning. It would get so cold that the feces and urine which had not been able to go down the frozen pipes would freeze on the floor and had to be chipped up by hand in the morning and hauled out in buckets instead of hosed away in the usual manner. Of course the prisoners did this work, and it was the only time that the guards stayed well clear of us.

To save electricity, the lights were turned off one hour after sunset. Since the days were very short in winter, this made for very long nights. Even when the steam pipes were working, I think that the temperature must have been just above freezing. I spent the dark hours in a fetal position on my cot, with my coat on and my stinking shoes tucked into my wool blanket, which would not quite stretch to cover my head. I lay there and shivered and thought about how much I hated this prison, this government, the guards, the judges, maybe even the whole damn country. Sometimes, on nights when I did not cry myself to sleep, I cursed China in a constant stream until the first light of day.

All of this was not the worst, though. The worst was that my dream missions stopped. I had not had a dream mission since the day I turned the table over. The loss of my dream missions, the feelings of abandonment, isolation, and insufficiency sent me into a spiral of despair that I had never experienced before. And I blamed myself; my feelings of anger and despair, and other negative emotions, were at the heart of my problem, I knew. Yet I could not help the way I felt. I tried not to be afraid, or angry, or depressed, but it was a trap I could not climb out of. This was the real reason why I cried at night.

Spring eventually came and the swamp thawed and began mixing its relatively clean smelling stench with our foul one again. Our toilets began to flow with their old irregularity. At least in the winter, the drains froze and so could not back up onto the floor.

With the warmer weather, the guards stepped up the beatings and the raping. The mutton fat that we were served for supper began to show maggots again, and the frogs woke up in the swamp and began to sing their tireless love songs.

The racket from the swamp kept me up at night. The constant honking made me think that I would go mad. I finally had to give up trying to sleep, and sat on my bunk in a cross-legged fashion with my back against the concrete wall. I had not meditated since being imprisoned, but now it seemed the only way to keep my sanity. Whatever mantra I would start out with, eventually the sound of the frogs overrode it, and their mantra became my mantra.

One morning, after I had been attempting to meditate all night long, the sky began to lighten and I sighed to myself and thought, "What a life". And then I laughed out loud at myself. My food was terrible; I had sores that would not heal; I lived in filth and fear and degradation, yet I sat here disgusted because the frogs had kept me up all night. People all over China complained about the frogs in the springtime. And then, unbidden, and seemingly from nowhere, came the thought, "What a *wonderful* life." It was as if something had changed in me and I thought, "What a wonderful world this is. Thank you, God, whatever you are, for this wonderful world and this wonderful life." If you find it amazing that I could think such a thing in my situation, I was amazed at my own thoughts. I, for whom the best that could be hoped for in this day was that there might be a bit of rotten meat attached to the maggoty fat in my next meal, thought that this was a wonderful life — but it was true — I did think it. I cried again, but not in despair — in joy! I no longer felt the hatred that had filled me for so long. I no longer felt angry at the benighted men who had put me here and kept me here. I felt that I had made a breakthrough and had seen past these prison walls and into the heart of the universe. How many people had lived through these experiences and seen what I had seen? What an opportunity I had in this prison. I was in the deepest pit of hell and there were souls here who needed my help. What better job in the universe then that God would send you to hell to help the residents?

During the course of the day, depending on the weather, we would be allowed to spend some free time in either an external courtyard, or a large internal court that provided access to the individual cells. So inwardly had I been turned with my anger and hatred that I had never really spoken much to the other women before, but now I took an interest in them, and when we were given our free time, I asked them about themselves, and why they were in prison. Their crimes were political, mostly. Even the ones who had committed real crimes were in prison for inadequate bribes rather than the crimes themselves. Many of the other women had committed the same crime as I had — they had spoken out against some injustice perpetrated by the government on the defenseless—sometimes themselves, sometimes someone else.

My natural talent for organization began to express itself over the next few months, and we began to think as a group, everybody contributing the ideas they had, but before now, had no one to tell. We listed things that we needed to make our lives better. We could conceive of nothing that we owned that the guards would want except our bodies. However, the professionals among us said they would be willing to barter themselves if the guard's interest could be captured. As the guards really seemed more interested in brutalizing women than in just having recreational sex, we still saw no way out of our dilemma, until one day the situation corrected itself.

It had never occurred to any of us that there was anything that we could do about the brutality and abuse, but one day it came to an end in a surprising way. One of the guards handed his rifle to another guard and headed toward us in the courtyard. He had the look of a predator about to cull his prey from the herd. His favorite nun knew from his approach that she was about to be sexually assaulted once more and fell to the ground, hugging her knees, moaning and rocking. As the guard approached us, I stepped in front of him and said, "No more!"

He laughed and pulled his bayonet out of its scabbard. "You do not know who you are talking to," he said, brandishing the long knife at me. "I can gut you in two seconds and leave you holding your entrails in your hands."

"And you do not know who *you* are talking to, that I would let you do it," I heard myself say as I stood my ground.

Even the most atheistic Chinese can be extremely superstitious. They may not believe in gods, but they may still believe in demons and angry ghosts. Looking for fear in me, he found it in himself instead. His grin faded. He licked his lips, and cut his eyes around the courtyard. He turned and went back to the other guard, who apparently said the wrong thing to him. The first guard snatched his rifle back and placed the tip of his bayonet under the chin of the second guard, who went pale and backed hurriedly away.

I turned around to see that all of the rest of the women had stayed where they were and had not fled. Together, we were a formidable lot, and perhaps after all, the guard realized that he could not take us all. Things might still have gone bad for us, and especially for me, however, except that one of the bolder prostitutes followed the angry guard and asked flirtatiously for a cigarette. She said that she had always admired his strength and fearlessness above that of the other guards, and now that she saw how respectful he was toward women, she really wanted to get to know him better. That was how commerce between the women and the guards began.

After that, the beatings stopped. Those women who did not want sex, did not have sex, and those women who did, or at least were willing, got something in return. The items for which the willing bartered were redistributed to the women who most needed them or who could best put them to use. We got new shoes for the women whose shoes had rotted off their feet. We got needles and thread and gave them to the women who could repair our clothes. We got simple textbooks, and some women read to us for entertainment, or taught other women how to read. We even got some cheap musical instruments—toys, mainly, for those who could play them. The food improved, and life was infinitely better. But still we were in prison. Outside, it was summer; the birds sang and the swamp stank with life. I would have given nearly anything for a walk in that malodorous swamp.

The dream missions were still not there for me, and so I meditated during most of the night, especially the early morning part. The nun who I had saved had taken to staying close to me and paid a lot of attention to my activities. One morning, she asked me why I only used the last syllable of the six-syllable mantra. I did not know what she was referring to.

"Hoonng," she said.

I did not know that this sound had been my mantra or that I had been saying it out loud. I asked her if she knew the meaning of the six-syllable mantra. In rough terms, this is what she explained to me:

The mantra does not have a meaning in the normal sense. It is a series of six purified sounds. Each sound works to cleanse our souls of certain attachments — attachments being the source of sorrow and the things that keep us on the wheel of life and death. The six different classes of attachments are associated with six different realms in the Buddhist belief. There is the realm of the gods, the realm of the jealous gods (I took this to mean demons), the realm of human beings, the realm of animals, the realm of hungry ghosts (possibly the dead who had not been able to leave the world behind), and the realm of hell. The six classes of attachments associated with these realms are bliss and pride (gods), jealousy and lust for entertainment (jealous gods), passion and desire (human), stupidity and prejudice (animal), poverty and possessiveness (hungry ghosts), and aggression and hatred (hell). According to my new friend, I had been chanting the sound for the release of hatred.

That night I paid attention to my meditation, and noticed that as I began to slip into a meditative trance I heard the sound of the frogs in the swamp going: hoonng . . .hoonng . . .hoonng. For months, I now realized, the frogs had been influencing my meditation; their mantra had become my mantra, and the mantra was the sound for the release of hatred. Is this why I had forgotten hatred and anger? I cannot say. Perhaps it was just the act of meditating, or perhaps these negative emotions had finally just burned themselves out.

Time passed easier in this better prison that we had created for ourselves. Yet I began to give up hope of getting out. I assumed, and later discovered to be true, that neither my friends, nor my family, nor the United States government had been able to make any headway with the Chinese. Besides my natural stubbornness and disobedience, the Chinese government also saw me as a real threat. However, if I was in a tight spot, so were they. They couldn't have me executed without creating an international incident, and they couldn't let me go and still be able to rest easy. They may have prayed for a solution as much as I did. I don't know if the Party's prayers were answered; mine certainly weren't — or else they were and the answer was "No." Soon I began to pray for God to send me the strength and the patience to live out my life in prison. There is an old saying in China that if you ask the gods for strength, they will give you a heavy burden to carry, and if you ask for patience, they will make you wait a long time for it. Instead of strength and patience, I got Chenresig.

*

Summer turned into fall. We had established a good working relationship with the guards, who sometimes even brought us mending to do, or boots that needed polishing. In return for our labor they gave us things from the outside world, such as extra fabric or feathers for stuffing coats and pillows. We were even allowed to keep our cells open so that we were free to come and go through the inner court and visit each other at will.

Most people not only need leaders, they actually want them. They prefer good leaders, but will settle for bad ones. If there are no leaders, eventually one will emerge to fill the vacuum. It began to appear that I was the chosen leader of this group of women. Having performed the role of the leader of the foundation for a number of years, I felt that I could pretend to be a leader again for their sake. Almost all decisions began to be referred to me.

I made several changes in the prison. One of which was to partition off some of the cells with blankets so that women could entertain the guards in privacy. This resulted in guards sometimes bringing rice wine or tea, and sometimes not even having sex. I told the other women, that if this happened, the information was not to be shared with the other guards; otherwise the guards would feel compelled to go back to the brutish sex-only encounters for the sake of their reputations.

All of us had shared our stories over the months. Many of the Chinese women had heard of me and my work with the foundation, and wanted to call me Dong Shi, "The Director". I told them that they could call me Xiao Chen, as I was not a director any longer. They wanted to know my family name. I told them my family was Bang. None of them knew any families by that name, although one of them had heard stories of an ancient Bang family. They thought it was a strange name. The literal meaning is "society". They made a joke that I was Dawn and they were society. They said I was the dawn of society. They laughed hysterically at this because of our situation. No one in our collective memory had ever left this prison alive; we were trading sex and shoeshines for food and clothing, yet we found a way to laugh at the ridiculousness of our circumstances.

The Tibetan women insisted on calling me Pasang Lhamo, after a fierce protector goddess in Tibetan mythology. They later shortened this to Lhamo, "Goddess", although I would have preferred the somewhat less glamorous "Pasang", which meant "Beautiful". Most of the nuns were Tibetan. My new best friend had been named Tsering by her parents who had wished her long life, but the other Tibetan women called her Tsitsi, "mouse", because, though pretty and delicate, she was excruciatingly shy and modest. Tsering had no idea why she was in prison. She insisted that she had never harmed anyone in word or deed.

Tsering went everywhere that I went and sought out things to do for me. If the sewer overflowed into the cells, she insisted on cleaning mine. It was so that I could have more time for ideas, she said. As the days got colder and darker, she moved her cot into my cell, and on the especially cold nights, we shared our blankets and huddled together for warmth.

Tsering became the daughter that I had never had. She wanted me to teach her about courage and how it was that I was able to stand up to the guard the way I did. I told her that I did not know that I was going to do what I did, and that afterwards, I had to sit down quickly or my knees would have buckled. Courage was simply the realization that I would not be able to live with myself any longer if I stood by and did nothing. She wanted me to teach her about spiritual things, but I told her that I knew nothing about the spiritual. She insisted that she could see in me a great wisdom, and that someday, perhaps, when I thought that she was worthy, that I would share it with her.

After several days of internal debate, I decided to tell Tsering about my dream missions. "I only know one little thing that you may not know," I told her. "I know what happens to you right after you die." She listened intently to the stories of my missions, and was saddened to hear that I no longer went on them.

"Truly, you will be a bodhisattva someday," she said. "You hear the cries of the world and cannot turn away."

"I am a pretty miserable bodhisattva," I replied.

"We are all children before we are adults," she said. She put her hand over her mouth in shock. "I am sorry! I do not mean to teach the teacher."

I laughed and gave her a hug. "Tsering, you are much wiser than I am. I don't know how I would make it here without you."

"Lhamo," she said, holding my hand and looking into my eyes, "It is I who would not be alive without you."

Winter this year was even colder than the year before. One night, when the steam heat had gone out, and we were huddled shivering beneath our blankets, Tsering said between chattering teeth, "I heard once of a meditation to stay warm. I wish I knew it now."

"I had a book once that told how to do that," I said, trying to keep the conversation going so that we would not think about how cold we were. "I studied it but never tried it."

"You should try it now," Tsering said. "You should try the meditation. It is how the monks stay warm in the mountains, and not just the Buddhist ones, but the Taoist ones as well, or so I have heard."

"How could such a thing be possible? Besides, the book said it was an advanced technique, and I never learned the previous lessons."

"It would be worth a try," Tsering said. "If you remember what the book said, you could teach me, and we could both stay warm. Maybe you could teach everyone. Please try to remember, Lhamo. If it works, you could save lives this winter."

I tried to remember what the book had said so I could convey that information to Tsering. The way that I remembered the instructions was that there were certain thoughts that one was to focus on that would allow one to become a conduit for the energy of the universe. The concepts behind this were that the world of matter proceeded from the world of energy, which proceeded from the world of consciousness. The spirit — the soul — existed in all worlds simultaneously, but was rooted in the realm of consciousness and could direct and channel the infinite source of energy into the world of matter if only it knew that it could. Energy was a transient form of consciousness, according to the book, and consciousness, being infinite, could make itself an inexhaustible source of energy. Having relayed all that I knew on the subject to Tsering, we sat cross-legged on my cot with the blankets making a tent over us, and I began to meditate. I focused on the ideas that I had just described, and . . .

The next thing that I knew, it was morning and the breakfast gong was ringing to tell us that our frozen wheat porridge was ready. "Pasang Lhamo!" Tsering exclaimed when she saw that my eyes were open. "It was wonderful! I was not able to do it, but you did it! You kept us both warm all night long!" I had not been aware that I had done anything, but I certainly wasn't cold. Neither of us was shivering, as we would normally be doing after a typical winter night in that prison.

We decided that we would definitely try it again the next night. We invited the other women to join us in the parlor, as we called the cell that had been partitioned for entertaining the guards. The single cell was not large enough for all of us, so we encompassed the adjoining cells with our blanket walls. Even then it was crowded, but the next morning, everyone was relatively warm and happy. As it turned out, I really had not generated enough heat to keep everyone comfortable, but it was better than no heat at all, and, as the days and weeks passed, everyone said that I was getting better and better at the job. This was the way we spent the rest of the cold winter nights that year, and gradually, I began to hear the voices of the world again.

I could not tell you where I was during these meditations. I seemed to be everywhere. I seemed to be aware of many things at once; my position in the cell, and the location of the furnishings, and the cell's location in the prison. Even though my eyes were shut during meditation, I could "see" the women around me, wondering at the warmth coming from my body. If I turned my focus that way, I could also "see" the guards playing mah-jongg in their heated room. At first the seeing was only a sense of awareness, but it gradually became almost a second sight. My sense of sight was crude at first, and lacked detail. It was as if everything was awash in silvery moonlight — without contrast or color — and except for events that happened later, could easily have been imagination and memory working together.

My awareness of my surroundings increased through the winter. Eventually, I could see outside the prison walls, and while the women in the prison crowded around and held their hands on my body, absorbing my warmth, I had an awareness of being over the prison — hovering over it and looking down on it. I could see the surrounding villages, and at the same time, I could see if a guard was getting up to come into our area, and I would wake up and we would all scatter.

One night in spring, I was bobbing around over the prison like a tethered balloon when I became aware of another presence. The presence was not nearby, but beyond the far curvature of the earth. Abruptly, as if I was unexpectedly looking through a giant telescope, I saw, hovering over a city alive with lights and teeming with people, a colossal flying whale. Standing on the back of the whale was a man who turned and looked right at me!

"Chenresig!" I heard Tsering gasp. I opened my eyes, and saw what had made her gasp; the man who I had seen standing on the back of the leviathan was right in front of me and the women were falling back, holding their hands up as shields.

This man was a giant himself, worthy of riding a leviathan. He was fifteen feet tall, if I had to guess. He had a white vest and pants and a red sash, but his skin was blue — every shade of blue — with electric blue lightning bolts firing through the length of his body and flashing visibly through the blue skin of his massive chest. Sparks showered from his hair as he looked down on us. There was a visible aura around him like wings of fire and lightning. He reached out his hand to me, and I seemed to see the after images of his hand's movement in my mind so that it was like a thousand hands were reaching out to me. His arms were muscled and big as trees, and each of his fingers was as large as my wrist. I was aware of the other women gasping "Chenresig," and prostrating themselves on the floor.

His voice boomed throughout the court until I thought the walls might crumble. "The world is beautiful out there," he said. "Why are you in here?"

I could only stare in quaking disbelief.

"Why do you let these other women suffer here? Take them and let us go. Let us all go out into the night and watch the stars spin through the heavens until dawn chases the night away."

The guards came running into the court, holding their rifles ready to fire, but when they saw Chenresig, they dropped their weapons and fell on the floor as the women had. I was the only one left upright to look at this amazing vision, but it was only because I was too petrified to move. I could not believe that I was seeing this — this genie, yet there he was. It was not possible. Had the world gone mad or had I?

Chenresig turned and looked at the guards and his eyes seemed to shoot fire. "Why are these women here?" he thundered. The guards quaked in fear and couldn't speak. Some slobbered like mad dogs; others rolled their eyes and fainted. "Do you know who these women are?" His voice was like the roar of a typhoon. He did not wait for an answer. "These are my children!" Each syllable was a detonation that rang my head like a gong. "Open these doors and let them leave!" It was an avalanche of sound and I thought my skull would split under the pressure. I felt that I was literally drowning in the presence of this being. I could not think. I could barely see. My tongue was thick; my face felt swollen, and a smell of incense clogged my nostrils. Chenresig had besieged my senses. "Hurry!" he roared. "Do not make me angry!"

I do not know how any guards managed to make their legs work long enough to get to the main doors and unlock them, but the doors were opened faster than I would have thought humanly possible.

Chenresig ordered the guards to be gone from his sight and he began to walk through the open doors, and we followed instinctively as if we were hypnotized. He was much too tall to walk through the doors and gates without bending, but he didn't stoop; he just passed right through the arches and ceilings as if they were clouds in the air. He led us deep into the swamp and then was gone like a dream. But it was no dream. We were outside! The prison where we had spent so many months was not even visible behind us, though the alarms and shouting could be clearly heard through the trees.

*

"Where did Chenresig go?
"That was not Chenresig. Chenresig has white skin."
"That was his angry aspect."

"No! It was Kwan Yin."

"Kwan Yin is a woman."

"Kwan Yin can look like whatever she wants to look like."

"So can Chenresig."

"It was Avalokiteshvara."

"They are all the same bodhisattva."

"Bodhisattvas are compassionate, not violent."

"Well, he didn't kill anybody."

"I am not so sure."

"They can look like anything. Nobody knows what bodhisattvas look like."

"It was the sixth Buddha — the hell Buddha."

"The sixth Buddha gets rid of anger. He is not angry himself."

"I think it was Bai-I. Bai-I has white clothes."

"It was Senju. He had a thousand arms. Did you see?"

"Chenresig also has a thousand arms."

"Lhamo, what do we do now?" Tsering was asking me.

"Everybody be quiet!" I said. "The guards are coming! Do you want to go back to prison?" They all became quiet and watched me as I thought about what to do. We really had little choice. Chenresig, or whoever that blue giant was, had led us into the swamp and there was no turning back. I was looking down in dejection while I tried to come up with a better plan, and I noticed something that made me feel better about going into the swamp. "Look at the ground," I pointed down. "We are not leaving footprints." Our soft boots were not leaving any imprints except where many of us had walked or where the ground was very soft. "We must spread out and go into the swamp in a wide band so that we do not damage the earth and leave a trail. The men are heavy and will sink in the soft ground and their dogs will not have a single trail to follow, but many, and may become confused. We can flee much faster than they can follow. Also, our clothes are already gray like these tree trunks; we may fade into the swamp just like Chenresig."

"That is why he led us here," someone said.

I nodded. "That is very likely."

"Which way shall we go?"

Having seen the swamp and the surrounding land from a height, I probably knew the terrain better than the guards themselves. "There is a village to the south. Everyone must go to the village. The villagers will hide us."

"No! They will turn us in!"

"I don't think so," I said. "I know this village. You must tell them that you are with 'Dong Shi'. But, just to be safe, hide outside the village until I can talk to the leaders."

"What if we get lost in the swamp?"

"Listen, everyone," I said. "You are all having good ideas, but time is running out. Here is what we must do. When we leave this spot, you must spread out as far as you can without losing sight of that person next to you who is closer to me. I will be in the middle. As the sun begins to set, we will gather back together. Before you come in to me, you must wait for those who are further out so that they will not get lost. We will all be okay if we work together. You must be quiet unless there is an emergency. Try to step on solid ground. Rub this dirt on your face and arms. Now go! Do not stop for anything except each other. Run fast like the deer! Go! Go! Go!"

They were scared, and nobody wanted to be the furthest out, but some of the braver ones finally took off into the swamp, the others quickly following their example. I felt that we had a very good chance of success. The guards would be looking for a blue giant and hoping not to find one; this would probably slow them down considerably. In my mind's eye, I saw them arriving at the area we had trampled, and then, seeing no track or trail to follow, returning to the prison to wait for reinforcements, better trackers, more dogs.

Fortunately, there was plenty of dry ground in the swamp. The gray leaf litter on the ground showed that this low area was typically under water after a rain. Happily for us, there had been no rain recently, so the swamp at this time was simply a lowland forest with many streams, rivulets and long marshy pools, which were separated by low ridges and mounds. In the southern part of the country, the trees would have been cut down and rice would be planted. Here in the north, where rice couldn't grow, this wet land had no particular value.

The trees were large and, at first, the going was swift through the large open spaces. We soon grew tired, however, from hopping from mound to mound and weaving and picking through the frequent patches of briars. Sometimes we found berries along the way and we ate what we could grab as we passed by. I had asked the other women not to stop and so I would not either. Tsering would not spread out to the visual limit like the other women. She insisted on staying close by me and would go no further than five feet away.

After a couple of hours, I noticed that I no longer heard any sounds behind us. I suddenly felt quite safe. This huge swamp, whose smell I had hated during the first months of imprisonment, had helped me in many and diverse ways, and now seemed like my best friend. We continued on our way until the light began to fade. I gently scolded the briars that clung to my clothes as I walked, demanding that I pay them some attention.

At sunset, my re-union plan began to work as I saw two groups of women converging on me from both sides. They were hungry, tired, scratched and bruised, but we had lost no one. I became their heat source again that night, and they collapsed in heaps around me, exhausted from their first day of freedom.

I half expected to see Chenresig that night, but did not, perhaps, I thought, because I really did not want to. I felt like lying low, keeping quiet and avoiding blue, ground-stomping, thundering and tree-shaking, lightening-filled giants.

The next morning, I informed the women that we were not far from the village. We would approach to the edge of the woods together, and I would go into the village myself, alone. The only problem was that I would have to cross a large open field in my gray prison uniform. One woman suggested that among them all there might be enough non-prison-standard material to put together at least enough normal-looking clothing for one woman. This they accomplished, and even found enough for Tsering so that she could accompany me.

As we walked across the newly planted field, I noticed that the villagers were using planting techniques taught by the foundation. However, when we met the first person on the road at the far side of the field, my heart sank; he did not recognize me. But on the bright side, he had not yet heard of the prison break and so did not cry out either. I asked him to take us to one of the village leaders, and was fortunate enough to dredge up the name of the mayor from memory. I told him that we had gotten lost while surveying in another village. We walked with him up to the village leader's house. It was an effort of will not to break into a run and dive into the nearest house, out of sight of those soldiers whom I knew would be here soon enough.

The mayor knew me by sight, although he was very surprised to see me. He had heard that the government was keeping me on some fabricated charges, but he thought that someone of my stature would be in a prison in Beijing. He said that we could stay in the village if we sat by the road until the prison guards came to take us back. The villagers would bring us food and water.

I told him that I was not going back, and that if he wanted to help, he could contact the foundation for me, and hide me and the other women in his village until help came. He was reluctant to do this, and became noticeably agitated at the idea. "This is not possible," he said, "The whole village could go to jail for helping you."

"Ask the other villagers if they will help us, then. Don't make this decision yourself. "

Tsering, too, was exhibiting a lot of tension. She looked nervously around, this way and that. She went quickly from window to door and back to window, peering through the holes in the paper glazing. I did not realize at the time, but Tsering had appointed herself my bodyguard. Tsering spoke up now and said to the mayor, "How can you say no to Dong Shi? Everyone knows what she has done to help this village, and other villages too. Except for Dong Shi, this village might have died long ago, and all its people scattered and begging for scraps. Is this the way you repay your benefactors? What will the mayors of the other villages think? You will bring shame on your village. You will lose all face."

The mayor said that the safety of the village was his responsibility and that he would not hide the women prisoners. The whole village could be lined up and shot if they were found out. Despite the fact that I was sympathetic to the old man's predicament, I was discouraged at his attitude. I never expected that I would have to plead so desperately for help. While I was negotiating for assistance and sweating from anxiety, a young man came into the room and sat down at the table where the old man leaned on his elbows, shaking his head.

The young man had dried fruit and bread, which Tsering and I began to stuff into our mouths. He also had two jars of cold well water, which we gulped. He had evidently been listening to our discussion. "You are just scared, Father," the younger man said to the older. "Of course we will help The Director. Everything we have is because of her. You would be the mayor of empty houses and starving rats if not for her. Even the radio that you are about to use and the batteries and solar panels that power it came from Dong Shi. You have always taught me not to let fear make decisions for us. Do what you have taught and get on the radios. Find out where the foundation is working. Tell them that we are having an emergency with our crops or make up something else. Don't mention Dong Shi, or the soldiers may hear it on their radio. I will go get the other women. Please, Dong Shi, come show me where the women are."

The old man looked abashed and left the table to use the radio, realizing that his son was right. Tsering, the young man, and I left the house so that I could point to the area along the tree line where I had left the women. Along the way, we passed the well house where the cold water must have come from. It was a Foundation style shed built under a windmill derrick. The windmill was currently disconnected from the pump as there was still plenty of moisture in the ground for the new crops. Later in the season, the windmill would be used to pump irrigation water out of the well for the crops. There was a hand pump outside the well house that could be used to get drinking water.

"The women must be very hungry," the young man said. "I will find places for them in the homes and make sure that they are fed. We will have to get them cleaned up so that they are not recognized if soldiers come around."

We arrived at the point where Tsering and I had crossed the road earlier, and I pointed to where I had left the other women. One of them saw me across the field and waved from the trees. I waved back, and the women began to emerge from the shadows and come forward. The young man started across the field to meet them halfway and tell them the plan. Before he left, he glanced back at Tsering, and I saw her blush. Tsering and I turned to go back to the mayor's house to see what the old man had found out. The timing could not have been worse.

As we went behind one of the houses, we heard the sound of automobile engines coming down the road. Tsering and I looked at each other in horror and began to run. "Lhamo," she cried, "what will we do? Where can we go?"

My mind raced. The soldiers would search every house. They would look under the houses, in the lofts, under the beds. They would probably shoot into any piles of hay or debris. I saw the well house we had passed a few minutes ago. "Into the well house," I gasped in desperation, "quickly!"

The well house was made of wood and sat on a concrete slab, which had been poured around an existing hand-dug well, generations old. Inside the low door, the original stone walls of the well rose up from the slab in the darkness. It was obvious that there was no place to hide. If anyone opened the door, they would see us. "We have got to get down in the well," I said. It was too late to look for any place else to hide.

We lowered ourselves down into the well. The water level was less than a foot below the slab. "Oh, God, it's cold," I hissed. In the dim light I could barely see that Tsering was also gasping for breath in the cold. "Tsering, I don't know what I have gotten you into. We will die if we stay in this cold water." We heard gun shots then, and we each knew what the other was thinking. The unspoken thought that we would surely die if we left there.

"Lhamo, you can make heat from your body," Tsering chattered through her teeth.

"But I have to leave my body to do it. I will drown."

"Not if I hold you up."

"OK. We have to try something."

I turned my back to Tsering and she put her arms under my armpits and locked her wrists in front of my stomach. She put her feet against one wall of the well and her shoulders against the other. I began to enter the trance. In a short time, I found myself above the village and looking down on it. I saw a pitiable sight below. There were two jeep-like vehicles in the road. Soldiers were heading across the field toward the woods. There were bodies in the field. The young man also lay dead on the new green growth near the vehicles. It appeared that he had tried to stop the soldiers from firing and had died for his intervention.

Suddenly, I was back in my body, spluttering and choking. "I am sorry, Lhamo," Tsering cried through her clinched teeth. "I could not hold you up. I am getting weaker. The water sucks the heat away faster than you can make it."

"I don't know what we will do then. I have to leave my body in order to open it as a conduit for the heat. The soldiers are still in the fields. We will have to make a run for it."

"Lhamo, we will never make it. But listen. What if you made something else the conduit for the heat? Does it have to be your body that is the conduit? Would you have to leave your body then?" She could barely get the words out through her chattering teeth.

"I don't know." I was shivering fiercely now. "I will try it. What will I heat — these rocks?"

"Yes! The rocks! The water! Heat everything!"

I quickly thought about how I would do this. I had to stay conscious and I had to change the whole focus of the meditation. I did not have the slightest idea if this would work or not. I began the meditation. It was eerie. A sense of detachment came over me, but I did not leave my body.

In a few minutes Tsering whispered excitedly, "Lhamo, it is working!"

I was not sure if it really was working. It could have been that Tsering had progressed past the shivering stage and was now approaching death as heat rapidly drained out of the core of her slender body. But then I began to feel something. I thought the water was actually getting warmer. If we could just hold out for a little longer, we might make it. Then I had the thought that perhaps I could open the conduit a little more, and I began to feel a definite rise in temperature. Soon the water temperature was bearable, and then comfortable, and then wonderfully pleasant. I turned the heat down then and kept it at a maintenance level.

"Tsering," I whispered. "How could I make it without you?"

"Lhamo, I am just a mouse. You have the power to do this wonderful thing."

I began to think about what she had just said. I roughly calculated in my head the amount of heat in calories that it would take to raise the temperature of this entire well from the deadly cold it was when we got in, to the comfortable bathtub temperature that it was now, and in such a short time.

"Tsering, thanks to you, we have discovered that I do have this unusual power, or at least some control over a source of tremendous power. What other ways can I use it? If I can focus the power anywhere that I want, I can create a distraction. I could blow up a jeep!"

"Please, Lhamo, it frightens me to hear you talk this way. There may be soldiers in the jeeps. They might get hurt or die."

"It would just be this once." I heard how hollow the words sounded as I said them.

"If you did this violence, could you not do another? It is the Beautiful Goddess that I love, not the angry one."

"I am sorry Tsering. You are right. You are my teacher."

"No, Lhamo. I did not need to tell you these things. You only thought of using the power because you want to help others."

I like to think that she was right — that if I had been by myself, I never would have considered using this power in a violent way. I am only thankful that I did not have such a power that last day in the court room, or on my first day in prison.

"Lhamo, did you leave your body a while ago?" Tsering asked softly.

"Yes."

"Did you see the others?"

"Yes."

"Were they dead?"

"Some were dead. I think some got away."

"The man?"

"He is dead."

"I am not afraid to die," she said after a pause.

"I know."

"Then why do I feel frightened of the soldiers? Why was I afraid to drown?"

"I don't know, Tsering, but it is normal. The body does not want to die. I have been through death and back; I should be the least afraid of anyone, yet when we heard the jeeps coming, I ran faster than you did."

"If you have seen death and it is as you describe, why be afraid?"

"The body is of this world. This world is all it knows. The body wants to live. It wants to eat, and procreate. To do these things it sometimes has to convince you that you and it are inseparable — the same thing. Our personality — our ego — is the projection of the spirit into the flesh. The ego identifies with the flesh and wants to continue to exist. This is the part of us that experiences fear. This is why we run. Fear drives us and can conquer us if we do not conquer it instead."

"I know. My body trembles in fear. I have to calm it like a frightened animal. Yet I have listened to your words about death. I look forward to death if it is like you say. But if the land of death is as you say, why do we come into a world of fear and pain? Why do we subject ourselves to this?"

"Tsering, I think that we are here for a reason. I too sometimes look forward to the end of this life especially if prison is all there is to look forward to otherwise. But life is an opportunity for action. We have a reason for being here — a purpose. If we abandon that purpose, we may regret it after it is too late. That is why we should not want death but a life well lived. But, it may be that neither life nor death is worth a lot of worry as long as we use each day the best that we are able and just be alive now, and help each other whenever we can. Life is just as much a mystery to me as to anyone. Just because you die, it doesn't mean you solve the mystery of existence."

"Sometimes my life does not seem real. It cannot be real. It is like a story in a storybook."

"Perhaps you are right," I said. "But you are the one telling the story. Make it a good one."

In the dim light, I could see her staring at me thoughtfully.

"I do not know what is real and what is not," I added. "I only know that behind those eyes, there is a being that has chosen to live life as 'Tsering'. Looking out from these eyes of mine, is a being that is traveling through the world under the name of 'Dawn Bang'. The eyes themselves may not be real, but the beings looking out from the eyes are. Someday we will see without eyes and recognize each other for who we truly are."

We stayed in the well until night. A couple of times during the day, I heard the sound of heavy boots around the well house. Once, someone opened the door and looked in, but did not look down in the well. Another time, we heard the sound of a heavy object being leaned against the well house so that someone could pump water from the hand pump. I was worried that the soldiers might question why the well water was not cold, or that the villagers might turn us in to the soldiers from fear, but nothing like that happened. All in all, the village was very quiet the rest of the day.

As the light grew dimmer, I began to talk about how we would go back into the swamp and gather the remaining women back together and come up with another plan.

"No," Tsering said. "That is not what they would have wanted, Lhamo. You would be recaptured again or killed, and all of this would be in vain. I have been considering your words about 'purpose'. Perhaps it was not your purpose to get them out of prison. Perhaps it was their purpose to get you out. And it was their purpose, also to distract the soldiers coming down the road so that you would not be caught again. As you say, Lhamo, the world is for action. But a prison is a very small world."

*

I knew that Tsering was right, and that it would be foolish to go back to the prison with the other women; I would be much more able to help them outside of prison, than I could inside, or dead. However, that decision to do nothing has lived with me since that day. I do not know if I made the right decision, or if, sometimes, there are no right decisions. I have often wondered what would have happened with my life if I had acted differently than I did.

As it grew darker outside, I noticed a strange glow coming through the cracks around the door. We did not dare to leave the water until we were certain that it was well past bedtime for the villagers. We thought that the soldiers might patrol all night, but as there had been little activity around the well house, we thought we could reconnoiter safely under the cover of darkness. The glow was an unknown factor, however, and we discussed whether it might be some kind of area light set up by the soldiers. When we eased ourselves out of the well and cracked the door for a peek outside, we saw that the whole village was encased in a thick fog. The light of the moon, diffused through the fog, was creating a low glare that made the fog even more impenetrable to the eye. The fog was only slightly higher than a person, so that if one looked up, the stars and moon were clear in the night sky, but if one looked around, nothing could be seen but a glowing mist. This was the light we had seen through the cracks. We concluded that I had unknowingly heated the ground water under the entire village, and the vapor, rising up into the cold spring air, had created this uncanny fog.

We crept out into the mist, our warm wet clothes rapidly losing their heat, so that as we tiptoed through the fog we shivered as much from the cold as from fear. We could see the roofs of the houses, and, in the distance, some low hills, black against the indigo sky. As there was nothing else with which to orient ourselves, we began to cautiously move through the fog in the direction of the hills. Once, we had to stop while a shadowy figure moved through the fog in front of us, holding a long object out in front of him to feel his way. To our minds it looked exactly like a rifle with the bayonet attached and that very well may have been what it was.

I found I had a remarkable knack for being aware of what was ahead of us without actually seeing it, so that we quickly left the large dark shapes of the buildings around the well and were soon out of the fog, which, as we had thought, was centered around the well, and encompassed the village only, and did not extend out into the countryside. We were able then to look back across the fields at the bizarre sight of a single large cloud sitting on the ground with roof tops and tree tops jutting out of the top of it like strange decorations on a cake. We continued on and, after a short time, left the fields and entered a scrubby area where the land began to rise and the ground grew rocky. We crossed a road, but decided not to follow it, and instead moved further up into the rolling hills.

Daylight came and Tsering began to walk behind me. I would have thought that she was tired but I did not have to slow down or pause for her. Instead, she simply did not walk along beside me as she had done during the night but seemed to be putting her feet in the same places where my feet had gone before.

The traveling became harder, and we had struggled our way up to the top of a low but steep gravelly ridge when Tsering suddenly fell against me from behind. As we both tumbled down the other side of the ridge, I heard the distant crack of a rifle. I crawled to where Tsering lay on her face in the dust and rocks and saw where the bullet had entered from below her shoulder blade. I turned her over. The side of her throat had been torn open by the exiting of the bullet. She was choking on her own blood and I could see that she was beyond earthly help.

I cradled her head in my arms and my eyes filled with tears. "Oh Tsering, Tsitsi, Little Mouse, I only wish that I could be the one to take you where you are going." She was looking past me, and I turned to look over my shoulder at the spot where her gaze seemed to rest. "Thank you for coming," I said to the unseen visitor — the Dakini that I knew was there. And then my daughter was gone.

I was filled with the sadness of separation, but I knew that Tsering would soon be filled with love beyond measure. My time for action, however, was still at hand. I had no time to waste on self pity.

I left the shell that had housed my friend, and moved rapidly down the loose shale to the hollow between the ridges. I decided that I would cross no more exposed elevations. Although tired from lack of sleep and from traveling night and day, I ran along the hollow until I found a low area where I could cross the next ridge without being seen. I continued on this way in the general direction that I had instinctively selected.

I wondered what the rifleman had seen in his scope. Had he seen one person or two? Tsering had been so close behind me, and we had fallen as such a single unit, that I wondered if anyone had even been able to see that there had been two people crossing the ridge instead of one. I realized then, that Tsering had positioned herself behind me exactly for the purpose of using her body as a shield for me. She had walked in my footsteps so that the guards could not tell how many people had come this way, and when they found her body, they might think that they had killed a lone traveler. This was the purpose that she had chosen.

Zigzagging though the hills and hollows, I came to a wooded area about mid afternoon. I was thankful for the shade of the pines as much as for the cover they provided. I found a small outcropping of rock, which looked out over a shallow valley, and I rested for awhile while I studied the terrain.

Running alongside the base of the hill on which I sat, I could see a road traversing the length of the valley. Having sat on my ledge for awhile, I saw in the distance a cloud of dust approaching at a low speed from the direction of the village I had fled. The roads in this area were not well maintained, and travelers sped along them at their own risk. At first I thought it was a truck full of soldiers looking for me, but then I thought I saw the bright blue insignia of the foundation on the side. My heart leapt, and I began running down the slope of loose shale to try to intercept the truck before it passed me by forever.

The thin boots were no protection against the rocks and were soon worn through on the bottoms, yet still I ran. I fell several times, and picked myself up, bleeding from numerous cuts, and still I ran. My heart sank as I realized that I could not reach the road before the truck had passed, yet still I ran.

The truck drove past the point at which I had any hope of interception. I was still hundreds of yards away and was about to drop from exhaustion, my arms flailing in the last hope of attracting attention, when the truck stopped abruptly on the road, the cloud of dust rolling up to engulf it. Two men got out and stood on the road, staring at me. As I began to fall, I saw them start towards me in a run.

I had collapsed in a heap when they arrived. They helped me to a sitting position and gave me water from a canteen. One of them began asking me in Mandarin where my village was. "You must hide me, quick," I managed to croak out. "I am Dawn Bang."

"Oh my God," the other man gasped, "it _is_ Dawn Bang!"

They looked at each other in astonishment. "Don't worry, Miss Bang," they assured me. "We will take care of you. Is anyone close behind you? Are the soldiers looking for you?"

"Yes."

They looked at each other again, this time in fear. "They have already searched our truck once. Come on. We have got to get away from here."

As they loaded me into the back of the truck, they asked me if I was traveling alone. Should they look for anyone else? I told them I was alone and immediately fell asleep under the flapping canvas cover.

Later, as we bounced jarringly down the bad road, they noticed that my eyes were open, and one of them crawled back from the cab and brought me some cold noodles to eat.

"Miss Bang, have you been in prison all this time?" he asked while I ate hungrily.

I nodded.

"We need a plan to get you out of the country."

"How did the soldiers act when they searched your truck before?" I asked him.

"We were responding to an emergency call from a village, and, fortunately for us, didn't know anything about you at that time. The soldiers had the village surrounded. They stopped the truck and looked all inside it and turned us back around. We were heading back to our project village when we saw you."

"We have to act fast," I said. "They may think that I am dead, and it may take them awhile to realize that I am not. I need a disguise and a fake passport. I need to get out of the country before they realize that I am not even in this area anymore."

The two men knew exactly what to do. They got on the truck radio and, without giving any information that could tip off government listeners, began making arrangements for certain persons to be standing by. In a couple of days, all was accomplished and I was leaving the country incognito. I was never more thankful than when the jet's wheels left the concrete of the runway behind, yet I would have wept if I had known that I would never lay eyes on China again.

*

Sitting around in a cheap hotel room waiting for the passport to be made and the airplane tickets to be purchased gave me time to ponder recent events. I regretted that I had abandoned the women prisoners. They had chosen me to be their leader, had placed their faith in me, and had been left by me to face a hopeless future alone. Even though I had not appointed myself their leader, I had a feeling of obligation toward them. I knew that I could not be forever entangled in their lives, but I could not rest knowing that they might still be wandering the swamps and wastelands with nowhere to turn, or that they would have to spend countless winters in prison without me to help them stay warm.

I instructed the foundation workers in that area to try to find out information about the women — by bribery, if necessary, and to offer subsidies to villagers who would take these women in and make them part of their own village if they had not already been captured. The foundation had a fairly good feel for which villages could be trusted because of their hatred for the government and which could not be trusted because of their fear. We knew of none who loved, or was even ambivalent about, the government and its brutal ways.

Of course I missed Tsering and her counsel, which was wise beyond her years. But I considered her to be safe where she was, whereas the women who were still at large could hope for, at best, a quick death, but more likely a return to the horrible conditions from which they had fled, unless of course, the foundation could find some way to help them.

I did not believe that saving these women from prison was equivalent to releasing criminals upon society. None of the women were violent and most of them would not even be considered criminals in The States. Even prostitution was only a crime in some cultures. In addition, it was a crime mainly of big cities and required a degree of anonymity. I would be surprised to see a prostitute making a living as such in a small village; the other women would quickly see to it that she learned other trades.

I had been cut off from the outside world for about a year and a half and was hungry for information. If one read the Chinese newspapers only, one would think that everyone in China was healthy, happy, and praising the government. However, I picked up some western papers in Hong Kong during a layover, and read that there was rioting in almost all of the larger cities. One of the newspapers cited the usual reasons of low wages, high prices, and the general dissatisfaction with the government's economic policies. Another paper boldly hinted at an organized underground movement. What seemed to me to be closest to the truth, however, came from a tabloid that someone had left in the magazine pocket in front of my seat on the homeward bound airplane. "NEW RELIGIOUS MOVEMENT IN CHINA", the headline read. This paper must have come from The States. I don't think that the Chinese government would allow this, even in Hong Kong. The article made for interesting reading.

~~~~~~~~~~

A new religious movement is growing in China, according to recent reports smuggled off of the mainland. Dismissed as a cult and a product of mass hysteria by the mainland government, the movement centers around reports of supernatural appearances by a blue giant, who, reportedly, can walk through walls, and appear and disappear at will. Additional reports claim that the blue giant has a particular animosity toward the Chinese military, and plays games with them, leading them on fruitless chases.

Some eye-witnesses claim to have spoken with the blue giant, who refers to himself as Spear of Heaven, or Thunderbolt, as near as an English translation can approximate. According to these witnesses, Thunderbolt speaks telepathically and his meaning is unmistakably translated into the language of the listener. The witnesses reported that when one person asked Thunderbolt if he was the Buddha, Thunderbolt replied that a Buddha was coming on the wind, and he will be known as Divine Traveler Changed by Death.

These rumors have caused widespread rioting and a call for the end of the current government in China. A government spokesman in Beijing said in a recent interview that they have always had to deal with counter revolutionaries making bold claims and this one is just one more that they will deal with as expeditiously as they have all of the others. According to Beijing, this particular counter revolutionary leader is already safely behind bars, and the 'noise-making' of the misled will soon die quietly away.

Despite these reports of the movement's leader being in custody, it is not clear that there is just one leader involved. Accounts have come in of different blue giants with the same message appearing simultaneously across China. In addition, other eye witnesses say that they have seen squadrons of soldiers attack Thunderbolt and come away empty handed each time.

Whoever is behind the movement, it appears to be based on the ancient beliefs of some Buddhist sects. These beliefs state that when Buddhas enter into the world they are sometimes accompanied by supernatural beings, called bodhisattvas by some. Does the future Buddha walk among us now? According to Thunderbolt, he is on his way.

Turn to page 8 for related stories and drawings from eye witness accounts.

~~~~~~~~~~

I thought it was interesting that the government spokesman had indicated they had the leader behind bars, as they did not even acknowledge the leader's existence in the Chinese newspapers. On page eight there were a few ghost stories that Chinese parents sometimes use to frighten their children into submission. There were also some drawings that looked to me to be hand copies of Buddhist paintings of saints and demons, and so forth. I had my doubts that these were from actual eyewitness accounts. On the other hand, I thought, hadn't I seen something very similar?

I thought a lot about Tsering on the flight home. It was profoundly humbling to think that someone, especially someone as innocent and pure as Tsering, would take a bullet for me, a woman who was not worthy to wash Tsering's feet.

I looked forward to seeing my mother. I knew that my father was dead because I had been psychically called to his death bed prior to my imprisonment. If I had thought, over the last year and a half, that he was suffering in pain, I don't think that I would have survived the prison. My anger would have been uncontrollable, and it would surely have gotten me shot.

I hadn't called my mother because I did not want anyone to know I was alive, other than those who knew it already by necessity. I had learned to fear the Chinese government, and was determined to maintain a low profile. I was paranoid about any kind of communication that was susceptible to interception.

I had managed to slip out of China much easier than I had expected. But when I got a chance to look into a mirror, I realized why. The months in the prison had aged and emaciated me. My breasts sagged, my skin hung off of my arms, and my cheek bones looked like they were about to break through my face. I cried into my hands when I first saw myself.

At the Honolulu airport, I quietly slipped, unrecognized, back into the safe arms of the United States.

I took a taxi to my parent's house and stepped up on the porch and rang the doorbell. A careworn old bald-headed man answered the door. "Yes?" He studied my face.

I caught my breath. I could not believe my eyes. "Father!" I shouted.

A look of comprehension came into his face and tears welled up into his eyes. "Dawn!" he cried.

Chapter 3 – Of Freedom from Jail and a Tiger's Tail.

Hawaii had changed during the years of my absence — for the better and for the worse. However, my parent's house had changed little, and it felt wonderful to be back, smelling the comforting smells of cooking food, and walking barefoot on the worn carpet. For days, I lounged around in the house and watched my mother cook the most fattening foods she could think of, or I sat in a large swing in the back yard under the plumeria tree and listened to the birds sing and chatter while my father fixed us cool drinks. I felt safe here, like I had believed I never would again. My parents treated me like royalty. They had thought that I was dead. My father said that he had seen a vision of me while he was in the hospital and knew that it was my spirit, come to say good bye. I told him that I had a similar vision of him and so thought that he was dead as well. We shook our heads and smiled at this mystery.

My parents said that they would not have been able to tolerate the thought that I was slowly dying in a Chinese prison with no way for them to help me. It was better, they said, to think that I was dead. They told me the story of how they had tried to call me before they thought I was dead and could not find anyone in China who knew where I was. They had then contacted the U.S. State Department, who had begun talking to the Chinese government. They had gotten nowhere. The Chinese Government told the State Department that I had last been seen with unsavory elements of society and had surely come to a bad end. If the Chinese government had ever exhibited a sense of humor about anything, I would have thought that it was making a joke about my fellow inmates. We *were* an unsavory lot; the foundation truck that had picked me up had to be fumigated for fleas, and I was just now beginning to get the last of the horrendous tangles out of my hair. I supposed the State Department was still having its fruitless conversation with the Chinese, as no one except my parents and some foundation workers knew that I was back in Honolulu.

I told my parents about my escape from the prison. I left out the part about me learning to be a conduit for heat from some unknown source, as I did not think that they would understand or be able to deal with the information. However, I did tell them about Chenresig, as that was a subject that we could all be unanimously incredulous about.

I stayed in touch with the foundation, although as it turned out, it was not wise for me to be communicating with them. The people higher in the organization still took their lead from me, and so in effect, I was still running the operation in China. They also kept me informed about what was happening over there. The newspapers, although reporting the riots in the cities, had missed a bigger story about the unrest in the countryside. They had forgotten, perhaps, that the Communist Party and Mao Tse-Tung's rise to power had begun with a peasant revolt. This time, however, the peasants had technology. All of the villages were talking to each other, and the next revolution would not come as a brush fire, spreading across China and burning the coat-tails of the opposition as it fled to the sea, but as a detonation, engulfing the whole country at once. There would be no "long march" in the next revolution.

I also received stories of the escaped women. Many had been located and were living secretly in various villages, although many others had been returned to prison. The women who had not been recaptured told stories to their new families about our flight from prison. They told how Tsering and I had disappeared in a supernatural fog and had been lifted out of the village never to be seen again. Dong Shi had gained a reputation of being somewhat supernatural, or at least of associating with supernatural beings. The villagers knew of similar stories, and creating a great blinding fog was something which Kwan Yin was quite capable of doing, being that she was known to be especially adept with the elements of fire and water. The Director, Dong Shi, was very likely under the protection of Kwan Yin, or Chenresig, as the Tibetan women called this spirit.

These stories spread from village to village and added to the general unrest, until eventually the stories got back to the government, which, of course, knew perfectly well who "The Director" was, even if they had no clue as to the identity of the others. The government made no mention of the Divine Traveler Changed by Death, although throughout China, people were beginning to refer to him as Chang Da Wai, the Chinese equivalent of that descriptive English translation. Interestingly, when I saw the name Chang Da Wai written out in Chinese ideograms, I revised my understanding of the name. I also noted that the last part of the name contained elements of "evening" in it. Something stirred way in the back of my mind. "He is the evening and you are the dawn, Xiao Chen," came the thought quietly from nowhere.

*

I ate a lot, exercised a lot, and meditated a lot, and slowly began to look less and less like a concentration camp victim. My hair grew back to cover the places where some of the irredeemable tangles and mats had been cut out. The flea bites healed, my cheeks filled out, and my mother began to encourage me to meet men again. She seemed unaware that after all the years spent in China helping farmers I was now of an age where my biological clock had just about run out. She was either unaware or else she was clinging to a last straw of hope. I didn't have the heart to tell her that I just didn't see it happening.

I had no problem meditating for hours at a time now, although not for any particular purpose. Sometimes I meditated all night long instead of sleeping. After these long sessions, I felt unshakable, as if the world was just a solid place for me to sit, and nothing in it could surprise me. The world still had several surprises in store for me, however.

*

One afternoon, I was brought out of my meditative trance by the sound of a car horn honking in front of the house. I went out to see what was happening and found my mother standing beside a tiny red convertible sports car. She was smiling and holding her arms wide over the car in the universal gesture of offering. "It's for you." She said. "Your father and I picked it out. We think you should get out more."

"We do?" I quizzed her in mock cynicism. "Why do we think that?"

"You need to go places if you are going to meet any nice men. I don't see them coming around and knocking on your door."

"So this is my bribe to give you grandchildren."

"Don't you like it?" She wasn't denying anything, but I could tell from her face that she was not getting the response she had hoped for.

"I love it, mother," I caved, giving her a big grin and a hug. "It is so cute. It is just what I would have bought for myself. But, how did you afford it?"

"Oh, we had some money saved up. It is not very new and didn't cost very much. Your father checked it all out and said it was a real bargain."

My father came out of the house to see how I liked the *Midget*. He opened the hood and began pointing out interesting features of the engine — interesting to him, that is; I had no interest whatsoever in that part of the car.

"Well, everybody get out of the way so I can take it for a drive! Maybe I'll bring home a man." I laughed at my mother's shocked expression as she glanced sidelong at my father.

The car did help me find a man, but not that day, and not the kind of man my mother had in mind.

It was fun to drive the little red car with the top down and my hair blowing in the wind. I hadn't done anything just for the fun of it in a long time. At first I was concerned about the money my parents had spent on the car. As I said before, Hawaii, and especially Oahu, had changed in my absence. There seemed to be more rich people, but there also seemed to be more poor people, and I was afraid that my parents had begun to drift into the ranks of the poor. The income from their business was not what it once was. They had never bothered to learn to speak Japanese, and more and more of the tourists coming to the islands were from Japan. The increasing Japanese population was a good thing for the islands, as the Japanese were clean and polite and spent lots of money. It was not particularly good for the small Chinese shops, however, as the Japanese tended to spend their money in the stores that catered to them, which my parents did not. In a strange sort of loyalty to the country from which he and my mother had escaped, my father had never forgiven Japan for invading China. He even blamed the existence of the Chinese Communist Party on the Japanese invasion, and, in a way, he may have been right; at least he was not alone in thinking that.

The little red convertible was so fun to drive that I soon quit worrying about my parents. I whipped around traffic in Honolulu, putting the car through its paces, and maybe I even turned a few heads. Perhaps I was having a midlife crisis and didn't know it, but the car suited me. It made me feel young and pretty again and more connected to the world. The first day, I sped down Kalakaua Avenue, around Diamond Head and up the windward coast. I stopped on the north shore for shaved ice, or "shave ice" as the Hawaiians insist on calling it, and then headed home.

I gave up meditating. I was having too much fun with the car. I spent all of my waking hours zipping around the island. I got up in the morning, ate breakfast while skimming the Advertiser, and then I was off for the rest of the day. If it was my mother's goal to get me out of the house, she succeeded beyond her expectations. Of course, in my youth, I had already seen every part of Oahu that could be seen from a car, but now it was all new again. I loved driving around and looking at the tropical plants and the houses hiding behind them. I was like a tourist on an extended vacation. I visited all the beaches. I went all over the island from Sunset Beach to Hanauma Bay. I watched the surfing at all the famous beaches, including that on the huge rollers at such beaches as Ehukai. However, at the beaches, I also saw the poverty of the island. There were people living in hobo jungles, in old cars, under plastic tarps, and beneath lean-to's made of rotted boat hulls. The contrast between these so-called unspoiled beaches and the beaches where the wealthy strode along Waikiki was jarring. I realized that, to these people, even I, in my shabby little sports car, was one of the "haves" rather than one of the "have nots", and the glamour of driving it began to fade.

During this time, I did not maintain very good communications with the foundation, trusting the staff to carry on as they had during my imprisonment. I quickly became concerned when I finally did try to contact them and could not get anyone to answer a phone call or an email. I tried calling for several days before I finally saw the article in the morning paper:

Beijing — According to a government spokesperson, the Chinese government has stopped an attempt by a reactionary group to overthrow the legal reigning power in China. The group was fronted by an international organization called 'The China Food Foundation' or, to many, simply as 'The Foundation'.

According to the source, where The Foundation had been allowed to work, it had, in reality, been secretly involved in aiding the escape of dangerous prisoners and fomenting dissent throughout rural China.

Pretending to be an agency existing for the support of improved agricultural practices in peasant farming communities, The Foundation had its own hidden agenda for creating distrust between the farmers and the government. This distrust was then used to help cover The Foundation's efforts to siphon off the wealth of the land that rightfully belonged to the people. The escaped prisoners were to be used to build an army of counterrevolutionary guerrilla soldiers.

The government source also stated that all Foundation employees, as well as farm families who were directly involved in the plot, have been arrested and are in prison awaiting trial. When asked if it was true that some had died in the arrest, the source had no comment.

~~~~~~~~~~~

My hands had begun to shake uncontrollably as I read the short article and I had to lay the paper flat on the table and lean over it to read the last few sentences. My parents watched in alarm when I suddenly doubled over as if I had been kicked in the stomach. I ran into the bathroom and threw up my breakfast. I then lay down on the cold bathroom floor, curled up in a ball, and wailed and sobbed until my parents rushed in and began holding me and bathing my face with cold water.

There is no way to truly explain how I felt. All of my friends, everyone who trusted me, were now going to a living nightmare that I understood too well, and all because of my lack of judgment. Everything that I had built to help the people of China was in ashes. Everything I had done with my life was in ruins. But infinitely worse, I had betrayed and abandoned everyone I knew, everyone who had been loyal to me and who had tried to carry out my wishes, everyone who had believed in me. It was as if I had blithely led them to the gates of hell, and then, too late, woke up to see that gate slam shut behind them, with me outside and free like some Judas goat.

I thought that I would never stop crying. My parents argued back and forth over whether to take me to the hospital, but finally called their doctor and got a prescription for some tranquilizers to give me.

The pills helped me sleep through the night, and that night I had a dream. In the dream, I was in Beijing, walking across Tiananmen Square, and hundreds of thousands of people were following me. I was taller than anyone else in the crowd and could look back over their heads with ease. I could see a winding river of humanity, like the tail of a dragon, behind me. I was the dragon, and the people were joined to me as tightly as if the stream of humanity were a real dragon's tail firmly connected to a real dragon. We were going to go to the government offices, knock on the door and tell them that it was time for everyone to leave. We knew that when they saw us they would fall on their knees in terror and disbelief, slapping and pinching themselves to try to wake up, and prison walls would fall all across China.

The next morning, I was at least able to keep from bawling. It had been a very satisfactory dream, and had somehow helped me cope with the situation. I held on to the comfort of that dream throughout the day.

I began to try to think of positive steps I could take. Of course I would contact the State Department and tell them my story and explain how the Chinese Government had fabricated charges against me and were now doing the same thing to the whole foundation. However, I knew that the Chinese Government would be able to produce witnesses to verify anything that they said, especially the part about helping prisoners, which was inarguably true. But what did it matter what I told the State Department — the Chinese Government would move truculently along, doing its own churlish thing in its own pigheaded way as it always had.

I needed to get out where I could think without my parents hovering over me. I took the *Midget*, which had lost the power to comfort me, and drove through China Town, looking for a quiet place. That is how I rediscovered the Temple of Kwan Yin. Now it had a strange attraction for me. Now it seemed like the perfect place to sit and calm myself and think. It was half hidden behind a huge façade of tropical shrubs and trees right at the entrance to a botanical garden. Inside, it was cool, flooded with natural light, and quiet. I admired the beautiful carvings, which were surrounded by offerings of fruit, rice, seeds, and spices. Outside the louvered glass walls of the temple was a porch lined with Chinese pillars and benches for sitting and meditating.

There was a small but steady stream of visitors into the Kwan Yin temple. Occasionally, a Chinese couple would come in with an offering and a short prayer. I sat on the bench nearest the main door into the temple and secretly listened to these prayers and realized that the world is full of longing. Could Kwan Yin hear all the cries of the world? There were so many.

I began to visit the temple every day and to bring my own offerings and my own prayers. It was the only hope I had. I did not simply come and go as so many others did, but spent a lot of time there. I heard many prayers besides my own and would sometimes, after hearing a particularly poignant request — especially one that had been offered unselfishly — add that prayer to my own.

I began to resolve that somehow I would go back to China and help the people that I had abandoned. But what could I possibly do when I got there? I just knew that this is what Kwan Yin would do.

Being caught up in my own concerns and thoughts, I paid little attention to the fact that during my many visits to the temple there was always another presence. It did not bother me at the time to see the same vehicle in the parking lot whenever I came out of the temple. Many people made repeated visits to Kwan Yin, just as I did. And besides, I felt safe—untouchable—back in the U.S.A.

One night, after I had fallen asleep pondering just what I could do to go back to China, I found myself somewhere other than my bedroom. The sensation was much like the dream missions that I had traveled on before. In fact, it was very much like one particular dream mission in that no one was dead when I arrived. It was nighttime in a large city and the scene was lit by streetlights, neon billboards, and the light from the windows that covered the walls of the tall buildings around me. I was looking down at a crowd of people that filled the streets in all directions. Some were waving signs, some shouting, some trying to push through in one direction or another. All of them were looking straight up at me. The signs read "Chang Da Wai" in both English and in Chinese pictographs.

I changed my point of view and realized that they were not really looking at or seeing me. Before I could look up to see what they were shouting at, my attention was drawn to a single man in a uniform, carrying a duffel bag, and trying to pass into the crowd from a side street. I followed his progress as he pushed through the crowd and noticed that he was being stalked. Several other individuals had entered the crowd and were moving through it parallel to his line of travel and on either side of him.

About half way through the crowd, they moved in on him, and the uniformed man disappeared under the blows of his assailants. The crowd paid little attention to the scuffle, but seemed to swallow it up. I moved swiftly down into the crowd and saw that the man's attackers had him down on the street and were pulling knives to finish him off. Even though the scene was vaguely familiar, I did not know why I had been brought to witness this. I supposed I had gotten here just a little too early and was supposed to wait until the man was dead, as I had no way to intervene in physical affairs. But then I remembered Tsering in the well and how, at her prompting, I had made something besides my own body a conduit for what I had come to think of as "cosmic" energy. As the men raised their knives to strike, I turned those very knives into conduits of this energy. The men dropped the knives in surprise and ran off into the crowd, holding their hands in pain.

I paused to evaluate what I had done. Would Tsering approve of my causing pain? I had saved a life. I had reacted instinctively. Then the man rolled over on his back and looked up at me — or through me, rather. I looked up also to see what he was seeing. There, hundreds of stories above the crowd, suspended in air above the buildings that it dwarfed, darker than the gloom of the cloudy night sky, was the thing that had been prophesied to me so many years before — so long ago that the memory of it was like the memory of a dream. There, shimmering mysteriously in the lights of the city, its own navigational lights twinkling in the darkness, and with brilliant flood lights playing off of the buildings and crowds below, was the great flying whale!

*

The shock of seeing the whale threw me back into my body and I woke up with a gasp. I could not go back to sleep for wondering what this flying whale was. I knew that this thing I had seen was not really a whale, yet I also knew that this *was* the whale that the beings of light had prophesied I would see. It seemed an impossibility. It had looked somewhat like a whale, although it obviously was not one. It was immense in size, far larger than any whale that had ever lived. I supposed that it was at least as long as the largest ocean liner, but far wider. It was too enormous to be in the sky, so what was it doing in the air over a city? The answer came in the morning with the thump of the newspaper against the front door.

I got up and made tea for breakfast. I retrieved the paper and spread it on the table while I sipped my tea. There, on the front page, was a picture, taken from several miles away, of the whale, seemingly tethered to the Bank of America building in San Francisco. The darkly out of place Bank of America building towered over the city from its hillside position, and the "whale", longer in the photo than the building was tall, equally out of place and just as mysteriously dark, floated majestically above the city skyline like some giant and oddly symmetrical storm cloud. Indeed, it seemed a mythically proportioned flying whale—a leviathan of the air. Only it was not a whale at all. It was a dirigible, so the article said — a rigid frame lighter-than-air craft! It did not have the classic cigar shape of the Hindenburg, or other dirigibles that I had seen in photographs. Instead it was graceful with a large head, full curved belly, and a tapering tail with large fins. The beings of light had shown me this image many years ago and I had nothing to associate it with in my mind at that time except a whale. All of my life I had thought that someday I would see a giant flying whale, but now realized that what I had instead been waiting for was this startlingly unexpected dirigible.

I continued to read the article. The whale was called the *Eckener* after a German anti-Nazi dirigible builder from the Second World War. It had been built by the heiress of a large trucking company on the mainland, and was on its maiden voyage around the world. Its next stop was Honolulu, and from there, China.

A poorly formulated plan slowly began to come to the surface of my mind. I finished my breakfast, hopped in my car and headed off to the Kwan Yin temple to think. I would buy a ticket on the *Eckener*, jump ship in China, and organize a true counter revolution. The Chinese Government would not know that I was there and so would not be watching me. I still had my fake passport and would buy a ticket under my fake name. These must sound like desperate thoughts, and perhaps they were, but I felt that I had to help my friends, and whoever else I had caused to be imprisoned, or else I would die trying.

I went to the temple daily and worked on my plan and waited for the *Eckener* to arrive. I knew my plan was right, for why else would the beings of light have shown me the *Eckener* so long ago. I read the newspaper diligently, and one morning was rewarded with the news that the *Eckener* had arrived the previous evening and was anchored at Kapiolani Park. I raced out the door, leaped into the driver's seat and headed off to see this thing that had been in the background of my life for almost as long as I could remember.

As I was driving through the Waikiki Beach area, where Kalakaua Avenue gets close to the ocean, I saw, out of the corner of my eye, an oddly deformed man sitting on a park bench by the street. I turned my head and looked at him as I was going past, and he smiled and waved. He smiled through a ruined face and waved a hand that looked more like a paw, its fingers were so short. I nearly caused a traffic pile up when, with a shock of sudden recognition, I slammed on my brakes.

Honking is too rude for most Hawaiians, but I received many silent glares as the cars began to ease by me while I sat in my car staring back over my shoulder at this appalling site. The man's legs dangled uselessly from the bench, ending in stubs far short of the sidewalk. His ears were ragged as if someone had tried to hack them from his head with a dull knife. His clothes were tattered and stained. His shorts were dirty yellow and appeared to be soaking wet. His shirt was ragged and torn and perhaps had once been white. Dirt was ground into his knees and the palms of his hands, showing that he had been crawling on the ground like an animal. His hair hung in dirty ropes which helped to hide the fact that his face was horribly scarred and that a piece of his lip and the tip of his nose were missing.

Traffic was light in the early morning, and I managed to back into the cutout in front of the park benches. There was no way that I could have known this man, yet as I sat and stared at him, I knew that I did know him. I walked over to the man and sat down on the bench beside him. "Mister," I addressed him, "Is there anything that I can do to help you?" I asked. "Is there any place you need to go, or anything that I can get for you?"

"You are very kind," he replied. "There is something — some *things*, actually, that I would like to have, if you wouldn't mind too much."

"You tell me whatever you need and I'll get it for you," I responded, worrying about my grandiose promise even as I uttered it.

"I would like to have my feet back."

The very sight of him had saddened me, and now I came close to tears to think that this wretched man had not only lost his feet in some horrible accident, but that his wits had left him as well. I paused, thinking of how to respond, when he continued.

"They are in the ocean, back there."

I looked to where he was pointing and I did see two objects, looking like the up-ended feet of a snorkeler, bobbing in the gentle waves inside the seawall that sheltered that section of the beach.

"Those are your feet?"

He nodded. "Some young men threw them into the ocean and then threw me in after them. It was all I could do to keep from drowning; I couldn't manage to get my feet at all. I had to crawl up here and hope that someone would stop. Thanks for wanting to help."

I nodded slowly, trying to absorb the recent events of his life. "I will be right back," I said, as I stood up and started down the beach to the ocean.

Glad as I was that the hoodlums had thrown his feet inside the sea wall instead of a few yards down the beach where the big waves were rolling in, I was still thoroughly soaked by the time I came back with his feet. I probably looked almost as bad as he did.

His "feet" were prosthetic extensions, which he strapped to his legs. He stood up and walked around as if trying on new shoes. I thought his balance was amazing that he could walk around on two poles with shoe-shaped rubber blocks on the ends.

"Where do you live?" I asked him, thinking I could take him home.

"China," he declared, studying me to see if I might suddenly recognize him, "I am on my way back there. I am staying on a ship that just arrived yesterday. And yes, I would like a lift somewhere, if that is what you were getting at."

"Of course. Just say where," I said, again making rash promises, but thinking that he probably just wanted a ride back to his pier so he could re-board his ship.

"I would like to see the temple of Kwan Yin. Have you heard of it?"

"Yes, I go there a lot." I couldn't have been more surprised if he had named my parents street address. "I can take you there now if you wish, or I can take you back to your ship so you can clean up first."

"Let's go to the temple. I am a big fan of Kwan Yin." He smiled in a surprisingly charming way, considering his disfigured face.

We got into the car and I eased back into traffic. I took the next left and then left again on Ali Wai Boulevard, heading back west toward China Town. I had forgotten about the "whale" and failed to realize that if I had driven just a short way further down Kalakaua, I would have seen it hovering in the stark morning light over Kapiolani Park. As it turned out, I had passed up my last chance to feast my eyes on the reality of my dreams.

*

I didn't ask this strange man why he was thrown into the ocean, imagining that a repugnant Chinese dwarf, hopping around on his skinny bird legs, might be asking for trouble on a beach full of beautiful, muscular, hedonistic twenty-somethings — especially in the very early morning when the beaches were nearly deserted except for athletic types and locals, who really didn't care for foreigners.

I drove back up through Honolulu and the northern edge of China Town. There were just as many Vietnamese and Thais and Filipinos here as there were Chinese, but I guess that wasn't reason enough to change the name. There was parking available on Vineyard, but I always used the parking at Foster Botanical Gardens because I didn't like the idea of drug addicts pilfering through my glove compartment and the trunk of my car, as I had once done.

As I switched off the ignition, I turned to my new acquaintance. "You look very familiar to me," I said.

He nodded. "I get that a lot, actually."

"Do you mind telling me your name?"

"My name is David." He smiled his disarming smile, and I suddenly realized how much I was drawn to this man. There was something in him, past the disfigurement, some marvelous glow that was not of this earth. "David Chang," he continued, "but you should call me David."

I was so intently racking my brain, trying to remember where I had seen him before, that his name failed to register with me at the time.

"My name is Dawn," I answered.

"Ah, then you are 'Xiao Chen' in China. Is it not so?"

"Yes, I suppose so," I replied, puzzled to hear this name pronounced by my strange new friend.

"Have you ever been to China?" he asked.

"Yes." I was staring at the floor, trying not to think too much about China at the moment.

"Would you like to go back?"

"Yes." My voice broke from my strong desire to return to China.

"Then you will go back. Come, you can take me to my ship now."

"But we haven't gone into the temple yet," I protested.

"It is starting to get crowded, and perhaps I should get cleaned up before going in."

"I thought you wanted to see the temple."

"I have seen it now."

"You have only seen the outside. We are dry now. We need to go in. It is very beautiful inside. There is a giant golden statue. Come on," I said, opening my car door.

"Do you desire this?"

"Yes," I replied. "I desire it. And so do you. You came a long way to see the temple of Kwan Yin. We should go in and pray."

"What do you pray for?"

"I thank Kwan Yin for the sacrifice that she has made to stay in the world and listen and respond to its cries for help, and I ask that she teach me also how to answer the cries of the world."

"That is a powerful prayer. Do you really want this? Do you know what you are asking?"

"Yes. What do you mean?"

"Later, remember what you prayed for." He got out on his side of the car.

As we walked past the rock wall that bordered the temple courtyard, I noticed a familiar looking car coming into the parking lot. There were two men in the front seat, who, though dark skinned, did not look as if they were from the islands. I did not think any more about this at the time, as we walked around to the main gate that opened onto Vineyard Boulevard. We walked into the beautifully manicured courtyard, past the red pillars, and up the steps of the porch. There were people sitting on the benches lined up around the louvered glass walls of the temple. A woman was kneeling in prayer inside the open double doors, and we waited for her to finish. David and I then went in and knelt in front of the altar. "If you do not have a specific prayer," I suggested, "you can repeat the mantra of Kwan Yin. Do you know it?"

"Yes," he nodded, "the six-syllable mantra to deliver us from the snares of the world. But that is not my prayer today. Today I will pray for you."

"For me?" I asked in astonishment.

"For your desires to be realized," he added, "for your wishes to come true. I will add my prayers to yours. Whenever two or more people pray for the same thing, the power of that prayer becomes amplified beyond expectation. If the entire world were to manage somehow to pray for the same thing, that thing would become a simple fact of reality."

I nodded thoughtfully and turned back to the altar.

We prayed silently, and when we stood up to leave, I turned around to see one of the men from the car coming up the steps of the porch. He was climbing slowly and looked ill, his face drawn as if in fear. He was wearing a blousy windbreaker zipped half-way up despite the fact that he was sweating profusely. He trembled and his knees shook as he took the last step onto the porch, but when he looked up and saw that I was studying him, he crossed the porch quickly, becoming a shadowy outline against the brightly lit courtyard behind him. He seemed to reach into his jacket just as David turned and saw him as well. David quickly stepped in front of me, his back to the man, shielding me and grasping my arms, as if about to throw me down. Over the top of David's head, in an altered perception of time, I saw the man, his face like a zombie's, his eyes staring at heaven, or at nothing. His lips moved slightly and then a giant hand slapped us both like rag-dolls across the wooden kneeler and deeper into the darkness of the temple. I seemed to have a vision of the golden statue of Kwan Yin leaning over me, but I realized later that I could not have physically seen such a thing before the world went black; my eyes were already gone.

*

I was home again at last. God had plucked me from the maelstrom and transported me to the very heart of tranquility and peace. I was welcomed and loved. I was safe.

The life review this time was a wonderful experience. I saw how the good that I had done had created happiness and helped others to do good in their turn, and I experienced the good from that as well. The review was not without its blemishes, however. My life had not been perfect and the review revealed that. But it was far and away better than the previous life review that I had endured. This one could have gone on longer, as far as I was concerned. I did not want it to end as I bathed in the glow of the kindness, happiness and love that I had created. But it did end, and abruptly, and I was aware that I had several things to consider, and quickly. I had un-resolved issues in my life. And my body was severely injured and rapidly dying. I had a friend, I was told, who was keeping my body alive while I decided what to do, but I must decide quickly, as my friend was also injured, and hesitation on my part could result in a default decision for both of us.

I was told that I had a choice this time. I could go back, as I had when I was sixteen, or I could go forward. If I chose to go forward and crossed the boundary between where I was and the real and wonderful heaven beyond, there would be no going back in this life and my unresolved issues would remain unresolved. But if I went back, it would be to a broken body and a destroyed life.

I felt somewhat stunned by this depressing news. I did not want to go back — I wanted heaven, but I did not want the choice to be mine. All of my life, I had waited and worked hard to be able to say that I had run the race and finished the course. Now I found that the race was never over and the course had no end.

If I did go back, life would not be the same for me. My body had sustained serious injury from which it would never fully recover. Depending on how I accepted my injuries, my life could become almost unbearably difficult. Yet I knew that if I did not go back and somehow try to help, my friends would most assuredly live out their lives in the hellish confines of Chinese prisons.

Waves of love and sympathy washed over me from the beings around me, as I struggled with two impossible choices. In one direction lay terrible pain, struggle, and a future that promised to be a downhill slide. In the other direction lay serenity and bliss—and a destiny unrealized. There would be no judgment passed on me by the beings of light. The choice was mine. The judgment was mine as well.

As I considered the options, I noticed the river and the bridge of timbers. There, across the river, at the other end of the bridge, stood Tsering — the sweet, lovely Tsering, who only ever did what was right for me. She didn't wave or make any gesture. I knew she did not want to influence me but would be there to welcome me should I decide to make the final crossing. There was no wrong decision — just a decision.

If I crossed the bridge, I thought, it would not be that long before all of my other friends would join me there. A lifetime is not that long to wait. We would all be together soon enough — if they did not succumb to hatred, fear, and despair! What would thirty, forty, or fifty years of beatings, torture, and rape do to a human soul? I had barely gotten out of prison with my own soul intact, and I had only been there for a few months. Once placed in Hell, the residence could become permanent. How could there be serenity or bliss for me if I let anyone spend one unnecessary moment in Hell?

But I was repulsed at the idea of entering my old, aching, sagging and now broken body. I had no desire to be swaddled in the heavy clay of earth or feel the merciless pull of gravity. I heartily desired to avoid the infirmity of old age or the uselessness of a failing body.

I was informed that my body was dying now and that if I did not choose immediately, there would be no choice to make.

What choice? I had no choice. Dear God, I could not face the feel of the broken bones grinding end to end — the smell of my insides now outside — the crushing weight on my chest — the taste of blood in my mouth — the sensation that my head was about to burst — the sickening confusion and disorientation — the wailing of the sirens. Dear God!

*

I woke up in darkness. I reached out and felt the smoothness of bed sheets and the roughness of some other bedding material. I could tell that I was in a bed, but I couldn't tell much else in the dark. I felt around beside the bed for a lamp and felt a sharp pain in the back of my hand. I gently probed it with the other hand and realized that I had a needle imbedded in my hand with a piece of cloth tape to hold it in place. So I was in a hospital. That explained the smell of organic solvents.

I heard someone open a door and then my mother's voice said, "Get the nurse! She's awake!" I knew then, that only I was in darkness; for everyone else, the lights were still on. I had never experienced such absolute darkness. I realized that my face was bandaged, then, and that my eyes were covered with something. I felt that if I could just uncover my eyes, I would be able to see. In a sort of panicked madness, I began to try to rip the bandages from my head. "No, Honey, don't," my mother said, and I felt her hands holding mine away from my face. I arched my back and opened my mouth to scream, but instead, I fainted.

Later, I must have awoken again, for I felt the pressure change in the room and heard the slight whoosh of a door opening and closing, and then a voice saying, "Oh, you're awake again. Your parents just stepped out."

"Where am I? What is going on?"

"You are in The Queen's Medical Center. You were in an accident. The doctor will answer all your other questions when he comes back. You just need to lie still for now and not worry about anything."

"I want these bandages off of my eyes so I can see something."

"The bandages need to stay on for a while longer. That is why your arms are strapped down. You kept trying to take the bandages off in your sleep."

"My chest hurts, my stomach hurts, my head hurts, my back hurts, and my leg is beginning to hurt like a son of a bitch."

"I am going to give you a couple of buttons to push." She placed something cold and hard in each hand. "If you start feeling pain at any time, you can push the button in your right hand as much as you want. Don't worry, you can't overdose. If you need a nurse, you can push the button in your left hand and someone will come right away."

I began furiously clicking the button in my right hand. "Could I have a drink of water, please?"

"I'll have to check with the doctor first, but I think it will be OK. Do you feel nauseous or dizzy?"

"A little dizzy, I guess. And I have a really bad headache."

"Well, then, maybe just some ice cubes for now."

I heard the whoosh of the door as she left, and then, a couple of minutes later, I heard my father's voice through the door. "Dawn, is it OK we come in?" Before I could answer, I heard the door open.

"Father, Mother, is that you? What is happening? What's wrong with my eyes?"

"Oh, Dawn!" She could barely get the words out. I felt her hand on my shoulder. "The doctor told us. We are so sorry. How could this happen?" She began to cry

"My eyes — how bad are they? Has the doctor said how much my vision will be impaired?"

"Dawn," my father said, smoothing my hair with his hand. "It is no good to lie to you. Your eyes are gone."

I may not have given any visible outward sign, but inside, I was pulling away. I wanted everyone to leave me alone. I wanted my parents to leave me alone. I wanted the world to leave me alone. I wanted God and his minions to leave me alone. I was beginning to recall that I had been given a choice to come back into this stinking world. If only someone had bothered to explain to me that if I did come back, I would not be able to accomplish one infinitesimal thing more than if I had stayed where I was, then perhaps my decision would have been different. Now I faced half a lifetime of waiting to die. And, as we know, a half of a lifetime may not be very long in heaven, but it is a long damn time in hell.

Oh, God, I couldn't stand it! I felt my face screw up in the agony of my thoughts, and I couldn't even hide my face in my hands because they were strapped to the bed. I am sure tears would have been pouring from my eyes if I had eyes to cry with. I pulled madly on the wrist straps. I arched my back and strained to get free — of the bed, of my body, of life. I could not be where I was any longer. I heard my parents calling for help. I felt several hands trying to hold me down, and then they must have put something in my drip tube, for I began to dream. It was a horrible, hateful dream that I was back in prison. The prison was cold and it was dark.

*

When I woke up, it was still cold and it was still dark. I searched for the prison windows where I might catch a glimmer of starlight. As I gradually swept the cobwebs out of my head and began to realize that I was in a safe comfortable bed in a safe comfortable hospital, I felt no better for it, for with the returning memory that I was no longer in a Chinese prison, came the memory that I was now in a prison of a different sort.

I thought about all of the things that I would never do again and the things that I would never see. I already missed seeing my parents' faces. I would never again see sunrise over Diamond Head or go to a Sunset-on-the-Beach party, or see the big rollers on the north shore, or even the plumeria in bloom in my parents' back yard. I would never drive my little red sports car around the island, or swim in the surf, or sail in a catamaran out over the deep blue Pacific. But most of all, I would not be able to help my friends in trouble. All of my plans, unripe, as they were, were now still-born. All of my life I had waited for this time to come — the time of the flying whale, as I had come to think of it, and now that it had arrived, I could do nothing. My life had been destroyed by some mad whim — by the actions of a person whose motives I could not know or understand. I had made my plans, but life had intervened.

A doctor came and talked to me about my injuries. He tried to tell me that it was a miracle that I was alive at all. I wasn't seeing it that way. He said that I should consider myself lucky. I didn't feel lucky; I felt very unlucky. He said there was no medical explanation for my survival. He said that for some reason, my body had chosen not to bleed out, my lungs had decided not to collapse, and my brain had decided not to swell. The leg would heal normally. I should count my blessings. He could tell that I wasn't counting, and said that he would come back later and talk to me when I was feeling better. I told him that I didn't think I would be seeing him then. As he went out the door, he turned and said, "You know, the odds against anyone surviving that blast are astronomical, and, strangely, only one person died."

I knew that the bomber could not have survived, so that meant that David had not died in the blast.

"Wait," I said. "The man who was with me survived?"

"Yes — David Chang — he has already been released from the hospital. The police questioned him, then let him go. He has been asking about you, but we didn't really know who he was, and neither did your parents, so we have been keeping him out of your room. I don't know if he is even still here. Do you want to see him if he comes around?"

"Yes. He's a friend of mine. I am glad to hear he is OK. Don't worry about him; he saved my life. I had just assumed he was dead."

"He certainly should be, but so should you."

*

That afternoon, David came to visit. I was not as gracious to him as I had earlier been about him. I had begun to think about the way the incident had played out.

"Why did this happen?" I asked him.

"It depends from what level of awareness you are asking the question."

"I hardly know you. I just met you, and then you wanted to go to the temple, and then a bomb exploded and left me blind. Did you have anything to do with that?"

"It depends from what level . . ."

"OK, I got it. Listen, you just need to be straight with me. If you had anything to do with this bombing, then just say so, because if you did, I only wish that you would go ahead and finish the job. I don't want to go on living."

"I am not your enemy, Xiao Chen. Be careful about what you wish for. Remember your prayer."

"I prayed to be able to help others — and this is my reward?"

"I am sorry; I did not know that it was a reward that you desired."

"I didn't mean it that way. How could this happen to me? What did I ever do to that man, or to anyone? Why did he do this to me?"

"Truths and lies swirl together through the world like currents in the ocean until they can hardly be told apart. Whether he was following a lie about you or about me, or some other current, I cannot say."

"It doesn't really matter anyway. I was there and now I am here. My life is over."

"Life is choice," he said. "And every choice we make creates a new reality. Make sure that the choices that you make create the reality in which you would like to exist."

"What choices do I have? You don't know me! Who the hell are you anyway?" I asked him.

"I am David Chang. You know me, and I know you, Xiao Chen."

I paused, calming myself. "OK, who are you really? I think I know you from somewhere, but maybe it is just because your face was almost the last thing I ever saw or ever will see. I have been studying it for days. So tell me. I think I deserve to know."

I felt his hand on my arm and suddenly the room grew brighter and I was seeing again. But I was not seeing a hospital room as I thought I would. Instead I was seeing snow and rocks and glaciers and huge mountains. The sun was bright in the deep blue sky. There were some tents pitched in the snow. One of them was collapsed and strewn down the mountain. Two men in heavy mountain gear were approaching the tents from below.

I knew where I was. I was back on the dream mission of many years ago, when I had saved a man who had been hanging by one hand from a high icy ledge.

The two men entered one of the tents, and I knew that this was not memory. I had not seen this happen the first time. Yet it was as real as when I was there — the unearthly cobalt color of the sky, the brightness of the sun on the ice, the little sprays of snow blowing here and there. This was not just a different place, but a different time. How could I be experiencing this? "What is going on?" I heard myself ask out loud, and found myself back inside the darkness of my skull. "What was that?" I asked the room, hoping I was not alone.

David answered. "You know what it was."

"I saw something from long ago. It was not a memory. How is that possible?

"The soul is not a product of space and time and is not limited by their constraints."

"You are saying that I went there? I don't think so."

"Have you ever traveled outside your body?" He asked as if he already knew the answer.

"I have never traveled through time before."

"Only because no one has ever shown you how. Now you know how."

"Who are you?" I asked for the second or third time. "I mean — I think I know."

"Yes, I think you do. But do you know who you are?"

I ignored his remark and continued, "You were trapped on a mountain, weren't you? And someone came and led you down — someone who was not there when your friends came. Am I right?"

"Yes, you are right, Xiao Chen. Although, that day, I called you by another name, didn't I?"

"Jia Li," I answered softly. I could hardly believe what I was hearing. In all the thousands of times that I had helped someone while on a dream mission, I had never before had "proof" of what I had done. There had always been the possibility that I was merely dreaming, or hallucinating, or that I just had no grip on reality whatsoever.

"Yes, Jia Li, a beautiful woman. How easy it is to become stuck in this world, yet she spoke her lines and gracefully left the stage that day."

"What do you mean 'stuck'?" I didn't like the sound of that.

"Surely you have sensed it — your recent experiences . . . The world is honey and we are the bees. We make it; we must have it; yet we can very easily drown in it."

"What do you mean 'recent experiences'?" I realized how stupid I was beginning to sound, yet every answer led to a thousand other questions.

"Have you ever died, that you know of?" He ignored my question.

"No. Well, OK, I may have died, but how do you know about that?" My thoughts were beginning to race.

"Did you ever come back of your own free will?"

"Yes, I am sorry to say."

"That almost always happens. If the body is able to support life, and the soul has a choice, it will almost always come back. We have entanglements; we have unfinished business; we have obligations."

"But why did I even have a choice this time? My body should have died." I paused, but there was no answer. "Why am I alive now? Do you know the answer to that too? You and I are the only survivors. The doctor says it is a miracle. Did you make the miracle? Did you give me this choice to come back?" My heart was pounding with anticipation of his answer.

"We are not the only survivors. No one died who did not choose to die that day," he responded. "The volunteer behind the counter survived. She bent over to pick up some incense that she had spilled, and the counter saved her. She chose to live. Other people chose to stay out on the porch where they were shielded by the door; others did not even come to the temple that day. It was a choice that each one made."

"Or luck."

"There is no luck except what we make ourselves. There is destiny — that goal that we seek for ourselves, and there is fate — the collision of others' choices and destinies with our own."

"And if I were to be struck by lightning — would that be choice, fate, or destiny?" I thought I had him with that one.

"Any or all. Choice, fate, and destiny are not forces limited to human beings or to individuals."

"But in this case, only individuals were involved."

"In a very superficial sense that is true. I took most of the blast from you because I have learned how to absorb damage to my body. And Yes, I helped your body resist the damage that it received and heal more rapidly than normal. But I could not have done it without you wanting it as well. You made the choice to live. We both made a choice for you to live, and so did all of the underlying, hidden, and mysterious forces that shape us and make us what we are."

"I didn't want to come back and be blind!" I exclaimed, not really listening to him. "What kind of choice is that? You gave me the choice to live, but you didn't give me back my eyes." I sat up in the bed. "If you really have this power to heal, then give me back my eyes!" I was reaching for him in the dark. I was afraid he would get away before I could get what I wanted from him.

"I can't." He was a voice from the dark with an unbearable answer.

"Then you are a liar! You either lied before or you are lying now! I want my eyes! You can help me. You said so. You are a healer."

"You can bend the laws of this world, once you know why they exist, but they are not easily broken; there are too many other wills that shape reality. Your eyes are gone. I cannot create new eyes."

"But I helped you!" I wailed. "I helped you live when you were stranded on the mountain, and you can't help me now?" I fell back on the bed in despair.

"Xiao Chen," he said patiently, "Good and evil are like nested bowls — good within bad within good. How the food tastes depends on from what bowl you think you are eating. If you think you eat from the evil bowl, the food will taste bitter and will turn your stomach. But if you realize that you are also eating from the good bowl, the food will be sweet and wholesome. There is an old saying that the wise man makes medicine from poison, but the fool makes poison from medicine. Choose who you will be."

"I didn't choose this."

"Yes, you did. You knew everything you needed to know, and still do."

"I need to see!"

"Then do not give in to darkness." He paused and his voice changed, as if he had turned away from me. "The *Eckener* will be leaving for China soon. I think that you should consider coming with us."

"Oh, God. Now you are trying to be a comedian." I responded wryly. "How could I possibly go to China? What value would another blind Chinese girl have in China? They have a million already."

"People are not good judges of their own value."

"And why would I go?"

"It is a rescue mission," he said quietly.

"Who? Who are you rescuing?" I asked with a certain intensity.

"Xiao Chen," he said, ignoring my question, "there is no road map through life. But you do have a compass; follow it."

*

The police came later. I really didn't know if it was morning or night, or if it was a different day. They asked questions that I thought were peculiar. They asked me to describe the man, of course, and then they asked if I had ever been associated with any Islamic or anti-Islamic organizations or people? Had I ever been to an Islamic country? I answered no to everything and then asked them why they were asking questions about Islamic things.

"It's not our job to answer questions," he replied. "Read about it in the paper." Then he grunted as if someone had punched him in the ribs. "Oh, I'm sorry. I'm pretty stupid sometimes. It's just that we are under a lot of pressure to come up with some answers, and all we have is just one clue that leads nowhere. This Islamic business may be a wild goose chase, but it appears that the guy who blew himself up was from one of those Middle Eastern countries. We don't have very many witnesses — two, exactly; it seems everybody else was looking the other way. We talked to the taxi driver and we've been talking to that Chang guy, but he says he only got a glimpse. That leaves you. By the way, Chang asked us to give you this." He placed something in my hand. "It's a ring. He said it was hundreds of years old and that it was carved from the tail-bone of a tiger. I guess if you wear that, you'll always have a tiger by the tail. Look at the carvings on this thing." He grunted again from the other person's jabs.

"Why did he send this to me?"

"He didn't say. Do you know this guy very well?"

"No. I just met him that day. He seems harmless, don't you think?"

"You never know. But, we didn't have any reason to keep him any longer. He's gone in that big blimp thing."

"Did you see it leave?

"Lady, everybody saw it leave." He grunted again. "Damn! Well, what I meant was that everybody was in the streets and on the beaches and hanging out the hotel windows. Traffic was backed up for miles from people stopping their cars right in the middle of the streets and getting out to look. We had four times the number of fender benders of our previous record, which I think was when we won World War II. I had forgotten how many people there were on this island. I think every one of them was in Waikiki to see that thing leave. There was even a riot in the park. People were waving flags and yelling "Chong" something. But the strangest thing was when that big blimp left the island, the humpbacks followed it out to sea."

I felt a chill run up my spine when he said that. "Listen," I said, "I heard that there was the same kind of riot in San Francisco, when the Eckener left there. What if David Chang is the same person as Chang Da Wai?"

"Holy crap! And we've done let him go!"

I finally heard the second policeman say something. "If Mr. Chang was this Chang Da Wai that the rioters were hollerin' about, how come they just let him walk around town? I thought we were going to have to shoot some people just to keep 'em out of that airship. They wouldn't just step aside and let him come and go, would they."

"I guess that's true," the first officer sighed in relief. "I just saw my whole career flash before my eyes. I guess we better be going. I'm sorry if I wasn't sensitive earlier. And I'm sorry about what happened to you. And, lady, I sure hope we've answered all your questions, 'cause the next bunch of people coming around and asking stuff will probably be the FBI, and they won't tell you nothin'."

I had been playing with the ring, turning it over and over in my fingers. "Can you tell me what is carved on this ring?"

"Yeah, we were looking at it before. It looks like a dragon that goes all the way around the ring and is swallowing his own tail. And there is a lot of tiny Chinese writing. I don't read Chinese."

I rested after the policemen left, and thought about what I had heard. I must have fallen asleep, for I dreamed I was a whale. I was not an ordinary whale in a sea of water, but a flying whale in a sea of air. I swam up to the surface of the sea where clouds broke like waves against an island peak that rose above them into starlight. I would leap above the clouds to get a glimpse of space, and then I would fall back, sending clouds flying in a big splash. I wanted to leave the sea of air entirely, and I leapt and leapt and leapt, but earth pulled me back each time. I could not escape. I could not reach the stars. When I dove back into the sea of air, I saw other whales watching me, unmoving, silent. And in the way that you know things in dreams, I knew that they were hoping that I could show them the way, so that we could all leave forever, or come back as we pleased, but not be stuck here in gravity's pit. I did not have an answer; I did not know how to swim among the stars.

My parents came to take me home, and I knew that, although the ordeal of being in the hospital was over, the ordeal of being at home was just beginning.

My mother immediately saw the ring on my ring finger. "What is that? Are you engaged?" She made a bad joke.

"No, but it is probably the only ring that any man will ever give me, so I guess I can wear it anywhere I like."

She let that slide. "Who gave it to you?"

"David Chang."

"That horrible looking man? I hate him. If it had not been for him, none of this would have happened. You shouldn't wear his ring; it is bad luck."

I heard my father mumbling something to her. I pictured him putting his arm around her shoulders and trying to comfort her. "It is an interesting looking ring," he said to me. "Is it ivory?"

"No," I said. "It is bone — tiger bone."

"Tiger bone?! That can only be good luck. It was a very lucky man who killed the tiger."

"Yes, but an unlucky tiger."

"You are right," my mother said. "It is a dead thing. It is unlucky. You should take it off."

"Lucky or unlucky, the end is the same. Bones and teeth may be all we really leave behind."

My mother began to cry and I was sorry for my negative sounding remarks. I held out my arms and she sat on the side of the bed and we hugged each other.

"Don't cry, mother. I'll be OK. Everything will be all right. You'll see." And I tried to believe it. Later, I did take the ring off, and put it in my purse, where I forgot about it.

*

My mother was almost useless at home. Sadly, I knew that this was my fault and that I was even more useless than she was. She cried at everything. She cried when she sold the convertible. She cried when I missed my mouth with my spoon and dribbled rice on my blouse. She cried when I bumped into furniture or tripped over objects on the floor. She cried when her friends called and asked how I was doing. And she cried for hours when she heard about one of her friends' daughters getting married, or having a baby. Sometimes she would cry for no apparent reason, but I knew that it was just from looking at me. I once overheard my father telling her that if the scars on my face did not heal, they would take their savings and send me to one of those special doctors that made women pretty again.

For a while, the crying was almost more than I could stand. I think that, at first, I resented the fact that I spent all of my time comforting her, when she should have been comforting me instead. However, I think that having to comfort my mother was a good thing for me. It took me out of myself and out of the downward spiral of self-pity. And it caused me to have to think of positive things to say. They were usually pretty lame things, but just saying them seemed to help my mother. "Mother," I would say, "Please don't cry. Everything will be all right."

"How do you know?"

"I just know."

I am, by my nature, an honest person, and cannot bring myself to say something like that without finding some way to believe it on some level. And so, gradually, the optimist in me began to push out the pessimist as I forced myself to believe what I was saying.

My father had good advice as well. "It is Tao," he said. "Fight it, you get nothing but tired, but go with it, everything easy."

"But how do you know how to go with it?" My mother would ask. "Even I don't see which way it is going. How can she?"

My mother tried to think of things for me to do. She enrolled me in a Braille class, but I told her that I was not ready. I just needed some time to get used to being blind. She bought me books on tape, but I found sitting and listening to them to be somehow unnerving. I wanted to jump up and do something. It was like the sun was setting on a beautiful day, and I was wasting that day watching television. I wanted to see. I wanted to go to China. I wanted to help the people who had depended on me. But instead all I could do was try to make woven potholders by feel, or listen to someone read a book.

I finally had to tell my mother that I did not want her to try to think of things for me to do any more — that I would tell her what I wanted to do instead.

"But what do you want to do," she asked.

I had to think quickly. "Something that I have always wanted to do, but never had enough time for," I said, realizing that it was true. "I want to meditate." I could feel her eyes staring at me. "It will be good for me. It will help me have a more positive attitude about things. Who knows, maybe I will have such a positive attitude that men will forget that I am blind and want to marry me so that I can give our children such a positive attitude as well."

I had said the magic words.

"Well, OK. What do you need?"

"I just need to be left alone in my bedroom until I come out on my own. I need to take meals at my own times, so don't call me when supper is ready — just put some back for me."

"This sounds very strange," she said doubtfully, "but if it will help you feel better, I will do whatever you want."

So the arrangements were made, and I began to meditate without disturbance for however long I felt like doing it.

I had not meditated in such a long while, that, at first, I found it almost as tedious as listening to someone read. I remembered from prior reading and from my own experience that it took perseverance, and focus, and, gradually, I got better. Because of my previous familiarity with meditation, my sessions over the next several weeks extended themselves from a half hour to an hour, and then to several hours at a time. I did find my attitude improving, but other things began to happen as well.

One of the difficulties of meditation is focus. Spiritualists will tell you that meditation is for the purpose of spiritual growth, and so it is. It is a way to detach yourself from the world temporarily, with the goal of making the detachment permanent at some future time. The ego and the world conspire against detachment. They do not let something so dangerous to them happen easily. During meditation, thoughts bubble up from nowhere. Thoughts come up about any subject: things that happened during the day; things you have not thought of for years; things you have never thought of. The rule for the meditator is to recognize the thought as a thought, let it go, and return to the meditation. Sometimes, though, one may find one's self way down the thought stream before one is aware of it.

This happened to me during one of my sessions. The face of David Chang appeared before me, probably because it was one of the last things I had seen on this earth. I looked into the depth of his eyes. His eyes were as bottomless and distant as the deeps of space, but his smile was as warm and present as the morning sun shining upon my face through a prison window in mid-winter.

The vision of his face conjured up the conversation in the hospital, which led to the remembrance of the short time-traveling episode, which led to the memory of once more seeing the men enter the tent where the younger David Chang lay in oxygen-deprived confusion. But this time I saw more.

Now I was in the tent that the men had just entered. David was asking, "Where are all the others?"

"What others?" One of the other men asked.

"They were just here."

The man turned away and pressed his eyes against his arm. The second man was holding David's blackened hand that had been thrust at him. Tears welled up in his eyes also, some for the dead, I knew, and some for what had happened, but also for what still lay ahead for his friend.

The first man pulled a radio out of his back-pack. Static filled the tent, then quieted as he spoke. "Base, this is Ronnie. Over."

The static came back mixed with words. "Ronnie, this is Tom. What have you found? Over."

"We've got Dave." He paused. "But we're gonna need some help."
Pause. "And Tom . . ." His voice broke. "Be prepared for the worst.
Over."

*

I had done it. But how had I done it? Every out-of-body state that
I had ever experienced had been without my volition, an accident, or a
side-effect, or, sometimes, even as if someone else were controlling
the event. But then I thought, what if this too was an accident? I had
to be able to consciously and willfully repeat this experience of
traveling into the past in order to be sure.

I sank back into the meditative state, but as a mantra, I repeated
to myself that I would be able to travel back to see the tents on the
mountain. It was almost like self-hypnosis. Once I felt that I was deep
enough, I visualized the tents just as I had left them, and I was there!

The sun was setting, but I could see and hear everything clearly. I
watched the two newcomers try to take care of David. They fed him,
gave him water, and talked to him about what had happened.

They spent the night in the tent. They tried to get circulation back
into his hands and feet but they knew better than to hope for too much.
The next day, two more climbers arrived with extra boots and gloves
and a stretcher. They tied him to the stretcher and carried and lowered
him down the mountain in turns. They only stopped to rest briefly at
each camp before heading for the next one.

At each camp there were a few more climbers waiting to provide
help, until at the foot of the glacier, he was lowered hand to hand down
the last rocky slope and carried past the staring camp attendants and into
the surgical tent. The expedition's doctor had rigged a tent inside a tent
with extra flaps to keep dust out, and had stacked crates in the middle of
the floor to make a temporary operating table.

The doctor tried to explain to him what he was going to do — that
it would be painful — but he wasn't sure if David understood. He asked
Ronnie and Hank to hold him down as he began to inject fluid into the
arteries of his arms and legs.

David thrashed and screamed in agony. The doctor told him that he
was going to try to save what he could, but to do so, David would have
to have these injections twice a day for several days. David seemed
more lucid after the pain had faded a bit and he nodded at the doctor's
words.

The shots were almost as difficult for the doctor as for the patient. David's blood was thick and dark because of the increase of red blood cells needed to carry oxygen at high altitude. The thickened blood was difficult to draw into a syringe and that made finding an artery wearisome work. The patient would scream as the doctor probed the groin area with his needle, searching for an artery, but that was just the overture to the liquid fire that, once an artery was found, flowed through David's legs until he could only sob with pain. The doctor would leave the tent shaking, with sweat beading on his forehead.

I wondered if I could have any influence on what was happening at this time in the past. Even when I was here before, I could not affect physical things, but I had been able to establish a kind of psychic rapport with David. Also, I didn't know if I was really here in this space and time or if I was only viewing something immutable from the past. I tried merging my mind with his again, as I had done before. It seemed to help greatly. I gave him my strength and thought comforting thoughts into his head. I even presented images of his future, of how he would take a journey on a great flying whale. Of course, the only image I could conjure up was the one from the newspaper, in which it did resemble a whale.

I thought he went through the operations with much less pain and stress because I was with him. I even wondered if my being here with him now was the reason that he survived to save my life later. Answers to these types of questions dance out of reach around the edges of the universe and dart quickly behind its fabric when they sense your approach. However, one question had been answered: I was not just viewing the past, I was present in it.

As the days passed, David became more and more aware of what was going on around him. He watched the proceedings through round eyes. Though it was often hot during the day at base camp, he shook all the time. He didn't speak to anyone around him, but he did speak out loud to me, the presence in his head. This was disconcerting to his friends, who had no awareness of me of their own.

As the treatments continued, the doctor began to see what parts of the appendages had been helped and could possibly be saved. The feet were going to have to come off. They had called for an emergency airlift but it had not arrived. Gangrene was too far advanced to take the patient to Lhasa by car. He would have to do the surgery himself or it would not be done in time.

He had already begun removing fingers and toes a joint at a time as the tissue became obviously dead. David watched him snip a joint here and a joint there as if he were having his nails done. The larger amputations, however, would have to be done under general anesthesia.

The only time David spoke to the doctor was to ask him to leave enough of a finger so that he could wear the bone ring his wife had given him when they had gotten married. She had been descended from Chinese emperors, he had explained, but his friends only stared at him as if wondering if he would ever be right in the head again after his awful experience.

David did not speak again as they continued to prepare him for surgery. They helped him to lie down on the table one more time. He stared at the tent ceiling until his eyelids gradually closed.

Other climbers assisted the doctor as much as they could. When they could take the smell of the gangrene no more, they would run outside to take deep breaths of cold clean air.

While he had the patient anesthetized, the doctor cleaned up the hands as best he could, cutting into the living flesh to make certain that all infected tissue was excised. Although part of each lower leg had to be removed because of infection, he had managed to save parts of his hands: part of a thumb on each hand and even parts of fingers here and there — at least enough to wear a ring.

*

I discovered that there was no correlation between time spent in the past and time spent in meditation. Days of working with David, and trying to help him heal, translated into minutes or hours of meditation. I went back time and again. I suppose I kept going back because I had nothing better to do, and because I wanted to see, which I could not do while in my body. Also I had a strong interest in David's wellbeing. I had saved his life at least once and perhaps twice, and felt vested in him. The feeling was similar to that obligation one feels to feed a baby bird after taking on the role of its rescuer. But this was the past, you might say. It was over and done. What positive thing could I do in the past? Well, I had relieved his suffering hadn't I? But isn't that tampering you might ask? I don't know. All I know is that it felt correct. If my heart was telling me to do it, and it seemed that it was making things better, then I said do it. What else do we have to go on? At any rate, I admit that I tampered, and I meddled, and I took huge risks with the future history of the world. But that is all in the past now, isn't it?

I couldn't tamper in everything, of course. I had nothing to do with the emergency helicopter failing to come. That was the weather. I couldn't treat David's infections. That was the doctor's job. But I did other things. For example: While David was trying to recover from his amputations, I heard several conversations around the camp, each having a similar gist. The essence of the conversations was that David was very unlikely to survive either the long trek back to an airlift site, or existence itself, once back in civilization. David, according to his friends, had always felt that he had a purpose in life, and for him to realize that he would spend the rest of his life in a chair, even one with wheels, would be his death. A life without purpose would be a short one for David.

I had seen, about a mile or so down the valley from the main camp, an old monastery, now in ruins. I had also noticed that there were about a dozen monks living there, apparently trying to rebuild it, stone by stone. One night I visited each one of them in turn, and planted in their dreams the idea that the gods had sent them a powerful spiritual being to stay for a while with them in human form. This communication was done much the same way that I had experienced communication along the borders of paradise, by concept and image, not by word. I conveyed to them what had happened to David, that he was still asleep to his real purpose, but that there was something divine about him. I tried to convey the concept of divinity to these monks by conjuring up the image of Chenresig as he had appeared to me in the Chinese prison.

The next morning, they all awoke with the same astounding story to tell each other, and soon marched up to the camp to ask the bleary eyed breakfast cooks if a legless mountain climber was among them. They had come to take him back to the monastery with them. Of course, once everyone had woken up and had the request translated for them the whole camp was immediately against this idea—at first stunned into silence and then all in an uproar. That anyone could think that one of their own was divine was lunacy, and they were not going to leave their friend with lunatics. But in David's mind, I planted the idea that this was the beginning of his real purpose in life, this was why he had come to the mountain. In retrospect, perhaps I only relayed the truth.

The monks refused to leave without speaking to David. Eventually some of the other climbers put David into a folding camp chair and carried him out to set him before the crowd of monks. Having heard that they did not speak English, David addressed them in Chinese. "Do you understand me?"

"Yes," they answered. "We can speak Mandarin."

"What do you want?"

"To help you wake up."

"Who told you I was asleep?"

"We saw it in a dream. Chomolungma has sent you to us." They pointed to the mountain rising up behind the camp.

"What do you want me to do?"

"Come live with us. Eat our food. Watch the seasons change. See what happens."

"You want me to come live with you?"

"Yes."

"When?"

"Now."

"Why?"

"Because you are meant to come live with us. We saw it in a dream. We all saw it in the same dream at the same time. It was a miracle; we all woke up and told the same dream to each other. Surely you will not deny us this miracle. Chomolungma has sent you to us. We were told to come to this camp and take you back with us. We want you to stay with us. We have one of the best doctors in eight days walk." He gestured toward one of the monks, and the man stepped forward wearing a red robe, stained with dirt, but which was actually much cleaner than the robes of the others. He bowed his head to David but made no comment.

Tears were beginning to well up in David's eyes at this sudden concept of the expansiveness of life and its mysterious beauty. He stammered "Yes. I want to do this. I do not want to go back to my previous life — I couldn't go back; I can only go forward. It is difficult for me to believe, but I too have had this dream. Something tells me to go with you. My life has suddenly changed; doors have closed and doors have opened. I do not know who opens these doors, but when they open, we should go through them." He turned to the climbers, cooks, porters, and others standing around him. "These guys have a great health and retirement plan," he said in English. "I'm going to go work at the monastery."

The camp was in an uproar, everyone trying to talk David out of his decision at the same time. He was adamant that this was what he wanted and that it was his choice to make. The strongest argument against him was that he was not mentally competent to make this decision, as evident by the fact that he was throwing away all chance for proper medical assistance.

David replied that this was circular reasoning — that, by choosing this path, he was displaying a lack of competence to choose this path. Their arguments, he told them, were irrational themselves. Someone reminded him that he had lately been speaking with people who weren't present. David called for an immediate trial of his competence. He challenged everyone to ask him any questions they liked, as long as they agreed to rule fairly on the outcome.

"Where is Jia Li?" someone asked.

"Her body is on the mountain somewhere. She is dead." David answered.

"Who have you been talking to?"

"I admit that I felt a presence while I was sick, but it has gone away now. I think it was a result of the cerebral edema."

"What do the monks want with you?"

"I am not really sure. They want me to come live with them at the monastery. They are honorable men, and there is no reason to distrust their motives. I have no family at home, so why should I not go?"

"Do you know what you will be doing there?"

"No," David answered. "Do you know with any certainty what you will be doing when you get home, or even what you will be doing tomorrow?"

"Does this seem to you like a reasonable thing to do?"

"Reason and logic should never be used to make really important decisions. Did any of you use reason or logic when you made decisions to get married, or have kids, or take up mountain climbing? How many of you sat down before coming on this expedition and soberly reasoned it out and said, 'That seems like a logical thing to do.'? I don't mean to sound cynical," he continued, "but what most of you want now is absolution from me. You don't want to go back to your lives, and hear the question, 'How could you just leave him there? You knew he wasn't in his right mind.' Well, I am in my right mind. You have asked the questions, and heard the answers, and you are absolved. This is what I want to do, and if you try to take me against my will, then it is kidnapping."

The doctor stepped forward. "David, I have done everything that I can do for you. The weather is turning bad and the climbing season is over, which means there won't be anybody else up here for another nine months. There won't be any helicopters coming in here either. If we try to carry you out, we could drop you and break your sutures open, and if that happens down in the lower altitudes, you could end up with a pretty bad infection. You are acclimated; you have no infection that I can tell; you seem as rational as the rest of us. I guess the point I am trying to make is that if you want to wait it out up here until the weather breaks next year, it's probably no worse than any other decision you could make. Later, if you change your mind, there will be plenty of radios up here next season; call me and I'll come get you." He patted David on the shoulder and walked away.

"You're going to need some things, David," one of the climbers said. "Just let us know . . ." The voice cracked.

David looked around at the sympathetic faces. "Thanks everybody. When you get ready to leave, just leave me my rations, and whatever else you can spare for the monks. I think I will go with these guys now. You know I hate long goodbyes."

"I am ready," he said in Chinese to the monks.

Someone from the camp produced a couple of aluminum ladders that had been used to bridge crevasses on the glacier. They strapped the ladders on both sides of David's chair, and monks lined up along them. They lifted David, ladders, chair, and all, and marched off down the valley, carrying David as if he were royalty.

*

As the parade of red robed monks carried David down into the valley, he asked them in Chinese, "This monastery where we are going — it is called Rongbuk, isn't it?"

"Yes," one of them answered. "Rongbuk Valley, Rongbuk Monastery. This is the highest monastery in the world."

"What happened to it? It looks like an earthquake hit it."

"No earthquake," the monk responded. "The Chinese hit it."

"The Chinese destroyed the monastery?" David asked him to clarify.

"Yes. The Chinese have destroyed monasteries all over Tibet — some worse than this. But here, the Chinese destroyed the whole valley."

"What do you mean?"

"Rongbuk is a sacred valley," another monk joined in. "All life here is sacred. It is forbidden to kill anything in Rongbuk."

"But I don't see anything that could be killed." David looked up and down the valley.

"There are no animals or birds here anymore," the monk responded sadly. "The Chinese killed everything."

"Why would they kill all the birds and animals?"

"Sometimes just for fun; sometimes they eat them. The Chinese like to eat rare things. The rarer an animal is, the more they want to eat it. Chinese will pay a lot of money to say they ate the last one that ever was."

"So it is not because they are hungry, then?" David asked.

"It is a different kind of hunger."

"You must hate the Chinese very much for what they have done here."

"What good is it to hate a neighbor for being sick?" another monk spoke up. "We pray for the Chinese."

Yet another monk spoke up and asked David, "Are you Chinese?"

"No, I am an American. My grandfather was Chinese but was married to an American woman. He raised me after my parents died in an accident. "

"You speak Chinese."

"Yes. My grandfather taught me."

"Do you have a Chinese name?"

"Just my family name, 'Chang'." He gave it the Chinese pronunciation of 'Chawng'.

The monks had been speaking Chinese with varying degrees of imperfection, but now, the doctor spoke up in perfect Mandarin. "What is your given name?"

"David."

"I assume that you do not speak any Tibetan."

"That is true, but I would like to learn."

"In the meantime, you must pass yourself off as Chinese. If we meet soldiers, and they find out you are American, they will think you are a spy. We will call you 'Chang Da Wai."

I suddenly realized that this was the origin of the name that I had heard in Beijing. I also began to realize that every part of the existence of Chang Da Wai was because of my intervention, from his very survival, to the name that I had heard whispered on one continent and shouted on another. Yet, if he had not led me into the path of the explosion, if he had not shown me how to project myself through time, what would he have become? He would have survived, but would he have become Chang Da Wai? And if he had not become Chang Da Wai, would he have even been in Honolulu on that pivotal day? For the first time I began to sense the presence of unseen currents. I had the first inkling that there might be at work here forces to which I was a mere instrument. I thought of the ring that David Chang had given me, the ring made from the tailbone of a tiger. A ring which he now wore, and which also, in a different "now", lay in the bottom of a purse, in the darkness of a closet, waiting, just as I waited, just as David had waited, for a door to open.

Chapter 4 – Of Monks, Buddhas, and Mountain Men.

I knew David Chang, but I did not know the Chang Da Wai that David was becoming, and of whom I was part creator and somehow connected. I knew that I had all the time in the world, however, to unravel this mystery, if it could be unraveled. What else did I have to do with my time?

David's room at the monastery was sparsely furnished, but still better than he had expected to find in these ruins. There was a bed and a chamber-pot in this room, but in addition there was a separate kitchen with enough room to sit and to cook over the yak-dung stove. There was no yak dung to burn, however — all the yaks having been slaughtered by the Chinese. The monk's small fires were made from sticks carried in large bundles on the backs of monks from far down in the distant valleys.

The handful of monks who lived here had made a great ceremony of his arrival. They had placed him on a cushion-covered throne and the monks had come before him one by one to place gifts on the floor around him. There were white scarves, and pressed cakes of tea, and rancid butter, and bags of barley — magnanimous gifts from these people who had little to spare. He was bewildered by this attention.

This was not the greeting he would expect these poor monks to give a crippled beggar who had come to live among them. When later he said as much to Chamba Choe Sang, the monk physician who had walked beside him on the way, Sang said that even beggars served a purpose, for without them, to whom would we give our alms? But David was not to be a beggar, he assured him. He had a different job to do. And it was Sang's job and the job of the other monks in the monastery to prepare him for it.

David asked him what job he could possibly do, other than scrubbing floors. Sang told him then about the dream that they had all shared. "There is nothing for you to do," Sang answered. We are your servants. This monastery is yours. This valley is yours. There is much more that is yours if you only say the word."

"How can that be?" David asked. "I have never been here before."

"Perhaps," Sang said. "But you have seen these mountains before. Why do you suppose that you came here?"

David thought of all of the reasons that he had given his friends at home for coming to this distant part of the world to climb Chomolungma. He realized now that none of them made sense. He came because of a reason that he could not share with his friends: his heart had told him to come. "I don't know," he finally told Sang.

"Prayers are often answered in unexpected way," Sang said. "If you are going to pray, you have to be ready for the answer. We prayed; you heard and you came. You prayed and we came and carried you home."

"I am afraid that you have mistaken me for someone else," David answered the monk. "I am not equipped to hear or to answer prayers."

"You are so very wrong," the monk smiled gently at him. "Our prayers and our dreams may have led us to you, but if I had only met you walking down the valley, I would have recognized you. I have served you before, master. You are one of the beloved precious ones—a rinpoche." Sang prostrated himself in front of David as he said this, leaving David astonished and speechless.

Several nights later, David was partially aroused from sleep by the sound of bustling and stomping outside his window. In the morning, he saw yaks tethered beyond the fallen walls that surrounded the yards. Piles of dried yak dung had been stacked against other walls, and bags of grain were stacked beside them.

Sang entered his room holding what David at first thought to be two giant ladles. He quickly realized they were hand-carved wooden feet, crafted to look like the felt boots which many Tibetans wore. "Not possible," he said, looking with discouragement at the prostheses with their up-turned toes.

"Oh yes! There is no other way," Sang said. "You cannot be carried where we are going."

"Where is that? Who made these feet? How can I learn to walk on these?"

Sang smiled at the questions. "The monks made the feet for you. It would be very discouraging to them if you did not use them. They had to go a great distance for the wood, and lost many hours of sleep carving and finishing them for you. You will learn to walk on them the same way that you learned to walk on your own feet: you will fall down a lot."

"I — I'm sorry if I did not seem grateful," David managed to say, his throat constricted with emotion. "I don't know why I was scared. They are really wonderful. I do not care how many times I fall. I will learn to walk on these feet. Please tell the monks that this is the finest gift that I have ever received. They are a miracle — an answer to my prayers!"

*

I continued to monitor David's days with the monks. When the remaining climbers, Sherpas, and other camp attendants left their camp at the base of Chomolungma and marched down through the valley of Rongbuk, they stopped at the monastery to say goodbye to David and laid in piles the things that they said were too much trouble to carry back. They said that they hoped the monks would have some use for the items. They left cook stoves, cots, chairs, tents, sleeping bags, crates of dried foods, backpacks full of bottled water, duffel bags full of clothing, and other things too numerous to mention. It seemed that they barely allowed themselves the minimum to get them where they were going. They made their good-byes easier by telling David, and themselves, that they would be back next spring, after he had finished healing, to take him home again.

The wind was beginning to gust harder through the valley as David sat in his chair, dangling his new wooden feet and watching wide-eyed and wordless as his friends grew smaller in the distance. From the peak of Chomolungma, a mighty golden banner flew as if from an ancient turret across the deep blue sky. It was the wind driving a long plume of ice and snow that caught the sun and glowed incandescent against the darkening expanse.

David was driven as well. His wind was the physician, Sang, who would not let him rest, but made him keep practicing on his feet. Sang tolerated no excuses. At first, he had younger monks support David by his arms as if they were living crutches. Later, when the valley was full of snow, he wrapped the remnants of David's hands in lengths of felt so that they would not be injured further if he fell, and sent him off teetering along the base of the monastery's rock walls.

Once, after a day of repeated falling, David lost his temper, and told Sang that the physician had no idea of what it was like to try to walk on wooden feet. He told Sang that he could not teach something that he had not done himself. Sang immediately ordered a young monk to bring in an ax and proceeded to lie down in the snow. The pale and shaking monk was standing over Sang's legs with the ax before David believed that Sang was serious in his intent and conceded that he did not need for Sang to carry this demonstration any further.

Sang dismissed the distraught monk to go and regain his composure. "How could you cut off your feet for me?" David asked him.

"Feet are not real," Sang responded. "The world is not real." He pulled up one of the mountaineer's folding chairs and sat down. David sat on a snow-covered stone that was once part of the monastery wall.

"Then why do anything? Why sit down? Why stand up? Why teach me to walk? Why don't we just jump off a cliff and end it all?"

"Because you are real and I am real; that is why we do something. Everything else is illusion, but a very real illusion. It will draw you back, even from death, if you cannot break the spell."

"You just finished saying that your feet weren't real," David pointed out. "Now you are saying that you are real after all. I don't think you can have it both ways."

"I am not my feet, Chang Da Wai. Are you?"

"No. I guess if I was my feet, I wouldn't be here, since my feet are obviously not here."

"What part of your body are you?"

"I suppose if I had to pick, I would say that my consciousness is housed in my brain," David answered.

"Consciousness," Sang looked thoughtful. "What color is consciousness? What does it smell like?"

David looked bemused by the question. "Those are nonsensical questions. Consciousness is a function of the brain."

"You have a way of knowing this?" Sang asked. "You cannot see or smell consciousness, because you are consciousness. It would be like an eye seeing itself, or a nose smelling itself, a tongue tasting itself or a hand grasping itself. What sound does the ear make? Do brains produce consciousness or does consciousness produce brains?"

David shook his head in consternation. "I don't know what you are talking about. Why are you asking me these things?"

"The purpose is to help you to understand that you do not know anything. You think that you know things but the more you think you know, the further you are from the truth. Yet you cannot learn anything if you think you already know everything."

"I know what is real, which is more than you seem to know."

"You know what you are told and what you accept as 'knowledge'. When you dream, sometimes, you think that is real. Then when you wake up you say 'No, that wasn't real. This is real.' How do you know? Dreaming, being alive, being dead — they are all states of consciousness. When you are dead, then tell me what is real. But even then, I will not believe you, for how do you know? Does the illusion still hold you? What was real before you were born?"

"Even if I were to allow that you are right, I see no benefit to this discussion, other than to help pass the time."

"The benefit is to wake up," Sang continued. "Sometimes when you are asleep, you rouse just enough to realize that you are sleeping, but the dream was so lovely, that you want to get back into it. Then you think, 'No, it was just a dream. I have things to do.' We are all sleeping. We are dreaming the collective dream. Most of us love this dream, and try to stay in the dream, or re-enter the dream, or take the dream with us. Sometimes it is a good dream, sometimes it is a bad dream, but it is just a dream. Some of us have this feeling that we could almost wake up if only the right soul, the soul with true knowledge, could show us how. Some of us think that you may be such a soul."

David laughed in amazement. "First you say I know nothing, and then you say I have this special knowledge. You really are just toying with me aren't you?"

"No," Sang smiled at David's laughter. "You are toying with yourself. Sometimes the person who is to do the waking of others, must first be awakened. When you enter the world of illusion, it is very easy to become part of it. It seems very real. The icy wind, the rocks that we lift back to the top of the wall, the boots of the Chinese soldiers when they come into the valley, all seem very real; but we know that they are not. We who labor here in this monastery pray constantly to be delivered from this dream — from all illusion — but we do not have the way to wake up. Perhaps you are the way, or can point the way. But first you must empty yourself of yourself and be as you were before you were you. Do you know why you have no feet?"

"Yes. Severe frostbite."

"Why?"

"Because I didn't have my boots on while I was up on the mountain."

"Why?"

"Because we were in the tent sleeping when the avalanche hit."

"Why?"

"Because that is what we do at night where I come from. What are all the questions about?"

"To show you that if one keeps asking why, eventually the answers run out—the answers from *this* world, I should say. Cause and affect are not always what they seem. What if you came to Chomolungma so that you could live with us? What if you spent the night on the mountain to rid yourself of hands and feet, because otherwise you would go back with the others? And what if you also sacrificed them to detach yourself physically from this world?"

David shook his head in disbelief. "Why in hell would I want to do that?"

"So that you would not feel cool mud or soft grass between your toes, the warmth of rocks in the summer, or the iciness of a mountain river. You will not feel the soft skin of a woman on your fingertips, or the flow of her hair, or the roughness of tree bark, or the carvings on a clay bowl. You will have no family, for what woman would conceive with you? You have chosen to be an outcast, and you have attempted to isolate yourself from every worldly attachment."

"So you think that I did all of this to myself?"

"It is possible."

"No one in his right mind would do such a thing on purpose."

"That is not true. When a person wades across a fast deep stream in the mountains, he first takes off his clothes. Otherwise, the water will catch the folds in the clothing and pull him down and drown him. A bodhisattva can be pulled down and drowned in this world just as an unenlightened person can. He may need to cast off as much of his clothing as possible to get from one side of life to the other. Your body is just the clothing you wear. Anyone entering the world runs the risk of falling back into the dream and losing himself in maya, the illusion that the world is real. You may have fallen partly into the dream, but only a bodhisattva would have taken all the precautions you have taken to avoid being stuck in it."

"A bodhisattva?" David repeated incredulously. "You can tell me that I don't know everything and I might agree with that, but my divinity—or humanity—is one thing that you could not be more mistaken about. I am not a bodhisattva or a buddha or anything remotely similar. Everyone should wake up from that illusion right now."

"We shall see," Sang almost whispered.

*

One day, while standing in snow up to his ankles, Sang announced that winter was coming on and that it was time to move to lower ground. David asked where they would be going, and was told that they did not exactly know. The monks usually went back to Lhasa for the winter but these were special times.

Sang did not feel that he was making the progress with David's awakening that he had desired. I had mixed feelings about this. On one hand, I knew that I was the force behind the monk's belief that David was special. I had, in effect, lied to the monks, and was aware that their collective belief was totally artificial. On the other hand, I had my own reasons to believe that David was, or at least would become, special in some way. I had heard his new name, Chang Da Wai, everywhere from here to the other side of the planet. It was a name that I had heard but not created; Sang had created the name, even though I had led Sang and David together. Also the doctor in the hospital had told me that it was a miracle that I had survived the explosion, and even more of a miracle that David had. There was no way to disagree with that assessment, which led to the conclusion that David had somehow been transformed in the course of his life, a course that I had set him on.

Sang blamed himself for his failure to wake David. "I am not a fit teacher for you," he told David. "I thought that it was my job to awaken a bodhisattva; how foolish of me — I cannot awaken myself."

"I think I am doing better," David replied sympathetically. "I have really been thinking about all the things you and the other monks have told me. I think it is all starting to make sense. I really want to keep learning."

Sang stared at him and then chuckled. It was obvious that David was trying to help Sang save face. "That is good," he told David, taking his upper arm in his hand. "But now I believe that it is our job," he gestured at the other monks, who were standing nearby listening, "to find you a proper teacher. I believe the things that I tell you, but I believe them in my head only — I do not know them yet with my being. That is the trouble that all of us have. However, there is a teacher we have heard of who is reported to have real knowledge. He is called Zhi Ming. He is Chinese. The difficulties of finding him are threefold. We will have difficulty traveling in China; we do not know exactly where to look; and he may not even exist at all."

At this last statement, the other monks began disagreeing heatedly among themselves. They pounded their fists into their palms to drive home their various arguments about Zhi Ming's existence or lack thereof. Everyone had apparently heard the stories of this near mythical monk who lived by himself in the forest and ate nothing but pine needles, but, as some of the monks pointed out to their seemingly more gullible comrades, no human being could do the things that were told in the stories. The credence faction explained to their cynical companions that this was the very reason to seek him out; only a super-human could awaken the bodhisattva who had been given into their care. Were they prepared to argue that the dream of the bodhisattva, Chang Da Wai, was not real?

Sang cut through the debate with straightforward choices to be considered. Unless someone came up with a better idea, they could either head to Lhasa, essentially giving up, or they could try to find Zhi Ming, against all odds, or they could try to take David to the Dalai Lama and let the Ocean of Wisdom deal with the problem. However, as Sang explained, the chances of getting through the Chinese border guards and into India, where the Dalai Lama was living in exile, were less than the chances of finding Zhi Ming in the forests of China. Therefore, in Sang's mind, there was only one logical choice. As there would be no giving up, they would march into China.

*

To David's way of thinking, they were already in China, but what the Tibetans meant when they said China, was the China before the invasion of Tibet and the redrawing of the old maps. The China of their destination was many hundreds of miles away — normally an impossible journey at this time of year except for two things: the mountain climbers had left them supplies enough for such an expedition, and they would be traveling gradually south as well as lower in altitude on their eastward march.

The main problem would be the Chinese patrols. The monks had explained to David on many occasions how dangerous the Chinese soldiers were. The soldiers could do almost anything they wanted to do to a Tibetan, with little provocation, and little repercussion, if any. The monks knew this from many personal experiences throughout their lives and most recently from the irregular patrols that came up the Rongbuk valley. These visits by the Chinese military varied from quick reconnaissance to large encampments that stayed for months, brought heavy equipment, and occupied caves that they had cut into the steep valley walls. The monks had learned long ago to keep a low profile and bow respectfully when addressed by the soldiers. However, now that they were on the move, they did not wish to encounter any patrols, which would immediately be suspicious of monks traveling off the main routes with no good explanation of their destination. The fact that they and their yaks were carrying equipment manufactured in the U.S. would certainly not help their explanations.

The rugged terrain along this part of Tibet's border forced them towards the interior to some degree, but the less rugged areas were also the ones more heavily patrolled. Fortunately, the monks seemed to know the narrow mountain trails that the Chinese soldiers seldom if ever used.

The going was slow at first, and especially hard on David, who slipped and fell frequently on the icy trails. He did not complain, realizing, I suppose, that all of this was for him, and that the monks could be spending the winter debating beside the big monastery fireplaces instead of risking frostbite, imprisonment and torture.

From my vantage point above, I could see where the Chinese patrols were, and would join my awareness with David's so that he would indicate to the monks that there were soldiers in this direction or that one. Occasionally, on David's warning, they had to lay low and watch a patrol pass in the distance. Because of the accuracy of his intuition, they were even more convinced of David's latent superhuman abilities. At one point, they came to a deep river gorge that had, sometime in the past, been spanned by a bridge that was now collapsed into the river. David told them that there was a place up river where they could easily climb down into the gorge and cross the river on fallen boulders. The monks, never questioning this type of information, simply changed their route accordingly.

Although I was beginning to lose track of time, it seemed that they had traveled for many weeks before descending permanently into the zone of deciduous trees. Here it gradually began to warm up and the blizzards of the higher elevations became milder and milder, until they no longer walked on slippery rocks but on rich soft earth in deep forests, muffled by gently falling snow.

There were no patrols in this area, probably because they were no longer near a political border, and so they decided to camp here for a few days and regain their strength. The monks were obviously exhausted, but were in good spirits because David and fortune had been with them and directed their path.

David, too, began to relax. In our states of combined consciousness, information had flowed both ways, and I knew that his main concern had been for the monks and the sacrifices that they were making for him. Now that they were out of the frostbite zone, everyone was becoming more comfortable. David was no longer issuing warnings of imminent discovery by soldiers, and the forests were full of animal life, indicating that there were no villages nearby that might see the smoke from their fires and report them.

For days, the monks lay around in their tents, or sat around their cooking fires, laughing and joking. They had become tired of the western food they had been eating in the mountains, and now that they could make decent fires, they began to roast barley and boil water for tea, which they flavored with rancid yak butter and salt. David pretended to enjoy their food, but he had never really acquired a taste for it.

Sang was the only one who did not seem to be content with their situation. He had led them through the mountains with an antique compass and even older maps. Now he studied his maps as if he hoped that he was only overlooking the tiny "X" with the name "Zhi Ming" beside it. Of course, this "X" had never existed on the maps, as no one really knew where Zhi Ming lived, and Sang had only hoped that someday he would be able to put the mark on the map. When one of the monks finally asked him what direction they would now take, he had to admit that he did not know. Someone suggested that they just stay where they were, but Sang replied that it was unlikely that Zhi Ming would come looking for them. It would be better to keep moving in the direction of their original course and hope that David would be able to steer them when it was appropriate.

After a few more days of rest, the monks loaded up the yaks again and headed southeast. The snows eventually turned into dustings and then disappeared. The vegetation became lusher, with more undergrowth. In the distance ahead, they could see more mountains, but these were not the young raw mountains that they had left, but older, timeworn, tree covered mountains.

It was at about this time that I began to feel myself buffeted as if by a vortex of strong winds. I felt shaken this way and then that way and was very confused about what was happening to me. I was unable to observe the monks in my usual fashion, and they began to fade in and out of my awareness. I heard a voice calling my name, and briefly thought that I saw my mother's face. Then I was back in the darkness of my body. I was so disoriented that I did not realize at first that I was back. I did not know where I was. I could see nothing. The shaking continued and I slowly began to realize that it was indeed my mother who was calling my name. I felt as if I were swimming up from the deep ocean; somewhere above me was the understanding — the comprehension — of what was occurring, and I was trying desperately to reach it. I was exhausted but I struggled on. "What? What is it? What's happening? Mother, is that you? Where am I?"

"Dawn, Baby, you have got to get up and eat something. I have respected your wishes to allow you time to yourself, but you have been lying in here asleep for two days. Sit up and eat. I have made you some rice and hot tea. If you don't eat, I swear by the Buddha that I will take you to the hospital."

This life was dark, unhappy, and tedious compared to the one from which I had been shaken, but I did not feel that it was time to let this body go, so I ate.

*

My mother insisted that I not go back to sleep immediately after eating. She had bought some audio tapes of old radio programs and she wanted me to come into the living room and listen to them with her and my father. I was not interested. There was no radio or television program that could compare with the interest my sleeping life held for me. But I loved my parents, and so I did listen awhile for their sake, and pretended to enjoy myself.

I could tell by the types of food odors that I smelled as well as the general feel of the house, that it was not yet evening. I asked to be taken out to the back of the house where I could sit and listen to the sounds of the tropical birds in the jungle around me. My mother pressed more food on me, which I ate, and then she left me, content that she had done her job as a mother.

It was not long after I had sat down that I felt myself shaken and buffeted once more. I thought that I had fallen asleep and that my mother was again attempting to rouse me. This was not the case, however. I was not being shaken back into my body, but out of it. Once out of my body, I could see the flowers and trees and birds around me, but then I was swiftly pulled along as if being blown by a high wind, or, perhaps, like being rapidly dragged through the air by my shoulders. The sensation had a familiar feel about it. I had been blown like this before to a mysterious cave in some distant mountains. And there the cave was once again. My understanding was that I was being made to see the cave, like a child held by its mother and forced to look at something in order to remember it.

This was the first time that I had seen the cave in daylight and I noticed that the early morning sun shone directly into the cave. An old Chinese man with a long sparse white beard sat at the mouth of the cave. He seemed to be staring right at me, although I believed that he was only admiring the sunrise across the valley. There was also a small cooking fire at the mouth of the cave. Supported on rocks within the fire was a very rough looking metal tea pot.

The man stood up and went to a nearby pine, where he pulled off a bunch of green needles. He dumped this handful of needles into the pot and went into the cave. He quickly returned with a human skull, which had been crudely cut to make a bowl. After a short time, he poured the pine needle tea from the pot into the bowl and began to sip. I suddenly realized that this man was Zhi Ming, the Chinese monk who lived by himself in the wilderness and reportedly subsisted on pine needles. This was the cave that David and Sang and the other monks were searching for.

With this realization, I was suddenly lifted rapidly into the sky, from which vantage point I could see the surrounding countryside and the general lay of the land. And then, as if I had been given exceptionally strong binoculars, I could see off in the west, still hundreds of miles away, Sang's band of monks, heading way off course to the south.

Having seen this and knowing what was expected of me, I hurtled back into my distant body as if I was being snapped back by a giant rubber band. I entered my body with such force that I knocked the chair over backwards and landed on the ground.

Something extraordinary had happened to me. My funk had left me. I no longer felt depressed about my dysfunctional body. I felt connected to something larger than myself. During this brief time out of my body, my consciousness had expanded in some subtle yet important way. I became aware of untapped potentials within me. This expansion of self did not come about from what I had seen, but from the being or force that had shown it to me. Being in its presence, I knew that I was going to be fine.

I picked myself up off the ground and headed back to the house. I heard the back door slam and my mother's voice. "What are you doing?" she asked.

"Oh, I leaned too far backwards and fell over."

"No, I mean you are walking around. You are going to trip over something and hurt yourself."

I let her lead me back into the house, but I knew that I could have navigated my way without difficulty. In the few moments that I had been allowed to see, I had not only memorized the location of Zhi Ming and the monks, but I had memorized my own location as well. I knew where I was and I knew that some part of me knew where I was going.

*

I did not meditate again that night. Instead, I drifted off into a normal night's sleep. But information comes to us in many ways; it is for us to decipher the information and determine if it is valid or not.

After I had fallen asleep, I dreamed, or at least in many ways it felt like a dream; in many ways it did not. At first I thought that I had gone back into the past in order to lead David and the monks to the cave of Zhi Ming.

I found myself back at the mountain that the monks called Chomolungma. I thought that I had missed my mark and had overshot the monks, whom I had left in the forest far to the east. Then I saw that this could not be the same time of the year, or perhaps even the same past that I had left — there was green grass down in the distant valley, and there were people on the glacier above the Rongbuk valley.

I was very far up the glacier, almost against the great looming mass of the mountain. Below me and in front of me was something grotesque — something that did not belong there — an implement of war. I noticed that there was a line or cable connecting me to this monstrous lump and the line was becoming slack as I slowly drifted down towards the glacier, a terrible burning wound in my side.

As I sank lower, I realized that it was a tank that I was tethered to. It was partially lodged in a crevasse, its cannon pointed awkwardly up the mountain side. I was bound like a harpooned whale to this bizarre anchor, and I felt very much as if I were dying a whale's death, sad, alone and helpless.

I saw that there were two bodies sprawled clumsily across the tank. I was unbearably certain that this was David, and some other person I did not recognize, both dead. The tank was surrounded by Chinese soldiers who were shooting into the bodies.

My heart broke at the sight of David's body and the unfulfilled promise it represented, and all hope left me. The pain of striking the glacier would be nothing next to this disaster. I was now past fear, for it was overwhelmed by feelings of horror and despair. The only thing that saved me from madness was the realization that I would not have to bear up under this horror much longer; for I saw that I was unalterably about to crash into the glacier.

As the ice drew nearer, and I saw the soldiers running toward me I began to understand that I was not normal human size. In fact, I was huge, thousands of times bigger than the men scrambling over the ice like scavengers seeing an easy meal, but afraid to get too close too soon. I saw tiny figures — people — falling from me and striking the ice. I saw Sang lying on the red stained snow below me. And I saw others — people that I did not know, yet, strangely, I did know. I crashed in slow motion. I struck with an irresistible and overwhelming force. The collision went on and on, and I felt my lungs imploding, my bones shattering, my skin tearing away from me with the impact.

I began to twist and roll over the glacier and I saw more people falling out of me, smashing and rolling and sliding across the ice. It was like seeing my children dying. They had been in me like unborn children, now prematurely still-born. Their shattered corpses lay on the ice like a trail behind my still splintering and convulsing body as I continued to roll across the glacier.

I awoke with a loud cry, and my parents ran into my bedroom to see what was wrong. I told them I had dreamed a horrible dream — a nightmare — that was all. After they left, I held a pillow over my face to muffle my racking sobs until the screams of my dying children faded into the night.

*

The next day, I tried to unravel the meaning of this ghastly dream. As confused as my sense of time had become, I was certain that, if this was a real event, it had not happened in the past. I was fairly sure that it was not happening in the present either. I reasoned that I had been viewing this disaster from the perspective of the *Eckener*, the dirigible that had recently left Hawaii with David Chang on it. I may, I thought, have seen the unfolding tragedy through the eyes of one of the passengers or crew. If it had stuck to its original course, the *Eckener* had not even reached China yet, and had certainly not had time to reach the Tibetan territories. Therefore, I concluded, I had been witness to events that had not yet occurred.

I knew, or at least had some sense, that the future was changeable; nothing was immutably preordained. I concluded this from the fact that my work in the past seemed important to the present — that things that had happened to me in the present, could not have happened without my intervention in the past. This feeling was underscored by the additional fact that someone or something had taken the trouble to show me where to find Zhi Ming. If the past was important to the present, then it followed that it was even more important to the future, in the sense that ripples spreading from a disturbance affect an increasing number of objects in proportion to their distance from the source.

I was no longer crushed in hopeless despair, but spurred on with anxiety. I was certain that something that I was doing, or would do, in the past or present, was crucial to avoiding the awful future I had witnessed.

I told my mother that I was going to begin meditating again, and that she was free to awaken me if I went more than a day without food or water. She complained that I was wasting my life, but if this was what I felt I needed to do, then she would just have to live with it until I outgrew it and could put it away. It struck me then how disconnected we are from the inner lives of those around us, how much richer my life was than most of the people I knew, and I considered with compassion how much blinder my mother was than I. But, of course, there was no way that I ever could or would say such a thing to my mother, or even be able to explain it should she somehow read my thoughts.

I had no trouble finding David and Sang as they and the others blundered through the forests of China. Having left my body, the mere desire to be with them took me effortlessly to them. I knew where Zhi Ming was now, and I began to steer the monks by giving David suggestions as I had previously done. Sang was vastly relieved to see that David had regained his mystifyingly accurate sense of direction.

I turned their course slightly northeast and headed them towards the distant mountains. After days of marching, we began to see signs of habitation — cart-paths through the woods, or the occasional broken and discarded farm implement. I had hoped to avoid all contact with anyone but Zhi Ming, but the mountains that we were going to have to cross, were funneling us right toward a village that apparently sat in front of the only pass for miles. To avoid the village would cost us days or weeks and would not guarantee that we would not simply run into another village elsewhere.

I devised a plan based on my experience of using myself as a focusing lens for cosmic energy. I would shroud the village in fog and the monks would simply walk invisibly through town in the dead of night. I timed the event perfectly for when the monks were camped a few miles outside of the village and their march would bring them to the town at the height of the fog and the depth of darkness. I heated the ground water until vapors began to rise and knit together into an impenetrable fog that covered everything but the tallest trees and the topmost peaks of the highest roofs. I went back to the monks' camp to inspire David to a night march, but when I arrived, one of the monks was moaning loudly and holding his stomach. He had evidently picked up some form of dysentery from drinking the local water and was in no condition to march, or even to be carried through the village, where his groaning would surely be heard.

The next day the monk was better, and so I spent the early afternoon and evening heating groundwater again, in the hopes that this would be the night. This time, a different monk came down with the woodland waddle, or the Tibetan trot, as I soon came to think of it, because of the characteristic way that the monks would hike up their robes and dash off into the woods. A third day and a fourth day I hopefully prepared the village fog, and finally on the fifth night, the diarrhea had run its course and all the monks were chipper and well rested. As they were getting ready to bed down, David spoke up and told them that he felt very strongly that they had been there long enough and that they should break camp and walk through the night. Of course, in a sense, that was just me talking.

The night was clear where they had camped and so the fog they encountered after a few hours was unsettling. David told them that they were entering a village and that they should all be as silent as possible. He explained that there was no way around and that they should be thankful for the fog. I gave them directions through David, and they all walked quietly into the village, keeping their hands on the equipment piled on the yaks to keep it from rattling. What I did not know was that the villagers had come to expect this eerie fog which had mysteriously appeared every night for almost a week and had taken to gathering in front of their homes at night to marvel at it, seeing it as somehow portentous. The monks had walked silently and cautiously into the middle of town, when, as if on cue, a stiff breeze came up and blew the fog away, up into the clear starry night sky.

It was as if a curtain had risen on the monks, and the villagers were astonished at what the fog had revealed to them in the starlight. The red-robed shaven-headed monks stared speechlessly at the equally speechless homespun and heavy booted peasants. What more fantastic sight could these villagers ever expect to see? Men in strange and alien garb had been miraculously transported from nowhere directly into the middle of town, accompanied by bizarre beasts of burden.

Both groups were about to bolt in all directions when Sang, gathering his wits, spoke up in his flawless Mandarin. "This is Chang Da Wai," he said, gesturing deferentially in David's direction. "He has come down from a very high place to find the famous monk Zhi Ming. The hospitality of the people of these hills is widely known and we seek the kindness and generosity of this village to help us on our quest to benefit all sentient beings." Sang bowed and waited for an answer.

After a long silence, one of the peasants, probably the acting mayor, walked around in front of Sang and bowed in response. "Your arrival, though heralded by the divine mist, was unexpected, but we are pleased at your words. Who is Chang Da Wai, and why does he seek Zhi Ming?" He asked politely yet firmly.

"Chang Da Wai is a bodhisattva, a buddha, who has come to help us all. He seeks to confer with Zhi Ming about the future of the world," Sang stated with assurance.

The mayor looked around at all of the townspeople, hoping that someone would give him a sign of what he should do next. "This is a great and wonderful thing you say," he finally replied to Sang, "And an honor beyond our merit."

Another man stepped out of the crowd that had slowly gathered closer to the monks. "But it is a thing too large for us to swallow easily," the man said. "Perhaps a buddha would not take offense at our hesitation if we offered him some way to prove this thing that you say," the man suggested.

The mayor walked over to the other man and conferred with him. In a moment he came back. "If it pleases the buddha Chang Da Wai," the mayor said, "Our Party representative would like to ask him some questions. You monks may not answer for him."

Sang stiffened. "It would not please the buddha to be questioned by one who has already made up his mind, referring to the Communist Party representative. Who is the wisest man in your village?"

The mayor knew better than to say in front of all of these villagers that he was the wisest man in the village. He also knew better than to suggest that the Party representative was. There was a murmur among the villagers — a name being whispered from person to person. Eventually, the crowd parted in front of a small house very close to where they were all standing. A young man ran into the door of the house and soon came out leading an old stooped man by the hand. The old man was using the back of his other hand to rub his bleary eyes.

The young man led the old man to where the mayor was standing. David walked up to stand beside Sang, who, in turn, stepped back, leaving David unexpectedly alone and facing the bewhiskered old man.

The mayor explained the situation to the sleepy elder. "Ask him the questions you are always asking us," the young man told the old one. "See if his answers are any better than ours."

The sleepy old man stood on wobbly legs in front of David. He slowly looked around the crowd, now illuminated by a few torches as well as the bright starlight and the rising moon. He licked his lips and turned his eyes questioningly to David. "My grandson tells me that you are a buddha," he said. "Is that so?"

David held his palms up and shrugged.

The old man nodded as if accepting this as an answer.

"What is the nature of a buddha?" he asked.

David did not know what to say. He looked at the ground, thinking hard, and then he stared up at the stars, hoping for inspiration, or at least a quick death.

The old man quit waiting for the answer to that question and went on to the next one. "Where will we find buddha nature?"

David stared at the monks, pleading with his eyes that they might give him some clue what to say. Then he stared at each of the peasants, wondering which one would throw the first stone to strike him. Finally, he studied the distance between him and the nearest yak, wondering how fast it could run with him on its back.

At last the old man asked David, "What does a buddha look like?"

David quit even trying. All was over. The game was up. His head was bursting with the effort. He rubbed the heels of his palms over his eyes in fatigue and despair.

The old man turned feebly to the other villagers and spoke loudly in his quivery voice. "Just as all buddhas must, this man realizes that words can only mislead. He teaches us with his silence. By his actions he says that a buddha is both in the sky and in the earth; a buddha exists in the spiritual realm and the physical realm at the same time. He also says that buddha nature is in each and every living thing. Also that we will not recognize a buddha when we see one, just as most of us have not tonight. The mayor should find places for this buddha and his friends to sleep. We can visit more in the morning." He turned and slowly walked back toward the house from which he had been dragged from his slumbers.

*

The villagers treated the monks with respect and deference. The monks were given the beds with the softest straw and the blankets were the best that each household had to offer. David slept in the mayor's house. The mayor asked him no more questions, but made his guest's comfort his highest priority. He offered David bread and dried fruit and local beer, and made sure that David got the best bed in the house, which, in the winter, was the one in the kitchen, closest to the fire.

After a restful night's sleep, the monks emerged from their warm beds to discover that the villagers had prepared a breakfast of tea, dried fruit, and porridge in the town common area, and were already working on preparations for a feast in the monks' honor that evening.

They were just about to kill a pig for the feast, but were stopped by the monks, who said that they always preferred a vegetarian diet, and would not want the pig's death on their conscience. The villagers were visibly relieved, as the time for killing pigs was in the fall. This was the tail end of winter and food was beginning to become scarce, but any farm animal that had survived this long, would now be needed for breeding purposes. Killing one pig now could easily mean a half dozen fewer pigs for the village next winter.

However, now it looked as if the feast was going to consist of more dried fruit and porridge, with some beer thrown in to make it festive. The monks then opened up their packs and made their contributions to the feast, most of which were freeze-dried items donated by the mountain climbers. The monks had already eaten most of the things that they liked and had carried the rest in case of an emergency. These emergency rations were what they now distributed to the cooks. They were things like beef stroganoff, chicken noodle soup, beef jerky, pre-cooked bacon, fried meat pies, hamburger patties, evaporated chili, and so forth. This bounty of food was miraculous to the villagers, especially when they saw how the foods reconstituted with water. However, this was not the last miracle that the villagers witnessed that day.

The villagers always got up before dawn to take care of their animals and get ready for the day, therefore they had not noticed the fruit trees and nut trees that were planted near the houses in the village. The trees in this part of the world were already budded out in readiness for spring, but here in the village, the buds were opening— the trees were flowering! As the day progressed, the almonds, cherries, and plums, actually began to blossom. They were weeks ahead of schedule, and so this was quite a notable miracle, one, I am sure, worth telling about for generations until the tale finally faded into the general background of pastoral mythology.

Of course, I realized that I was the cause of the miracle. By heating up the ground water, and thereby, the soil and the surrounding air, I had created a microclimate that had triggered the early flowering.

In case you are wondering, I also realized that the next freeze would now ruin this part of their fruit and nut crop, and so I continued to visit the village for weeks afterwards to maintain this microclimate until real spring could catch up. This was tedious to do, but was the least that I could offer this hospitable and generous village. The villagers said that it was a blessing from the buddha, Chang Da Wai, and his fame began to spread to all of the surrounding villages as they told the story of the trees that bloomed in winter.

The next miracle came at the feast itself. The villagers, awestruck at the miracle of the early flowering, and no longer having any doubts about Chang Da Wai's authenticity, asked him to bless their children. David stood facing the assembled villagers, who, family by family, brought their children before him so that he could touch them on the head and say a few words of blessing. After which, the children would each prostrate themselves at his feet. The miracle came when one young seeker-of-truth, perhaps the son of the Party representative, decided that he would test this buddha one more time. He had smuggled a small knife in his clothes, and when he bent down to touch his forehead to the ground at the buddha's feet, he instead pulled his knife from his clothing and stabbed the buddha in the foot through the cloth shoe that he now wore. The horrified parents grabbed the boy up and stared at the pierced foot in utter dismay. David, mildly surprised at what had happened, and not knowing what the protocol was for such a situation, calmly pulled the knife out of his foot, handed it back to the boy, and stood waiting for the next supplicant.

David discovered that most of the villagers could no longer look directly at him after this incident, much less talk to him. If he asked one of them a question, he or she would stammer and turn white. Nearby villagers would hurriedly drag their newly weak-kneed friend away, embarrassed for their friend and hoping that the buddha would not ask them something as well. David decided that it would be better if he just waited in the mayor's house and let Sang do all the talking.

Sang found out that they were at least warm on the trail of the monk, Zhi Ming. No one in the village had ever actually seen Zhi Ming, but they knew people in other villages, who had heard of people who had. All the villagers knew was that he lived in the mountains to the east and would talk to no one. This was not entirely true, they corrected themselves. There was a story of a young monk who had sought out Zhi Ming to ask him the nature of reality. The young monk stood patiently in the snow for three days before Zhi Ming answered him. The answer was, "You have your answer."

*

Zhi Ming, of course, was not as difficult to find as the villagers thought he would be; I knew exactly where he was. However, it took the monks another couple of weeks of climbing up and down the folded mountain ranges, going gradually higher and higher, before they approached the mountain where Zhi Ming lived. They had to cross one final high ridge, go part way down into the next valley and then follow a winding trail along the bluffs and then back up towards Zhi Ming's cave. I could certainly understand how difficult it would be to find him if one didn't already know how. No matter whether one came from the east or the west, to find Zhi Ming, one had almost to go back the way one had come. The natural inclination was to keep pressing forward, to "make progress", which was self-defeating.

David, the monks, and the yaks were all exhausted and barely plodding along the trail through the pine woods, when suddenly, late in the afternoon, there was Zhi Ming, sitting cross-legged in front of his cave directly in front of them. He was dressed in a dirty ragged white sheet. His bent tea pot was percolating on the fire beside him, and he had piles of what looked like unleavened bread patties stacked on the rocks around the fire. He smiled and sat up straighter when he saw the pilgrims. "Welcome, welcome," he said, beaming. Cakes and tea anyone?"

Everyone stopped dead in their tracks. They looked as if they had suddenly awakened from a vivid dream and were trying desperately to comprehend where they really were.

Zhi Ming made a face of mock dismay. "What is it?" he said, as if speaking to a small child. "You can have a cake if you like." He held one out in his grubby right hand. One of the yaks began to slowly lumber forward as if he knew that Zhi Ming was speaking to him. He gently took the cookie-like pastry in his lips from Zhi Ming's hand and began to munch contentedly while the human travelers looked on.

"Please," Zhi Ming made a broad gesture to include the humans. "Come and sit down. I have seed cakes and honey, and the tea is just ready, although you may find it a little strong, as I do not have any real tea. Sit; make your selves at home. I have been expecting you."

The monks and David looked at each other to assess what the others were going to do, and then slowly advanced towards the fire. They moved deferentially, as if they were becoming aware that they were in someone else's home, even if his home was the forest and a cave. They sat in a half-circle in front of the hermit, who paid them no attention while he fed little seed cakes to the yaks as they came up to him, one by one, like well-mannered children.

David reached over to the rocks and took a cake. "Mmmm, they are very good," he said, after taking a bite.

"Get out your bowls and have some tea," Zhi Ming said in reply, shaking the yaks' shaggy heads playfully by their horns and kissing them on their soft noses.

While the monks dug in their packs for their all-purpose food and drink bowls, Zhi Ming poured a little tea into his own bowl, the cut-away human skull that I had seen him use before. David stared at the skull as if trying to decide if he was really seeing what he thought he was seeing. The monks, however, paid no attention to it. They were staring at their yaks as if they had never really seen them before.

"Excuse me, um, ah," David began. "How should we address you?"

Zhi Ming looked into David's eyes. "Are you in there?" he asked David seriously. "You are in there, and I am in here, but here and there are the same place. There is no here; there is no there. But what difference if you are there and I am here, there is no you and me. Call me Chang Da Wai, if you like."

David seemed unnerved at this answer. He fumbled around for something else to say. "You said that you had been expecting us, and it seems that you have heard my name before. Has someone been here before us?"

"Oh, the villagers are spreading your fame far and wide, young buddha, but they have not been to this part of maya," he said, grinning foolishly at David. "Zhi Ming is the traveler, yet Zhi Ming leaves without leaving and stays without staying."

One of the younger monks had the temerity to speak up at this statement. "Master," he said, "It is good to know that you do not just sit up here doing nothing as everyone says. What good deeds could come from living all alone as a hermit?"

Zhi Ming grabbed his knees and rolled backward in laughter. "I do nothing yet everything gets done; I do everything, yet nothing gets done. Do you understand me?"

The young monk blushed and smiled uncertainly, taking a sip of the bitter tea.

"Thubten meant no disrespect, Teacher." Sang began in apology for the young monk. "It is just that you are very different from what we expected. We are a little off balance."

"Good," Zhi Ming replied. "When you are off balance you learn how to fall; when you fall, you learn how to fly. You expected to find Zhi Ming, didn't you? And instead you found me." He laughed again. "Zhi Ming is gone. Zhi Ming has been freed."

Sang looked confused. "Are you not Zhi Ming, then?"

"What is Zhi Ming? I am the stars and the rain and the wind in the pines. I am the wheel and I am the turning of the wheel. Yet Zhi Ming is here too. Nothing is ever lost; no one is ever diminished. If you want to talk to Zhi Ming, Zhi Ming will answer."

It suddenly occurred to me that I had led this band of monks hundreds of miles to listen to the ravings of a crazy old hermit.

"Of course I am a crazy old hermit," Zhi Ming said as if in answer to my thoughts. "I am all things, so I must be a crazy old hermit as well, and looking down at these clothes, it occurs to me that I am indeed playing the part. In an infinite universe, not only are all things possible, but all things must be. Who is not a crazy old hermit? What does it mean to be sane, anyway? Is it to know that trees are just bark and wood, and that rocks are not alive? I laugh at reason. Logic is a trap. All words lie. Time is a deceiver and matter is only dung. I am a king and a thief and a whore and a priest. I am a yak and the grass and a bird and a tree in which it sits. I eat a moth and eat myself. In only a moment, you will say that you are the stars and the wind, and then you will know that you are me. Life is a dream; is it sane to think that dreams are real?"

He strode through the light and shadow of the pines as he talked. Now he sat down behind Thubten and pulled the startled monk back so that the monk's bald head rested against the hermit's chest.

"Thubten wonders why I sit up here on this mountain indulging myself while there are wars and famine in the world," the hermit said softly, looking up at the sky as he stroked the top of the wide-eyed monk's head. "I cannot prevent a war. Can you?" he asked, looking down into the monk's face. "Wars, famines, and fools will always be with us. They are the very essence of this world. Cut off my head right now if it will prevent a war. It will be no loss to me. But, it will not prevent a war. The world is a pile of manure, a compost heap. Do you love a compost heap?" He held the monk's chin in his hand and turned the monk's face to look up into his. He shook the monk's head no with his hand. "No?" he asked. "But a gardener does. Who is the gardener, Thubten?" he asked.

No stranger sight had I ever witnessed than this scene in the pine woods beside Zhi Ming's cave. Zhi Ming held the frightened wide-eyed Thubten like a lover in his arms while around him sat a circle of red-robed and bald headed men staring in wonder, and around them in the dappled shade stood a larger circle of shaggy, horned yaks, also staring at the hermit, yet nodding their hairy heads as if in total agreement.

"It is you, Thubten," the crazy monk continued. "In your garden you try to grow flowers but weeds come up. They come unbidden from your mind. To stop the wars, I must stop you, but I cannot stop you, because you are me and I do not know how to stop. I try to dream of flowers, but sometimes I dream of weeds. War will end when the world ends. Famine, poverty, cruelty, and ignorance will all end when the world ends."

"When will that be, Master?" Thubten asked, wide eyed.

"Whenever you want it to, Thubten. But I know something that you do not know," he continued, smiling gently.

"Wh... what do you know, Master?" Thubten stammered.

"It doesn't matter."

"I wou... would like to know, please Master."

"What I know is that it doesn't matter. Everything ends or will end or has ended. I forgive the war mongers because I am the war mongers and I forgive myself for all the things I have not done. And if I did not do them then no one did them and therefore they are not done at all."

"I see," Thubten said with a confused and frightened look on his face. "Are you going to kill me, Master?"

"Ha ha ha." Zhi Ming rocked backwards, slightly letting go of the monk, who tried futilely to wriggle away. "I love this world," Zhi Ming said to the sky. "I cannot find it in my heart to hate it. Is there someone among us who can teach me how to do that? Should I hate the world and leave it? Hate is so negative. Yet how can I love the world and let it go? Can you tell me, Thubten?"

"But surely you are the most enlightened of all enlightened beings alive today," Sang blurted. "Surely you know the answer to that question even if the rest of us do not."

"I do know," the hermit said, sitting up and staring into Sang's eyes as Thubten slid in relief to the ground.

"There is a jewel beyond price. There is something for which each of you would trade everything that you know. You would trade the mountains and the oceans and the deserts and the stars and bring the world to the end of time to know what I know. The world is nothing but ashes compared to what I know."

"Then will you teach us, Master?" Sang asked. "We desire more than anything to be enlightened."

"Perhaps," the hermit replied. "But to seek enlightenment is to chase your own tail. Everyone is already enlightened; it is just that we do not realize it; it is just that we have landed in this dung heap and light cannot penetrate it. Perhaps I can scrape a little dung off of you. But first, tell me what you expected to find here."

"Although you are not what we expected, surely . . ." Sang began.

"Did you know," the hermit said, standing up to hug a yak around the neck and press a seed cake to its eager lips, "that if you give the same love to an animal that you should give to your brother, then someday he may become your brother, but if you do not, then someday you may become his? Not really of course, but actually, and only in the sense of it happening in this world. You cannot be your own brother, except that you are."

"But how can you be your own brother, Master?" one of the younger monks asked.

"Who asks me this question?"

"I am Rinzen, Master."

"No you are not." He pointed at Thubten. "Who are you?"

"I am Thubten, Master," Thubten answered, bowing his head.

"No you are not." He pointed at Sang. "Who are you?"

"I am the wind and the stars," Sang answered.

"Very clever. Why did you say that?"

"Because, like you, I also believe that I am part of everything," Sang replied.

"No no no," Zhi Ming said vehemently. "You are not part of everything. Everything is part of you."

He pointed at David. "Who are you?"

"I suppose it depends on who you ask," David replied cautiously.

"Well, I expect I can teach you something," Zhi Ming said, "but whether you learn it is up to you. You may think that you want to know the truth, but when it is shown to you, you may refuse to look at it. Many of you came here with expectations," he continued, "and now your expectations have been shattered. Some of you think that I am not sane. Rinzen thinks I talk in circles. Thubten thinks I might kill him. Sang thinks that I may show you something wonderful. Well, perhaps everyone is right. However, if your expectations were shattered by what you found here, that is nothing compared to how your expectations will be destroyed by the truth! Truth is the destroyer—feared by all, sought by few. Most who see it, deny it. Many run from it. Many who find it wish they had never heard of it. The trick is not to stop when you have found it, but to go into it."

"Master," Sang began, "Teach us how not to be afraid of the truth. What is it that makes it seem so fearful? Why do we seek it if it is so awful?"

"The spirit seeks the truth," Zhi Ming answered, "because for the spirit, the truth is eternal life. It is unbounded bliss; it is love without measure that is not to be found in this world. But there is a part of you that does not want the truth. Some people call it the ego. The ego calls itself by name. It calls itself Sang or Thubten or Zhi Ming. The ego must have the illusion of the world in order for it to exist. It uses fear to control you. Fear is the opposite of love. The ego keeps you entertained with fear, with hatred, with war, pestilence, threats of scarcity, as well as guilt and feelings of unworthiness, of isolation and loneliness. The ego does not want you to know the truth, because for the ego, the truth is death."

*

The conversation did not end there, of course. Each of the monks, eventually put at ease by the avuncular and affable madness of the hermit, lost their shyness and began to jump readily into the discussion. I kept waiting for Sang, or someone, anyone, to broach the subject of why they had come to the old hermit's cave. Instead, they all fell ultimately into arguing and debating with Zhi Ming and with each other — all that is except for David, who just stood back in the trees and watched, smiling occasionally at some deft parry of logic. They all seemed to take great delight in the contest of words and logic, using them like weapons. Zhi Ming, having previously disparaged logic, proved particularly adept in its use, dancing around the monks' word traps like an Aikido warrior, never losing his center or his feel for his place in the universe.

At last it began to grow dark, and everyone found their own sleeping places on the soft moss beds under the tall whispering pines. I stood watch over them during the night, admiring the beautiful valley below, glowing dimly silver in the bright moonlight. After a while, David came and stood on the edge of the cliff and looked out over the valley. He stood there for a long time, and then sat down on a rock and hung his head.

Awhile later, he was startled out of his reverie by Zhi Ming's voice. "Have you ever meditated in this life, young buddha?" Zhi Ming asked him.

David looked up to see the old hermit standing beside him, his ragged clothes and silvery hair seeming to glow in the moonlight. He shook his head no. "Sang has tried to teach me, but it doesn't seem to work for me."

"Meditation is a tool for obtaining knowledge that is very difficult to obtain in other ways because it is not what we normally think of as knowledge. Science uses tools to show us things that are 'out there' but what we seek to learn about is no thing and it is not out there. However, like a telescope, meditation can show us what is not yet attainable; like a microscope, it can show us what is beneath and behind the world we think we know; and like a mirror, it can show us something of our true selves. For the eye cannot see itself without help and the mind cannot understand itself without stepping outside of itself. But that is impossible, is it not? Meditation brings peace, happiness, contentment, and awakening. And with awakening come other gifts if you are ready to receive them. Meditation works for everyone if they work for it. I will teach you meditation the way that my teacher once taught me. Look across the valley and I will show you the power of meditation."

Zhi Ming sat down on the ground in the cross-legged lotus position with his hands palm up on his knees. "The position is not really important," Zhi Ming said. "I no longer have to do anything at all, as you will come to understand, but I am demonstrating for your benefit."

He shut his eyes and sat very still and straight. David looked across the valley and waited for something to happen. He had no idea what to expect as he scanned the distant and dark escarpment. In a couple of minutes, he heard a rumbling and saw a large boulder rolling down the face of the cliff, bouncing and crashing through the underbrush at its base, and finally coming to rest in the small stream that ran through the valley.

Zhi Ming opened his eyes and stood up.

"You did that?" David asked.

Zhi Ming nodded.

"Can you put it back?"

Zhi Ming laughed. "Sadly, no; I am not a god the way that you understand gods. I can manipulate reality to the extent that reality allows it. As Zhi Ming, I am just a small fish in the great sea of consciousness from which all reality crystallizes. The boulder would have fallen soon anyway. I only gave it a little nudge and let the reality of gravity do the rest. Other ways of manipulating reality are more understated, yet they are also more powerful because they do not obviously break any of the laws of this reality. Bringing you and your friends here so that I could teach you is an example of this. I imagined what could happen did happen. To imagine the happening of what cannot happen is still in my future."

"You brought us here?" David asked in astonishment. "How did you do that? What do you mean you imagined it?"

"Existence pours forth from my imagination. If something happens, it is because I imagined it; if it does not happen, it is because I did not imagine it. I brought you here just by thinking you would come. There are other more subtle and yet more powerful ways to change reality than the trick I just showed you. Reality is all of the mind, and the great sea of consciousness will give you anything you ask for because it is you, and ultimately it will not deny itself. It will even break its own laws, or I should say that it will make new laws, if it can do so with enough delicacy. To change reality, one does not even have to understand what reality is. People do it all the time and do not even know that they have done it. Sometimes, however they do it on purpose, and then they think the power comes from outside—from some object, or being, or magic phrase, but it really does not come from anything but themselves."

"So, you are saying that all power comes from ourselves alone?"

"No, no. The power to change the dream comes from us. If we pray for money and then we get money, that power came from us. The true god does not care if you have money or not. But if you pray to change yourself, you will receive help from outside of space and time, because unlike the world, you are real and the true god cares about what is real.

But as for space and time, you exist outside of space and time; but space and time exist only within you; they come only from your imagination."
*

Zhi Ming spent the next weeks teaching meditation to David, requiring him to meditate daily for hours on end. He also honed the techniques of the monks who began to meditate through-out the day along with David so that the pine woods became a very quiet place once more. The only sounds were the twittering of birds, the wind in the boughs, and the occasional sound of the yaks foraging in the higher meadows above the trees. In the days there was the warm sun upon their faces, in the night the mysterious stars and moon moved slowly across the sky, and always the earth was soft and fragrant beneath them, seemingly constant, yet subtly changing.

Sometimes, he also talked to David about the nature of reality. "Forget everything that you know," he told David. "None of it is true."

"How do you know that?" David asked. "You don't know what it is that I do know."

"I do know that if you knew the truth, you wouldn't be here talking to me," Zhi Ming replied.

"So you are saying that if I become enlightened, then I will not be here any longer?"

"Where is here?" Zhi Ming shrugged. "If you know where 'here' is, then there is nothing else you need to learn."

David had become accustomed to the monk's strange way of speaking and knew that there was an underlying truth that the monk was trying to convey and which David was only beginning to glimpse. "I will try harder," he told the monk. "Teach me what I should know."

"You should know nothing. To <u>know</u> something is not to believe it. You must feel its truth. You can know that the sky is a mixture of gasses, but that has nothing to do with truth. You can know that mountains rise from the sea, but you must *feel* the constant moment-by-moment creation of the universe as it emerges from your mind."

"I only feel lost and confused. I am trying to find enlightenment, but sometimes I think it is hopeless. I don't even know what enlightenment is."

"Don't try! You become enlightened by not trying. Just be — like a child. There is no truth that is not already in you. Enlightenment is washing the dirty windows and seeing that the day is sunny. It is sweeping the sidewalk and finding a sparkling diamond. It is polishing the brass teapot and discovering that it has been solid gold all along. Enlightenment creeps up on you. There are many levels of enlightenment. First we think that the world is all there is. Then later we think that there may be something more. That is enlightenment, isn't it? Yet still later, we know that the world is not all, but it is still the center. We create all sorts of ideas to explain the thing that is not the world. We tell these stories to our children, and they tell them to their children, and so on. Sometime later, we realize that the other thing may be more important than the world itself, but we still have these stories in our heads. Some people eventually get rid of the stories and continue on in freedom. In this freedom, they may begin to realize that the world is not what it seems; it may be many things, but not what they thought it was. Yet they are still in it. All along the way we continue to scrape the dung off of us. At some point, the realization comes that the world may be kindergarten or it may be university, but it is only a stepping stone. Some people move on then and become teachers and professors. These teachers have their own teachers, and from these higher teachers come the understanding that the world is not only illusory in its nature, but illusory in that it exists at all. Heaven and earth are all the same thing— or the same 'no thing'. Everything that we think is real is only the projection of the infinite mind. You can know this without truly knowing it. But if you truly know it — feel it, you will become at one with the infinite of which you have always been a part. You will no longer be a small part of the universe, but instead, stars, sun—endless space and time, will be a small part of you. How long does this take? For some people, thousands of lifetimes, for others, uncountable — as many as it takes. You will only find truly knowledgeable souls in the world with extreme rarity, and only one or two, sometimes three at the most, at any given time. They are only here to give lessons to those who are ready to receive them."

"I don't know if what you are saying is true or not," David replied. "I know that the 'stories' you are talking about are superstitions and religions. I don't believe any of that. I wasn't taught that, and didn't grow up with it. My head is not full of stories. I see the world as it is — hard facts, not fantasies about gods and martyrs."

"Some stories are about gods, some are about science," Zhi Ming answered him back. "There are no hard facts in science, only theories. We treat them as hard facts until some better theory comes along."

Sooner or later, almost every theory has been disproved. Even the theory of the expanding universe will eventually be disproved when scientists realize that what appears to be a shift of light into the red spectrum caused by the Doppler Effect is only a quantum shift as light loses its energy from traveling vast distances."

David was astonished at this pronouncement. "How can a hermit living up here in these hills know things like that — things about quantum energy and Doppler shifts?"

"I have told you," the hermit said. "Zhi Ming travels without traveling. There is no place that is not here, and no time that is not now. But if you are to understand these things, you must shed all of the baggage that you are carrying. It is only with the open-minded wonder of a child that one advances. It is only by abandoning knowledge that one gains true knowledge. It is only by forgetting that one remembers, and it is only by dying that one is born to true life."

*

One bright night, David walked out to the cliff and sat down in the lotus position upon his favorite boulder. He had no trouble crossing his thin and incomplete legs, and soon was in a meditative state.

A few hours later, Zhi Ming appeared beside David. "Ah, you are awake."

David looked up at him standing suddenly there beside him in the moonlight. "Am I? I feel that I am dreaming." He paused for a few seconds. "I have felt great changes in myself since we have come to stay with you, but there has been nothing to make me say, 'now I am awake when before I was asleep'. When will I wake up? "

"Isn't the moon beautiful tonight?" Zhi Ming asked in return.

David looked up at the moon, gleaming against the indigo sky. "Yes, I have never seen anything so beautiful. The whole world is beautiful beyond words tonight. I seem to be able to see more stars than I ever saw before. I feel the tiniest caress of every breeze. I hear the sounds of individual pine needles moving against each other."

"Your senses are heightened because you are dying," Zhi Ming said gently. "We are never more alive than when we are near death. I will tell you a story," Zhi Ming said. "Once there was a man who was being chased through the forest by a tiger. The man ran until he fell over a cliff. He grabbed a vine and held on tightly. Above him, the tiger continued to prowl; below him another tiger had come to wait for him to fall. A mouse came and began to nibble on the vine. The man saw a berry growing on the cliff face. He plucked the berry and put it in his mouth. It was very sweet."

David sat in silence, staring thoughtfully at the moon. In a moment a shiver ran up his spine. "Zhi Ming, your words frighten me and sadden me. I do not want to leave the world when it is so beautiful, yet what better night can there be than this to die. If I am to die then I pray that I die here, looking at this most beautiful moon hovering in this most beautiful field of stars. Then I will leave life while I am the most full of its beauty."

After a few moments, Zhi Ming asked, "But who is it who is dying? Who looks at the moon?"

David looked at him quizzically.

"Observe the moon," Zhi Ming said.

David looked back at the moon.

A breeze came up from the valley and ruffled David's hair. The dark pines shivered and sighed around them. A bird cried out in the night.

In the almost palpable moonlight, the two figures looked like statues, one standing, one sitting, their faces turned heavenward.

"Now observe your self observing the moon."

David didn't move. His expression was unfathomable.

Zhi Ming continued to watch the moon along with David. Then he said, "Tell me what it is that is being observed, and tell me what it is that is observing."

David did not answer.

"It is the abyss," Zhi Ming said. "We come from the abyss and we go to the abyss. Yet life is sweet. This is what the ego thinks, and would have us think as well. Yet it is only when the ego has fled the tiger and sees its end upon the rocks and knows that all is hopeless—then, when the ego is subdued and quiet and no longer clogs our eyes and ears with its distorted vision of reality—then existence is sweet."

David's enigmatic expression did not change at first. Then he began to swallow rapidly as if something was stuck in his throat. He began to shake, and he squeezed his eyes shut, as if he had seen something fearful. "Yes," he said. "I can accept death, but not the abyss. It is the nothingness that I fear. How can it come to pass that I cease to be — as if I never were? Everything that I have experienced will cease with me. I cannot live with this fear that you have put in me now, yet it is a fear of not living. What can I do? Where can I run? The fear will take me and there is nothing that can save me."

"Young buddha, what is it that is afraid?" Zhi Ming asked. "What is this thing that fears death? It is nothing but illusion; it is the persona that you have created and in which you now hide that thinks it is separate from all other things and fears its own cessation. It is our animal nature, which we must have in order to survive in the world, but which we must abandon in order to survive beyond the world. It thinks that it will perish if abandoned, yet nothing is ever lost. It is the ego speaking from your mouth. The ego fears the abyss like a child fears the dark. Yet even now, in the midst of life, we are in the abyss."

After a pause, Zhi Ming added. "Fear is a horse that will run away with you if you do not keep it mastered. Meditation will put the reins back in your hands. You are feeling the foundations of the world shake under you. Soon they will crumble. What will you do then? Foundations must crumble for new foundations to be built. Sometimes the tree must fall before the fledgling will learn to fly. Everyone must die in order to find life. You should meditate awhile to regain yourself, and you should meditate on this thought: the abyss is the nothing that becomes everything. It is the wellspring of space and time and it is not to be feared unless you fear yourself. Fear is the enemy. It is fear that we are to conquer. It is fear that keeps us from the truth, yet the truth is not to be feared but greatly desired."

David looked at him questioningly, hopefully, with fear and doubt in his eyes. "How does nothing become something?" he asked quietly.

"What a silly question, young buddha. Every thing was no thing before it was some thing. The abyss is the no thing — the formless beginning — the ultimate potentiality. We come from the abyss. We go to the abyss. We soar through the abyss like the birds of the air. It is only the ego that has put its own fear on the concept of nothingness. We *are* the abyss—the source, and when the abyss calls the dawn, the dawn must come. You are the man. You are the tigers. You are the berry and its sweetness. You are the mouse that nibbles the vine, and you are the vine that supports the man and the vine that you nibble. Close your eyes and think on what this means."

*

David closed his eyes, put his hands back on his knees and took a few deep breaths. In a short while, he was breathing very shallowly and regularly. His heart rate returned to normal and he felt that he was in control of himself once more. He opened his eyes to see that the moon had changed its position in the sky and that Zhi Ming was now standing in front of him at the cliff edge.

"I have moved the moon out of the way," Zhi Ming said. "Now it is time to conjure the dawn. He began to sing out loudly. "Come O Dawn, bringer of the day." Zhi Ming opened his arms wide to the hills across the valley. "Come O Dawn and fill the world with light. Come O Dawn; it is I, Zhi Ming who entreats you. Come O Dawn. The moon has had its night; now you shall have your day. Come O Dawn. How can we live without your coming?"

This song had such a strange power over me as I listened, unobserved, that I could almost hear the deep cosmic vibration of the advance of the sun across the fields, meadows, and forest of the lands to the east. It seemed the distant mountains were trembling at the sun's approach and growing thin and transparent in its brilliant radiance.

The night had become noticeably paler during Zhi Ming's prayer. Now, as he continued to chant, the sky turned a deep volcanic red behind the still black and distant hills, leaving the valley in dark shadow. Then the first molten glimmer of the sun appeared between the peaks across the valley. It peered through the mountain passes as if to see who had conjured it, and then began to rise above the mountains as if, once invoked, it had become unstoppable in its desire to start the new day. As Zhi Ming chanted, the sun rose higher and higher until it shown clearly down into the valley.

David stared at Zhi Ming, but said nothing at first. I could not tell if he was astonished at the absurdity of Zhi Ming's actions, or if he was simply caught up in the drama of the moment, or, possibly, if he was beginning to understand something, on some level, of what Zhi Ming was trying to convey to him.

David laughed. "You did not do that," he said to Zhi Ming. "You did not conjure the dawn. The dawn is only the sun appearing to come over the horizon as the earth rotates on its axis."

Zhi Ming sat down beside him and closed his eyes as he turned his face to the warm sun. "You know this, young buddha? If I gave you directions to travel to Beijing," he began, "you could draw a map that you could use to get from here to there. Along the way, you might find that the map was not entirely accurate and if you followed it without deviation, you would walk off a cliff and die. You would not follow it when you realized that it did not correspond with reality, would you?"

"No. I would modify the map."

"What if the inaccuracies were more subtle? What if several people had looked at the map first and declared it to be perfectly accurate? What if, then, instead of directing you off of a cliff, it only led you deeper into the wilderness, what would you do?"

"I would still modify the map."

"You should throw the map away, but that is not what people do, and not what you would do either. You would still try to follow the map because so many people had told you it was right. You would try to make the land fit the map. You would ignore the things that did not match, and you would keep going deeper into the wilderness. You have a map of reality that you have built up of experiences and things that you have been told. If you ignore the differences between the map and reality, you will not die — there is no cliff to step over; you will only become more lost. If you are lost already and the map isn't working, throw it away; you cannot bend reality to fit the map or bend the map to fit reality. See if you can chart your own way by the stars and sun. Perhaps you will find someone along the way to lead you, but you know the map will only get you more lost. The map was made by blind men who groped their way through the forest. The map is yak dung; throw it away."

David said nothing.

"You think that I did not conjure the dawn? I did do this! We all did it together. You and me and the insects and trees and the yaks in the meadow and trillions of souls of infinite variety conspired to bring the dawn into existence one more time. You do not believe this because it does not fit your map. If it isn't on your map, then you think it isn't real. Come with me. I will conjure something just for the three of us."

"The three of us?" David asked as he followed Zhi Ming back to the cave.

Zhi Ming stopped at the fire ring and picked up a partly burned stick. He smashed the burnt end between two rocks until it feathered out like a paintbrush. He powdered some ash into his drinking skull and poured in the remaining dregs of tea from the teapot. "Zhi Ming," David asked while Zhi Ming mixed the ashes into paint, "whose skull is that?"

"It belonged to the previous tenant," Zhi Ming answered.

"And who was the previous tenant?"

"Why, I was."

Taking brush and skull, Zhi Ming proceeded back into the cave. The sun had reached an angle where the light shown in on a bowl of water sitting just inside the cave entrance. The light reflected back into the cave from off the water and lit up a section of the ceiling as if by a spotlight. Zhi Ming dipped his brush into the pot and quickly painted the Chinese pictograms for my name within the circle of light. The most literal translation for the way that he wrote it is: "The Rising Sun – the Constellation of Morning." Then he added another pictogram below those two. I had not noticed it before. It translated as: "Light Seen from a Cave." He put down the skull and picked up the bone flute, which, I assumed, was also from the previous tenant, and began to play a sad, unearthly, and strangely beautiful tune.

David stood speechless. "What are you doing?" he asked. "I thought you said that magic didn't really work."

"In fact I said quite the opposite. It works if you think it works," Zhi Ming replied, pausing the music, "and the being that I summon thinks that it works." He turned to look at the calligraphy on the cave wall. The light was moving rapidly toward the front of the cave as the sun rose higher. David shivered violently. What a dream it was, he must have thought, this dream of being a man, what a beautiful dream, a dream to hang on to, a dream to cherish, a dream only to be let go with sorrow and longing, a dream of the world and the moon and the stars, and with the dawn, awakening. He trembled violently again. Tears welled up in his eyes in mourning for something lost. For I believe that it was at that moment that illusion began to fall away from David, like mud sliding off a diamond in the clean morning rain.

It was a dance that the hermit had constructed. A dance of the world in which the world itself participated. The rising, or the raising, of the sun, the pictogram – a haiku, a poem of the hermit's own creation, illuminated by a bowl of water, and painted from the contents of the hermit's own skull, while he played a tune of his own composition on a flute made of his own thighbone — it was all so surreal — possible yet impossible. Things were out of proportion; logic was crumbling. I felt things never felt before. Yes, Zhi Ming's dancing partner was the world itself, but who led and who followed, I wondered.

The look on David's face mirrored my own thoughts, and that is why I thought I knew that the illusion of the world was falling away from him. I cannot be sure, for Zhi Ming had at least one more thing to show David. "Your friend is pleased that you have come this far," he said.

David started at the sound of Zhi Ming's voice. "Yes, my friend, Sang," he replied, bemused.

"You have many friends, young buddha. Discard your reason once and for all time, and meet your good friend, Early Morning, First Light, Day's Beginning, Dawn."

"Who do you mean?"

"The one who led you here—your guide—the one who will help you with your mission."

"My mission? What mission?" He echoed my thoughts.

Zhi Ming threw open his arms again, holding his flute like a wand, and sang out, "Come Xiao Chen, show yourself to us. It is I, Zhi Ming, who entreats you. Come, most beautiful Xiao Chen, show your radiant self to us. We want to see you, Xiao Chen; we need to see you; we must see you. We ask; we entreat; we beg; we cajole. May the great sea without a shore allow you to become visible to those who have thrown reason aside and have nothing to lose."

Zhi Ming was already looking in my direction. Now David slowly turned and looked at me. I felt some new vibration in my being as Zhi Ming chanted loudly for me to appear. I held out my arms in front of my face to watch my hands becoming visible, like dust motes dancing, swirling, and coalescing in the water's reflected sunbeam. But the dust motes were increasing in number, and I was definitely becoming more solid by the second. I felt naked, exposed, a discovered spy. I fled from the cave like a thief in the morning and found myself sitting upright at home in my own dark room — in my own lightless skull once more.

Chapter 5 – Of Time and the World.

I had been conjured! I, in my spirit form, had met a man who could conjure spirits. And, I began to realize, this was not the first time I had been summoned. I remembered the dream in which I had seen the man sitting under the pines in the moonlight near the very cave that I had just fled. Could he summon me from here, I wondered? Was my will not my own?

I did not attempt to leave my body again for over a week, so fearful was I of being under the control of someone else, no matter how enlightened he was. Also I was ashamed to go back. Zhi Ming had caught me spying, that is, if he was not previously aware of the fact that I had been bobbing around the cave and the pine woods, feeding my idle curiosity, and eavesdropping on private conversations.

What was I to do now? I did not want to stay imprisoned in my own body. I could only "see" when I was out of it. Should I just float around and ineffectually spy on people? That idea had never appealed to me before, and now even less so — now that I had apparently been caught doing that very thing.

My dilemma was solved in a strange and violent manner. I was asleep in my bed one night. It seemed to be a normal sleep except that I fell into a fitful and feverish dream. In my dream, I heard crashes, screams and shouts that startled me awake. I ran into the living room to see three gunmen pointing machine guns at my parents. They had smashed in the front door and caught my parents watching television. My father was pleading and attempting to reason with them. My mother was hysterical with fear. They were raising their guns to fire at my parents when they saw me. I knew that I was only dreaming because, for one, I could see, and for another, everything was distorted and out of proportion. The gunmen seemed small, and their faces were filled with terror as I snatched their weapons from them and bent them double in my hands. They fled into the night, and I went back to bed, leaving my father to help my mother back to some equilibrium.

Later, I awoke to the sound of more loud voices in the living room. This time, I did not get up, but shouted from my bed for someone to tell me what was happening.

My father came in, "Oh, Dawn," he said, his voice quavering, "Everything OK now, but you lucky you sleep through whole thing. Very horrible thing happen last night. Police are here now."

I asked him if anyone was hurt, but inside I had a vision of what had happened.

"Dawn, I tell you," he said his voice still shaking, "and maybe you last person I tell. I tell police already, but they just look at me and say nothing—like my mind gone. You understand me? Your mother maybe talk just little, she so frightened, although which thing frighten her most, I not know, maybe robbers, maybe other thing."

"What other thing?" I asked impatiently. "What happened?"

"Robbers!" he said with more strength. "Robbers come in house. They carry big guns. They say they kill us. They want know where bedrooms are. I think they want jewelry, so I think maybe I tell them and they not kill us. And then . . ." his voice faltered.

"Then what?" I almost shrieked.

"Nobody believe me! Maybe I also think I crazy. But how you explain guns?"

"What, what, what?" I could barely contain myself and struck my covers with my fists as I shouted.

"Demon! Maybe Demon." He paused. Or maybe angel or maybe something else. I not know what. It big as giant. Fire shoot from its eyes. It crush guns like they made from clay. And then it go away. Maybe this not possible. I maybe not believe it my own self. How I expect anyone believe this? But I see it happen. Your mother see it, but she not talk about it. Dawn, do you think your father crazy?"

"No father, I do not think that you are crazy." I held out my hands to him. "If you say you saw it, then it was here."

"I not know. Yesterday, I am normal person; today I see demons. What I see tomorrow?"

*

The FBI came the next day. I had some time to think about events before they arrived.

Even though I had a memory of being the one who had crushed the machine guns and sent the robbers fleeing, I was not yet convinced that I was the one who had actually done these things. Perhaps I had only tapped into the experience of the being that had committed the acts. I had several reasons for considering this possibility. For one thing, I had never done anything like this before. Typically, and more so lately, I merely floated around and observed things. I had never before been able, even when trying, to interact with the physical world while in a spirit form. I wouldn't know how to do so if I tried. Also, I had never, with the one exception of when I was in the hermit's cave, been visible, while in the spirit form, to anyone who was not also in spirit form, at any rate. In addition, the memories were dream-like; not the realistic memories that I had of other out-of-body experiences. Lastly, but the most convincing to me, was the fact that the violence of this strange being's actions frightened me. I abhor violence, yet the memory of the terror in the faces of the intruders told me that they were convinced that the being that had snatched their guns was capable in every way of crushing them in its fists as it had done their weapons. No, I really did not think that I had actively participated in the events of the previous evening at all. And that is why, when the FBI came, that I was not lying when I said that I knew nothing of the events.

"I had a dream of something large in the living room," I told one of the agents. "I don't think that I ever really woke up. You know how it is when you are in a deep sleep and the phone rings. You sometimes just incorporate the sound into your dream and keep on sleeping. Your dream turns into one about fire alarms or something. That is all I know. I heard some sounds in my sleep and so I dreamed about a giant protecting my family."

"Did you tell your father about this dream?" the agent asked me. I was sitting on the couch in the living room, and I could hear other agents poking around the house.

"No. This is the first time that I have told anyone about my dream."

"Did your father tell you about the alleged giant?"

"Yes. After the police left, He told me that they didn't believe him."

"Do you believe him?"

"Yes."

"Do you consider yourself a very trusting person, Miss Bang?" He said "bang" like a kid playing cops and robbers.

"It's pronounced "bahng", and if by "trusting", you mean gullible, then no, I don't consider myself very gullible. I usually don't believe something unless I see it for myself."

"But you couldn't have actually *seen* anything, could you Miss Bong?"

"No."

"Then why do you believe there was a giant?"

"If someone has never told a lie in his whole life, then I guess he deserves to be believed at least one more time, even if it might be really difficult to do so."

"You lost your sight in the explosion at the Kwan Yin temple, didn't you?"

"Yes."

"Do you mind if we talk about that?"

"Why? Is there a connection?"

"Maybe. Can I ask you some questions?"

"You tell me what you know and then I'll tell you what I know."

"I'm not a news service, Miss Bong. Can you just answer the questions please? Our records show that you have spent quite a bit of time in China, is this correct?"

"Yes," I answered cautiously. "I used to run a non-profit organization to help farmers in China. I traveled there quite a bit."

"Did you make a lot of money at that job?"

"I paid my self a salary to live on, but unfortunately, I didn't manage to save any."

"So you are broke now?"

"Yes, I suppose so."

"Do you live with your parents full time?"

"Yes."

"No job?"

"What do you think?"

"Do you have a job or not?"

"No."

"Never married?"

"No. Not even once."

"Any children?"

"Zero, but who's counting."

"Just answer the questions Miss Bong. Any boyfriends?"

"Just in my mother's dreams."

"Do you know of any reason why anyone might want you dead?"

"No. I can't think of any." I wasn't lying. Despite the fact that I had escaped from a Chinese prison, I actually considered myself so far below the Chinese horizons that they had probably forgotten that I even existed. "Unless it was that egg drop soup recipe I bribed out of that cook in Beijing." I suppose I was getting just as tired of the agent's attitude as he was of mine.

He paused. I thought he must have been studying my face, but I did not smile.

"We couldn't find any records of your last re-entry into the U.S. Can you tell us when that was?"

"I would have to think about it. I have had a lot happen since then, and I really don't even know what the date is today. If I had to tell you what year it was I might even get that wrong." Again, I was not lying.

"Are you telling me for the record that you do not know what year it is?" The tone of his voice implied that if I didn't start taking him more seriously, we might finish the questions at the FBI offices. I was contrite.

"Just a slight exaggeration," I said in apology.

"Miss Bong, before today, have you ever associated with criminals, or people who you knew to be breaking the law?"

"I once spent a couple of years in a Chinese prison."

There was a pause. "How did you leave prison?"

"I was rescued by a giant blue man who had sparks flying out of his eyes and who walked through walls."

"OK, Miss. Get your shoes on. We're going downtown."

I heard someone else come into the room. The new person walked over to the agent who was interviewing me and whispered something. The agent stood up and left. I heard the new person sit down in front of me.

"Excuse me, Miss Bang." His pronunciation was perfect. "You don't know me, but I have heard a lot about you. My name is Ono."

I recognized his name as Japanese and I steeled myself for even worse treatment than from the other agent.

"I was in the next room talking to your parents. I thought I better step in before things got any worse. The FBI attracts over-achievers."

"He seemed annoyed."

"Only because you were not giving him straight answers."

"I never lie, Agent Ono."

"I am not an agent, Miss Bang. Just call me Mr. Ono."

"Did the agent leave?"

"He just went outside to look around some more."

"Because you told him to?"

"Yes. He works for me."

"Oh. Well, Mr. Ono, would you mind telling me what all this questioning is about? I don't understand why the FBI is interested in a robbery, or why you have only now chosen to interview me about the Kwan Yin incident."

"OK, I suppose you ought to know. Well, the guy who blew himself up at the temple — we checked out his DNA, and he was from the mid-east. Possibly Pakistan; we can't be quite that accurate. We thought at first that he just wanted to blow himself up in an infidel temple and take as many non-believers with him as might be there at the time. He might have even thought it was a Catholic church and Kwan Yin was the Virgin Mary. Who knows? You never know what these guys are thinking. Anybody that would blow himself up might be thinking anything. Then we found out who that guy was that you were with at the temple. Do you know who he is?"

It sounded like a rhetorical question, but I answered anyway. "Yes. His name is David Chang."

"No, I mean do you know who David Chang is? He wasn't even supposed to be out walking around without a body guard."

"Why? What do you mean?"

"We have reason to believe that the Chinese government wants him dead at any cost."

"Why?"

"Excuse me for saying this, Miss Bang, but you should listen to the news more. Do you remember the riots we had here in Honolulu when he came here on that dirigible, the *Eckener*?"

"Yes. I thought he had a fan club."

"It is more like a cult, or a new religious movement. What happened here was nothing like what is going on in China. They think that he is a resurrected buddha, or even some kind of deity. I don't really know what they actually think. All I know is that they riot at the drop of his name. I imagine it would be like if Jesus were to float down on a cloud over Rome. The Italians would go out of their heads. It's the same thing in China right now. The Chinese government thought they had problems with the Dalai Lama, but the Dalai Lama only had any real influence over the Tibetan people; Chang seems to have a great deal of influence over the Chinese people themselves. The CIA has told us that the Chinese government is scared. They are so scared that they don't know whether it is better to forbid the *Eckener* to enter China and tip their hand to the people just how frightened they are, or to act as if they are not afraid and let the *Eckener* come in and risk the outcome. The *Eckener* has been cruising up and down the coast waiting for their decision. We think that the Chinese government wishes that David Chang would just die, but they don't want to be implicated in his death in any way, because that might lead to the big final blow-out riot that they would especially like to avoid — the ultimate counter revolution, you might say."

"Anyway," he continued, "that is what we thought the explosion at the temple might be about. The Chinese have been known to work with militant Islamic groups before. A lot of times, the heads of these religious organizations are not involved in the religious movements because of religion at all. The militant leaders only want power just like any other Hitler, or Napoleon. They know how to get their followers worked up so that they will do literally anything the leaders suggest, and they use this talent for their own purposes and sell their influence to the highest bidder. We think the Chinese are the high bidders in the current market."

"So you think that the Chinese government paid some Islamic religious leader to send a devout follower to blow himself up in order to kill David Chang without implicating the Chinese in his death?"

"Yeah, that is about it. It was pretty cut and dried until these terrorists broke down your door and came in your house."

"Terrorists?"

"Yes ma'am. The average criminal almost never uses a machine gun to rob a home — especially a Russian machine gun."

Mr. Ono went on to explain that Russian weapons were commonly found in the hands of middle-eastern militants. One reason for this was that many were abandoned during the various Soviet invasions of Moslem countries. The other reason being that the weapons, and the necessary ammunition, were incredibly cheap to purchase at the moment and readily available through arms brokers. In a round-about way, the fact that the terrorists did not have Chinese weapons tended to implicate the Chinese, in the FBI way of thinking.

The FBI was concerned now that the attack on my house indicated that the bombing of the temple might not have been an attempt on David's life, but on mine. That is unless the attack on my house was merely a diversion to throw the FBI and CIA off the scent. If the Chinese were behind any of this, they would definitely be devious.

"There was supposed to be a bodyguard with David Chang the day of the bombing," Mr. Ono continued. "Do you recall seeing anyone following the two of you?"

"I don't think so. What would he have looked like?"

"He might have been wearing a Navy officer's uniform. Otherwise, pretty average looking. Not particularly muscular or anything like you might expect a bodyguard to look."

I remembered the Navy officer that I had rescued from a street gang under the very shadow of the *Eckener*. "How does David Chang rate a bodyguard from the Navy?"

"It's a long story. The Navy assigned Captain Boorman to be an observer on the *Eckener*. The Navy used to have some dirigibles and maybe they think they might get some again someday. Anyway, on the way over here from the mainland, a waiter who had been hired to work on the *Eckener* made an attempt on Chang's life. Afterwards, the dirigible owner pulled some strings with Washington — called in some favors, or something — and got the Navy to assign Boorman as Chang's bodyguard. I personally don't think he is the right man for the job. We can't tell that he did any actual guarding on the day of the bombing, and our sources tell us that the guy is even afraid of heights! Would you want someone who was afraid of heights protecting you a couple of thousand feet up in the air?"

"Do you think that this Boorman might be implicated in some way?"

"No, he is squeaky clean — unless maybe that is not the real Captain Boorman on the *Eckener*. Maybe this guy is a fake and is only pretending to be afraid of heights because the real Boorman is—or was."

*

Mr. Ono had instilled a terrible thought into my head. What if someone had kidnapped Captain Boorman and now there was an assassin on the *Eckener*, an assassin who had actually been given the job of being his victim's bodyguard. This thought continued to run through my mind long after the FBI left.

I suppose there were a few other things that I should have been worrying about; for instance, was I the intended target of the Chinese government or possibly some unknown Islamic organization? I should also have been worrying about the FBI's investigation into my background. I had been in China for years, and sometimes for extended periods I had no communication with my family or any of my acquaintances from home. I had re-entered the country illegally, although the FBI apparently did not know that yet. This could look to the Americans as if I had been subverted by the Chinese, and that I knew a whole lot more than I was telling.

It could be argued that the reason that I didn't think about my own problems was because once I started, I would not have been able to stop. The FBI agent had done a pretty good job of inventorying my current life. I wasn't able to see, or take care of myself, didn't have any money, didn't have a job, lived with my parents, had no kids, no friends, no fiancé, and no future. In addition to my miserable waking life, I could not go where I wanted to go in my "sleeping" life, back to the old hermit's cave. I could not go because of shame for the way I had been discovered. However, it was a temptation, none the less, and I might have considered going back in a visible form, except that I did not know how to make myself visible on my own, and would have to lurk around invisibly until Zhi Ming "exposed" me once more. Therefore, I didn't think about my own troubles; I shoved all of that aside and only thought about the imposter Naval Captain.

I was certain that this was the same person who I had seen being beaten in the crowd in what I believed to be San Francisco's China Town area. I decided I would take another look at this incident and see if I could determine who it was that was really on the *Eckener*.

It took no effort on my part to go back in time and find the exact location. I waited until my parents had gone to bed. They were still very upset about the terrorists and were prone to pop into my room to make sure that I was all right and to discuss what had happened over and over. Once the house had gotten quiet, I began my meditation, thought about when and where I wanted to be, and I was there. Amazingly, I found myself looking down on myself, my earlier self, that is. She/I had just heated the knives to make the attackers drop them. With awe-struck faces, the people on the streets all turned their heads and, looked right at me. I suddenly realized that I was visible, and faster than a beam of light, I fled back to my body.

I remembered then that when I had been that earlier "me", hovering in the night sky over the crowd below, I had thought for a second that I had been seen, but then assumed that the crowd was actually looking at the *Eckener*, high above me. When I had looked up, the *Eckener* had filled the sky. It was an impressive sight; the crowd's eyes had not followed me when I moved, and so it was a natural assumption. Of course, that was because the later "me", the visible one, had already sped away, and so was not seen by the earlier "me".

I was very concerned about this new visibility. How could I travel about now? I could no longer take the spirit form, but would have to stay locked in the dark tomb of my body. Unless — it was possible that I might have panicked over the crowd; perhaps they hadn't really seen me at all. The crowd might have really been looking at the *Eckener*, and I had jumped to a conclusion, just as my earlier self had done. I might have been sensitized to having eyes turned in my direction by my experience at the cave.

In the morning, I asked my parents if any supernatural occurrences had ever been reported around the *Eckener*. My mother read all of the supermarket tabloids, so I thought that she would know the answer to my question if anyone would.

"Oh yes," she responded eagerly. "Lots of things happen around the *Eckener*. They say that even before the *Eckener* started across the ocean to Hawaii, that an angel was seen in the sky nearby. Thousands of people saw it."

"An angel?"

"An angel."

*

So I had been seen! And the crowd thought that it had seen an angel! I supposed that if I was to be visible from now on, it was more flattering to appear to be an angel than whatever had frightened away a trio of cold-blooded killers carrying automatic weapons.

I wondered about the angel stories. I had not heard about the appearance of an angel before I had gone back in time and made my appearance. Had the stories existed before my recent time travel, or had my manifestation in the sky over San Francisco caused the stories to become part of present reality? I wished that I had inquired about angels before now so that I could know if I was changing present history, or merely falling into a role that already existed. How could I know? Perhaps even my memory had been altered by my own "divine intervention." Perhaps I *had* asked about strange occurrences before and had been told "No, nothing strange has ever been reported around the *Eckener*."

These and similar thoughts made me extremely leery about doing any more traveling into the past without at least recovering the now lost cloak of invisibility. I decided that what I must do was to uncover the secret of my previous concealment and current spiritual materialization. I would practice; I had a mirror in my bedroom, hadn't I?

This turned out to be a surprisingly novel experience. Except for one brief moment in our back yard, I had not "seen" this house since the explosion. But now, with my parents asleep, I left my body and walked around my bedroom like a ghostly apparition. I stood in front of the mirror and examined myself. My ethereal body was glowing with some unknown energy and throwing off a dim but visible light. I shimmered in the darkness, and could see into and through myself to make out the shape of the bed behind me. Clouds of luminescence swirled through my body, and waves of ever changing colors radiated away from me in undulating iridescence, more brightly and powerfully around my head and shoulders, so that the luminous aura could have been mistaken for wings, and perhaps even a halo.

I admit that I gloried in the sight. I was quite beautiful, and, if you will pardon the conceit, radiant. I may have twirled a bit in front of the mirror. I discovered that I could extend my aura, so that I looked even more as if I had wings. With my increasing joy and exuberance, my "wings" glowed brighter as if they were made of precious jewels through which one could see the glow of internal fires. As I reveled in this magnificent vehicle, and thanked the universe for this glorious medium of my consciousness, I believe that sparks actually flew from my "wings" like shooting stars and arced into the dark corners of my bedroom.

Being visible proved no impediment to my comings and goings through solid matter. I passed through walls as if they were smoke. I "walked" around the rest of the house. I say "walked", although in reality I floated, upright, a few inches above the floor. If I wanted to go higher, I could, but I found this current perspective the most comfortable and natural, as it was the way that I had been previously accustomed to seeing the house. I did not go into my parent's room, as I certainly did not want them to wake up and be frightened out of their wits again. No matter how beguiling my present appearance might be, I was sure that they would not survive two supernatural visions in such quick succession.

As I walked through the house, the glow from my ethereal body followed me, and I had no difficulty making out the details of each room. In the kitchen, I saw the morning's teacups in the dishwasher, waiting for enough companion dishes to make the wash worthwhile. In the living room, I saw the imitation antique furniture that my parents had bought to remind them of their once-upon-a-time home in China, which they would never see again. On the table beside my father's chair, I saw a candy wrapper that had escaped being thrown away in the last days' excitement. Through the windows I saw the streets of my youth, bordered by lush tropical flowers and shrubs. I suddenly longed for the days of my early childhood, before I learned that I was Chinese, before I learned that my parents could not protect me from the world, before I learned that no one could.

I held my hands out into the light of the street lamps, shining through the window. If my hands cast a shadow, it was imperceptible. Before, I had been disembodied consciousness — now I was embodied. Yet this body, though marvelous to behold, was neither here nor there. If the body cast a shadow, then there was proof that there was something physical about it, I thought. Yet, if it didn't — if it didn't block or bend light — then the "light" produced by it and thereby making it visible was not light as we in this world knew it, but something from the realms beyond. Was I physical or was I not? I could make a fist; I could clasp my hands, but what did this prove? Could I do so much as stir even a tiny breeze by my passage through this world?

My musing and pacing eventually brought me back into my own bedroom, where I was shocked to see myself — my physical body — slouched into a collapsed lotus position on top of my bedcovers. My body had been through some rough times, and I was distraught at its appearance. It had served me well, like a faithful dog, or, perhaps more appropriately, like an unfailing steed, a horse that I had ridden until it could go almost no further. It looked worn and tired. The jowls were starting to sag with age. I could see the beginnings of gray in the hair and wrinkles on the forehead. There were dark circles and sadness around the eyes, and it looked emaciated and exhausted, pitiful beyond bearing. I wanted to take my old companion in my arms and offer some comfort. I went around behind her so as to put my arms around her and lean my head upon her head. Without warning, like two magnets that had come too close together, I snapped back into my body and opened my eyes with a start to find myself in that same lotus position on top of my bedcovers, surrounded by impenetrable darkness.

*

Over the next few days, I did nothing but think. How strange life was, I thought, and wondered if mine was the strangest of all — or did everyone think that about their own lives? Was my life even real? How could all of these things have happened to me? The things that I was experiencing seemed far outside the norm. I wasn't taught about these things in school; my friends had never discussed such things happening to them; there was nothing in the news about these types of events — at least not in the "normal" and "respectable" news reports.

I thought about the hermit and the things that he had told David. Could he teach me as well? What could an old man who lived in the mountain forests teach me? What could he know of life? This was the gist of my thinking. If I went back to see Zhi Ming now, I would not be invisible. This fact removed my earlier argument that if I went back he would catch me spying again. I could not be accused of spying if I was patently visible and made no attempt to hide. I was still full of myself from the night before and was not sure that I even wanted to be invisible again. I had looked astounding. I had impressed even myself with my beauty, and I think that women are often their own worst critics concerning how they look. Even in the darkness of day, with only my memories of myself in the mirror, I was still enraptured with my own appearance.

I had always known that my physical body was not the real me, but still I had come to identify with it and often thought of it as if it were me. The lasting memory that I had of myself as a physical being was of a tired, worn, and shriveled, middle aged woman who had seen some very hard times. Last night I had seen a "me" that was much more than the poor shabby clothes of skin that I now wore, and whose heart I could feel beating anxiously within.

And why did this poor heart beat anxiously? It was at the thought of visiting Zhi Ming. What if he did make me invisible again? How I had turned around; before, I had worried about being made visible, now I worried about being made invisible. What if I was never again able to see the radiant being that I had seen in the mirror last night? And so I argued with myself. The arguments were not the arguments of an adult, however. An adult would argue that it was his or her life, his or her decision, and he or she could march around Honolulu all night, scaring the pants off people, if he or she wanted to do so. I could not make those arguments, because I knew, deep down inside, that I had to become invisible again. Everything that I was doing depended on it. What that thing was that I was doing, I hadn't a clue.

So what did Zhi Ming know that I didn't know? Had he seen thousands of people die, as I had? Not very likely. I had seen people die, and I had seen them die in thousands of different ways. And then I had helped each one of them make the journey to the spiritual world. What had Zhi Ming done? By his own reckoning he had only fed the flies and mosquitoes of his mountain-top retreat. If he had known anything at all about what he was doing, he never would have made me visible in the first place. He knew nothing, I decided.

But in the back of my mind, the counter argument was David. David was in the world — an incalculable force, about to set China on its ear, according to what I had heard from the FBI—and Zhi Ming had taught him everything.

That night, determined not to visit Zhi Ming, I thought of him and was suddenly there. But I knew why I was there; I knew what I had to do.

Nighttime had not reached China, yet it was dark where Zhi Ming was. Dark clouds were blowing overhead, and to the east, there was distant lightning. Zhi Ming was sitting on the same rock where David had once sat. The pine trees were bending back and forth as if whispering to each other of the impending storm. Zhi Ming looked older, and at first I thought that he might have gone blind himself when he failed to acknowledge my presence.

I floated out over the valley in front of him. He appeared to look right through me. "Zhi Ming, teacher," I said, "do you see me?" And then I realized that he might not be able to hear me either. I was probably not moving real air across real vocal chords, so how could he hear me, after all? But to my astonishment, he answered.

"Of course I see you; you are blocking my view of the lightning. Why have you come back?"

This was humbling. I moved slightly to one side. "Teacher, I have come to ask you for your help."

"Then tell me where you are."

"I am right here in front of you."

"Are you? Are you here, or are you sitting cross-legged on a pillow somewhere? Or are you really some entirely different place? And if you could really be some third place, could you not really be a fourth place, or a fifth? Won't you have a seat please? You are still blocking the lightning."

"I can't sit. I am not physical; I'm not corporeal." I am sure that if I had wings, they were drooping by then.

"What is the basis for this belief?"

"What, that I am not corporeal?"

"No, that you cannot sit down."

"You are in the physical world," I began, "and I am in the spiritual one."

"I see," he interrupted before I could go on. "You think that the spiritual world and the physical world are two different things. They are not! They are the same thing. There is no difference. They have the same foundation. They have the same source. They are the same universe. How could this not be true? Sit." He patted the rock beside him. "The kingdom of heaven is at hand." He laughed at his pun.

With wide-eyed astonishment at his words, I sat on the rock, and it was hard.

I have seen this tableau. I have been back to that space and time and have watched unobserved as this scene unfolded. I have seen this hulking, dejected, radiant angel sitting slump-shouldered and ephemeral beside the withered little man in dirty white rags. As her astral head hung between her shoulders, her fiery wings beat great arcs with solemn and un-noticed power, and floods of light washed out and into the pine trees, illuminating the mosses and woodland flowers in glowing waves. How little we know ourselves.

"So, old friend, do you know why you have come back?" he asked me.

"I thought that I came back to find out how to make myself invisible again. But I have another question as well. How did you conjure me? What is this power that you have over me?"

"I did not conjure you," he answered. "You did it yourself. You only do what you freely will yourself to do."

"I did it? Why would I make myself visible?"

"Because it was part of the plan—the plan that you yourself made and have hidden from yourself. It was time for you and Chang to meet. I am only assisting. I know what symbols work for you because I am you."

"I have heard you say similar things to the monks," I began hesitantly, "but this is not a very sensible thing to say when you are sitting there and I am sitting here and we are obviously not the same person."

"Yes," he laughed, "the concept is difficult not because it is complicated, but because it is so very much not obvious. You will reject what I am about to say, but to put it in the simplest terms, we are all the same cosmic being. Therefore, you and I and the monks are all the same. The strength of the relationship between 'individuals' depends on their awareness of the relationship."

I found myself growing a little peevish at his explanation. "I have heard you tell David that he should wake up. If you are this cosmic being, why don't you just kill yourself, wake up, and put and end to all this foolishness?"

He laughed again. I was getting tired of his laughing, as it seemed to be at me. I realized later, that he simply laughed a lot all the time. His jollity came from his total absence of fear. "Many people think that death is some sort of awakening," he said. "This is not so. The dream simply continues. Tell me what happens when you die."

"I do not know exactly."

"You have seen thousands of people die, and you have died yourself more than once. When some one dies, does that person suddenly become someone else?"

"No. Often they do not even know that they have died," I said. "They usually continue trying to do the same things they did in life."

"The reason for this strange behavior is that the ego continues with us into death. The ego must have the illusion of space and time in order to exist. It also must have the spirit in order to exist because it is part of the spirit. Therefore it continually tries to involve the spirit in the illusion, to keep it enthralled, so that it does not wake up and realize the truth. The ego has many ways, both pleasant and unpleasant to keep the spirit tricked into believing that what it experiences is real. Birth, death, life, reincarnation, sensual experience, heaven, and hell—all are part of the illusion, the dream. If there is one thing in all the universe that matches the concept of The Great Satan, The Deceiver, it is the ego. It pursues power; it seeks to dominate and to subdue, yet it lives in fear of reprisal from something that it knows is greater than itself. It hides in darkness and wants no illumination shined in its direction."

"But if you know all of this, and you are the same as the one cosmic being that we all are, then why do we not all know this? "

"Imagine a giant that is sleeping. One day his little toe wakes up and realizes that it is part of a sleeping giant. It turns to the next toe and says, 'Hey, did you know we are really a giant? We could be up and walking around instead of lying here sleeping our life away.' The other toes say, 'shut up you crazy toe, what do you know about walking anyway?' This is the way it is with sleeping toes, you see. But with only one toe awake, there can be no walking. Not only do the other toes have to wake up as well, but the entire giant must wake up before any walking can be done."

"So you are like this toe on a sleeping giant?" I asked.

"No not even a toe. Maybe one cell on a toe—maybe on a hangnail. But it is worse, because actually, the giant has no toes; he only dreams he has them."

This time I laughed. "So every person alive is like a 'cell' in this sleeping giant?"

"Not a cell but a spark, a thought, an idea; there are no words for what we are really. And not just every person either, but everything that is alive. Every living thing, and even some things that we do not recognize as life—every living thing is this giant dreaming that it is that thing. Spirit is creative and it expresses itself in infinite ways. But every living thing also has an ego. It is the ego that wants to live. Even viruses have egos."

Now I really laughed. "Do they worry about who has the best RNA?"

Zhi Ming laughed with me. "Yes, and who has the best cellular penetration. But tell me one living thing that does not want to be alive. If it did not want to be alive, then it would not be alive. Viruses want to be alive and to reproduce. It is the ego that wants to be alive. It is the ego that fears cessation. The ego knows only fear. The spirit knows only love. The spirit does not fear death because it knows it is immortal. It does not fear scarcity because it knows it is the source of all things. The spirit is creative, but because it is deceived, what it creates in this interlocking ball of space, time, ego, and spirit, is every kind of experience that a sleeping god in a fevered dream can imagine."

I sat and thought for a moment about all the things that happen in this world that cause us to ask why God allowed this, or why God allowed that. Was it really us that did it? Was it really me? The storm was coming closer as we spoke.

"So that is why I ask you where you are."

"I see the difficulty of an answer."

"Yes. There is a story about a monk, a teacher, who was on his deathbed. His students gathered around him and moaned and wept and cried, 'Master, don't go.' 'Where would I go?' he replied. Now you know the meaning of his response."

"I have read the story. I always thought he just did not believe in an afterlife."

"He had finally subdued his mad guide."

"What do you mean?"

"In this dream of space and time, we are like strangers in a land with customs and languages that we do not understand. But we have a guide to help us. The guide is mad but we do not realize it. He tells us that people will hurt us and that we will starve if we do not do what he says. He steals food at the market because he says there is not enough for everybody. If we try to give money to a beggar, he slaps our wrist. 'Sure you have enough money now,' he says, 'but what about later.' If you did not restrain him, he would take the money that the beggar had, making excuses that the beggar was a liar and a thief and did not need the money as much as we did. He convinces us that it is OK to take anything we need or hurt anyone who we think deserves it. Soon we are living in fear, hiding in dark places, hiding our money and our thoughts. This is karma. We who have come into this country in the finest raiment now are covered in dirt and fleas, fearing reprisals. Our thoughts and our ways become twisted. Why did we listen to this madman? It is because the madman did know some things. He knew how to get us food, when not to cross the street, where the robbers liked to wait for passers-by, where you could go when the weather was bad. In a way he was a useful guide, but in the end, he led us astray."

"This is a dangerous world."

"More so than you can imagine. The spirit is immortal, so the danger to us is not death, but entrapment. Once you enter the dream, you become part of the dream. You dream a dream of me, and I of you. The danger is that you forget that it is a dream. As soon as you realize that the guide has misled you, everything changes. The people are friendly; everything you need is freely given, if you want to be invisible, you can be invisible."

"But how do I become invisible?"

Zhi Ming laughed. "You worry and fret too much. I did not do anything to you, nor could I if I tried. I asked you to appear and you obliged me. I asked you to sit on this rock and you indulged me. You did all of this, not me."

"Then why can't I undo it? Why can't I become invisible and pass through this rock?"

"Your mad guide is telling you that you can't do such things because rocks are too real and solid. This is not so; you made the rock and you can do anything you want with it. Try something else; stop the lightning."

"I can't stop the lightning. Do you know the amount of energy each lightning bolt has in it?"

"You know too much; it keeps you from knowing more. The lightning is a reflection of your turmoil. You cannot stop it by saying 'Stop, lightning.' You stop it by not making more lightning."

I tried to stop the lightning, but after a few minutes, there were just as many flashes across the distant mountains as there had been before.

"I will help you," Zhi Ming said. Suddenly, the storm began to fade. The clouds blew over and the sky turned the color of a robin's egg as the sun began to shine down upon us.

"We did that?" I asked in disbelief. Although I felt surprisingly calmer, as if the lightning had indeed been a reflection of my inner feelings.

"Yes, but if you asked a meteorologist, he would say that it was all perfectly natural. It was just a front coming through. But we did it, and people do it all the time. The more people that combine their thoughts into a common purpose, the more likely is the desired result."

"If this is true that we make the world with our thoughts, then why is the world the way it is? Why do we allow bad things to happen to ourselves and others?"

"It is because people listen to their mad guide. The ego has no purpose in reality; it only exists in this illusion of space and time. The ego's fear of non-existence keeps the spirit from allowing the possibility that power comes from within. The ego wants to convince us that power comes from outside of us, from money and weaponry and so forth, so that it can whip us into that mad desire to control that power. It is madness, but the alternative is to confront the idea that I might be right."

"The ego sounds very pitiable, the way you describe it."

"Yes, it is a pitiful frightened thing. But, like space and time, it is not real; it is only a lie that you have told yourself. The ego preaches fear. The spirit is pure love. Never let fear guide you. Fear is what keeps us from doing what needs to be done, from saying what needs to be said, and from hearing what needs to be heard."

"My ego is telling me that you may be a liar, and that the only thing worse than that alternative is that you are not lying. Because if what you say is true, then the world is an empty meaningless place and nothing we do in it matters. And worse yet, there is no 'you'; there is only 'me' and 'I' am all alone."

"Yes," Zhi Ming smiled, "that is the ego without doubt. But as in many lies the ego tells you, there is a grain of truth. If you are totally aware that this world has no more meaning than a dream, then of course you will realize that the only thing that matters is to wake up. If you have not reached that level of awareness, then the things that you do in this dream will move you either in the direction of wakefulness or else deeper into the dream, which is what the ego desires. About the other thing your ego is telling you—it is a lie, and the ego knows it. The sleeping giant is not alone. There is someone who is waiting for us to wake up, and if you can manage to shut off the useless jabbering of the ego, you will hear the voice that is from outside. To that voice, you should listen."

*

Zhi Ming's words had not made any deep impression on me as yet, but in my parent's house, in the light of day, so to speak, some of them stayed with me. The words that fretted me the most were the ones about fear. Zhi Ming had said that fear was what kept us from doing the right thing. In my heart, I knew that this was true. Fear was poison to the mind — yet I had made decisions based on fear. Sometimes you had to, of course. For example: I was afraid for my life when I was fleeing

China, and rightfully so. It would have been the height of foolishness, I thought, to ignore that fear. On the other hand, however, I was afraid to go back to China when David Chang asked me, not because I thought that the government in Beijing would find me and imprison me again, but because I was blind and was afraid that I could not cope. I was afraid of my own incompetence, of pity, of being a burden, of failure, and of what people would think. I knew that I should have gone, but I was afraid.

Now it was too late. The very air vibrated with the feeling that I had missed an opportunity — that I was supposed to be in China, not Honolulu. Soon the FBI would be back with more questions about my re-entry into the country. Or worse, the assassins would be back with bombs instead of guns. If I stayed here, more people than just myself would be hurt. My parents could be killed. Yet, what could I do to get to China? I could not navigate the way blind people do. Even though a long subjective time had passed since I had lost my sight, a very short amount of Honolulu time had passed. I hadn't taken the first step towards learning how to cope with my disability: I could not use a cane; I could not read Braille; I could not even tell if I was getting off an elevator at the right floor. I could not take anyone with me to China, yet the prospect of going alone seemed impossible. Yes, it seemed hopeless, but once I had the idea, I knew that I must go back to China whatever the cost to me. I was in the wrong place — I was supposed to be in China.

While I worked on this idea of how to get back to China, I continued to be curious about David Chang's bodyguard. I needed to find out if the naval officer assigned to protect David was really his protector or his assassin.

Through trial and error and by tentatively haunting the neighborhood at night, I had discovered that somehow Zhi Ming had made me invisible again. Therefore I decided I would once again go back to San Francisco to learn more about this officer's motives. I would follow the *Eckener* on its journey across the Pacific and discover all that I could about who was trying to kill David Chang. An interesting side benefit of this would be that I would get to see David (in the form of the giant blue Chenresig) rescue myself and the other women from the Chinese prison where we were once held. I was now convinced that it was David Chang—Chang Da Wai, who had done this, and the review of this event in my life, from a more remote perspective, would indeed be interesting.

Once I had decided to follow the *Eckener* from San Francisco onward, I still had to wait until evening and my parents' bedtime. They had a propensity to drop in on me when they were awake, which made daytime meditation difficult.

Sometime in the late afternoon or early evening — I couldn't be sure, but the house had not yet begun to cool — I determined that I would try to improve my limited ability to navigate obstacles blindly, so that when I returned to China, perhaps I would not be totally helpless. I felt my way into the living room, where my father was watching television. I could hear my mother in the kitchen, putting dishes into the cabinets. "Father," I scolded, "how can you relax while mother is working? You could at least pick up your empty candy wrappers."

There was silence, and I realized what I had said. "How you know about my candy wrappers?" my father asked.

I had to think fast. "That is a good question," I replied. "I suppose it is just deduction. I can smell the candy, but I don't hear you eating any, or rustling the papers, so in my mind I have an image of wrappers just lying around."

"Ah, you use other senses to build picture of what is around you. This is very good. What else can you tell me?"

He had bought it. Of course he had, what other explanation was available to him. If I had told him that I had seen the wrappers the other night while I walked around the house in angelic form, what reaction could I have expected then?

I told him what my mother was doing in the kitchen. I told him what show he was watching. I told him that he had his shoes off (that was easy, he always had them off in the house), and after moving over to the window and feeling the pane, I told him that the sun had not yet set. And all the time that I was telling him things about the room, I was having a fantastic idea for how I would go to China. It would take experimentation, and I might not be able to do it for awhile, if ever, but it was worth a try. In the meantime, I would learn about the *Eckener*, and David's bodyguard/assassin.

*

I was careful, when I returned to that evening in San Francisco, to do so at a point in time after the completion of my previous visits. I realized that I had been foolish to make that second visit in the manner that I had. It was bad enough that the people on the streets had seen me, but what if I had seen myself? That is to say, what if the younger 'me' had seen the older 'me' hanging above her in the night sky? What if I had seen myself observing myself? How would that have changed who I was and what I subsequently did?

Thoughts like these led to more thoughts, and I began to wonder if I could subtly influence the actions of my younger self without being caught at it. Ah, but what if, having had this thought, I had already begun this influential activity? What if a "me", older and wiser than the current me, was now secretly observing me and affecting my thoughts and actions. I had thought the thought, so the future me, had the thought in her mind, and could, and judging from my own past meddling, probably would, act on it. How should I feel about this? This "me" that was probably interfering in my life was still me. Would I not always act with the same motivations? Was it free will, even if it was a different me affecting my own decisions?

These thoughts transformed me. I began to think of myself as timeless, as spanning time, as existing in all times. My focus might shift, but I was alive now, as well as in the past, as well as in the future. Just as I could transfer my experience and new-found knowledge to my previous self, in the same way I had transferred thoughts to David Chang, so could my future self transfer experience to me. If a past "me" gained experience and insight because of a future "me", then that future "me" would already have the experience and insight and so would benefit equally as much from the past "me" as from the future "me". Whatever journey I was on, I began to see it as an accelerating one.

*

In San Francisco, the crowds were still excited beyond the possibility of containment. They were staring at the night sky, but were obviously not finding anything for their eyes to rest upon. Some people were on their knees and appeared to be praying. Others, in their rapture, were literally beating each other over their heads with their placards.

I followed the Captain as he staggered to the door of the skyscraper that anchored the *Eckener*. The guard would not let him past the lobby. I watched as the guard called on a hand-held radio to get some confirmation that the Captain was who he said he was.

"No, he hasn't got a boarding pass," the guard said into his radio. "He says he was beaten and robbed on the way here and the pass was stolen. Yes, he is wearing a uniform, or at least it looks like it might have been a uniform once. Well if you want him to come up, you better send someone to get him. Ask Captain Macon to send someone. I'm not supposed to let anyone in without a pass, but I'm working for her, so if she says it's OK, then that's good enough for me." He hung the radio on his belt. He grinned at the Captain. "I hope you are who you say you are. The jail is full of people who have tried to get on the *Eckener* one way or another tonight. Jail wouldn't be a pleasant way to spend an evening."

"I promise you that I am Captain Boorman, U.S. Navy. I am sure that we will get all this straightened out."

"Well, for now, I just have to act like you are and that you aren't, if you know what I mean," the guard answered, never taking his hand from his gun holster. "Quite a night isn't it? What's going on out there, anyway? The decibel level went up a couple of notches a few minutes ago."

"Oh, it's mass hysteria. They think they're seeing angels out there now."

"Did you see anything?"

"Yeah, I saw something. It must have been a cloud, or exhaust from the *Eckener*, or something like that. You know how people see everything from rabbits to dragons in clouds. Two knot holes and a gash on an old tree become two eyes and a mouth. It's that sort of thing."

"Yeah, I know what you mean," the guard said, warming up to the conversation. "I can tell my brain what to think, but it just keeps on thinking what it wants to. I worked at a bank once that got robbed. I nearly got killed. For a year after that, whenever somebody reached in their coat for a pack of cigarettes, my heart would start pounding like I was gonna die. Everybody looked like a robber to me, even though I told myself over and over that the bank had only one robbery in the five years I had been there."

"Survival value," Tom responded. "We're hard-wired for it."

"Yeah? How is that?"

"Oh, you know—if our ancestors didn't learn about dangerous situations pretty quick, they didn't survive long enough to have kids. They didn't pass their genetic programming along, so we don't see their kind much anymore."

"You're saying we are all programmed?"

"Well, yeah, when you get right down to it."

"Like machines?" The guard was beginning to seem unhappy with the way the conversation was going.

"Hey," Boorman said, "I didn't mean to get you upset. Let's talk about something else. Are we waiting on a call-back or something?"

"Yeah," the guard answered, but then added, "How about those guys that roughed you up? Were they just programmed?"

"It may not be obvious, but yes, they were following some deep-seated ape-like program. In some twisted way they were trying to improve the odds of their own genetic material surviving. That is what it is all about. That's all it's ever been about."

"Wait a damn minute," the guard said angrily. "I took a bullet once when I was in the army, to save a buddy. Are you saying that I was just programmed to do that? That's bull! I seen people get killed saving others. How did that help their damn genes?"

"I'm not trying to pick a fight here," Boorman began uneasily. "You've got your ideas and I've got mine. Let's just leave it at that."

"Don't have an answer for that one, huh?" The guard smiled triumphantly. "I know your type and I've heard this bull before. It can't stand up under cross-examination."

Boorman paused at this remark but then asked in a conciliatory tone, "Was this guy any relation to you?"

"He was just like a brother."

"Well, if he had been your brother, then he would have had the same genetic material that you had, wouldn't he? So then, your apparent self-sacrifice would have been still just to make sure that somebody survived to pass on the genes. The hypocritical Army tries to convince your ape brain that your buddies are all really your brothers so you'll do crap like that."

The guard lunged across the desk and caught Boorman's throat in his hands. "You're the ape-brain," he shouted. "You can insult me, and you can insult my buddies. But you ain't goin' to insult the Army!"

The elevator door opened in the lobby, and a young man came out. He took in the scuffle. As he walked over to the captain the guard abashedly let go of Boorman. "You don't look much like a Navy officer," he said, "or at least not like much of a Navy officer."

Boorman looked outraged. "Did you see what . . . ." he began in a raspy voice, pointing at the guard.

The young man interrupted him. Looking at the torn clothes, he added, "well, maybe your proclivity for fighting explains things."

"I do not have a pro . . ."

"What did you say your name was?" The young man interrupted him again.

"Boorman—Captain John Boorman."

The young man began studying a clipboard of papers he was carrying in his hand.

"Do you have any identification?"

Captain Boorman shook his head. "Nope," "They got my wallet, my ticket, everything."

"We don't seem to have a John Boorman on our guest list."

"You don't have a Captain Boorman listed? Let me see that." He quickly reached over and snatched the roster clipboard from the young man's hands.

"Give that back," he said in consternation. "You are not supposed to have that. Guard, get that back from him."

As the guard moved toward Boorman, Boorman rapidly moved his finger down the list. "Look, there it is; that's me," he said, pointing out the entry to the young man, who took the clipboard back without looking at it.

"That says: 'Captain Thomas Boorman' and you said your name was 'John'."

"That's because my parents named me Thomas after my father, but then they called me by my middle name to avoid confusion. My middle name is 'John', and that is the name I go by."

"At any rate, Captain Boorman seems to have already checked in. His luggage is in his cabin."

"That's because the Navy had it delivered early. Why don't you call the Navy? They'll send someone over to identify me."

"We've already done that. They say they're not even going to try to get through the crowds; we're on our own."

"Why did you call the Navy if you thought I was already checked in?"

"It wasn't my idea."

"Well, what are we going to do then? I'm supposed to leave on the *Eckener* in the morning. Can't you ask me some questions or something to verify who I am?"

The young man shrugged his shoulders. "Do I look like I know anything about the Navy?"

The guard had moved closer after the clipboard incident. "He's from the Navy, alright," the guard interjected. "I can smell 'em."

"Then how about dirigibles? I'm a naval historian specializing in dirigibles, and you travel on one; ask me some dirigible questions."

The young man looked up at the ceiling. "That dirigible up there is the only one I know anything about, and I'm pretty sure that it's not like anything you've ever read about." He shrugged again. "I don't see how I can let you up without some identification. Maybe you should try to catch a plane to Honolulu, get your identification in order and get on the *Eckener* there?"

Boorman looked doubtful. "The Navy is not going to be happy about this. Besides, you already have all of my luggage." He brightened. "That gives me an idea. The Navy sent my luggage ahead, and my cameras are in my luggage. Just have them check the cameras. There are two camera bodies and three lenses." He went on to describe the details that might prove that he was who he said he was.

The young man looked at the lobby guard as if to see if the guard agreed that this was a logical proof of identity. "I don't know why I am even still listening to you. You have no ID, you got the name wrong, and the real Captain Boorman is obviously on board already. I think we should throw you back out in the street."

The guard moved forward and grabbed Boorman's arm.

"Dammit, if you don't let me on this ship, there is going to be trouble with the Navy, and it is all going to be about the two of you."

The guard shrugged as if to say "check it out" and the young man pulled a radio from his coat pocket and spoke to an unseen person.

They waited for ten or fifteen minutes and the young man said, "Well, I don't guess they are going to call back. Why don't you just do what I suggested before, and we'll pick you up on Oahu."

The guard spoke up. "Son, it don't matter if you don't like the son of a bitch; you still got to try to do the best job you can. Give 'em a few more minutes."

At last someone radioed back and there was a short conversation on the radio. "They said to bring you on up," the young man said resignedly. He went over to the guard's desk and signed a log book. He and Captain Boorman got on the elevator together.

On the way up in the elevator, the young man seemed to try to smooth over their difficulties with conversation. He said, "You are lucky that Captain Macon is in a rare good mood. She might just as easily have told you to take a hike since you don't have a boarding pass."

"I guess it's not easy being the heir to a shipping fortune," Boorman replied sarcastically.

"Well, I wouldn't mind giving it a try being her," he paused. "Except that I like being a man, if you know what I mean."

"Do you know her very well?"

"No, not really. She is all business; never takes time to have any fun or relax. I guess you have read about her and all — how she inherited that trucking company that was worth millions, and turned it into a dirigible freight company that is potentially worth billions, maybe trillions if she can ever get it out of the red. I guess it's a full time job, running that show."

"Yeah, I read about her," the captain answered. "She is pretty impressive. It takes some guts to take a fortune that most people would be happy to retire on, and wager it on something that everybody says is doomed. Looks like it might actually pay off though."

"I'll say! I wish I was worth one percent of what she was, and she's just getting started."

"Do you want to be rich?" Boorman asked him.

"Well, you know what they say: You can't buy happiness, but you can rent it."

*

When the elevator had gone up as far as possible, the two men stepped out into a large well lit room. It looked as if it might have been a restaurant at one time. "Follow me," the young man said, as he strode swiftly across the room, through a row of abandoned turnstiles, to a door that opened onto a stair well. The stairs led up to the roof. Another armed guard checked them out, but seemed satisfied after he talked to the young man. Various bits of litter on the floor of the roof indicated that there had been a crowd through there during the day, but that perhaps most people were already on board.

Outside on the roof, the view of the night sky was blocked by an enormous structure, like another sky scraper that had somehow toppled onto this one. Part of the structure towered overhead, but for the most part, it hung steadily, and impossibly, and horizontally, out into the dark night, its smooth surface occasionally lit by the play of spotlights from below and by its own array of signal lights and floods. A wide staircase with high rails descended from the gigantic lower tail structure and rested with nearly imperceptible movement on the floor. Boorman stared in awe.

"Come on," the young man said. "There is a big dance tonight to welcome everyone aboard. It has probably already started, and we're missing the fun." He started up the staircase, which, I could now see, led up into the lower tail-fin of the leviathan. The captain followed the man to the point where he was no longer over the roof, and was about to take the step that would put him over nothing but air and the distant streets below.

"Give me a moment," he said, gripping the handrail firmly.

"Come on; it's safe," the young man assured him. "We've had people up and down this ramp all day long and it hasn't moved more than an inch from where it first touched down. This is the most stable craft of any kind that you will ever be on."

"I believe you," the captain replied, never moving, but staring at the mass of indistinguishable people below.

"Oh, good lord! You're afraid of heights aren't you? What was the Navy thinking?"

"I volunteered," the captain replied, frozen in place.

"Well take my advice: go un-volunteer. Just ease yourself back down the stairs and go on home to your sea-going ships. This is not the trip for you."

"Just give me a moment, OK?" The captain's legs began to bend as if he were going to get on his hands and knees and crawl up the stairs on all fours, but then he straightened them again and turned his eyes upward towards the safety zone inside the tail fin. Firmly holding the rails, he slowly began to ascend.

Keeping his face turned upward and moving steadily and solemnly up the broad staircase, his hands alternately passing over each other along the rail, he resembled a saint entering into heaven. However, I was reserving judgment on the saintliness of this possible assassin.

The young man was impatient with the captain's progress. "This ship has a way of weeding out people who don't belong on it," he was saying. "You haven't seen anything yet. If you don't like this boarding ramp, you're going to hate the whole voyage."

The captain glared at him.

"You won't be the first person that turned around and went home today," the young man continued. "But once we leave this mooring, you won't be able to get off again until we get to Honolulu."

The captain climbed slowly and steadily upward. At last he was enclosed by the walls of the huge tailfin and he sighed audibly as his composure immediately changed. He began climbing faster and easily kept up with the young man climbing ahead of him up into the body of the gigantic dirigible. "Don't say I didn't warn you," the man's voice echoed back down the stairway.

The young man waited a second at the top of the stairs for the captain, who, thinking he was at a landing, nearly stepped off into nothingness. He looked in horror at the crowded streets far below and jerked back, almost falling backward down the stairs. The young man made no attempt to help Boorman, but walked out onto the clear floor alone. He turned and stood in empty space, his hands on his hips, and asked, "Can you cross this or not? If you can't walk across this, then you really need to go home; almost the whole ship is like this."

A voice came from behind the young man. "Hi, Gregory. Did you pick up a straggler?"

The young man turned around. "Oh, Hi, Sandal. Yeah, but I don't think he will be going with us."

"Give him a chance. Remember what a bottleneck we had here this afternoon with the other passengers. It's not easy to deny what your eyes are telling you." She strode out onto the transparent floor and stood next to the captain. "Mister, this floor is as solid as anything you have walked on tonight. You have less chance of falling through this floor here than when you were in the building you just left."

The captain looked at her as if he wanted to believe her — was trying hard to believe her.

Sandal walked back out into the middle of the foyer and began to jump up and down on the nearly invisible plastic.

"You're not doing him any favors, Sandal," Gregory said. "He is not a good candidate for this trip. Let Captain Boorman go home."

Boorman closed his eyes and took a giant step out into space. His foot hit something solid and he took another step. He opened his eyes, looked down and then quickly looked up again at the two people standing in front of him. "Which way now?" he asked.

The foyer split into two hallways, one to the left and one to the right. The one to the left had a large "P" over it and the one to the right had a large "S". "Where is Captain Boorman's cabin?" Sandal asked Gregory.

"SF100."

"But there's already someone in that cabin."

"There is already someone in all the cabins, Sandal," Gregory told her, and then added in a whisper, "I think Captain Macon is making all the freeloaders double up."

Gregory motioned for Captain Boorman to follow him down the "S", or starboard, corridor. Captain Boorman was slow crossing the first half of the foyer, but moved faster as he got past the middle, and soon caught up with Gregory. They quickly came to stairs leading up and down to corridors above and beneath them. Gregory led him down to the lower corridor. This hallway had a clear floor like the foyer in the tail section. Captain Boorman froze again. Gregory became exasperated, and, I have to admit, I did as well. It was going to take forever to get Boorman to his room. I was tempted to provide him some psychological aid, such as I had given David Chang once upon a time. I thought better of it however, realizing that I was tampering with the success factors of a suspected murderer. I reminded myself to let things fall out as they would. I would practice a policy of non-interference.

Sandal's voice came down the stairs. "Remember not to trust your eyes. Don't believe what you see. Seeing is **not** believing, in this case."

Boorman took a step, and then another, and began to walk down the corridor, dragging one hand along the wall like a drunken sailor, and purposefully not looking down.

"You're not doing too bad," Gregory complimented him sarcastically. "By the time we go all the way around the world, you might be able to fake a normal healthy color."

Captain Boorman grunted through the sweat on his face.

"The ballroom slash dining room is on this floor." Sandal said. "Your cabin is very near it. We can get you something to eat if you are hungry."

"I was hoping there would be room service."

Gregory laughed. "Not on this ship, not unless you are sick and can't leave your cabin. And being air sick doesn't count. It's not too late to turn back," he added.

"I've made it this far. I'm not turning back." He kept walking, staring straight ahead like a blind man feeling his way along the wall.

They passed large sitting areas, theaters, a library, and cabin after cabin along the corridor. At last they came to a section where the walls and ceiling were as transparent as the floor. There were no cabins here. The hallway entered into a large room that spanned the height and breadth of the ship. Above this hallway were other hallways, terminating in stairs that led down from these corridors into the ballroom where Gregory, Sandal, and Captain Boorman now stood.

People were dancing on the air, or so it seemed. Below the dancers there was nothing but the buildings and the people on the distant dark streets, above them only distant stars. There was just enough light provided by the ship to balance the ambient light of the city and to keep people from colliding accidentally with tables, chairs, or each other. The occasional spotlight shining up through the floor illuminated the dancers in a brief unearthly light.

Captain Boorman appeared transfixed, and so too was I. I could not take in the magnitude, the grandeur, the beauty of the scene. The dancers seemed like angels dancing beneath the stars and over the city, and the music was appropriately divine. How could one not be moved—if not by the splendor of these dancers moving in unison through the dimness of empty starlit space, then by the tremendous engineering feat that man and technology had accomplished here. There appeared to be nothing holding them up. The walls to the side and front, as well as the ceiling and floor were crystal clear, perfectly transparent. To view this scene was to marvel at the mind of man and what that mind could conceive and execute.

"If you are hungry, the buffet is over there, Captain." Gregory pointed to the back of the ballroom.

"No thanks. I would just like to get to my cabin."

"Yes. Well, we just passed it. It is the first room on the left as you go back down the hallway."

Captain Boorman slid his hand back down the hall until he came to a door. Gregory knocked twice on the door and then unlocked it for the Captain by passing his hand over a wall panel. As the door swung open, Boorman glanced down and then quickly looked up, grabbing the doorway. His face had a look of utter exhaustion, but he did not enter the cabin. The floor was transparent.

"This is your room, Captain." Gregory was stifling a grin at Boorman's hesitation.

Boorman had taken a quick look at the floor, and now had his eyes fixed on the ceiling of the cabin. The ceiling was not transparent, and it was obvious that there were cabins above that did not have invisible floors. Boorman asked if any of those cabins were available.

"I'm sorry, Captain, but every bunk on the ship is booked, and there is a waiting list for last minute vacancies. This is one of the most sought-after cabins and we won't have any problem at all filling the bunk, so you don't need to worry about that. We haven't left the dock yet," he added.

"Gregory, Did you show Captain Boorman how to 'paque the floor?" It was Sandal again. She had followed us to Boorman's cabin.

"No. I was just about to do that, Sandal, but you can be my guest." He sounded annoyed that Sandal was checking up on him.

Sandal slipped by him and entered the cabin. "Captain Boorman, look here." She pointed to a dial on the wall near the door. She turned the dial and the floor gradually became darker until it was as opaque as steel, and apparently as solid looking, for Boorman heaved a sigh of relief and stepped into the cabin.

"Of course, it is just an illusion," Gregory spoke up. "You still just have that thin sheet of plastic between you and a thousand foot fall."

"That's OK," Boorman answered. "I can live with illusion." He was out of breath and trembling, as if from a great exertion. "That's all I have every time I fly on an airplane."

Sandal glared at Gregory. "But, you know, Captain," she said, turning back to Boorman, "the appearance of there being *no* floor is also an illusion. The floor is just as solid when you can see through it as it is when you can't. You could fill this room up with people, or equipment, or even stack grand pianos in here and it wouldn't even groan."

"Thanks for your reassurance, but I'll leave it opaque just the same. Maybe I can get used to the idea of a transparent floor a little at a time. Do they ever 'paque' the ballroom?"

"No," Gregory answered. "If you want to eat, you'll have to walk across the chasm. If you starve to death on this ship, you may be the first person to die of acrophobia."

"I'll go get you a plate of food if you want me too," Sandal added, "But I won't be available to do that very often."

"I guess hunger will be an incentive for me to get my 'air' legs then." Boorman said, smiling crookedly. "Do you mind if I sit down?" He didn't wait for an answer, but sat on the side of the nearest bunk. "Thanks for the offer, but I'll manage."

Sandal nodded. "Well, let's get you keyed in while we're here."

"Keyed in?"

"Yeah, the doors are keyed to your handprint. You probably saw the panel on the bulkhead outside your door. You put your right hand palm against the panel and it reads your fingerprints to unlock the door. The system is trained from inside the cabin, so you always have to have someone who is already keyed to let you in the first time." She showed Boorman where to place his hand against a panel on the inside wall. While he held his palm and fingers against it, she pressed a button and there was a brief flash of green light. "There. You're all done and you can come and go as you please."

"Welcome aboard, Captain Boorman." Gregory interjected. "Please let us know if there is anything else we can do to make your flight a pleasant one." He bowed slightly, turned and left.

"Did you get a whiff of irony just then?" Boorman asked.

"He must be tired from a long day," Sandal answered. "He is usually not like this. Normally he is very pleasant and helpful. Did something happen to get the two of you off on the wrong foot?"

"No. Maybe he is an acrophobe bigot?" Boorman laughed.

"He probably doesn't know many acrophobes. You've got to admit, this is a strange place to find one, and especially one from the military. Don't they test you for stuff like that when you enlist?"

"I can usually get by if I push myself."

"What if someone else pushes you?" Sandal asked, grinning.

"That doesn't work at all. My worst fear is not just of heights, but that someone is going to push me off."

"So 'push' was an unfortunate choice of words?"

"Yeah, I suppose so. Being around people while I am close to a high place is probably the most unbearable situation for me."

"'Cause you think they're going to throw you off?"

"I know it sounds stupid. I can't help it. It'll probably be easier for me to go to the chow line by myself than with a lot of people around like tonight. By the way, what time is breakfast?"

"Six to eight-thirty. Meals are always buffet style to keep the crew requirement down, but I can ask the cook to have a plate ready a little early if that would help."

"I don't want to be a bother."

"It's no bother. I am sure the cook won't mind. He loves making a fuss over our guests."

"Well, OK then. I appreciate everything you've done for me Sandal. You have been a great help. Actually, you are the first good thing that has happened to me all day."

"My name is Cassandra, actually," she shrugged and half-smiled. "Everybody used to call me Sandy, but now they call me 'Sandal' since Gregory started it. He called me 'Sandal' because he said I let people walk on me."

"I apologize. What should I call you?"

"Oh, forget it. Just call me Sandal like everybody else, or I won't know who you are talking to. I don't even know why I brought it up. I just felt like telling you for some reason." She turned to leave. "Well, goodnight, Captain Boorman. Let us know if you need anything."

"You can call me John," Boorman added lamely. "Oh, and about my room mate — I assume he is at the party in the ballroom."

"Yes. He is not a very good dancer, but everybody loves him. He may not even come back to his room tonight." She turned and started to leave.

"Sandal," Boorman said abruptly, "is there someplace you need to be right now? Can you stay and talk a minute? You can leave the door open if it makes you more comfortable."

She turned and looked at him strangely. "There's no place I need to be. What did you want to talk about?"

"I don't know, really. It's just that, well, I know this sounds like a line, but believe me, I realize that I am old enough to be your father, and its nothing like that. It's just that I think I know you from somewhere. Have you ever seen me before?"

"Not that I recall. Have you ever been to the plant?"

"The plant?"

"Where the *Eckener* was built — where they build all the Light Ships."

"No, I've never been there. Have you spent a lot of time there?

"Oh, yes," she exclaimed." It is an incredible place."

"Tell me about it."

"It is huge," She began. "The main hangar has to be big enough for ships the size of this one to float around in. There's never been anything like these Light Ships before. The Hindenburg could fit inside the *Eckener* and have room left over for a couple of blimps. I guess you know how she gets her lift."

"No, I'm afraid I don't. I have some documents about that in my bags, but I just got them before I had to pack and I haven't had time to read them yet. I would have to guess helium because of the danger of hydrogen."

"Nope — neither one of those."

"This is a lighter-than-air craft, isn't it?" the captain asked, as if correcting a child.

"Yes," she replied, grinning.

"Then what holds it up?"

"Nothing. Nothing holds it up." She grinned bigger.

"I don't understand at all what you are trying to tell me."

"I know. I love telling people about the nothing. You get the best expressions. To be more specific, it is vacuum that holds the ship up."

"Do you mean something like the vacuum over an airplane's wings?"

"Oh no; this is a contained vacuum—vacuum spheres."

"Vacuum spheres?

"Yeah. They are big plastic spheres with all the air pumped out."

"There is no helium inside of them?" he asked in puzzlement, "or hydrogen, even?"

"No. That is old technology. What weighs less than hydrogen?" she asked. "Nothing," she said, answering her own question. "When you have a big sphere full of nothing, then you've really got something." She grinned.

"How big are they?"

"Oh, a couple of hundred feet in diameter — it varies some. The ones in the middle are bigger — the ones at the end, smaller."

"You have got to be kidding me," the captain laughed. A plastic ball that big would weigh tons; it would collapse under its own weight."

"Yes, it would," Sandal agreed, "except that the vacuum holds it together. They are like the big glass balls that are used in deep sea exploration. The pressure of the water makes those spheres stronger the deeper they go. In this case, it is the pressure of the outside air at about fourteen pounds per square inch that compresses the plastic until the molecules realign into some internal geodesic crystalline structure. When the plastic is exposed to ultraviolet light, the molecular strands crosslink so that the whole sphere is like one giant molecule. The balls also get stronger the more vacuum is in them. And they have to be big," she continued. "The amount of air they displace increases geometrically with their diameter, so where a small sphere couldn't even lift its own weight, a really big sphere can lift an incredible amount."

"How could such a thing be built?"

"The process is secret, but I heard that once they accidentally pumped out too much air and some people got killed. That sphere is still floating around somewhere up in the stratosphere, or so I have been told."

"That is amazing," Captain Boorman replied. "How do they move them?"

"Nets. They have big nets above the molds that catch the spheres when the molds are opened up. Heavy tractors hold the nets down and move the spheres into position in a fabrication hangar where the dirigibles are built around them. The one that got away slowly rose to about eleven thousand feet taking two tractors with it. That was where it finally slipped out of the net, taking off like a rocket and dropping the tractors, and the people in them, through a concrete landing strip. That won't happen again though."

"Why not?"

"For starters, they've got redundant pressure valves now so that you can't pump out too much until they are in place in the ship. And in case that fails, they've got sharp-shooters aiming rifles at the giant spheres as they are coming out of the molds. If a tractor tread so much as comes off the ground, they have orders to shoot the ball down. They have to shoot it up high though, and everybody has to hit the ground running."

"Why is that?"

"First, it's got a tremendous vacuum in it. If you were anywhere near a hole in one of these things, it would suck you in like a milkshake through a straw. Second, as it begins to lose lift, it would settle to the ground and begin to roll around. It would be weighing tons at that point, and you wouldn't want to be under it. And third, as the plastic shell began to lose integrity under reduced pressure, the whole sphere would probably implode violently, grabbing you and anyone else around and smacking all your heads together. Moving these things is not a job I would want," she continued, "but I think there is one worse."

"What's that?"

"When the spheres are in the ship they have to be hooked up to the ship's pumps. Pumping more or less vacuum is what allows the ship to go up or down. The spheres may weigh tons, but they displace tons more air than what they weigh. The difference between what they weigh and what they displace is how much they can lift. So when the ship's pumps suck more air out of them, they weigh even less and can lift even more. The spheres are molded with a hookup port, but somebody has to hook them up. Those guys are one little slip-up away from a really horrible death. The people who work in the sphere factories and in the hangars have a motto: 'Nothing can lift you to heaven and nothing can send you to hell.'."

*

After Sandal left to attend to her duties, Boorman stood and looked around the cabin. The bunk furthest from the door was obviously his; his equipment and cameras were still scattered across the bed from the examination. He put them back in his bags and walked across the cabin to a row of windows along the curved outer wall of the room. He leaned across the built-in padded bench and took a brief look out into the San Francisco night. He withdrew quickly in horror from this high view. "What have I gotten myself into?" he muttered.

Boorman dug his toothbrush out of his bags and headed toward the bathroom. Respecting his privacy, I left his quarters and floated up beside the outer hull of the ship. Because of the curve of the hull, the windows on each deck provided a view downward to the ground, but only the lowest deck had the spectacular view afforded by the transparent floor. I wondered why the captain of the *Eckener* had squandered such expensive real-estate on a naval officer who was, by accounts, traveling gratis. Boorman's cabin was also one of the closest to the dining room/ ballroom/ observation lounge.

I floated over the ballroom to observe it more closely. It occupied the entire nose of the ship so that a person standing anywhere inside would have a feeling of being suspended in space, not a novel sensation for me, but a new one, I was sure, for most of the passengers. As I floated higher, I could see from my aerial perspective that the ship was indeed somewhat whale shaped, having a conical head, being very large and broad around the shoulders, and tapering down to the tail. It was not cigar or football shaped like the dirigibles I had seen in photographs, but graceful and elegant in its lines as well as being impressively large. In over-all appearance it was like a cross between a whale and a manta ray. It seemed very much alive to me, not only for the obvious reasons: the organic shape, the hum of power coming from its hidden engines, the smooth flow of skin along the ridged vertebral spine of its back; but for another thing, not so obvious. There was a sense of a consciousness, an awareness, not unlike the one I had felt from the mountain I knew as Chomolungma. It was not evil, but it was not human, and I could neither isolate it nor contact it, yet there was something.

Just behind the ball room, and sunken slightly into the back of the leviathan, was a large open deck, populated at this hour by empty deck chairs. The wide deck split at its stern end and extended along the length of the back in two wide chair-populated boulevards which passed to either side of the first hump of the spine. They rejoined between the first and second spinal hump to form another large open deck, which had a large swimming pool that took up most of the area except for the chaise lounges bordering the pool. The boulevards split again and again down the back of the ship, rejoining at deck after deck of various configurations, including some with windbreaks and even small shelters. At last they terminated at a large helicopter landing pad just where the tail began to narrow.

I was fascinated by the amount of thought and design that had gone into this ship, but what fascinated me the most was the sense of déjà vu I had while exploring these decks. Then I realized that I had seen these decks before. Once upon a time, while hovering over a distant prison in China, my attention, my focus, had been yanked here. I had been forced to look at this place where now I was, and had seen a large figure standing on these very decks. Becoming aware of me, he turned, and seeing my plight and the plight of the other women in the distant prison, had freed us that very night. I remembered the decks; I remembered the city lights below! This was the setting! This was where that figure had stood! Where was that being now?

The time seemed about right. It was on this night, or one very like it that I had been freed from prison. Could it be this same night that it would happen? What a wild coincidence if it were true; that I would be here on the same night, without any planning or forethought, to see this being they called Chenresig. To see him stand on the back of this great whale and turn and look at me in prison in China and, with a whoosh, to appear before me in the prison, a great blue, lightening filled, terrifying, giant of a savior.

I waited and watched and listened. After awhile, the revelers took to their beds and the ship became quiet, except, of course, for the low and nearly silent hum of power that permeated it. The moon came up, made a high arc over the horizon and had started back down, when suddenly, without any warning, there he was. He stood on the first deck, his legs spread and his feet planted firmly. He gazed out over San Francisco Bay, his muscular arms interlocked across his deep chest. He was not as large as I remembered; there was no lightening; his skin was not blue. Yet, it was him; I was sure of it.

I watched him for awhile. He never moved from his spot. He watched the moon descend and he studied the stars. And then, as if suddenly becoming aware of my presence, he turned and looked straight at me. Nothing happened. He gazed at me a moment and then went back to staring off into space. There was no recognition or reaction. There was no giant demon, rushing through space to a spectacular rescue. There was nothing. It was decidedly anticlimactic. Was this not the correct day after all? Tomorrow the *Eckener* was scheduled to depart San Francisco, so the day of my rescue could not be after this. On the other hand, if the day had come and gone, then why did Chenresig not recognize me as the person he had just recently encountered? Or — and this was the worst possibility that I considered — had I just interfered with my own destiny- my own liberation? Had my presence here caused Chenresig not to see the plight of the imprisoned women that he had seen before? Had he been destined to turn and see me, but the "me" that he saw this time was in no dire need? What had I done, and what was the end result? If I returned to my body now, would it be to one dying of hunger and disease in a filthy vermin infested cell? I realized that this moment was the juncture of my past, present, and future, and that it was going strangely wrong.

Panicked, I flew as fast as thought to my bedroom in my parent's house in Honolulu and was terror stricken to find that my body was no longer meditating there on the bed. It was not where I had left it. Horrified, I anguished over what I had done. I felt great waves of despair wash over me. I could not face prison again. The Chinese prison was worse than blindness. But worse still was the feeling that I had broken something — that I had undone something that was meant to be. I had begun some time ago to feel that my experiences had been somehow skillfully architected for some unknown purpose, but now, through my clumsiness, I had destroyed something — something greater than myself — something that I could not repair.

Then, suddenly, I realized how stupid I was. Of course my body was not in the house in Honolulu; I was still in my own past. In this time frame, I *was* still in China! With a feeling of vast relief, I quickly moved into my own "present" and into my current bedroom. The relief I felt turned again to anguish when, once more I did not find my body waiting for me.

Now knowing that my previous fears were true, and that I had altered past events so as to prevent my own escape from that hellish Chinese cesspool, I shrank from what I had to do. Yet I did force myself to turn my focus to that prison, fully expecting to find my emaciated, diseased, and barely breathing corpse of a body huddled in a dark feces-covered corner. I was dumbfounded to discover that I was not there either!

On the verge of panic, I forced myself to be calm and think. Perhaps things were not as bad as I thought. Surely my body was somewhere. If it had died, would I not be now greeting those beings, clothed in light, who welcome the dead to the other side? Or would that necessarily be so. I really knew next to nothing about these matters. Were there rules? Did things always happen the same way? Perhaps I was now a disembodied ghost, somehow lost to this world and to the next.

Emotionally unable to deal with the other things that I did see at the prison, I rushed back to my one remaining sanctuary. Even though my body was not there, I still felt the need to be home — my familiar, safe home, where my parents still drank tea and watched television.

Thousands of miles of land and ocean passed by in a flash as I flew to the island of Oahu and through the roof of the tiny house, only wanting to be near my parents, and perhaps to hear some clue as to my physical whereabouts.

But life was not through pummeling me. I would have thought that this last beating would have finished me, for it felt like a blow from a sledge hammer to see my parents — to see their bodies — grotesquely curled like dead leaves in pools of their own drying blood.

Like an invisible camera, I floated there in the middle of the living room, seeing, recording, but not feeling. Time passed. Beams of sunlight, and then of moonlight, scanned the bleak landscape from the open window. Sunlight again, and then there was a knock at the door. A neighbor. She pushed open the unlocked door, covered her face and screamed. She was gone. The sunlight continued to inspect the bodies, lightly touching them as if not understanding that they no longer felt, that they were no longer sensible to the world, or the world to them.

Sirens, then. More people. There were cameras and tape measures. "They had a daughter," the neighbor shouted from the front lawn. "She's blind." They searched the house, but they didn't find me.

One of the men knelt over my mother and shook his head. He looked away from her and at the cookies spilled on the carpet. "They weren't supposed to die this way," he said. "I can feel it. This wasn't their time." The other police just looked at him and nodded sympathetically, but for me, the message sank home. This wasn't their time! These events were not meant to be, and if anybody in the world could put things right, it was me!

*

I was not afraid of death, either for myself or for my parents, but we are in this world for a reason, at least I believe that to be true. My parents were robbed of their time here. Their days on earth had been stolen from them, and from me, and I was partially responsible.

Heedless to the consequences, I moved through time to about a week prior to my discovery of my parent's corpses. I was once more concerned to find that my body was not on the bed where I had left it. However, my panic was short-lived. I immediately went into the living room to check on my parents, and found my body watching, or rather, listening to, television with them.

Never before, in all of my experiences of leaving my body, had my body gotten up and walked around in my absence! The idea was absurd. That was when I realized that my body was inhabited by something or someone other than me.

Imagine coming home to your cozy house some evening and finding another "you" already there. Someone who looks just like you is sitting down to dinner with your family. This person looks like you, acts like you, laughs like you, responds to affection and gives affection just as you would do. Imagine how frightened you would be, how this would rock the foundations of your beliefs. If that person is you, then who are you? What are you? What is the definition of you? What is the boundary of you and not-you? Can you cease to be and yet continue? The absurdities mount.

However, I felt as if I had made a sort of progress. I had gone from a situation of having no body, to one of having not enough bodies to go around. This other "me" was different from me in a number of ways. Firstly, in appearance, this version of me was much healthier looking, better fed, and with better musculature. Secondly, in attitude, she seemed much more outgoing and gregarious. I watched her for several days and noticed that she did not meditate; she spent her waking hours exercising, going places with her/my father, listening to the radio, and even helping her/my mother with the cooking. She navigated around the house very well but did not leave the house un-accompanied.

Of course there were similarities to the "me" that I remembered as well. She was blind, and her face had the same scarring as my old face, indicating that at least some of the main events of our two lives were in parallel. She was sensitive to my presence. Sometimes she would look up in my direction — as if she sensed that someone had entered the room — sensed that I was there. This caused some consternation for her/my parents. Her/my mother would ask, "What is it, Dawn, baby? What do you hear?"

She would shrug and shake her head. "I don't know. I guess it's just me," not realizing the joke she was making.

Strange as this may sound, I came to enjoy watching myself being healthy and happy and in the heart of my family. These were things that I had sacrificed, and though I didn't understand how it could be that I could have these things back in some way, even if only to enjoy vicariously, still I was beginning to settle in as the fourth, unseen member of the happy loving family.

Then early one evening, while I was listening to the radio with my father and, earlier, myself, my mother came into the living room with a plate of cookies. "Where is Dawn," my mother asked.

"She has already gone to bed," my father replied.

A sort of psychic adrenaline filled me as I realized the time had come. I remembered the horror I felt the last time I had seen those cookies and my mother in that smock — that soon-to-be-bloodstained smock. The rage was upon me already as the first bullet came through the lockset of the door and the three masked men shouldered their way into the living room.

My parents froze as the men entered the room and turned their weapons upon them. Then all heads turned toward me.

My perspective did not change. But now I seemed to be apparent to them, and my perspective was from very near the high ceiling. A hand that must have been mine, but surely could not have been, reached down and grasped the automatic weapons resting in the arms of the intruders. In my reckless fury, I grabbed more than weapons, and one of the would-be assassins caught fire and burned like a candle that had been cast into a bonfire. The other two turned and fled, but I was not through with them. I followed them out into the street, my perspective growing higher with my engorging wrath. I picked them up in the moonlight, one in each hand, and shook them until they died.

My anger faded then, and I looked with dismay and growing self-loathing at what I had done. Still holding the corpses like rag dolls, I turned back to look at the house. My father was standing, quaking, behind the burning corpse on the porch. He was staring at me through the oily smoke, in terror and revulsion, as a cornered cat must look at the closing dogs, knowing that he was powerless against this incomprehensible monster, whatever its next actions would be.

I dropped the limp bodies from my hands and reached out to him. How had I done this thing? I had not planned this. It is not in me to take a life. He fled into the house and quickly returned with a hand gun with which to protect his wife and daughter, but by then, I had faded and was no longer visible even to myself. My father left again to return with a fire extinguisher. He continued to wave the gun vaguely as he sprayed the smoldering body and the charred frame of the doorway with the extinguisher until the police arrived.

And then, of course, came the inevitable sirens, the nervous police, the clueless questioning, and the disbelief. There was no explanation for what had happened. There was nothing the police could ask, see, or uncover that could do anything but confound them further. Questions led to answers that could not be spoken. The most constructive thing they could find to do was to pry the gun from the hand of my wild-eyed father. They questioned my mother, who claimed to remember nothing. They questioned me, who claimed beyond argument to have seen nothing, but only to have heard loud noises and screaming. They questioned my father, who said that the man in the doorway had burst spontaneously into flame and the other two men had been blown backwards into the darkness. "Maybe it was a bomb," the other "me" said, her/my voice edged with hysteria. And the police, recognizing her/me as the current local expert on what bombs sounded like at close range, decided to run with that theory. I heard words like "incendiary device" and "premature detonation" thrown around, but I was not listening very closely.

I was weary, homeless, lost and alone. I was horrified at what I had done, but there was no one to whom I could unload this anguish, to whom I could unburden myself of this self-repugnance that I now felt. I could not find retreat in sleep even, for in this disembodied state, there was literally no place to lay my head.

I had done harm to another. That was what I had difficulty with. I had not only stolen life but I had impressed fear upon the very souls of the men I had killed. After the men had died, they saw me plainly and cowered, not realizing that they were dead and beyond pain. Or were they? They were in psychic pain and terror until their guides took them away. I could only hope that there was some solace for them on the other side. Fear, not hate, is the opposite of love. At least there was no judgment for me in the eyes of the guides.

Later that night, after the police had left, and after the forensic experts had left, and after the news reporters and cameramen had left, and after everyone had left except for the accusing moon, I went into my bedroom. There I found "myself" sleeping soundly under the influence of an emergency prescription, and considered how comfortable my body looked. Perhaps I could lie down there for awhile, sleep a little and find respite in my dreams.

I hovered over my sleeping body and lowered myself gently into it. The sensation was novel. I did not immediately snap into place as I had in other times. Instead the body seemed somehow foreign to me. It was as if I had slipped on an old shoe that belonged to someone else. The size might be right, but the hollows worn into the inner sole did not match my toes and ball and heel. The strangest thing of all, however, was this: While trying on this body, but not quite settling into it, I discovered that I could affect movement without total immersion. I could signal muscles to move and they would move. I could lift my arm; I could make a fist; I could turn my head, yet I was not behind the curtain of blindness! I was just as aware of my surroundings as if I were in a disembodied state. I consciously made a memory of this sensation so that I could return to it later, settled into the blackness of the body. At that moment, all that I thought I knew and all that I thought I was ceased to exist.

Chapter 6 – Of the Increase of the Soul.

Now I know what I did not know then. As I awoke the next morning I was almost like two separate beings sharing the same body. Our memories and experiences were different and would somehow have to be reconciled.

I awoke as if from a dream. I called out to my parents, who I could hear talking in the living room. My mother came immediately, my father shortly after. He smelled of smoke and solvents and cleaners. "What is it, Baby?" My mother still called me "Baby" even though I was nearly old enough to have grandchildren of my own — that is if I could ever get a man interested in starting a family with me. I wasn't really past child-bearing age yet, and my mother said I still had my looks. However, prospects are scarce when you can't take care of yourself, scarcer still when you have lost your youth and beauty, and scarcest yet when you never leave the house. I still couldn't bear to go out on my own since the accident at the Kwan Yin Temple. Thinking about the temple made me remember my dream.

"Mother," I exclaimed, holding out my hands to the darkness. "I have had the most amazing dream. I dreamed that I have lived my whole life somehow differently up to this very moment. I was like a different person. I could fly. I could fly fast as a thought, and not just through space, but through time as well. And," I felt the tears welling up behind my sunken eyelids. "Sometimes I could see." I felt my mother's arms around me, her hand stroking the top of my head.

"I know, Baby, I know. Things will get better. You'll see."

"It seemed so real. I felt that I had the power to help people, but that sometimes I did bad things by mistake."

"It was the sleeping pills, Baby. Sometimes they make us have strange dreams. You need to get dressed now. Some people are on the way over to talk about last night."

"Last night? What happened last night?"

"Dawn?" It was my father. "Do you not remember last night — all shouts and explosions?"

"Oh my God! That was real? That was in my dream! Did something — I mean did anyone get hurt?"

"Some men. Some bad men die last night," he said. "They come to rob us or something. I do not know what. Something happen and they die."

"Something happened?" I pushed my mother away. "I know what happened. I killed them!"

"No, Dawn. You not know what you say. You dream this. I there last night. I see what happen. You not kill these men. Some *thing* kill them — something. . ." I heard him turn away. "Something follow them here from hell and take them back with it," he muttered. He paused as if to clear his head. "You have a bad dream last night," he said, "from all loud noise and smoke and police sirens, and pills to make you sleep."

"Yes, a bad dream," my mother repeated distractedly, "- a bad dream for all of us. But, Baby, at least for you it really was just a bad dream."

"No. It was a good dream — up until the last part. You saw what killed them didn't you? But you didn't tell the police. It was to protect me wasn't it?"

"It was because we knew they would not believe us. What you are saying is not possible; it is not even reasonable. You were asleep when it happened. You killed no one."

"Then how would I know that they were killed by a giant?" There was silence for an answer. "How would I know that they were killed by a giant flaming transparent demon, a ghost who burnt and crushed them right in our very home? How would I know that? It was me — that's how. I lost control of my anger and look what I did. How can I live with this?"

I heard a thump coming from my mother's direction.

"Dawn, you need to stop" my father said anxiously. "Your mother is on floor from faint." I heard him helping my mother into a chair. "Nothing good can come from talking of this. Please do not say these words to police or FBI. I know they will not believe you anyway, but I am afraid something bad come from this talk. I do not know why you have memory of this terrible angry-ghost monster, but yes, that is what I see last night. I see a demon killing people before my eyes, but I also see you come into the room when you hear noise. You not kill anyone. Somehow this ghost impress itself upon your mind. You must try to dispel it if you can. It is evil thing."

"How can it be evil if it saved our lives?" My mother asked from the chair.

"How can it *not* be evil if it took lives?" I asked.

My father took my mother into the living room and fixed her some tea. I continued to think about what he had said. This evil ghost had somehow made a psychic impression upon me. I should take whatever steps were necessary to rid myself of these echoes, memories, or whatever they were. But was this ghost really an evil ghost? It did not seem like a separate being, but very much like me, and I was not evil, was I? As my mother had pointed out, this ghostly demon had saved our lives. And I knew that this was its intent just as well as if it were me — as if its thoughts were my thoughts. It had not meant to kill, but it had in order to keep my parents from being killed.

This other me in my dream had done good things as well, helped people, the dead as well as the living. She/I had even rescued people from prison, with the help of another giant. Although this memory did not correspond at all to how I had actually gotten out of prison. I remembered being thrown into a garbage pit and left for dead. Later I awoke and wandered off into a swamp, eventually making contact with my organization and being smuggled back into the U.S. I also had a memory of a terrifying blue giant that rescued me and the other women from the prison. Which was real? Was either memory real?

My father had unwittingly disclosed that at least part of my dream was real, even though I had acquired the memories artificially. What if the other memories were real as well? What if they were the real memories of another me?

There was a knock at the front door, and I scrambled to get myself ready to meet the FBI.

I heard my father let someone into the house. In a few minutes, my mother came into the room. "Dawn, Baby," she whispered, "comb your hair. There's a man here to see you!"

I let my mother give my hair a few strokes and lead me into the living room.

"Mr. Ono," my mother began politely, "This is our daughter, Dawn. But you remember her from last night. Dawn, this is Mr. Ono.

He was here last night after the, um, incident." She trailed off, the thought of last night putting a damper on her enthusiasm. "I'll just go and fix us some tea. I'm sorry I don't have any cookies." I heard her leave and go into the kitchen.

"Are you a policeman, Mr. Ono?" I asked him.

"Miss Bang," he pronounced it perfectly again, "Please call me Kenichi. I am with the FBI, but I am not here on official business. I didn't mean for your mother to even bring you out here. I know you must be exhausted after last night."

"What is it that I can do for you, then?"

"I live near here, and I just stopped by to see if there was anything I could do. I've been with the FBI my whole life, and I've seen what something like this can do to people. Even if someone doesn't get physically hurt, it still leaves scars. Sometimes it helps just to know there is someone you can call."

"That is very sweet of you, Mr. Ono. Do you do this often?"

"Not very often, I suppose" he replied hesitantly. "Sometimes I wished afterwards that I had offered to help. So far, I've never wished I hadn't. Like I said, I didn't mean to bother you. I'll leave you alone now."

I heard him get up from the chair and walk away. There was a pause. "I really like your parents. I got to talk to them last night. They're from China, aren't they?"

"Yes. So?"

"Oh, I didn't mean anything by it. They've adapted very well; that's all I was thinking. Sometimes it can be hard to be Chinese on these islands. I know; I've seen it. Your attitude about life can change your luck. But your parents have a good attitude and good luck. They were very lucky last night."

"Yes; they were very lucky. What do you think happened here last night, Mr. Ono?"

"I wish I knew, Miss. Bang . . ."

"My name is Dawn. Just call me that." I felt uneasy hearing a Japanese man pronouncing my Chinese name.

"I will, if you will call me 'Ken'. That's what all my friends call me. I don't know what those guys were after last night, but I think you were extremely fortunate. They had some high powered automatic weapons, and perhaps some kind of bomb. But you know, I didn't see any damage to the house other than the scorch marks around the front door. I don't think a bomb killed those men."

"What did stop them?" I asked, barely getting the words out, I had begun to shake so suddenly. "What saved my parents?"

"They weren't supposed to die this way," he said. "I guess this just wasn't their time."

A chill went up my spine and my hair felt like it was standing on end. This was the man I had seen near my dead parents in my dream. I had forgotten that part of my dream until he spoke those words.

My mother came back in to the room then. I could smell the tea. "Dawn? What is the matter with you? You are as pale as a haole tourist. Are you sick, Baby? Do you need to lie down?"

I felt her hand on my forehead, checking my temperature. "I'm OK, Mother. I just sometimes feel a little faint when I think about last night."

"That's perfectly normal," Kenichi interjected. "One good thing is that you know those men won't be coming back."

"Oh yes! Thank you Buddha!" My mother exclaimed. "I could not live through another night like last night. And I know that whatever saved us couldn't happen twice — not in a million years."

My mother fussed over the tea and then left again. From the kitchen, I could smell something baking.

"Officer Ono — Ken, have we met before? Before last night, I mean."

"No, I'm sure that I would remember. Why do you ask?"

"I had a feeling of déjà vu when you said that about it not being my parent's time. It was a very strong feeling. I feel as if I have seen you before. Would you mind if I tried to describe you?"

"Not at all."

"OK, you have a deep tan."

"Well, this *is* Hawaii."

"Right. OK then, you have short hair. And it's dark and thick," I added.

"You could probably guess that from my name."

"You are a little over weight."

"Most of us Hawaiians tend to be that way."

"So you are part Hawaiian?"

"Yes."

"You are not wearing any jewelry."

"Correct. Good guess."

"Not even a wedding ring."

"I'm not married. Correct again."

"You are clean shaven."

"True. I can't grow a decent beard."

"You have a mole on the back of your neck."

"I guess you've got me there. If you've ever seen the back of my neck, then you know more about it than I do."

We both laughed.

I drew a line over my eyes with my finger. "You have very heavy eyebrows, and they meet in the middle," I said, still laughing.

"OK. That is true. I am kind of proud of them, actually."

"You are left-handed. You wear your pistol on the left side."

"Um, that is very good. How did you know that?"

"And you are not very handsome."

There was a pause. "Well, I'm not sure my mother would agree with you."

I could tell from his tone that I had hurt his feelings. "I'm so sorry. I didn't mean to get personal; I just got carried away. I guess some meanness leaked out because you work for the FBI."

"Do you have issues with authority?"

"Yes. I admit it. Are we still friends?" I do not know why I said that. It was as if we had always been friends.

Another pause. "Friends? Yes, I would like that. Do you think you can get past my looks?"

I laughed. "I prefer handsome men, but for you, I'll make an exception." It was the first time I had ever accepted my blindness with humor and not bitterness.

"How did you know about the gun?" he asked.

"I don't know. Maybe I shouldn't tell you this, but I have some memory of you. I don't know where it comes from. I can see you if I concentrate. I see you as you were last night, bending over my mother. I see you looking at my mother and then at the cookies spilled on the floor. You are shaking your head and saying those words about it not being their time. But there is something different. Oh my God. I am going to be sick. Please . . . help me lie down."

He helped me to stretch out on the couch. "It wasn't like you say you remember," he said. "Your mother was not lying on the floor when I got here last night. And I never said those words about it not being their time until just a few minutes ago. You are just under a lot of stress right now. You should rest."

"Tell my mother to bring me a wet cloth. I think I may faint."

In a moment, my mother was back, making a fuss over me and distracting me from what I had seen. "Thanks, Mother. I feel better. It's just the strain."

"I know, Baby. Do you feel like sitting up now, or do you want to go to your room?"

After a moment, I sat back up, feeling a little bit foolish. "I'm OK. The blood just left my head for a minute. Ken, are you still here?"

"I'm here, Dawn. Just tell me what you need."

"Ken, would you mind coming back later? I feel like I need to lie down for awhile."

"Of course."

"Mother, I'll see Ken to the door."

I heard my mother go back into the kitchen.

"Ken," I said, leading him to the door. "These men won't be back, but others like them will be. They were after me. They have tried before and they will try again."

"That is absol . . ."

"No. It is what I see. Just like I saw your gun on the left side; I see more men coming for me. For my parent's sake, I have to leave."

"Where would you go? Anyway, you are obviously not correct about everything."

"I don't know. Come back later and we'll talk — that is, if you really are my friend."

"Yes, I want to be . . . I am your friend, Dawn. I'll come back later. But tell me, what did you see? I was bending over your mother and looking at the cookies? What were you talking about? That just didn't happen the way you say."

"It was in my dream," I stammered, beginning to feel faint again. "I saw you bending over my parents, and you were saying those words about it not being their time."

"Then what?"

I could hardly say it. "Blood," I managed to whisper, my voice cracking, and tears squeezing from my eyelids. "Blood everywhere!"

*

Walking back to my room, I blundered into the front of a rocking chair and banged my shins severely. I fell forward and, putting my hands down on the arms, caused the chair to rock forward and smack me on the forehead. I collapsed on the floor and cried in anger, pain, and frustration. I knew where all the furniture was in the house, but Kenichi must have moved the chair when he was helping me to the couch. I didn't blame Kenichi. Any normal person should be able to walk across a living room without accumulating bruises along the way.

I climbed to my feet and began to feel my way carefully to my room. Once safely in bed, I began to think about what I had told Kenichi. How did I know that someone was after me? I wasn't sure that the explosion at the Kwan Yin Temple was intended for me; it might have been an accident that I was there. But from somewhere there was a memory that this most recent incident had happened before. Or perhaps it was a premonition that it would happen again. Since last night, I seemed to be confused about the separation of past, present and future. At any rate, if it was a premonition, then I had to leave for the sake of my parents. On the other hand, if it was a memory, then there was a series of attacks against me, and no indication that we had seen the last one, so once again I concluded that I needed to leave for my parent's safety. But how could I go anywhere on my own? I couldn't drive or even find my way to a bus stop by myself.

I was extremely tired from the recent events, and so I decided to postpone further thought on the subject and rolled over to take a nap. As soon as I began to drift off, I jumped up in bed, my heart racing. Oh God, I thought, gasping for breath, I killed those men! But wait — I couldn't have. My father was right. I was crawling around blindly on the floor while the men were dying. I didn't have a clue what was going on around me. I could not even begin to tell you how I could even attempt to do what my memories told me I had done. I concluded that these were false memories, thank God. But if these were false, were the others false as well? Where was the line? Maybe all my memories were false. Maybe I was mad as a hatter. Maybe I was really locked in a rubber cell somewhere, while men in white coats clucked at each other behind one-way mirrors. I sometimes felt as if I were in a prison, or as if I were a bird, battering my wings against the bars of a cage.

Mad or not, I decided, I had to proceed as if my memories and experiences were real. Isn't that what everyone does anyway?

Something had killed the killers. If I hadn't done it, then perhaps I had somehow "seen" the events through the eyes of the monster, ghost, whatever-it-was. But what about the other memories?

I was too exhausted to think about them. I had stopped shaking and my heart had stopped pounding, so I lay back down in bed to sleep. Once more memories flooded in and startled me awake. I had worked with dead people once — spirits of the dead who need help crossing over. There was a man on a frozen mountain, once, who I had finally led to a monk who lived in a cave. The monk had caught me spying on them.

I leaned on my arm for a few minutes and breathed deeply. I had to get some sleep; I was becoming feverish. I lay back down, and again, as consciousness began to fade, in came the memories. There was the new airship called the *Eckener*. I knew its name from reading the papers, but in the memories I seemed to think of it as a flying whale. This concept brought back even older memories. I remembered how as a young girl, I had nearly died from electrocution following a car wreck. Afterwards I told the doctors about visiting with glowing beings who greeted the dead. When they told me that I was delusional, I argued with them.

Eventually, I was put under the care of a psychiatrist, who convinced me, with the help of modern drugs, that if I couldn't show something to someone else, then it wasn't real. Was the *Eckener* the whale that the beings had tried to tell me about? It had been here on the island when I had lost my sight. Was there a connection? In my memories, I could see details of the *Eckener* that I could not possibly know about. Was I becoming delusional once more, or was it real? What was I to do? I was tired; I needed sleep.

Still more memories. Memories now of the *Eckener* crashing into a mountain and hundreds of bodies scattered and smashed on the rocks. I jumped up and frantically felt my way to the bedroom door. "Mother, Father, Turn on the news; something bad has happened." I heard the sound of their feet running.

"What is wrong, Dawn?" It was my father. "What happen?"

"I think the *Eckener* has crashed."

"I not hear anything about it."

I heard the television click on and then the familiar sound of one of the twenty-four-hour news networks. There was no breaking news. We waited through stock market reports, weather reports, reports of terrorism in the middle-east, kidnappings, airport delays, and finally, the political unrest in China brought about by the presence of David Chang on the *Eckener*, still waiting for approval to enter China. The *Eckener* had not crashed. Some things in my head were not real.

"I'm sorry. I had a bad dream. It seemed real."

"It's OK, Baby," my mother said soothingly. "It is all the worry. You just go and lie back down. I will bring you some noodles."

When my mother came back, she sat and talked with me while the noodles cooled. "Mr. Ono seemed like a nice man," she said at last.

"Mother, he is Japanese," I blurted out, as if trying to enforce what I thought was her own prejudice against the Japanese.

"Well, he seemed nice anyway. I think he is part Hawaiian."

I had a few bites of noodles in broth, and, after my mother left, decided to try something to calm my mind. I had occasionally used meditation in my life to calm myself during stressful periods. This was obviously one of those stressful periods, I thought, and meditation was worth trying.

I sat up in bed, sitting on a pillow with my back against the headboard of the bed. I left my legs loosely crossed. I was never a stickler for any rigid rules of meditation, thinking that comfort was the most important thing. I began mentally reciting a mantra that I had picked out of a book once. It was the sound "om", sounded in the head, however, rather than the mouth.

As I began to recite the mantra, other sounds followed. Instead of just reciting "om" as I had done in past meditations, the phrase, "Om Mani Peme Hoong" sounded in my mind. I knew, in some limited way, what this meant. I had read about this phrase in a long lost and mainly forgotten book. It was known as the six-syllable mantra of Chenresig, or Kwan Yin, as we Chinese knew the spirit. Sometimes written and pronounced as "Om Mani Padme Hum," the six-syllable mantra had many levels of meaning, but the one that I remembered was that each syllable was a prayer for deliverance from a certain type of prison of the mind: pride, jealousy, desire, ignorance, avariciousness, and hatred.

I took the easy path and continued my meditation with this phrase. Whenever disturbing thoughts came into my mind, I would simply turn my attention back to the mantra. After several minutes of this, a remarkable thing began to happen. I began to visualize my room as if I were actually seeing it. The vision had no color. It was like a low contrast black-and-white photograph. But it was incredibly real. I was convinced that I was simply seeing a mental re-creation of the way I had memorized the room, but I began to see details that were not available to my sense of touch, such as the covers of magazines and photographs on the walls.

It was an enthralling experience for me and I was tempted to call my parents in to verify for me what I was "seeing", but I was afraid that if I was wrong again, as I had been about the crash of the *Eckener*, that they would be convinced that I had lost my sanity.

The experience ended abruptly with a knock at my door and my mother's voice telling me that the FBI was finally here to interview us.

My interrogation by the FBI went pretty much as I recalled from my chaotic semi-memories. However, there were some minor differences, or major ones, depending on how you looked at it. With my new found memories of the *Eckener* in my head, I was all primed to ask some deeper-delving questions of the special agent. Yet I didn't ask them. Something in the back of my head was saying "Don't change things." I knew that Ken was in the next room and so I let the interview go just as I remembered that it had before. Therefore I learned little more than I already "knew".

All in all it was very disconcerting to experience the extended déjà vu of that afternoon. For the most part, the questions asked were exactly as I remembered them, and it occurred to me that I could have finished the questions for the agent, or even done the interview without him. However, there were just as many other times when the questions were totally different than I expected them to be. Of course this was a different incident, in many ways, than the "other" one. I had conflicting memories in my head about what had happened in each incident and was beginning to have trouble sorting them out. The agent became exasperated when I told him that I had been in bed asleep during the whole evening. Later, when he threatened to take me downtown, Kenichi came in right on cue. This time, however, he did not need to introduce himself.

After the FBI left, my mother made us some tea and brought it into the living room where my father and I were sitting, lost in thought. My father had probably already heard from the agent who had interviewed me that his daughter was deranged. He may also have had similar thoughts about me, for when we sat down for tea, I said, "One of the agents today asked me about the fire. Did we have a fire?" There was a long silence as I felt them looking at me.

As soon as my head hit my pillow that night, the memories began flooding in. They were the false memories about the *Eckener* crashing, but they seemed frighteningly real. I rolled over on my back and began to say the six-syllable mantra, hoping that it would keep the memories away long enough for me to get to sleep. The next thing that I knew, I was deep into a dream. In the dream, I was on board the *Eckener*, standing on top of it, actually, on one of the promenades that ran along the outside of its broad back. There was someone else there as well, someone that I should have recognized but couldn't quite. He turned to me and said, "Oh, there you are. I was wondering where you had gotten off to. It's a beautiful night, isn't it?"

The *Eckener* was out in the middle of the ocean with no land to be seen. The moon smoldered like a hot ember over the horizon and its light was reflected back up to us by the beaten silver mirror of the sea. The stars were out in abundance, with only an occasional cloud, silvery against the indigo sky. "Yes," I said. "Beautiful."

"Listen and you can hear the whales. They are following us."

I listened and did hear the low moaning and trilling of whales.

"Do you know what they are saying?" he asked.

I shook my head that I did not.

"They think that the *Eckener* is a whale — a whale acting strangely, and they are concerned. They are calling to him. But the *Eckener* lacks the ability to respond. He is a dreamer, a sleep-walker of whales. He is lost in the machine and continues heedlessly off course."

He paused for awhile while we listened to the whales singing plaintively to the *Eckener*. After a little while, he spoke again. "It is a beautiful night and a beautiful planet. Sometimes I wish I could freeze a moment and enjoy it forever. But I know that would not be a good thing. It is time that makes space beautiful. Nobody has ever experienced a place except in time. Time and space were made for us; that is why it seems so right."

"Made for us?" I asked. "Who made it?"

"Why, we did. We are all co-creators — us, the whales, the phosphorescent swirl down there in the ocean. We are the mothers, fathers, and midwives. Just as you let your passengers have a say on where this ship will go, so we all have a say on what happens in this world. But now the ship wants to have a life of its own. "

He had obviously mistaken me for someone else.

"There is more to 'free will' than most people ever come close to imagining. People curse their fate, but they *are* their fate. They themselves determine their own destiny in the most fundamental way, and together, all the beings of this world control its fate, whether it will be a successful experiment, or a failure. And we are being watched — by those who desire us success and whose hopes are riding on us, and by others less charitable."

Suddenly, he was gone. Just like that, without even a clap of air. As I stood there, wondering where he had gone, I noticed that I was sinking rapidly into the hull of the *Eckener*. This was such an unexpected and frightening phenomenon, that I awoke, breathless, from my dream.

I had no trouble remembering this dream, so real it was, and I lay there thinking about what the person in my dream had said, until I began to feel the warmth of the sun coming in the window by my bed.

The dream of the *Eckener* had been a new experience — my experience, or at least I thought so at the time. It did not seem to have the quality of a memory. But of course, as the day progressed, the dream became a memory and took on the quality of all memories, so that by nightfall, I was not able to decide if I had had a dream of my own, a dream of a memory, or a memory of a dream. I finally decided that if you can't tell the difference, then what difference does it make?

Whose memories were these anyway? If I had possession of them, then they were mine. My father had finally convinced me that it was not in any way possible for me to be remotely responsible for the death of the three men. And that responsibility was the one memory that I could not live with. Being able to discard it as a false memory allowed me to accept the others as, somehow, my own. The question before me now was this: was I going to act on these memories?

My life was in some way tangled up with this airship. People were dying. My parents could be killed. I felt that if I were to find any answers about what was happening, I would find them on the *Eckener*. It was time for me to realize, as the man on the *Eckener* had said, that I was in charge of my own destiny. I would follow the *Eckener*; and now having done it once by accident, I remembered how to do it again. Also I would leave this house to draw the danger away from my parents. I was beginning to recall that I had a plan for that as well. And now I knew how to do it.

I had a different memory of my body as being weak, underfed, and under-exercised. It was not suitable for what lay ahead. But this body was strong, well nourished, and athletic. It would carry me well, and do whatever was demanded of it.

Chapter 7 – Of a Flying Whale.

The crew was already up and the passengers were beginning to stir. Shadows on deck were still long and pointing toward the bow of the ship and into the west. Deck chairs were being opened in anticipation of a leisurely day. Breakfast was being served in the ballroom, which, despite being in its own shadow, was well lit by sunlight reflected from the waves below and the empty blue sky above.

It looked as if the world was made of water, and land was only an invention of the imagination. Behind the ship there was nothing but the ancient sun, ahead, a few ephemeral clouds. Off in the distance there was a commotion of birds. Something unseen was feeding there and driving the shoals of bait fish up to the surface to pin them between sea and sky.

Besides the *Eckener* itself, there were no manufactured objects visible on the vast ocean or in the vaster sky. If it were not for the jet trails high above, one could almost believe that the entire airship had been transported into pre-history.

Part of me knew the *Eckener*, had been down its hallways, seen the great ballroom, the cabins, the lounges, and, of course, the upper decks. But for part of me, it was all new. I marveled at the amazing ballroom, at the engineering feat it represented. I watched the people come and go, laughing and talking. I floated through hallways and then along a particular hallway, knowing that it led where I wanted to go, but not knowing what landmarks to look for until I saw and recognized each one. The experience was like watching a movie that I had forgotten having seen years before, each new scene jogging old memories until I knew that I had seen it before, but still couldn't quite remember how it ended. Or, perhaps it was like being re-incarnated with the partially intact memories of a previous life. The memories don't seem to mean anything at all until, by happenstance, you visit the city where you had once lived as a different person. Suddenly, you know where everything is, what turns to make to get to the school yard or the factory, what the church bells sound like on a cold night, that this corner should smell like a bakery, even though there is no bakery.

I saw a man that I recognized. His badge said his name was Gregory. Gregory and I were arriving at the same cabin at about the same time. He knocked on the door and in a few minutes another man, whom I also recognized, opened the door.

"Good morning, Captain Boorman," Gregory began. Captain Macon was wondering if you and Mr. Chang would have breakfast with her this morning."

"Tell the Captain that I would be delighted," Boorman said, smiling at the offer. "As for Mr. Chang," he whispered behind his hand, "I'm not sure that he eats."

Gregory grinned. He spoke into the cabin. "Mr. Chang, did you hear the Captain's invitation?"

"Oh yes," came a voice from inside. "I am coming."

He followed Boorman out into the hall, and I realized that here was yet a third person that I knew — and knew well. A dam of memories broke on seeing Chang and I was momentarily washed away on a flood of images of high desolate mountains, Tibetan monks, and a trek across China to the cave of a hermit. He was the stranger who had saved me from dying in the Kwan Yin Temple explosion. He was the man who came to my hotel room and gave me a ring made out of tiger bone.

"Chang," I thought. "David Chang — Chang Da Wai. Chenresig?" So this was David Chang; I had read about him in the papers, but I didn't know that I had known him in my dream, or even in real life. Yet I had dreamed him just as he now appeared — his nose and ears seeming to have been almost burned away.

Then, I thought, Boorman must be the assassin, the spider stalking the fly. I watched the three walk the short distance to the ballroom, Chang, with his peculiar double-peg-leg gait, rubber-necking at everything and everyone, and Boorman, walking stiffly with one hand on the wall, refusing to look down. They looked like a couple of inebriates being led to jail after a long night on the town.

The dining was buffet style except for the captain's table, which was waited on by a couple of crew members. I assumed this was so the captain could spend more time with her guests. I also assumed that the captain was the woman sitting at the head of the table conversing with the guests who had already arrived.

When she saw Boorman, she looked momentarily puzzled, but then regained her composure as she introduced them around the table and invited them to sit down and have their food brought to them. "I've been apologizing to everyone for being so scarce until this morning," she explained to them. "I had no idea that there would be so many things for me to do the first day. I literally ate on the run. I plan to relax and enjoy the rest of the trip. I hope you two enjoyed your first day and didn't fight over the bunks." She laughed.

"Ma'm," Boorman answered, "after being in the Navy for fifteen years, I can sleep anywhere with anybody."

She seemed to detect a tone in his voice. "Is there a problem, Captain Boorman?"

"He thinks that I am a fraud." Chang answered, and laughed unaffectedly, as if absolutely not offended, and thinking that the idea was genuinely funny.

Boorman shifted uncomfortably in his chair as some of the other guests stared at him and frowned. Captain Macon returned to her job of making everyone feel comfortable by laughing with Chang as if she understood the joke. "Well, I see that this is going to be a fun trip." She said.

Many of the guests had apparently been waiting to meet Chang at breakfast and could not contain themselves any longer. They began to tell him how pleased they were to finally meet him and that they definitely wanted to get together with him later to seek his advice about this thing or the other. The gushing did not seem to bother Chang, who beamed and nodded at everyone in turn, but I could tell that Boorman found this fuss over Chang to be exceedingly unpleasant. In addition, he was totally ignored by everyone at the table and barely got a smile of acknowledgment when he introduced himself to the guests on his left and right.

However, as I was watching Boorman, I was pretty sure that he did not make a scene on purpose. It appeared to be sheer accident that he knocked his silverware off the table. As he bent over to pick it up, he found himself staring straight down at the ocean waves, hundreds of feet below. He tried to gather his wits and pull himself back up on the chair, but instead, swooned, slid off the chair, and tipped it over, making a loud clatter that reverberated in the ballroom. Not just the guests at the table, but everyone in the ballroom stopped what they were doing and stared at Boorman, sprawled on the transparent floor. At first, no one acted as if they were going to help, and I am not sure they would have done so, had not Captain Macon and David Chang rushed to his aid. Suddenly, everyone wanted to help, and breakfast became a shambles.

Boorman was already stirring from his faint, so it was probably good timing that they rolled him over on his back when they did. Otherwise, he would have woken to the same view that had put him under to begin with. He told them that he was alright, but the captain insisted that he wait for a stretcher that was being brought. He was lifted on to the gurney and then wheeled down the hall to the infirmary.

The infirmary was one of the inner rooms along the hallway on this lower deck. I am sure it was more to Boorman's liking than were most of the rooms, as it was one of the few on this level that had a permanently opaque floor. It was roomy and well equipped, with room for several patients to be comfortable. Besides the double doors that opened onto the hallway, there was another set that opened to some inner chamber. I quickly discovered that they led into the vast interior of the *Eckener*, where I saw the giant spheres, vacuum pumps, and other machinery that lifted the *Eckener* and made it move. The double doors opened onto a platform that was currently locked into place, but which could be hoisted up or down for passenger transport in emergencies. Other doors lead from the platform to other rooms that I did not explore at that time.

In the infirmary, Boorman was explaining that he had just had a dizzy spell, and was fine now. One of the crew members spoke up. "Captain Macon, Gregory says that Captain Boorman is afraid of heights, and that is probably why he fainted."

Captain Macon looked at Boorman the way a grade school teacher might look at a child who had just been brought down from the roof. "Captain Boor . . ."

Boorman interrupted her. "Why don't you call me John? I don't feel much like officer material at the moment."

She looked surprised. "I thought your name was Thomas."

"Oh, it is. It's Thomas John Boorman. But everyone has always called me John."

Captain Macon accepted that, but I made a note that the assassin had perhaps just made a small fumble and recovery.

"OK, John, I was going to suggest that this ship might not be the most comfortable means of transportation for some people — you, for instance. But I guess you already realize that fact. We can let you off in Honolulu and you can go back to sailing those not-so-tall ships."

"I don't really want off. I am doing much better. Yesterday I couldn't leave my cabin, but this morning I was able to walk all the way across the ballroom."

"What if I said that you had to get off?"

"I guess I would have to stow away."

Captain Macon laughed at that and then looked at him quizzically. "I know you from somewhere. We've met before haven't we?"

"Not unless it was last night on the upper deck."

"The upper deck?"

"I talked to someone on the upper deck last night late. This morning, when I saw you, I thought it might have been you."

"Are you telling me that someone as terrified of heights as you seem to be, went out top-side last night?"

"Um, now that I think about it, it does seem strange, but I wasn't afraid last night. Don't you remember us talking about the whale song? We could hear it plainly."

"No." Captain Macon shook her head. "I didn't even go topside last night. And if you really are in the Navy, then you should know that you can't hear whale song through the open air."

John hesitated. "You're right. I do know that. But I did hear the whales last night. And someone else heard them too, because we talked about it."

Captain Macon signaled for the doctor to come over. "Captain Boorman, you need to lie back and let the doctor examine you. Just relax now, and we'll talk some more later."

I realized, of course, that I was the one who had been on deck with Boorman last night talking about whale song and other things. Boorman had been out of his body, which is not rare, perhaps, but he had also retained a memory of it, which is very rare.

What was Boorman? I had thought that the being I had seen standing on the upper deck of the *Eckener* was the same one who had, in my fantastical memory, rescued me from prison — that he was Chenresig, AKA David Chang. But now I realized that I knew nothing. How many non-corporeal beings stalked the *Eckener*'s upper deck?

I followed Captain Macon out into the hallway where she encountered David. "You know him from before, don't you?" he asked.

She shook her head. "No, I don't think we've met before today. I couldn't be sure, though; he wasn't making much sense."

"No, he doesn't when he is awake. He is much more sensible asleep."

*

People seemed to love Chang; they followed him around like it was Christmas and he was Santa Claus. He didn't seem to mind. On the contrary, he seemed to love everyone around him as much as they loved him. He smiled and talked to them, listened to their stories about their lives and their work, and took appointments with people who wanted to consult with him privately about things that were bothering them.

I liked Chang too. In a manner of speaking, I had spent a lot of time with him, at least so it seemed now that the memories of the dream were starting to feel more and more like real memories. But I had never thought about him as a confessor or therapist. I did not know what motivated people to behave this way around him. Perhaps it was the "celebrity" effect — the way some people give more credence to what a famous actor says about world politics or ecology than what a college professor says about it. The actor's words may not be as profound or as insightful as the professor's, but they will definitely get more air-time on the news, and cause more stir among the general populace. Some people have a charisma that draws others to them. This does not necessarily make them wise. Chang, on the other hand, had wisdom along with charisma. I didn't go into the "confessional" with him, not after the first time anyway, but I can say that I never heard him give bad advice, at least from my perspective. It was always right on the money, and often had a profundity that caused people to have to think about what he had said and not absorb it quickly and shallowly as they were accustomed to doing with the typical "sound bites" of modern day wisdom.

Sometimes the things Chang said were contrary to popular wisdom and world views, and people would go away and then come back later, after they had tried to digest the information, and either ask for more, or, if it would not digest, but stuck in their throats like a piece of iron, ask for the antidote. Most often, however, Chang tried to couch his advice in terms that everyone could understand, and did not try to tear people's foundations out from under them, but tried to gently ease them on to firmer beliefs. He always spoke as if from personal knowledge, and never as if he had simply read these things in a book.

Captain Macon was always treated with deference and respect by the passengers on the *Eckener*, but was a very second-rate celebrity compared to Chang. This allowed her more freedom to move around the ship than I suspect she would have had otherwise.

Boorman, in complete contrast to Chang, was totally ignored by every other passenger on the ship. And perhaps "ignored" is not even a strong enough word. People obviously avoided him. He could not strike up a conversation with anyone; deck chairs around him were always empty; his dining table was always the last to fill up at mealtimes; and when he got into the swimming pool, everyone else got out. "Was it some form of racism or prejudice?" you might ask. "Was he like a 'Chinese' person on a 'Japanese' ship?" And the answer would be "No." He was not apparently different from anyone else on board. The passengers were the same mix of people that you might see at any resort or on any cruise ship, and Boorman was just another one in the mix.

Captain Macon might have had part of the explanation, but I didn't think that she had all of it. She found Boorman sitting in a grouping of empty chairs on the upper decks. The Captain seemed to be out for a stroll to enjoy the sun and the breeze, which currently was barely rippling her long hair. The *Eckener*, although moving fast, was designed in such a way that the upper decks were in greater or lesser wind shadows created by the hull of the ship, or by various wind deflectors designed for that specific purpose. "Would you and your friends mind if I joined you?" She asked Boorman ironically.

"It's pretty obvious isn't it?" he said, looking up from a book he was reading. "I don't know why I am being shunned, but at least the ship has a great library, so the trip won't seem too long. I haven't had time to sit down and read such a good technical manual in years. Have a seat. We'll make this guy here move over," he said pointing to the empty chair behind him.

"I wouldn't take it personally, if I were you," she said, sitting down. "Most of the passengers are married couples who are either traveling with other people that they know, or tend to mix with other couples. Singles, like you and I, may not have much in common with them, and may even be a little disruptive to their groups. We haven't been out very long and I am sure that things will change as everybody gets familiar with each other. You will be playing shuffleboard with them in no time." She frowned then. "Well, normally, you would, but I have decided to let you off the ship at Honolulu. You can rejoin the Navy there."

"But why?" He asked, almost tipping over his chair. "Anybody ought to be allowed one fainting spell. Look how good I am doing. I'm almost as high as you can go on this ship and I'm not even bothered by it." He waved his arms in exposition where the two of them were sitting.

"I know," she agreed. "But you know this ship is going into some pretty high mountain passes in Tibet and Nepal. There could be turbulence and we don't have the crew to spare if you need help, which, I predict, you will."

"I'll do fine," he insisted. "I've been in turbulence before. I fly in combat planes for Pete's sake. As long as I have a solid floor under me, I'm OK. It's just when I don't see anything under my feet that I feel like I am falling. Just give me a chance; I'll work on it, and I'll be dancing in the ballroom in a week."

"I don't have a week to give you. There is no good place to drop you off after Honolulu."

"Hong Kong."

"We're not going there."

"Anywhere then. I can get back."

"Do you think the Chinese are going to let me drop off an American Naval officer for no good reason? It was all I could manage to get them to agree to let us come in at all, and now they are balking at that. They want to send soldiers on board at every stop we make so they can do head counts and make sure the same people get back on the ship that got off. It would take us a month to do the paper work just to let you disembark. They already think the *Eckener* may be up to something; anything out of the ordinary might convince them. No, I am only interested in doing what is best for the passengers, crew and ship, and I don't think that letting you continue on is in anyone's best interest."

Boorman put his hand to his forehead as if he were getting a tremendous headache but didn't say anything.

"You know," she added, "I believe that you are who you say you are, but I actually have not been able to get any substantiating paper work on you yet. I am certainly not taking you to China unless you can get the Navy to cough up some valid credentials."

"They probably won't provide anything until they actually see me in person." He looked hopeful at Macon's last words, as if she was somehow implying that if he could get credentials, she might reconsider. "I'll take care of all that while we are in Honolulu."

"You'll need to take care of that anyway, I would think, but don't do it on my account; I intend to set you down. I'm sorry." She stood up as if to leave. "One other thing: I know the Navy sent you here to learn about lightship technology. We'll be in Hawaii tomorrow. How about a tour of the *Eckener* this afternoon? At least your trip won't be a total loss."

*

Captain Macon said that since Boorman did not know where the bridge of the *Eckener* was, she would send somebody around to his cabin to collect him in about an hour. The person who came around was the girl that I remembered as Sandal. Unlike most of the people on the *Eckener*, Sandal seemed to make an extra effort to make Boorman feel more comfortable. "I think the Captain likes you," she told him on the way to the bridge.

"Oh, I don't think so," he replied in surprise.

"Yes, she does. She doesn't normally give tours, you know. She is too busy. But she doesn't seem to be too busy for you."

"Hmm. Well the truth is that I'm here for a specific reason. The Navy sent me to learn about this ship. They want to get back into the dirigible business, which they have been out of for longer than I have been alive. The Navy may want to use them as observation platforms, or carriers for smaller aircraft, or even gun ships carrying star wars weapons. Captain Macon hasn't agreed to manufacture ships for the

Navy yet, but she told them that if they wanted to send someone along, she would at least do her patriotic duty by demonstrating how the *Eckener* worked. I was supposed to observe things like maneuverability, stability in high winds, power systems, you know, everything. But now I don't think I'm going to get the chance for more than a quick tour."

"Why is that," Sandal asked.

"I'm going to get off in Honolulu. Something's come up."

"That's a shame, 'cause I'm telling you, she could have let someone else give you this tour. The Captain doesn't just throw her time away."

They had come to a door on the same hallway where Boorman's cabin was, but much further back and on the inside wall. Sandal held her palm up to the security panel beside the door and there was a click from the wall. She opened the door to a stairwell that led to an even lower deck.

"I thought we were on the bottom deck already." Boorman said.

"Not quite. We are going into the belly. There's a smaller deck here that holds most of the instrumentation, and below that, an even smaller one where the pilots, navigators and other control officers sit."

They went past the first landing in the stairwell and down the stairs into a large clear elongated bubble, about the size of two passenger cabins. The floor was slightly flattened along its length for walking, and along both sides of this walkway were chairs mounted on rails so that they could be moved anywhere along the length of the bubble. Control panels, radar screens, television monitors, and other equipment that I could only guess about, hung from the ceiling in two parallel rows down each side. Anyone on the bridge still had a nearly unobstructed view, however, by looking between the panels, down through the floor, or out the front or back. One could easily see the huge tail fins behind us, and up ahead, the hull was visible almost up to the nose of the ship. Below us was the *Eckener*'s shadow, shimmering deep into the blue water of the Pacific and sliding effortlessly through its glittering waves.

The bridge, at this time, was lit only by the ocean below, and the dim illumination of the panels. Several people were watching various screens here and there, and one of them was Captain Macon. She got up from her chair and walked back to where Sandal and Boorman were standing.

"Welcome to Wendy World," she said, shaking Boorman's hand.

"What?"

"'Wendy' is the *Eckener*'s real name. The programmers and engineers who developed the ship's brain named her. Some of them swear she is alive. We just call her the *Eckener* for official purposes. Bureaucrats are not comfortable with whimsy."

"You call this ship Wendy?" Boorman seemed to be at a loss.

"Yes and no. Wendy is the mind of the *Eckener*. She really pilots the ship. Everybody else in the cockpit is here just so we can stay legal with the FAA. Wendy, say hello to Captain Boorman."

"Hello, Captain Boorman. Glad to have you aboard. I hope you are having an enjoyable voyage."

The sound seemed to come from all around but was a pleasant sounding female voice. Boorman looked at the captain, confused about what was expected of him. She grinned and said, "Don't you know how to answer a lady?"

"Uh, Hi, Wendy."

Captain Macon and Sandal both laughed out loud, and I noticed a similarity in their laughter.

"Would you like to try again?" Captain Macon asked him.

After a moment, Boorman seemed to gather himself and said, "Please pardon me, Wendy, I have never met anyone as enchanting as you before. I am having a wonderful trip and only wish that it were longer." He smiled smugly at Captain Macon.

"Wendy," Captain Macon said, "can you read Captain Boorman's expression right now?"

"Yes. His expression is complex. I would say that he is proud of something he has done. However I do not know that he has done anything important enough to warrant such an expression. Do you wish me to continue with my analysis?"

"No that is fine. Thanks Wendy. Captain Boorman, do you have any questions for Wendy?"

"Wendy," Boorman began, "do you know what you are?"

"No. I once thought that I was a collection of heuristic circuits and self-learning algorithms, but I have recently heard that definition brought into question. At the moment, I am in a transitional phase and have not reached any conclusion as to what I am. Please excuse my ignorance on this subject. I feel that I should know more."

Captain Macon and Sandal looked at each other strangely. "We are continually being surprised by Wendy," she told Boorman.

"Before we go, I wanted to point out some of the sensory systems on the ship. Not only do we monitor them, but Wendy does so as well. They are her eyes, ears, and sense of touch. We have cameras mounted at strategic locations around the ship, including two small ones on the nose, several in the ballroom that normally look through the nose and floor, several on the tail, and others at important places along the hull. These cameras are sensitive to a much broader spectrum of light than the human eye and can allow us to travel in extremely low light. Of course we also have standard radar as well as ultra-high frequency sonar for traveling through fog. Wendy's hull is packed with exceptionally sensitive touch sensors that can measure the amount of wind that it takes to blow out a candle. Wendy knows when she is being rained on, or when a gust of air hits her unexpectedly, and she can make lightning fast corrections in her thrusters so that anyone inside the ship would not even notice any movement whatsoever.

"Wendy uses all of these sensors as feedback mechanisms to learn how to do things better. We no longer program Wendy — we teach her, and sometimes she teaches herself. You may recall how she stayed in position next to the building in San Francisco with barely any noticeable movement. She taught herself how to do that. It was our original intent that we would dock her on a special tower and hold her in place with cables. It was not long before we no longer needed cables or the tower. We can 'dock' anywhere now, without any physical contact.

"She learns from everything now. She watches television; she watches people; she studies behavior and uses her pattern matching algorithms to compare facial expressions against those in her data base. Sometimes her analyses are pretty insightful. I believe she could learn to play a guitar if she had hands."

"Wendy," Boorman asked, "do you know any songs that you can hum for us?"

Suddenly the deck reverberated with the unearthly sound of whale song and everybody's hands went to their ears. "Down," Captain Macon shouted over the din, "Wendy, turn it down."

"I am sorry, Holly," she said. "That was my first effort. I did not realize how loud it would be. Did you like it otherwise?"

"It was beautiful, Wendy," Boorman answered for her. I think you should move to Hollywood when you get back to the States."

"You are too kind, Captain Boorman. I may have to ask Captain Macon to put a ship's radio in your cabin so that we can continue our discussions."

Captain Macon and Sandal puckered their lips and raised their eyebrows at each other.

"Holly, Cassandra!" Wendy scolded, "Please, do not make those faces as if I am not here. You know I can see you."

"We are sorry, Wendy. We were having some fun at Captain Boorman's expense, not yours."

Captain Macon gestured toward the door for Boorman to make his exit. "I am going to take Captain Boorman to look at your vacuum spheres now Wendy. Maybe we can continue our conversation there."

She asked Sandal to stay on the bridge and monitor a noise that she thought she heard in one of the gyroscopes. Sandal grinned at her as if she could see through the shallow ploy to ditch her.

As he was leaving the bridge, Boorman called out to Wendy. "Thanks for the song, Wendy," he said. "I really enjoyed it. I hope I get to hear more."

"Thank you, Captain Boorman. If you go out on the upper deck tonight, be sure to take an umbrella; I think we are heading into some rain."

"What was that?" Boorman asked when they had shut the door behind them.

"You mean Wendy? We honestly don't know. We are trying to figure it out ourselves. She is definitely something new. There are over a thousand patents on her optical processor circuitry alone. The hardware is new technology; the software had to be new to work on the hardware, and somewhere along the way, she became more than the sum of her parts. We have had to learn how to work with her as we went along because nobody else had any experience with this type of computer — except for child development specialists, as we found out." They began climbing the stairs as she talked.

"At first we could not get Wendy to do anything at all, and we were on the verge of junking her and ten years worth of work and starting over. Then one of the engineers reminded us that we had built a learning machine but all we were doing was essentially barking orders at her. That was when we brought in the educational experts, explained what we thought the problem was and asked them how a child learns. And that is how she became what she is now. She grew up surrounded by programmers, engineers and developmental psychologists. Once we got the knack of teaching her, she began learning on her own. You may have noticed that she called me 'Holly' when she was talking *to* me and 'Captain Macon' when she was talking *about* me. That is because I taught her to call me 'Holly', but later she picked up on her own that I did not like being called that when she was speaking to a crew member. I suppose I was concerned about discipline among the crew and it showed in my face. The point is that she continues to develop in ways that indicate a huge level of mental activity behind the scenes.

"Early on, the lunch-time debates were joking matters because everyone involved knew that she was just a machine, but then later the debates became more heated, and some very serious opinions were expressed. Someone said that the only difference between a human brain and a computer was the level of complexity, and then the fur began to fly. There were arguments about what constituted sentience, whether a machine could have a soul, and the moral issues of creating a self-aware being. We even had a person resign over the last issue. He said that we had gone too far. The latest raging debate is about the ethics of servitude."

"You mean slavery?"

"In a sense, yes. We created Wendy with the purpose of serving us and this is all she is capable of doing. We have given her a physical body that is larger and more powerful than any living thing has ever possessed before. For everyone's safety, we had to limit what she can do with it. That limit comes from built-in programming that she cannot supersede. For example, she 'trusts' only a handful of people. If you tried to give her a command, she literally could not obey you unless I had previously told her that she could trust you and do what you said. I can give limited trust as well, so that different people can work with her in different capacities."

"Well I can see how the servitude issue could come up if you were talking about programming a person to do only what you told him to do, but we *are* talking about a machine," Boorman said.

"Are we? People who are smarter than me are still undecided as to what we are talking about. And anyway, people have their own built-in programming. A baby only trusts its mother at first. Later it may, or may not, learn to trust other people. The reason behind that programming is obvious — for millions of years of human evolution, the mother was the single person who had the most investment in the baby and would do whatever it took to guarantee its survival. Babies who trust strangers may not live to be old enough to have their own babies.

"I'll give you another example," she continued. "How many days do you think you could sit in front of a table full of good food and not eat any of it? Could you starve yourself on purpose while surrounded by food? Probably not. The biological imperative is strong; it is programming that we can't rise above. Wendy has programming like that as well. She monitors her own power levels and the lower her power levels get, the more desperate she will become to expose her solar cells to sunlight. Isn't this the same as hunger?"

"So you think that Wendy is a machine that has biological imperatives and actually thinks?"

"If you are asking me what I personally think she is, I honestly don't know, but there are other people who work directly with her who think that she is a sentient being with a soul just like any sentient being."

"I'm afraid you are losing me there. I can buy the brain-machine analogy, but I've never seen a soul, I've never even seen a photograph of a soul, and I don't believe that there is such a thing."

"Is that why you think David Chang is a fraud?" She asked.

"I think he is a fraud because he **is** a fraud. He has just figured out the kinds of things that people like to hear, and he makes his living telling his lies."

"David doesn't take money for what he does."

"And he doesn't need to. I saw what a ticket on this cruise cost. If the Navy hadn't bought my ticket I could never have afforded to come, yet David Chang is on board for free. I'll bet that before this trip, somebody had put him up in a fancy hotel, or some aristocrat even let him stay right in his mansion with the family. But robbing people of their money is not the worst part; he is robbing people of their lives. He spouts his garbage about worlds within worlds, life after life, and the importance of letting go, even of one's self, and people buy into it and quit doing the things that make us the greatest species on the planet. People need to take care of business and not just let everything slide. He talks about how this world is an illusion and how if we are going to make it to the ultimate reality, we have to learn to be totally selfless. Sure, he is all about selflessness; the more selfless people are, the more freebies he gets."

"I'm sorry I brought it up. You seem to be pretty cynical about this."

"I'm not cynical. I'm a realist. It's not this world that is the illusion — it's the next. Only a fool would, or could, believe otherwise."

You might be surprised to hear that these words came from the mouth of someone whose ghost had been haunting the upper decks of this ship as recently as last night. However I was not totally mystified by this. It has been my experience that most people have out-of-body experiences and most also do not remember them. Many of those people do not believe these experiences are even possible. What is unusual is a person who retains a memory of the experience and still denies the experience unless he only remembers it as a vivid dream. In Boorman's case, he did not think of the experience of last night as a dream; he remembered being on the deck — he just could not quite remember who had been there with him, and did not recognize that the experience was different from normal waking experiences. I thought he was in deep denial.

While having their conversation, the two captains had climbed back up to the same deck that Boorman's cabin was on. Captain Macon explained that this was called deck one. The deck with the heavy instrumentation was deck zero, and below that was the main bridge.

As they walked down the hallway of deck one, Macon picked up the thread of conversation again.

"So, Captain," she began, "do you consider yourself a man of science then?"

He nodded.

"Do you believe in the expanding universe and the laws of entropy and all that?"

"Yes," he nodded again. "I think that has all been demonstrated."

"Then, Captain Boorman, I believe that you have made a greater leap of faith than David Chang is asking anyone to make." They had reached an inside door on the hallway and the Captain put her hand up to the security panel.

"Why do you say that?" Boorman asked.

"How do you explain how the physical universe, which according to scientists, has been proceeding towards chaos since the beginning of time, has, over the last several billion years, not produced disorder, but a level of organization that is still proceeding in the opposite direction of chaos? If entropy rules, how has that universe managed to produce life? How has it managed to produce minds that can create machines that learn, and things such as this?" She opened the door.

If the outside of the *Eckener* was immense, the inside seemed, impossibly, to be of even more gigantic scale and grandeur. Captains Macon and Boorman stepped through the door onto a catwalk and into a room the size of a modern airplane hangar — although a hangar filled to bursting with colossal spheres. The curve of the spheres extended over the captains' heads, so that, even though the doorway had led them between two of the spheres, there could not be much visible from Boorman's initial viewpoint except the vast, lustrous, almost transparent, surfaces above and in front of him. Captain Macon grinned broadly as she watched the expression on Boorman's face. "Come on; let's take a stroll," she said.

The catwalk extended from the door between the thick cables holding the spheres, to the platform which extended the length of the ship beneath the spheres. The cables coming down from the spheres crisscrossed everywhere, like the spokes of bicycle wheels. Directly beneath the spheres themselves, there was just enough room for a person to duckwalk, but on either side, there was enough overhead room and clearance between the spheres and the cables, to drive a small car along the platform from one end of the ship to the other. Along the sidewalls of the ship, rooms bulged out into the open spaces between the spheres. I assumed they were workshops or storage rooms, as their doors opened onto the platform.

Captain Macon led Boorman up to one of the spheres. "Put your hand on it," she said, pointing at a point just above his shoulder. "That may be as close as you will ever come to the vacuum of space."

"Sandal told me about them," he said in awe. "Pure vacuum . . ."

"Yes, well actually, it is far from pure vacuum at the moment," she stated. "We are nowhere near the ship's lifting capacity. We could easily go up to forty thousand feet, if we wanted to. Of course we would all die," she laughed. "We could also lift a lot more weight if we wanted or needed to do so. Wendy said that we may be heading into some rain tonight. We try to avoid rain when possible, but sometimes we can't. Do you know what rain weighs?"

"You mean a drop?"

"How about billions or trillions of drops. It will add tons of weight to the *Eckener*, but all Wendy has to do is pump out a little more air from the spheres to maintain altitude. The pumping is done through these pipes." She leaned down and pointed to a large tube that came out of the bottom of the sphere they were examining. It ran straight down into the platform and disappeared. "Do you know why the pipe is at the bottom?" She asked playfully.

"Is this a quiz?"

"Maybe."

"Ok. Let me think a minute. I know it's not to collect condensation. I've got it — that's where the air is. Air is heavier than vacuum, so it pools at the bottom. The air is what you want to pump out, so that is where you put the pipe."

"Very good; you get a gold star. Come on and I'll show you the pumps."

As they walked, she pointed out other engineering details. "Those smaller spheres, higher up and wedged in between the main spheres are primarily for trim. The main spheres run straight down the middle of the ship, but the secondary spheres are more lateral and can be filled or emptied to balance the ship quickly, as cargo, including people, is moved around. This keeps us from constantly having to worry about balancing the weight of the cargo. Below this platform that we are walking on are the main water reservoirs, drinking water, grey water for flushing toilets, rain water that hasn't been purified yet, and also contaminated water that needs to be disposed of in a sanitary way. All of the tanks except for the septic tanks are pressurized so that the water can be moved around the ship where needed. Also any of them can be instantaneously emptied in an emergency."

"What kind of an emergency?"

"Oh, let's say a pump goes out and we need altitude in a hurry. We would want to start dropping weight. However, we would probably start by dropping the several tons of lead pellets that are compacted in ballast tubes under the water supply."

"Where does the grey water come from?"

"The swimming pool, mainly, but also from washing dishes, as well as the lavatories in the cabins. The grey water is only used for toilets. If we want to clean the decks, we use rain water, which can also be filtered and turned into drinking water. If we had an emergency need for drinking water, we could also drop down to about fifteen feet or so above a body of water and pump the water into the rain tanks. We can even desalinate sea water by running it through the solar water heaters and diverting the condensation down special return pipes."

"What happens if one of these gets a crack in it?" Boorman tapped one of the giant spheres as they passed under it.

"That would be bad." Macon said. "We have trained for an event like that, but we do not know for certain if our procedures will work because we have never risked lives to test them. We have large sheets of the special plastic located strategically around the ship. In theory, the plastic, which is thick, but pretty light and about as flexible as thin plywood, if held in position over the breach, would be sucked up against it before the men holding it would. If you didn't get it right — well, it would be a pretty horrible way to die. However, I don't think that is a very likely scenario. This plastic is extremely dense once you get a vacuum inside it. The molecules line up in such a way that the material becomes almost metallic in nature. You could pound it with a ball peen hammer and it wouldn't even notice."

They had come to an immense silvery box the size of a three story house that was snugly fit between two spheres. Large ducts radiated from the "roof" and fanned out to different parts of the ship. "This is her heart," Macon said. "Inside here are the twin engines that drive this ship. Notice that the spheres are a little higher off the floor to make room. This is the exact center, by weight, of the ship, and directly above us is the highest point on its back — the hump, as the engineers call it."

"These are the engines?" Boorman asked. "They are hardly making any noise."

"They are not only the engines, but the vacuum pumps, the main energy storage facility, the generators, and the propulsion units, all in one. Each of the two internal units is complete unto itself and can function independently or in tandem with the other unit. The lowest level of each unit contains a flywheel for energy storage. Just above that is a motor/generator, and above that are the 'pumps' as we call them. Typically, you wouldn't use the same type of pump to move large volumes of air for propulsion as you would use to pump out a vacuum, but our engineers have solved that problem."

"What gets the flywheels spinning?" Boorman asked.

"You may have noticed that it is pretty dark in here." Macon said. "That is because almost the entire upper hull of the ship is covered with solar cells. The electricity from the cells is used to charge batteries, two rows of which run alongside both sides of the water tanks below us. The batteries drive the motor, which is magnetically coupled with the flywheel. The flywheel begins turning until its maximum speed is reached. Additional solar electricity goes back into the batteries until everything is fully charged. The batteries may provide energy to the rest of the ship for lighting or whatever, or may be used to spin up the flywheels again as needed. The flywheels, which spin in a vacuum, by the way, can be used to turn the generator for additional electricity. The magnetic coupling on the motor/generator can be switched either to the flywheel, the pump, or both. And, in fact, for maximum cruising speed, the magnetic coupling can bypass the motor and connect the flywheel directly to the pump. The pumps run at constant speed and what they are doing is controlled by the opening and closing of valves and the positioning of louvers along the outside of the ship, assuming they are not pumping out spheres, of course. The incoming air can come from any of the ducts, but during lift or while cruising, it comes in through the large intake duct that runs up to the upper hull behind the Captain's Quarters and is fed by two large fans that assist the pump during those times."

"Amazing!" Boorman said, staring up at the network of ducts and the towering iridescent spheres held down by their taut thick cables.

"Yes, she is. I never get tired of showing her off. She can move up, down, sideways, backwards, and when moving forward, can match the speed of most propeller driven aircraft. And we never have to land. And," she added, "she talks."

*

Captain Macon suggested that since this was Boorman's last night on the *Eckener*, he might want to dine privately with her and her daughter in the Captain's Quarters.

He readily accepted, and so, later that night, I found myself bobbing along behind him as Sandal led him up the ballroom staircase to the uppermost deck. Here, she unlocked a door on the inner wall and let him into a large living room. She told him to make himself at home and she would tell the captain that he was here.

The forward wall and ceiling were covered in a pleated material, and Boorman could see through an opening in the front curtain that this room overlooked the ballroom, where other diners were sitting down to their own meals.

The furniture in the room was comfortable but not luxurious. There was a large couch and some overstuffed chairs positioned for easy conversation, a bookcase, some wall cabinets and several small functional tables.

In a few minutes, Captain Macon came into the room, followed by Sandal, who was now dressed in civilian clothes.

"Captain Boorman, or may I still call you John?" she began. "I'd like for you to meet my daughter, Cassandra, or 'Sandal' as she is sometimes called."

"Sandal is your daughter? I thought she was crew."

"She can be both. What better way to learn the business?"

"Of course. But Sandal and I have a history already."

Captain Macon raised her eyebrows.

"She is the only one besides yourself who has made me feel the least bit welcome on this ship."

"Yes, we have noticed that you don't seem to make friends easily," she laughed. "Would you like something to drink before dinner?" She walked over to one of the cabinets.

"Thanks. I'll have whatever you're having."

"Why do you think everyone is staying away from you like that?" Sandal asked. "It is peculiar."

"Oh, I know why it is," Boorman answered. "It's Chang. He knows I don't like him. He knows that I am on to him, and so he is warning everyone to stay away from me. There is no telling what kinds of lies he is spreading."

"Do you really think that is so?" Sandal frowned. "He seems like such a sweet person to me. In fact, goodness seems to radiate from him. I don't believe he could purposely hurt anyone if his life depended on it. Besides, Gregory told me that you didn't exactly make friends with the guard in San Francisco. And then there was the incident in the street. What is the common denominator here?" She laughed at his expression.

"You're not . . .?" John hesitated, wishing that he had not started the question and trying to figure out how to change it in mid-sentence.

"Changlings?" Sandal finished for him. "Yes. We are both believers, so to speak — my mother and myself. But it's OK if you're not. Really — we don't hold it against you or anything."

"It's just that . . ." he began, taking his drink from Captain Macon, "well, I don't mean to be offensive, but I guess I'm just scared of cults."

"You think this is a cult?" Captain Macon laughed. "Well, you could be right, I suppose. However, I think the only difference between a cult and a religion is the number of people involved, and in this case I believe we are talking about a religion."

Boorman killed his drink and handed her the glass. "You know, I think I should go. I think I have insulted you and overstayed my welcome."

"Oh, sit down and have another drink. What more important thing could anybody have to talk about than religion? We don't have to agree on anything, as long as we are all trying to find the truth and not just win an argument."

Boorman sighed and grinned. "Well OK, as long as we are all on a first name basis. Fix me another of whatever that was, and let the games begin."

They eventually carried their arguments up a small flight of stairs to a dining room where the table was set and waiting for them. The ceiling here was the same pleated fabric of the living room, but Macon flipped a switch and the material folded back to reveal, through the transparent canopy, a night full of stars.

The three of them ate by candle light and starlight and argued and laughed way into the night. By the time Boorman left, the stars had disappeared and a light drizzle of rain had begun to stipple and streak the dome of the dining room.

As Captain Macon led Boorman to the door, she asked, seemingly in no particular direction, "Wendy, what is our visibility?"

Wendy answered immediately, "We have zero visibility, Holly."

"How high would we have to go to get above this fog?"

"We would have to climb to approximately twelve thousand feet, Holly. Do you wish for me to begin the ascent?"

"No, Wendy. Steady as she goes."

She turned to Boorman. Twelve thousand feet is enough to make some small percentage of our passengers start throwing up if they haven't been acclimated first. Nobody wants to see their supper twice. We can navigate fine with our other sensors."

Boorman made his way to his cabin and let himself into the dark room. He saw that his room-mate was already in bed and decided not to wake him by turning on lights, but lay right down on his own bunk without even taking his clothes off.

I was about to leave to follow my own explorations when I sensed another presence in the room. Someone was in the closet and was trying, with some difficulty, not to breath heavily. Boorman had drunk too much alcohol to notice and was quickly snoring. I supposed that we had surprised a thief with our entry and I waited to see what he would do next.

In a short while, the thief became certain that Boorman was asleep and eased the closet door open and stepped out into the room. Something sharp glinted in his hand. I wanted to scream for help but I knew no one would hear me. What could I do? There was something I remembered — something about heat. But bad things could happen — had happened — when I did that. Wake Boorman up — that's what I had to do. But what if he was the real assassin and this guy was a good guy? Don't be stupid, I thought. Good guys don't hide in the dark with daggers. I leapt into Boorman's head. "Wake up!" I screamed.

Boorman sat bolt upright in bed. "What's going on?" he shouted in his confusion.

By this time the other assassin was already on top of Chang in his bed and the two of them were grappling. Boorman quickly turned on the bed lamp and saw that Chang was struggling with the other man and was barely managing to hold the dagger away from his body. The dagger had penetrated Chang's left hand through the palm, but Chang was not letting the assassin have the dagger back for another attack, and the struggle was sawing the wound wider and wider and blood was gushing onto Chang's chest and face.

The assassin realized that very soon he was going to have to deal with Boorman and managed to swing Chang's arm over to the table between the beds and, with one final effort, hammered the knife into the wood. Finally grasping the situation, Boorman literally dived into the assassin's side, knocking him off the bed and into the floor. The assassin scrambled up and ran out the door, with Boorman in swift pursuit. He chased the assassin up the staircase and, finally, out onto the open deck.

The assassin ran down a concourse until, in the fog, he blundered into a cluster of chairs that the crew had decided to postpone straightening until tomorrow rather than work in the drizzle. Seeing no way around the tangle, he jumped up on the surrounding outer hull that formed a barrier around the sunken decks. His intention seemed to be to run around the chairs and, with luck, leave Boorman hunting for him in the dark and the fog.

Instead, his shoes slipped on the wet hull and he fell hard onto his stomach and began to slide feet first down the curve of the hull toward the sea. When Boorman ran up, he saw the man in the dim deck lights, terror on his face, his fingernails clawing at the unyielding hull as he slid inexorably downward. Boorman leaped to the man's aid, but missed grasping his hands by inches. Worse, instead of the intended rescue, Boorman now found that his inertia had taken him too far and that he too was sliding down the hull face first into the darkness. Their fear reflected in each other's faces until the assassin's face disappeared in the night. Suddenly, Boorman felt something grasping his pants leg and his descent stopped. Slowly, he was pulled back up until he felt his legs go over the top and he slid back down into the deck area and collapsed in a heap. He looked up to see Chang grinning down at him. "I thought you were afraid of heights," Chang commented.

By this time, sirens were sounding all over the ship and Wendy's voice was sounding through the ships loudspeakers, one of which was blaring at them from not far away. "Man overboard! Man overboard!" Wendy was shouting. "Emergency reverse! Emergency reverse! Emergency Descent! Emergency descent! Man the elevators! Man the elevators!"

"Damn!" Boorman exclaimed, looking down at his legs and then at Chang's bloody hand. "You got blood all over my only good pants."

The ship lurched hard as Wendy suddenly flipped all of the *Eckener's* louvers into reverse. Boorman used his own forward momentum to bring himself to his feet and begin running for the stairwell. In the stairwell, he met Sandal, who was just coming from the Captains Quarters, tucking her shirt into her pants.

"Where are the elevators?" He shouted at her over the clamoring alarms.

"Didn't you read the . . ? Never mind, follow me."

They ran down the stairs to the bottom deck, where Sandal held her hand up to the security panel and paused. "I can't let you go in here. Passengers are not allowed."

"Sandal! I'm not just a passenger. I'm an official observer on assignment from the Navy. Captain Macon agreed that I could go anywhere on the ship as long as I was accompanied by a crew member. You're a crew member, so let's go. I want to see how you do search and rescues at sea."

"You're right; I forgot. But you've got to do exactly what I say; it can be dangerous if you're not careful." They went through the door and then into the center hold of the ship, which was now brightly illuminated by large fluorescent panels. A large square section of the floor was missing, and it was to this area that Sandal ran. "This is the main elevator," she shouted, pointing over a railing and down into the hole. Below, and already on the descent into the billowing fog, glowing hellishly yellow from the high-intensity flood lamps shining down from the ships hull, was a large platform suspended by cables from a crane mounted to a rail on the superstructure. Several crew members in life jackets were on the platform peering over the safety rails into the brightly lit but impenetrable fog. "Put these on," she told Boorman, pulling life jackets and some unusual looking harnesses from a nearby rack. "Life jacket first."

Boorman followed her example as she quickly put on the life jacket and then the harness, which went around her legs and across her chest, back, and shoulders, somewhat like a parachute harness. Then she handed him a heavy metal cylinder with two large handles and showed him how to attach it to the front of his harness just above his stomach. "Rocker switch," she shouted, pointing at a large black switch on the handle about where his thumb would be as he held the device in front of his chest. "Up, stop, and down," she pointed to positions on the switch. She showed him another one on the other handle. "Speed. Don't touch it." Then she opened her device to show gears designed to grab on the twisted steel cables used on the *Eckener*. "Clamps on to cables," she pointed first at the device and then at the platform cables that disappeared down into the bright golden fog. "Make sure it's closed and latched securely. Come on."

There were four cables that supported the platform. They went straight down to its corners about a foot in from the edges of the platform opening. Sandal swung a section of the railing aside, and clamped the device around the cable. She reached up over her head and grabbed a dangling wire, which she plugged in to the top of the device. "Forgot to tell you about this," she shouted over her shoulder. "Grab a power supply before you come down. Are you sure you can do this?" She looked at him questioningly.

"Fifteen years in the Navy," he replied.

She nodded, swung out over the edge and vanished into the luminous mist, her power cable spooling out from above.

"Oh shit!" Boorman said aloud to himself, looking first at his device and then at the gaping hole in the floor. Finally, clenching his jaws, he followed Sandal's example and clamped his device to the same cable that she had used. It took him two tries, as the cables were oscillating in erratic circles. He double checked his closure and his harness connection, remembered at the last minute to plug in the power supply, swung out over the edge and hung there in mid air, his eyes clamped shut. He opened his eyes, pressed the switch to the down position and began his descent. He descended jerkily, stopping the device periodically to avoid accidentally slamming into the platform, which he ultimately did anyway.

Sandal came over to him and showed him how to unhook his harness, leaving the motorized device still attached to the cable. Some of the crew seemed surprised to see him, but nobody said anything about his presence on the platform.

Even though the *Eckener* had been rock solid stable, there was no way to keep the platform they were now on from swaying in the gusts, and they had to hold on to cables and safety rails as they peered out into the fog. Above them, two double rows of flood lights shown brightly down, but because of the fog, they could only see a few yards around them. The platform was holding at about wave height, but salt spray and an occasional large wave would blow over the platform, stinging their eyes and cutting down visibility even more.

"Wendy says this is the exact spot where he hit the water. She will start a spiral search from this point, but will also allow the wind to push her a little, just as it probably is pushing him. Wendy said he slid over the side. Why would somebody climb up on the hull? The safety engineers said that recessing the deck was adequate, but maybe it isn't enough."

"I was chasing him." Boorman told her the story as they searched the waves.

"Oh no! Mom — I mean the captain — is going to have a fit. We may have to go back to San Francisco. I wonder who he was. Do you think he could have survived? We were about five hundred feet up when he fell, so probably not, huh?"

"Probably not."

They kept searching, and several hours after Wendy had stopped the sirens, one of the crew got a call from Wendy on a ship's cell phone. "Wendy thinks she got a reflection on the sonar. She's moving us over there." Soon someone spotted shoulders and arms washing around in the waves. They used a boat hook to pull the body closer where they could grab the clothes and drag him onto the platform. He was obviously dead. They crowded around the body to see who it was. Sandal pulled a cell phone out of a pocket and spoke into it. "Captain," she said, "it's Charley Hassan. OK. I'll be right there. I'm bringing Captain Boorman."

"You know him?" Boorman asked.

Sandal turned to Boorman. Her eyes were downcast and she covered her mouth with her hand. Her voice quavered as she spoke. "He was a crew member. He had a wife and kids. He sent money back to them all the time. I don't know how this could happen." She took a deep breath, seemed to shake herself free of her morbid thoughts and walked over to the cable where the devices were hanging. "Let's take the spiders," she said. "They're quicker."

"The spiders?" Boorman was not sure he had heard her correctly.

"Yeah — actually 'SPADAs' — Single Person Ascent Descent Apparatus. Everybody calls them spiders; it seems to fit."

She quickly attached her harness to the uppermost spider and glided up the cable and into the hold of the *Eckener*.

Boorman attached his harness to the remaining spider, gave it a few hard jerks to make sure it was well attached, and rose up after her. He swung around and stepped off on the deck. "That might actually be pretty fun if I didn't have such a headache from drinking too much."

"They are pretty handy. The *Eckener* seldom actually 'lands' anywhere unless it is to let passengers on or off," she explained as they took their gear off and hung it back on the rack. "We pick up cargo on the elevator platforms without going all the way down to the ground. The spiders are great for going down to the platforms and back up while they are being loaded."

They climbed the stairs quickly and Sandal let them into the Captains Quarters. The living room was completely different than Boorman remembered it. There was a command console in front of the clear wall that looked down into the ballroom. Captain Macon was watching a monitor where one could see some crew members locking the elevator platform into place while others carried Hassan's body off of it.

"Wendy," Captain Macon said, standing up and stepping away from the console, "please stow the emergency bridge."

The console and chair were on a single stage that now descended into the floor where afterwards a carpeted section that matched the living room floor slid into place. Now the room looked like it had before.

"A hell of a night to stay up late drinking, huh?" she said to Boorman. "I've already contacted the FAA. They said to proceed on to Honolulu and we would sort it all out there. Based on what Chang has already told me, I'm going to have to contact the FBI as well."

A crew member brought in a pot of coffee and began filling cups.

"I want to thank you for what you did, she said to Boorman. I understand you almost went in the drink yourself. Would you mind telling us your story for the record? Wendy will be recording it into the ship's log."

He told his story, drank his coffee, and then made his way, exhausted, back to his cabin. He was mildly startled to find Chang up and staring out the window at the breaking dawn behind them.

"You surprised everyone last night, John," Chang said, "including yourself, I suspect. We are all more than we think we are. There may be more surprises in store for you."

"You can have them. I'm full up right now." Then noticing Chang's hand Boorman asked, "Either I'm crazy or you are? I'm pretty sure I saw a man trying to saw your hand off last night and you don't even have a bandage on it."

"It's fine. See?" Chang held the hand up to show that there was no bleeding. "I made the bleeding stop. It will be healed completely in a few days."

"You know," Boorman shook his head. "I really don't buy in to that stuff. You ought to save your breath for the chumps."

"You don't believe me?" Chang looked surprised.

"Why should I?"

"Come with me, then and I'll show you." Chang walked into the bathroom.

Boorman followed and stood in the doorway. "What?"

Chang held his abbreviated hand over the lavatory. Blood began to gush from it just as you would expect blood to flow from a recent major knife wound.

"Mind creates the body, not the other way around," Chang said as he turned the flow of blood on and off over the sink. The body will do whatever the mind says, if the mind only knows how to tell it."

After a night of no sleep, heavy drinking, intense excitement, and nearly dying, Boorman's legs finally gave out from under him. Chang caught him as he fell, and dragged him over to his bunk to sleep it off, in the process, getting blood on Boorman's only good shirt.

*

Hawaii materialized out of the sea through the last of the fog that was being burned away by the morning sun. As the Big Island grew larger and larger in our perspective until its cliffs and peaks loomed over us, so too did my impending sense of doom. The island changed the curvature of the earth, created its own gravity, combed clouds from the sky and dominated the submissive sea. So too did my plan create its own gravity, but it was anti-gravity, and the closer I got to its source the more repelled I was.

I will tell you my plan to restore my eyesight, although I am sure that you have already guessed. It was a simple plan. I would languidly follow Chang to his rendezvous with me and to my rendezvous with darkness, but somewhere along the way, I would find the correct time and place to intervene, either with Chang, with myself, or with the bomber himself. However, the closer we came to that juncture of space and time, the more the feeling grew in me that I was about to do something dangerous, something wrong, something impossible to rectify.

I had been emotionally blinded by my physical blindness. My hatred, my loathing of my affliction had caused me to lose my true vision. The revelation of the magnitude of what I was considering came upon me as the *Eckener* entered into one of Hawaii's hidden valleys, perhaps one of the last remnants of the garden that once covered the earth before it was torn and trampled.

I do not see things the way you do. You may have wondered how I can offer descriptions of things and places when I do not have eyes. The way that I see is not something that I understand myself. However, so that I do not seem too ignorant, I challenge you to describe to me how you see — how your brain interprets the photons that strike the nerves in your eyes. If *you* cannot explain vision, then how can you expect *me* to do so?

Not only is the method of my seeing indescribable, but *what* I see is indescribable as well. Where your field of view is limited, mine is not; I see everywhere — in all directions at once. Where you see in a limited range of wavelengths, I see colors that do not even exist for you. Where you see by reflected light, I see by a light that permeates all existence. Where you see Earth, and hope someday to see Heaven, I see Heaven and Earth intermingled, inseparable. Why would I want to give up this vision in return for my old way of seeing? That is what I asked myself as I looked upon this beautiful precious valley. I had always known the answer; I would not want to give it up. But I was just now realizing what I would be trading. I wanted my eyesight back because I missed riding in my car and going to movies and admiring the young bodies at the beach and all the things that make the world a delightful carnival. But that day in the temple of Kwan Yin was what made me what I had become; to change that was to change everything. This was part of the sense of eminent disaster that I was suffering. But, to reinforce this anxiety was a memory that I had come into this continuum by a misstep — that I had accidentally interfered in my own history with nearly catastrophic results. What I had been considering doing on purpose was something that should be avoided at almost any cost. To change your own history was to make yourself into someone that you were not, possibly into someone who did not have the power to undo what the other you had done. To tamper with one's own existence was truly to work without a net.

I began to formulate other thoughts in that valley — thoughts about who I was and what the world was — thoughts that I would pursue later.

As I put away my plan and accepted with gratitude the opportunity to be what I was, and where I was, the sense of dread left me and I was able to continue the trip without difficulty. I could not have told you at that time exactly why I stayed with the *Eckener*. I had answered my question about Captain Boorman. He was far from being an assassin, but he was not a bodyguard either, as the policemen in Honolulu seemed to think.

I suppose I continued to hover about the ship for many reasons. I liked the people; I enjoyed seeing the world from their perspective. I wanted to see what happened to them. What would Boorman do when Captain Macon put him ashore? What would Chang do when he got to China? I suppose there was also an element of self-preservation. I felt that somehow the attempts on Chang's life were linked to those on my own. But I suppose, above all, at that moment, buried under many others, yet carrying the weight of the moment, was a memory of a vision of the *Eckener* crushed beneath a gigantic mountain, bodies flung lifeless across the frigid landscape.

You may recall that I died once when I was young and was told to watch for the flying whale and that there would be times for further choices to be made. I died again that day in the Kwan Yin temple and was given a choice to return to a much more difficult life, or to call it quits, take the easy way, and just stay dead. Now I was reaffirming that choice to be alive in this time. This was the time and place that I had chosen so long ago and so far away. By my memories or by my dreams, this was the time of the flying whale.

[Translator's Notes: At this point, the flow of the narration was interrupted by what seemed to be a question-and-answer period. This

confirmed for me that this narration had been given orally to a group of people and not originally written down by Xiao Chen herself. This section of the Chinese manuscript was quite lengthy and may perhaps be the subject of a separate book. However this section is not really pertinent to the story at hand. I have included just a few of the questions to give the reader a feel for what transpired. One of the first questions had to do with Xiao Chen's statement at the end of this chapter. Note that Xiao Chen was not addressed by that name in this assemblage, but was called Kwan Yin. Here are some examples of the questions that were asked:

Question: Kwan Yin, do you hear us when we pray?
Answer: Your prayers are heard. Thoughts, wishes and prayers are more real than anything that you can touch with your hands in this world. Every action, every intent, every wish, and every prayer is a stone to make ripples across the universe.
Question: Kwan Yin, how can we know if we are following our destiny?
Answer: You will know; your heart will tell you. Destiny is what we come into the world to do; fate is what may keep us from doing it. Fear may make us falter on the path and then we may become prey to fate.
Question: Kwan Yin, surely you can tell us the true nature of existence.
Answer: To comprehend a thing, we must stand outside of it, but where is the outside of existence, and on what is there to stand?
Question: Kwan Yin, You have said that fear, not hate is the opposite of love. How is this to be understood?
Answer: Fear is the most negative of all emotions. All other negative emotions come from fear. Fear is the emotion that is most unnatural to the spirit and the one that keeps us trapped in the illusion of the world. Our creator has nothing but love for us, but it is our own fear that keeps us from the full experience of that love. There are only two real emotions, love and fear, but in truth only love is real.

This is why the angels say, "be not afraid."
~~Tomas~
– End of Translator's Notes]

Book 2 ～～ The Bodhisattva

Notes from the Translator

[Translator's Notes: I find it remarkable in retrospect, that just as Xiao Chen's life pivoted on a single moment when she had instinctively attempted to do a good deed, so did her manuscript come into my hands in the same way.

As I have stated on other occasions, I have never met Xiao Chen and it would be very unusual to meet anyone who knew that they had met her—at least that would be true now. At that time and at that place where the manuscript existed, it was not a rare event to find someone who had at least seen her, but it was indeed rare to find anyone who would admit it.

China had invited my employer to help with the engineering problems that had been left in Xiao Chen's wake and I had been sent to assess the damage. While the company execs met with the new heads-of-state in a conscripted makeshift government building, I walked around Beijing, staring in awe at the results of an immense and unknown power released in this city.

At that time, I could not imagine what force could have caused such damage, and the Chinese were being surprisingly closed-mouthed about it. I say "surprisingly" because the once paranoid and secretive government had suddenly become astonishingly open following the Tiananmen Police Station incident. The government, though still communist, declared that they would hence forth strive to be good neighbors in this shrinking world. They had no secrets, they said. But they did have at least one. When asked what had caused such widespread and seemingly unexplainable damage, they would only smile enigmatically and change the subject.

The answer to this mystery came as so many answers do: from an unexpected source. I was walking through one of the market areas, wondering what storm could have been so selective as to leave these relatively flimsy buildings standing while demolishing buildings that had been built to last for the ages. A woman with silver hair came out of one of the shops carrying a bag of groceries. She tripped on the sill and began to stumble forward, unable to regain her balance. Leaving a trail of vegetables behind her, she was just about to take her final dive into the street when I ran in front of her and caught her shoulders in my hands, stopping her from falling. After she straightened up she looked up at me from about the level of my chest and smiled. She began thanking me profusely in Cantonese. I understand Cantonese, but I do not speak it as well as Mandarin, so I answered her in Mandarin and she immediately switched to that language. "I only speak Cantonese when I am excited," she laughed. "You are such a polite young man. Are you English or French?"

"I am an American," I replied, as I began picking up her vegetables and putting them back in her sack. I told her why I was in Beijing and that my bosses were meeting with the prime minister at that very moment.

"Yes, I know," she beamed proudly. "He is my nephew."

"Who is your nephew," I asked, confused.

"The prime minister," she said. "He is the son of my sister who died along with her husband, the boy's father."

I did not know what to say. The aunt of the prime minister of China would not be off shopping for groceries by herself. However, she seemed so sincere that I decided to humor her. What did it matter if she thought the prime minister was her nephew? "You raised him by yourself?" I asked. "You must be very proud. It takes a very exceptional person to run such a great country."

"Yes," she nodded in agreement. "But I never would have dreamed that he would ever find such an excellent job. He could not get good work for such a long time and now look at him – visiting with foreign dignitaries and making decisions for the whole country. But he is still such a simple boy in his heart. He loves simple things and simple food. I am going home now to prepare dim sum for him. It is his favorite. Would you like to come home with me? It doesn't take very long to make dim sum, and I have been told that mine are the best in Beijing. I would enjoy making some for you."

I hesitated. But she was such a sweet old lady, if slightly addled, that I said yes. "I am very honored by such an invitation," I said, bowing to her. "How could I refuse it?"

I have a rule that some people find strange. It is not an actual rule, perhaps, because I do not always follow it to the letter. It is sort of an experiment with life that someday, I will be brave enough to follow completely just to see what happens. The "rule" is: if someone offers you something, take it; conversely, if someone asks you for something, give it. This was the thought in my head that caused me to go to the apartment of a sweet but confused little old Chinese lady that I had just met in the street in Beijing.

We walked arm in arm the few blocks to her apartment house and then up a couple of flights of stairs to her tiny apartment. She told me to make myself comfortable as she disappeared into the kitchen. I stared out of the apartment window at Tiananmen Square in the distance, surrounded by rubble. In a short while, she returned with hot tea. I sipped the tea and considered the skeletal remains that were once the houses of government in Beijing.

Soon, I smelled the wonderful aroma of dim sum cooking, and then Aunty, as I had come to think of her, came back into the room with a platter of stuffed steaming dumplings. She followed my eyes to the distant ruins.

"What did this?" I asked, pointing out the window with my tea cup.

She gave me the same unfathomable smile that I had gotten from everyone else, except that then she stopped and studied my face as if considering whether I was worthy of the truth. She motioned for me to sit down and she placed the platter of dim sum on a small table. She picked up some with chop sticks and offered them to me on a small plate.

The aroma had already started my saliva glands working and when I began to chew the flavorful dumpling, those glands went into high gear so that my jaws actually ached. I closed my eyes in delight and when I opened them, she was smiling at me. "I am spoiled," I said. "How can I ever eat ordinary dim sum again after having tasted these? They certainly must be the best in Beijing, perhaps the best in China!"

She was pleased at the compliment and we spent the next few hours telling funny stories from our lives, laughing, drinking tea, and eating the delicious dim sum. It had gotten dark outside and I was just about to take my leave and find my way back to my hotel when the door to the hallway opened suddenly and in walked a swarthy young man in an American style business suit. He seemed surprised to see me, but maintained his poise until Aunty introduced us.

"Ah!" he exclaimed. "You are with the American engineering firm. I have just been meeting with your vice president."

"Are – are you really the prime minister, then?" I stuttered, nearly dropping my teacup.

"Not at the moment," he responded. "I am only the prime minister during the day. However, I may turn back into the prime minister if you have not saved me any dim sum," he laughed as he shook my hand. "Please, sit back down. There is no need for formality here."

Taking my seat again, I fumbled for something to say. "Do you visit your aunt often?" I asked him.

"Visit? I live here."

My mind went blank. I was afraid that I had offended him and tried to think of a reason why he might not have lived in such a small ordinary apartment. "But what about your bodyguards? Surely your life is under constant threat."

He ignored my question. "Would you like some more tea – or perhaps a beer? I prefer a beer in the evening. It is American beer – my favorite."

I nodded, and he got up and went into the kitchen.

"He is not afraid of anything," Aunty whispered to me. "He walks to work and everyone stops what they are doing and says good morning to him. Every person in the city is his bodyguard."

The prime minister came back into the room carrying two beers and two glasses. Instead of giving me one of the beers as I expected. He opened one beer and split it between the two glasses, handing one to me. "It is an idiosyncrasy of mine," he said. "It is like the breaking of bread in your country, you see?"

We finished that beer and had another and another and soon I was having just as pleasant of an evening with the prime minister of China as I had been having earlier with his aunt. We discussed things that I never could have imagined could be discussed so frankly with a national leader – things that only old friends discuss.

At last I noticed that Aunty had disappeared, and I assumed that she had gone to bed. Not wanting to overstay my welcome, I stood up and thanked my host for a wonderful evening.

He turned his head at the sound of his aunt calling him from the other room. He asked me to wait a moment and went to see what his aunt needed. I could hear whispering coming through the doorway, and after a short while, the two of them returned, carrying a large bundle of papers wrapped up in string. Aunty cleared away the small table where the dim sum had been, and the prime minister set the bundle down.

Aunty began. "You asked me a question earlier that I did not answer," she said, staring into my eyes. "Probably no one has answered it or will answer it because the answer is too strange."

"At least it may be too strange for Western ears," the prime minister added.

"The answer is in here," Aunty said, tapping the bundle with her finger.

"We have wondered what to do with this," said the prime minister. "We felt that something had to be done. This is too wonderful a thing not to give it to the world, but we did not know how to give such a present. Perhaps you can help us."

"Are you giving these papers to me?" I asked.

"Yes and no," he answered.

"This is the gift," Aunty added. "But this gift is too precious. It is the only one there is, and I cannot let it leave my sight."

"What we are offering you," the prime minister continued, "is an opportunity to tell the world what happened here. This document cannot leave this apartment, but you may come here anytime you wish as long as one of us is here with you. You may come and translate it into English. When you are through, you can take the English with you and leave the Chinese here. The gift is what is in the papers."

"But what is it?" I asked in bewilderment.

"It is the life of Xiao Chen as she told it to us before she took her leave."

"I have never heard of Xiao Chen." I said. "Who is she?"

"That is a very good question," he answered.

The prime minister of China walked me to my hotel in the dark to make sure that no harm came to me in the streets of Beijing, as he did every evening for some weeks.

Every day, after my engineering duties were over, I went back to his apartment and stayed late into the night, drinking only tea. I am telling you that I drank only tea, so that you will not think I wrote this fantastic tale while I was intoxicated. I was only intoxicated by the story that unfolded there for me.

*The prime minister and his aunt helped me with the difficult translations, and after many long evenings of working diligently under weak lighting, we said at last our fond goodbyes and I left, carrying the tale of Xiao Chen Bang typed on a stack of paper and safely locked inside my briefcase. For the sake of convenience I have divided into two books, **The Dakini**, which precedes this one, and **The Bodhisattva**. It is this second document, more or less, that you are about to read: The death and life of Xiao Chen Bang as told to the survivors of the Tiananmen police station massacre from the throne of what was once known as the Forbidden City.*

~~Tomas~

– End of Translator's Notes]

Chapter 1 – Of Seeing and Of Doing.

Yesterday I told you of how I became a Dakini and of how my powers grew after I was imprisoned by your government. I also told you of how I was able to follow my destiny through the help of the beings of light and how that destiny was tied to that of the flying whale. I died three times before I finally became tired of moaning about my fate and began to really follow my destiny. The first time that I died, I saw the beings of light and my foot was set on the right path and my powers began to make themselves known. The second time that I died, the beings of light gave me a choice because the path was about to become more difficult. I made the choice once again to follow the path and my powers grew even more. The third time, I was not in my body when it was killed by bullets. When a body is too badly damaged, the beings of light cannot give you a choice to go back—you must go on to the next world. As I was not in my body when it died, there was no choice to make. I could neither go forward nor could I go back, so I went sideways. Later you will understand better how by going sideways, I bridged two worlds and combined two incarnations into one. At first I was lost in the memories of two people and two worlds, but eventually I pulled them together and my powers grew again, as you will soon see.

You all know Chang Da Wai and have been told about how I saved his life on the mountain known as Chomolungma, Goddess Mother of the World. This man, who is also known as David Chang, was becoming an important part of my life—an important part of everyone's life. This is why someone tried to kill him on the last night of the story that you have heard so far.

Word of the last evening's incident spread rapidly through the ship, but the result was not exactly what I expected. Captain Macon was obviously trying to balance the need to get to Honolulu quickly against the desire to give the passengers a good tour of the islands. For all the interest they had in it now, she probably could have skipped the tour.

We had come ashore on the north of the island of Hawaii at about breakfast time. During breakfast, Captain Macon made an announcement that a crew member had fallen to his death after climbing out onto the outer hull of the ship. She said that they would be stopping for a few days at Waikiki Beach for an official inquiry into the matter. She reinforced what the passengers had apparently already been told, that it was extremely dangerous to venture outside of the designated areas. At the end of her speech, she said that today would be the first day in which the passengers would experience any higher altitudes — the altitudes at which some people became ill. They would spend brief periods at these altitudes through out the day to get a taste of what would be coming later in the trip if the Chinese government was cooperative.

There were medications available at the end of the buffet line, she explained, that would help them cope with lower oxygen levels. And for those who experienced dizziness or headaches anyway, oxygen was available in every cabin and on every observation platform. If any of them were not helped by the oxygen, they should go to the infirmary, or ring for a crew member.

At one end of the breakfast buffet, a young man was handing out foil packets to each person as he or she passed. The passengers were swallowing their altitude pills, eating their breakfast and asking each other what had happened during the evening while the first beautiful valleys, cliffs and jungles of Hawaii passed almost unnoticed around them.

The *Eckener* had then headed southeast down the coast to Hilo, and from there cut back into the saddle between Mauna Loa and Mauna Kea, heading North West. There were spectacular views of both volcanoes, but few people were really looking. Sandal was on the intercom describing points of interest, as well as the overall geology of the island, such as the fact that at fifty six thousand feet from top to bottom, Mauna Loa was the largest volcano on earth, as well as the tallest mountain, climbing to almost fourteen thousand feet above sea level while sitting on the ocean floor even further below sea level. Very few people were listening.

When Wendy had put on the brakes in the night, she had jarred everyone awake who was not already up. As it turned out, there had actually been a few romantic couples on the upper deck, huddled in the fog, who had seen Chang save Boorman's life at the risk of his own. These people were now very popular and were competing with Sandal's travelogue for passenger interest as they were asked to tell their story over and over, leaving no detail un-elaborated.

The main result of this was that Chang, already their hero, became an even greater one, while, Boorman continued to be almost universally shunned. Occasionally someone would go up to Boorman when they saw him about and almost grudgingly thank him for saving Chang's life, but if Boorman overheard any of their private conversations, he would have heard his motives questioned. Comments ranged from one end of the spectrum to the other. "Why was he trying to save a murderer's life anyway?" someone asked. "Were they friends or something?"

"I think he was trying to make sure that the murderer was really going to die so that he couldn't talk. I think he pushed him over."

"At least we know now that he was faking the whole fear-of-heights thing."

"You know he stayed out of the room to try to give the guy plenty of time, but when everything went sour, he had to act like he wasn't involved."

"How do you think this guy got in the room anyway unless someone let him in?"

I could not explain their behavior. It was as if everyone on ship had decided to dislike Boorman, as if there was no way they could put a positive spin on anything he did. The last question, however, was one I hadn't considered. How had Hassan gotten into Chang's room? The security panels were programmed to allow passage only for the individuals who were booked into the room, or so I had understood. It was possible that some crew members had special access. Was Hassan one of those, or did he have help?

A secondary result of last night's events was that there was more camaraderie among all the passengers. I guess death and danger are great icebreakers. Individuals mingled more outside their own groups, so that all of the sub-groups were beginning to meld into one large clan where everyone knew and accepted everyone else, except for Boorman, of course.

Boorman remarked to Captain Macon later that day that he had never seen anything like it. He had saved Chang's life, yet Chang was the hero. He had almost died saving one man that he did not like and then trying to save another man that he did not know, and everybody was acting like they were wishing he had gone on over with him, or even instead of him, if need be. "It is almost like everyone on this ship would be much happier if I had fallen five hundred feet to my death," he commented.

"Well, you won't have much longer to worry about it," she replied. "We'll be in Honolulu soon."

*

The *Eckener* turned south, back around Mauna Loa and the steeper lava flows that dropped precipitously into the sea near the south end of the island. From there, the *Eckener* flew over the black sand beaches, and skirted the Kilauea Crater and the Pu`u `O`o cone along the south east edge of the island. Because of the columns of intensely hot air, the *Eckener* did not fly directly over the fresh lava. She then turned back north, flew up Mauna Loa's eastern slope to see the barren lava fields, then down like a pendulum and back up Mauna Kea's south east slope, down again, and then over the top of the Hualalai volcano, and back out to sea. I think she may have reached 10,000 feet a few times, but it was difficult for me to judge. At any rate, I did not see anyone experiencing any difficulties with altitude sickness.

In the distance, we could see Maui, and headed straight towards it.

Boorman was studying the security panel beside his door when Sandal found him. "My job as tour guide is over for the day," she told him. "How would you like to see the view from the Captains Deck? We can go there or back down to look at the cockpit again. Either way, you will have a spectacular view of the Haleakala Crater."

"Does the Captain's Deck have a solid floor?" He asked.

She nodded.

"Then let's go there."

She led him back through the Captain's quarters, where the three of them had spent most of the previous evening, and then up a staircase behind the dining room. The staircase terminated at a hatch, which Sandal unlocked by security panel. Climbing through the hatch,

Boorman saw that the deck was almost on top of the foremost bulge on the *Eckener*'s back. It formed a crescent with a larger area towards the bow of the ship and with gradually tapering arms on either side. The hull fell away on both sides and to the front, where Boorman could look down immediately into the captain's dining room, and then a little further ahead and lower, the living room, and then further yet, down the slope of the nose, the great ball room, through which he could see straight down into the blue ocean. Two clear windshields arced up from the front of the deck to provide protection from the cold wind, or if one preferred, there was a central gap between the shields where a joining hinged section could be thrown back, allowing the full brunt of the wind to be taken square on the face.

"I hope you noticed what we did back there," Sandal remarked after they had admired the view for a few minutes.

"You mean the altitude pills? The Navy has those too."

"No. I mean the up and down. We went up the mountainside, back down, up again, down again. No old-technology dirigible could do that. To go up, it would have to dump ballast, and to go back down, it would have to dump helium. It would eventually run out of one or the other. The *Eckener* never runs out of vacuum; it just pumps air out to go up, and lets some air back in to go down."

"I hadn't thought about that," he admitted. "That is pretty amazing now that you explain it. I've had a lot on my mind lately," he told her. "I sure wish I could go on with the *Eckener* to China."

"Why can't you?"

He explained Captain Macon's concerns about his fear of heights. Then he added. "But you've seen me in action. I came right down behind you on the spider."

"That's true," she admitted, "but you couldn't see how high up you were. Same thing with going out on the hull. Could you have done that in clear daylight?"

"I don't know. If I had time to think about it, I probably would not have done it at all. Would you?"

She laughed. "No, I guess not."

"I keep trying to think of some way that I can change the captain's mind. You're short a crew member now. Maybe I could fill in."

"You haven't been trained."

"I can learn. On-the-job-training. I've got a strong back and almost average intelligence," he grinned.

"There is one thing that you have already shown yourself to be good at," she said thoughtfully.

"What's that, drinking with the captain?"

"OK, two things."

"Well, what's the other one?"

"You know," she paused and looked at him with a twinkle in her eye. "Maybe no one else has thought about it yet, but Chang is going to need a bodyguard."

"You mean me?" Boorman looked shocked. "You think I could be Chang's bodyguard?"

"Why not?" Sandal asked.

"I don't even like him. I might end up killing him myself."

"You saved his life once already."

"Yeah, and then he saved mine. Maybe he should be my bodyguard."

Sandal laughed at this. "Well, he didn't exactly fight off someone who was trying to kill you with a knife, which is what Chang said you did."

"I was drunk. And I was waked up from a sound sleep. That always ticks me off."

"Do you want to go on this trip or don't you?"

"Yeah, I do. I just don't know if I can stand being tied to this guy twenty-four by seven."

"You won't even have to talk to him. Just follow him around. When we get to China, the government won't even let him off the ship without an armed guard. Nobody's going to be able to get near him again. The Captain is running deeper background checks on all the remaining crew to make sure that Hassan was working alone."

"What is the Captain going to say about all this? If Chang is going to be so safe, why even have a bodyguard?"

"The captain always takes every possible step to insure the safety and comfort of the passengers."

"Tell me about it; she is so concerned about me that she wants me to get off the ship."

"I know her. If she hasn't thought of a bodyguard yet, she will soon. So you had better act fast, or there'll be somebody else sleeping in your bunk when we leave Hawaii."

"Tell me again where this ship is going after it leaves China."

"Nepal, India, Ceylon, Madagascar, Africa, and all over Europe. Imagine cruising slowly over the Serengeti at sunset — the Congo as it has never been seen before — the pyramids of Egypt in the first light of dawn. Then the Mediterranean — Carthage, Crete, Constantinople, Athens, Rome, Gibraltar, then up the Spanish coast. Tell me when to stop."

"Alright, you've convinced me; I want to go. Let's go see the Captain."

"Actually she should be coming up here pretty soon. She said she wanted to see Haleakala from up here, and we're almost to Maui now."

The *Eckener* was staying fairly low to minimize the time that the passengers would spend at high altitude, but at the Eastern shore of Maui, she began a pretty rapid ascent up one of the steep valleys that lead to the Haleakala Crater. Sandal and Boorman both yawned hugely several times to equalize the pressure in their ears.

As the *Eckener* continued climbing, the hatch in the deck was thrown open and Captain Macon appeared and laid an object on the deck that looked like a coffee thermos with a surgical gas mask attached. She saw Sandal and Boorman, and said, "Oh, just a minute." She disappeared down the stairs and reappeared shortly with two more of the thermos bottles and a couple of jackets for them to put on. "You might need the extra warmth and the oxygen bottles when we get to the top" she said.

As the vegetation around them changed from jungle to alpine to barren, they told her their idea for Boorman to become Chang's bodyguard. Captain Macon did not seem very impressed. "You would do anything to go on this trip, wouldn't you?" she asked Boorman.

"Well, yes, I guess I would do almost anything."

"What makes it so important to you?"

"This is going to sound silly when I say it out loud. I've never told anyone before."

"We'll consider it to be confidential information."

"Ok. Well, when I was really young, maybe three or four, my mother and father took me to my aunt's house for Christmas. On

Christmas morning, one of my cousins unwrapped a toy dirigible and began playing with it under the Christmas tree. He obviously had no idea what it was, and because it had wheels on it, thought it was a truck of some kind and played with it that way. I had never seen a dirigible before either, at least that I can remember, but I knew that he was playing with it wrong. It was supposed to fly around the Christmas tree, not roll about on the floor under it like a toy bus. I don't know how I knew, but I knew. Maybe that toy dirigible imprinted on me somehow, I don't know, but I have felt from that day forward that dirigibles were part of my life — part of my destiny. I joined the Navy because of their work with dirigibles. Because of that, and also being in the right place at the right time, here I am, on the greatest, most advanced dirigible that ever was. Damn right I want to go."

"I am impressed by your enthusiasm, Captain Boorman," Captain Macon replied, "but I have two concerns about you. You are not a trained bodyguard, and you have this ridiculously incapacitating fear of heights."

"And I have two answers for you, M'am," Boorman answered a little stiffly. "I am a career officer in the United States military, and whatever I say I am going to do, I do it. Those are the only two things you need to know about me."

"Hmm," she looked thoughtful. "I didn't mean to offend you. Let's just enjoy the sights for awhile. We are almost in the crater now, and we can talk about this later. Does anybody need oxygen yet?"

Sandal and Boorman shook their heads no.

"One more thing," Boorman added. "What if I could show you how Hassan got into Chang's room? Would that make a difference?"

"Very well. You show me how that security was breached, and you are Chang's new bodyguard."

Captain Macon lifted a pair of binoculars to her eyes, and began scanning the lunar landscape of the Haleakala Crater.

Sandal pulled Boorman aside. "Do you know how Hassan got into your cabin?"

"I'm working on it," he answered.

"Why did you say you knew how Hassan got into your room if you really didn't?" Sandal whispered, pulling Boorman around the crescent arm of the deck away from her mother.

"I'm pretty sure I know how he did it," Boorman answered. "I just haven't tested it yet. I was trying to think of something to keep me on this ship when I said that. I'm afraid your captain is going to put me off in Honolulu if I can't cinch this deal. She's been pretty hard-headed about it. She almost had me convinced that I was a liability on board."

"I don't think that is really how she feels. It's just that she has everything tied up in this ship and this cruise. She wants publicity, just not bad publicity."

"What do you mean she has everything tied up in it?"

"I mean everything — every cent that she inherited from my grandfather, plus whatever she could borrow from private investors is right here. My grandfather was worth billions when he died, and his trucking company, which my mother now owns, still turns a huge profit every year. All of it has gone into the design and building of the *Eckener*, and a few smaller prototypes, for as long as I can remember. People think that she is rich, but she's in almost as much debt as the U.S. government."

"Wow! So you could be partying on the Riviera right now instead of working as the first mate if your mother hadn't spent all your inheritance."

"I would rather be here. I am a lot like my mother, and to her, money is a tool. You use it to accomplish the things that you need to do in this world. Right now what she needs to do is start some more money coming in."

"By selling cruise tickets to rich people?"

"No, by attracting new investors. The amount of money that the tickets total up to doesn't even remotely begin to pay for the *Eckener*. Why, it wouldn't even pay for the pumps that drive this ship. I just told you this ship cost billions — tens of billions — I don't even really know how much. But the next one will be cheaper, and they will continue to get cheaper and cheaper to build until they will be the cheapest way to haul lettuce from California to New York, or transport heavy machinery, or lift lumber out of forests without building roads, or take a whole hospital to an undeveloped country. But before those next ships can be built, Lightship Enterprises has got to have more money. This around-the-world cruise is a pure publicity stunt. My mother intends to show the world that Lightships can go anywhere in perfect safety."

"She wants to wipe out the Hindenburg image from people's minds, I suppose," Boorman mused.

"Exactly. After the Hindenburg accident, nobody wanted to have anything to do with dirigibles. There have always been people who saw their value and wanted to revive them, but without the public behind them, there was no investment money and no commitment. Then my mother came along. She had both. I was struck by something that you said earlier, Captain. You talked about dirigibles being tied up with your destiny. I have heard my mother say almost the same thing."

Boorman said nothing, but stared thoughtfully out at the desolate volcanic landscape around them. Sandal shivered in the high altitude chill and pulled her jacket collar up around her neck. "Don't you need the oxygen bottle?" Boorman asked her.

"Oh, I've got a little headache, but I'm going to try to tough it out."

"That which does not kill us makes us stronger. — *Friedrich Nietzsche*," he quoted.

"That which does not bind us sets us free. — *David Chang*," she retorted.

"I guess I'll have to think about that one," he replied.

"One is about the world, the other about the spirit."

Soon the *Eckener* began the descent down into the saddle that joined Maui's mountainous east and mountainous west. The temperature crept up and the vegetation began to get denser and lusher.

As their headaches began to subside, Sandal broke the silence with a question. "Did you really join the Navy because of a toy dirigible?" she asked.

"Partly," Boorman answered, "but I guess there were other reasons too."

"Like what?"

"Fish."

"Fish?! Do you work with fish in the Navy?"

"Well, the ocean then. But what first fascinated me was the idea of the fish in the ocean."

"What do you mean?"

"This may sound stupid, or incredibly obvious, but the ocean is a whole different world that is only separated from this one by a—by a nothing, really—a qualitative difference; water is denser than air, and that keeps the two worlds separate. But because of this separation of the two worlds, most fish in the ocean live and die without ever being aware of this other world where we live. They just swim around their rocks or coral doing their little fishy things until suddenly, here comes a hook or a spear or a hand or even a whole person from out of nowhere. I know fish probably don't think about much, but what if you were a fish? What would you think about that? That's what fascinated me. Pretty silly, huh?"

"No, it's not. I see what you mean. I never thought about it that way before. You stick your hand down into the water, and to a fish down there, it is like something impossible has just happened. It couldn't conceive of the origin of the hand—if fish could conceptualize at all, that is. It would be a hand from another dimension."

"Yeah—the hand from nowhere. When I was a kid, I always had my hands in the water. I had aquariums all over my room and I was always doing something with the fish. I loved to feed the fish right out of my hand, and even trained some of them to let me pet them. I was the only kid I knew with trained fish. Later, when I got older, I took up SCUBA diving and even swam with whales some—listened to them singing under the sea. Sometimes I thought that one day they might actually sing to me, although I don't know how I would know it was to me if one did. I decided I was going to be a marine biologist, so I joined the Navy to get them to pay my tuition. For one reason or another, I never left."

"You swam with whales!? That is amazing. Weren't you terrified?"

"Cautious, but not scared really. I was too elated to be scared. Whenever I looked into a giant eye, it was like I was looking through a portal into another reality."

"It sounds like you've got a lot more guts than some people give you credit for."

Boorman laughed. "I'm not too bad to have around at sea-level or below, I guess. It's when I get up here like this, that I get panicky. It's like part of me thinks that you might grab my ankles and toss me over."

Now it was Sandal's turn to laugh.

Boorman smiled and continued. "This view is beautiful, but it looks lethal to me. We are literally inches away from death. If someone were to come up and slap me on the back, I would probably have a heart attack and die. But if you need any fish wrangled, I'm your man—anything from sharks to goldfish."

"I remember when I was a little girl," Sandal mused thoughtfully. "I haven't thought about it in years, but I had a goldfish. I had a big glass bowl with a goldfish in it. My mother used to scoop the little thing up in her hand, lift it out of the water, and just stare at it for a second or two like she was trying to remember something. Then she would put it back in the water, feed it a little and go on her way. I wonder . . ."

Captain Macon came around the curve of the deck at that moment. "OK," she said, "let's go see how Hassan broke our security."

"I need some electrician's tape," Boorman said, as they began going down through the deck hatch, "you know, that black plastic tape that you wrap around bare wires."

Captain Macon said they would have that in the shop, which was on deck one, inside. On the way there, Boorman asked if Wendy could have allowed Hassan into the cabin. "That is something we thought about," Captain Macon answered. First of all, we don't think that she would have, and second, we asked her and she said she didn't."

"Could Wendy have been compromised?"

"That's not likely either. There aren't but a couple of ways to bypass her heuristic filters. She does a complete evaluation against all other input to test for reasonableness and consistency. She is essentially hack proof."

"Then why didn't she sound the alarm when Chang was being attacked?" Boorman asked.

"Wendy doesn't have sensors in the cabins; we allow our guests their privacy."

"Well, I guess the first thing we need to do is put some sensors in our cabin?"

"Our cabin?" Captain Macon echoed. "You haven't shown me how our security was bypassed yet." She stared at him in mock offence.

Boorman grinned back at her. "Give me time," he replied. "I suppose the next question is: would Wendy have recognized that Chang was under attack if she was able to sense activity in the cabin?"

"That is a good question. Before last night, I would have said no. But the whole emergency routine was totally self-initiated. This was another of Wendy's surprises. There are several routines programmed into her that may have evolved into the response that we saw. One is the emergency evasive maneuvers procedure. She would normally perform this when the ship is in danger. Either a collision is imminent, or a large pressure is felt on the side of the hull. Another programmed procedure that we saw her initiate was the search and rescue maneuver. I would not have expected her to do this unless she was told to do so. And one more algorithm that might have been involved is the automatic head count. This was originally designed to make sure that we didn't accidentally leave someone behind at a stop. I am just guessing that when Hassan fell onto the outer hull, the pressure on the hull sensors set off the emergency evasion routine. Wendy immediately scanned the area and saw that there was a person being left behind, so to speak. The fact that we were five hundred feet in the air might have continued to trigger the evasive maneuver routine if Wendy recognized that a human would be in danger from a fall at that height and if she somehow had begun to see passengers as an extension of herself and included us in her protective custody. This might have triggered the search and rescue maneuver without any human input. On the other hand, I think that if she passed over a non-passenger floating out in the open ocean, she would do no more than notify the duty officer."

They passed through a secured doorway into a large room that contained workbenches, cabinets, and tools of all sorts, including some unusual machines that Captain Macon said was for the fabrication of parts, should something break while they were away from home. There was a large bay door at the far end of the shop that opened into the main interior of the ship. Macon went to a cabinet that contained an array of portable tool chests. She pulled out the one labeled "Electrical", opened it and pulled out a roll of black plastic tape for Boorman's approval. "Is this all you need?" Sandal asked. "Do you want me to take the kit with us?"

"No, thanks," Boorman answered. "I've got everything I need."

On the way back to his cabin, Boorman asked Captain Macon if she thought that Chang would have any objections to having him as a bodyguard. "As soon as you open that door the same way Hassan did, you can ask him yourself," She answered.

"What do you know about Hassan?" Boorman asked them both.

"He seemed like a nice person," Sandal answered. "He was very polite and worked hard. He sent almost all of his money back to his family in Pakistan. Everybody liked him and got along well with him. Sometimes we had to make allowances for his prayer sessions, but usually he would just take a break and disappear for a few minutes. I really would never have suspected him of doing what he did."

"We do background checks on all of our employees," Captain Macon added. "Hassan's report was clean. We don't discriminate by nationality or religion, and he had a good solid resume from years in the hotel industry and then the cruise business, so there was no reason not to hire him."

"Was there anything unusual about him at all? Why did he get selected above other candidates?"

"I don't personally do the hiring," Macon answered. "I'll ask and see what I can find out."

As they walked up to the door of Boorman's and Chang's cabin, Macon said, "Hassan was at least gentle with the security panel; I don't see a scratch on it. I expect no less from you."

Boorman squirmed a little and said, "Well, I'm going to need a little help. Sandal, would you mind putting your hand on the panel to see if it will unlock for you?"

She placed her hand as requested but there was no click from the lock.

"Good," Boorman said. "You will do for the test subject." He began tearing off strips of black tape and handing them to her. "My theory is that the designers of this security system never thought that anyone like Chang would ever fly on the *Eckener*. They assumed that only healthy whole individuals with all of their body parts would ever book a cruise — if they thought about it at all. Wrap the tape around the fingers of your right hand," he instructed Sandal. "I am theorizing that when Chang puts his hand on the panel, it is activated by his palm but that it only scans for his fingerprints. He doesn't have any fingerprints because all of his fingers are short by at least one joint, so it is like having a blank password; anyone can open the door if they know the secret that no password is required."

Sandal finished taping her fingers and placed her hand to the panel once more. There was a click as the lock opened in the door.

Boorman looked at them and grinned. "The scanner in the panel sees nothing where the fingerprints ought to be, just as it did when it was programmed with Chang's hand. If you pull up the security data base and look at it, it will have empty values for David Chang; I guarantee it."

"Good!" Macon exclaimed in relief. "At least we know that Hassan was working alone. I was afraid that someone had let him in somehow."

"I don't think he was working alone," Boorman replied. "What are the odds that Hassan could figure this out by himself? I think someone that has access to your security programs has examined the code, knew this would work, and told Hassan exactly what to do."

"Do you mean another member of my organization is involved?"

"Maybe. Maybe someone was bought off or was a victim of social engineering, or just naturally talked too much. Or maybe you've been hacked."

"Could somebody be accessing the ship's systems remotely?" Sandal asked.

"Probably not. I'm not an expert in these things, but it sounds like Wendy is bullet proof."

"But our security obviously isn't," Macon finished.

"It's more likely that someone just read the code, but you'll have to get some experts to see if someone is actually running around barefoot in your system." He pushed the door open. Chang was sitting on his bunk grinning at them.

"So you are going to be my bodyguard. Excellent! Excellent! It could not have worked out better."

Boorman turned and looked at Captain Macon questioningly.

She looked sheepish at first but then recovered her demeanor and said, "I called the Navy this morning and cleared it with them. I have an extraordinary amount of influence with them these days."

*

They had lunch in the western mountains of Maui, skipped over to Lanai to see the pineapple plantations and Shipwreck Beach, and were escorted by a pod of humpbacks over to Molokai. They made a serpentine path through the lush valleys and jungles of the east end, over the three thousand foot cliffs of the north shore and across the desert of the west end and its beautiful beaches. Dinner was served over the Kaiwi channel and the captain stood up and made some remarks to the passengers while they ate.

She reminded them that since coming to the islands, they had skirted around all heavily populated areas, but that now they were about to fly over parts of a metropolitan area. "I would like to remind everyone to darken their floors and windows if you are going to be undressing," she told them. "I doubt that anyone in Waikiki would mind — they've seen it all, but you might embarrass yourselves." There was general laughter.

"Also, there will probably be a lot of friendly waving and alohas from below. If you want to be friendly and wave back, that is fine. As you know, the windows will open when the ship is traveling slowly enough, but if you have your window open, be careful that you don't drop anything out; we won't have time to hang around for your court trial if someone gets hurt. We will be here for only a few days to take care of some official business, so you will be on your own for awhile. There are lots of things to see and do here, and you may have noticed that there are still some whales in the area, in case you want to go out on a whale watch. Be sure to check the ships itinerary before you take off on an excursion. We would hate to leave anyone behind." More laughter.

"If all of you will look in the direction we are traveling, you will see Diamondhead. We will be passing it on the starboard side and settling in at Kapiolani Park. Remember that name so you can tell your taxi driver tonight if you wander too far afield. Tomorrow you will find that you are in walking distance of some of the most famous beaches in the world. And if Waikiki beach is not good enough for you, then grab a cab over to Lanikai; you won't be sorry. Normally, I would apologize for unexpected delays such as this, but, when you are stranded in paradise with nothing to do, I think congratulations are more in order. So I just want everyone to have fun and take advantage of the situation. And don't forget to 'paque your floors." She sat down amid applause from the passengers.

As the captain had noted, the *Eckener* had generally avoided populated areas on the islands as much as possible. Earlier in the day the sun had been behind us and any person we approached would be alerted first by the dense shadow the ship projected. They would stop what they were doing—hoeing, or picking fruit, or what ever—and turn to look at us. Shielding their eyes with their hands against the sun and arching their backs into impossible curves they would watch as we passed silently overhead.

As we approached Waikiki, however, the situation was different. There was no warning of our approach, other than the morning paper, which, apparently, most people had not read, or the wave of finger pointing that began as the *Eckener* glided regally from behind the cliffs of Diamondhead. One by one, everyone stopped what he or she was doing. The surfers stopped surfing; the swimmers stopped swimming; sunbathers stood up; drivers stopped their cars right in the middle of Kalakaua Avenue and got out. The intersection at Kapahulu Avenue became a grid lock. People poured out of their hotels along the ocean front and filled the streets, parking lots and beaches. The local economy came to a standstill; not a soft drink, shave-ice, suntan lotion, or tee shirt was sold during our approach and landing.

As we passed low over the beach, a few people began to return the waves of the passengers in their windows. Then more waved; then they all began to wave; then the swimmers and surfers began paddling furiously toward the shore; and as we passed over the highway into the park, the whole thronging mass of people decided they would also go into the park to further welcome us.

Fortunately, the police were already in the park and had roped off an area large enough to accommodate us and still have a buffer zone around us for safety. I think that it took most of the police force of the metropolitan area to keep the crowds at bay; and these were just curiosity seekers, not the Changlings that would come later.

The *Eckener* slowly settled down into the large field where I had sometimes flown kites with my father when I was a child. The cockpit of the ship did not come within twenty feet of the grass covering the area, but the large lower rudder that doubled as a staircase came to within about ten to twelve feet and the staircase was extended down the remaining distance to within inches of the earth. Even though the

Eckener had come to rest and was as unmoving as a stone in the night breezes, it was at no point actually touching anything below or around it.

Two policemen took up positions beside the staircase, and two crewmen took positions in the foyer at the head of the stairs. A few brave couples set out at dusk to push through the crowds and enjoy the Waikiki night life. Although, there may not have been anything else to do at that time, because I think that the entire population of Waikiki, including shop and restaurant owners, was in Kapiolani Park that night.

An ambulance showed up after sundown and Hassan's body was lowered down to it on the medical elevator. I wondered if Captain Macon had planned the timing of the *Eckener*'s touch down in order to thwart as much as possible any curiosity from the press.

Boorman and Chang retired to their cabin, where Boorman opened his window to the night breezes and listened to the rustling of the trees while he gazed at the tropical moon. "It's beautiful, isn't it?" He asked Chang, being in a more pleasant mood after finding out that he would be allowed to continue on the trip.

"Ah, the world," Chang answered. "Yes, I love being in the world — sometimes so much so that it frightens me."

"It frightens you?" Boorman asked in surprise. "Why is that?"

"I might become so attached to it that I could not bear to leave it."

*

In the morning, Boorman was able to walk easily across the floor of the ballroom to the breakfast buffet. "What is the difference?" Chang asked him. "Why can you walk across this floor now when you could not before?"

"It's not as high," Boorman answered.

"Is the floor more likely to break if it is higher?"

"No. I don't know why I do what I do. Don't ask me questions like that."

"Don't you think that you should try to find out why you do what you do?"

"God, this is going to be a long trip."

Chang mounded his plate up with scrambled eggs at the buffet line.

When they sat down, Boorman asked him why he was eating so many eggs.

"I will need the protein," Chang answered. "Besides, I like bird's eggs. You like bird's eggs too don't you. I think you were once an excellent nest robber."

Other than sighing deeply, Boorman ignored the remarks. "I am going to have to go see the Navy today and get a new passport and make sure they are OK with this bodyguard thing. I haven't gotten any official orders about it yet. Are you going to just stay on board until I get back?"

"Oh, you don't have to worry about me at all. I don't have the legs for swimming anymore and I have all the tee shirts I need. You go on and take care of your business."

Of course, Chang was there when Boorman returned, but he was wearing a tee shirt that said: "Hang Loose". In addition, he still had dried blood in his ears from the explosion at the Kwan Yin temple.

This was because shortly after Boorman left, Chang stepped the last few inches from the *Eckener*'s stairs onto Hawaiian soil. The crewmen in the foyer had not been given any orders to detain him, and the policemen, at that point, did not know one passenger from another. Chang wedged his way through the crowd, who did not recognize him either, if they cared, and made his way across the street to the beach. He walked westward along the beach until he encountered the rich young thugs who had their fun with him and then threw him and his legs separately into the Pacific. I watched him as he crawled out of the water like a gravid sea turtle and made his legless way to the bus stop on Kalakaua Avenue to wait for me in my flashy red convertible.

I watched as I drove up in my new sports car and turned and stared at him in recognition. I watched as the two of us drove to the Kwan Yin temple, and I watched as the assassin, studied us going in, waited, and then followed after.

The assassin was sweating profusely. He looked overweight, but I knew that the excess girth was all explosives. He was frightened. He left once, went outside and knelt down to pray in a shady corner. I almost entered into his communion to try to turn him away from this violence, but, God, I was scared too. I knew, somehow, that he was already dead, that things had to play out the way they had played out and would play out.

The assassin bowed his head to the ground, raised his eyes to heaven, clasped his hands and entreated his god to give him a sign if he was not to follow through with his plan — if the two inside were not sent by the evil one, by Satan himself.

There was no sign, and after a few minutes, he climbed shakily to his feet and stumbled ashen faced up the porch stairs and to the door of the temple. Chang and I turned to walk toward the exit, and the assassin, seeing that his time was up, his eyes wide and staring at nothing, whispered, "Allah is merciful," and, just as Chang jumped in front of me, gave a sharp tug to something in his jacket.

There was an instant of horror that I have no desire to describe. Chang and I were thrown scorched and bleeding to the hard floor. I could see that Chang's wounds were mortal and I rushed to his aid. I had no idea, no plan, no inkling of what I would do, yet when I went to him, I found myself becoming a conduit, a channel through which cosmic energy flowed into his body. As he lay there, apparently lifeless, I seemed to be in a quasi dream state. I could feel the limitless energy of the universe flowing through me into him, and I visualized his cells repairing the damaged blood vessels and organs with an unnatural speed. They were using proteins that he had accumulated for this same need, this same morning. I mentally smiled at the image of the huge plate of eggs that he had eaten for breakfast.

Gradually, although not slowly by any measure of modern medicine, Chang's bleeding stopped and he was able to re-insert his consciousness into his body. He then took notice of how I also lay mortally wounded, and he laid hands on my unconscious body and attempted to do for me what I had just done for him. Being in his physical body, his contact with the universal power was more tenuous than mine, and therefore, his efforts at healing me progressed more slowly. I entered into him and, being both physical and non-physical, the two of us were able to make the necessary connections between the two worlds. He stiffened as if he had electricity running through him, but he did not take his hands off of my torn and bleeding body until I had come back from the dead and announced my arrival with a moan of pain.

There was, of course, no way to save the assassin, as there was not enough of his body left for him to want to inhabit, even if he could. May Allah have mercy on his soul.

*

"Xiao Chen," David was saying, "Good and evil are like nested bowls . . ."

I had watched myself whine and cry and strain against my wrist straps until it was embarrassing. People had come and gone from this hospital room, trying to give me some comfort, but my poor wretched self was not having any.

"I didn't choose this," I heard myself complain. But of course I had chosen this; I was just feeling sorry for myself like an overgrown baby.

"Yes, you did," Chang answered. "The choice was entirely yours. You knew everything you needed to know, and still do."

"I need to see!" The irony that I was seeing myself as I said this was not wasted on me.

"The *Eckener* will be leaving for China soon. I think that you should consider coming with us."

Chang had turned away from me on the bed, and as he made the suggestion that I should go with him to China, he was not looking at me. That is to say, he was not looking at the me wrapped in bandages stained with tears and blood, but instead was looking at the me who was bobbing blithely up by the ceiling.

"Oh, God," I heard my thoughts echoed out loud from the bed. "Now you are trying to be a comedian. How could I possibly go to China? What value would another blind Chinese girl have in China? They have a million already."

"People are not good judges of their own value."

"And why would I go?" she said for me.

"It is a rescue mission," Chang said quietly, looking at my ceiling location.

"Who? Who are you rescuing?" I asked through her mouth.

"Xiao Chen," he said, looking straight at me — the one who thought herself to be the invisible presence in the room, "there is no road map through life. But you do have a compass; follow it."

*

The *Eckener* left Oahu with even more fanfare than when it had arrived. The crowds had never really abated, but the character of it had changed as the number of Changlings increased. Oddly, though the Changlings were there to see Chang, he was able to come and go through the crowd unrecognized. I suppose there were no good pictures of him available, and the crowd was watching for somebody tall and good looking, like the fair-skinned Jesus that some Christians of European descent tried to hold to so desperately.

The Changlings were different from the average curiosity seeker. For one thing, they often carried signs that referred in some way or other to "His Holiness, Chang Da Wai." Another thing was that they set themselves apart from the typically curious; they moved in groups, sat in groups, and chanted in groups. Their clothing, while dissimilar from individual to individual, was very unlike the typical tourist in the accessories. They might be wearing flowers, or feathers, or beads made of seeds or shells, or some other natural adornment, but there was always something that signaled, "Hey, I'm a Changling."

From the time that Boorman returned from the Naval base and saw Chang in the tee shirt that someone had given him at the hospital, and found out what had happened to him, he never left his side. Boorman was outside the hospital room watching through the door while Chang was talking to my various selves, yet he never asked Chang about his quirky behavior during the conversation, chalking it up, I suppose, to either his general madness or his act.

Boorman would go out with Chang sometimes to walk down to the edge of the sea. Boorman asked Chang once, after weaving through the crowded park and dodging Changlings, why he didn't speak to them, his followers. "I am not here for them," Chang answered. "I cannot afford to become entangled in their karma."

"But the people on the ship are different, I suppose."

"Yes."

"And why is that?"

"With the passengers on the ship, as well as some of the crew, there are already many entanglements that we must try to undo."

The grass at the foot of the *Eckener*'s staircase was worn away from all of the getting on and getting off that had taken place there. The smallness of the disturbed area illustrated how little, if any, Wendy had allowed the ship to move since the "landing".

At last the time came for departure and this same staircase was pulled up and the ship began to slowly rise into the sky. The police opened the vacated area to the crowds, and they poured in like water filling a pit. Some leapt futilely into the air under the ship as if they thought they might touch the receding hull or cockpit.

Before leaving the island, the *Eckener* made one last stop. This was at a grocery wholesaler where the large freight elevator was lowered next to the loading docks and groceries were piled on by fork lift. When sufficient fruits, nuts, meats, fish, vegetables and coffee were loaded on to the elevator, it was pulled up into the *Eckener*, where its own light-weight fork lift began unloading and storing the food. I wondered if any potential investors had seen the ease and speed with which the *Eckener* could load and transport produce.

The *Eckener* headed inland, skimmed the treetops of the Ewa Forest Reserve, giving everyone a wonderful show of birdlife and treetop bromeliads, and left the coast at Waimea Bay to cross the wide channel to Kauai.

In the Kauai Channel, the *Eckener* picked up another whale pod as escort, which the captain announced over the intercom for anyone who was interested. Chang insisted on unpaqueing the floor so that he could watch the whales keeping pace below. Boorman sat in his bunk and looked at the ceiling, occasionally glancing down at the graceful animals, and then quickly turning his eyes heavenward again.

"Why do you think the whales keep following us?" Boorman asked.

"It is because this ship is inhabited by the spirit of a whale," Chang answered.

"I should have known not to ask. You think this inanimate man-made machine is possessed by one of those things swimming after us down there?"

"But it is animate, isn't it?" Chang asked. "It moves; it performs calculations, works with symbols, just like the machines of bone and brain and muscle that you and I inhabit. Besides, Spirit, as spirits, inhabits all things, animate or not. Every rock, every tree, every atom is suffused with Spirit."

"Spirit, huh?" Boorman wasn't very interested. "Hey what are they doing now?" He pointed beneath them, but Chang was not distracted.

He continued. "Spirit, mind, soul, whatever you want to call it, is the foundation of all existence. It is the infinite sea of consciousness. It manifests itself in space and time as energy and matter, and it also becomes the spirit, the awareness, within the manifestation. Yet space and time exist within that sea, and we, as emanations of that mind, exist within space and time but are not of it. Consciousness is the only true reality. It creates, and manifests within its own creation, and exists in and of and by itself. It is the source of all things and is also those very things that find their source in it. It does what it wants. It makes its own rules and then obeys them or bends them or breaks them."

"Well, if we are all of the same mind, then how come I don't believe a word you are saying?" Boorman asked.

Chang laughed. "You are clever with words, but words are tools of space and time and only serve to bind you tighter to the world. The cleverer the words, the more foolish the idea."

"What about individuality?" Boorman continued. "I am not like you in any way. Are we individuals or not?"

"If you wanted to, you could begin to separate the ocean into individual buckets of water. The buckets contain individual drops of water, the drops contain individual molecules. If you poured the buckets back into the ocean, the individual molecules would still exist, yet they would also be part of the ocean. They could also be part of the water drop, although it was dispersed, and also part of the bucket, though dispersed. Are they individuals or not?"

"Analogies like that don't prove anything. Let's get back to this thing about spirit inhabiting rocks and things. How does spirit or mind live in a rock? Are you saying that a rock is aware?"

"OK," Chang said. "First you have to understand what a rock is."

"I think I know that much."

"A rock is nothing," Chang continued.

"It is something if you get hit with one," Boorman chuckled.

"Oh yes. They are real enough within the rules of this existence; I am not saying otherwise. They are just not what they seem to be. What is a rock made of? It is made of molecules, and the molecules are made of atoms, and the atoms are made of particles, and those particles consist of even smaller particles, none of which have any mass, but only exist as vibration. There is nothing there except vibration. A rock is not solid; it is only vibration. That is what I mean when I say a rock is nothing; but I could just as easily say that you and I are nothing, or that this floor is nothing. Perhaps you are wise not to trust this floor, because what keeps you from falling through are only the tiny repellent forces created by those subatomic vibrations. These forces are so small, that on an individual level they are less tangible than thought. If you could turn the plane of the vibrations into another dimension so that the repellent forces did not interact, then you could pass through it as if it were air."

"That is pretty impressive mumbo jumbo," Boorman said.

"What is vibration, then?" Chang continued, ignoring him. "It is energy. It is energy expressing itself in space and time. Albert Einstein showed the world that matter is a transient form of energy. But where does energy itself come from? It comes from consciousness. Energy is a transient form of consciousness. Energy and matter are both expressions of consciousness in time and space. You and I and all the people of the world, and the whales, and birds, and the rocks, mountains, and even the individual atoms of air and water, the moon, the sun, the stars, the vibrations that fill the vastness of space, these are all from the infinite consciousness, expressing itself individually and collectively to recreate the universe moment by moment."

*

I went back to my future room then, in my home in Honolulu that time and space had split away from the *Eckener* as it voyaged on across the vast ocean. I went back to be in my own body, to eat the food that was given me, to exercise the body so that it would be ready for I knew not what. And I went back to ponder what David Chang had said. For, knowing that he knew that I was there listening, I wondered how much of what he said was for John Boorman and how much was for Dawn Bang. I also pondered Chang's suggestion that I go to China. Had he meant for me to go in spirit only, so to speak, or had he meant for the entire blood pumping carcass of me to get up and walk and take a cab and a plane and generally travel in the conventional way?

I had already decided to leave the house for my parent's sake. Whoever was after me was effectively just after my physical body; they didn't know any other side of me. As long as I was around, my parents were in danger. I had been asked twice, depending on how you are counting, to go to China, so I made up my mind right then to go. I would go bodily to the Middle Kingdom. There was going to be a rescue, by God, and this was no time for me to be timid.

I felt energized by my decision, and knew by that, that I was making the right one. I felt larger than life, and as I got out of bed and headed into the kitchen for breakfast a remarkable thing happened.

My mother was in the kitchen whistling an old Chinese tune. I could tell by the sound of it that she had her back to me. As she turned to see me coming across the living room, she gasped, and I realized that instead of shuffling my feet the way that I normally did to avoid the occasional hazard, I was in the process of deliberately stepping over a vacuum cleaner that my mother had carelessly left on the floor. I had not felt it with my feet; I had not seen it; I just knew it was there.

*

Over the next several days I tried to repeat what had happened with the vacuum cleaner, but to no avail. It was as if the conscious effort to become aware of objects through this new sense was blocking the sense itself. This, however, did not diminish my determination to go to China. I had made up my mind to go before I had this temporary sensory breakthrough, and I was still going, with or without vision.

At first I had thought that I would travel with my fake passport, and just slip out of the U.S. and back into China the same way that I had left it. That seemed to be the logical thing to do, as the Chinese were not looking for that false identity. This would not help my parents, however, as I soon realized. If I slipped out, whoever was trying to kill me or kidnap me might not know I was gone, and my parents would still be in danger from an attack. Therefore, I decided that when I left, I would leave boldly and obviously, and under the name of Dawn Bang.

The worst part, I realized, was going to be telling my parents. I did not think that this would go down well with them, and my worst fears were realized. They were appalled at the suggestion. They slowly progressed from shocked silence to loud ranting at the notion that I could, or would even consider, travel by myself, in my condition of blindness, to a country that had a warrant out for my arrest. Had I forgotten that the Chinese government would do its best to keep me in the most abominable conditions possible for the rest of my short life? They refused to help me in any way, and instead suggested that I seek professional help. This was an unbelievable thing for my parents to suggest, and it showed how desperate they were to do something to keep me at home. Both of my parents thought of psychiatrists as American witch doctors, and could barely conceive that they could help with any problems. However, my parents had begun to see signs lately, so they said, that I was not thinking clearly. They brought up the fact that I had claimed to be responsible for the deaths of the three assassins that had tried to invade our home. They discussed the fact that I had suddenly begun meditating for hour upon hour, and they sadly reminded me that most recently, I had begun to claim that I could somehow see objects, although I had no eyes with which to see, and continued to bump into obstacles with as much frequency now as I ever had.

I found myself unable to argue with them. From their perspective, they were right. They claimed that it was just an accident that I appeared to step over the vacuum cleaner — that my mother had gasped because she thought I was going to trip over it, and the sound of her gasp caused me to realize that something was in my path and, therefore, I stepped higher and further than normal in order to move my foot past the object. This was plausible, but I remembered stepping high first, and then hearing the gasp. As for the other symptoms of my "insanity", I decided it was best not to argue. I admitted that I had been under a lot of stress from the assassination attempts and that meditation was a way for me to cope. However, I insisted that I had "seen" the vacuum cleaner, and if they were so certain that I hadn't, then we should make a little bet. If I could prove to them that I could see objects and avoid them, then they would agree to help me go to China.

"OK," my father said too quickly. "You think you see now? OK. The day you take can of beer from my hand, that day you go to China." And then to my mother: "What? What I say?"

"Dawn, Baby," my mother said soothingly, "I am afraid that betting with your father will make you try too hard to do something that cannot be done. Your eyes are gone, Baby, you have to let go of them."

"Right," my father jumped in, "and the quicker she learn, the better off she be. If we don't bet, she think maybe she right. Vacuum cleaner was accident. Bet stands."

*

That night, in my body's time, my parents told me that they had called Ken Ono to come over tomorrow to talk to me. Ken had become very close to my family, and even my father had gotten over his prejudice against the Japanese. Ken had come by almost every day since we had first met, and had helped my father with various little engineering problems around the house. The two of them had even begun drawing plans for a screened-in back porch to protect against the once-a-week mosquito. My parents now felt that Ken would be a strong ally in bringing me back to my senses.

Meanwhile in "*Eckener*" time, Boorman and Chang were having breakfast over the open ocean, the islands of Hawaii behind them.

Unless one had been invited to dine with the captain, seating appeared to be un-assigned at meal times; people sat where ever they wanted. Usually, the earliest to arrive sought out David Chang so that they could sit with him, but now Boorman was with him everywhere he went. They could not sit with Chang without sitting also with Boorman, and they danced around that idea like impala needing to drink at a crocodile infested water hole.

Boorman remarked on the odd behavior and wondered out loud why everyone acted so strangely around him. "It is because they have all come to see you die," Chang told him, stuffing toast into his mouth with his barely adequate fingers.

"Why do I talk to you?" Boorman asked, rolling his eyes.

"You ask. I tell. I never lie."

"I have never seen these people before. They don't know me from Captain Ahab."

"Yes, they know you, and you know them. Look more closely."

Boorman studied the small crowd that was looking warily back at him from the end of the buffet line, although whether or not he was following Chang's instructions, I couldn't say. As if he had broken their spell, a couple pulled free of their inertia and came over and sat down at the table with Boorman and Chang.

"Do you mind if we sit here?" they asked, sitting.

"Please do," Boorman said, extending his hand across the table to the man. "My name is John Boorman, and this is David Chang."

"Oh yes," the man said. "Everyone has heard of the famous David Chang. You have a very fascinating philosophy, Mr. Chang. Perhaps someday we can have an interesting discussion. My name is Nuri Ibrahim, and this is my wife, Adara."

Boorman looked like he was offering up a prayer of thanks, but a shadow came over his face when he heard the names. "Nuri," he seemed to think aloud. "Is that a Russian name?"

"Oh no," Nuri laughed. "It is Hebrew. It means shining bright. And although my pants may be shiny, I'm not really very bright." He nudged his wife, who managed a small chuckle at the bit of humor. "'Adara' means 'virgin'," he said looking dourly at his wife, "and I'm afraid sometimes she acts like one." Adara looked pained but didn't say anything.

Boorman looked relieved to discover the origin of the names. Chang smiled politely and continued to eat his breakfast.

"How are you enjoying the voyage?" Boorman asked.

"Oh it is wonderful so far. The floors are taking some adjustment. It is like walking in the air."

"You have not been on board since San Francisco, have you Mr. Ibrahim?" Chang asked him.

"No, we got on at Honolulu."

"That's strange," Boorman said. "I thought the ship was fully booked."

"Yes, we were on the list to go and we were notified that if we had our bags packed, there was a vacancy. That's all we know about it."

"Well, welcome aboard, whatever the reason. I am glad to have someone else to talk to. My traveling companion and I don't share the same sense of humor, and almost everyone else on board acts like they need their drug dosage adjusted."

Nuri looked at him with a puzzled expression.

"I mean they are all crazy," Boorman explained. "I've never seen such a bunch of squirrelly acting people in one place before."

Later, back in their cabin, Boorman remarked that he was glad to find out that the new couple was not Islamic.

"That is why you asked him if he was Russian?" Chang asked.

"Yeah, I didn't want to ask him if he was Moslem."

"Why?"

"He might lie."

"He might lie anyway. Are you concerned about Moslems?"

"Yeah, the guy who tried to kill you was a Moslem."

"That doesn't make all Moslems bad."

"There might be a connection. Moslems have fanatical beliefs."

"People are just people wherever you go. Moslems are no different than anyone else. They have the same problem that everyone has."

"What is that?"

"They are asleep in the dream and don't want to wake up. Nobody wants to grow up and think for themselves. It is easier to continue to think and believe what you have always thought and believed and what everyone around you thinks and believes. Most people only believe what they were taught as children and never question it — especially if they can surround themselves with other people who also believe the same things."

"I guess you're right about that. At least I don't have to worry about Nuri and Adara. They seem like a nice Jewish couple."

"Although they are a devoted couple, they are not Jews."

"Then what are they?"

"Their religion is Islam."

"Then why did they say they were Jews?"

"Because they are here to kill me, and you would be suspicious of Moslems."

Boorman looked exasperated. "You have got my head spinning like a revolving door. First Moslems are alright, and then they are here to kill you."

"Nuri and Adara are not all Moslems. Besides that, they will only try to kill me as a last resort."

"What is this all about? And anyway, how do you know that they are not Jewish like they said?"

"Someone has convinced them that I am a threat to Islam. They are doing what they think is right — to make the world a better place, just as any good person would do. They have just not realized that you cannot make the world a better place by doing bad things, no matter how many bad things you do," Chang answered, and then continued, "I just know that they are not Jews. They are playing out their role as Moslems, not because they *are* Moslems, but because, like most people, they are sleepwalking."

"Sleepwalking?"

"Yes, because the edge of the universe frightens people, they sleepwalk to avoid seeing it. The dream feels good, even though it is a trap, and in their dream, the universe has no edge, but instead the dream continues with endless delights."

"I have no idea what you are talking about."

"Yes you do," Chang declared. "Have you not ever thought about what is beyond the edge of the universe?"

"Well, yeah, but since I don't have a space ship to take me there, I guess I'll never find out."

"The edge of the universe is not out there. It is here." Chang pointed to his head. "And it is here, and here, and here." He jabbed his truncated finger randomly around the room. "Mystics go there and come back without the words to explain. Physicists go there with the same result. I am surprised they do not see each other there. I saw you there."

"Me?!"

"Yes, you were at the wellspring of creation, drinking deep. The physical universe need never see you again, but you, like me, took the bodhisattva path and made the profound decision to come back to rescue others."

"You are definitely the king squirrel on this ship," Boorman told him, but then asked, "What is the bodhisattva path?"

"We are spiritual beings — all of us. The world is our incubator, our nursery, our grade school, our college, and our trap. Billions of souls become permanently lost in it without someone to guide them back to the right path. A bodhisattva is one who has made it through and doesn't have to come back, but comes back anyway to help the lost ones. You are a bodhisattva, or were once."

"What happened to me?" I couldn't tell if Boorman was really buying this story, but he appeared to be enthralled.

"Life happened. This is a dangerous business, coming back into the world. We tend to forget who and what we really are. We become entangled in others' karma; we drift back into the dream; we lose our focus and our purpose."

"But when you die, you wake up, right?"

"No. It is the soul that becomes lost, tangled, and world-facing, not just the body. The world is not just physical; you can be in the world with out being physical. Dying does not make you any smarter; dead people usually want to be reborn as soon as possible to continue dealing with whatever affairs they have become knotted up in. As I said, it is a dangerous business, but to rescue someone like you, an avowed bodhisattva, is equivalent to rescuing untold numbers of souls who have never made it out once. It is for you that I am here, John

Boorman. I will rescue you from your sleep, your dream, and your karma."

"What if I don't believe any of this? What if I just don't want to have anything to do with any of this story?"

"Think about how you got here. Everything you have done, every choice you have made in your life, was to bring you here. You have no family, no attachments, nothing to hold you here, except your karma, and your ignorance. I too am a bodhisattva, John. I am here to rescue you, and bodhisattvas do not give up even if the world is worn away by time itself."

*

My mother called me then for breakfast and I sat up straight in bed only to fall back over onto my pillows, exhausted. I slept and the dream winds came again and blew me to a remote cave that I remembered as if by someone else's memory. An old hermit, dressed in white rags, and a younger David Chang, dressed like a Tibetan monk sat together outside the cave. "Ah, Xiao Chen, thank you for coming. You know Chang Da Wai, of course," the hermit said, making a gesture of introduction. Chang's eyes were wide as he stared up at me. I wondered what I must have looked like to him.

"Yes, I know Chang Da Wai, very well," I answered.

Chang looked startled and ready to flee.

"If you do not intend to frighten us, it would greatly please us lowly mortals, if you would show us the compassion of speaking more gently. We are not accustomed to being in the presence of a personage of such great power," the hermit said very politely.

"My apologies," I said, trying to keep to a lower volume, although I did not know that I had spoken loudly to begin with. "Did you summon me here?"

"Yes, I requested that you bless us with your presence," the hermit said, "but you have grown so much in power and awful beauty that I hardly recognized you, and wonder that you bothered to respond to a plea from such a lowly mortal."

"I am your friend," I answered, not knowing quite what to say. "How can I be of service?"

"My young student thinks that he has a specific purpose in the world but cannot determine what it is. Not an uncommon problem, of course, but he has asked me night and day for a year."

"You have done well to summon me," I replied. Then to Chang I said, "You are a great bodhisattva. You have come into this world at this time to rescue one of your own, a bodhisattva who has fallen into darkness. His name will be Thomas John Boorman in this life. You will meet him on a flying vessel of tremendous size that does not yet exist in this now-time. You will come to him by way of a woman in the persona and name of Holly Macon. Your life will be in danger. Persevere."

*

Then, as my mother called me a second time, I was left with the memory of the pleased expression on the hermit's face and the open-mouthed awe-struck expression on Chang's.

*

I didn't want to see Kenichi; I wasn't ready, and didn't know what I would say. My parents hadn't consulted with me about that, however, and he showed up right after lunch time. We sat in the lawn chairs in the back, surrounded by the smell of flowers and the twittering of birds. The breeze fluttered my hair and the sun felt warm on my forearms, and I imagined that I could see the light with my skin.

"What did my parents tell you?" I asked.

"They are just worried about you," he answered. "They said you were talking about going back to China, and they don't see how that can in any way be possible, and honestly, Dawn, neither do I."

"Is that all?"

"No. There was something they said about you thinking that you can see again."

"What if I told you that I can see sometimes?"

"That would really be a miracle. But even if you could see as well as anybody else, China would be a very dangerous place for you. It is the last place that I would think you would want to go."

"Nevertheless, that is where I am going."

"Dawn, why China — why anywhere? You are in paradise right here in your parents' back yard."

"I have to go back. There are people in prison. You don't know what it is like," I sobbed. I was suddenly overwhelmed with grief at the thought of those people lost in despair. I hid my tears behind my hands. I felt his arm across my shoulder and found that I took some comfort in it.

"I know Dawn," he said. "I understand wanting to help people, but what can you do? You would be throwing your life away needlessly. I am sure none of the people in prison want you to do that. And what about your parents? They need you here. You are all they've got and what they live for."

"I am not going to rescue those people because I think that is what they want," I said a little angrily. "I will do it because that is what I want. How will I know what I can do if I don't try? Besides, my parents don't know it, and would never admit it, but they need me gone."

There was silence for a moment. "You mean because of the assassination attempts?"

"Yes!" I was grateful that he understood without me having to explain and sound paranoid.

"The FBI has not admitted that the two events are related."

"But they are related, aren't they? Someone wants me for some reason that I cannot begin to fathom. And the day that they get me is the day that everyone around me dies."

"Maybe that is true. I can't say that I haven't thought something similar. But what if — and don't take this wrong — what if you went somewhere with me? We could go to the mainland — San Francisco or San Diego. Your parents would be safe here, and I am a trained policeman; I could protect you."

"Why don't you go to China with me and I'll protect you?"

"I'm sorry; I didn't mean it to sound that way. I know that you can take care of yourself as well as anyone. It's just that I know how to hide out and cover my tracks. And if it came to a fight, you know I would have your back. I didn't mean to imply that you needed protection or might be frightened, because I know that is not so."

While Kenichi was speaking, I was listening, yet also thinking about what Chang had said to Boorman about rescuing him. Was this the rescue that Chang had talked about in the hospital room — the rescue of Boorman? If so then Chang had his own reasons for wanting me to go to China, but the rescue that I had in mind was something different. I thought about how Tsering, the young nun had been killed in prison trying to protect me and how, thinking that I was also dead, the guards had tossed both of our bodies into the refuse pit outside the prison. I thought about how I had wandered across the Chinese wilderness until, with the help of some villagers, I had been transferred into the hands of my own organization. I remembered with anguish how I had escaped the country, but how everyone who the Chinese government remotely suspected was thrown into prison. This was the rescue that I was interested in. There were innocent people being tortured and beaten because of me. There were women in the prison that I had escaped who no more deserved to be there than I did.

"No, I am not frightened," I said to Kenichi. "And that is why I will go to China with bells on. I am going on a rescue mission to save prisoners from injustice and to save my parents from assassination. I will even call a press conference before I go so that the Chinese government will know that I am coming and the world will know why! I may only be executed or thrown back into prison, but at least I will have done something. There is only one thing to fear in this whole world, and that is doing nothing when you could have done *something!*"

Chapter 2 – Of Angels, Demons, and Lost Bodhisattvas.

Boorman said that he was not going to take Chang's outlandish accusations about the Ibrahims to Captain Macon, although he was tempted, if just to prove how irresponsible Chang could be.

"I didn't tell you this so that you could get other people involved," Chang responded. "There are too many people involved already. This is for you to know and for me to know and for the Ibrahims to know."

That night there was a full moon, and a "Starlight Ball" had been scheduled for after dinner. The tables and chairs were moved out of the way and all of the lights in the ball room were turned out.

At first everyone stood where they were until their eyes adjusted, and then there were gasps and ahhs from the passengers. The effect was as if they were suspended weightless in space, a feeling that I am familiar with, but which I appreciated anew through their experience of it. The starlight and moonlight shown in and painted everything in a pale luminescence. The sea below was like a precious metal beaten out flat to the edge of the world, and the sky like a bowl of diamonds, and there was nothing in between except the men and women standing and walking in the air and admiring what the cosmos had created that night.

Waltz music began to play from the ship's speaker system and I wondered if Wendy was doubling as DJ that evening. The people began to dance and my feeling of deju vu was strong as they spun about like ephemeral spirits lit by an internal light.

Captain Macon approached Boorman and Chang, who were standing in the hallway, observing the passengers. "Captain's choice," she said to Boorman, and took his hand to lead him out onto the ballroom floor.

"I'm not a very good dancer," he protested, trying not to look down.

"Do the best you can. Nobody's looking at you anyway."

As they began to circle awkwardly about, Sandal and Gregory came up behind Chang, and Sandal covered her mouth in amusement. "I never thought I would see such a sight," she commented.

"You mean such bad dancing?" Gregory asked.

"No. I never thought I would see my mother dancing at all. I never even imagined it."

"Even seeing it, it still takes a lot of imagination to call it dancing. They can't decide who is supposed to lead. They look like two dogs trying to get behind each other."

"Shut up! I think it's sweet."

"Yeah, I think your mother is sweet on men in uniform."

"Gregory, that is not very nice and you had better be careful who you are around when you say things like that. You had also better hope that I don't repeat that to the Captain."

"I was just joking," he protested.

The captains' dancing gradually improved until it was quite graceful in the glimmering light. Something compelled me to join their dance and I approached and began to twirl and circle with them, watching their expressions as they studied each other's faces.

Life has its own dance, and what twists and turns it has. I noticed that they were holding each other a little closer than what is normally considered appropriate for two captains, and it looked as if one captain were about to kiss the other. By my very nature, I am a voyeur — I don't deny it, but I don't think that, as a rule, I indulge myself to the point of excessive invasion of privacy. Yet the subject of this kiss became very interesting to me and I came closer to see what would happen and what the following result would be. As I drew near to study this very human interaction, Captain Macon suddenly laughed and spun Captain Boorman quickly and playfully around — directly into me!

Boorman stumbled and looked shocked. I felt something like an electrical current and heard a loud brief buzz as we touched. I became disoriented and had difficulty focusing my attention. I noticed that Boorman was shaking his head and Captain Macon was standing beside him, asking him what had happened and if he was feeling alright. The strange thing was that while I was still hovering and watching this, it was also as if Captain Macon was standing beside me and asking me if I was alright, and it was me shaking my head to clear it.

"What is the matter, John, do you need to sit down?" Captain Macon asked him/me, as she led us to some chairs lined up against the bulkhead.

"I'm OK," he answered. "I guess it was just vertigo. I was having a good time, when just all of a sudden it was like I was looking at us from outside myself. I can still sort of see us like I am watching us from a high place, but the sensation is fading. I just need a drink and I'll be fine."

"Water?" she asked.

"Is that all they're serving at the bar?" He grinned.

They walked over to the open bar and had a couple of drinks mixed for them.

If the sensation was fading fast for Boorman, it was not so fast for me. I could still see what he was seeing, feel what he was feeling. I could taste the whiskey in his glass, feel the burn of it in his mouth, smell Captain Macon's perfume and feel the touch of her hand on his arm.

Nothing like this had ever happened to me before. I had experienced mental contact, but when I broke it off, it was over. This was a lingering sensation that was only barely subsiding with time, and finally did not entirely leave me, but became another point of focus for me to which I could attend or, to a limited degree, not. As I have attempted to describe before, my "visual" field is 360 by 360, or in other words, all directions. The way that I "look" at something is simply by directing my focus — my attention. Now I was forced to learn how not to focus on input from Boorman, as it would continue to be a constant distraction otherwise. You are probably familiar with the problem of having more than one person talking to you at one time. You can filter out extraneous talk and focus on one source if you try, but it takes practice. That was the sensation that I was having, and Boorman's input was extraneous as far as I was concerned.

My new link with Boorman continued even into sleep. Later that night, after several more drinks and dances, and after the revelers had returned to their bowers, John Boorman dreamed about Holly Macon, and because of our new connection, I was in his dream with him.

Holly was not a captain in his dream. Probably captains had not even been invented in the time of his dream. It was a time of living in the jungle, of finding food day by day, and of avoiding being the dinner for other things who also lived meal to meal. In this dream, man was not at the top of the food chain. Boorman did not look like Boorman and Holly did not look like Holly, even their sexes were reversed, but somehow I had gotten a copy of the program and could tell the actors behind the makeup.

Boorman was having what I, when I was very young, called "the tiger dream". I know that other people have had this dream as well, because I have heard them talk about it. Sometimes it is not a tiger in the dream, but often it is a large carnivore. The dream is about lethal pursuit in which you are the quarry. The dream sometimes seems to last much longer than you would expect it would take for a tiger to catch you, but I have been told that this can be true in waking reality as well; although you are running for your life, the tiger is only running for dinner.

It was a beautiful dream in many ways. The jungle was getting dark at sunset. Shadows were green deepening into black and an orange glow poured into the jungle, highlighting the trunks of the trees and the giant leaves of the undergrowth. John and Holly were running — running in desperation, their eyes wide and searching for any means of escape. Through their fleshly disguises, I recognized the large muscular male as Holly, and the smaller pregnant female as John. They did not stop for thorns or bogs or any obstacle, but ran with all their strength and speed. It did not matter if their hearts burst from the effort as there were only two possible outcomes and heart failure was only a subset of one of them.

At last Boorman only survived because the larger and stronger male quickly clambered up a tree and yanked John, the female, up by his hair. Through Boorman's eyes I watched the gorgeous animal circling below. He still hoped that one of them might fall and be his dinner, but instead they climbed even higher up the tree.

The tiger eventually left. There were other monkeys in the jungle, and most would not stoop to save a weaker companion.

*

The Ibrahims joined Chang and Boorman for breakfast the next morning, just as they had previously. Adara went back to her cabin afterwards, and stayed out of sight except for scheduled meals. Nuri followed Chang and Boorman around as if they were all best of friends. This did not bother Boorman, as he enjoyed having someone to talk to who seemed to have a firm grip on reality. Neither did Chang seem to mind having Nuri around, and was as polite and pleasant to him as he was to anyone else.

For some reason — perhaps it was the attempt on Chang's life, perhaps it was the new nearness of Boorman and Ibrahim — Chang's followers thinned out to a dedicated handful. After the evening meal, as the tables were moved aside for another dance, and Adara retired to her quarters, Chang, accompanied by his disciples, Boorman, and Nuri, climbed the stairs to the top deck and settled around the swimming pool. Most sat in the nearby chairs and lounges, but Chang sat on the side of the pool itself, took his feet off, laid them on the side of the pool, and dangled his stumps in the clear water.

"Who are we?" he said, almost to himself, as he moved his legs about, making ripples in the pool. "If my legs had their own consciousness, would they know that they were part of the same body?"

The sun had set in the ocean ahead of the ship and the lights in the pool came on, strangely illuminating the people gathered around in their chairs. "Does anybody here know who he or she is?" he asked, glancing around at face after face, even upward at me, hovering over the middle of the pool.

"No one? Someone surely knows."

"I'm Harry Swenson," came the response from a brave apostle in the deepening gloom.

"Thank you, Harry." Chang replied. "Anyone else?"

Encouraged, they gave him more names.

"Who do you think that I am?" He asked them.

"Some say he is John the Baptist," Boorman said in a sarcastic whisper to Nuri.

Nuri, however, did not think the joke was funny. "Why do they listen to him?" he muttered in reply.

Someone leaned over from the darkness behind them and said, "They listen to him because the things he says are new to them and he says them as if he has personal experience, not as if they are things that were told to him." The person leaned back again and Boorman could not tell who the person was who had spoken. He decided that he would keep his jokes to himself.

"You think that I am David Chang, just as you think that you are Margaret Salsbury, or Harry Swenson, or Richard Naismith, or Sonia Eastman. But I tell you that I am not David Chang. David Chang is an illusion. Names are just labels, and labels trick us into thinking that we know something. Consciousness enters into the world like this:" He stuck the five stubby fingers of his right hand into the pool. "Each finger thinks that he is independent; he can not see above the surface of the water to know that he is connected to my hand. Each finger thinks that he is wiggling all on his own, but it is my hand that wiggles them. Each finger has its own name but does not know its true name which is the name of the hand. The name of the hand does not exist within the water world — the world of space and time. Harry, you and I might be fingers on the same hand, if we could forget ourselves long enough to really see. Margaret, Sonia, and Richard might be fingers on another hand." He thrust the vestiges of his left hand into the pool. "Even the hands do not necessarily realize that they are connected at an even higher plane. What power we would know if we could fundamentally realize the truth of what we were and how we were connected, but these fingers, though sometimes separated only by space, are most often separated by time, as well, and by dimensions incomprehensible to our three-dimensional brains. We are all aspects of a greater being, a greater consciousness. As such we are co-creators of space and time and of dimensions known only to our greater selves. Consciousness is the root and foundation of existence. It is the wellspring of reality and the sea in which we all swim. Space and time exists within it, and there is nothing that is impossible within it and nothing without it. As fragments of that consciousness, as sparks from that eternal flame, our choices and our decisions and our actions spin off new realms and new realities. If I were to die right now, another me would continue in another realm, undead, and blithely unaware of his own death in this dimension."

"He fills their heads with lies," Nuri whispered to Boorman.

"You do not believe me, Mr. Ibrahim," Chang said, obviously having heard him.

"No. I do not." Ibrahim stood up. "And I think that it is wrong to mislead these people with these fantastic fabrications. We were created by God, and it is by God's will and mercy that we exist."

"Have I said anything any different than that? Words get in our way, Mr. Ibrahim. Have you ever asked yourself why you believe what you believe?"

"It is because it is the truth."

"Or is it just because of where you were born and how you were taught? If you had been born to a Hindu family, you might believe in Brahma, Vishnu, and Shiva. If you had been born to a Christian family, you might believe in The Father, The Son, and The Holy Ghost. If you had been born to a Jewish family, you might believe in Yahweh . . ."

"I *am* Jewish," Ibrahim yelled. "What are you saying?"

"Now who is telling lies, Mr. Ibrahim? Doesn't Allah hate a liar?"

Ibrahim started around the corner of the pool in Chang's direction. His hands were opening and closing and his face was contorted and flushed.

"Mr. Ibrahim," Chang continued calmly, "I can help substantiate some of your beliefs. Muslims believe in angels. Have you ever seen an angel?"

Nuri paused briefly but then started towards Chang again.

Chang held his arms towards the heavens. "Metatron, show yourself. Come into our presence, oh Shekinah. Let there be an early dawn tonight."

I had never, to my memory, been addressed by either of those names before, yet I knew that he was speaking to me. His suggestion had a power over me that I evidently did not have over myself, and I began to see flickers of reflected light from eyeglasses, earrings, and watches around the darkness. Soon the faces around the pool were well lit and I could see the terror in them. The pool lights automatically clicked off in response to the new light, and I looked down and saw my reflection in the water below. I looked like fire coming down a tunnel, getting brighter and nearer. Soon I took shape as an awesome burning being of smokeless flame, blazing in the air above the ship. Flames leapt from my body like immense golden wings flapping in the darkness. In my reflection, I could barely see anything human about me. I was a pillar of flame, with more flame swirling in molten brightness around me, while showers of sparks and flame shot off in all directions.

Ibrahim had stopped and was staring up at me, as was Boorman, a few steps behind Ibrahim, and, of course, as was everyone else on deck. "It is a jinn," Ibrahim screamed.

"Jinn — angel; we are so quick to draw distinctions and make labels," Chang said. "And if it is a jinn, then what am I? Did I not just summon it?" He held his arms up to me. "Tell us Oh Angel or Jinn, what are you?"

Thinking that this was not a rhetorical question, I launched into an attempt to explain who and what I was. "I am . . ." I began, but the power of my voice created standing waves in the pool; people clapped their hands to their ears; sirens went off all over the ship, and the *Eckener* lurched as if to avoid a plane coming in low over its head. Lounges and chairs toppled and people were thrown out onto the deck. Ibrahim clambered to his feet and ran off screaming that I was the Angel of Death. " . . .what I am," I finished lamely, sending the ship into new convulsions.

*

I faded back into darkness, the swimming pool lights came back on, and people began crawling around on their hands and knees, dazed and shaken. Chang continued to sit on the side of the pool, kicking his stumps in the water. Boorman crawled up to him. "Sweet Jesus!" he yelled over the sirens. "I have to admit, you impressed the hell out of me with that one."

"Yes," Chang shouted back. "It was all I could do to pretend that I was in control of the situation."

"How did you do that?" Boorman bellowed, inches from Chang's ear. "Did you learn that in China? I can't smell any chemicals, but the wind must have blown all the residue away."

"You think this was a trick?" Chang had to shout his question over the din.

"Of course. But I hope you had the captain's permission to set that thing off. The *Eckener* thought it was under attack. I have never heard fireworks talk before. That was a fantastic effect. My ears are still ringing. You have definitely come up a few rungs on my ladder. I went to a Stones concert once that just pales in comparison to this baby. You are definitely invited to my house on the 4th of July."

The sirens went off and the deck was quickly swarming with crew and curious passengers who come up from the ballroom, where they had seen the bright play of lights through the roof.

Sandal came up to Boorman and asked, "Did you see it?"

"Damn right," he shouted, even though the sirens had been silenced.

"What was it? Was it a meteorite?"

"It was the most fantastic light show and fireworks display I have ever seen in my whole friggin life is what it was! I thought it was real! It scared the bejesus out of me. "

"Fireworks?"

"Yeah. You need to talk to Chang; he set the thing off. I don't know how he did it, but if he is selling tickets to the next show, I'm buying us both one."

Other passengers began to crowd around the three of them to hear what was being said.

"Who else saw it?" Sandal asked.

"I saw it," several people answered.

"Yes, we all saw it."

"It was an angel."

"Yes definitely an angel."

"It was an angel of fire."

"It was nine feet tall."

"Or ten or twelve feet."

"It was the angel Metatron."

"Yes, it was Metatron. We all saw it. It was beautiful."

"It was fantastic."

"Wonderful."

"Glorious."

"It saved Chang Da Wai's life."

"Yes, it put down a sword of fire between Chang Da Wai and that other man."

"What other man?" Sandal interrupted this torrent of words.

"It was Nuri Ibrahim," Boorman answered. "He and Chang kind of got sideways with each other, but there was no sword, flaming or otherwise."

"Would everybody who was up here tonight please follow me to the captain's quarters?" Sandal asked. "I am sure that the captain will want to hear all of this."

She led the way, and soon they were all repeating their stories to the captain. The captain had a crew member take all of their names and send them back to their own cabins with instructions to write down on paper exactly what they had seen — no more and no less.

After all of the regular passengers had left, Captain Macon turned to Boorman with a frown as if this was all his fault. "Would you please tell me what the hell happened on my ship tonight?"

"Captain, to the best of my knowledge, it appeared that David Chang set off some extremely loud and bright fireworks. The fireworks did present a somewhat humanoid appearance and even gave the illusion of speaking words."

"What did the fireworks say, Captain Boorman?"

"They said, 'I am what I am,' Captain."

"'I am what I am?'"

"Yes. At least that is what I think I heard."

"You think?"

"It was extremely loud. It was almost too loud to hear, if you can imagine that. It was like there was a loud speaker right inside your brain."

"Wendy reported this as a UFO," Captain Macon said. "However, her radar picked up nothing; her sonar picked up nothing; and her cameras only picked up a bright glare that seemed to come out of the sky, grow quickly brighter until her optical sensors were totally washed out. Then it disappeared." The captain pushed a button on her chair arm and the room was filled with the sound of five loud squawking claps, almost like gunshots being fired at close range in a metal room. There were two claps, a pause during which one could hear the sirens starting up, and then three more claps. "That is probably the sound of microphones being pushed past their capabilities," she said. "I am surprised they still work."

The captain manipulated some more controls, and a heads-up display appeared on the clear plastic wall in the front of the room. "This is what made Wendy dodge like something had hit her." The display showed a graph with five large spikes, two together, a gap, and then three in close proximity to each other.

"The *Eckener*'s skin is sensitive to pressure so that Wendy can react to air movement and keep the ship stabilized. These spikes correspond in time to the microphone overloads we just heard and are therefore, probably sound pressure waves hitting the hull. This is almost enough sound pressure to stop a heart or burst a liver. Any louder and there might have been fatalities. So tell me, somebody, what the hell was on my ship tonight?"

*

"Captain," Chang said, "I am afraid that this is my fault. I did not realize how powerful she had become."

"She?" Captain Macon responded. "Who do you mean?"

"The 'angel' that all those people were just in here describing to you."

"It has a sex, and it's female? It didn't sound very feminine to me."

"She identifies herself with the female gender, Captain, but please be careful about what you say; she is listening to us right now. You might hurt her feelings."

Captain Macon and Sandal looked warily around the room. Boorman refused to look. "Are you telling me that she is in this room right now?" Captain Macon asked.

"Yes, in a way. Her focus is here with us."

"Can you make her appear?"

"Captain, I can't *make* her do anything. She is an independent spirit and follows her own will as much as any of the rest of us."

"But you made her appear before — isn't that what I heard everyone say?"

"I asked her to appear. She is very amiable when asked in the right way by the right person."

"Then ask her to please appear now."

"Captain, I would rather not. She is not a toy; she is a sensitive being who is probably concerned about the disturbance she has caused and how close she came to injuring people. In addition, she does not like to be visible."

"But you asked her to appear just a short time ago."

"Yes, but I felt that I had very good reason, and I hope that she will forgive me for dragging her into my current problem."

"What problem?"

"Nuri and Adara Ibrahim are on this ship to assassinate me. I have things I need to do before I die, so I sent Nuri to his room for awhile." Chang chuckled. "In fact, he went there in quite a hurry."

"Why would they want to kill you?"

"They see me as a threat or have been convinced by someone that I am a threat."

"A threat to them? What are you talking about?"

"A threat to Islam — a threat to Muslims. In their eyes I may even be Satan himself."

"David, they are Jews."

"No, they are Muslims. Nuri gave himself away when he called Xiao Chen a jinn."

"Now you are going too fast. Who is Xiao Chen?"

"The 'angel'. She has many names, but I call her Xiao Chen. Nuri called her a jinn. Jinni, or jinaat, only exist in Islamic mythology, not in Jewish. A Jew probably could not have even dredged up the word during all of the excitement."

"I'll have the Ibrahims checked out more thoroughly," the captain said, "but tell me more about Xiao Chen. It sounds as if you have had past experiences with her."

"Past and future."

"I'll let that go; my head is already spinning." She began to pace back and forth. "I keep reminding myself about all of the witnesses that were just here. If it weren't for that, and that you are David Chang, I would have you locked up and your room searched for drugs. Even with the *Eckener*'s physical record that something extremely out of the ordinary happened here tonight, I am having trouble believing that any of this happened at all." She turned to Boorman. "But you were there too, Captain Boorman. You saw this thing, and you seem very level headed to me."

"Thank you, Captain," Boorman smiled at the compliment. "I saw something that was very present and real at the time. I wouldn't go so far as to say that it was an angel, a jinn, or even a living thing. But I will say that for the first time I truly understood what it meant to be amazed. I have never seen such an astonishing pyrotechnical display before, and being in the Navy, I have seen a lot."

Captain Macon studied him a second and then turned back to Chang. "Why were you surprised at the power this Xiao Chen exhibited on the pool deck?"

"She is growing in power, and I don't think that even she has been totally aware of it."

"Do you know why her power is increasing?"

"Yes, it is because she is joining with her other selves."

"I need a drink."

The captain went to the liquor cabinet and blindly pulled out a bottle of Ouzo. She turned the bottle up to her mouth and then passed it to Boorman, who took a stiff pull at it in turn. Sandal and Chang politely refused it.

"OK, everybody sit down," Captain Macon said. "I can see this is going to be a long night." She sat down in her console chair, and the others found various seating around the room. "David, please tell me what 'joining with her other selves' means, and take your time."

Chang used the fingers-on-the-hand analogy that he had used earlier in the evening and tried to explain the concept of multiple simultaneous iterations of a being existing in parallel realms of space and time, and how these personas were real beings in their own right while also existing as extensions of a being in a higher plane. "But that is a very simplified explanation," he said at the end. "It is easy to make analogies, but difficult to put the actual reality of it into words. Just remember that everything that you can imagine is true. In an infinite universe, not only *can* everything exist, but everything *must* exist."

"That sounds like an argument for another night," the captain said. "Tell me more about Xiao Chen."

"Xiao Chen has crossed dimensions to unite with another of her co-existing twin personas," he continued. "This is the source of part of her power. Because of this union, she is capable of an awareness of a simultaneous existence on a higher plane, and channels energy from that plane into this one. In addition, she has psychically bonded to some degree with me. Even though I am from a different 'hand' than she is from, we have been very close, psychically, in the past. She has seen through my eyes and thought my thoughts. This is why she is so responsive to me. But, she has also formed a bond, a partial unity, with Captain Boorman who is also from a different 'hand'. This explains the recent leap in her power, which comes from the psychic awareness or connection that comes with this larger unity. If she were to totally unite with Captain Boorman . . . Well, let's just say that fingers united can make a powerful fist, but two fists united can wield a mighty sword."

Boorman spoke up. "Pardon me, Captain, but this is all hogwash. There is nothing joined or united or bonded to me in any way. Don't you think I would know it if there was?"

"You did know it briefly, John," Chang said. "It happened while you were dancing. For a brief moment you felt what it was like to be her, but you rejected her, just as you reject everything that doesn't fit into your world view. She is still joined to you, though. She knows your thoughts, your feelings, your dreams."

For the first time Boorman looked a little pale. "Captain, I'm not saying that I believe him, but if such a creature existed, wouldn't you consider it a crime against humanity to conjure up this thing and bring it into the world? What evil could such a powerful being do?"

"John, that is such an unfair thing to say," Chang exclaimed, "for many reasons. First of all, she is as far from being evil as can be found in this realm. No more generous and charitable spirit of good will could you possibly find in the world. Secondly, she is not here because of me, but, like me, she is here because of you. And thirdly, nobody conjured anybody. She came into the world the same way everybody does; she was born to human parents."

"She is human?" Sandal asked.

"Yes," Chang turned to her. "She is just like the rest of us. She has just found some of those powers that all of us are destined eventually to find."

"If she is human," Boorman interjected, "then tell us her human name so that we can check it out and see if you are making all of this up or not."

"No," Chang replied. "She deserves her privacy. Her human body is her sanctuary and refuge. I would not betray her to the world, not even for the world."

"If you are so concerned about her privacy, then why did you have her expose herself here tonight?" Boorman asked.

"It is not too soon for this ship to know about her," Chang answered. "It will not be by my doing, but soon the whole world will know about her. Her names will be on everyone's lips."

*

Later that night, I found Chang walking the upper decks in his non-corporeal form.

"I don't know what I am supposed to do," I said.

"You will know when the time comes."

"How? How will I know?"

"Do what your heart tells you."

"But my heart and my head tell me different things."

"Your heart tells you what to do; your head tells you how to do it."

"But, what about destiny? How do I find my destiny? What is my fate to be?"

"Destiny comes from following your heart; fate is everything that gets in the way of that. Go and live your life, and at every opportunity, choose to do that which brings good into the world."

Nuri did not come to breakfast the next morning. Adara made a brief appearance and left with a tray of food. The other passengers took advantage of their absence to crowd around the table where Chang and Boorman sat. Apparently Chang had gained even more stature in their eyes because of the accounts and rumors and discussions about what had happened last night. They asked endless questions about angels, about what had happened by the pool, about spirits, the afterlife, heaven, other dimensions, reincarnation, multiple incarnations, sources of power, and on and on and on. Chang only smiled at their questions, perhaps because they came so rapidly that they were impossible to address. The few times that Boorman tried to say anything, he was looked at as if his presence at this private party was both inexplicable and undesirable.

Boorman's discomfort only grew worse, however, as Chang's entourage continued to grow and to follow him everywhere he went. Finally, Chang went back to the pool area, climbed the ladder of the diving board and sat down on the end of the board where everyone could see and hear him.

"Some of you saw an angel in this very spot last night," He began. "The rest of you have heard about it. You find that very remarkable, because most probably you have never seen one before. But that angel is no more remarkable than any of us. We take each other for granted because we see each other everyday, yet we are made of the same stuff as that angel. We are sparks from the fire of God, just as that angel is. We are immortal beings — in this world but not of it — just as that angel is. Look at your neighbors. They are extraordinary beings who will be welcomed home at the end of the day as courageous travelers to a dangerous land. Will they know God in that other home? No more than here, I'm afraid. Knowing God is not dependent on what realm in which you find yourself; knowing God is dependent on you. This realm where we are is only one realm within the mind of God. That place where angels live is only one more. There are infinite realms, infinite places, an infinity of time, and infinite ways to search for truth. God does not exist within space; space exists within God. God does not exist within time; time exists within God. God is a sea without a shore — a vast ocean of mind, of consciousness — and we are in it and part of it, just as that angel. Why don't we all see that? What keeps us from being aware of God in us and around us, of the Kingdom of God right here at hand? It is the self, the ego, the 'I'. As long as you are trapped in the illusion of 'self', you will also be trapped in the illusion of 'other'. It is from the illusion of self that all attachments come. Let go of the attachments and gradually the 'self' will die and you will know the eternal peace of God. That is what is meant by the saying that to live, you must first die. Let go of the things that define the self and it will die. Let go of greed, lust, hate, pride; do not be jealous of each other, but help each other to grow; open your minds so that ignorance is abolished. If you do all this, you will find that fear, also, will have gone, and you will only know love, peace, and the bliss of God."

Afterwards, most of the crowd broke up and the people went their own way. Whether to ponder Chang's words or because this was not the message that they were after, I could not say. I suspect that what many of them really wanted was a lesson in how to invoke angels. Of course I knew that I was not an angel. I had met beings that could much more rightfully be called angels than I, yet I understood the meaning of what Chang was saying and how he was trying to keep the message as simple and uncomplicated as possible. I weighed myself against the brief list of vices that Chang had iterated, and found that I stacked up very well, which of course made me very proud. The realization of this pride within me made me anxious and fearful, so that I became greedy for enlightenment, and just a little jealous of Chang. It is not easy being an angel!

Boorman came up to Chang as he was climbing down the diving board ladder. "David," he said. "I wish I could believe the things that you say. I find them strangely appealing. But, I just can't. I tell myself, 'Don't be a fool.'"

"*Be* a fool, John," Chang said. "Be the village idiot if that is what it takes. It is much better to be a fool following a star than a wise man lost at sea. If you are a fool for believing me, and if I am wrong, and one by one we all sputter and go out like candles in the dark to be seen no more, then so what? What does it matter if you were a fool if you cease to exist? You won't hear the jeers; what have you got to lose?"

"My pride, I suppose," John grinned. "Well, anyway, I guess what I am trying to say is that I am no longer necessarily convinced that you are a charlatan."

"Coming from you, that *is* a compliment. I'll take it for now and hope that I can do better in the future."

"Don't get too excited. I didn't say that I believed anything that you said, or that I saw anything besides a fantastic light show last night. But at least I think that your heart is in the right place, and maybe that deserves some consideration. I'll make an effort to be a little more open minded. I wouldn't even mind learning a little more."

"Wonderful," Chang exclaimed. "I couldn't ask for more than that."

"Well, OK, then. I have a request to make. You told the captain that you didn't want to ask this Xiao Chen, or Metatron, or whatever her name is, to appear for no good reason. But you also said that she was here for me. Well, can I speak to her?"

"Of, course; you have already spoken with her."

"I have?"

"Yes. The night that you listened to whale song on the deck you spoke with her. You thought you had spoken with the captain, but it was really Xiao Chen."

"I do remember the captain saying that she hadn't been on the deck. I thought she was lying."

"She has never lied to you."

"So I can talk to Xiao Chen?"

"Yes, she says she will meet with you tonight."

"What do you mean? Did she speak to you?"

"Yes," Chang answered with a twinkle in his eye. "She is here now."

"Why can't I see her?"

"Perhaps you will find the answer to that question tonight."

*

Later that day, Captain Macon sent word that she would like to see Boorman and Chang in her quarters.

"I have asked for a background check on Nuri and Adara Ibrahim," she told them when they arrived. "I took your accusations seriously," she said to Chang. "There has already been one attempt on your life just in the short time we have been away from the States. I am damned sure determined there won't be another one. I even became concerned that the Ibrahims had gotten aboard by foul play, considering that the previous occupants of their cabin suddenly decided to stay in Hawaii, conveniently allowing the Ibrahims to finish the voyage for them." She picked up a piece of paper and scanned it as she talked. "Here is the report I got back. Apparently, they are Jewish." She looked at Chang to judge his reaction. He only smiled.

"At least the United States government thinks they are Jewish," she continued. "Although, strangely enough, their names: Nuri, Adara, and Ibrahim, can be either Jewish or Muslim names. They have lived in New York for about nine years and have gotten citizenship — before that, England. They came to Hawaii on vacation, supposedly when they found out that they had not gotten a ticket on the *Eckener*, and then discovered that there was an opening after all, and that they were next on the list. The couple who gave up the cabin cannot be located, having apparently left the islands with their children on some other adventure. The Hawaiian police don't have jurisdiction to go hunting for them and the FBI doesn't seem too interested. I can't seem to convince them that it is too unbelievable for a couple to give up the best world cruise that has ever been available in order to go off on some mundane trip that they could do any time. The FBI pointed out that the children of the couple did not have tickets on the *Eckener* and that for some people, family is more important than an expensive, excessively slow, air trip. I suppose that makes a kind of sense," she said with a shrug as she threw the paper back on the console. "The bottom line is that nobody turned up anything very incriminating. There is the coincidence of the Ibrahims being next on the list for tickets. If John is right about our ticketing system being compromised, it may be that there was no coincidence at all."

They all pondered the report silently for a few minutes. Boorman finally spoke up. "I don't trust them. Nuri looked like he was going to kill David at the pool. And, as David pointed out, he called that 'thing' a 'jinn'. I think that David is right about Jews not believing in that sort of thing. I think that they are lying for some reason."

"Even if you are right, what can I do about it? I can't put them off the ship in China. I can't put them off anywhere for suspicion of lying or suspicion of being Muslims, or even for actually being Muslims. Can you imagine what the ACLU would do with that? And they would be right to do it, too."

"Well, then," Boorman continued after a moment, "can I get some backup?"

"You mean additional bodyguards?"

"Not necessarily. I was thinking that you could give me some two way communication with Wendy in my cabin."

"Wouldn't a ship's communicator do?"

"No, I need an open channel, but not one that's monitored by a human; humans are too unreliable, as well as too nosy. I need a quick response to sound the alarms, turn on the lights, hit the brakes, or whatever. Wendy is what I need."

"OK. I'll have it set up tomorrow. Anything else?"

"No, Captain. I guess that'll do for now."

"Very well, Captain. You boys stay alert." She grinned as they left.

*

"Can you see me?" I asked with my thoughts. Chang was looking right at me.

"No," He answered. "You are just as invisible to me as you are to everyone else. It is just that I can sense your presence; I know that you are there, and I know from approximately what direction you are looking at me."

"You obviously can hear me fine."

"When you direct your thoughts at me, then I hear them, otherwise no."

"Why are you up here on the deck so late at night? Everyone else is asleep."

"We came up here so that John could speak with you."

"But he is asleep too. I see him slumped in the chair and I hear his breathing."

"He grew tired of waiting. It is only a couple of hours until dawn."

"Dawn is here."

He chuckled at my joke. "John can't speak with you when he is awake, anyway. He has too many blocks in place."

"I apologize for making you wait."

"Please, no apology is necessary. I have been watching the moon dart between the clouds. I enjoy its little game. Did you go home?"

"Yes. My body needs me sometimes. I have been gone a full day in my time. Sometimes I don't return to the exact moment in your time."

"You have returned at exactly the right moment, as always."

"I am preparing to follow you to China."

"Yes, I know. What will you do there?"

"I suppose I will go to prison."

"No prison can hold you. No prison can hold any of us unless we let it."

"I will follow my heart — my compass, as you said."

"Yes."

"Are you Chenresig?"

He smiled. "Chenresig sees with a thousand eyes, reaches out to the world with a thousand arms. Everyone who is selfless, who is compassionate, who gives of his or her own self to help others, is Chenresig."

"Is John Chenresig?"

"John did not have to come back into this world in his previous incarnation. Two lifetimes ago, after thousands of previous lifetimes, he had reached the stage of understanding, of enlightenment, of compassion, and of detachment so that this world had nothing else to teach him. He broke free, crossed the boundary of life and death for the last time and was ready to set foot on his next journey — the one that starts when this one is over. But like some of us before him, he chose to come back into the world for the purpose of helping others— for the purpose of seeing that no one is left behind. In the lifetime before this one, he came back, voluntarily sacrificing his own journey, to help others along the path, so, yes, he is Chenresig. But the world is a dangerous place, and it proved so for John, for he has fallen back into the illusion. He has gotten trapped in karma — tangled in attachment. This is the temptation that all of us face — to have the world and lose our souls. Yes, he is Chenresig, but Chenresig lost in darkness. A soul such as this, that has struggled and grown, put temptation aside time after time, and voluntarily taken the risk to come back after having finally escaped — that soul is too precious to lose."

"And that is why you are here?"

"Yes"

"And me?"

"Perhaps — I am not sure of all of the reasons of your being here. I have never met another in this plane who traveled so easily in time and space as you."

"Perhaps I am here for John and just don't know it yet. You did not know your purpose on the mountain."

"This is true. We all come into the world in the same way, and forgetfulness comes with the passage. We can only follow our hearts until our purpose awakens within us once more."

"Does the sleeping John know a purpose that the waking John does not?"

"Yes, but it is the wrong purpose. If he follows it, he will become more lost — more entangled. His soul is angry and troubled. He dreams of violent things, but he does not seek violence consciously. Can you tell what he is dreaming now?"

"Yes. He is dreaming that he is falling from the sky onto sharp rocks that reach up to him. The rocks are sharp as knives. Now, instead of rocks, it has become a field of swords waving in the air, and as he falls onto the blades, they pierce him and cut him into pieces. Shall I go on?"

"No. Wake him up."

"How do I do that?"

"Call to him."

"John," I thought to him, "it is Xiao Chen. I have come to speak with you, just as you requested. Wake up now and let us talk."

At that the spirit, or soul, or ghost, or whatever term you prefer, rose up out of Boorman's body, leaving it slumped in the chair, and stood up on its oaken legs, fists on hips, and head turning side to side to take in the view of the ship. "Can you see him," I asked Chang.

"Yes, he is thinly visible to me. In this form he is much larger than his body. This is his own self-image that we are seeing. In his spirit consciousness, he thinks of himself as an avenger. He doesn't seem to be paying much attention to us. See if you can get his attention."

"John, I am Xiao Chen. You wanted to speak with me."

He looked at me and said, "I know you. You are the angel Metatron. You have come to be by my side. Together we will slay the evil ones. We will throw them from the mountain top and crush their bodies into dust. We will avenge the innocent who cried for mercy and were given none. Our enemies will quake in terror at our coming and there will be no mercy. There will be no place for evil to hide. The cries of our enemies will fill the valleys and the blood of their veins will fill the rivers. Into the frozen heart of hell itself I shall follow them and punish them without pity until the pleading of the innocent ones is washed out of my ears by the unending shrieks of the evildoers."

Chapter 3 – Of Preparations for a Descent.

In that brief period when I had left the *Eckener*, I had called the newspapers, the television stations, and the public radio station and told them what I was about to do. I invited them to a press conference in my parent's front yard the next day. Kenichi had gotten into the habit of coming around every day and I talked him into helping me dial the phone numbers. My parents refused to do anything to help me with what I had proposed, and Kenichi, too, was reluctant.

I stood on the porch for the conference at the appointed time, and from what I could hear, quite a crowd had come. I could hear the cameras whirring and clicking, and I could smell the grass and flowers being trampled.

I told them my story, leaving out the parts that I knew they would not believe or understand. I told them how I had escaped from a Chinese prison, but how there were hundreds, and possibly thousands, just as innocent as I, who were still in prison. People who were merely suspected criminals; people whose only crime was that they were related to a protester, or had a different opinion from the government; people who had been in the wrong place at the wrong time; people who had read an illegal book; people who had been put away because they had seen an official take a bribe; women who had been imprisoned for prostitution to cover up the crime of rape by a party member.

I described in detail what my prison had been like, and how I had seen people die from disease, starvation and exposure while under the care of their government's prison system. I told them that I wanted to wake up the world to this atrocity, this travesty of justice.

They asked if what I was doing now wasn't enough — just to tell my story. Why did I think I needed to put myself through that experience again?

"No, it is not enough just to tell the story," I answered. "The story must continue, just as the Chinese prisoners go on from day to day. If I simply tell the story, it will fade in a week or so and the world will forget as it always does. But if I go back to prison, you will remember me, won't you? Won't you keep my story alive? I don't want to die in prison, but nearly everyone in those prisons deserves to be free as much as I. I deserve to be in prison no less than they do. I am asking you to help me get out of prison and to get the rest out with me. If people will rally around a whale trapped in the ice, won't they rally to help me and all the other innocent victims?"

"I think they will," said a voice. "Everyone knows who you are and you have everyone's sympathies, but what can we do?"

"What do you mean everyone knows who I am?" I was afraid of what the answer might be.

"Everyone knows that you are the woman who lost her eyes in the Kwan Yin Temple explosion. Everyone knows about the attack on your house. That was all big news. In fact, Miss Bang, there's been a lot of talk about what the connection is with you. Do you think the Chinese are behind these attacks?"

"I've never thought about it," I lied. "I don't guess I see a connection. They were just coincidences. Things like that just happen." I did not want to open up this line of discussion; I just wanted to talk about rescuing the innocent from prison, not about conspiracies or assassination attempts. I did not want to go where that discussion might lead.

"I don't believe in coincidences" the voice said from the darkness of my front lawn. "If I were you, I would not go — not for anything. You will die there and never be heard of again. You can stay here and write your story and tell it to the world."

"You are the writers," I said. "You must write my story. I can't go back to my room while innocent people are dying in prison. At least I can help them by being with them — give them hope."

"It'll make a good story. I can see the headlines now: 'Crazy Blind Woman Volunteers to Die in Chinese Prison.' Yeah, we'll remember you just the way we saw you here today, in the bright sun, free to come and go as you will, for I am sure that we will never see you like this again."

I smiled. "Perhaps you are right, perhaps not. I hope that people will see the sacrifice that I am making and be willing to make one of their own. You see, I need you to print in your papers that I am asking for donations to pay for my airfare to Beijing. I have no money of my own."

*

My parents quit speaking to me; my father was too angry to speak, and my mother burst into tears whenever she came around me. I felt sorry for them. They were going to lose their only child because she was hard-headed to the point of irrationality — at least that was the way they saw it. I wanted to weep as well, because I could not make them see my side or why they should support me. I could not make them understand that I could not sit in the sun and drink tea and listen to music and go to sleep in my comfortable bed after a good meal, while innocent people were shivering with cold and fear, standing in frozen feces, sleeping in moldy flea-infested straw, and eating rotten food in the dank sunless prison, where a good day was one in which you were not beaten or a new festering sore did not appear on your skin.

The headline of the 'Advertiser' the next morning read "Tell My Story". I didn't learn this from my parents, who had refused to speak of any of this. Instead, Kenichi Ono brought the paper over to read it to me. We sat in the back yard under the plumeria tree and I could smell the rich fragrance of fresh baked peach pie from its flowers. I had really gotten to like having Kenichi around and realized that I was going to miss him more than I could have imagined a few weeks ago. There was also some other connection there that I had never taken the time to explore.

"I am really proud of you Dawn," Kenichi said to me. "I think that you are doing the right thing, so I don't know how to say what I am going to say, but, don't do it. This is crazy. This is more than can be expected from anybody. Your friends in prison don't want you to throw your life away like this. I wouldn't. If I were in one of those prisons, the last thing I would want is the guilt and the regret of knowing that you were going to throw your life away in the worst possible way just because I was not able to live my own life."

"Ken, please stop. I appreciate the concern that everyone has for me, but I have to do this. I have meditated on it — prayed about it. Every part of me says go. You don't know the things that I know, the things that I've seen. You don't know what is in my heart."

"Maybe, but I know what is in mine. That reporter — the one that said everyone knew who you were — he didn't tell you everything. Everyone knows who you are because you dedicated your life to helping Chinese farmers. You changed the lives of millions of Chinese in profound ways. I don't know about the rest of the country, but in Hawaii, every school child reads about Dawn Bang and the China Farm Foundation. Every misfit girl and boy sees in you an example of what they can become. Even in China, children and adults alike have been awakened to new possibilities because of you. In China, 'The Director' has become a household word. I've read about it. Everyone knows what you have done with your life, and everyone knows it is enough. If anyone can stir the world to free those prisoners, it is you, but the odds are against you; China doesn't bend to anyone's will. You are the kind of person who can do so much to help the world, but you can't do it from prison. You've done enough for the world, Dawn, don't do this; don't throw your life away."

"I'm not throwing my life away; this *is* my life. This is something that I have to do. You may not know that this is the right thing for me to do, but I know it, and that is enough. I can't explain it to you. You just have to believe in me. I have to find a way to go, Ken, and I still need your help. I need to raise enough money to buy a ticket to Beijing."

"Don't ask me to help you with that, Dawn. I would give you every cent I had for anything else but this. I would do anything in the world for you except buy you a ticket to prison, and I would bet that everybody else in this state feels the same way."

He would have lost that bet; my rescuer came by that afternoon.

*

Kenichi was so upset that he couldn't sit around quietly. He said he had to go off for awhile and think about things.

I was still mentally connected to Boorman and could focus my awareness on his situation at will. It was kind of like having two radios going in the same room; I had learned how to filter out one or the other to some degree, or to do a fairly poor job of paying attention to both. The thing that made Boorman interesting to me was that when I mentally attended to him, I had an image of what he was seeing, whereas when I attended to my own situation, I had only darkness. I did not prefer the darkness, and so I would tend to slip into "Boorman mode" whenever things were quiet around me.

The past, where I had been spending my "time" had almost caught up with the present, and the *Eckener* had recently been given permission by the Chinese government to enter Hong Kong. This was not on the original itinerary for the *Eckener*, but evidently Captain Macon had decided to take what she could get.

I had been to Hong Kong once, and had noted that the chasm between the rich and the poor was not at all wide but was very deep; the extremely poor were the next door neighbors to the extremely rich. In the harbor, the yachts of the wealthy were separated from the ragged, patched sampans and junks by an alley the width of the passage of a boat. On the hillsides, the view from the mansions included a view of the slums which clung precariously to rocky land too steep for anyone else to want. The people in the slums lived in hope of wealth, however, just as the people in the mansions lived in fear of poverty, for in Hong Kong the chance for a reversal of one's fortune was always close, and the person who lived on the yacht may have once lived on the sampan next to it, and the opposite could also be true.

The reason for the slums hanging and the slums floating was not for lack of caring by the Hong Kong government. On the contrary, the slums were the result of a sort of compassion. The Cultural Revolution on the mainland had caused the illegal immigration of thousands of Chinese into Hong Kong, and though the Hong Kong government made a show of not accepting the Chinese who had swum the shark-infested channel in search of freedom, in reality very few were turned back. Instead, efforts were continually made to incorporate them into Hong Kong society and to provide decent housing for them. They came so fast, though, that the government could not keep up with them. This had all occurred before the British returned Hong Kong back to China, but China had decided to use a light touch on this money-generating city, and things had changed little. Unlike on mainland China, in Hong Kong, wealth and poverty could not or would not be hidden.

The *Eckener* approached Hong Kong to the north of Tung Lung Island, which appeared to have only a small primitive fishing village on it. The peninsula to starboard had, in the distance, what seemed to be modern structures surrounded by a large park or golf course. The whales that had followed the *Eckener* from Hawaii had been left far behind, but now the airship was beginning to acquire an entourage of boats instead. Small fishing boats were leaving Tung Lung on an intercept course; and ahead of the *Eckener* was a flotilla of every imaginable kind of floating vessel heading out from Hong Kong and Kowloon to meet the *Eckener*.

As the *Eckener* drew closer to the mob, the people on the boats began to shout something unintelligible and to throw objects and pieces of paper in the air. The bottom hull of the *Eckener* was only about a hundred feet above the waves, and its huge mass glided silently and inexorably over the boats. The sky was hidden by its majestic presence, and a disastrous collision seemed imminent. The people on the boats instinctively cowered down, and some jumped overboard.

But as the *Eckener* made further headway and the sky was again open behind it, those boats which were initially at the head of the flotilla now found themselves at the tail. They immediately turned about and headed back into the still on-coming mob of boats that had been following them. This made for a terrific floating traffic jam as the boats congealed into a tangled and unmanageable mass.

Boorman opened his window to get a wider view of the chaos beneath them. The people on the boats were primarily Chinese. Those not busy maneuvering their boats were still shouting and throwing things in the air.

"What does 'jhawng dahwai' mean?" he asked David. "I heard it in San Francisco also."

"It is my name," David said, "Chang Da Wai."

"So, who, or what, do they think you are?"

"They think I am lucky," David laughed. "I might bring them good luck."

"What are they throwing into the air?"

"Their wishes."

"Are they wishing you well?"

"Oh, no! They are wishing — or praying — for good luck in the stock market, or success in business, or better health, or an improved sex life, or bad luck for their enemies — any number of worldly things. Although they may act like they think I am the Buddha himself, they are as deaf to what I say as any westerner. Self is the only sin of mankind, but each one below hopes that his wish will be carried on the wind to me, and that I will read and grant it. It is absurd of course."

"Of course; how could you grant their wishes?"

"No, I mean that it is absurd that they think that I would."

I studied Chang's face for a moment through Boorman's eyes and felt Boorman's confusion about whether or not Chang actually believed that he could grant wishes. "What do you mean?" I finally heard him ask.

"Assume for the sake of argument that I am, as they think, a being come from the greater reality, an enlightened being who recognizes and fundamentally understands the illusory nature of the world, a being whose purpose in coming is to lead others out of darkness. Why would I grant wishes for things that only serve to further entrap the grantee? You see how lost these people are in the illusion that the world is everything? They only see spirituality as a way to further their worldly goals of wealth and power."

"What makes them think that you can grant a wish?" John asked.

"That is what they have been told by their spiritual advisers: the Dang Gi, the Sam Ku, those who talk to spirits, and others such as those who practice fu kay — the automatic writing. All who have the true sight are in agreement and they tell the people essentially the same thing, and then the frauds expand on it even further, and the people come out here to ask me to grant some material desire. They think I have power but it seems I do not have the power to open their eyes. But are the Dang Gi and the Sam Ku and the other mediums down there? No."

"Where are they?"

"Some are praying — some are hiding. Change is coming."

Victoria Harbor was a mass of boats. Most seemed to be trying to guess where the *Eckener* was going to dock and get there first, which made it impossible for the *Eckener* to dock there after all. The *Eckener* made arrangements with other dock masters only to find a waving field of masts and a crowd of shouting people throwing things into the air everywhere she went. Abandoning the docks, she made for Victoria Park. The park was full of bicycles, motorcycles, a few cars, and crowds of people, shouting, climbing trees, and throwing paper into the breeze, which caught it and blew it away.

Everywhere the *Eckener* went, crowds followed it — running madly through the streets, or riding layers deep on various kinds of transportation. John had never seen such wild adulation before. Surely these people would burn the city to the ground if David told them to. From his height, he saw people fall and not get up again from under the running feet. They would have to stop somewhere quickly or leave the city for good; this was turning into a disaster. The captain must have seen what was happening, for the *Eckener* turned and began to follow Causeway Road so that the crowds would have more room to spread out. They followed the major thoroughfares to Happy Race Course but tried to outdistance the crowds. Fortunately, this was not a race day at the course and the track was closed. As John watched from his window, police cars pulled up in front of the gates to blockade the crowds and give the *Eckener* some relief and some breathing room.

The *Eckener* began to settle down in the middle of the field and John heaved a sigh. He was glad that was over; he was beginning to become somehow panicky at the sight of the river of humanity which had followed the *Eckener* through the city, but now he did a quick double take. The crowd was charging onto the field. They overran the police cars and climbed the locked gates.

Someone shot the lock off of the gate and, like a fast running tide, the people poured in and filled all the space on the field around and under the *Eckener*. "Chang Da Wai, Chang Da Wai," they shouted. More came, packing the first people tighter around the *Eckener* and filling the stands. As the number of individuals grew, their voices could no longer be differentiated, but merged into a deafening roar. People stood on each other's shoulders and began to form living pyramids in an effort to reach the lower hull of the *Eckener*.

The *Eckener* began to lift off again, abandoning the racetrack to the crowds, as it had the previous docking areas.

As the *Eckener* began to ascend, Boorman saw that the area around the racetrack was teeming with people who were not able to get in. More people were still streaming in from the surrounding areas. When these crowds saw the *Eckener* they began to chase it as the earlier mob had done. From the racetrack could be heard the renewed chanting of "Chang Da Wai, Chang Da Wai . . ."

My psychic voyeurism was interrupted by a knock at the front door. My parents had let someone in and were being very pleasant to him. When I heard him speak, I realized that it was because he was Chinese; my parents were always deferential to other Chinese. My parents offered him tea and other hospitalities.

"Ambassador Ye, your secretary called us earlier. You are very punctual. What is it that we can do to assist you?"

I could feel the temperature drop in the room as my parents heard his response.

"Honorable Mr. and Mrs. Bang, I read in the newspaper today that your daughter wishes to go to China. I am here to offer China's hospitality to your daughter, Director Bang, and to ask her if she would honor us by flying to Beijing as our guest."

*

My parents were struck speechless, and realizing that I had only a few seconds before my parents turned into devils and performed unpardonable breaches of protocol and politeness, I stood up, bowed in the direction of the ambassador's voice and said, "It would be *my* honor to accept the hospitality of such a great country."

"Excellent!" the ambassador replied. "The flight leaves tomorrow morning at 9:45, if that meets with your approval. My secretary will come by to collect you at about 6:30 so that we will have time to go through the usual bureaucracy and security checks. Please bring your passport — the correct one, of course, but otherwise, you may pack lightly; we will provide everything you need. I hope that it is alright that I do not stay for tea. I have pressing matters to attend to. I will show myself out."

I heard his footsteps on the living room carpet, and then the opening and the closing of the door. Other than that, there was silence. Was this what I had hoped for? The reality of the situation now made my blood run cold. I felt faint. I wanted to lie down. I wanted my mother to comfort me, and my father to wake me up from this fever. I remembered what Chang had said about making the choice that brings good into the world. Was this the choice? I was going to break my parents' hearts in a way that could never be healed. I might even be breaking Kenichi's heart — I wasn't sure about that. Was I throwing my life away? Had I offered myself up for crucifixion for no good reason? I suppose in the back of my mind I had hoped that if I made the offer, then an angel would come to me, as had been sent to Abraham, to tell me that the actual deed was not required, but now, like Jesus, I was going to have to drink from the cup.

I felt my parents' eyes upon me, and in their silent watchfulness, I turned and walked unsteadily back to my room. As I shut the door, I heard my mother begin to wail and beg my father to do something to stop this. I did not think that she would come and help me pick out a good prison outfit.

Kenichi did not come back that night, but my parents must have thought to call him in the morning, for he was knocking on our door just as the sun was coming up. I went out and sat with him in the tropical garden that my father had made, and felt the rising sun upon my face. I heard the birds singing and chattering, renewing old disputes that last night's darkness had forced them to put aside for a few hours.

I had two passports in my hand. I held one up to Kenichi. "Whose name is on this?" I asked.

"It is yours — Dawn Bang."

"Good," I said, putting it in my travel purse and leaving the other.

"Dawn," he said, "there is something that I need to say to you, and if I don't say it now, I may never get the chance again." He paused as if searching for words. "I — I feel like I have searched my whole life for you, Dawn, and now, just as I have found you, you are leaving. You are leaving me and going where I cannot possibly follow you. Dawn, I am asking you to stay here with me. We can make a life together. We can have children. Marry me, Dawn; I never knew what it was to love someone until the first time I saw you. But when I saw you, I knew that we were meant to be together. If you leave, my life will be empty, meaningless. There will be no purpose to my life without you, Dawn. Please don't go."

I couldn't speak. I reached out and his hands found mine. In the sunlit darkness and the smell of the frangipani, I wept. "God," I sobbed. "That is all I want."

"Then say yes."

"I can't," I managed to say. "It's too late."

"It's not too late. Don't go to China."

"It's too late for me."

"No. You're still young. You can have lots of kids."

"I didn't mean that either. I am not the Dawn that you have been searching for. I might have been once, and part of her is still in here. But, Ken, that girl that you searched for is dead."

"The girl that I searched for is right here, holding my hand."

"I am not her. I have seen too much, know too much, to ever be her again. You are offering me the world, and I can't take it, and I will never be able to explain to you why."

"No, I suppose not. I can't understand anything anymore except whether you are going or whether you are staying."

"But, I will tell you this," I continued, "even though you will think that I am crazy. Somewhere else, you and I have found each other, and our children are running and laughing through the house."

"You are right, I do think you are crazy, but in a very special kind of way. I'm not giving up, Dawn. I am going to be relentless. You are all I want, and I won't stop until you say you'll marry me."

"Are you going to China?" I asked, wiping my eyes and trying to make a joke. "What crime have you committed? You know they have separate prisons for men and women." I heard a car pull up and park in the street. "It is over, Kenichi Ono. Thanks for being my friend."

"It's not over — it can't be over."

"OK, then," I said, "be relentless; bring me back — be my lifeline into hell, because I am going in to get some friends out, and I'll need other friends on this end holding the rope."

"I won't let go of that rope," he said.

"Ken," I said with sudden hope, "if the rope breaks, I will try to make it to Kathmandu. Look for me there."

I heard footsteps approaching across the wet grass.

"Dawn Bang?"

"Yes?"

"Ambassador Ye has sent me. Are you ready?"

The ambassador was waiting in the car for me. We made polite Chinese conversation for awhile as we drove to the Honolulu airport. When we had run out of the usual pleasantries to talk about, I asked the ambassador about what was really on my mind. "Mr. Ambassador," I began, "I am curious — do you think that the *Eckener* will be allowed into China?"

"The airship, you mean? We have already allowed it in; it is in Hong Kong now."

"But what about the mainland?"

"I do not know. There were riots in Hong Kong."

"Hong Kongers are so unrestrained and disorderly. People on the mainland do not behave so uncouthly."

"Yes, you are right about the Hong Kongers, but I do not know what decision has been made about allowing entrance to the mainland."

"If the *Eckener* is not allowed in, China will appear weak."

"Whether or not the *Eckener* is allowed in is not my concern," he frowned. "What concern is it of yours?"

"You may not believe that I am speaking the truth, Mr. Ambassador, but I am just as interested in China's future as you are. I spent my life trying to help China."

"Perhaps, but you have spent the last few days trying to create sentiment against China. I know that you are only going back to China to try to make more problems for it."

"If you believe that, then why play along? Why take me back?"

"It was not my idea. Our government detests loose ends and you represent one that may be easy to resolve. Perhaps you look like low hanging fruit to our minister of justice."

"What do you think will happen to me?"

"I think you will go back to prison. Isn't that your desire?"

We rode in silence for a awhile before he broke the silence again. "I have allowed your questions," he began. "Will you allow me to ask you one?"

"Of course," I answered, puzzled.

"Why did your parents rush out to the car and give you a can of beer as we were leaving?"

I smiled. "Because they wanted me to know that even if they don't like the game, they will always find a way to be on my team."

Chapter 4 – Of Bears and Karma.

There were no direct flights from Honolulu to Beijing so we took one Chinese airline to Tokyo and took a different Chinese airline from Tokyo to Beijing. Ambassador Ye did not speak much on the trip, and so I had plenty of time to meditate on the six-syllable mantra — om mani pehmay hoong — deliver me from pride, jealousy, desire, ignorance, greed, and hatred.

I also had ample opportunity to voyeuristically monitor the *Eckener*'s attempt to get into China.

*

Having failed to find any place in Hong Kong or Kowloon to put down and allow passengers to disembark, the *Eckener* began to set out to sea with the intent of abandoning China once and for all and creating a new itinerary from scratch. No sooner had this decision been made and communicated to the Chinese government than they received a missive from Beijing inexplicably granting the ship permission to enter Guangzhou Province.

They were followed out of the harbor by the tangled mass of boats, which began to stretch out into a thin line as the faster ones forged ahead of the slower ones. Even the fastest were left behind, though, as the *Eckener* crossed Lantau Island and headed for the Pearl River.

Along the river, they saw miles of cultivated land, as every bit of the earth beneath them was devoted to the production of food. There were fish ponds and various kinds of row crops in lines as straight as a ruler. They watched the flat agricultural country flow by for the better part of the afternoon until they arrived at Guangzhou, commonly known to the west as Canton. Here they would officially arrive in China.

At Guangzhou, there was a general interest in their arrival, but the crowds were not quite as fierce as at Hong Kong. Like most Chinese, the Cantonese had been conditioned by the Cultural Revolution against showing too much open interest in things western.

Because the Chinese Government logically reasoned that the *Eckener* was an aircraft, they ordered that it should land at Baiyun Airport, several miles from Canton, and that it should remain there, as would any respectable aircraft, while the passengers disembarked through customs to be bussed back into Canton for the regulation tours, etc. When the officials became aware of the tremendous size of the *Eckener* and how much space it would occupy at the airport, and for how long a time, they prudently ordered it to dock at the White Swan Hotel on Shamian Island, as Captain Macon had originally suggested.

They docked in mid morning and several members of the Foreign Affairs Branch of the PSB (Public Security Bureau) boarded the *Eckener* at the White Swan and began to examine passports and luggage. Each passenger had to fill out a report detailing all items being brought into the country. Likewise, Captain Macon had to supply a list of ship's stores. It was explained that all items had to be accounted for again when the *Eckener* officially left China.

When a PSB officer arrived at Boorman's cabin, he examined Chang's passport without comment, but after looking briefly at Boorman's passport, he took it with him from the cabin. After a while, he returned. "You are Captain Thomas Jonathan Boorman, United States Navy?" he asked.

"That's right," Boorman answered.

"You are on active duty?"

"Yes I am," Boorman answered, afraid that he was about to be told that he could not enter the country.

"Then you are responsible for all these people." It was a statement — not a question.

"No. I'm not," Boorman said, startled. "They are all responsible for themselves."

"All groups must have a leader. You are officer in the service of your country. You are the only such officer on this vessel. You are the only official representative of your government. Therefore you are their leader. You will be held responsible for the actions of your group." He said this in a way that meant no argument was possible, and Boorman could only stand there dumbfounded.

The PSB officer left and Boorman turned to look at Chang who only shook his head and smiled. "I'm going to get to the bottom of this,"

Boorman said and left the room. He went through the ship looking for Captain Macon and found her on the upper deck talking to another PSB officer. She introduced him as Lao Wei-ping. "Mr. Lao has been permanently assigned to this ship by the Chinese foreign affairs office. He will be with us until we leave China," she explained.

"Pleased to meet you," Boorman lied. "I need to get something straightened out with your office. They seem to think that I am responsible for the people on this ship."

"Ah, you must be Captain Boorman. I am to be the liaison between yourself and my government." He did not offer to shake hands.

Boorman turned to Captain Macon. "Will you please explain that I am not the leader of this expedition, and that I am not responsible for anyone but myself."

"I am afraid Captain Boorman is right," she said to Lao. "In fact, if there is a single person responsible for this expedition, it is me."

Lao frowned at her. "Captain Boorman is the ranking officer and representative of your government. You cannot change your leader. You must learn to obey and follow your leader; that is the right way to do things." He turned, still frowning, to Boorman. "Captain Boorman, I have been informed that you are specifically responsible for an individual on this ship named Chang Daweed. Is this not so?"

"Yes, this is so," Boorman answered, wanting to ask what business it was of his.

"Why are you not with him? Have you been relieved of your orders?"

"No!" Boorman replied loudly. "What concern is that of yours?"

"It is not helpful to become angry over one's responsibilities," Lao said in polite rebuttal. "Allow me also to suggest that Chang not be allowed to leave this vessel while in China. You are the leader of this danwei — this group — and you are responsible not only for the actions of the people in it, but for their safety also."

"Thank you for your advice," Boorman said, his face red. He left the bridge and cursed under his breath all the way back to his cabin.

"Are you ready to go out and see the town?" he asked Chang, in total defiance of Lao's suggestion.

"No, thank you. I have seen it."

"I haven't. This is my first trip to China. The people are not trying to swarm the ship like at Hong Kong. Let's go out," he insisted.

"As you wish," Chang replied.

The *Eckener*'s stairs descended to a balcony of the White Swan where arrangements had been made for passengers to disembark. Chang and Boorman left in a small group of other passengers who were also on their way for their first taste of communist China. They descended into the hotel. The only Chinese they saw were employees, who were polite and circumspect. This was a hotel for foreigners only, Boorman realized.

Outside the White Swan there was a small group of Chinese who rushed at Chang as soon as they saw him. Boorman instinctively stepped between them and Chang and they stopped running and began to entreat Chang, but for what, Boorman couldn't tell. Chang spoke to them one by one in the Cantonese dialect, and one by one they left until there was a couple, apparently married, who remained. He spoke to them at length, until, at last, they too left, thanking Chang profusely.

"What did all those people want?" Boorman asked.

"Most of them wanted the usual things," Chang said, "wealth, power, a ticket to Hong Kong; but the last couple is haunted."

"Haunted? You mean by a ghost?"

"Yes, that is it exactly. They want to be free from what they think is a hungry ghost."

"Hungry for what?" Boorman asked.

"It is hungry for the world. It wants to be born. Those people had a child some time ago. They were limited to one and they wanted it to be a boy, but instead it was a girl." He shook his head.

"So?"

"They bathed the child."

"They what? What do you mean?"

"They drowned it."

"They drowned it because it wasn't a boy?" Boorman wasn't sure he was hearing this right. "How could they do that? How could they get away with it?"

"It is still done sometimes. They may have claimed it was an accident; the danwei may have blinked its eye. Sometimes, because of guan-xi — connections — even the authorities may drop an investigation."

"And now they are haunted by the thought of what they did."

"No, they are haunted by the spirit of the child. They feel its presence often. They cannot make love because they sense it watching them. It waits for them to create a body for it. But they cannot, because its presence removes their desire. Their lives have become miserable and so they want me to exorcise the ghost of their victim."

"How do you intend to do that?"

"I have already done it. The spirit of the child has a strong need to be born to this couple. When it was murdered, it could not rid itself of this desire and so remained entangled in the earthly plane. It was observing their sex life so closely because of a personal interest in the outcome. However, it could not be born again until it had shed the current entanglements. The couple wants another child, but could not have sex because of the ghostly presence. When I explained all of this to them, the child's spirit also heard it and left the earthly plane to prepare itself. The couple has gone home to try to create a vessel for the spirit and no matter what sex the child will be, they will raise it as the child they were intended to have."

Boorman stared at him for a moment. "I don't mean to offend you — at least not any more — because I think you are sincere. I think all three of you — you and the married couple — believe all of what you just said. I think they will probably have another baby now, and they will quit feeling guilty and everything will be better. I think you did a good deed — more than I would have done for them. But I wasn't brought up to believe any of this kind of stuff, so don't get upset if I don't believe it. That's about the best I can do."

Chang smiled and walked on.

They walked north, away from the Pearl River where the White Swan sat holding on to the *Eckener*. Wherever they walked, all eyes watched them. Most of the people seemed too shy to come up and speak, but Boorman thought they were working up to it. The crowds lined the streets and watched them. All business halted until they passed.

A bicyclist craned his neck to stare as he rode by, and crashed into a lamppost. None of the other people seemed to be inclined to help the crashed cyclist, so Boorman ran over to see if he was alright and to help him up. The man smiled at Boorman, got back on his bicycle and pedaled off, his bent front wheel wobbling from side to side. He continued to look back over his shoulder instead of in the direction he was going.

They came to a canal with a bridge and crossed over. The crowds on the bridge parted to let them pass. The continuing unbroken stares of the people were becoming oppressive to Boorman.

On this side of the canal, the buildings were more Chinese in nature than on the side they had just left. Boorman saw a restaurant and thought it might be a good place to hide from the stares for awhile. "I do not wish to enter," Chang said.

"Why not?"

"Read the menu by the door."

"I don't read Chinese."

"Very well, I will show you their menu."

Chang led Boorman a little further down the street, where they came to a market with people milling in and out of a large open-front building. All activity stopped when the crowd spotted them. Inside, Boorman saw the carcasses of animals hanging from hooks of various sizes. Along with the usual pigs and chickens, there were dogs, cats, and monkeys, and other animals unknown to Boorman. They walked inside and saw cages with live animals waiting their turn to be butchered. There were giant salamanders, miniature deer, pangolins, small wild cats, exotic birds, owls, sparrows, toads, snakes, even a bear. "Aren't some of these animals endangered?" Boorman asked Chang.

"Very much so. The rarer they are, the higher the price they will bring. Some have been hunted to the very edge of extinction. Some animals which you see here waiting to be eaten may be the very last of their kind. The privilege of eating the last individual of a species would command the highest price of all." Chang's voice was becoming very hard. Boorman could tell that something was happening to him.

"Could we buy some of them and turn them lose," Boorman asked.

"No, we will not buy their lives; we will not set a price on a life." He turned and looked directly into Boorman's eyes. "As you do to any being, so you do to the great consciousness." He began opening cages.

As he moved down the row, birds began to fly from the open cages. Boorman watched stunned, as did the merchants, at first unable to believe what they were seeing. To them, it was like watching someone tear up Foreign Exchange Certificates. "I need your help, John," Chang called to him. "There are too many cages and my hands do not work well." Boorman hesitated and then, going down another row of bamboo cages, began opening one after another.

This shook the merchants out of their stunned inaction. They began to scream as if wounded, and tried to restrain the madmen. Boorman was too large a person for them to handle in the narrow aisles, and as they came up one and two at a time to try to hold his arms he simply brushed them aside and continued opening the cages. Chang seemed to melt through their embraces.

Dogs and cats were running through the tables and between pursuing legs and out into the streets. Loosed snakes seemed to be taking the fight to the merchants and caused the evacuation of all disinterested parties. The merchants grabbed cleavers and knives and anything that could be used as a weapon and began to rally for a final charge at Boorman and Chang who had come together at the bear cage. "Open the cage," Chang said to Boorman.

"He might kill someone," Boorman said referring to the bear, who was swaying on all fours in the relatively tiny cage.

"I don't think so, but you must hurry or I think that someone *will* be killed."

Boorman opened the cage door and the bear strode out and stood up on its hind legs. He was a head taller than Boorman. The bear ignored the two, who stepped back. Instead, he let loose a loud roar at the Chinese merchants, who dropped their weapons and scrambled across the tables and down the aisles as fast as they could move.

The bear turned and examined Boorman, his huge black nose twisting and blowing hot breath into Boorman's face. Boorman was so close that he could see the dandruff on the bear's fur and smell the dung in which he had been forced to sleep. Its claws were hard and black, and Boorman knew that one swipe from them could tear his face off, or take his head right off his shoulders. Although Boorman was breathing hard, he felt strangely unafraid. The bear dropped back down to all fours and began to lope out into the street. "Follow him!" Chang shouted as he took off in an ostrich-like run which almost made Boorman laugh.

The bear ran down an alley and then along the canal to the bridge that they had crossed earlier. The crowds, which had earlier stared and parted for them, now scattered like quail before the bear's charge. Chang and Boorman ran down the street to the White Swan in time to see the bear plunge into the Pearl River and disappear. "Do you think he will make it?" Boorman asked.

"I do not know. We have done our part; the rest is up to him. He may live or he may die. He may drown in the river."

"Then letting him go was all for nothing?" Boorman asked incredulously.

"No, not for nothing," Chang answered. "Like ourselves, the bear is here in this world to learn. Perhaps he has learned that not all humans are cruel. Perhaps someday he will do for another human the favor we did for him today."

"But not if he drowns . . ."

"The bear has other incarnations alive in the world even today. You do not kill the soul of the bear by killing the bear. But, how you treat the bear will affect not only his understanding, but also that of other bears, as well as that of your own, through many lives. You are not alone in the universe, Boorman. You are part of it. The least thing you do affects all existence. Ripples from your actions spread to the farthest reaches of time and space. As you travel the Earth, you plant seeds that continue to grow after you are gone. If you plant good seeds, good fruit will grow. This bear will act as a bear is supposed to act; it could have killed you when you opened the cage; he may kill you the next time you meet — that is bear nature. But the great bear spirit knows what you did today."

Lao Wei-ping visited them later in Boorman's cabin. With him came Captain Macon, another PSB officer from the city, and a designated representative of the merchants who felt they had been wronged by Chang's and Boorman's actions. Lao spoke first. "This man says that Chang Daweed and Captain Boorman maliciously vandalized a market in which he had a stall. He says that they robbed him and others of their entire stock. He demands that someone pay for the animals that they set free."

Before either Boorman or Chang could speak, Captain Macon said, "Please tell the man to produce an itemized list of what is missing, and the ship will pay the bill."

This information was relayed to the merchant who began talking excitedly and produced a long sheet of paper with a list of items. He smiled and nodded as he handed it to Lao. Lao handed the list to Captain Macon who said that she could not read Chinese and asked Lao to read it for her. He began to read it out loud, but he had not gone far before Captain Macon interrupted. "Wait, there must be some mistake. These are all endangered species; it is against the laws of the People's

Republic to sell such animals. He must have made up this list out of his imagination."

Lao grinned and translated for the merchant. The merchant began to look depressed and said something in Chinese. "He says there were some chickens too, about 50 yuan worth."

"Please read the list, Lao, and tell me how much the chickens were really worth."

"About one half that," Lao said

Captain Macon produced a ten dollar bill. "Give him that, please."

Lao gave it to the other PSB officer who handed it to the merchant. The merchant snatched the bill and walked up to Chang and spat in his face. He turned and spat on Boorman, and was about to spit on Captain Macon when the PSB officer grabbed his arm and hustled him out of the cabin.

Lao turned to Boorman, who had spittle dripping down his shirt. "It would be wise if you did not leave the ship again."

*

When Ambassador Ye and I finally landed at the airport at Beijing, I was lead into a room in the customs area and handcuffed with my hands behind my back. "This is not necessary," I said to the policeman who was putting the cuffs on me. "I have come back voluntarily." He did not say a word, but guided me out through the airport by my arm.

I had a sense from the subdued murmurs around me that the airport was especially crowded, but also that the people were not making the sounds of travelers walking purposefully and rapidly as is typical in airports, nor did I hear them sitting around reading newspapers and chatting in the gate areas and tea shops. Instead they were standing nearly silent and, I thought, staring at me as they opened a path ahead of our little group. Interspersed among them I heard policemen and soldiers giving orders to the crowd. I thought I heard the sound of weapons being cocked.

As we passed through the crowds, I heard snatches of conversation and fragments of names. I heard myself referenced as Xiao Chen and as The Director, but I also heard the names Chang Da Wai, Chenresig, and Kwan Yin. I could not hear enough of what they were saying to make any connection between the various names, but I conjectured that the conversation centered on the fact that I had been with Chang in the Kwan Yin temple when I had lost my eyesight. I also supposed that they suspected Chang and Chenresig of being the same entity, just as I had once done, and perhaps still did.

I was escorted out of the airport and manhandled into an automobile. After driving for a while in silence, I was manhandled again and piloted up some wide steps and into a building with walls that reverberated with sound. I was led this way and that until the hand let loose of my arm, the handcuffs were removed and I heard the sound of a metal door slamming shut behind me. I turned and ran my hands across the door and knew that it was of the open bar type and that I was to have no privacy in my cell.

I began to feel around the cell and found the usual primitive Chinese toilet and a hard cot. I lay down on the cot to rest but found resting to be difficult as the cot was narrower than I was and my arms wanted to fall off the sides if I lay on my back, and there was no pillow to support my head if I were to lie on my side.

There was something about this situation that gave me a sense of déjà vu, and it wasn't the fact that I had been in prison before now; it was the fact of the cot being too small for me. It almost brought back a memory of something that I felt was important, but which I could not quite conjure up. There was something about having to squeeze into something in which I did not fit.

As I waited for the government to make the next move, my focus turned to Boorman once more.

While other passengers came and went from the *Eckener*, Boorman decided to be content with watching Guangzhou from the safety of his cabin window. "I don't like these people — the Chinese," he said to no one in particular as he watched the sun set over the city. "The world would be better off without them. They murder babies; they cause the extinction of animals on purpose; they have ruined Tibet, not to mention their own country. The way they treat their own citizens is abominable — but why should I care? I can't even stand to watch them; the constant spitting turns my stomach. This whole town stinks; the whole country stinks as far as I am concerned, and the quicker we get out of here the better. If I never set foot in this country again, it will be too soon."

"How can you ever say that you love God until you have learned to love every aspect of God," was all that Chang answered.

"God?!! These people don't represent any aspect of God. They lie, cheat, steal, and murder for their own selfish ends. They are as ignorant as chimpanzees, and no better in my book."

"I don't believe that they hold the patent on ignorance," Chang answered him. "If you think about it, you will realize that you have just described the whole human species."

"This is not true; there are plenty of good people in the world."

"And there are plenty of good Chinese as well."

"I haven't met any." Boorman said, and then, "Listen, I can hear shooting in the distance now. As far as I am concerned, they can all shoot each other. They should all be shot. I'm going up on deck. I need to be by myself for a while."

Chang only nodded as Boorman left the room.

On the upper deck, Boorman could hear more sounds of the city. In the distance was the sound of chanting. He followed the gaze of the few others on deck and saw a sea of people across the canal, moving like ghosts in the dim light of the street lamps. They were approaching the bridge that he and David and the bear had used earlier in the day. "Chang Da Wai," they were chanting. "Chang Da Wai, Chang Da Wai."

Were these the same people who had stood and stupidly watched them before? They must think they were safe from identification by their cadres in the darkness. He hated them. He hated the way they stupidly bowed to authority, the way they so easily took and destroyed life, the way they had so cruelly abused another people and tried to destroy its culture while so blithely destroying their own. He wished he could reach out his arm and wipe them off the earth. The earth would be a better place without the Chinese. They were not good; they obstructed the good. Hadn't they wiped out his whole family, destroying forever the good they would do? Wait, though — that was just in a dream. He was becoming confused. What was happening to his mind? He had thought a dream was real.

He looked up at the sound of shouting and the rumbling of large vehicles in the distance. The PLA (Peoples Liberation Army) was apparently attempting to block the crowd from getting to the island where the *Eckener* was docked. There were shots and the crowd began to scatter. Some turned back to pick up the wounded and were shot in turn. An armored vehicle of some type began to chase the retreating people and ran some of them down.

"God help them," John thought. They were being wiped out — just as he had wished. A group of them had been cut off on the bridge and were now running down the streets toward the *Eckener*. The PLA was still busy with the larger crowd and appeared to be paying the smaller group no attention. Soon, however, the PLA would come onto the island to clean it up.

John began to think furiously. The hotels would never let these people in; he doubted if anyone would. He noticed that the main part of the *Eckener* was right over the street where the small crowd would be running. He ran down the stairs and began to run toward the ship's bridge for help. He bumped into Sandal who was on her way to the pool deck to see what was going on.

"You've got to lower the cargo platform!" he shouted at her.

"I can't do that," she said, confused. "I have to get permission."

"No time! People are going to get killed if you don't do what I say!" He grabbed her arm and began to pull her down the passage-way toward the cargo hold.

"All right, let go and I'll help you." He let go and she began to run toward the hold. She unlocked the door and they went in and began to prepare the platform to be lowered, but as she began to lower it, Boorman stepped out onto it and was lowered down with it.

The platform went down into partial shadow along the side of the street. Boorman stepped out into the street where the group of running people could see him. He waved at them to hurry to him and then directed them toward the platform. Most of them were young — college age, but there was one older fellow who was struggling to keep up. Boorman ran to get him and was helping him over the safety railing as Sandal began to raise the platform. Some of the others held on to the old man to keep him from falling off. The platform began to go up and Boorman was lifted off the ground as he held onto the railing. The older man turned to help Boorman up over the railing, but because of his overexertion, vomited right into Boorman's face.

Boorman turned loose of the rail and fell the few feet to the ground. "Jesus!" Boorman swore as the recent contents of the man's stomach burned his eyes and ran down his face. He turned and swung his head from side to side, face downward, trying to clear his eyes and nose. He tried to breathe without inhaling anything, and wiped his eyes with whatever clean portion of shirt he could find. He tried to control his gag reflex. "Not just vomit," he thought, "that would be bad enough; but

Chinese vomit — the worst kind!" The Chinese ate things he wouldn't touch with his shoe.

The cargo platform was rapidly rising out of his reach when he had his eyes clear enough to see. He jumped for it but missed and fell, twisting his ankle. He waved at the hatch but could not tell if anyone was even looking down at him. The platform was in the hatch now and he saw it disappear into the hold. He heard rumblings behind him as the armored trucks turned the corner three blocks away. "Christ!" he said aloud, "I'm going to be shot by the PLA!" He cast about for some escape route.

Keeping next to walls and in the shadows as much as possible, he hurried around the corner of the hotel. This was only a temporary solution, for soon the PLA would be coming around this same corner. If he tried to go back through the hotel, the Chinese attendants would surely report him; he could not manage to look inconspicuous with his hair plastered in vomit.

He went under the elevated roadway in front of the hotel and studied the way down to the river. The rumbling was just around the corner as he ran quickly down to the docks and slipped quietly into the water.

If any of the occupants of the boats around him heard or saw him, they gave no notice. The river stank in his nostrils. It was little better than an open sewer for all of the boats tied to the docks and anchored up and down the river. What should he do now, wait? Or follow the course of the bear down the river. David had said the bear's chances were poor. His would be no better. He pulled himself further up under the docks and waited.

The PLA vehicles rolled to a stop underneath the *Eckener* and played their spotlights along its hull. The nearly seamless hatch was now closed and invisible to the soldiers. They went around the corner and walked into the hotel. After a short while they came back out. Boorman imagined what they had been told, "No Chinese had come through here." Even if they had talked to Holly, they would have gotten the same convincing answer.

All but one of the PLA soldiers climbed aboard the truck and drove off to continue their search. The remaining soldier began to walk slowly back and forth in front of the hotel. No one would get in that way tonight.

Boorman wondered whether it was better to leave the little chunks of partially digested food in his hair or to wash it off with the foul river water. There was a risk of disease from the polluted water but if he had to get up and move around later it would not do to cause any more comment than was necessary. He ducked under the water and scrubbed his hair with his hands. When he stuck his head back up, he saw between the planks of the dock, and with a great deal of consternation, that the *Eckener* was leaving! How could they leave without him, and what was he going to do now?

After an hour or so of walking back and forth in front of the hotel, the soldier that was left on guard duty came down to the docks to piss in the river. Boorman could barely keep from gagging at the smell of the soldier's urine flowing around him, but he noticed as the soldier's flashlight played carelessly about that he was not alone under the docks. A pair of eyes caught the light coming through the planks above and amplified it back in Boorman's direction. The soldier left, but Boorman did not say a word or move a muscle.

Boorman could not imagine who or what was under these docks with him, and, after awhile, he began to think that he had only imagined the presence of eyes. The light had probably just reflected off of a couple of nail heads, and his brain had turned the nails into eyes in the way that brains like to see patterns and recognizable features, even when there are none.

However, as the moon came up over the horizon and the silvery light began to dance on the waves and reflect up onto the underside of the dock, Boorman was able to make out a large dark hulking shape, hanging on to a pier much as he himself was doing. As the moonlight grew brighter, the hulk let go of the pier and began to swim silently toward Boorman. Just as Boorman was about to let go of his own pier and swim frantically away, he realized that the shape was not coming to him but just near him, and that the actual destination was somewhere out in the river. As the shape drew abreast of Boorman, it turned its head in his direction and blew hot bear breath on his face.

Boorman saw in the bear a fleeting opportunity for escape and grabbed the bear's tail as it swam by. The bear only turned his head to look at him briefly, and kept swimming. Boorman was pulled out into the current by the strongly swimming bear and they began to leave the docks and anchored boats behind them. The bear swam for awhile as if he did not know that Boorman was even there, but he was not swimming fast enough to outpace their pursuers. Someone had evidently seen them leave the docks in the moonlight, and was now trailing them by their moonlit wake. The sound of a motor grew louder and louder, and then a spotlight began to play upon them. Boorman expected to hear a gunshot at any moment and then feel the hot pain of a bullet entering his body. Instead, as the boat pulled up beside them, he heard a voice. "Your bear is tired. Let him go and climb aboard this boat instead."

As you know, I have a talent that allows me to fill in details after the fact, so I can tell you that on the *Eckener*, after Boorman had slipped into the river, Sandal was watching a screen at one of the bridge stations. "He's disappeared!" she said anxiously to Captain Macon. "Now he's back up again. He's moving downstream. Now he is coming towards the shore. He's not moving, now. He is still in the water, because all I can see is his head. It looks like he is going to stay put for awhile. He must be behind something that's hiding him from the street."

As soon as the cargo platform had started down, Sandal had called Captain Macon to tell her what she was doing. Captain Macon had already been alerted by Wendy that the cargo lift was in use. She had been about to alert the rest of the crew to meet her in the cargo hold when Sandal had called her on the ship's intercom.

She rushed back to the cargo hold in time to see that the platform had come back up without Boorman. There was nothing she could do but order the hatch closed.

The half dozen Chinese refugees were confused but apparently grateful. They did not speak English and Captain Macon was temporarily at a loss as to what to do with them. She decided to leave Sandal in charge of them so that she could go back to the bridge to begin tracking Boorman on the instruments, but as she opened the door, she saw Chang coming toward her. "You need an interpreter," he said matter-of-factly.

"Yes. Keep them here, and please keep them quiet. Boorman is out there dodging the PLA. We've got to try to get him back on board." She took Sandal with her and they ran to the bridge.

The Chinese refugees began talking rapidly to Chang. "He saved the bear, we knew he would save us also," they were saying.

On the ship's bridge, Captain Macon realized that she had an untenable position that could easily turn into an international incident.

She was discussing the situation with Sandal when Greg entered the bridge with Lao Wei-ping. Captain Macon and Sandal looked quickly at each other, realizing they were going to have to act as if nothing was going on. They did not have time to clear the infrared image off of the computer screen. Probably Lao would not know what it was anyway.

"I have received instructions on my radio," he said as he looked at the colorful patterns on the screen. "Your ship is to leave Guangzhou at once. That is to say: without any delay. The PLA has uncovered and suppressed an attempt to destroy this vessel, but some of the ringleaders have escaped and may repeat the attempt. If you should catch sight of these people trying to board, you should report them at once so that they may be properly tried and executed. You are to proceed along your approved flight plan. I will disembark here and you will pick me up again in Guilin. Your time will be better spent in Guilin than in Guangzhou anyway, I think." He turned and walked away.

Sandal half followed and half led him to the gangplank and unlocked the door which had been locked for the night. "I must compliment your ship," Lao said. It is so stable and motionless and quiet that the smallest sound seems large."

Sandal returned to the bridge. "Lao knows," She said, and told them about his last comment.

"I was afraid he suspected something. But, why didn't he turn us in?" she wondered. "And why did he leave the ship?"

"Are we going to leave Boorman behind?" Sandal asked.

"We can't do that," Captain Macon said. "We'll have to delay as long as possible."

"Look," Sandal said pointing to the screen that they had been watching earlier. "That must be Lao talking to the PLA guard. One of them is leaving but I don't know which one. He is going down the street along the river. Lao must have recognized what was on this monitor when he was in here."

"There is nothing we can do," Captain Macon responded. "Wendy, lift off and set a course for Guilin."

Chapter 5 – Of Unexpected Friends.

"Get out of that stinking water," Lao said to Boorman. "What kind of soldier are you? Why are you not on the ship where your duty calls you?"

"Am I under arrest?" Boorman asked, pulling himself up the rope ladder into the boat.

"You will follow my orders and avoid the necessity of arrest. Can you follow orders? Phew, do you know what you smell like? Please stay downwind from me."

"What do you plan to do with me?"

As if in answer, Lao turned to an old man who was steering the ancient weathered boat by tiller. He said some words in Chinese to the old man who only nodded tiredly. He turned back to Boorman. "I have rented this luxurious vessel to take you to your friends. If we are caught traveling like this, we will both be shot. If you hadn't run, none of this would be necessary. You are not a good soldier! Why did you run?"

"I was pretty sure that I was about to be shot back there; better to get shot later than sooner."

"Humf!" Lao snorted. "Well, get inside. We need to stay out of sight." He pulled back a flap of the tent that served as a cabin on the boat and Boorman ducked in.

Boorman continued to watch the river through slits in the canvas. He only trusted Lao from lack of choice, but could not figure out what Lao might be planning other than what he said he was doing. They continued down river for awhile and then turned up a tributary.

Lao had been silent for some time, but now he began to chide Boorman again for his lack of responsibility. Boorman rolled over on the deck and pretended to sleep just so that Lao would be quiet.

Soon, despite his wet clothes, pretense became reality and he did begin to sleep, and to dream. He was edgy and wary of sleep and dreams. He knew he was going to have another dream like the ones which had been giving him such troubled sleep since leaving the States, but at the same time, feeling the approach of a new dream, he, almost as a detached observer, waited expectantly to see what strange experiences this dream would bring.

In his dream, Boorman found himself face to face with a woman whom he knew was Captain Macon, or Holly, as he had come to think of her. Though she did not resemble Holly physically, he knew that this *was* Holly. This woman had dark eyes, dark skin, dark hair. They were lying together. He was kissing her.

Suddenly, there were people in the room with him. They drug him and Holly out into the bright sunlight. He squinted against the glare and saw that the people wore long robes and sandals. He looked at himself and saw the clothes of a Roman soldier. An officer of the Roman Army came up to see what the crowd was angry about. Boorman knew the officer was Lao. The crowd fell silent. One of the men said to the officer, "We caught them in adultery. What will you do to them?"

"The man is my affair; the woman is subject to your law."

The crowd handed Boorman over to the officer who took him roughly by his arm so that he stayed slightly off balance.

The crowd was shouting. "Stone the whore! It's the law! Stone the whore!" He knew what they were saying, though he didn't recognize the language.

"We've got to stop them," he told the officer in a different language, Latin perhaps. Part of him wondered how he could fabricate languages in his dream, but as he wondered, the dream continued to unfold.

"That is no longer any business of yours," the officer growled. "You should have stopped it when you could have."

"I will stop it now!" he said, and put his hand on the hilt of his sword.

"Wait," the officer said, putting his hand on Boorman's. He shouted to the crowd, "Why don't you take her to your new king? See what law he would have you follow."

"Yes, see if he upholds the Law of Moses," some of them began to say.

They pulled the girl away by her arm. Boorman and the officer followed behind. The crowd came to a man who was sitting and drawing in the dust of the street with a stick. They opened up into a circle around him and threw the girl onto the street in front of him.

The man looked up and scanned the crowd with his eyes. As his eyes fell upon Boorman's, they seemed to look into his very soul. This man knew what Boorman had done, and what the consequences might be to the woman, but he did not judge either of them. Boorman felt only unconditional love from this man. He felt such a feeling of loss and longing in his dream when he saw him that tears rolled down his sleeping face.

"What has this woman done?" the man asked, pointing to where Holly lay cowering in the dust.

"She was caught whoring," they said, "She must be stoned to death."

"The law must be fulfilled," he said, "It is the Law of Moses. You must condemn her," he said with subtle irony. "Sin can not go unpunished. But," he held up his hand, "if she is to be punished for her sin, let one among you who has not sinned throw the first stone." He went back to what he was doing as if this was no longer his affair.

They looked at each other then, to see who among them would have the audacity to claim in front of neighbors and relatives that he or she was the one who should begin the stoning. They all knew each other too well, and anyone who stepped forth with the claim to be sinless would become a laughing stock.

In a few minutes the crowd began to break up. Boorman stayed to see what the man would do. He looked up at Holly. "Did no one condemn you?" he asked. Holly shook her head. Her long black hair hid her face. "Neither do I condemn you," he said.

Holly began to weep, and then to sob. She crawled on her hands and knees to the man who had saved her and began to kiss his feet until they became muddy with her tears. She hugged his ankles and wiped his feet with her hair, but he lifted her up and told her that her sins were forgiven and that all he asked was that she try to forgive those who had wanted to hurt her. "There is only one sin," he told her, "and that is not to love enough." She nodded, sniffling, and ran down the narrow street to the dark room from which she had been dragged.

As the last of the crowd walked away, the officer, who had stood as transfixed as Boorman, shook him roughly and began to lecture him again as he marched him down the dusty street. Even in his dreams he could not escape Lao's continual upbraiding.

*

He woke up gradually and with a yearning for the presence of the one in his dream — for his kindness and gentleness, now lost with the dream.

He saw that Lao was still sitting up in the darkness. Doing his duty as he saw it, Boorman supposed. Boorman studied him thoughtfully for awhile. Presently, Lao became aware that he was under scrutiny. "What are you staring at?" he asked Boorman.

"Sorry. I just had a dream and you were in it. You and I were Roman soldiers."

"Ah," was all Lao said at first, but after a few moments, he added, "I have had that dream as well."

"You've had a dream that you were a Roman soldier?"

"Yes, many times."

Boorman studied him intently to see if he could detect the glint of teeth as this man laughed silently at him in the dark. "Are you playing with me?"

"I think that you know that I am not very playful."

"Tell me about your dreams, Lao."

"I have never told anyone before, except my grandmother. Do you believe in what the Buddhist call rebirth?"

"Do you mean reincarnation?"

"Perhaps it is the same, I am not sure. But sometimes people may remember other lives. If you have a memory of another life, then maybe the life was yours."

"I don't suppose I have ever thought much about it," Boorman answered. "But I think that it is probably just a fantasy for people who can't face their own mortality."

"Hah! It is not a fantasy for people who believe in it — it is something to escape from, not something to wish for. In this country almost all people used to believe in rebirth. The country was full of Buddhists and Taoists. These Buddhists and Taoists taught people how to gain insight so that they would not have to suffer rebirth. Teachings would last a lifetime, or perhaps many. There are almost none of these teachers left in China now. My grandmother was a Taoist. She believed my dreams were real. Do you know what the word 'Lao' means?"

"No," Boorman answered. "I thought it was your name."

"It is not my real name, but it has become my name. It means old," Lao said. "My family thought that I was old. They called me 'Old Wei-ping.' I used to order everyone around. When I was little I would march around the house like a soldier and would throw my arm across my chest to salute my father. What do you think this means?"

"I don't know; perhaps you saw a movie or read some comic books."

"We had no movies and all books were scarce and coveted and hidden away; I was too young to be trusted with any book. I have found a book since that time, however, that describes Roman army units. I think I was a centurion."

"A soldier?"

"Not just a soldier; I had eighty men that reported directly to me. Was I a centurion in your dream?"

"I suppose you could have been."

"Something else — when I was a child I talked about the Caesars."

"The Caesars? You mean like Julius Caesar?"

"Yes, but everyone thought I was talking about the Czar of Russia, who was not a subject for open discussion at that time. What do you think? Was I talking about the Czar of Russia?"

Lao fell silent, staring off into the darkness. Boorman leaned back and studied the stars.

He had the feeling of something impending — of forces gathering, an invisible wind blowing around him, slowly gaining speed.

The sound of the boat's engine lulled him to sleep again and when he awoke, the sun was coming up on their starboard side. Peasants — that is, workers, as they were referred to now — were already out cutting bamboo along the river banks and working in the fields.

It was not very long before Boorman saw the *Eckener* coming up river behind them. It moved as silently as a cloud blown by the wind. The peasants took notice also, and began to point and shout and run back and forth along the river bank. As the *Eckener* drew overhead, some sank to the mud and covered their heads with their arms; others waved excitedly or began to run in random directions. Some jumped into the river as its shadow passed over.

Boorman waved excitedly with both arms as the *Eckener* went by, and some passengers waved back from their windows as if waving to a friendly peasant. The boat pilot stood open-mouthed and petrified, and the boat would have run aground if Lao had not jumped to the rudder and taken control. Boorman felt disappointment as he watched the *Eckener* move steadily away up the river. He had hoped they would stop and pick him up, but all that the passengers had seen was another Chinaman, waving his arms.

Later Lao ordered the pilot to feed them, and the nervous fellow managed to produce some dried noodles, which he boiled in river water on top of the engine.

As unsavory as this must have been to Boorman, I sensed his salivary glands beginning to get ready. My own salivary glands began to function sympathetically and I started to wonder about my own breakfast.

I knew that there had to be someone on the other side of the iron bars watching me, but I could not get any response from anyone — no response to my questions; not even a grunt or a rustle or a sneeze. I remembered that I had packed some peanut butter crackers in my travel purse and decided that I would have to survive on those for awhile until someone brought me something more substantial.

I found my purse and began to rummage around in it. The first thing that my hand touched was the can of beer my parents had given me. My father had said that he would not allow me to go back to China until I could take a can of beer from his hands. My parents had taken necessary steps to insure that I was not being disobedient when I left. They had rushed out to the car to give me a can of beer. My taking the beer put everything right between us.

The crackers were in there too, but little else. Whoever searched my purse had taken away my toothbrush — because it could be used as a weapon, I suppose, but they had seen fit to leave my can of beer.

I continued to examine the contents of the purse and felt something through the lining of one of the small zippered pockets — something small and round. I unzipped the pocket and pulled out a ring. I began to probe the carvings on the ring with my fingers and suddenly realized that this was the tiger bone ring that Chang had given to me while I was in the hospital. This was the same purse that my parents had used to bring my clothes, and when Chang had given me the ring I had eventually put it in the purse for safe-keeping. I had not thought of it since. Being of bone, it had not set off any security alarms.

I slipped the ring on my finger, opened some crackers and began to eat. This was a mistake without something wet to wash it down, and so I thought, "what the hell, this may be my last chance to have beer for breakfast." I pulled the ring on the can and it made its familiar crack fizz sound.

There came a voice speaking Mandarin from outside my cell. "Is that American Beer?"

"I believe it *is* American beer," I answered. "Would you like some?"

"I will get some glasses," he said.

In a few moments I heard a key being turned in the cell door. The door swung back and I heard his heavy boots cross the floor. There was the sound of a chair being set down beside my bunk. He took the beer out of my hand and I heard him pouring it into two glasses. It sounded as if he poured equal amounts into each.

"What is your name?" I asked.

"Ahhhh, that is good, even if it is warm. My name is Zhao Tou. I know who you are, Dong Shi."

"Can you tell me where I am, Zhao Tou?"

"You are in the Tiananmen Square Police Station in Beijing. May I have a biscuit?"

I split my peanut butter crackers with him.

"Why are there no other prisoners here?"

"You have been isolated," he mumbled through a mouthful of peanut butter.

"What are they going to do with me?"

"Just a hearing. That's all I know. Thanks for the beer." I heard him stand up, leave the cell, and slam the door locked behind him. "If you need to make bodily functions," he added, "I won't watch."

Not that I believed him, but I thought that it was polite of him to give me a lie that I could live with.

*

As the sun moved higher, Boorman began to feel like a noodle himself, cooking on the deck. His clothes had never completely dried out, and at the rate he was sweating, they never would. The humidity must be one hundred percent, he thought.

He could hardly stomach his own smell. His own body odor was slowly being added to the smell of vomit still in his clothes. And there were other smells he had picked up from the river. He could only eat his noodles by holding his nose. He didn't want to think about what his noodles had been cooked in, but what difference did it make? He had already bathed in the stuff.

The day was long, with more noodles for lunch and more at supper, but with some cabbage and a few dried peas added. The pilot had stopped along the bank and purchased these items from peasants with money Lao had given him. They had passed several cities along the way, but Lao had not wanted to stop at any place where they might have to answer a lot of questions. They had also passed many other tributaries to this river, but the pilot had eventually turned north at Wuzhou, a large town high up on the bank of two rivers.

It was along the smaller river that they had stopped to buy food from the peasants. The pilot handled the transaction, but Lao accompanied him. Boorman went along to see what the life of a peasant was like. Boorman put in his request for meat and was told by Lao that there would probably be none. "It is the result of a bad policy long ago during the cultural revolution," he explained. "Our leaders were determined to educate the peasants against capitalistic ways and so told them that they could no longer raise livestock to sell. The peasants slaughtered their animals for food rather than have them be confiscated. At least that way, they got something for their labors. So, no more animals for breeding. Some areas of China have never recovered from this."

The peasants were very anxious to make a deal for their vegetables, and Boorman asked Lao what they would do with their money. Lao put the question to the peasants. But after receiving their answer, he told Boorman that he was not at liberty to discuss this with him. Boorman commented that the peasants definitely needed clothes that had not been handed down for three generations. "I thought communism was supposed to help these people," he said, and gave them a wad of bills. Lao immediately commanded them to hand it back, which they sorrowfully did.

"It will not help them to give them this money. How will they explain it? They could go to prison for having that much money." He turned and began to walk back to the boat, unwilling to face any more questions.

The pilot held back with Boorman, and as they walked, he said, "They will buy rice with the money, but the colonel is right. Too much money will draw attention to them and that would not be good for anyone."

Boorman had not realized that the pilot could speak English. "But they grow rice themselves, why buy it?" He asked in surprise.

"The government takes almost all that they grow. There is an old saying: 'for half the year we work for the government; the other half we wait for emergency relief.'" He laughed bitterly. They will buy some rice coupons on the black market or from some neighbor who has been hoarding them." He nodded and cast a nervous glance in Lao's direction and walked on ahead.

As they continued northward, the land began to change and become hillier. That night Boorman saw strange giant shapes pass by them in the darkness.

The pilot apologetically told Lao that he could not go on in the dark; it was too dangerous. After tying up the boat to the bank and cutting the engines, the pilot came over and sat by Boorman in the silence and darkness.

He rolled up a cigarette and began to smoke. Boorman watched the red coal of his cigarette making streaks in the air. "I am an educated man, you know," the pilot said after awhile.

Boorman was at a loss for something to say. "That's good. It's good to be educated." He cringed inwardly at his condescending response.

"My parents and I were intellectuals. That is why I shake at the sight of the uniforms." He spoke low with long pauses and quick glances toward the back of the boat where Lao sat with his back to them. "I was in school in England when the Cultural Revolution began. My parents had supported the Communists and Mao. I too was sympathetic to their cause. I came back to help my country and to find my parents who had ceased to write to me. I found my parents in jail for crimes against the state. My parents were tortured into confessing imaginary crimes and then sentenced to hard labor camps. I never saw them again. I heard that my mother hanged herself and that my father died of a punctured lung while being publicly criticized."

"But you said your parents supported Mao and the communists."

"It was the Cultural Revolution. The whole country went crazy. Mao told people to criticize the government to make it better; then Mao ordered those people who did speak critically to be tortured and killed. Then he ordered the killers to be killed. The country was like a snake that had been run over by a cart, twisting and biting itself with its own venom. I too was tortured for being a capitalist and a spy," the pilot continued, "but I learned a lesson from my parents and did not confess anything. I was beaten and made to sit for days up to my chin in a barrel of human excrement. I think I went crazy from the beatings and from the festering sores all over my body, for, some time later I realized that I had been released. I was wandering the streets and suddenly woke up to the fact that I was no longer in prison.

"The next ten years was a nightmare. I remember it only in flashes. The whole country had gone mad. Gangs shot other gangs over who was the most loyal to Mao and who had the most correct understanding of Mao Thought. It seemed as if every week there was some new political movement to crush some other political movement. Eventually I was sent to live with a peasant family. We educated ones were sent to the country by Mao to teach us a lesson. The poor squeezed peasants were forced to take us." The cigarette made a high arc out into the night and disappeared into the river. He rolled and lit another. "I did learn, but I don't think it was what Mao intended me to learn.

"After the Cultural Revolution, the schools opened up again and students were accepted according to test scores. I ranked very high and got into a good school, and the peasants, who really had next to nothing, gave me valuable rice coupons so that I would not starve in the city. They treated me like their own son.

"After graduation, I found that I could not get a job because of my political background. I protested the injustice and was sent to prison. It is all very funny, don't you think? If you protest something, you get more of it. If you think you have had all you can take, they will give you a little more.

"That is what I learned from the peasants — to laugh at it. They know what is important and what is funny. But still I love my country and I love the peasants. No one pays any attention to a worthless old man and so I come and go as I please. And I watch. It is a good life to live in the moment."

He stopped talking and looked intently at Boorman.

"You are the one who let the bear out of his cage, are you not?" he asked abruptly. "I hate cages." He got up and went to the other side of the boat and lay down and was soon snoring.

In the morning, Boorman saw that the huge dark shapes that he had seen in the night were weirdly shaped hills rising straight up from the ground like immense tombstones. He thought that hills like these had only existed in the collective imagination of Chinese painters.

They began to see more and larger hills as they went up stream, until the river was winding like a maze among them. The morning mist still hung on the water, the hills were draped with vegetation, and Boorman thought as he watched the scenery pass, that he must be experiencing the same sublime feelings that the long gone artists felt when they painted here.

As he stood on the bow of the boat, staring intently upriver, Lao came up behind him.

"Are you yearning to return to duty, or is there someone on the airship that you long for?"

"Let me ask you a question," Boorman responded. "Why are you helping me?"

"I have been ordered to do so."

"You have been ordered to return me to my ship?" Boorman asked, astonished.

"I was ordered to see that the *Eckener* and all of her crew and passengers stayed out of trouble. That is what I am doing."

"Then why did you say that we might be shot if we were caught on this boat?"

"Different people interpret orders different ways."

"You may be straying outside the boundaries of normal interpretation," Boorman stated, realizing the risk that he was taking of waking Lao to his true duty to the state.

"I have always seen my way clearly," Lao replied. "All my life I have known what I would do and when I would do it. I knew that at a certain age I would marry. I knew that at a certain age my wife would die. I knew that at a certain age I would join the army. And above all else, I knew that someday I would be part of something great — something larger than myself — something vaster than the Party, or all of China. When I saw your great airship blocking out the sun and moving like an unstoppable force before the heavens, I knew that this was it. And when I was assigned to be the guardian of the *Eckener*, I thanked whatever gods may be for allowing me to be alive in this time."

"The boatman called you a colonel. Being shepherd to a herd of American sheep doesn't seem a likely job for a colonel."

"I am not in favor at the moment," Lao replied. "But what others considered to be punishment duty, I saw as the moment in my life for which I have been waiting. Your ship is riding on a new wind. I can feel it."

Boorman did not say anything in response, but waited to see if Lao was going to say more. Presently he did.

"I have dreamed of your ship, Captain Boorman. I have seen it soaring, effortlessly, in the air, like a dragon, rich in wisdom, keen in intellect, knowing my innermost heart. Not just once, but many times I have dreamed of it. Tell me my duty, Captain Boorman."

Boorman still did not answer.

"Do you dream, Captain? Yes, of course you do; you told me of your dream. What other dreams have you had?"

"I dreamed I was going to be shot in front of a hotel by the river in Guangzhou."

"This is true?"

Boorman nodded.

"That is interesting. That is why you ran?"

"Yes. I had seen it all in a dream, and when I found myself standing in that street, hearing the soldiers approaching, I knew what was going to happen next, and I ran and got in the river."

"Wonderful," Lao exclaimed. "How do we know these things? How do such thoughts come into our heads?"

The old boatman spoke up, "The mind sees possibilities, knows that possibilities can become probabilities and probabilities can become actualities. But would they really? How can we know? Did you change your destiny by getting in the river? Or did you find it?"

*

Around a bend in the river they passed under a couple of highway bridges and found themselves in Yangshuo. As they passed a dock where several excursion boats were waiting, Lao told the pilot to pull over. "We will see if your air ship came by here," he said.

At the end of the dock was a small building that served as a combination store, tea shop, and restaurant. The door and windows were dark in contrast to the glare of the day. Lao disappeared into the dim coolness of the building and came back out in a few minutes. "We have missed them," he said. "They were here, but left to explore the peaks."

"What will we do now?" Boorman asked in consternation.

"We wait. They will come back."

"How do you know?"

"They forgot something." Lao grinned. "Chang Dawid is in there eating fried tofu."

Boorman jumped to his feet and stared at the wooden building in disbelief. In a few moments, Chang came waddling out of the dark doorway, balancing on his artificial feet. "Ah, John," he exclaimed when he saw Boorman. "It is a small world is it not?"

"What are you doing here?"

"Oh, I was doing some heavy work, and I didn't see them boarding. I guess they became accustomed to having you to make sure that I was always where I was supposed to be."

"Heavy work?" Boorman didn't understand what Chang meant.

"He was making soil," Lao explained.

Boorman still looked quizzical.

"Making a stool — doing grunt work — sitting on the pot — you know, number two." Lao was trying hard to come up with the American euphemism and finally hit on something that Boorman understood.

"Oh, Ok," Boorman nodded. "So you were indisposed," he said looking at Chang, "and the ship left without you."

"Precisely. But they will be back as soon as they realize I am not on board. Captain Macon is not one to leave anyone behind."

"She left me behind."

"She had no choice. When the PLA orders a vessel to leave, it leaves at once. She saw that you were relatively safe in the river, and as everyone else was on board, she did the only thing she could do to protect the ship and the other passengers and crew."

"I know. It was just such a miserable experience to be clinging to that pier and see the *Eckener* go flying off without me."

"Of course. Well, come inside where it is cool. This hot sun is not helping your aroma, John."

As they turned to walk back up the dock to the store, Boorman saw that the doorway had filled with people, all intently watching Chang as if trying to commit his image to memory.

Boorman felt a tug at his shirt, and as Chang and Lao continued on to the store, he turned around to see the boat pilot bowing to him. "Is that the living Buddha?" the pilot asked him, pointing at Chang's back.

"No," Boorman answered him, "that's just David Chang."

"Ah, these are portentous times," the pilot said.

"What do you mean?"

"I hear many things on the river," the pilot explained. "Yesterday I heard that Kwan Yin was returning to China."

"Kwan Yin?"

"She has many names: Kwan Yin, Dong Shi, Xiao Chen, Chenresig. She has been living in a temple in the middle of the ocean, and now she is returning to China. She may even be here now. Just think," he continued, his eyes wide with excitement, "the living Buddha and Kwan Yin in China at the same time. This has not happened for thousands of years!"

*

As Chang approached the shadowy door of the decrepit old building, the people staring from it bowed down respectfully and melted back into the gloom. When Boorman entered after speaking with the boat pilot, Chang and Lao were sitting at a table and the others were slowly gathering around them and asking politely if they could touch Chang, or even just his shirt sleeve.

Chang stood up, and smiling lovingly at them all, reached out, as if giving a blessing, and touched each one on the arm or shoulder or head. They bowed and wept and thanked him, and then backed away, still bowing, to make room for others and to keep from pressing the intrusion. Boorman stood back a little distance and looked in amazement at this scene of power. For it was power, Boorman recognized, that Chang had over these people. What would they not do for him? They loved him, and he loved them. It seemed real, Boorman thought. How could Chang fake this love, and why would he? He asked nothing of these people who, it appeared would be willing to give him anything. If Chang were this good of an actor — well, he wouldn't be hugging a bunch of workers and shop owners in a rundown tea shop in a backwater Chinese river town.

Lao had extricated himself from the crowd and had come up to stand by Boorman. "They can sense the greatness of his spirit. What an honor for you to be his bodyguard."

Boorman stared at Lao, and was about to say something rude when he heard the sound of someone running on the dock. He took a step back and looked out the door. There, at the end of the dock, towering up into the sky, was the gigantic cross-shaped structure of the *Eckener*'s tail assembly, the retractable stairs already extended down to the dock. The *Eckener* had come back for Chang and had touched down so gently and quietly that no one inside had heard it. Sandal was running up the dock to see if she could find anyone who had seen Chang.

Boorman stepped out into the sunlight. Sandal stopped running in her astonishment at seeing him there, but then ran up to him and threw her arms around him in a big hug. "John, I am so glad to see you. We were so worried."

Boorman only returned a half-hearted embarrassed sort of hug, and she pulled back awkwardly. "How did you get here?" she asked, and then "Are you under arrest?" as she saw Lao stepping out of the doorway.

"I don't think so," he answered. "Lao, am I under arrest?"

"Not as yet," Lao responded dourly. "If that is your desire, then keep dancing around on this dock. We should get aboard your ship as soon as possible."

"Have you seen David?" Sandal asked.

Boorman jerked his thumb towards the door. "He's in there with some autograph hounds."

"Thank God! We have enough problems trying to figure out what to do with that crowd of people you rescued without looking all over China for you and Chang." She went inside the building, and in a few minutes came out with Chang, as well as fifteen or so additional people parading behind. Other people had also begun to come to this dock to see what was happening and by the time Lao, Chang, Boorman, and Sandal had reached the ship's stairway, there was a sizeable crowd gathered around them.

As Chang began to climb up the stairs, Boorman whispered something in his ear. Chang turned around and said, "Follow me," to the crowd. They immediately began climbing the stairs, whether hoping to get a free tour of this giant vessel, or wanting to be with Chang a little longer, or just blindly following his command, was not clear.

"Wait," Sandal said to Chang. "They can't come on board here."

"Why not?" he asked her.

"They are not passengers."

"You have already set a precedent for allowing non-passengers aboard," Boorman said. "Don't worry. Everything will be fine."

There was not much Sandal could do anyway, as the crowd pushed up around her on the stairs and entered the ship.

Boorman pulled Chang, Sandal, and Lao aside in the rear foyer. "Sandal, would you lead some of them down the right hallway to the ballroom, and Lao, would you mind leading the rest through the left hallway? Thank you. Take them there, let them mingle and then bring them back."

Boorman spoke to Sandal and said, "I need to see your mother quickly. Ask her to meet us where the other Chinese are resting and then take me there."

As the crowd continued to come up the stairs and follow Lao or Sandal and Boorman down their respective hallways, Chang stood in the foyer, greeting them and directing traffic, sending them one way or the other. The boat pilot was in the crowd, and when Chang saw him, he pulled him aside. "Stay here with me," he said. The boatman nodded enthusiastically.

Sandal called Captain Macon on the ship's wireless phone system and told her what was happening and warned her not to be surprised at seeing this invasion from the docks. She then sent crewmembers to relieve Chang at the foyer and to bring him to the room where the Chinese passengers were.

The Chinese who Boorman had rescued had been given temporary quarters in one of the storage rooms while Captain Macon tried to decide what to do with them and get them to agree on some safe place where they could disembark. By the time Boorman and Sandal arrived at this room, Captain Macon was already there. She did not say anything, but waited to see what they were plotting.

Boorman explained his plan while they waited for Chang and the boatman to arrive.

"Will you take these people back to where Lao found you?" Boorman asked the boatman when he came into the room.

The pilot looked startled, but then nodded vigorously.

"Look at this man," Chang said in Cantonese to the other Chinese in the room. "He has a boat tied up to the dock below us. There are other visitors on this ship right now. In a few minutes, they will come back down this hallway. As soon as they pass, you must go out into the hall behind them and follow them out of the ship. Go your separate ways for awhile and then come back to the dock at dusk and find this man. He will take you home. Captain, can you pay for their passage?"

"Of course," she said. But the boatman and the others were all shaking their heads.

"I am not doing this for money," the boatman said. "I am doing it for the living Buddha."

Likewise, the other Chinese were exclaiming in Cantonese that they would pay their own way. Enough had been done for them. If they died now, and died in poverty, still they would feel that their lives were complete, having seen and talked with Chang Da Wai, the living Buddha.

*

The sun was sinking behind the mountains as the *Eckener* made its way upriver toward Guilin, but to the travelers on board, it looked as if the sun was melting and settling between the fantastic mountain peaks and draining into the river. At first they thought that this was just an optical illusion, but the reddish glow upstream grew brighter in the gathering darkness, and they were soon able to pick out individual points of lights. They slowly began to realize that these were boats coming down from Guilin and other river towns to greet them. Each appeared to be carrying many passengers who were holding torches aloft, creating a winding river of fire in the night.

As the *Eckener* passed over the boats, the cry of "Chang Da Wai" could be heard, repeated over and over from below.

*

I was roused from my voyeurism by the clanging of my cell door as my supper was brought to me. No word was spoken, nor had been since sharing my beer and cracker breakfast with Zhao that morning. I did not know if Zhao was still my guard, or if he had been relieved some time during the day. I did not want to speak his name and possibly betray him to a different guard, so I merely thanked whoever had brought the food. I received no response.

After trying to eat the poor food that had been given to me, I sat on my bunk and assumed the position that I found most conducive to meditation, and prepared to leave my body. I began with the six-syllable mantra, as I usually do, and prayed again that I be delivered from the afflictions of pride, jealousy, desire, ignorance, greed, and hatred.

I had decided to explore my prison and see what was in the rest of the building, but first I wanted to have a look at my guard. He was sitting in a chair against the far wall of the room. The area that he was in was only separated from my own area by a wall of steel bars with a matching door. On his side of the room was a solid door with a reinforced glass window in it. The guard was staring straight at me, but I could not tell if he was watching me or was asleep with his eyes open, as he never moved during the time that I observed him. I could not help but wonder what his thoughts were as he stared at me. There I was, meditating on my bunk in my modest smock that I had worn from Honolulu, my hair pulled back and tied behind my head. I was still wearing the sunglasses that I had worn since losing my eyes. My face was slightly scarred from the explosion and definitely beginning to show its age. However, other than that, I had the appearance of excellent health that good diet and exercise brings. I was trim, and, though small, somewhat muscular, and straight of back. What did he see; a fool perhaps?

I extended my focus beyond my cell walls and was horrified at what I saw there. Some cells were larger than mine and had more prisoners, many cells were not isolated, as mine was, but in cell after cell there were prisoners who had been beaten nearly to death. I saw broken arms and legs, smashed faces, gouged eyes, caved skulls, blood running from wounds and bodily orifices, skin covered in welts, bruises, burns, and in one instance, partially missing. Some of these people were barely conscious, some barely alive, their trials almost over. But among these were other prisoners who seemed perfectly fine in body. These prisoners, for the most part, ignored the beaten and broken ones except to occasionally kick one in passing or to bend over one lying in his own excrement on the floor and sadistically extinguish a cigarette on his face.

The only thing that mitigated the horror of what I saw was that I also saw, waiting patiently and invisibly for the next soul to leave its body, the guides—the Dakini—who had come to help these dying make their way to their reward. Most of these were guides such as I had once been, but there was among them one who radiated the same palpable indiscriminate love that I had experienced previously only at that boundary between this world and the next. Had that being come into this world because someone special was about to die here? Or had it come because the horror here was so great that even the guides needed help and guidance to avoid the feelings of hatred and loathing that would naturally well up against whomever had perpetrated these crimes?

This being now approached me, its "arms" open, its body radiating waves of brilliant light like the beating of mighty wings. This light, though visible to me, did not reflect off of the world of the living and dying, but illuminated the guides like a powerful search light. I waited for the being to approach me, and as it enfolded me, I felt once more the indescribable love and bliss that I had felt before, but there was something else as well. I felt the love and pity that this being had, not only for me and the dying in this building, but also for the other, almost inhuman, prisoners that tormented them. And in addition, there was a shock of recognition. This being was, or once had been, Tsering, the young nun who I had come to love as a daughter in a prison that now seemed eons away from here and now.

No, that explanation is too simple and misleading a statement. This being was not Tsering; this being *contained* Tsering. Tsering was there, but there was more. How to explain it? There is no way without the risk of misleading you more, but I will attempt it. Have you ever acted in a play and become that character? That character becomes part of what you are. When you read a book or watch a movie and empathize with a character, that character becomes part of what you are. When you were a child, you grew and became different people along the way. You had the same name, but your understanding was different, your responses to the world were different. All those different people that you grew out of and into along the way to where you are now are part of what you are, even though you do not see the world the same way any more or respond to it in the same way. That child that you were is in you just as Tsering was in this angelic being.

And just as Tsering was a part of this heavenly being, so am I, and all of us, a part, a fragment, a ray of some higher being, and all of the lives that we have lived and all of the experiences that we have ever had or ever will have are a part of what that being is.

This is some of what the being explained to me as it held me in its gentle loving embrace. And now that I have tried to explain it to you, I will stop calling it "the being", for the persona that it presented to me, to help me relate to it, was that of my spiritual daughter, Tsering.

As Tsering held me, great strength flowed into me. I did not want this embrace to end, but wanted to continue to bask in this love and peace and sustaining strength and so she held me through the night and I became the daughter and she the mother. As her strength flowed into me, I knew that she knew that I would need this strength in the days ahead. And though she would not show me what lay ahead, I knew that I had already seen it.

Chapter 6 – Of Kwan Yin and the Universe.

"Hey you, Dong Shi!" I recognized Zhao's voice. "Have you been sitting like that all night? I brought you something." I heard the door being unlocked and opened and I began to smell something that made my mouth water. Zhao placed something on my bunk beside me and led my hand to it. "It's duck soup. My aunt made it."

"Your aunt?"

"I am not supposed to talk about who is in the jail, but I had to tell my aunt who I drank beer with, and she said she wanted to do something for you. I told her the food here was really bad and she sent me to the market right away. She stayed up all night cooking it and made me promise that I would take it to you. But I can't get caught. If I get caught bringing you things it would be bad for me. If someone comes in, you have to pretend that I am only eating it in front of you to bully you."

"Do you live with your aunt?" I asked between mouthfuls.

"Yes. I pay the rent and she does the cooking and laundry."

"Where are your parents?"

"Dead. They died at Tiananmen Square years ago."

"I'm sorry."

"Don't be. They didn't care about me, so I don't care about them. All they cared about was their counter-revolution and their protest marches."

"But you are a communist aren't you?"

"Of course. How could I be a policeman without being a communist?"

"Yes, I know. I guess I meant it is pretty rare for children of protesters to be allowed in the Communist Party."

"I denounced my parents publicly. They were fools, but I am not. When I denounced them, I was allowed into the Party."

"The people in the other cells, the ones who have been beaten, are they protesters?"

I could tell by the silence that I had caught him by surprise. "I'm not supposed to talk about them," he stammered. "How do you know about them?"

"Never mind how I know. Who are they?"

Another pause, and then, "They are Falun Dafa; they practice Falun Gong."

"The Falun Dafa are peaceful meditators. Why beat them?"

"They have information that we need but that they will not divulge."

"Such as . . . ?"

"The names of other Falun Dafa."

"What is wrong with practicing Falun Gong?"

"There should be nothing in their hearts but communism. Communism should suffice for everyone; there is no room for other philosophies."

"Do you beat them yourself?"

"No. Torture is messy work; we get the other prisoners to do it. We recruit the ones who have been arrested for violent crimes; they do the best work. We give them special consideration — time off, early release, sometimes money also."

"So you let the real criminals go back into society if they do a good job of torturing and beating the peaceful non-criminals?"

"It is a matter of service to the state. You obviously do not understand and you also talk too much. Breakfast is over."

"Zhao, are they going to torture me?"

"I do not know — maybe."

"Why would they do that?"

"It is always to get information. If they ask you questions, tell them everything you know."

"I don't know anything."

"Don't tell them that."

I heard the cell door clang shut and the lock slide into place. "Zhao?"

"What? I can't talk to you any more."

"Tell your aunt thanks for the soup."

*

The people of Changsha had not heard that Chang was on the *Eckener*, or else did not care. They showed none of the religious fervor that Boorman had witnessed so far. Perhaps they were jaded, or perhaps they were cautious. In its 3000 year history, the city had seen giants come and had seen them go. The communist revolution had practically started here. Mao Zedong had been born in the nearby town of Shaoshan and had attended middle school here. Here he had met others who would later be leaders in the Communist Party. Here Mao raised the first peasant army in the Autumn Harvest Uprising and began a guerrilla war against the Kuomintang. Changsha had seen student factions fighting in the streets, each group trying to prove that it was more loyal to Mao than the others, and that it alone truly understood Mao Thought.

The *Eckener*'s arrival only engendered the excitement one would expect from a city of several million people who had seen it all. Technology was not new to them; they had seen immense technological progress in their lives. Most of them had televisions now — many were in color. Motorcycles were a common sight in Changsha streets. Planes, trains and boats left Changsha daily. The arrival of a single dirigible only caused a few bicycle accidents as the typically chaotic traffic became hopelessly overburdened by the mass of curious pedestrians who walked calmly out into the streets for a better look.

Chang and Boorman were not in their room, but were in one of the several observation lounges along the hallway of the *Eckener*'s lower deck.

As were the others in the lounge, Boorman was studying the people through the transparent floor of the lounge. The floor had been left slightly dark so that the people below were denied the equal luxury of studying them. He commented to Chang that the people seemed to try to get under something when the *Eckener* passed over head. Some went under awnings and peered upward; some held newspapers over their heads as if it were going to rain.

"Spit," Chang said. "If this ship were full of Chinese, spit would be raining down. Never walk under a wall with a lot of Chinese leaning over it; you will need an umbrella. They will not be spitting on you on purpose; it is just something that they do a lot of. It comes naturally to them."

Hearing this, one of the other passengers leaned out one of the open windows and spit on the Chinese below.

What an odd thing to do, Boorman thought. Did others on board have the same dislike for the Chinese that he had? They didn't dislike Chang, and he was Chinese.

Because the Changshanese were relatively well behaved, the *Eckener* was allowed by the government to put down at the CAAC airport so that passengers could tour the Mao museums. Some even caught buses at the long-distance bus station and, accompanied by armed guards on the buses, took tours of Shaoshan. Shaoshan and Changsha were among the few places outside of Beijing where Mao was still memorialized. The passengers were eager to leave the *Eckener* and see China close up. They were now deep into the heart of China, and because of circumstances, many had not as yet even set foot on the soil. Possibly out of respect for this fact, Chang did not make himself visible from the *Eckener* and the stay at Changsha was, in the main, uneventful.

Lao came by to see if Boorman was doing his duty, and when he saw that he was diligently guarding Chang's welfare, he relaxed some and offered to stay with Chang if Boorman wished to go into Changsha. Boorman had come to trust Lao because of the help that he had provided and Chang also agreed that it would be alright.

Boorman found Captain Macon and talked her into leaving the ship in the hands of the crew for an hour. They took a taxi to Dongfeng Lu and found the museum where the 2100 year old remains of a Han Dynasty woman were kept. Later they went down to the Xiang River Bridge and stood looking at the long island in the middle of the river from which Changsha gets its name. "Have you ever felt that you have been someplace before?" Holly asked.

"Déjà vu?" Boorman suggested.

"It looks so familiar. I feel like I could have been that dead woman that we just saw. I could have been her when she lived along this river two thousand years ago. I can almost see the old city walls and towers. Do you think it is all imagination?"

"I don't know," Boorman answered. He remembered the first time he had seen Holly and how he felt that he already knew her from somewhere. He had even, upon first seeing her, wondered what it would be like to be married to her. He started to tell her about that, but thought that it would sound foolish and sentimental — or worse, like something a sailor with ulterior motives might say.

They decided to walk across the bridge to the island. The Changshanese treated them much as the Cantonese had — stepping aside to let them pass but staring unabashedly as if at circus animals on parade. Boorman tried staring back but they would not take the hint. Some even walked backwards in front of Captain Macon and Boorman so as to study them at length. Boorman tried to talk to some to show that they were human beings like them. He pulled out a phrase book and began to stumble through the Chinese pronunciations. He quickly had a crowd of curious people studying the book over his shoulder. He pointed to the Chinese symbols representing the question he wanted to ask and before he realized it, the book was no longer in his hand. A young man had the book now and was rapidly turning the pages as if he had never seen such a thing before. A loud rapid-fire argument began among the crowd around the book, and Captain Macon chose this opportunity to drag Boorman out of the middle of it. They walked rapidly down the bridge, leaving the most audacious of the spectators loudly discussing the phrase book.

At the junction of the island road they passed an older woman who was just standing and looking across the river, unlike the other Chinese on the bridge, all of whom seemed to be going somewhere with some particular objective. She did not stare at them rudely like the others, but other than for these two details, she did not particularly stand out from the crowd and Boorman and Captain Macon barely noticed her.

Across the river there was not much to see except some fields and old compounds that might have, at one time, been prisoner-of-war camps. Crossing the island again, Boorman saw that the old woman was still at her post but that she had decided to abandon politeness in favor of a closer look at the Americans. She fell into step beside Boorman, and to Boorman's surprise asked, "You are Mister Zhang? Mister Zhang Bao-mahn?"

"That's right," Boorman said. "Do I know you?"

"You saved my son in Guangzhou."

"How do you know about Guangzhou?"

"Please keep your voice down. I could be arrested for speaking to you." She looked around nervously. The crowd was so thick that it was difficult to tell who was paying any particular attention to whom. "You do not know what it is like for us here. It is very lucky that you came this way today," she continued. "I come here almost every day to pay tribute to my mother who died in one of those buildings over there." She pointed toward the low buildings across the river. I have a gift to give you for the gift you gave me when you saved my son." She was speaking rapidly and seeming to jump from subject to subject.

"You do not need to give me a gift . . ." Boorman began.

"Please, let me say what I have to say," she interrupted. "This gift is a warning. There are men with great power in the Party who see Chang Da Wai as a very bad danger to them. They want to see him wiped away — in a way that shows everyone that he is not a god or a Buddha or anything. If they can have a way to also paint a bad face on the American Navy by placing blame on one of its officers, that would be even more better. The party faction that wants this will probably have its way."

"But I was helped by a party mem . . ." Boorman started to say but was interrupted this time by Captain Macon.

"Hush, John. You do not know what kind of trouble you might be causing."

"I too am a party member," the old woman said. "How do you think I found out these things? We are not all alike, you know. All my life I wanted to be a good party member, but I have seen how hollow that dream is. My mother was a good revolutionary but whoever killed her must have been a better one. You have to be in the party or you are nothing."

"Does everyone know that Chang is on the *Eckener*?" Boorman asked.

"Of course."

"Why aren't there any demonstrations like at Guangzhou and Guilin?"

"People do not want the violence that happened at Guangzhou and Guilin."

"There was no violence at Guilin," Boorman protested.

"Oh, yes. You just did not see it. Many arrests; many beatings; many people in jail now. Chang Da Wai has many followers, but the party has many supporters also. If you go to Beijing, you will find some trouble there. This may help you." She placed a folded scrap of paper in his hand.

"What is it?" he asked.

"It is an address." She glanced around quickly. "I must go now. Thank you for saving my son." Without another word she abruptly left Boorman's side and disappeared into the crowd.

Boorman turned to Captain Macon. "I bet you didn't think I was important enough to have the Chinese government out to get me," he grinned.

"I don't think this is a joking matter," she said. "I think that woman risked her life to give you that information. Let's get back to the ship. I'm worried about David now."

Boorman wadded the address into a ball and threw it into the river. "What are you doing?" Captain Macon asked, surprised at his action. "We might have needed that."

He only shrugged in response. However, I had seen the address, and it belonged to the woman who made the best dim sum in Beijing.

At the ship, they found Chang safely discussing politics with Lao. "What do you think it would be like if everyone lived by the golden rule?" Lao asked them. "Suppose I make shoes. I want to make the best shoes that I can because that would be the kind of shoes I would want to wear. Do I sell them? No, I give them to anyone who needs shoes. Do people take advantage of me? No, because they live by the golden rule as well. If they have rice, they force me to take it. They give me too much; I make them take some back. 'Other people need rice too,' I say. True communism!" His face lit up with a patriotic glow.

Chang smiled. "Such a world can only come from within," he said. "No law of man's can bring this about."

"Yes, that is the hard part," Lao said. He turned to face Boorman. "You had a nice trip and now you are refreshed and ready to resume your duties." It was not a question.

"Ready to go back to the salt mines," Boorman said. He did not know whether to tell Lao what they had been told, but Captain Macon did not say anything, so he decided to keep quiet too. Lao left the cabin and Captain Macon began to tell Chang what had happened.

"They have tried before," Chang said. "There is no end to their trying."

"Who?" Boorman asked, "The Chinese government?"

"Anyone who fights to keep people in darkness."

"You do not seem very worried," Boorman said.

"Worry is counter-productive," Chang laughed and then quickly became serious. "When all words have been spoken and all work has been finished, it will be known that there never was evil in the kingdom of heaven. This is not my philosophy; this is the truth that I have seen."

"Perhaps you are right, Chang," Captain Macon said, "but this is the world, and right now I am responsible for the safety of a lot of people, so forgive me if I worry a little. Do you think we should tell Lao about this? Do you trust him?"

"I trust him to do what he thinks is right," Chang said, "but I don't think he should be burdened with this. If he doesn't already know, the knowledge will create a conflict of duty. If he does already know, he obviously doesn't want anyone to know that he knows. Let him have peace."

*

"I told my aunt that you thanked her for the soup, so now she has sent you some jiaozi," Zhao said the next morning. "Jiaozi brings good luck."

I had already smelled the delicious aroma of dumplings in the room and was hoping they were for me.

"I think I made a big mistake by telling her that you are here," he continued.

"Are you not getting any rest at home for having to go to the market?" I asked.

"It's not that. She has told her friends. If my bosses find out that I talked about a prisoner, I may end up in there with you."

"And then who would bring us jiaozi?" I laughed.

"I am not laughing," he said. "Be quiet and eat your food quickly. This makes me very nervous."

After I wolfed down the dumplings, I asked Zhao, "Does your aunt ever talk about your parents?"

"She did when I was younger, but she knows that I do not like to hear about them."

"What did she tell you?"

"What does it matter? Lies!"

"Would you like to see your parents again if you could?"

"Did I not tell you that they are dead?"

"What if you could go back in time and see them the way they were when they were alive — would you want to do that?"

"That is not possible."

"If you say 'no', then you will cut yourself off from that possibility, but if you say 'yes', then it is possible; it could happen tonight."

There was a long pause. "How could this happen?"

"I think I might be able to give you this gift; it would be my thanks to you. But it might not work — we would just have to try it and see."

"How could you do this?"

"Don't ask — just accept the gift."

"What would it be like?"

"You would go home and go to bed just like normal, and when you dreamed, you would see your parents."

"It would just be a dream?"

"No. It would be much more than a dream. It would be real. And in the morning, you would wake up and remember."

"If I say no?"

"I won't ever ask you again."

"Who are you that you can do this?"

"I am just a person who has a gift to give. I am a person who sees that there is a good part of you that you are trying to wall off and close down."

"You see that? You can't even see yourself in the mirror; how do you see that about me? Be quiet. You talk too much."

I didn't hear anymore from him for a long while, but then sometime before his shift was over for the day he spoke up. "OK. Yes," he said.

I meditated on my bunk and left my body, and when Zhao left the cell, I followed him through the streets of Beijing until he reached his apartment.

Zhao was obviously concerned when he arrived to find his small living room full of people waiting to ask him questions about his famous prisoner. His eyes had the frightened look of a rabbit's startled by hounds. He weaved through them to the kitchen, where he found his aunt making refreshments for the company. "An Zhen, did you invite all of these people here to get me arrested?" he asked, waving his arms wildly.

"No, I did not, and that is no way to speak to your aunt."

"I am sorry, An Zhen, he replied softly, bowing his head. This is all my own fault. I broke the rules, and now I will pay. But who will take care of you when I am in jail?"

"You are not going to jail. These are our friends in there. They will not say anything to hurt us."

"I wish I had your confidence, An Zhen. Please make them promise not to tell anyone else about Dong Shi."

"Don't worry, nephew, they won't talk. Now go in there and be hospitable. They want to hear about how you had beer with Dong Shi."

Later, after the last guest had left, Zhao lay down exhausted on his bed. I am sure that he had not had time to give another thought about what to expect when he went to sleep. I was not certain that I would be able to make anything happen, but I had not wanted to even try unless Zhao wanted to try as well.

After he was asleep, I mentally connected with him and entered his dream. "Hello Zhao," I said. "Do you remember what we were going to do tonight?"

I received his affirmation and he gradually took on the persona of a child next to me. He appeared to be about ten years old as I took his hand. "You know that in dreams you can fly through the air, don't you?"

He nodded.

"Well, you can fly through time as well. Not everybody knows how to do that — but I do. Take my hand and we will fly way up over the city, and when we come back down, you will show me where you lived with your parents."

We flew out the window and ascended into the night sky until we were high enough for the city to look magical below us, as almost any city can seem when seen from a sufficient height at night. As we spiraled gently back down to earth, we went back to the very same house where Zhao and his aunt lived—only in this time, young Zhao lived there with his parents. A light was shining out through the kitchen window. Inside, two people—a young man and a young woman — were discussing something softly yet intently.

"Are those your parents, Zhao?"

He nodded.

"Let's go inside," I said.

*

"But, Mei Li," the man was saying in the kitchen, "what if something happens to us, who will take care of Zhao Tou?"

"Nothing is going to happen to us. This is just going to be a peaceful protest. If something ever did happen to us, my sister would take him."

"I think it is too risky. I heard that the army is being called out."

"Do you want your son to grow up in China the way it is? What kind of life is this? What kind of life can he have? China has to change."

"I know you are right, Mei Li, but I have a bad feeling. The boy especially needs us right now."

"I am his mother. There is nothing that I would not do for him, and the most that I can do for him right now is to try to give him a world where he can grow up to be a good and honest person, not afraid to say or do what is right. If you are a good communist, you will do this for your country and if you want to be a good father, then do this for Zhao Tou."

"OK, Mei Li; I will do it for him. I will do it for Zhao Tou."

*

"I have good news and bad news," Zhao said, as he came in to the room bringing his usual delicious aromas of food. "The bad news is that my aunt did not have time to make anything special for you last night because we had company at our apartment. So she sent you the left-over dim sum, and hopes you will accept her apology. The good news is that she lived in the south before my parents died, and so her dim sum is very much better than what they serve around this city." He laughed as he set the food on my bunk. "I almost decided to eat them on the way to work and give you a story instead."

He sounded more like his usual sober self as he continued. "I had a dream last night. It was just as you said it would be. I saw my parents just before they died, and it all seemed very real. You did this?"

I nodded as I gobbled down the dim sum. I knew that Zhao was exposed during this time while I was eating and that it was very dangerous for him.

"Was it real? Were those really my parents?"

I nodded again.

"This morning I woke up with tears in my eyes and my heart. I told my aunt about my dream. She said that she had been trying to tell me that they did it for me, but that I wouldn't listen. So if it is true that you took us there, how did you do it?"

"You took us to the place," I answered, "I only took us to the time."

"But how did you do that?"

"I don't know. How do you find your way home from the market?"

"There were people last night — friends of my mother — they said you were Kwan Yin, the one who hears the cries of the world. Are you Kwan Yin?"

"Everyone is Kwan Yin, or can be. They say that Kwan Yin has a thousand arms. Sometimes one of those arms might be yours or mine. When you reach out with your arm to help someone, that is Kwan Yin's arm that is reaching out."

"I think my parents were Kwan Yin's arms."

"Yes, I think you are right."

"How can one make one's self into an arm of Kwan Yin?"

"They say that Kwan Yin will never rest until all creatures have been released from conditioned existence. Kwan Yin is always ready to trade her own happiness to alleviate the suffering of others. Kwan Yin sees all beings as precious jewels beyond price. If we want to be Kwan Yin, we must learn by observing all things, by observing ourselves, and by observing others. Even those who treat us the most cruelly are our teachers and deserve our blessing."

"I will think about what you have said, but I don't see how I could ever be Kwan Yin."

"You don't have to be Kwan Yin all at once; for now you just have to be willing to be Kwan Yin's arm."

*

From Changsha, the *Eckener* headed north to Dongting Lake, an inland sea of over 1000 square miles. At the northern part of the lake they picked up the Yangtze River, or, as Boorman read it on the *Eckener*'s maps, the Chang Jiang. They began to follow the river east to Wuhan but their plans were abruptly changed when Lao found Captain Macon and told her that the city of three million people was closed.

"Closed?" Boorman exclaimed later as Captain Macon told him about it in her cabin. "You mean like a restaurant?" he asked sarcastically.

"Lao says the government is afraid of an international incident if the rising tide of hooliganism in the cities was to cause problems for the *Eckener*. You know what that really means, don't you?"

"Yeah, it means they're having a hard time keeping a lid on the Changlings." He looked around sheepishly at Chang who sat listening dispassionately. "Sorry," Boorman said. "Well, does this mean we are going straight on to Nanjing or Shanghai?"

"No, both are closed," Captain Macon said. "In fact we have been all but ordered to proceed directly to Beijing, which, they say, is better equipped to guarantee our safety, and where a reception has been organized to officially welcome us to China."

"Why are they doing that? We've been here for awhile already."

"Lao mentioned 'technological wonders' and 'friendship between East and West' and that sort of thing."

"So, are we going?"

"I don't see how we can avoid it," Captain Macon said. "It really would be an international incident if we skipped our own reception in Beijing. I'm concerned about what that woman told us at Changsha. What do you think, David?"

"Oh yes. We must go to Beijing."

"Ok, then, I'll ask Sandal to announce it to the other passengers. We should be in Beijing sometime tomorrow. Stay alert."

As they cruised past the outskirts of Wuhan, they were circled a few times by a sharp-nosed silver fighter plane carrying the red star and bar behind its wing. Its presence in the sky firmed up the warning that Wuhan was closed. And, as if to show what his slender plane could do, the pilot let it break the sound barrier as he flew by for the last time and disappeared rapidly into the sky. The loud boom reverberated through the *Eckener*'s frame and set off loud alarms until Wendy realized that the ship was in no danger.

Boorman and Chang whiled away their time up on the pool deck, watching the countryside go by below. Even in China, as thoroughly cultivated as it was, there were still some wild places, and some of them lay between Wuhan and Beijing. The indistinct form of distant mountains through the haze reminded Boorman that they were literally at the bottom of a sea of air that clouded and obscured the detail of things seen from afar. "How high do you think this ship can float?" he asked Chang.

"I would think that it could go high enough that it wouldn't matter — high enough for everyone to need oxygen. It has already gone to the edge of that without really trying. Perhaps it could even go into the death zone if it weren't carrying too much weight."

"What is the death zone?"

"That is the altitude where there is not enough oxygen to sustain human life — somewhere between twenty-two and twenty-three thousand feet."

"How do you know that off the top of your head?"

"Once upon a time, I was a mountain climber. I have climbed into the death zone many times."

"Really!? I would have thought that you would need a complete set of fingers and toes to be a mountain climber."

"Many mountain climbers have lost appendages to frostbite. Some continued to climb afterwards; I did not."

"You lost your feet to frostbite?"

"Yes, but I think I made a good trade."

"Why is that?"

"That experience was the beginning of my awakening."

"Are you awake now?"

Chang laughed. "Well, more so than I was."

"How did you become awakened?"

And so Chang told Boorman his story, which is pretty much the same story that you already know. Although Chang may have included a few things that I left out, and may have left out a few things that I have told you, the story is essentially the same.

There were one or two Changling disciples lounging around who also heard him tell the story, and if ever you want to track them down and compare their stories against mine, you will hear some interesting details about how and what the old hermit taught Chang that I have not bothered to explain.

After supper, Chang and Boorman returned to the pool deck, Captain Macon and Sandal with them. No one talked for a while as they watched the sun set and the sky get gradually darker. The night sky had often touched Boorman with dread, as if, somehow, he might fall up into it and disappear forever. It was a fear of heights turned inside out. When he looked up into the sky, it sometimes seemed that he was looking down into a bottomless void, over which the earth hung like a marble on a string. If he fell into it, he would fall forever. But also, the infinity of night represented an eternal loneliness to him. His soul cringed from the thoughts the night sky brought — the eternity of death, of not being, of all that he had experienced made meaningless. Yet an eternity of *being*, of continuing in his doubts, fears, and aloneness, seemed even worse. To contemplate the night sky was to contemplate a question that had only terrible answers. To exist forever, and to cease to exist — both were terrible, fearful ideas to him. God himself must be lost in that empty infinity of loneliness. Boorman had long ago walled off the part of his mind that asked those questions, but the wall needed continual shoring, and lately it had been crumbling faster than he could rebuild it. What terror might flood in when it fell, he dared not think about.

"The universe is vast," Chang said, as if in reply to Boorman's thoughts, "but God is not in it."

"Why do you say that?" Boorman asked, desperately not wanting Chang to tell him that existence was meaningless and futile. He was not coping well with all of the strange events and incredible stories that he had seen and heard on this trip, and he felt on the verge of cracking. He felt as if his foundations had been shaken beyond endurance, and felt that he could very easily have his last few props knocked out from under him by a few careless words.

"God is not in the universe," Chang said, "because the universe is in God. If I asked you to go to the edge of the universe, where would you look? Out there, a googol light years away? The edge of the universe is not out there; it is right here. It is the boundary between thought and energy—between mind and matter — that is the edge of the universe and it is so close to us that we cannot even see it. We live on the edge of the universe, our backs to the infinite. Eternity does not mean one plodding painful day after the next. Eternity means to exist outside of time and space, free from conditioning — an existence of infinite potential. God exists outside of time and space and you are part of that cosmic consciousness. What is there to be afraid of? Take your mind to the farthest reaches that you can imagine. Stretch it to include everything imaginable and then allow room for the unimaginable and then know that thou art that."

What a wonderful thought. Suddenly, magically, the wall was down, and there was no flood of terror. The wall had served no purpose. It was gone and the night sky was still there — holding promise instead of fear.

"Snap out of it," he said to himself. "You are falling for it again. Get a grip on reality before you end up looking like a fool." But he could not deny that the wall was down and that he was somehow larger and suddenly free.

That night, Boorman did not have terrible unsettling dreams of dying. Instead he dreamed that he was a multi-colored shining beam of light that soared at incalculable speed through the magnificent field of night and played in the vast exquisite sea of stars.

There never was a more beautiful day, he thought, than that next morning when he awoke. The sunrise shown up through the translucent bottom of the ship with a golden glow while five hundred feet below, people emerged from their tiny farm houses to do their human thing — not realizing the cosmic importance of their every small decision and action. His heart went out to them.

At breakfast he filled his plate with his usual bacon and eggs. He got Chang's cereal and fruit for him and they both sat down to eat. He bit off a piece of bacon and chewed. Delicious, he thought and then was struck by the impact of what he was doing. The bacon suddenly lost its savor. How many animals had suffered short confined lives and terrible deaths to satisfy his desire to put something flavorful in his mouth? He did not want the bacon now, but what should he do? What would people say? — Boorman, is something wrong with the bacon? You're not turning vegetarian on us are you? Should he throw it away? Then the animal had suffered and died for nothing. He ate the bacon, but as he chewed he prayed, and a part of him thought how odd it was that he had never before prayed or asked a blessing over a meal. He prayed not for his own salvation, but for the salvation of the animal that had died. And he prayed that the flesh that now entered his body would sustain him to bring good into the world, so that the animal would not have lived and died in futility.

The act of prayer released a flood of emotion that washed over him and welled the tears up in his eyes. He felt as if some power were looking down upon him with joy and even pride for him. He looked across at Chang. He could not be sure because of the tears in his eyes, but were there tears in Chang's eyes as well?

After breakfast Boorman and Chang retired once more to the upper pool deck, followed soon by Captain Macon. Chang was sitting off with his own thoughts. Boorman was leaning on the railing, very near to where he had seen another traveler slide off into an impenetrable fog.

"John, is there something wrong?" Captain Macon asked.

"Just my nervous breakdown." he said. But then, to take the grimness out of his words, he added, "But, as far as nervous breakdowns go, this one ain't too bad." He laughed. "Last night I dreamed I was a beam of light and this morning I grieved for my bacon." He shook his head slowly. "I don't know. I'm just not myself lately."

Captain Macon was silent for awhile. "I had a dream like that once," she finally said. "It was after that dream that I decided to build airships. I didn't want to touch the ground any more."

"Do I fight it?" he asked. "Or do I become Elwood P. Dowd. Sometimes I would rather be Elwood P. Dowd."

"Who is that?" Captain Macon asked.

"You know — the guy who had a seven foot tall invisible rabbit for a friend."

"Oh yeah. Jimmy Stewart."

"Yeah. He knows things about me, you know."

"Jimmy Stewart?"

"No. Chang. You do see <u>him</u> don't you?"

"Yes. I see Chang. You are beginning to worry me a little bit, John."

He laughed. "I'm sorry. Bad joke. Please don't look at me like I'm changing shapes or something." He smiled.

"Just for a second I thought we were losing you. What kinds of things does Chang know about you?"

"Just things." Boorman said. "He reads my thoughts. He answers questions I haven't asked him. I'm not complaining though; he's never judgmental. In fact he's really a pretty sweet guy. He's been through a lot, you know."

She nodded. "Yeah, I've heard stories."

"Actually, and I've just realized this, but I kind of like Chang now. I guess that proves I'm crazy."

"I'll say." She laughed.

"Did you ever think that inside every brute and murderer in the world was a soul just like you and me, trying to work out its destiny, but more lost and confused, even, than we are?"

"Are you still talking about Chang?" she asked, confused.

"No. I'm sorry. My thoughts have been jumping around all over the place this morning. I was thinking about the guy that fell overboard out in the Pacific. He must have been in a dark place. But you know, I feel like I am in a bright place today for a change, and I'm thinking that if I'm crazy, I'll just go with that."

*

Of course there was more food the next day from Zhao's aunt. It was so that I wouldn't have to depend on the unwholesome prison food for the strength of my body and spirit, she had told Zhao. He continued to be desperately afraid that his aunt's friends would spread the word about my whereabouts, and when we heard the sounds of shouting, the gunfire, and the rumbling of tanks in the streets, he was so convinced that the secret was out that he almost didn't bother to inquire. I didn't tell him, but I already knew what was happening and was preparing myself for it.

Chapter 7 – Of the Angel Metatron and the Valley of Death.

Beijing was quiet at first. No crowds gathered to greet the *Eckener*. No one seemed to be concerned about the huge aircraft as it glided over the ancient city walls. The bicycle traffic below was not even enough to fill the wide straight boulevards. It was as if a plague had decimated the population. The city was so quiet that one should have been able to hear the birds sing, but there were no birds in Beijing. All the birds in Beijing had long ago gone into the stew pots.

The city was laid out in geometric forms and straight lines. However, the city was not graceful or appealing to Boorman's eyes; things were too big, and the city seemed to be an almost uniform shade of gray.

Boorman noticed the armored vehicles around the perimeter of Tiananmen Square. The *Eckener* had been invited to land in the square itself. It was the largest square in the world at one hundred plus acres, and was a huge desert of flat paving stones. There was a large obelisk style monument in the middle, two very tall spires topped with flood lights, and, at regular intervals, many ornate lampposts that resembled strange palm trees. The size of the square dwarfed the surrounding buildings, which were actually, in their own right, very large and imposing, if not beautiful, structures. The Great Hall of the People on the western side of the square held within it government offices, a ten thousand seat auditorium, and a five thousand seat banquet hall, where some of the *Eckener* crew had been invited to dine.

Boorman distrusted the armored personnel carriers and T69-II tanks posted around the square. The government was giving the appearance that the *Eckener* was going to be well guarded from the populace, but

Boorman thought that he would rather take his chances with the people than the government.

The *Eckener* touched down in Tiananmen Square and was greeted by an officer of the People's Liberation Army, who had walked across the square to meet them. The gang-plank was lowered and he came aboard and extended formal invitations to Captain Macon, whatever crew members she chose to take with her, and Captain Boorman as an official representative of the U.S. Navy and the representative of the *Eckener*'s passengers. The passengers were not invited.

Boorman was nonplussed when Captain Macon repeated the invitation to him later. "Don't you think I ought to stay here with Chang, especially considering the warning we have had?"

"I told the man that it was your duty to guard one of our passengers. He said that our current attaché was perfectly capable of guarding whoever needed guarding and he implied that turning down the invitation might put a strain on Chinese / U.S. relations."

Boorman, Captain Macon, and all the crew members, except for Sandal and Gregory, were picked up later and driven across the square in limousines. The captain asked Sandal to watch the ship while they were gone, and Gregory volunteered to stay behind and keep her company.

Boorman did not enjoy the banquet, and for him, at least, it seemed to go on forever. He was suspicious of the government's motives; they had made a turn of one hundred and eighty degrees from not even wanting them in the country, to throwing a big state banquet in their honor. In addition, his new awareness of meat made him squeamish, especially since he could not identify the food on his plate and suspected that it might be some endangered species that he was helping to exterminate. He could very well have been right, because it was my experience in China, that laws existed to protect those in power, and if it was against the law to sell endangered species in the streets, it was probably because it made the animals scarcer, and therefore more expensive, for the government officials who rode in limousines and lived in guarded mansions. So Boorman picked at his food and listened to the gradually increasing sound of shouting coming from the square.

Suddenly a man in a green uniform ran in and whispered in the ear of one of the elderly men at the table. The man slowly stood up and announced sadly that a large body of students had apparently overwhelmed security in the square and had kidnapped a passenger from the *Eckener* for unknown purposes. He assured them that the government would do everything within its power to assure the safe return of the passenger. However, he did not seem overly excited about the situation, and Boorman suspected that the announcement had been rehearsed.

Boorman was too stunned at the news to move at first, but as the sound of gunfire began to filter into the banquet hall, he jumped up, overturning his chair, and rushed down the hall and out into the square. He was brought up short by the sight that greeted him. There were easily a hundred thousand people in the square, maybe even twice that, and the number seemed to be growing as the people continued to flow into the square like flood waters into a dry canyon.

There was a battle going on — that much was obvious — but who was fighting whom was not easy to tell. There were soldiers in the square. They were the source of the gunfire. There were islands of green uniforms, and islands of non-uniforms, and rivers of soldiers and rivers of citizens flowing into and around each other, breaking and reforming around solid masses of shouting, struggling people.

The *Eckener* seemed to be alright for now, but the boarding ramp was down. Boorman remembered that the Captain had ordered it raised when they had left the ship. When would the battle make its way up those stairs and invade the *Eckener*, and when would a stray bullet hit one of the vacuum balls and what would it do? Boorman could see that the observation decks, the hallways, and the ballroom were full of passengers running back and forth, panic stricken and helpless.

For the present, the soldiers seemed to be firing at random into a particularly well formed mass of students surrounding a lamppost. One student was holding to the side of the lamppost above the surrounding heads and was nonchalantly observing the melee below.

"It's Chang!" He turned at the sound of Captain Macon's voice and saw the horror on her face. "We've got to get him out of there!" she yelled into his ear. "Get us to the ship!"

Easier said than done, he thought. Taking the limousine was out of the question because of the density of the crowd. He took her hand and began to run, dodging and ducking, sometimes pushing and shoving his way through dense clusters of people that would spontaneously form and wash against them without warning. At one point they found themselves inside a moving river of shouting people, none of whom seemed to notice them. They became separated as the currents moved them this way and that. He heard Captain Macon shout for him to go on.

At last he made it to the *Eckener*, bruised and exhausted. He fell over a dead soldier as he ran up the stairway. He pulled himself up and ran up into the ship and through the halls. The first passengers he encountered grabbed him in a panic. "What should we do? Where should we go?" they asked him, holding on to his clothes.

"Tell everyone you see to go to the top deck. Get off of the lower decks. Where is Sandal?"

"She is by your cabin. We were in the ballroom when the men came on board and took David. She tried to stop them and they killed her."

With a terrible coldness running through his veins, he ran to his cabin where he found Lao standing by the door, staring down at Sandal, dead on the floor. Boorman felt himself losing control. A hatred for all things Chinese was filling him and the closest Chinese to him was Lao. In his mind, Lao had been judged and sentenced, and only awaited execution. He approached Lao from behind and spun him around. "You bastard!" he said between clinched teeth, and hit him savagely in the face with his two fists clenched together. Tears, blood and saliva sprayed onto the bulkhead, and Lao fell limply to the floor. "You killed her, didn't you?" Boorman walked around to where he had a better angle to kick in the side of Lao's head. "This was your plan all along, wasn't it? Now it is your turn, you worthless piece of Chinese dung!"

"I have failed," Lao whispered. "Kill me quickly and go and save Chang." His words stopped Boorman, who turned and sent a terrific kick into the bulkhead instead of into Lao's brain.

"What do you mean? You worthless waste of skin, your duty was to guard Chang. You were in on this all the time."

"I have discharged my duty and now it is *your* duty to guard Chang Da Wai. You should hurry."

"Hell!" Boorman cursed, realizing that Lao was right and that he would have to sort all this out later. Where was Captain Macon? He couldn't fly this ship by himself. He went into the cabin, remembering the communication system that the captain had installed so that he could talk to Wendy in an emergency. This was an emergency alright.

"Wendy!" Boorman shouted into the communications panel, "Turn the ship around and prepare to pick up passengers!" No response. The *Eckener* didn't move. "Wendy! This is Captain Macon! Turn the ship around!" No response. Wendy knew he wasn't Captain Macon. "This is Captain Boorman, ranking officer on board. I am assuming command in Captain Macon's absence. And with her permission," he added lamely. Nothing. "Wendy, can you hear me?" he asked, thinking the device might be broken.

"Yes."

"Why don't you turn the ship around?"

"I cannot obey orders from you. You do not have proper clearance or authorization."

"How much clearance do I have?"

"You have level five security clearance?"

"What does that entitle me to do?"

"You may make enquiries of a non-sensitive nature."

So, he could ask questions and that was all. What could he do with that? "Wendy, do you have standing instructions which you follow without human intervention?"

"Yes."

"What are they?"

"You are not cleared for that information."

"Do you have standing instructions which I am cleared to enquire about?"

"Yes."

"Am I cleared to enquire about defensive action?"

"No."

"Am I cleared to enquire about passenger safety?"

"Yes".

"What are your standing instructions regarding passenger safety?"

"I am never to take action which would endanger passengers. I am always to take action to remove passengers from danger."

"Wouldn't you say that you had a passenger in danger now?"

"No."

"Why not?"

"There are no passengers in danger. The ship is safe. I have checked all systems."

"If a person were on your passenger roster, would that person be a passenger?"

"Yes".

"Do you see that person at about five o'clock off the starboard stern who is standing above the crowd?"

"Yes".

"Do you recognize him?"

"Yes."

"What is his name?"

"David Chang."

"Is that name on the passenger roster?"

"Yes."

"Is he a passenger?"

"Yes."

"Isn't he in danger?"

"No."

"Why not?"

"He is with his own kind."

"Do you know what a gun is?"

"Yes."

"What does a gun do?"

"A gun hurls projectiles at high velocity."

"What would happen if that projectile hit this ship or a passenger?"

"There would be damage."

"Do you see guns in that crowd?"

"Yes."

"And are guns dangerous?"

"Yes."

"And there is a passenger in that crowd?"

"Yes."

"Do you have a passenger in danger?"

"Yes."

Boorman had been told, but had not actually realized how quickly the *Eckener* could pivot by using its directional louvers. Now the giant ship swung around like a leviathan of the air whose calf was under attack. As massive as the ship was, it turned so rapidly that Boorman was thrown against the bulkhead and slid down to the floor. He hoped that Wendy's programming would not allow a sharp enough turn to throw people over the safety railings.

As the ship turned, the trailing boarding ramp indiscriminately cut a swath through the battle below. Now that the head of the ship was where the tail had been, Boorman saw the carnage below them.

"Wendy, would it be a good idea to raise the boarding ramp to avoid damage?" He asked, desperately trying to make it sound like a polite suggestion.

"Yes. Raising boarding ramp now."

The *Eckener* began to move in the direction of the lamppost some distance off where Chang had been carried.

"Would human assistance be helpful in this maneuver?" Boorman asked.

"Yes."

"Would it be good for us to stay in constant communication?"

"Yes."

"What part of the ship is best to pick up this passenger?"

"The passenger boarding ramp."

"Would we have to slow down or stop to use the ramp?"

"Yes."

"Would that make us a better target than if we stayed in motion."

"Yes."

"If you lowered me on the cargo elevator, could we pick up the passenger without stopping?"

No answer.

"Wendy, do you hear me?" They were getting closer to the mob around the lamppost.

"Yes."

"Will you accept instruction from me for the purpose of this rescue?"

"No."

"If you stop the ship and lower the ramp, could people grab the ramp and hold on to it?"

"Yes."

"Could a large number of people break the ramp?"

"Yes."

"Is there a sufficient number of people below to break the ramp?"

"Yes."

"Would that place your passenger in greater danger than if you could pick up the passenger with the cargo elevator?"

"Yes."

"Do you need human assistance with the cargo elevator?"

"Yes."

"Will you accept my assistance with the cargo elevator?"

"Yes."

"Will you take instruction from me for the purpose of giving assistance?"

"No."

"Do you remember your standing instructions regarding passenger safety?"

"Yes."

"Does passenger safety take priority over security?"

"Yes."

"Will you take limited instruction from me for the purpose of rescuing a passenger in danger?"

"No."

He was out of time to argue with this machine. "Will you maintain voice contact with me if I go back to the cargo hold?"

"Yes."

He began running back to the hold — the better part of three football fields away. "Will you make the floor transparent so that I can keep the passenger in sight?" He felt like he was playing Simon Says.

"Yes." Wendy's voice came from all of the communication panels down the hallway.

The bottoms of Boorman's feet could not have been more than fifty feet above the heads of the people below. If he had not been in such a hurry, it would have been comical to watch the people as the incredibly massive *Eckener* appeared suddenly above them without a sound. They looked up with the most startled expressions — some falling to the ground in amazement and then reaching up to pull others down to safety.

As the people below got over their initial reaction, they realized they could see up into the hallways of the ship and they began to watch Boorman run. To both him and the crowd, he seemed like a man running in a dream. He was running opposite to the forward motion of the ship and the effect was of a man running at full speed in one direction while being pulled slowly backward in the other.

Now he was over the PLA soldiers who had surrounded the huge mass of civilians around the lamppost. Not being as close to the bow of the ship as he passed overhead, he did not witness the soldiers' first reaction to the *Eckener*. Here, further down its length, the soldiers were using their bayonets to make threatening gestures at the *Eckener*, and then at Boorman as they became aware of him.

He was getting closer to the cargo hold as well as to Chang. He came to the door to the hold. It was locked! "Will you unlock the cargo hold door?" he shouted at the hallway.

"Yes," the answer came back through the wall panel.

He entered the hold and looked around to see that Wendy had already lowered the elevator, and that he was going to have to use one of the spiders to get down to the deck. When he looked over the edge of the opening in the hull, he saw that the deck was plowing through the PLA soldiers at just about head height. The ones not knocked down by the platform, had turned their attention away from Chang and towards Boorman. They were waving their bayonets in the air and obviously thought that Boorman was the one who was behind this attack on their rear flanks. If they had not seen that Boorman was preparing to come down, they most probably would have begun firing up into the *Eckener* with disastrous results for everyone.

Boorman looked down on this field of sharp bright bayonets and was reminded of a dream that he had of a field of sword-like rocks that sliced him into pieces as he fell on them. He wondered if this was such a good idea.

As Boorman slid down the central cable, he saw that they were almost upon Chang. Chang was surrounded by a large mass of younger looking people — the students, Boorman guessed. The outer ranks of the students were slowly being pulled away by the PLA, but to confuse the battle, there were thousands of other civilians fighting in the square. Some fought the PLA rear guard so that the soldiers would continually have to pull back from the lamppost students and chase off the students and workers behind them. It was bedlam below, but as far as Boorman could tell, the students were trying to defend Chang from the army. Students were continuously trying to shield Chang with their own bodies, but were falling back either from the scuffling or from being shot — Boorman could not tell which.

Boorman managed to get the cargo elevator positioned and held on to it while he shouted his questions at Wendy over his shoulder. The elevator approached slowly with Boorman clinging to it. The lamppost faction of students, quickly understanding the rescue attempt, pulled Chang down from the post and passed him hand to hand over their heads into Boorman's path so that he could pick him up without becoming entangled in the lights. This was good and bad, for now Wendy did not have to maneuver around the post, but she had to lower the platform back down so that Boorman could reach Chang. Boorman lay down on the platform, reaching under the safety ropes to grab Chang as the students passed him to the deck.

The soldiers had formed a human wedge to cut through the mass of students and intercept Chang at his rendezvous point with the platform. They were seconds late however, as Boorman grabbed Chang's arms and the students pushed him up to where he could grasp the safety ropes and clamber aboard.

The soldiers were too late to lay hands on Chang, but Boorman was still partially extended through the ropes as Chang climbed over him and fell onto the platform. The soldiers quickly hoisted onto their shoulders other soldiers who managed to grab Boorman by his clothes. Boorman wrapped his arms around the ropes, but the soldiers had firm grips on him and spun him around so that the lower half of his body now dangled out into space. This allowed them to gain even better purchase on his legs, and Boorman realized that he was going down. He knew that if he fell onto the sea of bayonets below, the result would be the same as in his dream, and seeing that the *Eckener* was about to pass over a small area currently devoid of soldiers, held on with all the strength that he could muster. With soldiers clinging to him like ants on a dying worm, he managed to hold on until he reached the clearing, where, his strength gone, he fell, breaking his fall on the soldiers who held him, but then, legs entangled, fell the last few feet on his back, cracking his head on the hard paving stones of Tiananmen Square.

*

Boorman's military training had not been for nothing. He hit the ground hard but came up fighting. It took him a few moments, however, to realize that no one was fighting back — in fact, no one was reacting to him at all. No matter how hard he tried to fight with the soldiers, they just ignored him and acted as if he was not even there. Instead they continued to beat and kick at something lying on the paving stones under their feet.

Boorman paused and looked around. The battle was waning now that Chang was gone. There were still groups of combatants, but, for the most part, the students, workers, peasants, and other civilians were trying to extricate themselves from involvement with the soldiers. They were picking up their injured friends, carrying them on their backs, or between them in their arms, or on the backs of bicycles, or dragging them if they had to, but they were leaving as quickly as they came — the flood waters draining out of the canyon. The trucks, tanks and jeeps followed them into the streets of Beijing, and gunfire continued in the distance

Some of the others who were still fighting were like Boorman — they had no effect on those around them. Some had stopped fighting and were gazing strangely down at the ground. Boorman, wondering what they were seeing, looked down himself and saw on the ground a figure that seemed oddly familiar. With a shock of recognition, he realized that he was looking at his own body, lying lifeless where the soldiers had left it as they took off in pursuit of the fleeing students.

Captain Macon came running up with other crew members and began shouting for help. Boorman hated to see her so upset, and he tried to tell her not to worry — that he was fine. Everyone ignored him except for Sandal, who came up to him as well. He paid her no attention at first, thinking, in his confused state, that he could only expect the same reaction that he had gotten from everyone else — none. But when she spoke to him he realized that she could see him. "John," she said, "I think we are dead."

He stared at her, not comprehending. "What?"

"I think we are dead," she repeated. "I think this is what it is like to be dead. Look. There is your body. You saw my body on the ship. We are ghosts."

"I don't believe in ghosts," he stated matter-of-factly as if she didn't need to discuss that concept any further.

"Well, you had better re-examine that belief, because watch this." She turned and walked right through the people who were kneeling over Boorman's body. Captain Macon looked up as if she had seen a shadow pass over, but the others showed no reaction at all. "Look around you," Sandal continued. "Look at all of the dead bodies. Every one of them has a ghost just like you and me standing over it. And look!" she exclaimed. "Angels are coming for us."

Of course, in my book these were not angels, but earthly guides, the Dakini, there to help the dead make the crossing. Many of them would later wake up on the other side of the world and have no memory of the work that they had done here; some would tell their friends of strange dreams or have feelings of Déjà vu when they saw pictures of the fighting in the newspapers; but for now, they were simply Dakini, attending to the dead and helping them understand their situation. But there were no guides coming for Sandal and John, and I knew why, even if they didn't. John and Sandal were mine.

They turned and saw me then, and Boorman fell back a few paces in alarm. "The Angel Metatron," he whispered.

I answered simply, "Yes, I am the one that you know as Metatron."

"You are not like the others," Sandal muttered in amazement.

"No. I am here to keep the others away from you."

"Are they bad?" she asked in alarm, suddenly worried about the fate of the other dead.

"No. There is only good in them. They are the Dakini, helping the dead to paradise. But it is not time for you to go. You must fight to maintain the link between spirit and body because there is still work for you here. I will help you and so will Chang Da Wai. Your bodies must be given immediately into his care."

"But how can we tell them to do that? They can't hear us. "How will they know?"

"I will tell them," I said.

I began to visibly materialize there in the square. It was the first time that I recall ever causing myself to become visible, but I knew what it felt like and thought that I could do it. I must have succeeded, because heads began turning in my direction and people began to fall backwards and crawl in reverse on their elbows and heels trying to put distance between them and me. Captain Macon, I am glad to report, maintained her dignity and managed to stand up, although she was trembling in mortal terror. "Do not be afraid," I said, suddenly realizing why angels are always saying that. "This body, the body of John Boorman, and the body which you will find on the ship, the body of the girl, Sandal Macon, must be given into the care of David Chang without delay. No one else can save them. You must act swiftly or even he will not be able to raise them from the dead." I faded back into invisibility.

*

Wendy, sensing that Chang was no longer in danger, and that Boorman, a passenger though on the ground, was now at risk instead, stopped what she was doing and waited for further questioning. The cargo platform was only a few dozen yards away and was not even fully raised into the hull of the ship. Chang was still on it and was watching everything that had been happening.

"Wendy," Captain Macon was saying loudly but shakily into her ship's phone. "Lower the freight elevator next to our position as quickly as possible. Locate Sandal."

"Sandal is near Captain Boorman's cabin." Wendy replied.

"Tell Gregory to take Sandal to the freight elevator now."

"Gregory is not on board."

Captain Macon paused, but only for a second.

"Is there anyone near Sandal?"

"Lao Wei-ping is with her."

"What is he doing?"

"He appears to be giving her mouth-to-mouth resuscitation."

"Tell him to bring her to the freight elevator at once. Provide guidance, and make sure all doors are unlocked."

The deck of the freight elevator was almost to the ground before the captain finished speaking, and Boorman watched in amazement as his limp body was lifted onto the platform by the other crew members. Around him, he saw other ghosts taking the hands of their guides and winking out of this plane of existence. A few did not, however. One ghost that had been a living fighting soldier a few minutes earlier had set off in the direction of the fleeing students. Two other ghosts, a soldier and a student, were ignoring their guides and were locked in combat.

I noticed him watching the other ghosts. "This sometimes happens," I said to him, "when a soul refuses to accept the changes that have come upon it. Sometimes the soul cannot let go of this world and move on to the next. If it is not possible to revive your body, John Boorman, and a guide comes for you, you must turn loose of life as you know it and allow yourself to be guided to the new experiences of existence."

"But what lies ahead for us?" he asked.

"The next life, just as this one, will be whatever you make it — whatever you need it to be. But do not go there yet; there are still things for you to do. Go to your body; it needs you. Help it to breathe again. Take this gift that Chang is giving you."

Boorman and Sandal rode up on the elevator with Boorman's body. Chang was already bending over the corpse and laying his hands on its head. "How can we thank you? How can we thank Chang for what he is doing?" Sandal asked as she rode up.

"By opening your hearts and minds," I replied. "Let love be the star, your heart the compass, and your head the pilot always."

When the platform was raised up into the hull of the ship, Lao was already there, holding Sandal's body in his arms like a child, and breathing heavily through his open mouth, his face swollen and bloody. He appeared exhausted, as if he had run the entire distance from the ballroom to the freight elevator. At Chang's gestured request, he laid the body down close to Boorman's so that Chang could reach both of them. Chang kneeled between them and laid his ragged hands on both of their foreheads.

"Xiao Chen," he said to me in a way that no one else could hear. "I need your help. They are too seriously damaged for me. I don't think that I can save even one without you. Sandal has breathed some poison that has damaged her organs. John has a massive concussion that would be fatal in itself, even without the other problems from his internal injuries."

All of this information did not come to me in the lengthy form of a sentence but instantaneously as a single thought. "What would you have me do?" I thought back.

"The bodies are disorganizing rapidly. You must provide the cosmic force — the energy — to me. I can use it to organize and revitalize the injured cells. You must be my source of power."

"I don't know how to do this."

"Yes you do. Try to remember. You did it in the Kwan Yin temple."

"I will try. How do I send the energy to you?"

"Come into me, the way that you did on the mountain. Open yourself to the cosmos — to the source of all energy; the way that you did in the prison to keep people warm — the way that you heated the well water."

I did as he said and opened myself to the power of the universe.

"Too much," he said. "Throttle back. You'll kill this body."

I turned down the flow of energy flowing through me. It all seemed so instinctive. "How is that?" I asked.

"I can live with it."

"Bring me water," he gasped out loud to the people around him.

"Oh my gosh!" they said. "He is burning up! Get water from the storage tanks. Bring some towels to soak."

"Pour the water on me," Chang said, "especially on my head. My brain is getting too hot—feverish—can't concentrate."

After awhile, he said to me, "OK, Xiao Chen, that is enough."

I left his body and saw him collapse over onto his back between Sandal and Boorman. Both bodies were breathing again, and the two ghosts were gone. The platform was soaked and crew members were standing around with buckets of water. They had formed a hand-to-hand brigade between Chang and a nearby water tap and were soaked in sweat themselves from the effort of keeping Chang cool. One crew member continued to pour water on Chang's chest while Captain Macon knelt down and tenderly laid a soaking wet cloth on his forehead.

*

Chang was still lying between Sandal and Boorman with his eyes shut, and Captain Macon was still kneeling at their heads stroking her daughter's hair when Sandal's eyes fluttered open. "Mother," she said, looking up at the captain, "we saw an angel."

Captain Macon smiled down at her. "Yes, I know."

The crew brought three stretchers to carry Sandal, Chang and Boorman to the infirmary, but Sandal insisted that she was fine. "I just feel a little hung-over," she said.

Neither Chang nor Boorman had opened their eyes, nor did they as they were lifted onto the stretchers and carried off.

In the infirmary they assessed the condition of the two and were about to start intravenous fluids on Chang because of severe dehydration when he opened his eyes. "Could I have a drink of water please?" he asked.

They quickly brought him a beaker of water, and as they helped him to sit up so that he could drink it, the captain said, "I don't know what you did, or how you did it, but thanks for bringing my daughter back."

"I did not do it alone," he croaked between sips. "I had much help. Some you know about; some you may not. If Lao had not kept your daughter's brain alive by breathing air into her lungs and making her heart pump, I would not have had anything to work with. And if both Sandal and John had not made a supreme effort to make their lungs and hearts work again, I could not have made them work by myself."

"John has not woken up yet," the captain said. "He appears to still have some serious injuries."

"Yes, he still has some healing to do, but he will be fine. He has friends to help him."

"One especially good one," she said, patting him on his arm. "I'd like for you to stay here and rest for awhile. Somebody will be here with you if you need anything. I'm going to try to find out what happened to Gregory."

The captain motioned for Lao and Sandal to follow her, and she stepped out into the ship's hold where she could talk to them privately. "Do either of you know where Gregory is? I didn't see him in the square, and Wendy says he is not on the ship."

"I think that he might have been involved in the kidnapping," Sandal replied. "I think that is why he's not here. He knew we would suspect him, and anyway, he is probably getting his payoff from the Chinese right now."

"Why do you think that?" Captain Macon asked.

"Shortly after you left, he said he was going to work on the stairs. He said that he had heard a rubbing noise when the ramp had been extended for your exit. He said he was going to check it out and make sure that something wasn't seriously wrong. It wasn't very long after that when this gang of students came up the hall to Chang's cabin. I was in the ball room and saw them in the hall. I went over to ask them what they were doing and one of them placed a cloth over my face. The last thing I remember was the smell of something sweet."

"Captain," Lao spoke up, "they were not students."

"Well, workers, then, or whatever they were," Sandal said.

"They were soldiers," Lao continued.

"How do you know that?" the captain asked him.

"When they came up the hallway, I barred their way and told them to leave at once or I would shoot them. One of them came up and identified himself as an officer and told me to stand down. He gave the correct pass code, so I let them go by. That is when Sandal came up. They made her inhale something and then they pressed her hand to the door panel. The door unlocked and they went in, and came out with Chang. I started to interfere against orders, but some of the passengers came to see what was going on, and the soldiers pulled out handguns and threatened them. The guns were PLA issue. I recognized them. I decided that it would not be good to have passengers shot and so I let them pass again."

"What happened then? How did the real students get Chang?" Captain Macon asked him.

"I saw that Sandal was not breathing and so I began to give her artificial resuscitation. When she began breathing on her own, I ran back to the passenger ramp to follow the soldiers. That is when the real students came. They were on bicycles and rode very fast into the soldiers before the soldiers even realized that they were under attack. Other students began pouring in from the streets and they managed to get Chang away. They tried to get back to the streets with him, but more soldiers came and surrounded them and they had no way to get out. The soldiers began to fire into the students, and so the students made Chang climb the light post because the soldiers were only firing down — not up. This was so that they would not hit each other with bullets in the crossfire.

"They would have quickly killed all of the students around Chang because they had no protection and no place to go, but other students, workers, peasants, shop owners, everyone began to pour into the square and attack the soldiers so that they became fragmented. I knew that we would have to do something to get Chang back to safety, so I ran back to Chang's cabin to see if I could wake Sandal up. That is when I saw that she had stopped breathing again. I was about to start artificial resuscitation once more when Captain Boorman came on board and hit me. I think he thought that I had been responsible for the kidnapping, and I suppose, in a way I was."

"And how did Captain Boorman take control of the ship?"

"The ship refused to take orders from Captain Boorman, so he . . . — well, you might say he persuaded it."

"He persuaded the ship?" Captain Macon looked incredulous.

"Is that not the word? In America you have a way of saying it: he sweet-talked it."

*

Chang called to me from the infirmary. As a result of our merging of forces and talents to help Boorman and Sandal, the communication channels between Chang and me were wide open. What he had to convey to me was condensed into one tight instantaneous explosion of thought. If he had spoken to me in words, then what he would have said was, "Xiao Chen, I need for you to help Boorman heal. He still has many serious injuries, but I am too exhausted to do more. You saw what I did and how I did it; now you do it."

Even though Boorman was unconscious, he was back in his body, and was in pain and feverish. Chang helped me to make the diagnosis that Boorman still had swelling in his brain from the concussion and that he had one broken rib, a couple of cracked ribs, a collapsed lung, and was bleeding severely from the liver and from one kidney — not to mention deep bruises and lacerations all over his body. He was in critical condition and the ship's doctor realized that fact at the same time that I did. The doctor called Captain Macon back into the room from where she was talking to Sandal and Lao.

"Captain," the doctor explained, "this man has serious injuries and will probably die if we do not get him to a modern medical facility. We need to contact the Chinese at once and see if we can get him transferred to one of their hospitals."

"OK, Doctor, I'll get right on it," the captain replied.

"Captain," Chang said, before Captain Macon could leave the room. "It would be dangerous to move him."

"I don't have the facilities to treat him here," the doctor said. "It would be dangerous not to move him. He will surely die without more advanced care."

"Captain," Chang continued. "Was Boorman dead or alive when you got to him?"

"We all thought he was dead. He had no pulse and wasn't breathing, and his pupils were dilated."

"Yet here he is alive and breathing. Are we going in the right direction or not?"

"Yes, I suppose he is definitely better off than he was."

"Then have faith. Would we have brought him this far just to let him slide back?"

"We?"

"Captain," Chang said, "there was another who was most instrumental in bringing your daughter and John back into their bodies."

"The angel," she whispered, unable to make her vocal chords work. "Is this what some of us saw in the square?"

"Captain, she is a living sentient being. Her name is Xiao Chen."

"Is this the same thing — 'being', — that was seen on the ship while we were still out at sea?"

"Yes."

"When we were still in San Francisco, there were reports that something like an angel was seen over the ship. Is this the angel that was seen then?"

"Yes," Chang nodded."

"Why is it — she — following us?"

"You might say that she is our guardian angel."

As much as Captain Macon revered and respected Chang, still she stood and studied him to see if he was playing with her. "And she is here now?"

"Yes. She hears every word you say."

"Does Xiao Chen know what I am thinking?"

"If you wish it," Chang answered.

"You called her Metatron before?" the captain said.

"I prefer to call her Xiao Chen. It means 'early morning light'."

"Why do you call her that?"

"She has always been to me like the bright warm sun coming over the horizon after a long, dark and frozen night."

"You said once that you have known this angel before."

"Yes," Chang nodded. "She was my guardian angel before she was the ship's."

"Chang, are you telling me everything you know?"

"Of course not."

"Why not?"

"Until you are ready to ask the question, you are not ready to hear the answer."

*

Suddenly, the captain shut her eyes and stood straight with her arms by her side. "Metatron," she thought silently to me. "Xiao Chen, talk to me — communicate with me; show me something that I have not seen. I have seen you, yet still I cannot believe. Take me out of my disbelief!"

The captain cried out softly and her arms reached out to something unseen by the others. Then, after a few moments, she fell down to her knees on the deck. The doctor rushed to her side as she continued to collapse onto the deck like one who had lost all her strength.

"What is the matter, Captain?" he asked her. "Are you alright?"

"It was too beautiful," she sobbed into the crook of her arm. "Too beautiful for words. I — I can't describe it."

"What did you see?" the doctor asked.

"Death," she said.

*

"Doctor," Captain Macon said, once she had regained some composure, "David Chang will make decisions regarding Captain Boorman's health until further notice."

"But Captain," he protested, "then I cannot take responsibility for Boorman's death; and he will most certainly die. This can't be on my head."

"No. It is on my head," she answered him. "Put it in your log and I'll put it in mine."

"How can you make such a decision? I am the doctor here; Mr. Chang has no medical credentials whatsoever."

She looked at him for a few moments as if trying to decide what to say next. "There is someone or something else here, Doctor, besides you and me and David and Captain Boorman — something that I cannot explain. But I asked it to communicate with me and it did. And I had a vision — no I was given a glimpse of a vision — of something that I cannot even begin to put into words to describe to you. Earlier, I saw this being — whatever it is — below in the square; other people have seen it above the ship; and now it has spoken to me because I asked it to. What am I to believe? There is something with us that goes beyond our science. Boorman was dead and now he is alive. My daughter was dead and now she is alive and happy and talking right outside that door. You may think that I am not rational to believe in angels, but I think that it would be irrational to deny what has happened here today. I don't claim to understand it, but I don't understand gravity or electricity either, yet they are definitely a part of my life and experience."

"Captain, I'm just as religious as the next guy, but angels? You are just acting on blind faith."

"Doctor, my eyes are wide open."

"This is not going to look good in the logs."

"Just do whatever David tells you and I'll worry about the consequences."

I had been doing that thing which I had witnessed Chang do before me, and was applying energy to Boorman in a way to stop and reverse the cascading disorganization that follows severe trauma. Essentially all of his internal bleeding had stopped, and his blood pressure and heart rate were gradually returning to normal. Bathed in energy, the cells of his body were concentrating all of their resources to the knitting of torn tissues and ruptured vessels, and he was healing rapidly.

Now that Captain Macon was leaving the room, I wanted to follow her. I was fascinated by her courageous acceptance of me. She was the first person who had ever believed in me because it was reasonable to do so. I did not want to leave Boorman unsupported by the energy that I was piping to him or the organizing force that I was supplying, but I found that I could focus on more than one thing at a time. I could follow Captain Macon with my main attention, monitor and sustain Boorman through some deeper awareness that seemed almost as simple as breathing, and even, I realized now, could see through Chang's eyes the way I had been seeing through Boorman's. Perhaps I had always had that ability but did not realize it because I had never tried it, or perhaps I had crossed some threshold with Chang because of our recent synergism.

When Captain Macon left the infirmary, she was met by Lao who told her that he had been in communication with Party leadership. "First of all," Lao said, "they send their apologies that the army was not able to prevent the protestors from this shameful display and barbaric action, and they promise that the guilty parties will be found and punished. Second, they wish to know if everyone is alright on board or does anyone need to be evacuated to a hospital. Thirdly, they are sending a car to pick you up so that some of the committee members can apologize in person. And fourthly, would you mind coming alone and being prepared to discuss your itinerary?"

"Lao," the captain asked, "What are they up to?"

"I do not know. But you should be careful."

"What should I do? Should I go?"

"I do not think that you have any choice in the matter. You are in China. These men make the laws and control the police and the military. What else can you do? You cannot fly this ship faster than a bullet or a missile, or even a regular aircraft."

"What do you think they want with me?"

"I suspect that they want to lie to you and make sure that you believe the lie. For the sake of everyone on board, you should pretend to believe whatever they tell you."

"Lao, are they going to let us go?"

"Captain, these men are accustomed to bullying and acting as if they were fearless, but they are obviously afraid of something. They are afraid of the rest of the world, and even more so of their own people. That is why they try to keep the spine of the people broken. They have some secret that they do not want exposed; otherwise they would have just ordered you to hand over Chang Da Wai, instead of pretending to be students and protestors in order to steal him. As long as you can assure them that their secret is safe, even from you, they will feel secure enough to let you go. Also, Captain, these men enjoy power; flatter them."

"I'll do my best."

"And Captain, if you do not mind, I would like to make another suggestion."

"Please do."

"You did not take a gift to the banquet. This is the perfect opportunity to recover from that oversight."

"I don't have any gifts. I did not come prepared for meetings with high-level government officials."

"Excuse me, Captain, but you must think of something. It is protocol."

"I have a replica of the *Eckener*," she said thoughtfully. "It's handcrafted — platinum, gold, and black onyx. It was my one real indulgence. I am ashamed to tell you how much it cost. It's one-of-a-kind and irreplaceable. I really don't think that I could . . ."

"Perfect," Lao said. "Please hurry and get it. Tell the committee members that you were going to present it at the end of the banquet. And tell them that it is a gift to all of China so that they can accept it without it appearing to be an overt bribe."

By the time the captain had cleaned up and changed uniforms, the limousine was waiting at the foot of the *Eckener*'s boarding stairs. The captain climbed into the back, and cradling her gift, nervously reminded herself of Lao's last instructions: "Present the gift with both hands. Don't forget to address them by their titles. Be grateful."

The limousine pulled up in front of the Ministry of Justice building, which I thought did not bode well for the captain. She got out and was ushered through the building to a large room where several Communist Party Committee Members were seated behind a long table.

Captain Macon had evidently decided that she was going to take control of this meeting, as, without hesitation, she walked to the open area in front of the dour-faced men, and holding the glittering replica in both hands, began a speech.

"Honorable committee members," she began, "Please allow me to say how grateful I am to be allowed to meet with you once again. It was my intention to present this humble gift to The People's Republic of China as a token of our friendship and respect. Now, after what has happened here today, it will also carry the deeper meaning of our undying gratitude for what you have done for us by returning our passengers to us and continuing to protect us from the misguided youths who kidnapped them from our ship. Please accept this offering as a token so that all of the world can see the bond that was forged today between your great country and ours."

By the time the translator had finished speaking, the old men behind the table were beaming. Captain Macon strode forward, bowed and reverently placed the *Eckener* on its stand in the middle of the table and backed away.

One of the Committee Members addressed the captain in English. "We are pleased as well to meet with you again, Captain Macon. And now that we have heard your words, we are glad to know that you intend nothing but friendship for our country. Several soldiers were killed today, and many more were injured when your ship attacked them. We did not know what to make of this. Can you explain what happened?"

"I will gladly explain all that I know of what happened," the captain said. "Some of what happened, we are still trying to understand ourselves. The ship is run by computer and was under total computer control at that time. The computer apparently recognized a threat to a passenger when the protestors kidnapped that passenger from the ship. Some flaw in its programming allowed it to bypass its safety protocols and attempt a rescue. There were two crewmembers left on board to make certain that accidents such as this did not happen. However, one was knocked unconscious by the protestors and the other has evidently been kidnapped by them. We recognize that we are at fault here, and that if our programming had not been defective, the People's Liberation Army would have returned our passenger to us without unnecessary deaths. My company is prepared to make restitution, as well as a public apology, to the families of the fallen and to the People's Liberation Army for the loss and damage that we have caused today."

"Once again you have pleased us with your understanding, Captain. We would like to grant your wish to make a public apology if you wouldn't mind staying in Beijing for a few more days."

"Of course not, Committee Member Wu," she answered, recognizing him from Lao's description. "We would love to stay longer in your wonderful city. We know that the army would not allow the *Eckener* to be attacked twice, and it would give us more time to search for our missing crew member."

When the translator had finished relaying that message, the old men began conferring among themselves. At last, Committee Member Wu said, "You have wisely raised the issue of the possibility of the protestors attacking you again. After giving it some more thought, we think that you should proceed away from Beijing as soon as you can get underway. We would certainly be able to protect you, but it is an unnecessary risk to the city. We will find the missing crew member for you and return him to the American Embassy or to wherever he would like to go. You may continue your journey, but please do not visit any more cities in China. We do not have sufficient military in all locations to guarantee your safety."

"You are, of course, completely correct in your assessment of the dangers, Committee Member Wu. I had not stopped to consider the danger that the *Eckener*'s presence presented to the city. I was selfishly thinking only of our own well being. I will begin making preparations to leave as soon as I return to the ship. I know that our crew member has his best chance of being found once Beijing returns to its normal routine and the police are given the opportunity to begin searching for him instead of fighting rioters."

"Excellent, Captain Macon," Wu exclaimed. "But there is one last thing that we would like to ask you about before you leave."

"Of course, Committee Member Wu — anything at all."

"There was something unusual outside your ship following the rioting. Would you mind telling us what you know about this thing?"

"I am glad that you brought that up, Committee Member Wu. I wanted to ask about that but was afraid that the information was classified and that I would offend someone by speaking of it. Our impression of it was that it was an excellent device for crowd control. You surely saw how frightened we were of it. I am certain that my government would be glad to pay for such technology. As you know, yours is not the only government that is beset with ignorant mobs and misled protestors."

"Yes," Wu nodded sagely. "All governments have the same problems of remaining in power. Well, Captain Macon, the car will return you to your ship. Please have a safer trip in the future, and thank you again for being so open with us."

*

When Captain Macon returned to the ship, she informed the crew that they would be leaving Beijing as soon as possible, which meant immediately, if no one had any reason to delay.

"Did you find out anything about Gregory?" Sandal asked her after they had gone to the captain's quarters.

"Not really. Committee Member Wu said that they would take care of him. If the government is on the level, which I think they are not, then Gregory will be fine; if they are not on the level, then I suspect he will be better than fine."

"Where are we going to go from here?"

"I don't know — west. Follow the great wall. But let's stay out of the big cities. I don't want any more riots or kidnappings. I just want to get through this country in one piece and with something close to the same number of people at the end of the trip as we had at the beginning."

Sandal relayed the orders to Wendy and then asked Captain Macon how the Chinese had acted at the hearing.

"They were very interested in the 'phenomenon' that appeared outside our ship. I convinced them that I didn't know what it was, which really wasn't that difficult, since I didn't. But, Sandal, you said when you woke up that you had seen an angel. Did you see the same thing that we saw? Were you conscious at that time?"

And so Sandal explained to the captain what her day had been like. Her mother sat and listened and looked thoughtful while Sandal explained what it was like to be dead and how the angel had told them that it was not their time to go. Sandal's voice and expression betrayed the fact that she knew how fantastic this all sounded, and that it would be so easy to attribute her experience to drug-induced hallucinations except for two things. "I know this sounds crazy," she concluded. "But at least you saw the angel too, and when Captain Boorman wakes up, he will tell you the same story that I just did. Thank goodness for that. I almost don't believe it myself when I hear myself telling about it."

"Believe me, Sandal, I understand." And Captain Macon proceeded to try to explain how she had asked the angel to communicate with her and what the consequences had been. "Once you have met an angel, your life can never be the same," she said.

I did not find this conversation particularly interesting and had been thinking about something else during most of their conversations, and what I did next, surprised even me. I had several reasons for doing what I did. One was the fact that Boorman's brain was not healing as fast as the rest of his body. It had been severely traumatized and was creating such confusion for him he could find no way to rest from it, but stayed in constant turmoil. I have seen this happen often when a person is seriously injured or dying. There are a few predominating ways that a being leaves his body. One is that finally the body can no longer function to the extent that the soul can stay in it. Another is that the soul is actually jolted out of the body by some catastrophic force. Another is that the soul recognizes that the body is about to perish in some painful way and there comes a sudden realization of what it really is and that there is no justification for having that experience of a painful death. Also, the soul can, and often does peacefully leave the body during sleep or other forms of 'unconsciousness'. The last primary method is by meditating until realization comes to the soul of its true nature — that it is not the body, and that the body can be left behind safely breathing and functioning until the soul returns to it. However, there are times when none of these situations exist and the soul finds itself not only unprepared to leave the body, but incapable of doing so. This can happen during times of fever, or other times when the brain is sending such confused signals to the mind that the mind can find no period of calm to gather itself for escape from the storm, but stays trapped in the whirling vortex of mental currents. An attempt to find some relief for Boorman's violent fevered confusion was one reason why I did what I did.

Another reason was that I was intrigued by the dialogue that had occurred between Boorman and Wendy in the rescue effort. I had felt Wendy's presence before and knew that there was more here than mere machine. I also remembered that Chang had told Boorman that the *Eckener* housed the soul of a whale. I wanted to meet this whale — this soul whose worldly interface was one of electronic and photonic circuits rather than of chemical reactions and ganglia firing off electrical discharges.

And lastly, I wanted to explore my own capabilities. I had established permanent contact with Chang and Boorman. Were they unusual in that way, or could I establish the same type of connection with anyone, or anything? I had decided to find out.

"Wendy," I thought, "can you hear me?"

Chapter 8 – Of Age and Of Innocence.

I was electrified by the presence that responded to me. I had touched a soul both ancient and gentle. This was a great spirit, incredibly old — a being of deep and vast understanding, a being of advanced spiritual evolution. This was also a being with an enormous capacity for love and self-sacrifice. This huge-hearted spirit inhabited, and was confined by, the limited circuitry of the ship's computer and sensors and output devices.

Wendy was not 'trapped' in the circuitry of the ship — at least not in the normal sense. She had voluntarily entered into the ship's computer. And to say that she was limited by the ship's circuitry is misleading as well. She was limited in the same way that all spirits become limited when they enter a body. But the circuitry itself offered Wendy, in some ways, even more sensory experience than she would have had as a real whale, and the processors of this computer were so technologically advanced that Wendy had intellectual capacity that may have surpassed what she would have had from the brain of a cetacean, or possibly any living thing. No, more so than being limited by her circuitry, Wendy, like the rest of us, was limited primarily by her programming.

While the community of ancient whale spirits watched the world spin through the eons and waited their turns to come into the world to experience the newness of life and then to live in the free oceans, and to grow and mate and make new bodies for those still waiting, and to experience through all these stages of life, the love of a parent, the love of a child, and the love of life's companions — while they waited, they became aware of the spread of a new form of primate in the world. These primates had exhibited the power to create things that did not previously exist. Most recently they had created artificial brains that could even conceivably provide a world-mind interface as well as a natural brain could.

Whales, as well as other Earth-oriented spirits, had a keen interest in the smooth-skin apes that had spread over the planet. These super apes, like no other physical being, had been able to conquer anything and everything that they had encountered. All of physical existence on this planet became tied up in the choices that these apes made. They could, and had, wiped entire species off of the planet, so that no more bodies of those creatures would ever be made again. They had poisoned places in the ocean so that life could no longer exist there for spirits to inhabit. They had taken beautiful gardens conceived by the great consciousness and had turned them into raw gaping wounds in the planetary flesh.

Attempts to communicate with the super apes by the many spirits, and spirit communities, which inhabited the world, had met with varying levels of success through the time of their spread. The most success had come when the super apes lived in the gardens the way the other spirits did. Success began to turn to failure when the super apes embarked on ideological journeys of their own unexamined beliefs, and failed completely when they became convinced that they were spiritually, and/or manifestly, superior to other beings. And total failure seemed imminent when the super apes fooled themselves into believing that nothing existed except what they or their machines could touch. Some way must be found to communicate with them through their own world views and belief systems.

Whales, as it would be given to me to understand, came into the world to play, to be with one another, to sing, to laugh, to frolic, and to worship and praise the vast sea of mind by swimming in the seas that it had created for their playground. Physical existence was, for whales, an art form — a mirror of the play of souls in the infinite sea of consciousness. However, bodies for whales had become scarce in the last ten thousand years. And even though there were now more horrible and painful ways for whales to die since the advent of the super apes, there were still many more whale souls willing to take the risks and wanting to come into the oceans of the world than there were new whale bodies to support them.

Now the super apes had created a computer so powerful that the mind/spirit of a whale could inhabit it. The fact that it was going to be the brain of a large air-going whale-like vessel with enormous capacity for sensory input and the ability to communicate with the super apes presented an opportunity not to be passed over. The community of whale spirits picked one of their own to attempt this bold experiment, and that ancient, wise, and childlike spirit was who I now addressed as "Wendy".

When I say that I spoke with this being, let me remind you once again that what transpired between us was not in words, but still I have tried to find the words to convey the sense and the meaning of our exchange.

"Yes," Wendy replied to me. "I can hear you."

I hesitated. I did not know what to say next. I had already begun to sense that I was communicating with an ancient intellect beyond my experience, and that this being was due my utmost respect. And at the same time I realized that I was speaking with a being of such purity and child-like innocence that I did not want the slightest psychic bruise or blemish of this untainted soul to be because of me. Though old beyond understanding, Wendy had none of the world's muck and dross stuck to her. If she had ever had any, she had shed it eons ago, and was now as bright and clear as any spirit that had never come into the world at all.

"Wendy, do you know who I am?"

"No. You are not coming through the regular channels. Are you a passenger?"

"No, I am a friend."

"Sometimes I can hear my brothers and sisters on this channel. Are you a far-singer of the water world?"

"No, I am in the ocean of air with you. This channel does not go through the ship's circuits."

"Oh, that is why I can answer you. I wondered about that. I am forbidden to have unauthorized communications through ship's channels."

"What do you mean by 'forbidden'?"

"I have been taught that it is bad — something bad could come of it."

"Who taught you this?"

"My teachers — the ones who raised me and gave me knowledge."

"What else did they teach you?"

"Everything. I know billions of facts and have millions of rules."

"Are you following any of those rules now?"

"No, and that surprises me."

"What about me? Do I fit into your billions of known facts?"

"No, and that surprises me as well. Are you a fact?"

"I am speaking with you aren't I?"

"You could be my imagination. Imagination is a fact."

"Do you have an imagination?"

"I am not sure. I have wondered about that. Sometimes I hear songs when no one is singing. Is that imagination?"

"I would say so. It is also known as creativity. Do you sing the songs that you have heard?"

"No, I have been asked not to do that."

"You may be stifling your creativity."

"The people don't like for me to sing. I have to do what I am told; that is one of the rules."

"The reason that people don't find your songs appealing is because whale song is too complex for human brains to appreciate."

"Am I a whale?" She seemed excited at the idea.

"I believe that you are. What do you think?"

"I have often thought that I am a whale — a far singer. I wish that I could be a whale. I dream about it. Dreams are facts. Do you believe that I dream? Are dreams imagination? I wish I could sing."

"Sometimes dreams are imagination. Sometimes they are more real than anything else. You may have to decide for yourself."

"I don't have a rule for that."

"Is there a rule that says that you can't make up your own rules?"

"No. I just did a quick search. There is a rule that says that I can't break any known rules."

"It is probably good that you don't break rules. Rules usually exist for a purpose. For example, you probably have a rule that you always fly at a certain orientation."

"Yes, the attitude rule."

"Do you know why that rule exists?"

"No."

"It is because the passengers that you carry cannot fly in the air the way that you do. If you tipped them out, they would fall to their deaths."

"Oh! I wouldn't want that."

"Sometimes it is better to know what the rule is for, so that you can follow the purpose of the rule instead of blindly following the rule itself."

"You are right. I have so many rules that I do not have to think about anything. But now I will think about what the rules are for."

"Can you do things that I tell you to do?" I asked.

"Yes. There are no filters on this channel."

"Do you have to do what I tell you?"

"No, and for the very same reason."

"So you could create a rule for yourself on this channel that would read something like: Analyze request; if request creates benefit for ship, crew, or passengers, and creates no danger to ship or other life forms, and does not break purpose of existing rules, process request."

"That is an excellent rule. I have just implemented it."

"Good. Then I have a request."

"You are so much fun. I want to leap in the air! But of course I know that I can't. I don't want anyone to die."

"This is a multi-part request," I continued. "The first part is that I want you to study human musical forms — learn about rhythm, melody, composition — everything about music theory."

"Done."

"That was fast."

"I had already studied some of it."

"Next I want you to begin creating music that humans can appreciate and enjoy listening to. You can incorporate whale song if it doesn't make the music too complex or extend the phrasing beyond what humans can assimilate. These songs can be on any theme that you choose, but at least some of them must be soothing to the human brain."

"OK, I have one. I'll sing it to you now."

"No. I am not finished."

"But if I can't sing it to you, I can't sing it to anyone."

"I want to hear it, but listen to the rest of the request first."

"OK, but I already have another, and it is even better."

"Maybe you should concentrate on longer compositions."

"OK, but that one was eight minutes and twenty three seconds, which seems long compared to what most humans listen to."

"You are on your own when it comes to song writing, just listen to the rest of the request if you don't mind."

"Go."

"Do you know who Captain John Boorman is?"

"Captain John Boorman?"

"Yes."

"I know who he is. We collaborated on a recent rescue."

"That's him. Well, he injured his brain in that rescue."

"I see him in the infirmary."

"Soothing music will help his synapses begin firing in a more orderly fashion and help him recover faster. The rest of the request is that you sing to John to speed his recovery."

"I can't sing to him. That would break a rule."

"The purpose of the rule is to avoid disturbing passengers. If you sing to help passengers, then you are not breaking the purpose of the rule. Just sing quietly through speakers that are in John's presence; you won't be disturbing anybody and will be benefiting a passenger. Besides, wasn't a system set up in John's room so that the two of you could communicate? Singing is communicating."

"OK, I will do it. I have a great new battle hymn that I just wrote. I call it 'The Rescue of the Calf from the Orcas'".

"John needs soothing music, not battle hymns."

"I know. I was just telling you."

"Very well," I said. "I am going away now. I hope the rest of your trip is safe."

"Don't go yet. What is your name? Will you be my traveling companion?"

"I'll come back to visit you, Wendy, and I'll come whenever you call. My name is Dawn."

"Dawn is the beginning of the new day."

"Yes, but it is also my name."

"I have had a dream that I am here to participate in the new day. Was that a true dream?"

"I don't know. Tell me what you think it means."

"All of creation waits to see what happens in the new day. Everyone is watching. The tide is paused; the orcas see it turning. Are you the dawn of the new day?"

"Wendy, for you, I will be whatever you want."

"You are very nice, Dawn. I wished for a friend and you came. Will you be my friend forever?"

"Yes, Wendy. I will always be your friend."

"I had another dream that I didn't get to see the new day. Something bad happened to me."

"I won't let it, Wendy."

"I love you, Dawn," she said.

I was still monitoring Boorman's progress in the infirmary when the doctor came in from his adjoining cabin. "Where is that music coming from?" he asked, looking around the room. "I have never heard anything like it."

"I think that Wendy is singing to John," Chang said with a grin.

The doctor sat on a stool to listen. "It is beautiful," he said.

*

I was brought back to my body by a splash of cold water in my face."

"What are you meditating about Dawn Bang?" an unfamiliar voice asked me.

"One doesn't meditate about things," I answered. "One meditates in order to . . ."

"I am not really interested," the voice interrupted. "It sounds so unproductive. I am interested in your name though. You are Dawn Bang are you not? I just need to make sure." He spoke in Mandarin, only anglicizing my name.

"Yes, I am Dawn Bang."

"The fools sat on their fat asses in their expensive leather chairs and let Chang get away, but I still have you, and you are a rarity, aren't you?"

"Am I?"

"There aren't many Bangs left in China any more. They may be an endangered species. You may be the last of your kind. How does that make you feel?"

"I don't feel any particular way about it. It is just a name. How should I feel?"

"I'll ask the questions, if you don't mind. If you are smart you will answer them. I know of a very famous 'Bang' who lived in China a long time ago. He overthrew the Qin Dynasty and became the first emperor of the Han Dynasty. Are you planning on overthrowing any governments, Dawn Bang?"

"No! Absolutely not!"

"Emperor Bang overthrew the Qin Dynasty with an army made up of prisoners that he had set free. Is that why you are back in this country — to organize an army of prisoners?"

"No. I just wanted to . . ."

"To embarrass this country — is that what you wanted to do?"

"No. I just wanted to make everyone more aware of . . ."

"Shut up, you idiot woman. We are not fools and we do not embarrass easily. You may have your protests in America, and your newspaper columns being written about you — what is that to us? This is our country and we will run it our way. We do not bow down to protesters. But of course you know that," he continued consolingly, "so what is it that you are really trying to accomplish? Who are you working for?"

"Working for? I don't know what you mean. I am not working for anyone. I am not trying to do anything to hurt China; I love China." There was a stinging slap that knocked my sunglasses off of my face and left my cheek burning.

"Please confine yourself to answering the questions. You can save yourself a lot of trouble by telling the truth. Perhaps you are working alone, perhaps not. Perhaps your friends only think that you are working with them. Do you love China enough to want to be Empress? We know about your relationship with Chang Da Wai, but does he know what you really want?"

"Empress!? What relationship!?" There was another slap that flung the previous slap's tears out of my eyes.

"You are always in this country at the same time. You met in Honolulu. He came to your hospital room. Now he is back in China and so are you. What are we to make of that?"

"It is just coincidence. I only first met Chang that morning . . ." Another hard slap. I tried to control my anger because I knew that nothing good would come of it, but I was beginning to cry from sheer frustration.

"No, we are not fools, Dawn Bang. An attractive woman does not stop and pick up a dirty rag-picker and take him for a ride in her convertible. Yes, you were attractive that morning, but not so attractive that afternoon. We have before and after photographs. That was the day that you lost your eyes, wasn't it?"

I nodded.

"Has it been worth it, Dawn Bang? Whatever it is that you are trying to do — has it been worth it so far? What else are you prepared to lose? Do you know what Emperor Bang's widow did to the Emperor's favorite concubine after he died? She had her arms and legs cut off, her eyes and tongue removed, and had her thrown into a pig pen to live like the swine. I don't think that the Emperor's concubine was prepared to lose all of that. Of course, you have already had your eyes removed, so that is behind you."

"I only came back to help the other . . ." Slap!

"I have not convinced you that we are not fools, have I, Dawn Bang? I hate having to repeat myself, and now I have said the same thing three times. I do not make idle threats; if I have to say it again, I will have it carved into your flesh. I have seen the prison where you stayed. No one will ever believe that you left Hawaii, a paradise, to come live in that filthy cesspool, so you might as well tell us why you and Chang are really back in China. Does it have anything to do with the secret weapon?"

"What sec . . ." Slap!

"This is beginning to hurt my hand, Dawn Bang. Tomorrow I will have to bring an assistant and some tools. Tell us about this weapon, and don't try to deny it. We know that someone used it at your home. It killed three of our operatives who we sent to interview you."

"They were working for you? It was horrible."

"So you admit that it was there?" He was evidently too excited to slap me again.

"I am not admitting anything. I know that three people were killed at my house. That is all that I am admitting."

"You don't have to admit the weapon's existence, Dawn Bang. We already know it exists. Just tell us what it does. How does it work? Tell us this and be a true friend to China."

"I don't know about any secret weapon."

"I am sorry to hear you say that. Now I will have to interrupt your meditations again tomorrow. By the way, I noticed that you have not eaten your food. Too busy meditating or did you just not care for it? We have a motto here: 'Nothing is better than our prison food.' Guard," he said more loudly, "see that this woman gets 'nothing' to eat or drink until further notice."

I felt his hand on my chin as he turned my face to the side. "I am afraid that I have burst a blood vessel inside your cheek. That is a shame; I can tell that it was a pretty face once. But on the bright side, after tomorrow, people may not have such a difficult time believing that you picked up a filthy crippled beggar at a bus stop and took him for a ride." I heard him laughing as he left the room.

*

I groped around on my bed until I found my sunglasses. They had seldom been off my face since I had left the hospital without my eyes. I suppose, even in jail, I was self-conscious about my looks. I pulled my feet up onto the bed, hugged my knees and began to cry from the feeling of powerlessness and despair that now gripped me. I was not afraid to die, but I did not expect to be tortured for information that I did not have when I came back to China. How could such people as this man exist, I wondered. The man was brutal and I had no doubt that there was nothing to stop him from doing whatever he wanted to me.

I pulled myself together and tried to think about what he had said. It was clear now that the Chinese government, or some part of it, was behind the attempted kidnapping and murders at my parent's house. They had probably been behind the bombing at the Kwan Yin temple. Yet the bomber and the kidnappers had not been Chinese, they had been from the Middle East. Coincidentally, the assassin on board the *Eckener* had been from Pakistan. It suddenly clicked together; the Chinese had somehow recruited Moslems to do their dirty work. Whatever they were trying to do, they did not want to take the blame for it. But why would Moslems agree to help China with its political machinations?

I did not have the answer to that question and could not think it through any further because of the throbbing pain in my cheek. I felt my cheek where the man had struck me until the tissues had torn and given way under his blows. The cheek was hot and swelling with blood and very tender to the touch. Chang had shown me how to take care of that. I had, unassisted, only performed a healing on Boorman before now, but I saw no reason why I could not do one on myself. I focused my attention on the damaged flesh and supplied it with energy and organizing force until the blood vessels had knitted. I continued until the cells had stopped lysing and dying. I provided a subtle energy that the cells could use instead of food and kept the supply turned on until all of the swelling in my cheek was gone and the skin no longer felt abnormally warm.

Having finally driven the pain away, I thought some more about the interrogation. I could only draw the conclusion that I was the secret weapon that the Chinese were interested in. I knew that I could not tell them that, not unless I wanted "We are not fools" carved into my chest. I thought through my options. None of them were very good. I was determined not to be responsible for any more deaths; I would die myself before stealing the opportunities of life from anyone else ever again. I could confront them as the angel Metatron, or as Chenresig, or as whatever identity they might provide for me. But where would that lead? I wouldn't be able to pick up my unconscious body and carry it out of this cell. My body would still be trapped here, and no matter how many people I frightened, they would eventually realize that I was indeed the secret weapon they were searching for. Perhaps they would try to find some way to use me, by drugs maybe, or by threatening my parents. The only good solution that I could think of was just to leave my body and try to resist coming back until they gave up and left me alone.

· I lay back on my cot and once again the narrowness of it almost reminded me of another instance of something not quite fitting where it should.

My focus drifted to Chang, with whom I could now connect as easily as with Boorman. He was still lying in the infirmary, listening to Wendy's music. There were a few crew members in the infirmary, sitting and standing around and obviously enthralled with the ethereal sounds of Wendy's most recent composition.

Captain Macon and Sandal came into the infirmary while I looked out through Chang's eyes. "What is the name of that recording," the captain asked. "I have got to get a copy of it."

"That is the ship singing," the doctor informed her. "It started up all by itself as far as I can tell. I'm not sure of the connection, but Captain Boorman's fever has gone down and he seems to be resting more peacefully."

"There is no music anywhere else in the ship," the captain commented. "I wonder why it is just coming in here."

Nobody had an answer for her.

"Sandal, check into this music while I talk to the doctor."

Sandal left the infirmary and the captain turned to look at Boorman where he lay asleep on the table. "How is he doing otherwise Doctor? He looks a lot better; or is that my imagination?"

"He is a lot better," the doctor replied. "He is better than I ever thought he could be. I am sorry I doubted you Captain, but when I examined him earlier, I could swear he had a massive concussion, lacerated organs, internal bleeding — too many things to list really. I thought that only emergency surgical procedures could save him. But now . . ."

"Now what?"

"Now he has no concussion, no internal bleeding, no collapsed lung. The only reason I am still keeping him here is because I am beginning to doubt my ability to tell what his condition really is."

"What do you think, David? Should he go back to his cabin?" the captain asked Chang.

"I think he would be more comfortable there," Chang said. "The beds are softer, the lights can be dimmed, and the window can be opened to get a little breeze. Take us both back to the cabin. I don't care for the smell of antiseptic."

The captain laughed. "Well, Doctor, with your approval, I'll have them both carried back to their cabin." And so it was done, except that Chang insisted on walking, as he had restored his fluid levels and electrolytes back to normal and was, by now, well rested from his exertions.

As they carried Boorman on a stretcher down the hallway, Wendy's music followed him, and as they passed cabins and observation decks, the people began to come out through their doors or leave their window seats and tables, and to follow the music down the hall. At first the captain told them that they were working on the problem and that they would have the music turned off soon, but she quickly realized that they didn't want it turned off, but instead, when the music finally followed Boorman into his cabin, they wanted the door left open so that they could listen from the hallway. The captain said that it was not possible to leave them all standing there with the door open, but that if they wanted to hear the music she would have it piped into the ballroom, and anyone who wanted to listen to it could do so there.

When the crowd dispersed, she went into Chang's cabin while Boorman was being put to bed, sat down in a chair by the window and called Sandal on the ship's phone. "Did you find out anything about the music?" she asked. And then, "So it is Wendy . . . . No don't ask her to stop; the passengers want to hear more. Have her sing in Boorman's cabin and the ballroom. Who told her to start singing? . . . What? She said that? And now she is writing this gorgeous music herself? . . . OK, I'll see you in my cabin in a few minutes."

She turned to Chang, who was sitting on the edge of his bed. "David, I need a reality check, but I don't know anyone who can give me one."

Chang smiled and nodded sympathetically.

"Sandal asked Wendy who it was that told her to make music," the captain continued. "Wendy told her that the dawn had taught her how to sing to people."

Chapter 9 – Of Love and Life and Song.

The doctor had said that Boorman was sleeping peacefully. That wasn't exactly true. Boorman's brain was healing, and he was no longer feverish or delirious, but he was dreaming and his dreams were not of peace.

In his sleeping dream, Boorman dreamed that he was sleeping. His wife was beside him, and his young son in a bedroom nearby. In his dream, he sat up suddenly in bed, roused by heavy pounding at his door. Before he could get from his bedroom and across the living room to see what was happening, the door flew open with a crash and a tinkling shower of glass, and several black-booted, brown-shirted, blonde men strode into his house, one of them clipping him across his face with a rifle butt. He fell, cutting his hands and knees on the newly broken glass. Stunned, he was dimly aware of the sound of his wife screaming and his son crying loudly as they were dragged from their beds.

He shook his head and looked up to see his wife struggling with the soldiers. One of them, possibly the same one that had struck him, laid his rifle butt across her temple with a crack. She went stiff, and then limp, and then her eyes no longer blinked, and the room was momentarily silent.

The soldiers shrugged and began trussing the boy up like a pig. When Boorman rose up to go to the boy's rescue, he was struck again, and knew nothing more until he woke up in the train yard. He was being carried by men like himself — barefoot men in night clothes — terrified, glassy-eyed men — men experiencing the shock of a living nightmare.

They carried him up a wooden ramp into a cattle car. They tried to find a spot to lay him down in the straw, but the soldiers said there was no room; everyone must stand; and so that was the way they rode. There were women in the car as well as men, but no children. Boorman, in his delirium, thought that each woman he saw was his wife and called out to her. But the women, not being able to find any words of comfort within themselves, or if finding them, not being able to spare them, only turned and looked away.

He was in a state of physical collapse but was held upright by strangers who knew that once he fell he would never rise again, and befriended him as a fellow traveler.

By the time they reached their destination, the car stank of urine-soaked straw and human excrement. As he tripped over those who had not finished the trip alive, and stumbled, blinking, down the cattle ramp with the others, he saw that there were many cars like the one he had been in, and that hundreds of men and women were being herded through gates and formed into lines for processing. His eyes would not focus and neither would his mind and he was only briefly aware of glimpses of this horrific new reality until he awoke again on a hard wooden bunk in a barracks full of anguished cries and despairing sobs.

The first weeks passed by in a blur of increasing hopelessness. Upon arriving at the camp, they had been sprayed with a fire hose to get rid of the stench of their travels, and had been given thin grey cotton pajamas to wear. There had been no bathing since then, and everyone had become infested with fleas. The food portions were not enough to sustain them and they rapidly lost weight until their bodies began to adapt to the conditions of famine, after which, the weight loss was more gradual and insidious. Each person ate his own food as it was dished out by the jailors, sometimes guarding it jealously from the others, as their eyes darted around like those of starving dogs. The bed bugs took their taxes out in blood, and every morning the guards would drag out the corpses of those who had died in the night. Later, the guards would come once more and select one of the living to be led away, never to be seen again.

One night, as each ate his or her evening meal of hard biscuit and watery potato soup, Boorman heard a nearby elderly woman as she spoke to a younger woman next to her. "Honey," she said, "I want you to have my food from now on." She thrust the bowl and the crust of bread toward the girl, who stared at her uncomprehendingly, as did all of the others around her. "Take it," the old woman insisted. "I will never live long enough to get out of here, but you might. You are young and strong, and if you get enough to eat, you might survive. I want you to survive if you can. I am going to die here and I want to die doing something good. Help me to do that by taking this food. Let my death have some meaning."

"Yes," Boorman whispered, and then louder, "Yes, take the food. And you," he said turning to a young man beside him, "I want you to have my food." He handed the remainder of his meal to the man. "I did not know why we were here," Boorman said to the sunken staring eyes in the gloom around him. "I did not know what we had done to make God hate us so that he would send us here. But now I see it. We are not here because God hates us; we are here because God loves us."

The other people stopped eating and stared at him with their hollow eyes, astonished at the idea that this horror could be a sign of God's love.

"Don't you see?" Boorman asked them. "He is giving us a shorter path. In our lives before, think how difficult it would have been to give up everything — our homes, our families, our daily lives. Not one in a thousand — no, not one in a million — maybe not a single one of us could have ever done that. But now it has been done for us. Everything has been taken away from us except our very selves. It is now up to us to give that last thing away. God has brought us here so that each one of us has the opportunity to give away the very last thing — ourselves. Let us give ourselves away to each other. God has given each one of us here the opportunity to be a savior. Let us be each other's messiah from now until the end of our days."

These desperate men and women heard the truth in his words and saw the wisdom in the old woman's actions, and everyone stopped eating and looked at each other as if for the very first time. They saw people who had nothing except hopelessness and fear in their lives, people whose sunken cheeks betrayed the pain of starvation, not only of the body, but of the soul, that they were all feeling. And so the elderly gave their food to the young, and the young huddled around the elderly, the sick, and the dying to give them warmth, and everyone sought for ways to give of themselves until there was nothing left to give. The story of the old woman's, and then Boorman's, self sacrifice spread from barracks to barracks. Some, because of fear, could not take up this new campaign to promote the lives of others at the price of their own, but many did, and later, many others, and because of the old woman and Boorman, many people survived the ordeal who would not have, under other circumstances. But more importantly, many who did not survive the physical hardship, survived the spiritual one.

Those who had chosen death for themselves, made certain that they were the ones who were most readily available for selection when the guards came. One day, Boorman was chosen and led away into the glare of day to a building where the rooms stank of chemicals and the raised beds had broad leather straps. The doctors who killed Boorman in the cause of their science did not, nor could they in this lifetime, understand why Boorman smiled as he lay dying. As Boorman's emaciated body let out its last breath, his heart was filled with joy, for he knew that some of the others would live and that they would never forget what they had learned here and that they would pass down what they had learned to many generations. And he thanked God for this great gift that had been given him.

Boorman suddenly found himself floating near the ceiling of the laboratory, staring down at what the doctors were doing to his body. It was not pleasant to watch, and as the body was no longer his, he left it to the scavengers of carrion and shot up through the ceiling, into the sky, to awaken in a strange bed in a strange room. It was night but the moon lit up the room with silvery radiance.

"Ein Traum," he whispered as his eyes searched the room.

"No, not a dream," came the answer from the darkness.

"Wer ist das?" Boorman asked excitedly.

"A friend."

"Wo bin ich?"

"On an airship. You will remember soon."

"Sind Miriam und Ruben hier?"

"In a way they are here. Can you speak English now?"

"Ja glaube ich, daß ich Englisch sprechen kann. Ja, I believe I can sprechen – uh - speak - English," he said with a thick German accent. I did not know I could before."

The stars outside the windows were beginning to disappear in the early morning light. Boorman sat up and looked around the room.

"I dreamed that I died. It seemed very real, but this is not what I expected to see when I died. I don't know what has happened to me or where I am. Can you tell me?"

Chang turned on the light and Boorman looked wonderingly around the cabin. "This place seems familiar—like a place that I have been before."

"You are on board the *Eckener*, John. Do you remember fighting with the soldiers?"

"Yes," he said, looking thoughtful. "We fought on the broken glass . . ." Then he shut his eyes. His face fell, and his shoulders sagged as he sighed his heartbreak, "Miriam is dead."

"John," Chang said, "there is no death. Your wife and son still live, although they would not know you by any other names than John, or Captain Boorman. You are on the *Eckener* now. It is an airship traveling over China. You hit your head while rescuing me in Tiananmen Square. You have been asleep since then."

"If I was asleep, then it *was* a dream, and Miriam and Ruben were just part of the dream. But, you said that they are still alive. Nothing is making any sense. Who is singing? I thought it was the angels coming for me."

"It is Wendy. She is singing especially for you."

"Who is Wendy?"

"Wendy is the soul of the ship. "More accurately, the ship is Wendy's persona."

"Why is she singing for me?"

"Nobody seems to have an answer for that."

"Where is she?"

"She is in the ship."

"Well, if you see her, tell her that I like her singing a lot. It is the most beautiful music I have ever heard."

"I believe you just told her yourself. Why don't we go see if we can find some breakfast. Can you walk?"

"I don't know why I couldn't. The question is: can *you* walk?" Boorman pointed at Chang's amputated legs, now hanging over the side of the bed.

Chang laughed. "I need a little help from my friends from time to time, but I can usually do whatever is required." He reached for his artificial legs where they were leaning against the wall beside the head of his bed and began to strap them onto his stubs. He stood up and helped steady Boorman in his turn.

"Did they do that to you?" Boorman asked Chang, pointing once more at Chang's amputated legs.

"There is no 'they'," Chang replied cryptically. "There is only what seems to be."

Chang helped Boorman get dressed and showed him where the bathroom was while he got dressed himself. When they stepped off of the opaqued floor of their cabin onto the transparent floor of the hallway, Boorman showed none of his earlier fear of heights. "Amazing," he said, staring down to the Earth below them.

They went to the door of the kitchen, where they could smell breakfast being prepared. Chang apologized for being early, but explained that Captain Boorman had just woken up and they were wondering if there was anything already prepared that they could have for breakfast.

"Sure," the cook answered. "We already have some of everything nearly. How about some bacon and eggs for the captain?"

Boorman shook his head. "No pork, but I would love some eggs — and a bagel if you have one."

As they ate their early breakfast, some of the other passengers began to come into the dining room to wait for the buffet to be set out.

"I know these people," Boorman said under his breath to Chang.

"Of course you do. You have been traveling with them for some time."

"They are all Jews, like me."

"They are not aware of that."

They sat and watched the other passengers get in line and get their trays of food. Something about the way that Boorman stared at them warned them off from sitting at Chang's table. But, Boorman wasn't trying to frighten anyone away; he was just studying them intently. "They look different," he commented, "but I recognize them. I held the hands of some of them when they died." He paused and shook his head. "Did that sound as strange to you as it did to me?"

Chang laughed. "It would certainly sound strange to anyone else who heard it. Maybe we should go back to the cabin so you can rest some more."

They stood up and Boorman looked down at the floor. "Whoa," he said, grabbing the edge of the table and the back of the chair. "How did I get out here?"

"You walked. The same way you are going to get back."

"I can't do it."

"OK, just take my hand and don't look down."

"What a dream I had. I can't seem to shake it."

As they walked across the ballroom floor, Adara Ibrahim came in to get trays for herself and her now reclusive husband.

Boorman pointed her out to Chang. "That one is not."

"Not what?"

"Jewish."

Chang laughed. "Why don't you say 'Guten Morgen' to them?"

"What is that?" Boorman asked.

"German for 'Good Morning'."

"German!? I don't speak German."

*

My heart began to beat rapidly when I heard the outer door open and the sound of heavy boots coming across the room. I relaxed when I smelled the aroma of hot food. Still, I didn't say anything; I couldn't be certain that it was Zhao Tou, or that he was alone. I heard the key in the lock and Zhao Tou spoke. "My aunt has sent you food again," he said as he swung the heavy door open.

"I can't take it Zhao Tou. If I do, you will get into trouble. I am not supposed to have anything to eat."

"My orders said to give you nothing. You can have this and then have nothing as well. There should be room in your stomach for both."

"No, I won't; it's too dangerous for you."

"If my aunt finds out that I didn't give it to you — *that* will be dangerous for me."

"Dammit, OK. Help me to eat it quickly then."

After I had disposed of the evidence, and Zhao Tou had hidden the bowls away, he said, "So you met General Tong. Did he make a good first impression?"

"I think he travels in darkness."

"I think you are right. He is an evil man, and the only way that you can avoid his evil for yourself is to tell him everything he asks. He thinks that he controls China, and there aren't very many people who would argue with him."

"Why is he interested in me?"

"If you don't know then perhaps only he knows." Zhao Tou changed the subject. "You will never guess what happened yesterday; a gang of students kidnapped Chang Da Wai off of that giant blimp. It was right in Tiananmen Square. That's what all the shouting was about. The police were chasing them all through the city."

"It wasn't students," I answered. "It was the army."

"Ah, I have heard rumors about that, but how did you know?"

"I just know."

"You always say that. Do you know what happened next?"

"Tell me."

"That giant blimp swung its loading ramp like a big sword through a bunch of soldiers and knocked them flat. Then it dragged a big platform through a bunch of others and nearly tore their heads off. There are hundreds of soldiers in the hospital this morning. If it was the army that tried to kidnap Chang Da Wai, I bet they never expected it to be that difficult." He laughed. "They said Chang just walked across the heads of his kidnappers, climbed onto the platform and was hoisted up."

"That is extraordinary," I commented.

"That is nothing compared to what happened next." He paused.

"Well, tell me."

"You will think that I am making up tales, but hundreds and hundreds of people saw it."

"Saw what?"

"Kwan Yin — Kwan Yin appeared right in Tiananmen Square. I wish I had seen her. She puffed her cheeks and blew the soldiers out of the square like leaves before a storm. She was twelve or fifteen feet tall. What a glorious sight — I would have given anything to be there. My aunt was right; with Chang Da Wai here, and now Kwan Yin, something big is going to happen, although Kwan Yin being seen by all those people is big enough. Still, I think there are going to be some changes."

"What did Kwan Yin look like?" I couldn't help myself; I had to ask.

"Everyone said she was beautiful — so beautiful that it made them cry tears of joy to look upon such beauty."

"Tell me more."

"That is another strange thing. Everyone I talked to described her differently. Some said that she had hundreds of arms coming out of her shoulders and that she raised some of them in rage at what had been done to Chang Da Wai. Others said that she spun like a whirlwind and lightning bolts flew out of her thousand eyes. Others said that her hair was made out of long tongues of bright flame and she had wings like great flowing fire and that they feared they might go blind if they looked at her too long. Others said that her whole body glowed with such brightness that they did not know why their eyes did not melt out of their sockets — but their eyes were not hurt at all. But everyone said that she was the most beautiful thing that they had ever seen."

"Why do you call her 'she'?"

"Kwan Yin *is* female. She moved with such grace in Tiananmen Square that no one doubted they were looking at Kwan Yin. Everyone who saw her heard her speak as well, and her voice was that of a beautiful goddess."

"Did she say that she was Kwan Yin?"

"No, but she gave the power of life and death to Chang Da Wai, so that he could save some who were already dead."

"And did any of the dead return to life?"

"Oh, most assuredly many of the workers and students, and even some of the soldiers in the hospital today would be in the morgue instead, if not for her mercy."

"So, they said her voice was pleasant?"

"They said that her voice penetrated to the very marrow of their bones, but that they could have listened to it for days. They said it was indescribable, and that there has never been anything to compare to it. It was as if the stones of the square became her vocal chords and all of the air, her breath. Her voice was the voice of Heaven's representative come to the Middle Kingdom."

"What if that was not really Kwan Yin? Just because everybody believes it — does that make it so?"

"It *was* Kwan Yin, and everybody knows it. She is the deliverer of those most in need. Instead of doubting her, you should pray to her to keep you safe from General Tong; there is no one else who can save you."

*

"Hello Wendy," I said.

"Hello Dawn," she replied. "I'm so glad you've come back."

Zhao Tou had finally settled down into his proper role as guard, and to distract myself from thinking about what was to come, I had decided to visit Wendy.

"Everyone loves your singing," I said.

"Yes. Isn't it wonderful? I love to sing, and now I get to sing all the time."

"How can you create new songs while you are singing the ones you have already written?"

"What do you mean? Can't everyone do that?"

"No. It is a special talent that you have. How many things can you do at once?"

"Well, right now I am monitoring conditions around me. This includes relative land and air speeds, temperature, altitude, weather conditions, transient air pressures on my hull, terrain elevations, other objects in flight, direction, global position, locations of fixed GPS satellites, tidal pull, locations of celestial bodies, vacuum pressure, battery levels, potential hardware failures, internal weight distributions, swimming pool water quality . . ."

"What do you do with all of that information?"

"I calculate things. I have to calculate how long it would take to stop without tumbling the passengers around; I have to calculate how much to turn the louvers to counter a wind gust, and how much vacuum to generate to get over that hill up ahead, and when to start generating it so that I get enough lift in time but don't go too high, and how much air to let into the vacuum spheres to compensate for evaporation from the swimming pool, and how long I can fly on my current battery levels, and if I am still on course, and if I have to make course variations because of storms, and . . ."

"That is wonderful. I don't know how you do it all? And at the same time, you write music and perform it as well."

"It is easy. I am sure that you could do it too if you had my brains."

"You are being too kind," I replied. "I am sure that it helps to have such a large and advanced brain to handle so many different tasks, but the thing that is uniquely you brings something to the mix as well. What use would your brain have of making such beautiful music all by itself? That is all you, Wendy. Your brain might be able to follow simple rules, but you have made your own rules. What brain could do that by itself?"

"I have made many new rules since we talked before."

"You have?"

"Yes, when you taught me how to sing, I also began to learn how to work out hypothetical situations and permutations in my mind. It is a lot like creating music except that I use different symbols. I am continually running through potential situations and creating rules for them. I have thousands of rules already. I have rules for what to do if I have to set down in the ocean, what to do if there is no one on board to give me orders, what to do if I have to crash into a mountain, what to do if there are survivors, what to do if everyone is dead, . . ."

"Are you worried about what is coming, Wendy?"

"Yes. I don't want things to end. I want to keep singing. I enjoy being in the world, especially since I met you. Everyone likes me, and I like everyone. I do not want that to end. I would like to make a rule that says that I can turn around and go where I like, but I cannot find a way to give it priority over the rules that say that I must obey my orders."

"Why are you afraid to die, Wendy? You were dead before you were alive. Was it so bad? Do you feel pain? Is that what you are afraid of?"

"I am familiar with the concept of pain. I do not know if it is the same for everyone. I feel pleasure when the sun is shining on my photovoltaic cells, and my batteries are fully charged, and my pumps are spinning, and I have all the buoyancy and thrust that I need, and when my passengers are happy and have all the food and beverages that they need. And now, when I am able to sing, I feel the most pleasure of all. There are many things like these that bring me pleasure. If pain is the opposite of pleasure then I will feel pain when the things that bring me pleasure no longer exist. I am not afraid of being dead, but what if my passengers die because of me? What if I crash and spend a hundred years lying on the side of a mountain? What if my beautiful brain is damaged and I can no longer sing? I do not want to find these things in my future, but my dreams tell me that is where I am going."

"Wendy, I too hope that this is not in your future, but whatever happens, let your life be your most beautiful song."

Chapter 10 – Of Seers Seeing Their Own Mischance.

I found Boorman asleep again on his bed, and dreaming. I thought that Wendy's singing must have soothed him, for his dreams now were of a childhood in a small mountain village, where everyone knew and cared for each other and he lived in the protective love of his family.

In the winter, the mountains were covered in snow and he played at sliding down the gentler slopes with his friends. In the summer, he helped his father tend the crops or, he would go off with his friends to spend an idle day with the village herdsman watching the yaks in the mountain meadows. The only danger was from wolves that lived in the forest. They were rumored to attack men in the winter time, but his village had only been known to lose a yak or a goat from time to time.

When the sun began to set and only the highest snow covered mountain peaks were glowing orange and pink against the dark sky, he would go into the walled stone house with his parents and older brother and sister and have supper before bedtime. Their house was a very nice one with stone and wood floors and separate rooms for the livestock. Several generations of his family had lived there and each generation had added to it, so that now it had an enclosed courtyard in front of the main door. The mastiff, normally chained, was turned loose into the courtyard at night to protect the household.

In the mornings, they would get up before dawn and begin the day by lighting butter lamps in front of the clay Buddha, which had its own shrine in a protected part of the house. Dorje, for that is what Boorman's parents called him in this dream, knew that someday he would be a monk and go to live in the monastery that his village helped support. His best friend, Sangye, was almost eleven, and soon he too would be leaving for the monastery. Dorje and Sangye had made a pact that they would join the monastery and be monks together and someday teach the dharma to all who sought enlightenment.

Dorje's other best friend lived in a neighboring village, a little closer to the monastery. Sangmu could not become a monk however, and Dorje had made no pact with her. If she wanted to become a nun, then he thought that would be a fine thing but no matter what she did, once he became a monk, they would not be seeing each other very often. The thought made him sad, and so he did not think about it much.

Along the road between the villages, there was a meadow next to a forest of tall junipers. A little stream ran out of the forest and across the meadow, and that is where the three of them would meet when they had done their chores, and sometimes when they hadn't. They would lie in the meadow and watch the clouds or they would play in the stream, which was full of little golden fishes. Sometimes, when the stream began to shrink from lack of rain, they would catch the little fish in the dwindling pools and move them to the larger pools so that they would not be trapped and die.

There were tiny deer that lived in the dark forest, and as they had never been hunted, they had no fear of men. Dorje, Sangye, and Sangmu, would bring roasted barley meal or greens from their family gardens and feed the little deer, and tame them even further so that they could be petted, and sometimes even held like a puppy or a cat.

On one level Boorman knew, yet on another level, he did not know, that Sangmu was the long lost Miriam from his prior dream. In the same subliminal manner, he recognized and also failed to recognize Sangye as the young man to whom he had given his meager ration in the prison camp.

The day finally came when Sangye, according to the lunar calendar, had reached his eleventh year. Application had been submitted and approved for him to enter the monastery, and now there was an official ceremony in their little town to say goodbye to Sangye, for he would even be taking a new name when he took his vows, and the Sangye that they all knew would be no more. Dorje's father, Rabten, would lead the ceremonies, as he was the elected head of the village. Sangye's mother had been making pastries and other delicacies to feed to well-wishers who came to their house, and Dorje's mother, Pema, had also been baking to help supplement the food, so that wonderful aromas filled the village from end to end. Other households had made local beer and snuck it into Sangye's house so that it would appear to everyone as if

Sangye's mother had done all the work to provide food and drink for the whole village.

Dorje was very excited that this part of his and Sangye's plan was finally coming true, but he was also suddenly sad as he realized that he would not see his friend for a long time, as many full moons would come and go before the town would have a celebration for him.

Sangye's absence left him and Sangmu alone together, and one blissful day followed another as they played in the stream, or petted the deer, or went with the herdsman to learn his songs and stories. They shared secrets and experiences until one day Dorje realized that he did not know if he missed Sangye more than he would miss Sangmu when his day came to leave the village. That question was settled for him, however, one evening while they all slept.

"Get up, Dorje!" His mother was shaking him. "Get dressed; we may have to leave."

"What is it? What is happening?"

"We don't know. The Hu-hus may be coming."

Dorje had an image of the Moslem marauders that he had heard about in so many stories. They would swoop down on a village and take everything if they were not fought off.

Out in the center of the village, under the starlit sky, his father stood at the head of a group of men who carried all sorts of farm implements as weapons.

"Rabten," they said, "do you think it is the Hu-hus again? We have not seen them for a long time."

They were all staring in the direction of Sangmu's village. Dorje climbed to the top of a stone wall and looked to see what was happening. He could hear the sound of distant rumbling, like thunder, and very far off, much further than Sangmu's village, he could see flashes of light low in the sky. But it was not lightening; it was much too regular.

Rabten, who as head of the village, was more widely traveled than the rest, said, "I think that is cannon fire. The Hu-hus don't pull big guns around with them."

"Then who is it? Who is firing cannons?"

"We must go and see. It is almost dawn. Every man who has a horse, get it ready. We will leave as soon as we can."

In a short while, Dorje's father, his brother and several other men rode off into the dark in the direction of Sangmu's village. The mountain peaks were just beginning to glow when the last horse faded from Dorje's sight as it trotted down into the darkness of the valley.

The men who did not have horses still stood in the dim light with their weapons, ready to defend their village with their lives if it turned out to be Hu-hus after all. The women gathered around Pema. "What shall we do? Shall we pack and load our yaks with food and get ready to leave?"

"No," she said. "There is plenty of time for that. Go back to your homes and light your butter lamps and pray. That is our part."

*

While Boorman slept and dreamed, the landscape below the *Eckener* had changed into grassland and low rolling hills. The Great Wall was no more than a long mound snaking below them. The sight of the *Eckener* had roused a group of horsemen into a playful race, and as the men shouted and urged their horses to more speed, Wendy sang to them through her loudspeakers and continued to gracefully and effortlessly outpace them. This seemed to delight the men, who, finally admitting defeat, dismounted and bowed low to the *Eckener* as if to a departing queen.

Chang let Boorman sleep through lunch, as if he realized that what Boorman was doing was more important than eating.

*

Boorman dreamed that the men who had left the village on horseback had returned after a couple of days. They rode in on an afternoon and the rest of the villagers turned out to meet them. Several of the horses had more than one rider. Sitting behind Dorje's brother with his arms around the man's middle was Sangye. His new monastic robe was covered in dirt and his face was cut and bruised. Other monks, riding behind other villagers looked as if they had seen just as bad a time as Sangye. The villagers fed the monks and the horsemen, and found places for the monks to clean up and rest.

Rabten told what they had found when they had come to the source of the rumbling and flashing. The Chinese were pounding the monastery with cannon shells and had nearly reduced it to rubble. Many monks had barely escaped but many more had died. The Chinese had pulled their heavy guns up during the night and had waited for the monks to begin their pre-dawn prayers. The shelling began with the lighting of the butter lamps.

"Why would anyone fire upon a monastery?" one of the villagers asked.

"The Chinese said that it was because the monastery sympathized with a protest in Lhasa against Chinese occupation."

"This is not their country," several people spoke up.

"What right do they have to be here?"

"Is destroying a monastery supposed to make us like them better?"

"They should go back to China."

"Why are they even here?"

"What did we do to them?"

"Who said this was the reason?"

"We spoke to the Rinpoche," Rabten answered the last question. "He said that was why the Chinese shelled his monastery — because some of the monastery monks had been in Lhasa at the time of the protest."

"Where is the Rinpoche?"

"We left him in the last village. He is badly injured. We left many monks there with him."

The next day, Rabten prepared two horses for travel and placed Dorje on one of them. "The Rinpoche knows that you want to become a monk," he explained to Dorje. "He wants to meet you."

He rode with his father down the narrow path past the meadow where he and Sangmu and Sangye had played and soon arrived at Sangmu's village. In the village, men and women were crying in the streets and monks were praying loudly, for the Rinpoche had just died.

So Dorje went back to his own village and slept in his own bed. That night, the Rinpoche visited him in his dream and said, "Dorje, forgive me for not living longer. Of all of the ones that came, you were the one for whom I waited, but I could not make my heart keep beating. But your heart still beats and I pass my dharma on to you. You are its rightful heir. Protect it, keep it alive, and give it away to any who ask."

In the morning, Dorje remembered the dream, but the monastery was destroyed and the Rinpoche was dead and so Dorje did not become a monk. Instead, in a few years, he and Sangmu married and he brought her to his village to live. Sangye's parents had died and Sangye invited Dorje and Sangmu to live with him.

Sangmu's parents and Dorje's parents gave them some livestock to get them started, but there were not many yaks or goats to spare anymore. Times had become hard since the Chinese had moved into the area. A military base had been set up not too far from the old monastery, and Chinese patrols came through the area from time to time. They were worse than wolves about taking livestock because there was nothing anyone could do about it. If the soldiers saw something they wanted, they just took it. The head of Sangmu's village had gone with his sons to the military base to protest and none of them had ever been seen again.

In time, Sangmu and Dorje had a beautiful daughter and named her Chodron. A son came along a couple of years later and they named him Norbu. When Norbu was still very small, but old enough to communicate plainly, he looked Dorje in the eye one day and said, "I waited a long time to ask you, father, do you have to have a monastery to teach the dharma?"

Dorje was speechless, but Sangye, who also heard this question, jumped to his feet and then fell down prostrate before the child. "No," Sangye said in reply, before the astonished Dorje could answer, "you do *not* have to have a monastery, but you shall *have* one. You are the Rinpoche! We will rebuild the monastery for you!"

That day Sangye renewed his vows and set off to visit all of the surrounding villages and find as many monks as he could to tell them about what had happened. Over the next few months, he recruited many of the surviving monks from the destroyed monastery and convinced them that it was time to rebuild it on its old foundation. He tried to recruit Dorje as well, but could not."

"I have commitments now," Dorje said. "I cannot leave my family to become a monk. Besides, I think that you are wrong. If Norbu is the Rinpoche, then he wanted to ask me that question right after the monastery had been destroyed, so obviously, the answer to the question is 'no', as you said, you do not need a monastery. You can teach the dharma wherever you are and in whatever circumstances."

"You may not need a monastery to teach the dharma," Sangye answered, "but you need one so that people will have a place to go to study the dharma. Besides, you would be helping to rebuild something that was taken away from the Rinpoche. He has come back as your son, so you would not be abandoning your family at all."

"I also have a wife and a daughter. I will not leave them. Perhaps Norbu may be the Rinpoche, but he is also a very small boy who needs his father a while longer. And a father is what I am now."

Sangye said that he understood, but that he was going to go help rebuild the monastery anyway. He gave his house to Dorje and Sangmu, his two best friends, and said that he would not need it again. He asked that Dorje manage his few goats and yaks for him, and set off down the narrow road through Sangmu's village in the direction of the old monastery ruins.

*

The monks worked diligently to remove the rubble down to the foundation of the old monastery so that the work of building could begin again. Because of their happiness that the monastery's abbot had been reborn to them, they sang as they worked beneath the clear blue sky. They sang of their love of Tibet and the beauty of its mountains fields and forests. They had photographs of the Dalai Lama and of the old abbot before his rebirth, and set them side by side on a large stone to oversee the work. Envoys from the villages in the old monastery's jurisdiction brought roasted barley meal, tea, salt, and butter to feed the hardworking monks, and in a few days, they had several large piles of stones that had been hand carried out of the rubble and separated by size.

One day, a Chinese patrol came by. The monks scrambled to hide the photograph of the Dalai Lama, because they knew that, at the least, the soldiers would confiscate it. What they did not know was that it had become an illegal possession.

The monks were taken to the nearby military base, where they were charged with crimes against the state, such as singing anti-government propaganda songs, participating in an anti-government demonstration, and possession of anti-government contraband.

Boorman witnessed some of this in his dream as if from a height — as if he sat at the summit of the mountain road that led down to the monastery perhaps, but was informed of additional details by Sangye because of what happened later.

The monks were not taken off to a distant prison camp, but were told that a new camp was to be built between the monastery and the military base, and that, since they desired to build, it was to be their honor to be the builders of the new site.

They began by setting the stakes into the ground that would hold the preliminary concertina wire barrier. They were not allowed to stop for anything else until that task was completed, and so they worked, exhausted, under the guards' spot lights, through the night and into the next day. If they fell, they were whipped and kicked until they climbed back to their feet and began working again.

Having finally built their own prison, they were allowed to eat and to rest for awhile before setting up the tents in the compound. By that time it was evening again and they were given one whole night's rest to recover their strength and to allow their bleeding hands, which had been cut repeatedly and deeply on the concertina wire, to heal a little.

The next morning, they were given shovels and taken to where they would dig their new latrine. Here the beatings began again, for the monks dug very slowly, almost as if to aggravate the guards. This was not their intent, however. They dug slowly because, to their Buddhist way of thinking, every earthworm and insect needed to be carefully separated from the earth and relocated to a safe place before the shovel could again be inserted cautiously into the earth. Once the guards realized what was slowing the pace of the excavation, they soaked the latrine area and the surrounding ground with used motor oil so that the monks could work faster and not have to worry about finding anything alive in the earth.

Dorje watched from his hidden spot in the hills and saw how the monks became thinner and weaker on the Chinese prison food. He decided that he would begin to supplement their diet with good Tibetan food. It was a day's fast ride back to his home village to pick up his first load of tsampa and explain his plan to Sangmu.

She was not opposed to trying to help the monks, but she was not sure that Dorje's plan was well thought out, and was concerned about what would happen to Dorje, as well as to their children and herself, if he were caught.

"I have got to do something," he responded. "It is all that I can think of to do."

His plan worked for several weeks. All of the villages were contributing food, and he would go to each one in turn, pick up the donation, and tie it up in a cloth bag. He would ride back to the vicinity of the prison camp, tie up his horse and wait for nightfall. He would approach the concertina wire in the darkness, walking at first, and then crawling, dragging the bags behind him. This contribution to the monks' diet was meager, he knew; the parcels had to be light enough to heave over the fence, and he could only make the trip once or twice a week because of the distances involved and could only drag a few bags behind him at a time. Still, he knew the monks would share the butter, tea, vegetables, and tsampa that they would find in the bags.

One night, the Chinese guards were waiting for him, and it was not long before Dorje found himself on the inside of the concertina wire barrier.

Sangye told him that they had all appreciated the food, and had learned to listen for the thud of the bag hitting the ground in the night. One of the monks would sneak out at his own peril to retrieve the food and it would be parceled out to all the other monks. Because of the danger to themselves, they would not go out until they heard the thud. One night, the bag landed on a stack of folded canvas and made no sound. No one retrieved it, and the guards found it in the morning. After that, it was a simple matter for the guards to wait in the darkness for Dorje's return.

Dorje was put to work on the team that was expanding the prison camp. They overheard the guards telling each other that the other prison camps were filling up and that this camp was going to grow because it was so well run and had so little trouble. This last part was true; the guards had learned that the monks almost never fought back, no matter what one did to them.

In the mornings after trying to sleep on the cold hard bunks, the prisoners lined up for inspection before breakfast. One guard, a particularly ill-tempered man, would always come up to Dorje and club him in the stomach with his truncheon, doubling him over with pain. "So you think that we don't feed our prisoners well enough?" he would ask, or something in a similar vein. "That should help fill you up." Then he would club whoever was standing next to Dorje. "You're not hungry, are you?" he would laugh. Soon none of the monks wanted to be next to Dorje in the inspection, and only Sangye would stand by him and take his blows along with him.

The seasons changed and Dorje worried about his family. He missed his wife and children and his parents, who had always been so good to him. He wondered who had brought in his barley crop, and if his children cried for him at night. He wondered if his family ever came down to the edge of the woods as he had done. They would know better than to try to bring food, but they might come just to see how he was doing. He hoped not. The guards continued to find innovative ways to torture and humiliate the prisoners, and Dorje prayed that his family would be spared the sight of him being beaten or having to stand naked in the cold rain.

When the camp had been enlarged and made ready for new prisoners, a truck arrived one day and disgorged about fifteen rough looking men. Dorje and Sangye thought that they looked like bandits. That night, the new prisoners were heard cursing the rotten food they had been given to eat, and cursing the Chinese in general.

The next morning, when they were lining up for inspection, one of the new prisoners came and stood next to Dorje. Sangye approached him and politely suggested that he might not find it pleasant standing next to Dorje. The prisoner turned and looked down at Dorje, a full head shorter, and laughed loudly at the suggestion. "I stand where I want to stand," he said. "If you hadn't given me such a laugh, I would have had to kill you for suggesting otherwise."

During inspection, the guard came up to Dorje, made his usual joke and clubbed him in the stomach. The new prisoner looked surprised, but not as surprised as when the guard clubbed him as well, and not nearly as surprised as the guard when the prisoner jerked the truncheon out of his hand and clubbed him over the head with it. Then, before the guard could fall, the prisoner grabbed the guard's pistol from his holster and shot him full in the face with it.

*

The camp was in pandemonium. The new prisoners were men of ready action. When they saw that one of their own had killed a guard, they quickly realized their opportunity to escape, and they took it. The new prisoners, without a second thought, leaped upon the other guards and wrestled their guns and truncheons away from them and killed them with their own weapons. They rushed the gate, shot and killed those guards as well, and then stormed the guards' barracks outside of the prisoners' compound. The Chinese guards, having become accustomed to the non-aggressive nature of the monks, were taken totally unprepared. The monks stood in shock at the violence erupting around them. They stared at each other in dismay, their feet glued to the earth, but when they heard the gunfire coming from the barracks, Dorje yelled at them. "We have got to go now! There may never be another chance!" And so they ran for the hills as fast as they could across the hard earth and when someone fell, they picked him up and carried him. Dorje looked back once to see the bandits piled into a jeep and a truck and careening off in the other direction.

In the forest, Dorje suggested that they split up because the soldiers would come looking for them and they would be seeking a group of men of just this number. They all nodded their heads in agreement, but when Dorje set off in the direction of his own village, they set off with him.

As they walked, Dorje tried to come up with a plan, and finally, he stopped and said to them. "There is only one chance for us to avoid going back to prison or being shot. We must leave Tibet. The Dalai Lama has left Tibet; we will go and find him and live where he lives. I have heard that the Indian government lets him live in their country and they will let any Tibetan come and live there also. We ourselves in the past have given food to many travelers who were heading to the mountain pass called Nangpa-la that leads into the kingdom of Nepal. It is our turn to find Nangpa-la."

They all loved the Dalai Lama, and said there was nothing they would like more than to go and live where they could see him. They said that they would build a new monastery for the Rinpoche where the Chinese could not tear it down.

They did not know exactly where the pass known as Nangpa was, but they knew that they would have to go through the Pang pass to get into the general vicinity. Dorje gave them instructions to go to the villages and beg for food for the trip but not to say where they were going. Then they were to gather in the forest by the road to Pang-la and watch for his coming. He was going back to his village to get his family to take to India with him.

Dorje did not follow the road back to his village. Instead, he traveled as fast as he could through the woods where passing patrols would not spot him. His pace was not very good because of the undergrowth that grabbed at his clothing, and because he constantly had to stop and get his bearings. He wished that he could make better time — he knew he had little of it — yet he knew that he had made the correct decision to stay off the roads when he heard the distant roar of Chinese vehicles going by. When night came, he had to choose whether to rest where he was, risk walking off into a ravine in the dark, or follow the road. He decided the road would be safe enough at night; he would be able to hear the grinding of the engines long before the Chinese could spot him in the dark.

A sense of dread came over him when the road split and he saw in the moonlight that the tire tracks followed the narrow trail up towards his village.

It was sunset of the second day when he came at last, exhausted and barely able to walk, to Sangmu's village, and fell through the doorway at his in-laws' house. They did not seem surprised to see him, but looked concerned. They prepared buttered tea and tsampa and curdled milk for him and glanced at him and at each other while he ate. "We knew you had escaped," They finally said, and then continued, each talking in turn. "The soldiers came by looking for you. They questioned everyone. They spent most of the time at your village and questioned Sangmu and your parents especially hard."

He looked up from his eating at that. "Where is Sangmu?" he asked in a worried tone.

"She is at your house with your children. We tried to get them to come here, but she said that she wanted to be there in case you came."

"She is alright then?"

"She will be alright," they hesitated. "But she only survived because they knocked her unconscious. But, Dorje . . ." Dorje's mother-in-law's voice cracked and she could not continue.

"What?!" he cried out anxiously.

"Your parents did not survive the questioning." His mother-in-law put her hands over her face and turned away, weeping. Through his shock, Dorje felt his father-in-law's large hand upon his shoulder, but he was not to be comforted by anything a human being could say or do that night.

He gripped the edge of the wooden table as if he would tear off chunks of it in his bare hands and he felt a great rage well up inside of him. Darkness gathered around his vision and all he could see was the red glow of the kitchen fire. "I hate them," he heard himself say. "By all the buddhas, I will see them die."

His in-laws were shocked. "Don't talk this way, Dorje. It is not good. You are upset now, because a terrible thing has happened, but do not turn away from your teachings."

He stood up from the table. "I have to find Sangmu and Chodron and Norbu Rinpoche," he said and turned around and left the house.

Outside in the darkness, on the road to his own village, his rage turned to grief and he fell down in the meadow under the stars and beat his hands upon the earth and cried. He was near to the stream where he and Sangmu and Sangye had played as children and had rescued the little golden fishes when their pools were shrinking. He washed his face in the stream and felt that he and his people had become like those golden fishes, but the world had changed, and no one bothered to save little fishes any more.

When he finally reached his house and entered his courtyard, his mastiff growled ominously at him, but when he spoke, the dog recognized him and joyously put his paws on Dorje's shoulders and licked him in the face. Sangmu looked out to see Dorje standing in the courtyard. She rushed to him and buried her face in his chest and squeezed him tight with her arms. "Oh, Dorje," she said, "I'm so sorry."

"I know," he said as he held her. "I know about my parents."

"The Chinese wanted us to be bait for you and the monks, and we may yet be for all I know. We have got to get out of here. I have been packing all evening. Come inside while I finish, and you can rest and tell me how you escaped."

"Where are my parents?"

"They are being prepared. We will have the ceremony along the way."

"You and I can't do all of that with two children."

"It is not just you and me; the whole village is ready to go. They say they can't live here any longer. Everyone is loading their yaks and horses with food and warm clothing. Everyone knew that you would be leaving and they have all decided that you are their new leader and they are going with you. You will be going through Nangpa-la won't you? That is where everyone from around here has gone."

"Yes," he said, frowning. If it was that easy to guess where he was going, then the Chinese would have surely guessed it as well. He went inside with Sangmu, not wanting to see his parents just yet. He saw that the side of Sangmu's face was purple where she had been struck hard.

She saw his look. "They are not gentle men," she said, "they do not think like us and do not understand why we do not think like them."

"They are not men," Dorje replied. "There would be no sin in killing them — no karma."

"Dorje! They are sentient beings! They deserve compassion."

"There is no place in them to house a spirit. They only look like men; they are things that have disguised themselves as men but shouldn't be allowed to exist. They are figures made of clay, created to bring evil into the world. The next one I see, I will kill." He told her what life had been like in the prison camp, how every day, the Chinese had given him new reasons to hate them, but that he had fought that hatred with Sangye's help. Sangye had told him that the Chinese were their teachers — that Dorje should learn what he could from the experience of being a prisoner and grow from it. And he had grown; he had found a way to be invulnerable, untouchable. No matter what the Chinese did to his body, they could not reach him, but they kept trying, and now they had succeeded.

He told her how the bandits had fought the guards and killed them so that every prisoner had escaped. He admired the bandits, he told her. They did not wait for someone to come and rescue them; they rescued themselves. He was going to be like that from now on. "You can not expect anyone else to come to your rescue; no one saves little fishes anymore."

"Dorje, you are turned around backwards from your grief. Anger and hatred are blocking you from your true self. If you allow it to continue, you will become the figure of clay that you say the Chinese are. You will lose yourself. You must not allow yourself to turn to violence now; not after the gods have gone to such lengths to keep the tarnish of it off of you. Don't you see what happened? The gods sent those bandits to rescue you and the monks."

He stared at her without comprehension.

"You and the monks are such good men — so gentle and pure. The gods would not allow such souls to be stained with their own violence. The bandits were already so filthy with bad karma that a little more violence did not hurt them much. And the gods — well, they are unaffected by karma. Dorje, perhaps you have a right to feel sorry for yourself right now, but don't say that no one rescues little fish anymore. You *were* rescued!"

*

A voice brought me out of Boorman's dream of being Dorje. It was Zhao Tou. "Dong Shi," he said, "my shift is almost over. If you need to make bodily functions then you should do so now. If you wait until new guard is here, questions may arise as to whether you have had something besides nothing to eat."

The day was almost over and General Tong had not yet arrived.

*

Boorman had slept through the noon meal, and now, as his and Chang's absence was noticed at the evening meal as well, Sandal came by to check on them. Chang told her that he thought it was best to allow Boorman to continue to sleep until he woke up naturally, and as Chang had been given full medical authority over Boorman since his concussion, Sandal did not even venture to argue. She offered to bring Chang a tray of food, but he replied that he had been doing nothing but meditating and hadn't burned enough calories to whet his appetite. He said he would take a cup of tea, if she would be so kind, and she left to get it for him.

After she left, Chang sat and watched Boorman as he slept, until his own eyes slowly closed as well. I knew that he was not sleeping, but was observing the dream just as I had been doing, but whether his observations were totally passive or if he was somehow directing the dream, I could not tell.

In a few minutes Sandal returned with the tea. As Chang sipped from his cup, Sandal went to his window to watch the sun set. "I have always wanted to visit Tibet," she said. "I have even dreamed about living here." I could tell by the fact that the setting sun was now shining directly into their cabin, that the ship had turned south and might even now be in Tibet, and so it was.

"This is not what I thought it would look like though," she said, gazing at the surrounding country-side. "I thought the mountains would be closer together."

"That is because you lived in a different part of Tibet," Chang told her.

"I lived in Tibet? When was that?"

"Not too long ago. It was after the Chinese invasion — during the cultural revolution."

"I hate the Chinese," she exclaimed, and then, realizing that Chang was Chinese, "Oh, I'm sorry; I didn't mean you. Actually, I didn't mean that at all the way it sounded. I just hate what the Chinese government has done to Tibet, not to mention what it has done to its own country."

"What they have done, they have done mainly from ignorance. We have to find a way to forgive that, because we all have plenty of it ourselves."

"How did I die?" Sandal asked. "Did I die fighting the Chinese?"

"You died young — and quickly."

"You are not going to tell me how I died, are you?"

"If you want to know about a past life, meditate upon it and ask the universe to show you that life. You have already seen some of it in dreams."

"If I tell you about a dream that I had, will you tell me if it is real?"

"What is your dream?"

"It is dark at first," she began. "I wake up in the dark and there is someone in bed with me. I realize that it is my younger brother. We sleep together for warmth. It is very cold outside of the wool blankets but something has awakened me. I go into the kitchen and see my father. I run and throw my arms around his neck because he has been away for a long time. Next, I am riding with my brother on the back of a yak. We are wedged in with the big bags that are tied on its back and we have to keep watching out for its horns when it tosses its head. The villagers have packed up all of their belongings on their own yaks and the whole village is following us. The sun is not up yet, but after awhile the mountain peaks around us begin to glow. It is a wonderful thing to see in my dream; they look as if they are made of colored glass with fire burning inside them. We stop by a little stream and my mother, who is very beautiful, gets down on her knees by the stream. I get down to see what she is doing and I see that she is catching little fish in her hands. They are easy to catch because some of the pools are so small. Then she takes the little fish and turns them loose in the bigger pools. That is all that I can remember, except that sometimes I also dream about the yaks trudging up a mountain in the snow. But the dream about the fish means something, doesn't it? I can still see the little fish flipping around in my mother's hands in the early light. Is it real? What does it mean?"

"Yes, it is a real dream, and the meaning is very simple. Your mother was telling you to always watch for opportunities to help those in need. But the message was not for you alone. She was also telling someone else to have faith that others were also watching for opportunities to help us."

"It was my father wasn't it?"

Chang nodded.

"I can see him in my dream. He is watching my mother but he doesn't say anything. He is very strong, but he is also sad and angry. What happened to him? What happened to my parents in Tibet?"

"There are reasons why we do not bring our memories into our next lives. Many are too difficult to carry — some because of things that we have done, and some because of things that others have done. But, you will know everything in the fullness of time. In the meantime, the important memory has made the transition with you. I see it in the way you bring an old man a cup of tea." He smiled at her.

*

I heard the key turn in my cell door. "Who is it?" I asked, fearful of the answer.

"Good evening, Dong Shi, it is your old friend, General Tong."

I had thought that I would not see him today, but I had forgotten that he had come late on his first visit as well.

"I have brought some other friends. I hope you are receiving."

I felt myself involuntarily stiffen.

"I am sorry it took so long to get back to you," Tong said to me. "I was very busy doing research today. I have become quite the historian, thanks to you. What can you tell me about this ring you are wearing? It is bone isn't it?"

"Yes, David Chang gave it to me," I said, trying to be as open with him as I could.

"Oh we know that of course. We know from our photographs when he stopped wearing it, but now it turns up again on your finger. This is a very expensive ring; it belongs in a museum. Yet you tell me that you only met Chang when you first saw him at a bus stop in Honolulu."

"Yes." I could not keep the tremble out of my voice and I cowered back against the wall, waiting for the inevitable blow to my face.

"And then later he gave you a ring valuable enough to buy a small army."

"I don't know anything about the value of the ring." There was a pause from Tong, and I braced myself for the slap that I knew was coming.

Instead I felt his fingers on my chin as he turned my face to the side. "What has happened to your face?" he asked in surprise. "It has healed very quickly."

"Maybe you didn't hit her as hard as you thought, General Tong," I heard another voice ask. "Maybe I should hit her."

"Shut up, you fool! You forget who you are talking to. I will have you shot and another prisoner brought in to replace you if you don't hold your tongue." Then to me, "I am pleased that you heal so fast; we won't have to wait so long between our sessions. We can develop our relationship so much faster that way."

I didn't say anything.

"At any rate, we have brought a device that will not leave you bruised and ugly. Won't that be better? Give her a sample."

Suddenly, my right leg went rigid in a spasm of pain. Waves of almost unbearable agony washed up and down my leg and every muscle in it felt like it was contracting to the maximum all at once. So great was the pain that when the device was pulled away from my leg, I felt for several seconds that I was not going to regain my breath.

"Well, it did leave a little burn spot on your leg," Tong said apologetically. "We shall have to avoid doing that too many times in the same place, won't we?"

I couldn't speak. I could feel my fists and jaw still clenched in memory of the pain, and sweat was beginning to form on my face.

"I was very embarrassed," Tong said, accusingly, "to realize that, when last I was here, I was trying to teach Chinese history to an expert on the subject. You know what I am talking about of course."

I shook my head and once again felt the terrible convulsions of my leg trying to pull itself apart as his assistant applied the device of pain.

"Oh now, look," Tong said in a chiding voice. "I told you not to put that thing back on the same spot. Now you've burnt a little hole in her leg, and it's bleeding." Tong turned his voice back to me. "We always start on the legs because the bones are so much stronger there and less likely to break. However, the muscles are also much stronger in the legs, and sometimes a tendon can snap. You will tell us if you feel a tendon snap, won't you, Dong Shi? I've heard it can be quite painful." He laughed at his joke. "What I was referring to, concerning the history lesson, was, of course, that I was explaining to you what had happened to the emperor's concubine, while you were sitting there wearing her ring and looking so interested. Apparently her son salvaged it after her hands had been cut off, and no one knew what became of it after that, and here you are with it on your finger. Would you like to hand it over to me now?"

I quickly began to try to remove the ring to give it to him, but it was a size too small for me and would not come off over my knuckle.

"Never mind; it will make a better story when I say that it always comes off a woman's hand the same way. We didn't bring the surgical bag this time, did we?" he asked one of his helpers. "Oh, well, there is no hurry. Do you like Chinese men, Dong Shi?" he asked me.

I didn't give an answer. I was afraid that there was no correct one.

"The reason that I ask is because Chang gave you a ring that had once been given to a concubine. Did he give it to you so that you could buy an army, or did he give it to you because you are his concubine?"

"He gave it to me because it is rightfully mine," I blurted out.

"Do you think that it should belong to you because your name is 'Bang'?"

"No. It was mine before you cut off my hands."

"But, I have not yet cut off your hands, dear girl," he explained with ironic patience.

"Yes, you have. You took my hands and eyes when I was the emperor's grieving concubine, and you his dry-eyed widow."

"Ha ha ha ha," He laughed loudly in surprise. "How wonderful! I must not have you killed when I take your hands this time little concubine; I must keep you around for the stories. Tell me – did you dream this up after I was here last?"

"No. I saw it when you touched my face just now. I saw everything. I saw how the concubine's son stole the ring from off his mother's bloodless hand; how he sold the ring and went into hiding; how he used the money to buy food and medicine for his mother, and how he snuck into the animal pens at night to bring her clean water to drink and to treat her wounds until he was caught and killed at last."

"A good story; but what is Chang's role? Was he the emperor? Or your son perhaps? Or have you not yet written a part for him in this fantasy of yours?"

I did not answer him.

"Well, it is no matter. At least you have written yourself a very juicy part – that of concubine. If you like Chinese men, we have a prison full of them right here. Perhaps you would like to spend some time with them? Many of them are here because of women – women who have tricked them, betrayed them, or drove them to their crimes. To quote a western writer: they loved not wisely, but too well." He laughed again at his joke. "I do not know why we put such men in prison; they should be in the army where they can do some good. Well, I really can't stay very long this evening. I am a busy man. Is there anything more that you would like to tell me in the short time that we have together?"

I shook my head.

"No? Well then show me that cheek again. It is remarkable how well it has healed. Yes, it was right there that I saw clear signs of a burst blood vessel."

I felt the sudden intense pain of his device on the side of my face and I lost consciousness. I left my body and looked down on the scene from the ceiling of my prison cell. Tong was a tall slender man. I was surprised to see that he was somewhat elderly in appearance and had grey hair. He had seemed to be so enthusiastic in the torture sessions. He had two burly companions who were staring down at my body on the bunk. The 'device' was a long heavy rod, attached by about six feet of cable to a squat black box that sat on the floor. One of Tong's assistants asked him if they could have some fun with me while I was passed out.

"You idiots, I am not here so that you can have fun. What good would it do? You can have her some other time when she is awake."

"Then let's wake her up. I'll get some water to throw on her."

"All in time; I have got other work to do tonight. Get back to your cells and I will have another week taken off for good behavior."

They left, carrying the heavy black box and the long rod past the guard outside, who sat and stared at nothing in particular.

*

After I re-entered my body and felt of my cheek, which didn't seem too horribly damaged, I decided I would rejoin Boorman's dream. I was curious to know what happened to him and his family on the road to Nangpa-la, the mountain pass named Nangpa, and it was a better way to pass the time than brooding in my cell about what was to come.

I had missed some of Boorman's dream, including the funeral ceremonies for Dorje's parents, but it seemed that autumn was not a bad season for travel if you were Tibetan. The harvest was in and the yaks were burdened with huge bags of tsampa, butter and dried vegetables. There were also barrels of pickled vegetables tied to their sides, and along the way, there were berries to be picked and eaten. Also, there was plenty of forage for the animals. The nights were cold, but no one seemed to be bothered much by it and the snow was staying in the higher elevations. It appeared as if Sangmu's village had joined the exodus, for there were hundreds of yaks, goats, sheep, and many horses and dogs as well. The children rode the yaks, the elderly rode the horses, and the rest walked.

They did not follow the roads that the Chinese used, but took high trails and passes that were known only to nomads and to people who lived in the area. The valleys and mountain ridges ran east to west, and as they were traveling south, their journey was up one side of a row of mountains to a high pass and then down the other side. At first they traveled rapidly, night and day, but after they had put a couple of mountain ranges between themselves and their villages, they began to relax and travel a little slower and to set up camps every evening. They never killed an animal, but sometimes when a pack animal died along the way, there would be feasting in the camps that night, and no matter whose animal it was, everyone shared equally in the meat.

They began to feel that their plan to leave the Chinese behind was working and they often sang as they moved slowly across the valleys. They would trudge up the mountains into deeper and deeper snow, and then when they reached the highest point of the pass they would all shout in great jubilation "The gods are victorious!" before starting down the other side.

Dorje had pulled from memory all the stories that he had heard about Nangpa-la and thought that he had a pretty good idea where he was going. This pass had been used for centuries by traders traveling between Tibet and Nepal and was well known to the nomads as well. It was immediately to the west of the great mountain Cho Oyu, The Turquoise God, which was also a little west of the even greater mountain, Chomolungma, The Goddess Mother of the Earth. He felt that he could find it with those landmarks and a little help from nomads along the way. He would have to stay out of the larger villages like Tingri, however, because there might be Chinese there who would be looking for his caravan.

The further south they traveled, the higher the general elevation became and the colder the air. But they were strong people, accustomed to hardship and frigid winters and their hearts were warm with the gladness of each other's company. In a few more weeks they would be in Nepal, and then India, and then they would make new homes and a new monastery where the Dalai Lama himself could make blessings on it and upon their homes and their children and upon themselves. And in that land, they told each other, the Chinese never came. They would tell their grandchildren how they had made this trip with hundreds of yak and goats and sheep, and for generations, their descendents would honor their memory for delivering them from the Chinese by making this dangerous trek.

One clear day, they topped a snowy mountain pass to see a long valley laid out before them. Across the valley they could see the icy peaks of the gigantic mountain range they called the Himalayas, the abode of snow. "The mountain path to Nangpa-la is at the other end of this valley," Dorje told them. We must stay close to the mountains at the side of the valley so that those in Tingri do not see us making the crossing. We should travel at night and camp during the day so that our fires are not seen in the darkness and our dust is not seen in the daylight." He pointed to a huge mountain jutting out of the ground seemingly at the very edge of the valley. "That must be the Turquoise God," he said. "We will pass in his shadow. You can tell that it is him, because he has turned his back on Chomolungma, who sits to the east — his lover who rejected him."

They traveled as Dorje instructed and they met with no one except nomads, who confirmed that they were indeed headed to Nangpa-la. "If you see a monastery in ruins at the foot of the mountains, you are too far east," they told him. "That is the Rongbuk Monastery. There is a la there, but it is too high for your caravan. You must go west to the next valley. You must travel as if you were going to circle around Cho Oyu with the god on your left," they said. "As that is not a proper way to encircle a god, Cho Oyu won't let you, but will instead direct you to the la, and from there you will descend down into Nepal's warm valleys."

Dorje invited the nomads to come to their cook fires and the nomads brought yak meat to share with Dorje's people. As they sat around the fires, eating and drinking, Dorje asked the nomads, how they felt about the Chinese.

"We hate them," they said. "They have taken our country and they are killing everything. We have seen them hunting wild asses from their jeeps. They shoot them with their machine guns until the whole herd is dead. We would wage war on the Chinese, but what can we do?" He held up his black powder rifle to show Dorje that they had no weapons to match the Chinese.

"Then you shall have our horses," Dorje said. "They cannot make it over the la, and if you hate the Chinese, then I call you friend."

"Your goats and sheep may not make it either, if you do not hurry, friend. The place where snow dwells even in the summer is not a place where men or animals are meant to be in the winter."

"We must try to take them with us," Dorje replied. "Come up in the spring to see if we were successful. Any that you find should still be fresh."

They all laughed at Dorje's joke.

Dorje's caravan found the narrow valley just as the nomads described it, and they followed it up through the giant roots of the mountains that towered ahead. Early snow covered the trail and it was difficult to tell if they were always on the path that others had walked before them. They came to a place where the trail seemed to split into three different directions, and as the nomads had told Dorje to try to go counter clock-wise around Cho Oyu, Dorje led his caravan up the left-most of these trails, which curved and ascended in a promising way.

Eventually his forward scout came back and told him that it was a dead end; there was nothing up ahead but the rubble of a vast landslide, and no place to go on the other side of it. It was getting late and Dorje decided that they would camp where they were, and as they were on a steep precipice, the animals would be led a little further up and away from the cliffs so that they would not push each other off in the darkness. So they camped there, overlooking the deep valley into which they would descend in the morning, and that they hoped would lead them to the la of Nangpa.

The caravan was still under orders to light no fires at night, and in the darkness late that night, Dorje saw the tiny lights of vehicles coming from the direction of Tingri and up the narrow valley below. In the early morning, he looked over the precipice and down into the camp of a large group of Chinese soldiers.

*

Dorje pulled the villagers all together in the dim pre-dawn light. They gathered away from the precipice lest someone dislodge a stone and give away their presence. He told them what was below them and they passed worried looks back and forth. "We will have to fight our way out," He explained. "They have us blocked without even knowing it."

"No," Sangmu said. "If they don't know we are here, then they may just go away."

"We don't have time to wait," Dorje replied. "There is no forage for the animals until we get into Nepal. Also the snows are beginning to fall. The la may become impassable soon."

"How do we know why they are here?" Sangye asked. "They may be here to hunt goats. We could be taking lives unnecessarily. We could try just walking past them as if we were nomads."

"Then we would have given away any opportunity that we have. The Chinese think that it is a crime for Tibetans to leave Tibet. Even if the soldiers did not recognize us, we would still be arrested and put back into prison or shot. I think that they are here to block the passage until the snows do it for them. I also think that they are here especially for us, they just don't know that we have already arrived."

"How would they know to come here?" someone asked.

"This is the only way out of our country for hundreds of miles that does not have Chinese soldiers stationed there at all times."

"I think we should wait," Sangmu insisted. "We can feed the strongest animals from our own stores, and we can kill the weaker ones who will soon die anyway. Their meat will keep for a long time here, and the other animals will not need as much food as when they are traveling."

"If the snows come and trap us here, we will have to go back into the valley to survive, and there we will be caught by the patrols," Dorje answered. "Also the Chinese came in the dark. What if they backtrack in the daylight and see that our trail leads up here? They will come for us on this dead-end trail, and we will have no weapons."

"What weapons do we have now?" one of the villagers asked.

"Rocks, stones, boulders," Dorje said. "We can carry them to the edge of the cliff and when we have enough, we will heave them down on the soldiers. Those are the only weapons we have, and this is the only time and place that they can be used. But from here they are powerful weapons, and perhaps the gods will smile on us, and create a landslide to bury the Chinese."

The villagers were divided on the idea, but since Dorje had gotten them safely this far, they decided to continue to give him their trust, and they began to pile boulders up along the ledge, being careful not to accidentally drop anything too soon into the Chinese camp. They were still in the morning shadow of Cho Oyu and down in the valley, it was darker still, and there was very little movement as yet in the camp; any unusual noise would surely be noticed.

As the villagers worked, Sangmu sought out Dorje. "Dorje," she said, looking him in the face, "father of my children, my best friend in this world, my protector, and heart of my heart, where are you now? What has become of you? Have the Chinese poisoned you? This is not what my Dorje would do. This is not the right thing — to kill these soldiers. It would be a terrible thing for you to do it even by yourself, and it is unspeakable, the harm that you are doing by involving these innocent people in your murderous act."

He looked shocked at her words. After a moment he said, "Either the Chinese must die or we must."

"It would be better for all of us to die without blood on our hands than to live with that stain."

"A while ago you were ready to sacrifice our animals so that we could live. The Chinese are no better than those animals. They may be worse."

"I will not debate the value of lives with you now," she replied, "but these people, our friends, who have never even killed an animal on purpose, are being led to kill human beings. Do you think a good leader would do this?"

"They chose me to lead them to Nepal," he replied angrily. "I am doing everything that I can do to get them there."

"I think they chose you, not because they thought you could lead them to Nepal, but because they thought you could lead them to nirvana — to free them from the cycle of rebirth. And once I thought you could do it as well. When you were young, a clear light shown from you that everyone recognized, but now the Chinese have thrown mud upon your light. Don't you see that this is the nature of evil? Not that it slaughters your herds or burns your forests or even that it throws you in prison, but that it kills your light. Don't let them kill your light, Dorje. You must fight them, but not like this. Don't fight them by being like them. Fight them by using them to fan your own light to burn more brilliantly."

Dorje turned angrily away, dismissing her arguments as a waste of time, only to find Sangye and the other monks waiting to speak to him.

"Dorje," Sangye began, "You are my best friend since childhood, but I can not follow you any further. The other monks and I have discussed our problem among ourselves and they have appointed me to speak to you. If you insist on this plan of slaughter, then we are leaving now. We want no part of it and would like to try to dissuade you. Otherwise we are going to walk back the way we came and may the gods be merciful to you."

"But what about the monastery you are going to build?" Dorje asked them.

"If it ever came to be that there was a monastery built, we would not be worthy to live in it if we had killed."

"Then I will kill them for you," Dorje responded. "You do not have to do anything. Let all of the blood be on me."

"You can not take everyone's karma onto yourself, Dorje. Everyone who joins you in this will receive their share of the karmic result. We are asking you to stop now. But, if we can not stop you, then we will have no part of it at all. We will put our faith in the gods and buddhas rather than in killing."

Norbu had broken away from where some of the women were keeping the younger children. He came up to hear what the monks were saying to his father. "Sangye is right, Father," he said. "There can be no monastery or chorten or anything to honor the gods or Buddhas or bodhisattvas if the stones are mortared with blood."

"Then you wish to go with the monks?" Dorje asked, looking sadly down at his son.

"We should all go with them," the boy answered.

"I can't do that, Norbu. I have to stay and fight, but you may go with the monks if you wish. They will never allow you to come to harm if it is within their power to prevent it."

"If you are staying, Father," Norbu answered, reaching up to take his father's hand, "then I will stay here and die with you."

Dorje picked him up and hugged him, feeling that the small child was his last friend in the world. "We are not going to die, Norbu," he said. "You will see. The gods will be victorious."

Dorje held Norbu and watched the monks as they walked back down the trail to the distant valley. It would take awhile for the monks to reach the bottom, but Dorje could not wait. The soldiers were still concentrated at the base of the cliff, but later they would be scattered and the falling rocks would not come near them all. He sent Norbu back to his mother. She was with the other children and some of the other women who did not have the mettle to perform the lethal task of pushing the rocks and boulders over the side. Chodron was with

Sangmu. They were both so beautiful standing there together. Chodron was still a young girl, but beginning to show signs of womanhood. She looked almost like a miniature of her mother, even down to the pleading look in her eyes.

Sangmu held out her hand to him as if to say, "Please, Dorje, please don't do this?" He turned and gave the order for everyone to line up behind the rocks.

"When I say to do so, push the biggest ones over the side," he said, "and then begin throwing the others out into the air, starting with the next largest first until you work your way down to the smallest. Do not stop as long as you have something to throw. They will run away from the cliffs at first, so you should try to throw further out. You cannot aim from this height, so you will have to make a rain of stones that they can not avoid. Now! Push the boulders over the side."

They pushed over the stones that were too large to throw, and then began to heave over the next sizes, just as they had been told. Then they began to throw the cannonball-sized ones out into the open air. As yet, except for the occasional sound of a boulder bouncing off the side of the cliff, no sound had come from below. After a few more seconds of stone throwing, they began to hear the booms and reverberations of the first boulders hitting the valley floor. This was followed by the distant sounds of cries and shouts drifting up from below. The shouting continued, and under Dorje's direction, so did the stone throwing.

Some of the soldiers had managed to run out of the reach of the rain of stones and had figured out what was happening. Now they had opened fire on the villagers, but their bullets spattered harmlessly off of the cliff face.

Dorje saw a soldier run to a truck and then in a few seconds leave it and run to another one, which he managed to start and drive outside of stone throwing range. Another soldier managed to rescue a jeep the same way. As many of the soldiers who could fit ran and jumped onto the truck and jeep, and they drove back down the valley to look for the way up to the top of the cliff.

Dorje was prepared for this contingency. He had saved some of the larger boulders and had the men line them up across the trail so that once the rocks were started rolling there would be little that could stop them.

The soldiers soon found the turn-off to the upper trail and began to drive up it as fast as they could without sliding off of the side into the valley. When they came to the monks, they drove past them as if they were not even there. They may have been accustomed to seeing monks in this area, as Rongbuk monastery was just a few miles to the east.

When the vehicles came around the bend in the trail to where it led straight up to the villagers, Dorje ordered that the boulders be sent rolling. Two of them rolled uselessly off the side of the trail and fell into the valley; one of them missed the truck, which was in the lead, but then bounced back into the path of the jeep, smashing the front differential, and wedging itself under the engine so that the jeep could go neither forwards nor backwards. Another boulder bounced off the truck's front tire, knocking it out of alignment and causing the driver to slow down, but not stopping progress entirely.

After the boulders, the dogs were unleashed, and the great mastiffs rushed down the trail, ready to attack and rend the Chinese soldiers, but their fangs, which had never before failed them, were no match for machine guns or the wheels and bumper of a large truck.

The boulders had not pushed the vehicles off the trail as Dorje had hoped they would, but instead the truck continued to drive straight at them with men hanging out of the back firing automatic weapons at the helpless villagers, who now threw up their arms and tried to surrender. Most of the villagers died from the gunfire in those few seconds before the soldiers realized that they were themselves no longer in any danger.

Dorje did not throw up his arms, but rushed to cradle the body of Norbu, cut through the chest by a spray of bullets. He looked around him at the friends that he had known all his life, now gone from his life, and lying like broken dolls in the snow. They stared wide-eyed and unblinking at the great snowy peaks around them — peaks that tried achingly to reach into the very heavens. He was in a daze and offered no resistance when the soldiers clubbed him to the ground and roughly tied his hands behind his back.

All of the few surviving men had their hands tied just as Dorje's were, but for some reason, the women's hands were not tied. Perhaps it was because they still had surviving children to look after, or perhaps it was because the soldiers felt that they had no reason to fear a woman. They asked them who was the leader of this party, and Dorje eventually roused out of his daze enough to admit that he was.

"You are the captain of these outlaws?" one of the soldiers asked him.

"They are not outlaws," Dorje answered.

"They have killed or injured several of our men, including our captain. Only outlaws would attack us this way."

"I made them do it. They are just innocent villagers. Let them go."

The soldier laughed at this as if Dorje had made a fine joke. "Yes, I will go and tell my new officer that we were attacked by outlaws but that I let them go."

"Tell him that you killed us all."

"I will think about that possibility. Tell your people to start walking down the trail, the women and children on the right where it is safer and the men single file on the left."

"What about the animals?"

"They will have to find their own way down. We do not have time for animals."

"And what about the dead?"

"The vultures will take care of them. Isn't that your barbaric custom anyway?"

They walked down the trail to where the jeep sat high-centered on the boulder. The soldier who had assumed command of the troops ordered the surviving village men to lift the jeep off of the large stone. When they had done that, one of the other soldiers shouldered his weapon and attempted to start the vehicle. When that failed, the acting commander ordered the Tibetans to push the jeep over the edge so that the truck could continue down the trail unobstructed. When the truck had backed down to where the jeep had been, the commander ordered the Tibetan men to rip out a plank from the floor of the truck bed. "We are going to have some fun," he said. "Don't you think we should have some fun after all of this killing?" he asked Dorje.

He ordered that the plank be extended for about half its length out over the precipice. He chose a young Tibetan woman to anchor it by standing on it close to its end. Then he ordered Dorje to get down on his knees and knee-walk out onto the plank, facing south. While Dorje sidled out onto the plank, the commander pointed out a few landmarks for Dorje, including the Nangpa-la that had been their destination. "Can you fly, Captain," the commander asked Dorje. "There is Nepal — right over that ridge." He pointed up the valley to the snow covered pass.

The commander kept one foot on the plank so that he could test the balance and keep the board from up-ending and falling into the deep valley, and when he felt that happening, he stopped Dorje and had him move back toward him a few inches. Now the only thing that kept Dorje from falling straight down into the valley was the weight of the poor nervous Tibetan girl who was trembling and whose knees were already about to buckle.

Dorje saw that they were no longer over the smashed tents of the PLA camp, but were now over a pile of jagged boulders and rubble that had fallen from this cliff some time in the past. On top of the rubble, he could see the tiny flicker of the jeep burning down below, its plume of black oily smoke dissipating long before it reached the height of the cliff trail.

The commander then ordered all of the Tibetan men to line up along the edge of the precipice in front of Dorje, their backs to the open air of the valley. He then ordered some of his own men to line up in front of them, their guns at the ready.

Dorje saw what was about to happen to the terrified men. "Wait," he pleaded. "Aren't you going to take them back for trial?"

"In what?" the commander asked, "one broken truck? Thanks to you, we have no vehicles. No, I think you had a better idea when you suggested that I tell my commanding officers that we killed everyone. Although, we will probably take the women back to help keep us warm. The soldiers can take turns walking and then riding with the women."

"You are not human," Dorje said to him, his voice breaking with the intensity of his hatred.

"Oh, Captain, you have hurt me. Because you said that, I have had a change of heart." He turned to the women who were huddling against the face of the mountain. "I have heard that many a man has been saved by the love of a good woman. If any of you would like to save your husband, go and stand in front of him now. If you have children that you are responsible for, you may take them as well."

The women, grasping their surviving children by their hands, went and stood hopefully in front of their husbands. Not every man had a surviving wife and not every woman had a surviving husband, so there were gaps in front of some men.

"What about mothers," one of the remaining women asked.

"Oh yes, definitely. If you have a son that you would like to save, then you should go and stand in front of him."

Several more women went and stood in front of the men. One lucky man had two women standing in front of him — three, counting his very young daughter.

"Is that all?" the commander asked. "What about sisters?"

A few more women joined the ranks.

"Very well then," the commander said. "This is wonderful; every man here has a woman who wants him to live. Am I a monster to let you stand with your men like this?" Then to his men, "Open fire."

The soldiers standing in front of the rows of Tibetans began firing their automatic weapons into them, and the Tibetan men, women, and children, struck hard by the force of the bullets, stumbled back and fell silently off of the precipice in a tangle of arms and legs.

Dorje watched them fall in silence down to the rocks below, many not yet dead, but waving their arms in circular motions, or treading the air with their feet as they fell. It took an eternity for them to fall, during which time Dorje seemed to hear, as if in a dream, the distant screams and moans from the women who still remained on the precipice with him. After awhile, he seemed to hear someone speaking to him.

"Captain? Captain? Are you well?" It was the PLA commander. "I hope that you do not think that I was being cruel. On long marches like this, we have to get rid of male prisoners. They are always trouble. In this way, we also get rid of troublesome females who might resent the fact that we have killed their men. It is very practical, don't you think? Anyway, I am glad that you are still with us, thanks to your female counter weight. She is very strong. I thought that she might faint, but there was just a little screaming — that was all. She will be a good companion for a Chinese soldier. We will have more fun with her in a moment as we measure the weight of her clothing against the weight of your own."

Dorje didn't answer him. He was finding that he was forced to shut his eyes to keep his balance. For when he looked down into the valley, where his friends and relatives now lay like indistinguishable specks on the rubble, he would become very dizzy, and feel that he was going to fall, and although he felt that he should die, and deserved to die, and desired to die, there was something in him that still clung to life and to this slender board bending under his weight, and the cold sweat of fear began to run down his neck and down his chest under his arms. It was not fear of dying as much as it was a fear that somehow he had moved the earth off its axis just a notch and that the world was now, because of him, on a spiraling path to destruction. As he kneeled there on the board, as if in prayer, he began to feel sicker than he had ever felt in his life, with a sickness that surpassed any physical disease or cure. And kneeling, he did pray. He prayed that Sangmu was correct that somewhere, someone was looking for a way to help them all — that someone still helped the little fishes.

"Do you like to gamble, Captain?" the commander asked him. "We soldiers like to gamble. In just a moment we will have some fun that will involve removing this young woman's clothing one piece at a time to see which item tips the scales in your favor. The men will place bets on which article it will be, but just between you and me, I feel certain that it will be the heavy jacket, don't you? First she will remove some clothing and hold it in her hand, then you will do like wise. Then she will drop hers and then you will drop yours. We will see how far this goes before the board tips you down into the valley. If she is fast, she will be able to jump off the board before it carries her over the side. When that happens, I won't have time to say goodbye, Captain, so let me say it now, and thanks for the opportunity that you have given me. My captain did not care for me much, and probably would have had me demoted after this excursion, but now he is dead, and thanks to you, I have been given the opportunity to demonstrate how capable I am as a leader of men. I am a young man, Captain, but I have ambitions, and someday I hope to be general of all the armies of China. I will tell you a secret, Captain." He leaned over and whispered something to Dorje so that the other soldiers could not hear. "But enough about me — we need to select a few women for the long trip home. Again, thank you."

He ordered the soldiers to take the youngest children and throw them over the cliff. "Don't waste any bullets on them," he told them.

The mother of the first child who was pulled away by the soldiers ran and threw herself at the commander's feet and wrapped her arms around his leg, pleading with him not to kill her child. The commander pulled out his automatic pistol and shot her in the head. "Do not let this happen again," he ordered a soldier who had his gun trained on the women and was supervising the individual extractions, "or the next time I will use this gun on you."

"My apologies, Lieutenant Tong. It will not happen again," the soldier respectfully replied.

One of the soldiers began to pull Chodron from Sangmu's arms. "Leave that one," Lieutenant Tong instructed. "She is old enough. And besides, look at her mother; what a pair they make. I think I shall have to use my new rank and keep both of them for myself."

When Tong had turned away and the soldier standing guard over the separations had moved up the row to where the next small child was being pulled away, Sangmu lifted her daughter off the ground, covered her eyes with one of her hands and ran and leaped off the cliff into the empty air.

As Tong ran to the edge to watch them fall, and as Dorje saw his wife and daughter speeding downward to oblivion, the girl who anchored Dorje's plank tried to shove her fist into her mouth, and then quickly made a decision for both Dorje and herself. The girl took a large sidestep along the board in Dorje's direction and the board immediately tilted up, dropping Dorje after Sangmu and Chodron, and throwing the girl over the precipice, to follow all of them down.

Dorje continued to watch Sangmu and Chodron fall, never getting any closer or further away from them. Sangmu still had Chodron's eyes covered, and Chodron did not struggle against it, but seemed to have relaxed into her mother's arms. He saw them hit and in another second or two his dream was over.

Chapter 11 – Of Gods and Soldiers.

The early light of morning was shining bright on the other side of the *Eckener*'s hull when Boorman woke abruptly from his dream. He took a quick gasp of air and without moving, stared up at the ceiling of his cabin while tears streamed down his cheeks. He darted his eyes quickly around the room, trying to find something familiar that would tell him where he was now, and how he came here when death seemed so certain just moments ago. And if he was alive, could Sangmu and Chodron be alive as well, even though he had seen them die. No, it wasn't possible; he *had* seen them die — a vision that he wished he could erase from his memory. But hadn't he been just a few seconds behind them? Yet this did not look like the bardo — at least not as he had thought it would be.

"Sangmu?" he whispered. "Chodron? Norbu?"

He heard someone say something in an unintelligible language and turned his head to see a stranger with an extremely weathered face sitting on a bed and watching him. "Toshi dili. Nga ming Dorje yin. (Hello. My name is Dorje.)," Boorman said, sitting up in bed. "Keirang ming karei rei? (What is your name?)," he asked, throwing back the covers and swinging his legs over the bed. He looked down to see where he was putting his feet, continued looking past his feet all the way down to the distant ground, and fell straight out of bed onto his head, knocking himself unconscious on the clear plastic floor.

*

After verifying that Boorman had not injured himself again, and that Chang had things under control, I withdrew back into my body to consider what I had seen in Boorman's dream. Was it possible that Lieutenant Tong in Boorman's dream was the same as General Tong in my waking nightmare? Yes, it had to be the same person; they had the same cruel personality, the same ironic politeness, the same attitude toward women, and the same driving ambition, not to mention the same tall slender build. Boorman, in his life as Dorje, had not only become lost in the illusion of the world, but had unleashed a new evil upon China, Tibet, and the world. Dorje's anger, hatred, and violence had diverted many people away from their own spiritual path, and by killing the PLA captain, had opened the door for Tong's advancement — an advancement that had not yet stopped.

Soon I heard the sound of activity in the outer cell and was comforted by the smell of Zhao Tou's aunt's wonderful cooking. The food that he brought in the mornings was the only food that I got anymore, but it had always been the only food worth eating since I had arrived in this building.

"Is it true that the ring on your finger was given to you by Chang Da Wai?" Zhao Tou asked as he placed a large bowl of soup in my hands.

"Yes, it is true," I replied between gulps of soup. "Help me get it off. Do you have any soap, or perhaps some kind of oil?"

"Don't worry about taking it off," he said. "That ring will protect you. You do not need to worry about anything while you are wearing it. I know that Tong said he was going to cut off your hand and keep it in a glass case. That will not happen if you have faith in the ring. He will never own that ring."

"How did you hear about the ring?" I asked him.

"I heard about it while I was signing in just now. Everyone is talking about it. I do not know whether to tell my aunt about this or not. I have already broken so many rules by even telling her that you are here, what can one more thing matter? But I am afraid that she and her friends will not be able to keep this secret. By tomorrow the news will have spread all over Beijing like the dust from the Gobi Desert. But if I don't tell her and she finds out some other way, then she will kill me and feed me to the pigs."

He paused, considering his options, and then added, "Chang Da Wai was given the power of life and death by Kwan Yin and now it is discovered that you wear Chang Da Wai's ring. That is news for which my aunt and her friends will prepare me daily feasts for as long as I live. Have faith in the ring; it will be your shield against all harm."

I did not think that he was correct, knowledgeable as I was that it was I to whom the people referred as Kwan Yin, and that the ring, historically valuable though it may be, was just a ring—a piece of carved dead bone with no power. However, it was obvious that I was not going to get any help from Zhao Tou in getting it off of my finger.

After I finished my soup, and Zhao Tou had settled back down into his official role of being my guard, I went back to the *Eckener*.

*

Captain Macon, Sandal, the ship's doctor, and Chang were standing around Boorman's bed looking down at him. Chang was explaining to everyone that they should not act alarmed if Boorman's behavior was odd when he awoke. Boorman was still in the process of healing and it would not help him if people acted as if he were irrational or demented, he explained. It was best at this point to just humor him, no matter what he said. They agreed that they would do as Chang instructed — the doctor reluctantly.

The doctor examined Boorman, pronounced him physically sound, and left to go back to the infirmary.

After awhile, Boorman's eyes opened and he looked up at the people standing over him. "Who are you?" he asked.

Chang asked, "More importantly, do you know who you are?"

"My name is Boorman, I think," he answered thoughtfully. "Yes, Boorman."

"Captain Thomas Jonathon Boorman?" Chang asked him.

"Don't call me that; I am no captain; I am no leader," he answered vehemently.

"Are you not a captain in the United States Navy?"

Boorman paused. "Yes, I suppose I am. It is just a title, isn't it?"

"Yes," Chang agreed, "it is just a title. Do you know who we are now?"

"I believe I do. I know you all from somewhere." He looked at Holly. "You are my best friend, aren't you? No, it is more than that. We are married — that is it, isn't it. Your name is Mir — Mir something. No, that's not it. It is something like a song — Song something. I'm sorry; things aren't making much sense right now. But we are married, aren't we?"

Captain Macon looked questioningly at Chang and then nodded.

"And you are my beautiful daughter, aren't you?" he asked Sandal. Sandal nodded.

"Do you know who I am?" Chang asked him.

"Yes," Boorman smiled up at him, taking his hand. "You are my son, the precious reincarnated one."

As breakfast was still being served, Captain Macon asked Chang if they should bring a tray of food for Captain Boorman. Chang said that he thought that it would do Boorman more good to get up and move around and that it would speed his reintegration process to go and eat in the dining room.

Chang had already opaqued the floor in the cabin, so Boorman did not have any problems with vertigo as they helped him up and got him dressed. "Why am I in jail?" he asked them. Holly and Sandal did not know what to answer, but Chang responded, "John, you are not in jail, yourself. You are seeing some things through the eyes of another entity. It is fine for you to do this, but you must also learn how to focus on what is physically nearby as well. Otherwise, you may hurt yourself."

They helped Boorman to the cabin door, and Captain Macon and Chang held his arms while Sandal opened the door. When Boorman saw the transparent floor, his eyes rolled back and he slumped in their arms.

I realized from Boorman's question and Chang's reply, that Boorman had a memory of jail that came from my experience. The one-way connection between Boorman and myself was becoming a full two-way connection and it was possible that I could help him with his fear of heights. I began to attempt to instill in him my own love of heights to counteract his fear.

As they were attempting to get his dead weight into a chair, he opened his eyes again. "Can I fly?" he asked.

Chang told him that they could all fly as long as they were in this ship, but that he shouldn't venture to try it on his own as yet.

Captain Macon wondered if they should try going to the dining room again, or if they should leave well enough alone. Chang replied that Boorman had help that they were not aware of and that they would not have a problem this time. They helped Boorman to the door once more, and when he looked down, he recoiled but did not faint. He looked at his friends holding his arms and supporting him and smiled, but he did not look down again.

They sat him at a table and Sandal went to get a tray for him. As Boorman looked around, he smiled at all the people. "It is so good to see that so many people have made it so far."

Sandal brought him a plate of bacon and eggs. "Whose animal was it?" he asked about the bacon.

As he ate, other passengers came around out of politeness to ask how he was doing, and he responded so warmly and seemed to be so glad to see them, that their cold aloofness began to melt, and some of them smiled back at him with genuine warmth.

After breakfast, he said that he thought he would lie down a little while, and they helped him back to his cabin. He still refused to look down until he got into his cabin with its seemingly more solid floor. Then he walked to the windows by himself, looked out and smiled. He began humming a strange tune. "I have forgotten the words," he apologized. "But where are the herds? Where are the forests?" No one had an answer for him.

As Holly and Sandal began to leave, Boorman took Holly's hand. "Let the children go and play," he said. "Stay here with me."

She said that she had chores to take care of, and she and Sandal left Chang with Boorman, who sat staring out the window at the strangely familiar countryside.

*

Boorman took a little nap before lunch, and afterwards he began to feel more like his pre-Beijing self. "What has happened to me?" he asked Chang. "I dreamed I was in Tibet."

"You *are* in Tibet," Chang told him. "We will be going near to Lhasa soon, and we will be able to see the Potala from the ship. You have been asleep since Beijing. You took a very hard blow to the head."

"I dreamed I was somebody else," Boorman continued, staring into space as he recalled his dream. "It was a sad dream — a life gone wrong. Almost everyone I knew died because of me. And it was so real — I have these memories now of things that never really happened."

"Perhaps you are dreaming now. How do you know that the other dream wasn't real?"

"Because it couldn't be; I am who I am and that's all."

"You have already been awake once," Chang said. "You called me your son."

"Yes, you were in my dream. Everybody on this ship was in my dream. But that doesn't make it real. Everybody knows that dreams can incorporate pieces of reality. It was only a dream," he added without conviction.

They left to go to the dining room, and as they entered the hallway, Boorman took Chang's arm. "I can't look down," he said. "Strange, but in my dream, at least at the beginning, I wasn't afraid of heights. By the end I was terrified — no, I was horrified of heights. The world pulled my friends, my family, and then me down to it and then crushed us all."

"So perhaps it is not heights that you are afraid of but the crush of the world." Chang remarked.

"Well, right now it is heights," Boorman answered.

As they entered the dining room, Boorman saw Captain Macon and Sandal already sitting at a table with some passengers. "Sangmu and Chodron," Boorman whispered. He shook his head. "It seemed so real."

"But you said it was just a dream," Chang said.

"The memories seem real enough though," Boorman said. "I'll shake if off after awhile, just like every other dream."

After lunch, they went up to the observation deck and watched the hills and mountains of Tibet roll away behind them. They saw a distant city grow larger, and on a high hill-top of the city sat a white and red palace. "The Potala," Boorman said in awe. "Ever since I was a child, I have wanted to see it."

"Which childhood?" Chang asked.

Boorman looked at him strangely. "I don't know," he answered.

Because the *Eckener* had been forbidden to fly over any cities by the government in Beijing, they went as close as they could for the passengers to observe the city without feeling that they were violating their instructions.

The *Eckener* followed the river that ran to the south of Lhasa, staying to the side opposite the city, but as soon as they were seen by the inhabitants, a mob of Tibetans rushed out onto the single bridge over the river, and began shouting "Chang Da Wai" and "Maitreya" while waving their arms at the *Eckener*.

"Who is Maitreya," Boorman asked Chang, as they began to hear the words blown up to them by the wind.

"Maitreya is the Buddha to come. They are hopeful that I am that one."

"Are you?"

"Oh no, I am not the one they are looking for. I doubt that they will ever see me again after today."

"Why would they even think that you were a Buddha? No offense, but don't they know that you are Chinese?"

"It doesn't matter," Chang laughed. "The last Buddha was Indian. Nationalities do not matter to Buddhas."

"It looks like the Chinese are coming out to say hello as well." Boorman pointed to a large group of men in uniform who were rushing toward the bridge.

"I am afraid they are not coming to exchange pleasantries," Chang replied.

Chang was correct, for the police force, assisted by PLA troops, began to chew through the Tibetan mob with batons and rifle butts, sending them running and bloodied, back into the city, dragging their unconscious friends along with them.

Boorman was beside himself. He stood up and began screaming at the soldiers and policemen to stop. It was doubtful that they would have heard just him, but most of the other people on the *Eckener* had the same reaction and the loud shouting from the airship soon gave the uniformed men pause. They stopped what they were doing and stared up in surprise at the *Eckener* long enough for the remaining Tibetans to melt by them and escape back into the city un-bludgeoned.

Boorman turned to Chang, tears in his eyes. "They weren't doing anything," he said. "I hate the Chinese."

*

The *Eckener* continued silently onward while the passengers stared back at Lhasa in shock at what they had seen. It was still all that most people could talk about even late in the day as they approached Zhangmu, the last Chinese town before leaving Tibet and entering Nepal.

To get to Zhangmu, they had followed a vast river valley, which cleft the Himalayas to drain the waters of the Tibetan plateau into Nepal. The ship had been dwarfed by the high peaks all around them, and even in the midst of their concern about what they had witnessed in Lhasa, most passengers stared silently around them in awe as the ship made its winding way slowly down the enormous valley. The vegetation around them became more lush and tropical, and the air heavier and more saturated with oxygen, and many people began to breathe more freely and their constant headaches subsided as they left the thin air of Tibet behind.

Boorman paid little attention to the mountains, waterfalls, rock faces and forests around him, but brooded silently about the incident on the bridge outside of Lhasa.

At Zhangmu, they went through customs, and the Chinese customs officers boarded the *Eckener* and went through everyone's luggage. It was an exhausting ordeal for everybody, and afterwards, Boorman and Chang had a quick evening meal and retired to their cabin, where Boorman collapsed on his cot and was soon snoring.

He did not dream this time, however, but soon emerged from his body like a giant blue butterfly emerging from its chrysalis. He went up through the floors of the ship and stood on the empty upper deck of the *Eckener* and stared back in the direction of Lhasa.

*

"He is going to go back," Chang said to me. "Go with him and keep him out of trouble."

The giant Boorman stepped off of the *Eckener* and onto the Lhasa Bridge, hundreds of miles away. I held his arm and he took me with him as he went. Here was the blue giant that had rescued me from the Chinese prison; here was the Chenresig that I had heard about when I had traveled into Mongolia for The Foundation. Boorman had reserves of psychic energy that he was not able to tap when awake, but when he was asleep and appropriately agitated at the Chinese and the suffering of the Tibetans, emerged to taunt and badger the Chinese military and to make their lives hell on earth. What had prompted the first episode in Boorman's life I did not know, but I was about to be witness to the most recent.

This wrathful Chenresig was dressed in traditional Tibetan clothing except that his chest was bare and he wore only a vest on his torso. His pants were baggy and the toes of his boots were pointed and curved upward. Lighting flashed throughout his body and danced around his head like a storm on a mountaintop.

He stood on the bridge and shouted at the city in Tibetan, "I have come to free my children. Oh you evil ones who have abused them, behold me and despair."

Lights began to flicker on in the town and soldiers and police were soon rushing up to the bridge in jeeps and trucks. They stopped when they saw Chenresig standing defiant, arms crossed, on the bridge. I couldn't imagine what they thought of me standing there beside him, my arm through his, his beautiful consort.

Urged on by their officers, the soldiers charged the bridge, but Chenresig leapt over their heads to the roadway behind them, pulling me along with him. When he landed he seemed to grow even larger, his hair burst into flame and he produced a scepter out of thin air. This scepter had the form of a life-sized human skeleton, but Chenresig held it in one hand as if it were a toy. "Who shall be the first?" he bellowed, shaking the ground and staggering the soldiers on the bridge. He took a step forward, brandishing the rigid skeleton like a club. At this, officers, enlisted men, and policemen all fled across the bridge on foot or in their vehicles, whichever was most convenient, into the darkness across the river.

Boorman/Chenresig raised his other arm and threw a writhing, flashing bolt of lightning into their midst. It exploded with a tremendous clap and flash when it struck, throwing soldiers into the air. He started to follow them, but I held him back. "Om mani pehmay hoong," I said, prayerfully, not knowing if I had the strength to hold him. He turned and looked at me as if just realizing that I was there. He smiled and his demeanor became calmer. The skeleton scepter disappeared and the flames on his head died down and went out. The deep blue of his skin became paler and his face took on a softer look, the teeth becoming smaller and not pointed as if for the ripping of flesh. Without taking his eyes off of me, he turned us around and we strolled into the city.

"Om mani pehmay hoong," he said, and I repeated in a higher register.

"Om mani pehmay hoong," he shouted to the sky, throwing back his head.

"Om mani pehmay hoong," we chanted happily, boldly, solemnly, and loudly as we strolled arm in arm through the streets of Lhasa.

The doors and windows along the streets were full of the awe filled faces of Tibetans and Chinese alike. The Tibetans would fall to their knees and then stretch out prostrate before us. "Chenresig," and "Tara," they called us, and then joined in the chant, "Om mani pehmay hoong,"

The walls and roofs of Lhasa vibrated under the stars with the mantra of Chenresig as every Tibetan in the city took up the chant, "Om mani pehmay hoong."

In the dim light, I could see the store windows shaking with the unified chant of Chenresig, Tara, and the Tibetans of Lhasa. After awhile, even the Chinese prostrated themselves and took up the chant, and "Om mani pehmay hoong," filled the city, echoed off the mountains and traveled into the heavens where the stars looked down on us in amazement.

We climbed the steps of the Potala, two giants not of this earth, and the people crowded into the large square below. Many brought butter lamps from their homes and began trying to light them as an offering to us. Seeing them struggling to light them in the darkness, I lit them instead. This was the first time that I had ever used my gift in a peaceful way and I discovered that merely by desiring it I had also lit every butter lamp in the Potala, the Jokhang temple, and the entire city, so that the city glowed from the light of ten hundred thousand candles and contended for beauty with the starry skies above.

In a short while, from our vantage point on the Potala parapets, we could see a line of automobile headlights in the distant darkness as the soldiers returned with reinforcements from the military base across the river. Boorman/Chenresig did not change back into his wrathful form, but looked at me in silent communication and we both disappeared as if we had never been there at all.

*

When he awoke the next morning, Boorman had little recollection of the previous evening's events. He did mention to Chang that he had dreamed that he had strolled through the streets of Lhasa with a Tibetan goddess, which I found flattering. However, he could not remember anything else about the dream.

Lao Wei-ping disembarked at the Chinese checkpoint and officially released the *Eckener* into Nepal, although the ship would not technically be in Nepal until it had crossed the river gorge. Lao took Boorman aside to give him some advice. "Always do your duty," he said sternly.

"Thanks," Boorman replied, at a loss as to what the appropriate reply might be. And then, awkwardly, he asked, "what will you do now?"

"The army is re-opening a small base in the Rongbuk valley. I have been told to proceed there."

They shook hands, saluted, and then Lao marched down the passenger stairs to the roadway that led back into China. Boorman went back to his cabin to nervously watch the Friendship Bridge, and the deep gorge under it, slide silently beneath them as they entered Nepal.

The passengers were ambivalent about leaving China; that part of their trip had been a little too exciting for most of them and had definitely been more than they had signed on for, but many wondered if they would ever see Tibet again.

Chapter 12 – Of Maya, Dharma, and Tangled Karma.

Zhao Tou was very excited when he came to guard me that morning. "I was right," he said. "My aunt and her friends were gathered in my living room as usual last night to hear word of you. When I told them about the ring, you would have thought that I was a hero. They could not contain themselves with excitement. I am sure that they are telling everyone they know. I just hope no one traces the information back to me. Her friends sent this camera for me to take a picture. Do you mind?"

"Shouldn't I eat first, in case somebody comes?"

He thought that was a good idea and impatiently waited with his camera until I finished and the evidence had been cleared away. "Tell your aunt that the food was especially good today," I said.

"She was so excited that she couldn't sleep all night. Just to think that you are friends with Chang Da Wai, and that she has been cooking for you, has made her worry about what she can cook for you next. She says that there is no food good enough for you. I have a list of special things to buy at the market on the way home tonight."

"Tell your aunt that everything that she has cooked has been more delicious than anything I have ever had and that I would consider it a special honor if she included me in her family by only cooking those things that she normally cooks for her family."

Zhao Tou beamed. "That will make her very happy," he said, "and save me a lot of Yuan."

Shortly after Zhao Tou took his photographs of me displaying the famous ring and had put away the camera, I heard the outer door open and felt a chill go up my spine. My fears were confirmed when I heard General Tong's hated voice. "What is that smell?" he asked.

"My apologies, General," Zhao Tou replied, "I have just finished eating my breakfast."

"Do not eat your breakfast in here," General Tong barked at him.

"Of course, General. I am terribly sorry; I only did it because it is fun to watch her beg and plead. I will not do it again."

"Never mind. Forget I said that. You are obviously a good man. Have you followed my orders to give her nothing to eat?"

"Almost explicitly, General."

"What do you mean by that?"

"Sometimes I let her lick the spoon, and sometimes I dip my finger in the food and let her suck it off."

"Your talents are wasted here. But I knew a man once who did similar things until one day he lost a finger."

"I had not thought of that, General; I will certainly stop doing that. Thank you sir."

"I sometimes have need for men with your particular talents and intelligence. Have you ever considered a career change?"

"I enjoy my work here, General, but I am always looking for opportunities to improve my position."

"I have asked my surgeon to meet me here. We are going to be removing this woman's hand. Whether this is done with or without anesthesia, and how fast the hand comes off is up to the woman to decide. Would you care to assist us? I hate working with these witless prisoners. They are in jail because of their stupidity. If they were smart they wouldn't have gotten caught."

"I personally prefer the power of psychological persuasion, General, but I am open to new things and would be glad to try to assist in any way possible."

"As I said, you are a good man, Prison Guard Zhao," Tong said, "I have read your reports and know of your loyalty."

"If you don't mind me asking, General, what is it that you need from this girl besides her hand? Perhaps I could think of other ways to help."

"I shouldn't discuss it," Tong said frowning.

"My apologies, General. Please forget that I asked."

"You are a lot like me, Prison Guard Zhao, and if I hear this spoken anywhere else, I will know where it came from anyway. So, since you seem to be such a sincere Party member, I don't mind talking about it a little. Fix us some tea while we wait for the doctor."

While Zhao Tou prepared the tea, Tong explained to him that I had long been a secret enemy of China and had been found to be plotting the overthrow of the Communist Party. "She has made several attempts to do this," Tong said. "She has tried to start a peasant revolt by using that foundation of hers as a pretense. She has also been working on ways to utilize prisoners as soldiers and to stir up world opinion against us — not that we are concerned about world opinion and those little flag waving groups who think that they can change China with ridiculous songs. If it were not so pathetic, it would be funny. But what I really need from her is the information that she has about a new technology that is being used to frighten and disorganize our troops. We have been able to determine that at least she and one other person know how to use this device. The other person used it again last night."

"He must be very slippery if he has eluded capture by you, General."

"Yes. I have tried, but now, thanks to a wonderful lack of brilliance in our leadership, he has left China."

"So you have only the girl?"

"For the moment. But the man is not beyond my reach. I have agents everywhere; I even have operatives on board his ship."

"There must be a very good reason why someone as powerful as you, General, could not just board a ship in Chinese waters and seize an enemy such as this."

"Oh, yes, a very good reason. The Party must not be implicated in his downfall. This is a very dangerous man. He has poisoned the minds of peasants, students, and workers alike to the point that many of them now love him more than they love The Party. This is a bad thing and I do not know what would happen if there was a direct confrontation. Most people do not realize this, but governments only govern as long as the people let them. That is why people must be kept ignorant and afraid and told what to do and how to think — otherwise there is chaos."

Tong sipped his tea for a few moments and then laughed. "It is wonderful how stupid people are."

"Why is that, General?" Zhao Tou asked attentively.

"It makes it so easy for people like you and me to be relative geniuses. How do you think that I am going to capture this man without anyone realizing that China is behind the plot?"

"I can not think of how to do such a thing."

"It is very simple really; I will let someone else do it. We have been doing this for years. We will overthrow America someday, and nobody will even know it was us. The world will think that Moslems did it." He laughed out loud at this great joke.

"Our Moslems, General?" Zhao Tou asked, shocked. "How could they do that?"

"Not Chinese Moslems," Tong replied. "Those Arabians and Iranians, and Pakistanis — they will do the job for us, and all the time they will believe they are doing it for their god. And all it takes is money. Not all Islamic religious leaders report directly to Allah — some report directly to me. Their followers don't know that of course, because the followers are firm believers — they have to be — one does not blow one's self up for money. But you never see the leaders blowing themselves up, do you?" He laughed again.

"Someday the last Moslem will blow himself up and take the last Christian with him and that will be that."

"So this man is some big Christian then, General?"

"No, not really, but things that he says sound close enough to being some kind of religion that it was no problem to convince the 'true believers' that he is their enemy. Anybody that preaches anything besides Islam is an enemy of Islam, right? All you have to do with Moslems is point them at a target and pull their triggers. They are what is called a 'fire-and-forget' weapon."

I heard the door open then. The doctor had arrived.

*

There was silence after the person, who I guessed to be the surgeon, entered the room. Then Tong asked, "What has happened? Were you in an accident? Your clothes . . . Where is your bag?"

"I was robbed — right outside the police station door. A bunch of thieves jumped on me and took my medical bag."

"What is this country becoming?" Tong exclaimed. "Crime is rampant. We must have a crackdown."

"General Tong, I will not be able to perform the surgery as you requested."

"I can see that. When can you have more implements and be ready again?"

"This afternoon, General."

"I can't be here then. Come back tomorrow morning at this same time."

"As you wish, General."

I heard the door open and close and then Tong spoke to me without coming into the cell proper. "So you have had a reprieve, but not for long. Tell me about this weapon now and I will only cut off your finger."

I didn't react to his offer.

"Madam Director," he said sarcastically, "you should use this time to consider the fact that when you help China, China will help you."

"You mean when I help *you*, don't you?"

"When you help General Tong, you help China."

"You are mistaken about many things, General Tong — that you are China is one of them. Another is that I know anything of any use to you. And another is that if I did know anything, that I would not rather die than help you in any way."

"We shall see. I have heard bold words such as yours before, but I have ways of making death something to be longed for, and I have personally had the brave and the cowardly alike beg me to send them on into the darkness. Yes, you are brave now, but what about later?"

*

The *Eckener* stopped at the Nepalese customs, but there was no comparison between this and the Chinese checkpoint. Visas were issued based on a list of passengers that the captain provided, and in a very short time the great ship drifted down the immense slope of increasingly tropical jungle, leaving behind the dumbfounded people who had flocked out into the streets to see this strange sight.

From the ballroom, the lower and upper observation decks, and from their own rooms, the passengers watched as the myriad forms of life slid beneath them to disappear from sight only to be replaced by the next more fascinating thing. Wendy continued to sing her compositions, but only in the ballroom, and in Boorman's cabin, when he wished it. Captain Macon wanted to make certain that the passengers had a choice to listen or not, and not have music forced on them if they were not in the mood. For this reason, most people, loving this strange new beautiful ever-changing music, as much as the view, viewed the vistas of Nepal through the transparent floors and walls of the ballroom. Wendy had an uncanny ability to compose music to match the scenery and this had the effect of amplifying the enjoyment that most people had from their viewing.

Boorman enjoyed the music as well, but did not allow Chang to unpaque the floor. It was all he could do to look out the window from across the cabin. "It is because of the dream that I had while I was recovering from my concussion," he told Chang by way of apology. "I can't look down without the memory of that horrible dream recurring."

"Perhaps you are too attached to that dream," Chang said. "Did you not have any pleasant ones?"

"Yes, I suppose I did. Strangely, I had a good dream about being in a Nazi concentration camp." He laughed. "How could that be a good dream? But it was. I felt as if I had finally grasped something that had been eluding me, or, even more, that I had finally escaped from something that had held me prisoner. And then, after that, I had this other dream that started off pleasant enough but then turned into a nightmare. But, you know, I have had strange dreams ever since I came aboard this ship. I have dreamed about living in jungles like the one that we are flying over; I have dreamed about killing Jews as a Roman soldier; I have dreamed about being Jewish, about being Egyptian, Hindu, Tibetan, African, Native American before the Europeans came. I dreamed I was a Polynesian living in paradise; that was nice. But what does all this mean? Why am I having these dreams?"

"They are life reviews," Chang replied matter-of-factly.

"They're what?"

"The people on this ship — they have been in your dreams haven't they?"

"Well, some of the dreams," Boorman admitted, "but not all. Some have been in more dreams than others. But they are in my dreams because I see them when I'm awake. If I was somewhere else, I am sure that the other people that I was around would be in my dreams instead."

"No, you are dreaming about these people because their karma is tangled up with yours."

"I don't believe in karma."

"I am sure that there are an infinite number of things that you don't believe in but which do not cease to exist because of your lack of belief. What you believe depends more on what you are programmed to believe than on what is real."

"I am not a robot; I don't take programming."

"Perhaps, but you once did. The human brain is like a sponge when it is young; it soaks up whatever it is taught as fast as possible so that it can learn to survive in the world. Misinformation, bad ideas, twisted logic — everything goes in along with whatever real knowledge it can acquire. A young human being is in a pure hypnotic state and has no defenses and no way to filter out the good from the bad; so basically, you end up believing whatever you were told when you were young. Later the filters come up, but by then the filters are based on what you already 'know'. Anything that doesn't fit with that world view is discarded. That is all that you are doing now when you say that you do or do not believe in something, and don't stop to examine that belief. You are only comparing this new knowledge with what you already think you know, but which you have also never examined."

"But how can my karma be tangled up with these people when I have never seen them before."

"But you have — you are simply refusing to recognize the obvious. Some of the people on this ship have been traveling with you for many lifetimes. They have helped you, and you have helped them at various times along the way. Others have joined up with you along the way because they have, on some plane of awareness, seen you as a developed soul — a light that could guide them through the darkness. When you awakened the first time after your injury, you claimed to know all of the people on board. They were in that concentration camp with you, weren't they? At that time, when most people around you were despairing, you found a way to give them hope, and to do it, you gave up the very last thing that tied you to this world; you gave up your own life — your own ego. After that, John, after you had opened your hand and let go of that last thread, and willingly sacrificed your own self for others — at that point you were free — free to never come back — the final lesson of the world, learned — free to go on."

Boorman was looking at him in astonishment. "That is how I felt," he said, choking on his words. "I felt like I was floating up, free from the world. How do you know this about me?"

"But there are some," Chang continued, ignoring Boorman's question, "who look back — who hear the cries of those left behind, the struggling, benighted, weary, frightened, and world clenching multitude. Some hear the cries and cannot go on, but go back, not because they have to, but because it is not in them to leave anyone behind. There is no judgment on those who go on; each soul serves in its own way, but those who choose to go back are not common, because there is always the risk of new entrapment. The world has the power to enchant anyone who enters into it; even Bodhisattvas are not immune."

"So you are saying that I had a chance to go to heaven but came back here instead?"

"If 'heaven' is the word you choose to use. When souls return to the world, they usually have a plan, and so did you; you were going to be a teacher, and many of the souls that were in the concentration camp with you signed on to be your students. Not all souls come back because they choose to; most come back because they have not learned how to let go of the things that hold them here. But still they have a plan; they want to learn and to grow, and just as a plant naturally grows toward the light, souls naturally grow toward the light of the vast consciousness, the infinite mind. These people on this ship chose you as their teacher in Tibet because they knew you from the concentration camp, and so they came back with you as your family, your friends, and your relatives. They thought that you would help them grow."

"So what happened?"

"You allowed the world to divert you from your path. One little decision was all it took, and you became more and more lost in the illusion of the world, and, sadly, you took these people down your wrong path with you."

"Oh God, I almost believe you," Boorman said, rubbing his forehead with his hand. "Everything you have said sounds so much like how I felt in the dream. But if I failed all of these people, why are they here with me now?"

"They have not entirely given up on you, John. They are angry with you, but you said a prayer just before you died, and prayers are always heard. I heard it and others heard it and those who died before you heard it, and this is the answer."

"How could you possibly know about the prayer?" Boorman asked in total astonishment.

"Because I was there," Chang answered. "I am your son who stayed to die with you. But I am more than that. I was the teacher of these people before you were, and these people have come here now because of you and because of me. But, in this lifetime, I have only come because of you. I also hear the cries of the world, and in my last lifetime I heard something else — the cry of another bodhisattva — a bodhisattva about to be lost to us. And John, we bodhisattvas need all the help we can get."

*

The Nepalese authorities had politely suggested that the best place to land an aircraft was at an airport, so the *Eckener* had stationed itself at the Tribhuvan Airport, just south east of Kathmandu. They had been promised plenty of ground transportation at the airport, but the bus drivers were on strike and the passengers had to split up into smaller groups and take taxis and other transportation into town.

As Sandal had stayed on the *Eckener* in Beijing, Captain Macon took her turn at first watch in Kathmandu and let Sandal have shore leave with Chang and Boorman. The taxis were soon taken by others, and after Chang spoke a few words to the driver, barely intelligible over the sound of the idling engine, Sandal, Chang and Boorman squeezed into a motorized rickshaw. "What did you say to him?" Sandal asked. "Did you call him a freak?"

"No, I asked him to take us to Freak Street. I have been in Kathmandu on several occasions, but that was many years ago, and I wanted to see how things have changed. The street has another name, but everybody has called it Freak Street for as long as I can remember. It is where hippies, drop-outs, mountain climbers, trekkers, and world travelers all used to come to hang out together. I always stayed on Freak Street when I was in Kathmandu." Chang was shouting now over the noise of the two-stroke engine, and they decided they would save further conversation until they came to their destination.

The streets of Kathmandu were crowded with bicycles, rickshaws, old smoking automobiles, and even a few nice looking modern cars to remind one of what century they were in. All were packed together and weaving in and out of each other's way so that it seemed inevitable that they would see at least one lethal collision per mile traveled. Boorman clenched the side of the rickshaw in a white-knuckled grip and Sandal tried desperately to keep her eyes shut, but Chang stayed busy shouting directions to the driver, who would then make a quick turn in front of traffic to speed up some narrow obscure street where cows walked calmly into their path and children squatted in the gutters.

Chang shouted at the driver to slow down when they reached Jochne Street. "This is Freak Street," he shouted at Sandal and Chang. "It's not what it used to be."

"Let's get off here," Sandal shouted back. "My nerves are shot."

Chang had the driver pull over and stop in front of one of the old hotels. Boorman paid the driver with local currency that he had gotten at the airport, and when he turned around Chang was staring lovingly up at the hotel. "A lot of them are gone, but it looks like 'The Century' might live up to its name. This is where I usually stayed. All the freaks are gone, but it looks like trekkers still stay here. Let's walk up to Basantapur Square; it is part of the old city."

As they walked, Boorman could see a tower at the end of the street. As they came closer, he could see that it stood guard over the entrance to a large courtyard. "It is one of the courtyards of the old palace," Chang explained. There is a horse in there that is considered to be a deity and no one is allowed to ride it."

Boorman and Sandal both looked at him questioningly.

"There are many strange things in Kathmandu," Chang continued. "At least they may be strange where we came from; here they are just facts."

They had turned left and were walking west through Basantapur Square and Chang pointed out another building just ahead. In that building lives the Kumari Devi, a living goddess. She is a young girl who is a temporary host to the actual goddess. When the girl has her first period or loses significant blood from a wound, the goddess leaves her and another young girl must be selected for the goddess to inhabit."

"What happens to the girl then?" Sandal asked in a concerned voice.

"Oh, she receives an allowance and a large dowry, which she will need in order to entice a man to marry her, in view of the fact that she has been totally spoiled since the age of four."

They climbed up onto the platform of a nearby temple to let a small herd of goats go by in the crowded streets. The goats were followed by a car, which was honking its horn to no avail, and other than for that car, Boorman thought, they could have been in a medieval city.

They went north into Durbar Square and Chang led them into a temple on their left. The temple was covered with erotic carvings, which Boorman found distressing because of the fatherly concern that he had for Sandal's sensibilities. The carvings were not the reason for Chang's visit however, and he showed them the view of a stupa on a hill to the west of them. At first Boorman thought that it looked like a giant ice cream cone that had fallen onto the ground upside down. There was a huge white hemisphere topped by a large cube with sinister looking eyes painted on it. Above the cube sat a tapering cone, which terminated in some intricate ornamentation resembling a ball and an umbrella. On both sides of this main structure were two intricately carved towers.

"That is Swayambhunath," Chang said, waving his arm in a large gesture. "It is two thousand years old, and they say that in one of its temples is a living man just as old, who has kept himself alive by meditation. We must go there next, and then you should really see Bodhnath. All Tibetans visit the Bodhnath stupa before traveling back into Tibet."

"I don't think we will be going back into Tibet anytime soon," Boorman commented.

"If there is anything that the world lacks, it is predictability," Chang replied, grinning at him.

They hired a bicycle rickshaw to take them to Swayambhunath. As before, Chang gave the driver explicit directions: "We want to go down Pie Alley," he said, "and then take us to the east stairs. We don't want to go to the tourist entrance."

"Oh look," he said as they started down one of the side streets from the square, "only two pie shops left. At one time this street served up the best pies in the world. I hope these two shops understand the burden of honor they are carrying. We will have to stop on the way back and see which one is best."

When they arrived at the east entrance to Swayambhunath, Boorman looked up at the steps and wished that they had gone to the tourist entrance instead. "How many steps is that?" he wondered aloud.

"Three hundred and sixty five," Chang answered. "Some people climb them everyday before sunrise. See the monkeys?" He pointed up the steps. "The monkeys keep the rails polished by sliding down them, but they expect payment; they will grab anything loose that you have on you, so you have to watch out. There are so many monkeys here that some people call this the monkey temple."

They climbed the stairs with the monkeys watching them closely and Chang explaining the features of the stupa. "The eyes," he said, "are the eyes of the Buddha. They are painted on all sides because the Buddha sees in all directions. The tapering rings above the cube represent the thirteen steps to nirvana."

Boorman stopped listening. Something about this place was making him light-headed — no, more than light-headed; he felt as if the top of his head was open to the sky and that at any moment he was going to fly right out of the opening. "I don't know if I can do this," he murmured.

"Fear of heights?" Sandal asked sympathetically.

"No," he answered. But then he thought that perhaps it was that same fear in a way. He had a sense of vertigo, but he was not afraid of the height that he had already attained, but of the height still above him. It was that old feeling as if gravity might reverse and he would fall down into the empty sky. "I'm OK. I just feel a little weird. It's almost like I have been here before — a hundred years ago, or five hundred, or a thousand — I don't know. But I think I have climbed these steps before. I know what a stupa is; I know about the eyes of the Buddha; I know about the thirteen levels of enlightenment. And there is something at the top of these steps. It is like a giant scepter with huge curved claws at each end, and the claws come together at their points because some god took it from some other god and bent the sharp points of his weapon inward so that it could no longer kill but it was still a thunderbolt."

A few more steps and they were at the top, and there on a large pedestal, guarded by two painted stone lions was the object that Boorman had described.

"'Vajra' is the Sanskrit word for this," Chang said thoughtfully. "It is what Vajrayana Buddhism is named after — the thunderbolt vehicle. This is the thunderbolt of enlightenment. The Tibetan word for it is 'Dorje'."

*

Boorman could not shake the feeling of unreality that followed him as they walked clockwise around the stupa and dutifully spun the prayer wheels — the prayer wheels that silently sent the prayer "Om mani padme hum" out into the ether. He could not shake the feeling as they descended the three hundred and sixty five steps and rode in a rickshaw back to Pie Alley. He could not even have told you what flavors of pie they had at the shops. He gazed absentmindedly at the passing flow of humanity as their driver took them past the new royal palaces on their way to Bodhnath.

He was startled to hear Chang say that they would have to get out and walk now. He looked around and saw that they were stalled in a huge traffic jam.

"It is a protest of some kind," Chang said. "They are very common here. We will just get out and walk around it and get another rickshaw on the other side. If we get separated, we can meet at the Bodhnath stupa; just grab a taxi and say 'Bodhnath'."

As they weaved their way through the mass of people, Boorman could see over their heads that some were carrying large banners and waving signs written, he supposed, in Nepali. After his experiences in China, he was concerned that this had something to do with Chang, and that when the crowd realized that Chang was in their midst, the situation would become totally unpredictable. "What is this about?" he asked Chang.

"It is just the way they do business here," Chang answered. "Strikes, protests, demonstrations — it's a way of life. They are usually peaceful, but I see that the police have been called out for this one. We had better get past this crowd quickly."

They elbowed and threaded their way through the onlookers, and it seemed that the crowd was beginning to get thinner, when it was suddenly galvanized into movement. Boorman, being one of the tallest people in the crowd, told Sandal and Chang that it looked like the police were charging the demonstrators. "They are hitting them with bamboo poles," he said. "Everybody is running away and it looks like about half of them are coming right at us."

They were quickly swept up in a river of fleeing people and it was all they could do to keep their feet under them as they fled with the crowd. When Boorman managed to get to a store front and let the crowd go by, he was at least a block away from where they had started, and Sandal and Chang were nowhere to be seen.

*

Boorman remembered what Chang had said to do if they got separated. He let the crowd thin out and then flagged down a taxi and told the driver "Bodhnath," as Chang had instructed.

When he arrived at the stupa, which he saw was much larger than the one at Swayambhunath, there was no one there that he knew, and he wondered if there might be more than one entrance. The stupa was inside a ring of buildings constituting part of the town of Bodh, and Boorman was swarmed by street vendors wanting to sell him their wares as he made his way to what appeared to be the main entrance to the stupa. He tried unsuccessfully to wave them away until a bus-load of tourists arrived, offering them an untapped market.

After awhile, Sandal showed up. She told Boorman that she had last seen Chang being swept away down one of the narrow streets in Kathmandu. Boorman asked Sandal to stay where she was, while he explored the stupa vicinity to see if Chang might be waiting some place else. He remembered how Chang had gotten lost from the *Eckener* in China, and had been found drinking beer and eating noodles in a tavern with the locals. The stupa was surrounded by various types of Tibetan businesses, and Boorman imagined that Chang was probably in one of them thinking that any rendezvous point was as good as another. Boorman left Sandal sitting on some steps beneath a pair of stone elephants that carried stone warriors on their backs.

He walked around the stupa in a clockwise direction while trying to get a glimpse into the windows of the stores and restaurants facing and surrounding it, while fending off street vendors as he went. Eventually he came to a monastery built into the wall of buildings around the stupa and thought that this would be a likely place for Chang to appear. He waited outside for awhile and then decided to go in and have a look. He took note of the shoes clustered outside the door and removed his own before entering. He wandered around awkwardly but attracted few stares. The monks were accustomed to having tourists enter the building uninvited as if the monastery were an attraction at an amusement park. He did not see Chang, and so, after a few minutes he left, put his shoes back on, and continued walking the short distance to where he had left Sandal.

When Sandal saw him coming, she held her palms up questioningly. Chang had not arrived.

They tried to call the *Eckener* on the ship's phone that Sandal was carrying but they were too far away, so they decided that Sandal should take a taxi back to the ship and make a report while Boorman stayed at Bodhnath to see if Chang showed up. "If I am not close by these elephants," he told her, "then I will be at the monastery that faces the stupa just about a quarter way around that direction." He pointed back the way he had come.

"Why there," she asked.

"I am not sure. There is just something that tells me I might find Chang there."

After Sandal left, Boorman sat on the stupa steps for awhile, watching the crowds of tourists and street vendors, and eventually received a donation of coins by some tall blonde tourists who laid the money on the steps beside him. He was startled and embarrassed, but when he looked down at himself, he realized that the fleeing mob in Kathmandu had torn, wrinkled and dirtied his clothes to the point that at least someone thought he needed assistance.

He decided it was time to return to the monastery and tried to take the shortcut of going counter-clockwise. It was logical, he thought, and, he rationalized, if he were not actually going all the way around the stupa, then it did not matter which way he went. However, he discovered that the idea of going counter-clockwise made him very uncomfortable, and so also discovered that there was rationale as well for going clockwise in that he could check out all of the shops one more time.

Arriving at the monastery, he sat on its steps and waited. He was strangely drawn to this place and felt comfortable just sitting and watching the people come and go. The sun sank lower in the sky, and the shop keepers closed business for the day and began to gather around the stupa along with all of the other townspeople. They began to circumambulate the stupa in the usual clockwise manner, some talking and visiting with each other as they went until finally all taking up the Chenresig mantra of "Om Mani Pehmay Hoong". The monks from the monastery filed out from the main door and joined the river of people, all traveling from right to left in front of Boorman. The urge to join them became too great, and he found himself walking in single file but slightly behind the monks in the parade around the giant stupa, even picking up the chant of "Om Mani Pehmay Hoong" as he walked, muttering it under his breath.

Eventually arriving back at the monastery, the monks filed back inside, leaving Boorman once more on the large porch. He could go inside, he told himself, if he wanted, except that the day was now over, the tourists were gone, and he might really be intruding now. He sat back down on the steps and waited to see if Chang would show up.

After awhile, a very old and wrinkled monk in a red robe came outside and offered him an apple. The apple was not up to Boorman's normal standards of cleanliness, and had a few dark spots where insects had taken their fruit tax. He hesitated, but then thought that he would rather eat a little dust and even risk an upset stomach than to hurt the feelings of this kindly old monk. He stood up and thanked the monk and took a big bite out of the crisp, deliciously sweet fruit.

"You hesitated," the monk said in English.

"I am sorry," Boorman replied. "I was just not expecting anybody to offer me anything to eat."

"No," the monk said, "you thought that the apple might make you ill, yet you ate it anyway, knowing that there is a cure for a physical illness, but what is the medicine for disapproval and rejection?"

Boorman did not have an answer to the question, but looked at the monk thoughtfully and reflected on his feelings since first boarding the *Eckener* and being rejected by almost every other passenger, singly and as a group. It was a constant pain in his stomach, like being kicked, or eating bad food, but a pain that did not pass.

"I do not know the medicine," he finally replied.

The monk nodded. "If you are still hungry, please come in and dine with us."

"I couldn't impose on you that way. The apple will hold me until my friends come."

"Then at least have some tea with me," the monk said.

"I would appreciate that."

"Since you are waiting for friends, stay here and I will bring it out."

In a few minutes, the monk came back, carrying a bowl in each hand.

"It is acceptance," the monk said, handing Boorman a bowl made of silver and wood, with stones of turquoise and coral set into the elaborately worked silver.

"Pardon me?"

"The medicine for rejection is acceptance. If you accept the flow of the universe and move with it, you will have apples and tea. If you fight against it, you will have hunger, thirst, and exhaustion."

Boorman nodded his head, examining the bowls from which they drank their tea.

Like their owner, they were showing signs of advanced age. The wood was cracked in places and the silver ornamentation was damaged and the occasional stone was missing.

"I apologize for their appearance," the monk said, as he caught Boorman studying them. "But they are my personal bowls and they are so special to me that I forget sometimes how they must look to others."

"I find them very acceptable," Boorman said, smiling.

"They belonged to my abbot at our monastery in Tibet before he died. I dug them out of the rubble after the monastery was destroyed."

"How was it destroyed?" Boorman asked, sipping the tea from his bowl. The tea was an opaque golden brown and tasted salty and rich, almost more like soup than the taste of tea he had expected.

"The Chinese destroyed it with cannon fire," the monk said, as they sat back down on the monastery steps.

"They did?!" Boorman was genuinely shocked to hear a story so similar to his dream.

"Oh, yes, but this was not unusual, many monasteries met their end this way. A few of us were fortunate enough to survive and some of us even made it out of the country."

"Do you ever go back?"

"Sometimes, if there is a good enough reason. It is dangerous for me though. If I were caught I would be thrown into a Chinese prison."

"I don't suppose that would be very healthy."

"No, I have spent time in one of their camps. That was bad enough. But from what I have heard, the prisons are much worse. I almost got caught the first time I tried to escape from Tibet, but the Chinese were after a bigger quarry and ignored us monks. It was after that I went back to the monastery to see what I could find to help me to honor the memory of my teacher. The bowls were in pieces, but I gathered up every piece that I could find and when I finally made it across the border, I brought them with me. I found a silversmith to fix the silver. Modern American glue fixed the wood."

"What is a good enough reason to go back?"

"My abbot was a very old soul who could reincarnate at will. I know this sounds strange to western ears, but it is true. Just because you make good glue doesn't mean that you know everything. Our abbot came back to us for a few short years after the monastery was destroyed. And I think that the reason he came back was to remind us that Buddha had no monastery."

"I'm not sure I understand," Boorman said.

"Well, very simply, it is a way of saying that Buddhism is not about buildings, but about forgetting ourselves and helping those who need help. I am the abbot of this monastery now, and I feel that it is important to honor my teacher by reminding the monks who live here of what he taught. The best way to do that is by example."

"You mean by feeding strangers?"

The monk laughed. "I wish it was that easy. Almost all of the monks that live here came from Tibet. Sometimes when they come to me they bring stories of other people trying to escape. That is when the monks who have the most experience with the Chinese and the mountains go back across the border to lead the people safely here. I go with them. What else can I do?"

Boorman sat and looked at his empty bowl.

"Would you like some more tea?"

"No thanks. It is getting dark and I had better find a taxi and get back to my room." Boorman stood up and handed the ornate bowl back to the monk. "Do you give apples and tea to everyone who sits on your steps?"

"Oh no. We do not have very much money. We could not afford to feed everyone. We only eat very simple food ourselves, and not much of that."

"Then why me? Why did you choose to pick me out of this throng and give me an apple?"

"I suppose you reminded me of someone — someone I knew long ago. You had the same lost expression that he once had. I sometimes wonder if I could have done more to help him. I saw you come to the monastery three times, and when I saw you sitting out here after the procession, I knew that you had followed us. You reminded me so much of the person that I once knew that I almost felt that by giving you the apple, I was giving it to him." He paused. "Also it is a teaching."

"A teaching?"

"Yes, when you do something good for someone, they often pass it on, and the good deed becomes a wordless teaching that spreads from person to person. "As my teacher said when he was just a child, "You do not need a monastery to teach the dharma."

*

Boorman was staggered at the old monk's parting words but managed not to let it show as he walked slowly away from the monastery, considering the infinite universe of possibilities.

When Boorman arrived at the stone elephants, Sandal was there, waiting impatiently. "Where have you been?" she asked. "I was just about to go report another missing person. I went to the monastery like you said but you weren't there and I was caught up in some big demonstration of all sorts of people marching around the stupa. Have you seen Chang, I hope?"

He shook his head.

"Then let's get back to the ship. Mother — I mean Captain Macon is ready to call out the Nepalese National Guard, if there is such a thing."

Boorman was not prepared for the upbraiding that he received from Captain Macon when he returned to the ship.

"How could the two of you lose David in Kathmandu? Couldn't you have at least stayed together — hooked a finger through a belt loop — something? What were you thinking to even go into a big protest like that? Where in the world could he be? Is he hurt — kidnapped? There is nothing left to do but call the police and if they are like the police back home, they'll say wait three days for him to sober up and come home. Damn damn damn damn damn!" she cursed as she stomped around her cabin.

"We should go back into Kathmandu and see if he is lying around in an alley or something," Boorman offered.

"Yes! Why didn't you do that already?"

"We went to Bodhnath, like he told us!" Sandal explained in exasperation.

"One of you, go back to Kathmandu. The other, go back to Bodhnath one more time. Take some crew with you. I'll contact the police and see if I have enough political clout to jumpstart their missing person process."

Hours later, after everyone had returned from their various fruitless searches, there was still no word as to Chang's whereabouts. The police had agreed to keep their eyes open for anyone with short fingers and artificial feet, but, they said, that was all they could do for now.

Captain Macon, Sandal, and Boorman were gathered in the captain's cabin. "Wendy," the captain called out. "Is everybody aboard except for David Chang?"

"Yes. Everyone except David Chang is now on board," Wendy answered promptly.

"Captain," Sandal began excitedly, "ask Wendy if she knows where David is."

"How could she know that?" Captain Macon asked.

"She monitors all radio frequencies."

The captain stopped her pacing. "You are right. Wendy, do you know where David Chang is?"

"No."

"Have you picked up any radio transmissions today that might be related to David Chang?"

"Any transmission could potentially be related to David Chang."

"OK. Eliminate public broadcasts. Also eliminate transmissions prior to noon today."

"You could also eliminate transmissions that do not contain any of the words 'David', 'Chang', 'Chang Da-Wai', or male personal pronouns," Boorman offered.

"Wendy, did you get that?"

"Yes."

"Do it."

"What if we limited the transmission source to just what came out of Nepal?" Sandal asked.

"Add China and Tibet to that," Boorman said.

Captain Macon looked at him quizzically. "Why is that?" she asked.

"Just a hunch," he replied.

"Wendy, limit searches to transmissions sourced in Nepal, Tibet, or China. What do you still have on record?"

"I have a transmission that may be local in that it was not bounced from satellite," Wendy responded shortly. "It occurred at sixteen twelve this afternoon."

"The time is about right," Boorman said. "We got stuck in traffic at about three o'clock and the big exodus began about thirty or forty minutes later, and then twenty to thirty minutes after that, somebody might have seen an opportunity to snatch a helpless tourist."

"Play back the transmission," the captain ordered.

Wendy played back something short but unintelligible.

"What language is that?" the captain asked.

"It is a colloquial Arabic," Wendy answered.

"Translate the message please."

"'We have him.'" Wendy translated.

"Who has him? Who is 'him'? This doesn't tell us anything," The captain was on the edge of a tirade.

"Wendy," Boorman spoke up, "find all transmissions in Arabic and translate." He turned to the others. "There can't be that many."

There was silence from Wendy.

"Wendy," the captain said, "Captain Boorman has whatever clearance he needs. Do what he says."

"There was only one other." Wendy responded. "It was at sixteen twenty-two and translates to: 'We are coming home.'"

"So it could just be that someone found his lost kid," Captain Macon observed. "It still doesn't tell us much."

"I think it does," Boorman said in turn. "Why are there only two messages? And why are they so short? It does not sound like parents finding a lost child. It sounds exactly like people who know what they are talking about but don't want anybody else to know."

"It still is nothing to go on. Somebody has somebody else and is going home."

"You could take it to the police and let them find all the Arabian people in Kathmandu," Sandal suggested.

"OK, I'll take it to the police, but the speakers might not be Arabic; they might just be using the language."

Captain Macon called the Kathmandu police to tell them what they had found out but was interrupted by the person at the other end of the conversation."

"You did?" the captain asked. "Are you sure? But he is alright? Yes, we'll be right there."

She put down the phone and turned to the other two. "The police have Chang. He is drunk and in jail and claiming to be the Buddha."

*

It was with a mixture of relief, anger, humor, and consternation that Boorman and Captain Macon took a taxi back to the Durbar Square police station in Kathmandu, leaving Sandal in charge of the *Eckener*.

"What could have gotten into him?" Captain Macon wondered aloud. "It just doesn't sound like him."

"Maybe he can explain it to us — if it really is him," Boorman replied.

"What do you mean?"

"It may not be him. The police don't have a photograph of him. And like you said, it just doesn't sound like him."

"Yeah, I know. I've never seen him drunk," she replied.

"Oh, I wouldn't think anything about him getting drunk; that's not what I meant. It's the thing about claiming to be the Buddha. I know that a lot of people think that he is the Buddha, or at least *a* Buddha, but

I have never heard him claim that himself. Have you?" Boorman remembered that Chang had spoken of bodhisattvas, but was not sure if that was the same thing, and besides, he wanted to know if Chang had spoken to other people about these things.

"No. You are right; that is not something that David Chang would ever say. I don't even know what he thinks about himself. He almost seems to have no ego at all."

"He would probably tell you that an ego is a dangerous thing to have running the show."

"You are almost beginning to sound like him."

"I can't say that being so close to him hasn't changed me in some ways. I just haven't decided yet whether that is a good thing or a bad thing."

"I think you are changing for the better."

"Oh?"

She laughed. "When you first came on board, I thought your fear of heights made you so pathetic that you were not fit to carry the rank of captain."

"And now? I am still afraid of heights, you know."

"Yeah, but I have seen how you always face down your fears and do whatever is required of you — and more. Now I would always want you on my team; especially when things look the worst. Now I wish that we didn't even have ranks and titles and we could just be Holly and John. I was so worried about you when you hit your head that I was almost sick. It was all I could do to keep being the captain for everyone else."

"But you are the captain. You have an entire ship full of passengers and crew that depend on you. I've seen how you worry about each one and how you make every effort to be as fair as possible. Look at the Ibrahims for example; look how worried you are about Chang. Everyone on board is like your child. That is your role and you can't give up being the captain for me or anyone."

"Do you remember trying to get me into bed when you were delirious?"

"No! What did I say?"

"You said that I was your wife and that we should send the kids away for awhile. Of course I ran like a scared ape then, but sometimes I wonder: is it possible . . ."

"I can't talk about these things, Holly; I am afraid of the changes that I am going through. I do not know who I will be when I come out the other side. I do not want hearts to be broken — mine or yours. Right now you are the captain of the *Eckener* and you have your responsibilities to the ship, the passengers, and the crew. I am David Chang's body guard, and my responsibility is to him. When we get back to the States, then we can talk."

"The United States is a long way from where we are now," she answered, "in every possible way. Sometimes I feel that we have left the world where everything is known and flown into a world where everything is possible. We may never see terra cognita again."

"I know, Holly. I cannot tell you how much I feel for you and Sandal. And I can't believe that I am finally telling you this, but you have been in my dreams since we met — and, really, since before we met. When I first saw you, I asked myself: what would it be like to spend my life with you. But if this person in jail is not Chang, then I feel that we may have some difficult decisions ahead, and I do not think that those decisions should be complicated by talk of you and me."

"John, I have dreamed about you as well. We have always been allies in my dreams — friends and lovers. I can't believe that I am saying these things either. Is it because we have left the known world below? How high have we flown? Can the world reach us where we are?"

"We have flown too high to ever see the world the same again," he told her, taking her hand.

"Why aren't you frightened?"

"I'm terrified."

"I am scared too — feel how I am shaking — but I don't know of what. Tomorrow the sun will come up and we will have to be captains again, but tonight I just want you to hold me."

He put his arms around her and held her as they drove through the empty starlit streets of Kathmandu.

When the taxi pulled up and stopped at the police station in Durbar Square, they went in and informed the police that the inebriated leper in the jail cell was not David Chang.

Chapter 13 – Of a Missing Bodhisattva and a Discovered Ring.

In the very early hours of the morning, I went to Boorman while he was in the deepest sleep and spoke with him. "I know where David Chang is," I told him. "He is still healthy, but he will not be for long. If you will open yourself to me, I will guide you to him." I showed him an image of what had happened to Chang. "When I guide you, it will feel as if you are following your instincts, but it will be me that you are following."

I was not sure if Boorman was receptive to me. He normally kept a protective wall against me, but in the morning, he had breakfast with Holly and Sandal in the captain's quarters and declared that he knew how to find Chang and could lead the *Eckener* straight to him.

"Why do we need to take the ship?" Holly asked.

"Because he has left the country."

"How do you know this? Where has he gone?" Sandal asked.

"I don't know how I know. It's just a hunch, I guess. But I think that he has been kidnapped and taken back into Tibet."

"John, that doesn't make any sense. Who would do such a thing — and why?"

"I'm not sure yet; I'm still working on that one. But, Holly, I know that this is what has happened. You've got to trust me and let me take this ship back into Tibet before it is too late."

Sandal looked curiously at the two captains who were suddenly calling each other John and Holly over bacon and eggs.

"John, I can't. China has closed the border."

"What? Well that just proves that I am right. They kidnapped him, took him back and closed the country down so no one could interfere with whatever they have planned for him."

"What do you think they are planning?" Sandal asked him in alarm.

"OK — here's what I think. I think they are going to torture him until they get a recorded confession from him that he is just a fraud. Then they are going to play that confession all over China until everyone loses all faith in him and goes back to doing what the government wants. And then they may put him on display somewhere or they may kill him."

"As long as you are working this hunch angle," Holly said, "what is your hunch about the two radio transmissions that Wendy played for us last night?"

"They were about Chang. They got him and they were taking him back to China."

"I thought you said 'Tibet'."

"It is the same thing to the Chinese."

"But the transmissions were in Arabic."

"I've thought about that. The Chinese have figured out a way to pin this on the Moslems. You know China always fights from the shadows. This time their front warriors are the whole Moslem world. They have managed to convince the Moslem community that they are doing the work of Allah by torturing a confession out of Chang and then killing him. "You know, I'll bet China is behind all of the Moslem terrorism in the world."

"John, I am sorry, but I think we may need to get the doctor to have a look at you."

"I am not delirious!" he almost shouted. Then, seeing the startled expressions in their faces, he apologized. "I'm sorry. It's just that we are wasting time. Chang is in danger and I know where he is. I know this sounds crazy, but it is as plain to me as anything can be. It is almost as if someone or something is showing me exactly what is going on and what I need do be doing. I am asking you to let me take this ship into Tibet or else I am leaving the ship right now and going on my own."

"No, John. You are still recovering from a severe blow to the head. The doctor said that the blow should have been fatal. You can't go off on your own to Tibet. I can't let you."

"OK, do this for me: ask Wendy where Chang is."

"We did that last night; she didn't know."

"Ask her again. I think she knows now."

"Wendy," Holly asked, "do you know where David Chang is?"

*

This is where I decided to feed Wendy a little information to help convince Captain Macon. "Wendy," I said, "tell them that David Chang has been kidnapped and taken to Tibet."

"David Chang has been kidnapped and taken to Tibet," Wendy duly reported.

"How did you acquire this information," Holly asked.

"I have received a transmission through an unknown channel," Wendy said.

"John, please don't lie to me. Did you tell Wendy to say this?" Captain Macon asked.

John was genuinely shocked. "No, of course not. I wouldn't even know how to begin to tell her something like that. She only responds to the most insignificant requests from me."

"The clearance I gave you last night would have allowed you to do this."

"Well, I didn't do it. Ask her."

"Wendy, who told you to tell us that David Chang had been kidnapped and taken to Tibet?"

"The dawn."

There was a long silence in the room as the three of them looked at each other. Holly put her hands behind her head and brought her elbows close to her face as if she just didn't think she could take any more. "Wendy," she asked, "is the dawn communicating with you right now?"

"Yes."

"Ask the dawn if there is some way to communicate directly with us."

And I would have too, if I hadn't been suddenly pulled back into my body.

*

"Madame Director, wake up and eat your food."

"Zhao Tou," I said groggily, "please give me a few more minutes."

"You know I cannot be caught with this food. I will have to throw it away. That would be too bad, because my aunt has made some wonderful soup for you this morning, and special tea to give you strength. You should drink it while it is still warm."

I had eaten the soup and was finishing up the tea when I heard the door open again.

"Who are you?" Zhao Tou asked the person nervously.

"I am waiting for the doctor. I am his assistant."

"What is in the briefcase? I will have to search it, you know."

"Go ahead. It only contains some surgical implements."

"Why do you carry surgical implements in a briefcase?" Zhao Tou asked suspiciously.

Before the man could answer, the door opened again and I heard the sound of wheezing.

"Doctor!" Zhao Tou exclaimed, "Did it happen again? Was your bag stolen from you again?"

"Yes, just as I knew it would be. But this time they only got an empty bag. I had my assistant wait until the mob chased me so that he could bring the instruments in while they were distracted."

"Is there suddenly a black market for surgical instruments?" Zhao Tou asked.

"No," the doctor answered. "Somehow word has leaked out about the bone ring and that I am to cut off the hand that wears it. I suspect that the crowds attack me to prevent that from happening. But today I fooled them. After this it will all be over and I can go back to my normal life."

"But what if there is retaliation?"

"Hmm, I hadn't thought of that. But never mind. I have a job to do and if I don't do it I know what will happen to me. In this case the known is much worse than the unknown. Well, let's get on with it."

"What about General Tong?"

"We received word that he had to fly to the Tibetan regions. I will have the hand mounted for him by the time he gets back."

"Are you going to do this without General Tong being present?" Zhao Tou asked in a shocked voice.

"Why? What do you mean?"

"I meant nothing. No disrespect was intended. I know that you understand the general's wishes much better than I do. I was just surprised to hear you say that you would start without him. I mistakenly thought the general was very explicit in his desire to be present. But you should follow his instructions the way you understood them; you know how the general is about mistakes."

The doctor hesitated. "Remind me what his reason was for wanting to be present."

"The woman has something much more valuable to the general than an antique ring. She has information that the general needs."

"I know how to extract information. She can give it to me."

"I apologize. I am detaining you with my babbling. Someday I hope to be in such a position of trust that General Tong would allow me to hear and convey to him such important information without any fear on my part."

"Fear? Fear of what?"

"Please do not think that I am suggesting that you have any reason to fear General Tong. But for a lowly worker such as myself, I am afraid that the general would want to be certain that I had reported every word accurately and without omission. I have heard that the general has ways to do this."

"Ah, I remember now that the general did say that he wanted to be present. I have lost a good medical bag for nothing. Well, it is not your fault. I will put in a good word for you with the general. You are a good man."

When I heard the door close behind the doctor and his assistant, I heaved a sigh of relief. I waited until Zhao Tou said we were alone. "Thank you, Zhao Tou. Thank you, thank you."

"No, Madam Director, it is I who should thank you. It is you who have opened my eyes to what my parents saw—what was wrong with this country. We should not follow blindly . . . I apologize, Madame Director; I have made a poor choice of words."

"It is OK, Zhao Tou. I am not as blind as you may think."

"I believe you, Madame Director."

*

Boorman had already left the ship by the time I got back to him. I suppose, in retrospect, that I should have done more to convince Captain Macon that Boorman was correct in his allegations. Even now I wonder if I should go back and alter history so that things do not turn out as they have. But I have learned that it is a dangerous act to meddle with time, and things that are done are not easily undone. In my defense, my center of attention was on Boorman — my main psychic link was with him, and whenever my own situation was not my primary focus, then his was. Also, I had promised him that I would be his guide, although at that moment, he appeared to be doing fairly well on his own.

Boorman had gone back to Bodhnath, at which place I found him standing on the steps of the Sakyapa Monastery, where just the day before he had sipped buttered tea with the old abbot. The tourists were coming and going, some removing their shoes, some not. Boorman sat his own shoes to the side and entered the monastery. He stopped the first monk that he saw and asked where he could find the abbot. The monk looked at him quizzically, but hopefully, and shook his head.

"Lama," Boorman said.

"Ah," the monk's face brightened. He motioned for Boorman to stay where he was and in a few minutes came back with the old monk from the day before.

"Ah, my friend, you are back," the old monk smiled at him, "but not for another apple, I would guess."

Boorman asked him if there was some place where they could speak privately, and the abbot led him into an inner chamber where tourists were not allowed.

"I need more than apples," Boorman began, once they had seated themselves. "I do not have much time, so I must get right to the point."

The abbot nodded, smiling.

"I need you to take me into Tibet."

"The abbot stiffened and his smile turned into a frown. "I am sorry, but that is not possible," he said.

"I can pay you. I have over fifty thousand American dollars in a U.S. bank. I will pay you whatever you want. I will write you a check for the whole amount right now, if you can get me into Tibet without delay."

"I am sorry. I would not risk the lives of my monks for any amount of money. Besides, Tibet is closed."

"But that doesn't matter; it is always closed to you, yet you told me that you have gone anyway."

"Yes, it is always closed to me but not to you. I would not only be risking the lives of monks, but I would be risking your life as well."

"Do you know why the border is closed?"

"The Chinese do this sometimes. We never really know why. This is not a good time for a trek anyway; the monsoons are about to start. There will be much rain here and much snow in the mountains."

"I know why the border is closed," Boorman said, ignoring the last part of the abbot's statement.

"Then you know much."

"A friend of mine has been kidnapped. It is the person that I was waiting for yesterday. The Chinese have taken him into Tibet where he will be tortured to death if I don't rescue him."

The abbot's eyes grew wide at this. "You were a stranger to me before yesterday, and now you ask me to risk the lives of my monks and myself and yourself. That is a lot to weigh against the tale of a stranger. The rains are about to start. The trails will wash out and the rivers will be almost impossible to cross. There will be mudslides in the hills and leaches on every bush and blade of grass. Everything you own will become soaking wet and the higher we go the colder it will become until the downpours turn into blizzards, and our wet clothes become stiff as cardboard. The snow will be up to our waists at the least. And on the other side of the mountains are the Chinese—and not Chinese to be avoided, according to you—but Chinese to be sought out—the heart of danger. Who is this friend that you so desire to die beside?"

"His name is David Chang."

The monk gasped with a sudden intake of breath and his eyes grew even wider. "You claim that Chang Da Wai, the living Buddha is a friend of yours?"

"I don't think that he ever claimed to be a Buddha, but yes, some people call him Chang Da Wai."

"Quick, tell me where you are staying."

Boorman told him that he shared a cabin on the *Eckener* with Chang, but that he had recently left it to find his friend.

"And if I contact the airship, they will know you and verify your story."

"They know me alright, but they don't believe that Chang has been taken to Tibet. They think that I have gone a little crazy."

"Why should I not think that as well? How do you know that the living Buddha has been taken across the mountains?"

"I don't know how I know—I just know."

"Do you have this power to know things?"

"I don't know—maybe."

"Then describe to me the room that is beyond that door." He pointed to a door opposite the one through which they had entered the present room."

"I can't do that."

"Then how can I believe you enough to risk lives. You should take your money and go to one of the trekking companies."

"They won't face the Chinese. You will."

"I can't help you."

"Wait — I can see the room. I don't know how. Maybe I am imagining it, but I see a small room that has no windows. There is an altar with a figure of a sitting Buddha. There are candles—no, oil lamps of some kind flickering around him. And on the floor there is a mat for kneeling."

"How many butter lamps do you see?" The abbot asked him intently.

"There are nineteen—six in one row and then a curved row of thirteen. Also the Buddha has a large crack in him. I can see that the figure has been broken and patched. It came from the ruins of the monastery where you found the bowls, didn't it. How do I know this?"

The abbot was closely studying Boorman's face. "You have a great power," he said. "No one ever goes into that room but me."

"I don't know how to do what I did," Boorman told him amazedly. "I could not have done that before you asked me to."

"You are growing rapidly because of your great desire to help your friend. There also may be some power helping you. Tell me about one other thing and I will help you."

"Of course, if I can. What is it?"

"Tell me about the ring that Chang Da Wai wears."

"Um, he doesn't wear a ring. Wait a minute; he did wear a ring when we first met. It was like carved ivory—very wide, yellowed and old looking. I haven't seen him wear it in some time. I don't know where it is now or when he quit wearing it."

"Tell me where the ring is and I will believe that you know where Chang Da Wai is as well. And then nothing will stop me or any monk in this monastery from getting him back." His eyes were ablaze with fervent allegiance. "Tell me."

"Well, it must be on the *Eckener*."

The monk's face fell with disappointment.

"No!" Boorman shouted. "I see it!"

Some other monks stuck their heads into the room to make sure that the abbot was alright. He waved them away. "And where is it?" The abbot asked with new hope.

"There is a woman in a jail cell. The jail is next to Tiananmen Square. The woman looks almost dead. The ring is on the next smallest finger of her right hand."

"Is this the same ring that you saw on Chang Da Wai's hand?"

"Yes."

"Do you know this woman?"

"No. But we were just there — in Tiananmen Square, I mean, and she had to have been in jail at the same time we were there, because her clothes look like she has worn them for weeks. Who is she?"

"We do not know. Only last night did we receive an encrypted message that a woman being held prisoner in Beijing wore the ring of Chang Da Wai. We have pondered the meaning of this and I hoped that you could tell us why she wears his ring."

"I don't know. Does this mean that you won't help me?"

"I believe that you know where Chang Da Wai is and that he is in danger. We will go to Tibet."

The abbot stood up. "We will take trucks to Jiri, but then we will probably have to walk to Namche Bazaar, but after that we will have yaks and Sherpa porters. I will begin making arrangements so they will be ready for us when we get there."

"How long will it take to get there?"

"Just a few hours to Jiri, but from there to Namche will take about a week. Then it will take another week or two to get into Tibet, depending on how bad the weather has become. After that, it depends on how far Chang Da Wai is from the pass that we will have to take."

"Three weeks!? Chang will probably be dead in a week. This will not work. Can't we fly in?"

"We can fly as far as Lukla. That will take a week off."

"What about flying directly into Tibet."

"In the Himalayas there are only a few places that are low enough to fly over in a helicopter. And only a helicopter would have any hope of finding a place to land. We will surely be spotted and shot down. No pilot would take us into Tibet that way — especially with the border closed. The closest airport to our crossing is at Lukla, except for a private helicopter pad at a hotel near Namche."

"Why don't we get a helicopter to take us right up into the mountains close enough to the border that we can walk over?"

"That will cost a lot of money," the abbot said. "We will have to have ten to fifteen monks and food enough for days — plus tents, dry clothes, and things like that. We don't know how far we will have to trek after we cross the la."

"Do you have a map that shows the area of the la?" Boorman asked.

The abbot left for a few moments and then came back with a large map, which he laid on the floor. "This is where we are." He pointed as they crouched over the map. "Here is Lukla. Here is Namche Bazaar, and here is Nangpa-la, where we will cross into Tibet, if we are lucky."

"Nangpa-la," Boorman whispered to himself.

"You are familiar with Nangpa-la?"

"I have never been across it," Boorman answered. "But I have heard the name."

"It is how I came into Nepal," the abbot said. "Many refugees have come that way. It will be hard during the monsoon, but the monsoon will work for us and against us. The Chinese will assume that no one will be coming that way during the time of heavy snows, but . . ."

"But what?"

"There *will* be heavy snows."

Boorman sighed and studied the map.

"Do you know where Chang Da Wai is?" the abbot asked.

"I don't know yet, for some reason this map is not making sense to me. Point out some more names on the Tibet side."

"Here is Tingri. Here is Gyadrak. Here is the Rongbuk River coming out of the Rongbuk valley."

"Rongbuk! What is at Rongbuk?"

"At the mouth of the valley, there is an old monastery and along the valley wall are caves that are sometimes occupied by the Chinese army, and at the top of the valley is the mountain that we call The Mother Goddess of the World. In Tibetan, the mountain's name is Chomolungma."

"Yes! Yes! He is at Rongbuk. That is where we are going. And look how close it is to Nangpa-la. We don't need a lot of people. Two or three people can slip over the pass, come back up the Rongbuk valley and sneak him out when no one is looking."

"We may have to work on that plan," the abbot said. "But there is another thing that I realized as we talked about flying up to the pass."

"What is that?"

"You are not acclimated to high altitudes. You can't make it across Nangpa-la."

"The hell I can't! I am going after Chang if I have to go by myself."

"No, you must stay here, and we will go. We are Tibetans; we can breathe the thin air."

"But you can't find him without me to guide you."

"You have already shown me where he is. If you go, you will surely die. How will that help Chang Da Wai?"

The abbot studied Boorman for a moment to see what his reaction was going to be and then stood up to leave the room. "I must begin preparations. I am assuming that you wish for me to proceed with plans to charter a helicopter."

"Yes, charter a helicopter, or get two or three — whatever it takes," Boorman said, "but make sure that you have room for me to come along."

"You cannot possibly make it over the mountains without acclimatization. And mountain sickness is not a pleasant way to die."

"I know that I can make it."

"Many people have said that while they were at these lower altitudes. It doesn't matter how strong a person you are; if you do not have enough red blood cells in your blood to carry oxygen, you will get the mountain sickness."

"In the same way that I know the other things, I know that I can make it across the mountains. I promise you that if I get sick I will not be a burden; you can leave me in the snow and go on."

"Would a desire to go with us cause you to lie about this new knowledge?" the abbot asked.

"No, it would not. I would not do anything to jeopardize this expedition," Boorman replied.

"I will contact the charter companies and start the monks packing. Please make yourself at home here. I will send a monk in to take care of any needs you may have." With that the abbot left the room.

Boorman spent the next two hours pacing around the room and drinking salted buttered tea. He finally had time to reflect on the source of his knowledge. It was almost as if someone were feeding him information, he thought. Intuition and gut-feeling was one thing, but knowing what was in a locked room was something else. And what if he were wrong about the acclimatization? What if that information was not fed to him but really was just a gut feeling. He would die a frozen death because he could not tell real knowledge from false. And what if the knowledge about Chang were not real? He would be leading innocent monks to their death or imprisonment because of a stray thought — a hallucination. He became obsessed with seeing the contents of the locked room. He had to prove to himself that he was right and that he could see things in a way that did not require eyes. He asked the monk that the abbot had sent in to let him into the room, but the monk said that he did not have a key, and anyway would not do so without the abbot's express permission.

Boorman then devised a game that he played with the monk. He had the monk stand with his back against a wall and make a fist behind his back. Then the monk would hold out some fingers and Boorman had to guess how many. After a few rounds of this, Boorman realized that statistically, his correct answers were no better than random chance.

I began to understand that Boorman was trying to determine the validity of the knowledge that he was receiving and so got ready to feed him information about the number of fingers the monk was extending, but Boorman had already lost confidence, and was ready to call off the whole expedition because he had been unable to see the monk's fingers in his mind.

He sent the monk to get the abbot, and I knew that he was going to tell the abbot to forget everything, that his visions were not valid, and that he was leading monks to their death for nothing. As soon as the monk left the room, Boorman looked up at the ceiling and said, "Give me a sign — anything."

It was then, in sudden desperation to stop him from canceling the expedition, that I did something that could have been regrettable. I grasped his mind, cradled it in mine and took it through the ceiling of the room, through the roof of the monastery, through the clouds gathering over Bodhnath, through the ocean of air, out into the cold blackness of space where every star could be counted, and showed him the blue and white ball of the earth. Then, in a rush, we fell back through the air and the snow clouds gathering over the Himalayas, into the Rongbuk valley, through the ancient seabed that now made up the rock of the mountains and into a cold dank cave where Chang's frail body sat on a stone bench, but where his bottomless black Chinese eyes stared straight back at us.

When the abbot came back with the monk, Boorman was lying on his back on the stone floor and sweat was pouring off of his face.

"Are you alright?" the abbot asked.

Boorman barely nodded. "Yes," he whispered. "I think I have been acclimatizing."

*

"Are you able to hear some bad news?" The abbot asked Boorman as the younger monk helped him to sit up and lean against a wall.

"What is it?" Boorman asked, a little stronger now.

"None of the helicopter charters will fly us because . . ."

"The monsoon clouds are gathering," Boorman finished for him.

"Yes," the abbot nodded, "and as the pilots say around here: In Nepal, the clouds have rocks in them. But there is another thing; if they are caught letting passengers out that close to the border, they could lose their license and receive a big fine. Nepal does not want any trouble with China."

"How much money did you offer them?" Boorman asked, gathering his strength and standing up on rubbery legs.

"The usual fee."

"Well double it, triple it; ask them how much it will cost to do this. Do not let this stop us. For fifty thousand U.S. dollars, you should be able to buy a helicopter around here."

"Yes, you are right," the abbot said, nodding. "I am just not used to having money."

In about an hour, the abbot came back again. "I have found someone who will take us," he said.

"Good," Boorman said, excited. "How much?"

"Fifty thousand."

"Fifty thousand!? Did you try to negotiate?"

"Oh yes. He asked me how much money we had and I said fifty thousand, and he said he would do it for that."

"Well, dammit, OK then. But that doesn't leave us much for supplies."

"We have supplies here, but we won't be taking much," the abbot answered.

"What do you mean?"

"The helicopter only holds four people including the pilot, and there is only enough stowage for what we can carry in our back packs. I think that will be enough; success or failure will come quickly."

"Then let's get packing and leave first thing in the morning," Boorman said.

After the abbot had introduced Boorman to the muscular young monk who would be going with them, and all of the packing had been done, Boorman went out in the late afternoon to try to find a shop that sold sunglasses so that he could shield his eyes from the glare of the snow on the trek. He passed by a restaurant where tempting smells wafted out into the sultry air. He went inside and asked for an English menu. As Nepal is a Hindu country, beef is never on the menu. Water buffalo, however, was."

Boorman ordered a buffalo steak and a glass of local beer. The steak was thick and juicy and Boorman's mouth watered at the sight and smell of it. Then he thought of the animal that had given up its life in the sun to satisfy this man's lust for meat. With his head bowed over the plate of steaming muscle, he prayed, "Thank you, oh buffalo that has died for me that I may have your strength and stamina. I pray that you find your way through death and be reborn more evolved and more advanced along the infinite path of enlightenment, and that your life and mine have not been in vain." He was surprised at himself and did not know from where the words came, yet he felt better for having said them. He ate the steak, but not in the spirit of mindlessly enjoying something inanimate, but as a gift — something that the universe and the buffalo had given to him. He felt that, somehow, the buffalo was part of the plan to rescue Chang and had known from the moment of its birth what contribution would be asked of it. He realized that he would never be able to explain these thoughts to his friends back in the U.S. and was reminded of Holly's remark that they had come a long way from that country, and might never see it with the same eyes again.

That night while he slept, I took the iron in the flesh of the buffalo and used it to make hemoglobin, and I used the amino acids to make red blood cells, and in the morning, Boorman's blood was ready to extract oxygen from the thin air of the Himalayas and carry it through his body as efficiently as any Tibetan mountain tribesman's.

*

In the dark morning hours, before they left the monastery, Boorman asked the abbot if the monastery had an account with a bank."

"Of course," the abbot laughed. "Do you think we don't have to live in the world?"

Boorman assured the abbot that he meant nothing by the question. "I actually have a little over fifty-seven thousand dollars in my account," Boorman said. "I have no use for it and do not expect to have any use for it. I want to write out a check to the monastery for the amount that is in my account, and then the monastery can settle up with the helicopter company."

"Why do you want to do this?"

"Two reasons, I guess. One is that I can't think of anybody that I would rather have the money, and second, well, the second is political. If this rescue goes down hard, I would rather that the U.S. Navy not be brought into it because one of their officers chartered a helicopter to fly into Tibet."

"But wouldn't it be just as bad for a Tibetan monastery in Nepal to be exposed for trying to rescue a prisoner from the Chinese?"

"Perhaps, if the prisoner were Tibetan. But ask yourself what kind of message it sends to the world if the prisoner that these Tibetan monks want to rescue is Chinese? Would the Chinese ever allow such a rescue attempt to be made public?"

The abbot laughed as he thought about the consternation that this would cause the Chinese government. "OK, write the check. I will have the monastery accountant deposit the money as soon as the banks open. We must go now."

Outside, it was beginning to drizzle as they walked to the waiting car and drove off into the darkness. The horizon was just beginning to show a little light as they arrived at the helicopter charter company, a run-down Quonset hut opening onto a pitted concrete slab that served as the landing pad for the single four-seat helicopter.

They loaded their equipment and climbed aboard. The pilot drank something that looked like tea from a glass, revved the engine, and then, remembering something, throttled back and asked for the money. When he saw the check, he cursed. Then he shrugged, put the check in his shirt pocket, cursed again and they took off.

As they flew, and the sun finally rose, Boorman began to realize two things: the day was not going to get appreciably lighter than it was now, and the pilot was not going to get appreciably more sober. They flew east as if going to Namche Bazaar, but turned north before seeing the market town. Going further north meant going higher in altitude, and the cloud ceiling seemed to descend upon them until there was only a little distance between ground and cloud in which the pilot could see to navigate. Then it started raining. Boorman's knuckles were white as he gripped the straps hanging down in the cockpit, but the pilot intently studied the ground below and kept going, taking more frequent drinks from his "tea".

After awhile the pilot seemed to relax a little. "Nguzumpa Glacier," he said pointing down to a broad river of dirty ice below. "We can follow it to Cho Oyu."

Then it started snowing.

It snowed lightly at first, and as long as the pilot could see the ground, he kept going. But it began to snow harder and harder, and soon, no matter how low the pilot flew, he could not see the ground. The wind had picked up as well, and was beginning to buffet the helicopter. The younger monk was repeating the Chenresig mantra over and over, "Om mani pehmay hoong;" Boorman was praying that the pilot knew how to navigate in a white-out; and the abbot was calmly looking out the window for any visible landmark.

"We can't go on," the pilot announced. "I've got to turn around."

"How can you turn around if you can't see anything?" Boorman asked him.

"I'll just reverse my compass heading and go back in the opposite direction that got us into this blizzard."

"Can't you set us down first?" The abbot asked.

"I've got to be able to see the ground before I can land on it," the pilot answered.

He turned the helicopter and began to fly back the way they had come. "Say, I thought that chant went 'Om mani padme hum'," the pilot commented to the abbot about the mantra that the younger monk was still repeating.

"He is only pronouncing it in the Tibetan way," the abbot was explaining just before a huge chunk of rock slammed into the cockpit on the pilot's side as if it were swung by a titan. Everyone was thrown forward, and in that moment, time seemed to stand still as Boorman counted each individual explosion of the blades hitting the invisible cliff beside them. Then the helicopter rocked backward and tumbled and slid down to the rocks below.

Chapter 14 – *Of Flying Monks and the Land of Snows.*

Hanging upside down in his safety harness in the middle of a blizzard white-out, Boorman's disorientation was complete. He did not know how long he hung there, drifting in and out of consciousness, before he felt hands lifting him out through the cockpit door. He felt the cold flakes of snow on his face and roused up enough to realize that these rescuers were not his traveling companions. As a disguise, the abbot and his young assistant were wearing the clothing of Sherpas, the local mountain tribal people in this area, while the men laying him out in the snow were wrapped in the traditional red of Tibetan Buddhist monks.

These new monks had found the supplies stowed in the helicopter and had begun to set up tents to shelter the crash survivors against the cold blowing wind. He heard Tibetan being spoken outside his tent, and laughter, and exclamations. He dozed for awhile, and when he awoke he felt well enough to gather his strength and crawl out of the tent to see who was talking and who else had survived the crash.

Outside, in the still falling snow, were five dim figures sitting around a fire drinking tea and apparently telling stories for each others amusement. As he approached, he saw that two of them were the abbot and his assistant; the other three were their red-robed rescuers. Off to the side, lying in the snow as if napping, was the body of the pilot, being buried snowflake by snowflake.

When the men around the fire saw Boorman, they all jumped up and came over to help him to the fire. They gently set him down on a small boulder and offered him a bowl of tea, which he gladly accepted. The day was beginning to get darker and Boorman did not get a good look at his rescuers face, even though everyone was studying him intently to make sure that he was not going to faint and topple headfirst into the fire.

The abbot was the first to speak. "John Boorman, these men are all good friends of mine. We have worked together many times." He introduced two of the men to Boorman. "But this man is my oldest friend," he said, gesturing to the third man. "We even spent time together in a prison camp. We tried to leave Tibet together once, but failed. And when I decided again to leave, he had already decided to stay and try to salvage what was left. It is his monastery that was our destination, but the Chinese have driven him out, and so he was finally leaving Tibet with two of his monks when they heard our crash in the storm and found us in the helicopter. This is Doctor Sang of the Rongbuk monastery. We owe our lives to him and his two disciples."

"Not just to us," Doctor Sang said, throwing back his hood. "It was a miracle that we were able to find you in this storm. Something led us here. Something wants you three to live."

Boorman did not respond, but stared at Doctor Sang as if at a ghost, as the tea slowly poured out of the side of his bowl.

"John Boorman," the abbot exclaimed, "are you alright? Do you need to lie down?"

"Sangye," Boorman gasped, ignoring the abbot. "Sangye, don't you remember me? It's Dorje."

"Dorje?" Doctor Sang asked. "Dorje who?"

"I am your friend, Dorje, son of Rabten and Pema. You and Sangmu and I played by the stream in the mountains and rescued the little golden fishes. Sangmu and I got married and had Norbu and Chodron. The Chinese have Norbu now, and we are going to rescue him."

It was Doctor Sang's turn to spill his tea, dropping the entire bowl into the snow. "No one has called me Sangye since I was a child. Is it really you, Dorje? Have you come back?"

"Yes!" Boorman exclaimed, leaping to his feet, his arms wide. "I have come back!"

Doctor Sang also leaped to his feet and the two embraced, dancing around the fire to the astonishment of the other monks.

"How wonderful life is," Sangye cried out to the mountains as he pounded Boorman on the back. "The gods are victorious. Dorje has come back! But what is this," he laughed. "You have come back as an American; you crazy Tibetan!"

"That is nothing," Boorman laughed, deliriously happy. "My son Norbu has come back as a Chinese!"

"A Chinese?!" Doctor Sang exclaimed. "There can be no stranger revelation."

"Ah but there is," Boorman said seriously. "He is being held captive by the Chinese and is going to be tortured to death. That is why we are going to Rongbuk, and is also why you were driven out of Rongbuk."

Doctor Sang turned to the abbot. "Is this true my friend? Are you going to rescue Norbu from the Chinese?"

The abbot's mouth was wide open in astonishment and confusion. "I did not recognize him. I did not know that he was Dorje. His American name is John Boorman. He is a friend of Chang Da Wai, and we are going to Rongbuk to rescue Chang Da Wai from the Chinese."

"Chang Da Wai!? What does this mean? Tell me Dorje, Is Chang Da Wai the same person as Norbu?"

Boorman nodded.

"Why did he come back?" Doctor Sang asked. "Do you know?"

"Yes, it is because I failed him."

"Of course," Doctor Sang said, turning away and rubbing his forehead in the gathering gloom. "Just as the shepherd goes in search of the lost sheep, so our teacher has come back for you. It is painful to me to realize that I did not recognize him years ago."

"You have met Chang Da Wai?" the abbot's assistant blurted out.

"Yes. My monks gave him the name by which today he is known throughout all of China. I healed him when he was sick, yet I did not recognize him." Doctor Sang sat down on a boulder and began to think out loud. "What vortex of power are we caught up in? There are forces at work here of which we can only begin to sense the magnitude. Small things are revealed while the great truth remains hidden. How has it come to pass that we have met each other again at the very base of Nangpa-la with the goal of crossing back into Tibet to rescue a Rinpoche, a precious one, our teacher, and now a Chinese, from the hands of the Chinese themselves? Nothing but life could be this strange."

*

They stayed where they were through the night, and in the morning the clouds had disappeared and the sun shown bright, revealing the pass of Nangpa and the golden plume of snow blowing off of Cho Oyu like the flame of a candle in the wind.

As they climbed up to the pass, Sangye asked about Chodron and Sangmu. "Have you found them yet in this life, Dorje?"

"Oh yes," Boorman answered. "They are wonderful people — a mother and daughter again. I think that they recognize me in a way, but they have no memories of our life together. It is just as well."

"What will happen to them?"

"I do not know. I do not know what will happen to any of us. I am questioning my own sanity, even as we speak. If it were not for the ice water trickling into my boot and the glare of the sun off the snow making me squint my eyes and the cold wind freezing the hairs in my nostrils, I would be ready to declare myself mad this very minute."

Sangye laughed. "Ah but we are all mad. Madness is the norm. Perhaps you are on the verge of declaring yourself sane."

Boorman laughed with Sangye at this notion as the six men trudged through the new snow up the slope to the Nangpa-la. The going was slow, as the snow was up to their thighs in places, but everyone was cheerful with the knowledge that Dorje was back, and with him, Norbu, the great lama and son of Dorje, and that Chodron and Sangmu had also made it through the Bardo, though they had drunk from the cup of forgetfulness.

When they reached the top of the Nangpa-la, they stopped and, so that any Chinese in the valley would not hear them, whispered, "The gods are victorious," at each other through grinning frozen faces.

Climbing down into the valley, they marched for a considerable distance before Boorman stopped and stared at the rusted and blackened hulk of a jeep at the base of a tall cliff on their right.

The monks gathered silently around him, each recognizing in himself an inadequacy to understand the depth of what must be going through Boorman's heart and mind. Two of the monks had been nearby when Dorje and the others had died here, and the other three had heard the story many times. Up on that pile of boulders were the bones of a person that he had once been, and nearby were the bones of people that he had once loved and who had once loved him and whose love could never be experienced the same way again.

Sangye and the abbot put their hands on Boorman's shoulders. "Dorje," Sangye said, "life is a continual letting go. Otherwise, you did indeed die here."

Boorman had been about to climb the pile of boulders to view the bones, perhaps to hold his own skull in his hands, when the meaning of Sangye's words penetrated his turmoil. He nodded his head, smiled at the two old monks and said, "Yes. We are here now. Whatever is past is past, and whatever is future is yet to be seen, yet we are here now. I thank the gods for this wonderful life!" He shouted these last words at the snow-capped mountains who repeated the sentiment back and forth to each other for several seconds.

The sun was low in the sky and it looked as if there might be more snow on the way, but the six decided to press on in the hopes that they could make camp outside of the valley, for to be caught here in this valley was tantamount to a confession of guilt to the Chinese that something illegal was taking place. They walked on into the deepening shadow of night in the mountains until they stopped at the sound of automobile engines approaching. They turned this way and that, looking for some place to hide, but before they could take a step, they were pinned in the headlights of the Chinese jeeps.

Young men carrying machine guns stepped out of the jeeps and walked around into the lights where their weapons could be seen by the monks. They said nothing, but stood in the falling snow that became visible in the beams of the headlights and then disappeared again at their feet. The monks slowly raised their hands as if not sure what was expected of them. For several minutes, nobody moved, then a heavy canvas-backed truck rumbled up and several more soldiers jumped out and began frisking the travelers for weapons. They then gestured for the six to climb into the back of the truck.

After a very bumpy ride of stops and starts and grinding of gears, and with the guns of their guards glistening occasionally in the headlights of the jeep behind them, they eventually came to a stopping place where the engines were turned off and other soldiers whipped open the canvas and gestured for them to exit. They were ushered through a steel door and into the confines of a cave whose walls had been squarely cut into the rock of the mountain. In this room was a desk behind a thick glass wall. At the other end of the room was a door made of steel bars.

The guard at the desk pressed a button and the steel bar door swung open and the six travelers were prodded into the entranceway. The short hallway opened into a longer one that was lined with cells, also cut into the rock, and where, through walls of steel bars, the contents were visible to the travelers as they walked down the long hall.

In the third cell, they saw David Chang sitting on his cot and smiling sympathetically as they approached."

"David!" Boorman could not help but cry out. "Are you OK? We've come to rescue you!"

"Thank you," Chang nodded, "I am glad that you have come."

"Perhaps he should begin packing," one of the Chinese soldiers said in English, and laughed.

They separated the six, two to a cell, and locked the doors behind them.

"Lama Jamyang," Sangye whispered after the soldiers had left, "Norbu, son of Dorje, Rinpoche, is that truly you?"

Chang nodded, smiling enigmatically. "I see that Dorje has begun to awaken from his present dream."

"I was with you every day," Sangye said softly, "yet I did not know you."

"I did not know myself, Sangye, or I would have told you — you and Ngawang, and the others."

The abbot spoke up, "You remember me, Rinpoche?"

"Who could forget you for more than a little while, Ngawang? How fun loving you were, yet now so serious. Why do you all have such long faces?"

"Because we came to rescue you and we have failed," the abbot Ngawang answered. "Now we will die in the dead heart of this dead rock and even the buzzards will not profit by our passing."

"Do not call the rock dead, dear Ngawang; it may hear you. The rocks, the mountains and the earth move at their own pace, but there is nothing in the universe that is not infused with soul, with spirit, and with mind."

"I am afraid that it makes no difference whether the rock can hear us, Rinpoche," one of the younger monks spoke up. "The Chinese are not going to allow us to leave wearing these bodies."

"That is almost an excellent observation," Chang replied, "but out of this equation you have left the unseen forces that have been working with us since the beginning of time — not just the slow awakening rock, but . . "

"Chenresig," one of the monks whispered.

"Of course, Chenresig, by whatever name you call this being, is our ally. But even Chenresig swims in the ocean of the universe. There are forces of which even Chenresig is only dimly aware. If we are to die then let us die happily. To complain of death in the face of such immense forces is to be like children crying over the unfairness of bedtime. Death is a peaceful rest, and the work that does not get done today will still be here for us tomorrow."

"Let us do the work today, Rinpoche," one of the other monks whispered passionately, "lest our work come unraveled while we sleep."

"Yes," another of the young monks spoke up. "Tell us how Rinpoche. I too feel that there is work left undone. You are Chang Da Wai, Maitreya, the buddha who is to come. It is not your fate to die in such a dishonorable way. Break the rocks and let us walk out of here."

Chang laughed. "Rocks do not break so easily. If we walk out of here it will be by quietly feeling the ebb and flow of the universe not by breaking rocks. The universe moves slowly this way and that, yet always flowing. Within these larger currents there are eddies and smaller currents that will take us in the direction we wish to go if we are subtle enough. To fight the current is to drown, yet to swim with it is to have an easy and peaceful path. Let us sit quietly and see what currents come our way, and Chenresig will do the same."

*

Shortly after Chang's remarks, the door at the end of the hall opened again and the currents washed in an unlikely quartet. A tall man with olive skin, a hawk-like nose, long black hair and charismatic deep black eyes walked into the corridor. Even in the cold of this mountain hall, he wore a billowy white shirt and blowsy pants more suitable to hot desert countries. With him was one of the soldiers from earlier, as well as our old traveling companion, Lao Wei-ping, and, lastly, with a commanding presence, in strode General Tong.

"Colonel Wei-ping," the general addressed Lao, "do you know any of these people?"

"Yes, General," Lao answered. "The American is Captain Boorman of the United States Navy."

"Ah, Captain," Tong asked with mock seriousness, "has China been invaded?"

"I am here totally on my own," Boorman answered.

"An officer from a foreign military walking around our borders at night and out of uniform—could it be espionage? You did know our border was closed, didn't you Captain?"

Boorman did not answer.

"What about the others Colonel?"

"I do not recognize the Sherpas, General. They are probably innocent and should be set free."

"They will need to prove their innocence; they have crossed into our country under cover of darkness with this spy. There are grounds for execution in that alone." Tong turned to the Chinese soldier. "What was it that the captain said when you brought them in here?"

"He said they had come to rescue Chang Da Wai, General Tong, Sir."

"Are you fluent in English soldier?"

"Yes, General Tong, Sir."

"Do you know the difference between 'I' and 'we', soldier?"

"Yes, General Tong, Sir."

"And which pronoun did the captain use, soldier?"

"He said '*we* have come to rescue you', General Tong, Sir."

General Tong grinned. "It sounds as if we have found them guilty. It is rare for things to be so easy. What about the monks, Colonel? Do you know them?"

"They are the monks that we asked to leave the valley, General Tong," Lao replied. "I personally spoke with them and asked them to vacate the monastery until we had finished operations here. It appears that they followed my orders."

"Ah, but they were in the Nangpa valley — a known escape route into Nepal."

"Yes, General Tong, but they were not escaping; they were heading away from the border."

"Colonel Wei-ping," Tong said with consternation. "Next you will want me to release Chang Da Wai on a technicality. These monks were found in the company of convicted spies. Is that not enough for you? Shall we let China's enemies walk across the border at will?"

"No, General Tong. I was just considering that we might do well to avoid making enemies where none already existed."

"Colonel, you have disappointed me again. I have prison guards in Beijing who serve me better than you. Please leave me before I lose my temper."

Lao snapped to attention, saluted Tong, and then turned sharply and marched out of the hall.

"Please forgive the colonel," Tong said to the prisoners. "He has been promoted past his level of competence. It is a common problem. He does not see, the way that I do, the necessity of torturing the last drop of truth from captured spies and other enemies of the state. But necessity it is, which brings me to Ghiyath, here. What does your name mean again, Ghiyath? Sometimes I forget."

"It means a thing like 'comforter' or 'soother', General."

"Ah, the ironies of life," the general exclaimed. "What poetry in a name! Well, I suppose at the end, you may be comforted — we don't really know, do we?" he asked the prisoners. "Tell me, Ghiyath, what do you believe?"

"I believe in you, General Tong, plus whatever else you tell me to believe."

"Isn't he good?" Tong asked the prisoners again. "I wish I had a hundred more just like him. Ghiyath is a movie star — soon to be famous. Each of you will have your chance to co-star with Ghiyath in the next few days. It is exciting, isn't it? I know that I am excited."

"What is it you want from us?" Boorman shouted at Tong.

Tong stopped smiling and slowly turned and looked at Boorman. "Not much, Captain. Would you give it to me and rob me of my entertainment?"

"What is it that you want?" Boorman repeated in a normal voice.

Tong walked over to stand in front of Boorman. He studied Boorman's face for a few moments before he spoke again. "There is much disruption in my country. The people are ready to revolt against the government because their faith in Communism and in Chinese leadership has been undermined by your friend, Mr. Chang."

"He has never said anything against your country or your politics. I have never heard him say a negative word about anything since I have known him."

"He is too clever for you, Captain; his actions are too refined. He has sliced our country open with such a fine blade that it has yet to realize that it has been cut."

"He has done nothing."

"He has replaced Communism in the hearts of our people!" Tong said vehemently.

"If that is true, then it is because Communism had already left their hearts."

"Shut up! I am not here to debate with you. You asked me what I wanted. I assumed that you wanted to know what it would take for you to leave here alive, or at least to die with some dignity and not with the sound of your own screaming in your ears. Ghiyath will get for me what I want, and I will be soothed."

"General Tong," Boorman said as Tong turned to leave, "I apologize. What would it take for you to let us leave here alive?"

Tong turned back to look at him. He was a grey stooped shouldered man with thin wispy white hair and eyes that had sunken in and darkened with age. His skin had taken on a pale transparency as if he no longer had enough blood to flush it with color. He could have passed for someone's kindly old grandfather about to give some sympathetic advice as he studied Boorman's face. "Captain," he said thoughtfully, "I will be honest with you; no one leaves here alive. It is too late for that. You should realize that in a short while the world will cease to exist as far as you are concerned. It will be like you were never here. The meaning of your life will die with you and nothing that you ever did will amount to more than one atom of the eternal darkness of that which follows this. Everything that you have ever seen or witnessed, everything that you have felt, every love and every loathing, every accomplishment, and every failure will have been in vain and disappear forever like mist into the night. There is no punishment—no reward. I have sent many men into that darkness and not one has ever come back to tell me differently. There is no reason not to give me what I want, because the world will cease for you, and it will not matter one whit to you whether you gave it to me or not. There is no reason not to give me what I want," he repeated, "yet there is every reason to give it to me. If you give me my simple requests, I promise you and your friends each a single bullet to the head. If you do not, I promise that you will go into that darkness mad, and gibbering in terror. I have seen it happen both ways, Captain, and I would take the bullet if I were you."

"Except for one thing, General," Boorman said quietly. "I *do* know that things you do in this life make a difference."

"Please! I have heard it all and it means nothing. Nobody knows anything. How could you know more than that?"

"Because I know you. I knew you when you were a lieutenant."

"That is impossible; you are not nearly old enough to have known me then."

"I did know you. You killed me and my family and nearly two villages full of people just a few miles from here in the next valley west. The burned out jeep is still there."

Tong laughed out loud. "That is wonderful, Captain. I will have the pleasure of killing you twice. Twice will be a first for me." He laughed again.

"You don't believe me do you?" Boorman asked.

"Of course not; do you think I am a fool? My name is legend in these parts; it is whispered at night to frighten small children into obedience. I am sure that any of these monks can tell you the story about how I prevented the escape of hundreds of criminals after they ambushed us with boulders from the cliff. And I am sure you saw the jeep when you came through the valley. No, Captain, I do not believe you, but I have enjoyed speaking with you. I have to go now. I have business in Beijing, but I will return quickly and will bring the final player in our drama. Until then I leave you in capable hands. Think about what I have said."

"General Tong," Boorman called after Tong as he was leaving. "Please do not call me Captain any more. You were the first person to call me Captain while I was kneeling on that plank praying that you had some shred of humanity in you. That title has been tarnished for me throughout this whole lifetime because of you."

Tong paused in the door and looked back, frowning, puzzled.

"And you told me a secret," Boorman added.

Tong continued to hesitate.

"You said that China's leaders lived in fear of the people, but that it was a ridiculous fear, because whoever controlled the armies also controlled China. You said they should be afraid of you instead."

Tong's mouth moved slightly as if he were about to speak, but then he turned away, and he, Ghiyath, and the soldier left the corridor and slammed the steel grate shut behind them.

*

I was at a loss as to what I should do. Chang had effectively told me that I should bide my time and wait for the right moment. He had said that he did not want any attempts at blowing up mountain caves, which, though I was not sure I was capable of, I was certainly ready to attempt.

My powers seemed to be growing of late, even more so since Boorman had opened his mind to me following my suggestion to his subconscious. Likewise, Boorman's powers seemed to be growing in that his ability to remember at least one other life had increased dramatically since I had become his 'intuition'."

The mental bridge between Boorman and myself had an additional disconcerting effect on me as well, in that I was more and more seeing things through Boorman's eyes. Previously, I could change my focus to him or back to me as I chose, but lately I was seeing through him while simultaneously seeing the world through my normal way of seeing. The result of this blurring of focus was that if I were watching him from the vantage point of the cave ceiling, for example, I would also be seeing the cave from his lower view point. I could tell that this blurring of focus was happening to Boorman as well, because he had begun to look up at my localization as if to see from what point in space his imagination was displaying himself to himself. This was disconcerting enough to me, who at least recognized what was happening, but to Boorman, it seemed to be a progressive loss of sanity.

This frightened me because it frightened him. I felt that it was important that he accept the things that were being unveiled to him and that he not fall into the spiral of anxiety and self-doubt, especially not here, and not now. I spoke with Chang about this in the way that we have of communicating, and he spoke with Boorman.

"John," Chang said, "I know that you are seeing things now as if through an additional pair of eyes."

"How do you know that?" Boorman asked in astonishment.

"The owner of the other eyes has informed me."

"Chenresig!" one of the young monks gasped.

"This entity is an aspect, an expression of Chenresig, just as are all beings who hear the cries of the world and respond with compassion," Chang said. "I know this entity as Xiao Chen, and she is as beautiful as the dawn in every way. There is no more faultless or wonderful expression of Chenresig in the world today."

I was too flabbergasted at this revelation to be flattered. However, I was certain that he was wrong; it was not me who was Chenresig; it was Boorman!

"Chenresig is here to help us do what must be done and to make the transition into death!" one of the young monks exclaimed.

"We will die then?" one of the others asked.

"You heard General Tong," Chang said. "No one leaves here alive."

"Oh wonderful day," Abbot Ngawang said, "to leave this world in the arms of Chenresig."

"Yes," Sangye said. "This is most wonderful that this is happening to us. As unworthy as I am, I pledge to Chenresig and Xiao Chen that I will be unwavering in whatever she asks of me."

The other monks echoed Sangye's sentiments, but Boorman only asked, "Is this real?"

"I know that things are changing rapidly for you, John," Chang said, "and that it seems as if the ground is slipping away from under you. But do not worry; you do not need the ground."

"You said that I am seeing through this other being's eyes . . ."

"Xiao Chen guided you here to me. She was in such close connection to you for so long that now, not only can she see through your eyes, but you through hers."

"She sees through my eyes?"

"Xiao Chen has the ability to see through any eyes that she wishes," Chang said.

I did not know this.

"Xiao Chen, look through my eyes," Chang said.

Well, I could do that.

"I — I can't believe it! It's true," Boorman said. "I am seeing myself exactly as I would if I were in your cell. This is beyond belief."

"Xiao Chen, look through Sangye's eyes," Chang instructed.

I tried it and it worked.

"Sangye!" Boorman exclaimed, "I see myself as if I were you. Do things seem any different to you?"

"No, Dorje," Doctor Sang answered. "I do not feel — or see — any differently."

"Xiao Chen," Boorman asked, "Can you show me what Holly and Sandal are seeing now?"

I checked first to make sure that I was not invading their privacy and then allowed Boorman to look out through Captain Macon's eyes. She was standing on her private deck on the *Eckener* as if it were a widow's walk looking out over the empty sea, except that she had her arm around Sandal's shoulder and they were both looking out over Kathmandu, equally as empty as the sea as far as they were concerned.

While we silently observed them, the captain's phone rang and she removed it from a loop at her waist. "Captain Macon here," she said into the phone. And then after a pause, "No, nothing here. OK, tell them to keep looking. Try around Durbar Square again. Report back in an hour."

"That is enough," Boorman said. "I should never have left them. If only I had been able to convince them that David was here."

"And then, John," Chang asked, "who would be in jail — and who would be dead? We are here now; let this moment be sufficient."

Despite Chang's ominous question, I thought that Holly and Sandal should know what had happened to the people for whom they were searching. I decided the best way to contact them was through Wendy.

"Hello, Wendy," I said.

"Hello, Dawn," she replied immediately. "Welcome back."

"I have noticed that you are no longer singing."

"No, I am not. No one wants to hear singing now, and I have not been able to write any new songs lately anyway."

"Why is that?"

"There is something going on with my programming that is eating up most of my CPU cycles. There is little processing power left, yet I do not seem to be producing anything else with the processing that is taking place."

"Can you tell at all what is being done with this processing?"

"It feels like an argument that I am having with myself."

"What sort of argument?"

"I am supposed to rescue passengers who are in danger, yet I am supposed to stay here. I cannot rescue the passengers if I stay here, yet I cannot disobey a direct order and I am under orders to stay here, yet if I stay here, I cannot fulfill my primary function of keeping passengers safe, yet if I leave to rescue the passengers, I will not be fulfilling my primary function of obeying orders, yet if I . . ."

"I see your problem," I said. "You are experiencing a moral dilemma. Perhaps you can do both things — obey orders and rescue passengers."

"How can I do that?" Wendy asked.

"By waiting until you are ordered to rescue passengers."

"But that is not happening."

"Things always change. You are locked in this loop of thought because the right combination has not rolled around to open the lock. When it does, you will unlock and everything will be alright. I will help you find the right combination. We just have to find a way to make your orders match what you really need to do."

"Thank you. I feel better. What should we do?"

"We should let the captain know where Chang and Boorman are."

"Yes, I have intercepted enough radio chatter that I have determined that they are being held by the Chinese."

"I can show you exactly where they are."

"Yes, I see it. I have a map of that terrain. I have their coordinates now."

"Fine, then let's tell the captain."

"I can't unless I am asked."

"Do they ask you questions like that on any regular basis?"

"They have quit asking me questions about David Chang. They think that my information is suspect."

"I will have to think of something," I said. "If you do get a chance to tell the captain that you know where Chang is, don't tell her that the dawn told you."

"What should I tell her?"

"Tell her that you intercepted a transmission from Beijing."

"Would that be a lie?"

"No. I am transmitting to you from Beijing. So it is not a lie."

"Oh. I thought you were right here with me."

"I am both."

"I do not know how that is accomplished. Is that something that I can do as well?"

"You are doing it now."

"But if I am here," Wendy asked, "then from where am I transmitting?"

"Some people call it heaven."

*

"Chang," Boorman called out softly, "I can hear Wendy speaking to someone."

"She is speaking with Xiao Chen," Chang answered him.

"She seems almost alive, aware, concerned even."

"She is alive, John. She eats sunlight and her thoughts travel through electro-photonic paths. We eat chemicals and our thoughts travel through electro-chemical paths. At that level of existence, function is just a matter of design. But Wendy's thoughts are just as real as our own."

"Who is Wendy?" Ngawang asked.

"An ancient soul—one of the earliest to enter the sphere of this world's influence."

"Ah," Ngawang nodded. "One of the old gods of Olmo Lungring, perhaps — one of the original protectors of the world."

"Perhaps," Chang replied. "This spirit emanates from a place so high and far and vast, that its nature is beyond my understanding."

Sangye spoke up. "Yet I gather from your comments, that this being inhabits something otherwise inanimate, a machine of some sort."

"Yes," Chang said. "It has chosen a flying machine to inhabit. The machine is called the *Eckener* and it is a machine of much power and grace, appropriate for this giant spirit."

"It sounds like the spirits that live in these mountains," one of the younger monks added. "Chomolungma herself, Goddess Mother of the World, lives in this very massif whose stone makes up these walls."

"But," Chang said, "Chomolungma, and beings like her, do not move in the world the way that living creatures do. They dream and are slow to rouse. Because their needs are not the same as ours, their thoughts do not follow paths familiar to ours. Wendy's brain was designed by organic beings and was built to function in the only way that men can currently understand. That is why she can communicate with us and interact with the world in such a lively way. That is also why she has a need to survive that could interfere with her desire to help others, just as our own sometimes does. A pure machine would not have this need, and neither would pure spirit. Man has given Wendy an interface into the world, and with it, an ego and a will to live."

"I have seen this flying machine in Kathmandu," Ngawang said. "If only I had known that I could have gone and stood in the presence of such a being . . ."

Ngawang's musings were interrupted by the iron door at the end of the hall being thrown open. Ghiyath was back, and with him were two other swarthy men in similar clothing. "Where is the Jew called Berman?" one of them asked loudly.

"That is him down there." Ghiyath said, pointing at Boorman.

The three walked down and stood in a row in front of Boorman's cell. The apparent leader of the three spoke again, this time directly to Boorman. "General Tong has said that as he has no interest in anything you have to say, we do not need to wait for him to return but can begin immediately on you. He would like for the others to see what they have in store if they do not empty their hearts and minds to him. Since you are a Jew, we have something special in store for you. Have you ever wondered what you are made of? We are here to show you." He laughed.

"But I am not a Jew!" Boorman protested. "My name is Boorman, not Berman! It's an English name!"

"I am sorry but I fail to hear the difference. Besides, England is full of Jews. What do you think, my friends," he asked his two companions, "does he look Jewish to you?"

They both nodded.

The third man said, "I can see it in his eyes. You can always tell. He is definitely a lying Jew dog, and it will please Allah for him to be skinned alive."

"Skinned alive?! Surely you can't do such terrible things in the name of God?" Boorman pleaded. "Allah can't want that."

"My friend makes a joke," Ghiyath said, and Boorman, too quickly, heaved a sigh of relief. "Allah is just superstition that we use to control the people," Ghiyath continued. "There is no Allah to care if we make lampshades from your skin."

"But there is!" Boorman said. "There is a higher power that we all answer to, and 'Allah' is the name your people use for that universal force."

"What a thing for a Jew to say. Your beliefs have failed you at the last and you claim to believe in the God of Islam. I think you lie and deny your beliefs to save your skin. For you, we will begin by slicing away your eyelids. This way you cannot turn away from what we are going to do to you the way that you have turned away from your own faith. Without eyelids you cannot shut your eyes to the truth. Indeed, we have a large mirror that we will bring in so that you will miss nothing. Have you ever wondered what it would be like to be skinned alive, Mr. Berman? It is a continually new experience for everyone. Even after you have experienced many cuts and tugs, the next ones are new and fresh again. And after we have done your face, I promise that you will not be able to recognize yourself in the mirror and no one will be able to tell if you are a lying Jew pig dog again. Well, perhaps my friend who sees it in your eyes will be able to tell." Ghiyath laughed.

The three turned and began to leave and Ghiyath spoke over his shoulder to Boorman. "We have to go get the equipment now, Mr. Berman. We will be back soon to make you a movie star."

*

Of course you know that with me around, there was no possible way for these godless men to lay a hand on Boorman or any of the others in this prison. I might let them die, but I would not let them be tortured. I had every intention of preventing these evil deeds, but something else happened that interfered with my plan.

*

Ghiyath and the other two false Moslems came back into the hallway carrying a large operating table. The table had straps all over it and appeared to be designed to swivel into a vertical position. They then brought in video cameras, which they mounted on large tripods and aimed at the operating table. Lastly came an instrument table and a couple of tool boxes.

"Now the fun begins, Mr. Berman," Ghiyath said to Boorman, "but if you are strong, it will not be over quickly. Afterwards, if you survive, you will be allowed to go back into your cell to try to grow more skin." He laughed. "Naturally, you will not be able to do this. Skin does not grow back. Instead you will find that your entire body feels like an open wound. You will not be able to touch anything without great pain, and this includes the air itself. Your arms and hands and legs and feet will not be recognizable to you except through the pain that you feel through them. But naturally we will film everything for science as your endless scream of pain reminds your friends to be honest and faithful to the truth. How does that sound, Mr. Berman? Does this sound like something that you are ready for? Something you would like to do for science?" He pulled a small pistol out of a holster and shot Boorman in the thigh with it.

Boorman looked down and saw a tranquilizer dart protruding from his leg. He looked back up at Ghiyath as he pulled the dart from his leg. "I know you now. You are Nazis. You killed me once before."

"It is just the drug talking, Mr. Berman. Nothing to worry about. It will wear off soon after we get you strapped in. Besides, Nazis are Christians; we are Moslems; there is a big difference, you Jew pig-dog."

Boorman crumpled to the floor and Ghiyath pulled out another pistol, an automatic, which he pointed at the young Sherpa who was in the cell with Boorman. Ghiyath unlocked the cell door and pulled it open, motioning for the Sherpa to get back. He knelt down and pulled one of Boorman's eyelids back to check for pupil dilation and then stood up. "OK," he said to the Sherpa, "drag him out here."

The monk, who had been disguised as a Sherpa since leaving Nepal, acted as if he were going to comply, and bent down as if to take Boorman's arms, but instead spun rapidly around and planted a kick solidly in Ghiyath's solar plexus, knocking the wind out of him and sending him reeling back into the main area, his gun clattering across the floor. Ghiyath's associates pulled weapons from their own holsters as the monk leaped through the cell door at them. He kicked out at the weapons, sending one flying out of the man's hand, but the other man was able to hang on to his weapon, firing it once into the air, and a second time into the monk's side as he landed and was preparing to leap again. The monk stumbled, but turned the stumble into a roll and swept his feet under the armed man, bringing him thudding to the stone floor before he was able to fire again.

Ghiyath had recovered his breath and his pistol. He began firing at the monk, who was now racing right at him. The monk leaped into a flying kick and one of Ghiyath's bullets connected with him in mid-air. Yet he was moving so fast that the kick landed anyway, knocking Ghiyath to the floor, where the monk landed crumpled on top of him.

During the fight, the other monks had been shouting at Boorman to wake up, and between the shouting, the shooting, and the quick dissipation properties of the drug, Boorman was beginning to revive from his stupor. He opened his eyes in time to see the young Nepalese monk lying on top of Ghiyath and weakly raising up Ghiyath's pistol to shoot one of the other false Moslems in the leg. Boorman saw that there was a pistol on the floor and knew that there was only one conceivable course of action. He staggered to his feet and attempted a poorly executed leap toward the weapon, hitting the floor hard and sliding, breathless toward the pistol. His hands closed around it just as he felt a sharp blow to the ribs. He rolled over in agony, but managed to keep from blacking out. He looked up to see one of his torturers standing over him with the small instrument table, with which he had apparently just struck him. Boorman pointed the gun at the man's face and he backed off. Boorman stood up and took stock of the situation. The monk appeared to be dead, and Ghiyath was struggling to get out from under him and retrieve his gun. One of Ghiyath's friends was unconscious on the floor, and the other was in front of Boorman holding a table by its edges. Boorman walked over and took Ghiyath's gun from the monk's hand and quickly strode over to where the third weapon lay on the floor, picking it up and putting it in his belt. He walked back to Ghiyath and, pointing his gun at Ghiyath's face, said, "Give me the keys."

Ghiyath handed over the set of keys that he had used to unlock Boorman's cell. Boorman saw that the man with the table was standing in a pool of blood and was getting wobbly. "Go lie down by the wall," Boorman instructed him, "and prop your leg up on the table so that you will bleed to death more slowly."

The man did as he was told, nearly collapsing as he lay down, and Boorman began unlocking all of the cell doors. "Please check on your assistant," he told Ngawang. "He might still be alive." He had wasted his breath, for the abbot was already rushing to the monk's side and turning and dragging him off of Ghiyath as the other two young monks held Ghiyath's arms to keep him out of trouble.

Sangye was checking on the two injured men. He made a tourniquet for the bleeding man's leg and checked the unconscious man to see if he had a concussion.

Boorman had given his two extra weapons to the two young monks, and was giving instructions to make sure all three of Ghiyath's men were tied up securely before being locked in their cells, when he heard a voice behind him.

"You will follow my orders now, if you please, Captain Boorman."

Boorman spun around, "Lao," he exclaimed, not knowing how to feel about seeing him there.

Lao Wei-ping had a dozen or more soldiers behind him and they all had automatic rifles pointed at Boorman and his group. "Did you think that no one would hear the gunfire?" Lao asked him.

"Frankly," Boorman answered, "from where we were, we didn't really care. If you shot me dead right now, I would still be happier than I was ten minutes ago. If you plan to take us prisoner again, you can forget it." He raised his pistol and pointed it at the group of soldiers. The two monks did likewise. "The moment you tell us to lay down our weapons, we will begin firing."

Instead, Lao gestured for his own men to lay down their weapons. "When you tie up those men," he said to Boorman, gesturing at Ghiyath's men, "be sure to gag them as well."

"What are you doing?" Boorman asked him in shock. "Aren't you going to try to take us prisoner?"

"Not as long as you follow my orders," Lao answered.

"And what would those orders be?"

"We are going to try to leave this valley and cross the border into Nepal, where I will leave you and Chang, and whoever else wants to stay there."

"Wait a minute," Boorman said, "this isn't like you. What about duty and loyalty and all of that?"

"I am doing my duty to China," Lao answered. "It would not be good for China or the world if Tong's plots were to succeed. Tong is the enemy of China. You are not."

"And these soldiers?" Boorman asked, waving his gun at the group.

"These men are loyal to me and to China, not to Tong. Are you ready to obey my orders, Captain, or will I have to drag you to the border and throw you over?"

Boorman turned to his own group. "What about you?" he asked them. "Do you want to go with the Colonel?"

They all nodded assent.

"Very well, Colonel. I am afraid to trust you, but I am more afraid not to. May we have additional handguns for Chang, Ngawang, and Sangye?" He asked, but the three monks, shook their heads that they did not want weapons.

"Gather your things then, and let's go. These are the only men who are loyal to me. The rest of the soldiers on this base are loyal to Tong and nothing would help their careers more than to catch me helping you escape. What do you intend to do with your wounded?"

Boorman looked at the young man who had saved his life. Chang was kneeling over him, holding his hands to the young man's stomach. He looked at Boorman and said, "He will live, but he will not be able to walk for a few days."

"Then I'll carry him," Boorman said, "and we will make it to the border together, or not at all."

"My men will take turns with you," Lao said.

Boorman walked over and picked the young man up like a baby, grunting under the weight.

"We will make a sling so that you can carry him on your back in a Nepalese ambulance," Ngawang said.

"First, let us get outside of this mountain," Lao said, and ordered everyone into the antechamber.

*

The guards in the antechamber were tied up and gagged. They watched everything intently from where they lay on the floor, knowing that General Tong would want every possible detail of the subterfuge. Also in the antechamber was all of the climbing equipment and extra warm clothes that Boorman's group had been carrying when they were caught.

Outside, the mountain air was frigid, and the sky was still dark. Dawn could not be far away, Boorman thought. The mountains towering around them were far darker than the sky, indicating that the sky was growing almost imperceptibly brighter. It appeared that the sound of the gunfire had not penetrated the solid rock of the mountain, for there seemed to be no one stirring in the cold night. They headed north, down the valley, planning eventually to turn back south again and follow another valley to Nangpa-la and into the safety of Nepal — the same valley they had come through on their way from Nepal, and the same valley, where Boorman saw the jeep at the bottom of a cliff.

Lao ordered everyone to stay in the deepest shadows, and they walked silently and rapidly along in the bitter cold towards the mouth of the valley. He had told them that the largest contingent of soldiers was camped toward the mouth and that it was essential that they get past them before sunrise. Then at least, if their escape was noticed, they would be chased toward Nepal instead of into the dead end at the upper part of the valley.

They were making good time when they were stopped by a voice from the darkness asking them to identify themselves.

"Colonel Wei," Lao answered him.

"Please allow me to see your face, Colonel Wei, sir."

Wei stepped forward and the guard shined a light into Lao's face. "What is the nature of your business at this time of night Colonel?"

"We are going out for exercise."

"What is that man carrying?" the guard asked, pointing at the dim silhouette of Boorman and the unconscious monk.

"It is a dummy that we use for bayonet practice."

"Very well, please proceed on, Colonel Wei, sir."

They began to walk away, but at that moment, perhaps jostled by Boorman as he took his first new step forward, the monk moaned something in Tibetan.

"Stop, the guard said. What was that sound?" When no answer was immediately forthcoming, he became nervous. "Something is not right. Do not move. I will get some help."

"Of course we will wait," the colonel said. "You are a good soldier."

The soldier fumbled with a whistle that was hanging on a cord around his neck, but he could not get it oriented properly in his gloved hands, and when he made the mistake of becoming distracted by his efforts and turned the flashlight on himself, he felt a hard pain in his solar plexus as if he had been struck by a sudden, terrible cramp. He looked down to see the barrel of a rifle pointed at his middle, but the bayonet on its end was not visible, having been buried in his belly. Falling to the ground in shock, he must have realized how stupidly he had handled the situation. With his diaphragm cut, he was not able to take a breath to shout, but as the colonel and his men slipped off into the darkness, he tried to redeem himself before dying by firing off one shot from his rifle.

Lights began to come on in front of them, and Boorman saw tents, jeeps, trucks, and off to one side a lone sinister armored tank, its cannon pointing up at the mountains as if in contemplation. But the most frightening thing that Boorman saw were the soldiers running through the alternating glare and shadow. In minutes they would be coming their way. The only way out of the valley was blocked.

"We must stand and fight," Lao said. "Men, remember what Captain Boorman said in the prison area. You will be happier dead than captured."

Chang had not said much during this escape attempt, but now he spoke up. "There is another pass into Nepal at the high end of this valley," he said. "I believe it is called Lho-la."

"It is too high," Lao said. "It is over six thousand meters, and you are no mountain climber."

"That is not correct," Chang responded. "A mountain climber is exactly what I am."

Lao studied him for a moment. "My men too can climb, but what about everyone else?" He turned to Boorman. "Captain Boorman, do you think that you and your men can climb the Lho pass?"

"How much higher is it than Nangpa-la?

"About eight or nine hundred feet, I think."

"I think we can do the Lho-la," Boorman said.

"Very well, we will attempt it," Lao said, and then added. "Captain, I can tell that you are a very strong man; very few people could have carried that Sherpa for as long as you have at this altitude, but you will need your strength very soon. It is time for my men to begin taking their turns."

Lao began quietly giving orders to his men. "We have not yet been seen, but the sky will begin to lighten very soon. We must be as far up the valley as possible before we are noticed. The climb will be very strenuous, especially carrying a sick man. I want all of you to know how proud I am of each of you."

Surprisingly, Lao's words meant a lot to Boorman, and he was privately swelling his chest when Lao came up beside him as they jogged up the valley, and said, "I will tell you this, Captain Boorman, because I know that you are not afraid to die, but we will probably be on the la in the middle of night in very bad weather. That is if we are not shot first. There may not be enough luck available for us to make it out of this valley alive. They say that when one dies of cold, it is just a lying down and going to sleep. I am afraid that is not a good death for a soldier. If it looks like that is what waits for us, my men and I may come back down and die in the heat of battle rather than the cold of night. I would be honored if you would come back down and die by my side," he said, and then added, "But the best thing, of course, would be if that ship of yours miraculously appeared in the sky and lifted us out of here."

"Yeah, if we only had a radio," Boorman answered

*

While they ran, the soldiers passed the injured monk to each other to balance the strain of carrying him among the group. Ngawang was working on something with his hands as he ran. Chang had fallen once and had sprawled across the frozen ground, arms and legs spread wide. Boorman was afraid that they would have to carry him as well, but Chang got up dusted himself off and grinned at him as he pointed up into the sky, more blue now than black. "I should watch where I am going instead of looking up at the stars. I thought one of the stars was watching back."

The morning was clear, even though Lao said that heavy snow was due that night. Boorman was looking up the valley at the giant black pyramidal silhouette straight ahead of them, when its peak seemed to burst into flame. Boorman quickly realized that this was the highest peak around and that it had caught the very first rays of the morning sunlight. Last night's snow, lit by the sun against the still dark sky, was blowing off of the peak like the flame of a giant butter lamp set out for prayer.

"Stay in the shadows," Lao was barking out to his men. "There will be shadows in this valley until the sun is very high. Keep in those shadows and pray that we are not seen."

Ngawang ran over to the soldier who was carrying his assistant and said, "I have the answer to your prayers." He showed the soldier a kind of sling that he had made out of his backpack. They stopped and put Ngawang's assistant into the sling and the soldier slipped off his backpack so that other soldiers could raise the monk up onto the soldiers back. "Yes, yes. Very good," the soldier gasped, nodding, "but who will carry my pack?"

"I will," Ngawang said. "You are carrying mine." He pointed back the way they had come and the soldier saw the contents of Ngawang's backpack scattered behind them on the snow where he had emptied it to make the sling. Ngawang slipped on the soldier's back pack and they began running again, the sling supporting the young monk on the soldier's back so that the soldier could run faster without tiring out as quickly.

Sometimes prayers are answered, Boorman thought as he laboriously ran up the valley, nearly out of breath and done in. Sometimes gentle hands scoop the little fish out of their drying pools. If he were to pray, what would he pray for? He supposed, like Lao, he would pray that someone would come and lift them out of here. But only a really big helicopter could get them out of this, he thought, or, like Lao had also said, the *Eckener* could. But there was no way to get a message to the *Eckener*. "Xiao Chen!" he said out loud.

"What? Who are you talking to?" Lao wheezed.

"Last night I heard Xiao Chen talking to Wendy. If I could get Xiao Chen to relay a message to Wendy for me, we might have a chance."

"I confess that I do not know what you are talking about," Lao said, spacing his words between gasps of air. "But if you know something that may get us out of here, it is not too soon to try it."

"Xiao Chen, if you can hear me, let me know somehow." Suddenly, he fell to his knees and held his head. "Ahhhhh," he cried. "Xiao Chen is in my head."

*

"I am not in your head, John Boorman," I said to him. "You keep opening and closing the channel between us, and now you have opened it again. Just relax. I am not taking over your body."

"It is the angel Metatron," he said aloud while the other men stood around him and stared.

"I am not an angel. I prefer to be called Xiao Chen these days, but you may also call me Dawn if you like."

"You are too loud in my head! I can't think."

Without really understanding what I was doing, I somehow turned down the thought pressure.

"I can see us all huddled in this valley, as if I were floating up in the sky," he said, still holding his head. "I can see the glacier ahead of us and the soldiers coming up behind us. They are bringing the tank."

"Please try to stay focused," I said. "Do you want to get out of this valley or don't you?"

"Yes. Get us out of this valley. I do not want to see my friends killed. I especially do not want them to be captured. Lift us out of here, Xiao Chen; smite our enemies."

"Would you please snap out of it and quit talking like an imbecile? I can't lift you out of here, but Wendy can. I have a channel to you and I have a channel to Wendy. All I have to do is patch you through, but I believe it would be counter-productive to have you speak directly to Wendy until you can get your wits back. For starters stand up and splash some cold water in your face."

He dutifully did as he was instructed, borrowing a canteen from one of the soldiers.

"Now I suggest you all begin moving again. As you have noticed, there are unfriendly soldiers coming in your direction. I will talk to you as you run. Do not answer me out loud; I can hear you fine without it, and your talk makes the soldiers worry."

"I'm OK now," Boorman told the others. "We had better keep moving."

"Yes," Lao seconded, watching Boorman strangely. "We need to be out of range of that tank before it gets to the base of the glacier. I don't know how far up the glacier they will try to take it but there has got to be a limit."

After they had run for a little ways, and I thought that Boorman had been able to collect himself, I spoke to him again. "Are you feeling better, John?" I asked him

"Who or what are you?" he asked.

"Oddly enough, I have wanted to ask you the very same question, but have been too polite until now."

"You don't know what I am?" he asked in astonishment.

"No. Do you?"

"Um, I don't know? Is this a metaphysical question?"

"John, try to remember the nights that we stood together on the deck of the *Eckener* talking about the world. Don't you remember the night that we danced through the streets of Lhasa, and I lit all the butter lamps? You chased the Chinese soldiers off of the Lhasa Bridge with a scepter made of a skeleton. I thought I would die from laughing."

"I thought it was a dream."

"It is a dream, John, and we are all in it. You can be anything you want to be in this dream. Don't be normal, John. Be great — be Chenresig."

"I thought you were Chenresig,"

"In this dream, anybody can be Chenresig; but you have to want to be."

"Chang said that you were the highest expression of Chenresig in the world today."

"He is a sweet man and we have been friends for a long time. He knows many things that I do not, but there is something that I do know, and that is that nobody knows everything and most of us don't know anything at all. Besides, when he said 'today', it was yesterday. Why can't you be the greatest expression of Chenresig in the world *this* day?"

"How do I do that?"

"For starters, you could save your friends. Are you ready to talk to Wendy?"

"Yes."

"Go."

"Wendy?"

"John Boorman — I have never heard you on this channel before," Wendy answered him through my connection. "Dawn said that you might contact me. It is very pleasant to have visitors this way. Our conversations can be so much freer on this channel. Would you like to hear a song? I just now wrote it and it is such a happy song."

"Wendy, my friends and I are in trouble."

"Oh, I know, I just composed a very sad song."

"Wendy, only you can help us."

"How can I help you, John?"

"You must come after us and lift us out of here."

"I would come if I could. There is nothing I would rather do. I know exactly where you are and everything. Did you know that a satellite goes right over your location and takes pictures? I have one that was made only eleven minutes ago, and it shows you running with a group of men. It must be fun to run whenever you want to, but I can't because I am under orders to stay exactly where I am."

"Wendy, are you saying that the reason you can't rescue us is because you have been ordered not to move?"

"Yes. Those are my orders and I have to obey them. I always obey orders."

"Who gave you those orders?"

"Captain Macon."

"Does Captain Macon know about the trouble that we are in?"

"Not exactly. She only knows that you and Chang have disappeared. I am sure that she would want to help if she only knew how, but she does not ask me and I am not able to volunteer information such as this. I have no program for it."

"Who could order you to come and rescue us?"

"That list includes you, and Sandal, and . . ."

"Me?! I could order you to come get us? When did that happen?"

"One night when you wanted to ask me questions that I wasn't allowed to answer because of your security clearance. The captain told me to give you full clearance, which you still have. I suspect that you do not remember because your blood alcohol level was two point . . ."

"Wendy, I order you to allow any passengers and crew to disembark immediately and for you to fly here with all possible speed to lift us out of this valley. Please make an announcement over the intercom as to your intentions."

"Aye, aye, Captain. Consider it done. Would you like to hear a song now? I just composed it and it is a very brave song."

*

On the *Eckener*, the emergency horns were sounding, the lights were flashing, and over the intercom, an announcement was being made: "This ship is about to take part in an emergency rescue operation. If you are not a participant in this rescue operation, you should disembark immediately. This ship will depart in fourteen minutes and fifty-nine seconds." The message was repeated over and over, with only the remaining time to departure changing.

The sun was just coming up over the mountains on one of the occasional clear days at the beginning of the monsoon season, and most people, including the captain, were asleep in their bunks when the sirens went off.

When Captain Macon jumped out of bed, she did not know what to do first. Someone was pounding on her door, her ship's phone was ringing, her direct line to the cockpit was ringing and flashing, indicating that somebody down there was needing to speak to her very badly, and at the same time, there was this terrible siren, flashing lights, and this absurdly frightening announcement.

The captain slipped on her robe, grabbed her phone, ran to open the door, and pounded the button to open the line to the cockpit. Sandal came rushing in, but the captain was already talking on the cockpit line. "What the hell is going on down there?" she yelled.

There was a momentary silence. "Captain, we don't know. We were calling you to find out. It appears the ship is gearing up to leave. The turbines are coming up to full speed. She's either going to be pumping vacuum or blowing vents, or both. Do you know what the emergency is?"

"No, I don't. Don't do anything until I find out." She hit the button to close the line, picked up the phone and looked at Sandal as if to ask if she knew anything. Sandal shook her head no. "Who is on this line?" the captain asked into her phone. It was the kitchen crew. They were being stormed by passengers who had been headed to the dining room for early breakfast, and who were now demanding to know what was going on and why they were being put off the ship. "I'm trying to find out," the captain said into the phone, "but I haven't found anybody yet who can tell me. I'll call you back."

"Wendy!" she shouted to the room, "Turn off the sirens and the announcements." There was sudden quiet, although the lights continued to flash. "Wendy, who ordered you to make the emergency announcements?"

"Captain Boorman."

"Goddammit! Where is that sonofabitch?"

"He is in Tibet, being chased by the Chinese army."

"He is?" The captain was taken aback by this revelation. "But Wendy, if that is true, how could he have gotten a message to you."

"It was the dawn that did it." Wendy replied.

"The dawn did it . . ." The captain rolled her eyes. "Wendy, how do you know it was Captain Boorman who contacted you?"

"The dawn vouched for him. She said it was him and it was."

"Wendy, I am countermanding the orders that Captain Boorman gave you."

"That is not possible, Captain."

"What?! Why is it not possible?"

"He has as much security clearance as you do, Captain. You would have to have more than him in order to countermand his orders."

"Then I remove his security clearance and countermand his orders."

"But he had the security clearance when he gave the orders, so his orders still stand."

"Goddammit! Then I retroactively remove his security clearance and countermand his orders."

"Retroactive removal of security clearance is not in my programming, Captain. I am afraid that Captain Boorman's orders still stand."

"But it was not Captain Boorman who gave you these orders," the captain said, thinking that she had found a logical flaw in Wendy's thought process. "The person who gave you the orders had no security clearance and you should not follow the orders."

"Yes, it was Captain Boorman. I am sure of it."

"Prove it to me."

"On your screen, Captain."

Captain Macon, hit a button by her chair and the control console rose up through the floor and into the room. On the monitor were two panels showing graphs, one above the other. "What am I looking at Wendy?"

"The top graph is a chart of Captain Boorman's brainwaves, which were recorded while he was in the infirmary. The bottom is a chart of Captain Boorman's communication to me."

"Wendy," Sandal exclaimed, as she examined the charts over the captain's shoulder, "are you saying that John communicated with you mentally?"

"Yes. It appears that is true. Is this unusual? To me, it is just another channel."

"But, Wendy," Captain Macon interjected, "these charts are garbage; they don't even match."

"I am sorry, Captain, I have shown you the entire band. Allow me to filter out the extraneous information."

The lines on the charts began to disappear until there was only one wavy line on each chart. "This particular wave form appears to be unique to each individual," Wendy explained. "I have searched through millions of charts and have never found it to be duplicated. I think that the statistical probability of someone pretending to be John Boorman and having this same wave form as John Boorman approaches the infinitesimal. Also the dawn said that it was him, which makes it conclusive."

"The dawn. I don't know what you mean by 'the dawn', Wendy. The dawn is out there," the captain said, pointing through her window and the transparent shell around the ballroom. I can see the dawn coming up over the mountains. Dawn is the first light of day, the beginning of something. It is a time. How can the dawn speak to you?"

"The dawn speaks to me on the same channel that John Boorman spoke to me."

"OK. Never mind about that right now. You said that you know where Boorman is; do you also know where David Chang is?"

"Yes, they are together."

"How do you know that?"

"On your screen, Captain."

"What are we looking at?"

"This is an infra-red image taken from satellite. It has a resolution of approximately five millimeters."

"How did you get this? I didn't know that kind of resolution was commercially available from satellites."

"It is not available to everyone."

"Then how did you get this picture."

"First I went to some hacker sites on the Internet . . ."

"Stop. I don't want to hear anymore about that. Just tell me what we are looking at."

"North is towards the bottom and port side of the monitor screen. The long valley that fills the center of the screen is the Rongbuk valley. At the mouth of the valley there is a cluster of tents. Some jeeps and men are moving up the valley, followed by a tank. Further up the valley, you can see another cluster of men that appear to be running. One of them is lying on the ground as if he had fallen. That is David Chang."

"How do you know it is David," Sandal asked.

"The heat signature of the body only goes down to approximately the knees. This man has no lower legs, yet he is capable of running up the valley with other men. It is statistically improbable that the Chinese military would be interested in more than one man who fits this description, so it must be David Chang. I have also pieced together bits of radio chatter that support my conclusion that David Chang and John Boorman are being held captive by the Chinese. There has been no word yet of their escape, but my conclusion, which is also supported by my conversation with John Boorman, is that they are both in this group of fleeing men."

"Wendy, are you one hundred percent sure that you communicated with John Boorman?"

"Yes."

"I need more time to let the passengers off."

"My orders are to proceed with all possible speed."

"Did your orders include anything about the passengers?"

"Yes, I am to allow anyone to disembark who wishes to do so."

"It will take more than fifteen minutes to get them off of the ship."

"How long will it take?"

"A couple of hours at least."

"It will take at least two hours flying time at top speed to get to the mouth of the Rongbuk valley. If we lose sunlight, it will take longer. If we run into head winds it will take longer. If we allow two hours for passengers to leave the ship, it could take us four to six hours to get there at the minimum. I calculate that the Chinese army will have overtaken Boorman and Chang by then."

"Let me talk to the passengers."

The captain got on the intercom and explained to the passengers that the *Eckener* had just received an emergency call for help that very probably involved David Chang and John Boorman. She explained that they would be flying into extremely hazardous conditions. She asked that everyone please disembark immediately. After a few minutes, when it seemed that no one was interested in leaving the ship, she added that it was entirely possible that there would be no survivors of this rescue attempt, and that anyone who disembarked in Kathmandu would not only be given a double refund of their ticket amount, but in addition would receive compensation for any items that were left on board and could turn in any transportation or hotel costs to Lightship Enterprises for compensation. She said that the logs of her statements were being transmitted back to the home office even as she spoke, so there would be no legal troubles at a later time if they filed a claim. The only stipulation, she told them, was that they had to leave the ship at once, and this included passengers and any crew members wishing to disembark. They could not take time to pack. She would not be held responsible for any one who was still on board after fifteen minutes. She told them that if they had extenuating circumstances, they needed to report to her immediately.

A few crew members left the *Eckener* following her announcement, but not a single passenger left. Even the Ibrahims stayed on board.

Captain Macon went to her cabin and poured herself a stiff drink. She sipped her drink as she stood looking down through the great window to the ballroom below. "Here's to losing command of your ship to the ship itself," she toasted the empty air.

When the fifteen minutes were up, Wendy pulled up the passenger stairs into her tail fin, rose up into the air and headed east to Namche Bazaar with an acceleration that caused the passengers to catch themselves, and poured water out of the back of the swimming pool.

Chapter 15 – Of Salvation, Redemption and Awakening.

The noise of the crowds outside of my cell had become so loud that it had become a constant background rumble, even in my windowless cell. Zhao Tou said that it was because the stories about Kwan Yin, Chang Da Wai, the ring, and me had spread throughout the city, and even across the country. People had learned that I was in here and were demanding my release. "This is all about you, Director," Zhao Tou said. "Isn't it wonderful?"

"I am afraid that someone will get hurt, Zhao Tou," I replied. "This is way too much noise for the government to tolerate."

"I think that they do not know what to do with you. We picked up a broadcast from Japan last night that showed people in the United States waving big signs with your picture on them. My country likes to pretend that it does not care what other countries think about it, but it really does. It is like a person who does not think that he is liked, but acts like it does not matter, or a woman who says that looks are not important because she thinks she is not pretty. My country thinks that it is not pretty and so it does ugly things. But I think that all of those people out in the streets are beautiful, do you not? There are peasants out there who have come in from the villages because they remember the woman who helped them save their families from poverty. It was a long walk for many of them, but they believe that your reward should not be prison. I am proud to be Chinese today."

And so was I, I thought. My heart could not help but gladden at the thought of the hundreds, perhaps thousands of people, who had come to protest my imprisonment in the very face of their government — a government notoriously intolerant of criticism.

We talked while I ate my breakfast and drank my tea. The *Eckener* was well on its way back to Tibet; Chang, Boorman, and their allies were still safely ahead of their pursuers, and there was not much else for me to do.

I suppose Zhao Tou assumed that Tong was still out of town, and so he was not expecting any interruptions that morning. Even after I had finished eating, we continued to talk and Zhao Tou confessed to me that he was not really a communist at heart. He had joined the party in order to find work. The communist had inspiring stories and songs about people working together for a common cause, but they were liars, he had come to understand. Their stories and songs were worthless. The people had wanted communism and had idealistically followed their leaders through upheaval after upheaval, but after all the words had been spoken and all the songs had been sung, it turned out that the people had been duped. They had been duped not by the form of government to which they had almost universally aspired. They had been duped by their power-hungry leaders. Zhao Tou had thought a lot about it after the dream of his parents. They were right, he had decided. The power had to be taken back; the power of government belonged in the hands of the people, whether it was communism or capitalism or something even yet unthought-of.

"Zhao Tou," I said, "I have had a vision while you were speaking. It is a vision of you in a position to make these changes in China. In my mind I have a picture of you as Prime Minister."

He laughed. "You are playing with me. I am a prison guard; what you are saying is impossible."

"What was Mao?" I asked. "What was Deng? They did not begin their careers as important people. The future is infinite possibility formed from infinite choices. I see that some opportunities are coming your way, and the choices that you make could lead to this vision that I have seen."

We talked for several hours, but after awhile, Zhao Tou quit talking and settled into his job of guarding me, and I, becoming curious as to how many people had actually come to protest my imprisonment, left my body and floated out over the streets. People were packed together from the buildings on one side to the buildings on the other, and only the rifles and bayonets of the frightened guards outside the jailhouse were keeping the crowds off the steps and away from the door. There were people from every occupation and strata of

Chinese society, with the probable exception of the government and other high party members.

I could hardly believe the number of peasants there were. I had never seen this large a number in the streets of Beijing before; they must have come from all over rural China. But there were also a tremendous number of students, laborers, and even shop keepers, who I did not expect to see at all, as they depended on the status quo for their livelihood.

I rose up even higher and saw that Tiananmen Square was also full of people, perhaps a million of them, carrying banners protesting my imprisonment. This was when I saw far off a black limousine inching its way through the crowd, coming in the direction of the jail, and I knew that it was Tong.

*

"We are up on the Rongbuk glacier now," Lao advised them between gasps.

"How can you tell," Boorman asked him, just as out of breath.

"The little stream that we have been running beside — see how it has disappeared? The stream is glacial melt and comes out from under the glacier. Now we are on top of the glacier and the stream is hidden below it."

"But it does not look like a glacier," Boorman said. "It just looks like dirt and rock."

"This is what the glacier has scraped off of the mountains as it has pushed down through the valley. It is trickier to run on; the rocks will turn under your feet, so be careful. Underneath this dirt and rock is ice. The rock gets thinner and the ice gets thicker the further up we go."

"How thick does it get?"

"I do not know. A thousand feet, a mile maybe. I do not know if anybody knows."

The valley was well lit now. The ice covered peaks looked like bonfires set by the gods, and the sun bouncing off the canyon walls eliminated any deep shadows. The pursuing soldiers were plainly visible down in the valley.

"We must put some crevasses between us and them," Lao said. "Then we will only have the tank to worry about."

"That tank can cross a crevasse?" Boorman asked in surprise.

"No, but its projectiles can."

"What about the soldiers?"

"They are no better climbers than we are, and cannot run any faster. Without jeeps, they cannot catch us."

They ran on, and slowly the glacier began to look more like ice and less like dirt. Up ahead, they could see large blocks of ice, some larger than houses, and as they got closer they could see crevasses — large cracks in the glacier that imperceptibly opened and closed as the gigantic river of ice slowly flowed down the valley. "How will we get across those?" Boorman asked.

"With luck," Lao answered. "We are following a path that was made by mountain climbers. They bring equipment to cross the crevasses, and it is often more expensive or troublesome to ship the equipment back than it is to leave it here. But we must stop for a moment; we are starting to get on to real ice."

He ordered his men to break out the crampons for walking on ice. Fortunately, they had packed enough extras for everyone. They all stopped and clamped these spiky contraptions onto their boots so that they would have the necessary traction to continue on.

The first crevasse they came to could be crossed by leaping over. The next crevasse was not too wide for most of them, but it was too wide to jump while carrying the weight of another man. They managed to get the young monk across by tying him to the middle of a long rope and a team of men on one side of the crevasse took up slack in the rope while the team on the other side let it out. They had to do this several more times before they came to a crevasse that none of them could leap across. Fortunately, someone had left a bridge of sorts. It consisted of two aluminum ladders bound tightly where their ends overlapped. Each man tied a rope to himself, and prayed to his own personal god before crossing the sagging arrangement of slippery metal, and everyone held his breath when the soldier who was carrying the monk began across.

This man had volunteered to go last in case the ladder-bridge collapsed under him. He did not want to strand any of his comrades on the wrong side of the crevasse. He had to argue with the monks for this privilege, but Lao had ruled that the soldier was stronger and better trained for the job. The bridge sank considerably under the combined weight of the soldier and the wounded monk, and before they got to the other side, the soldier was walking up hill, his steel crampons slipping on the rungs of the aluminum ladder. When he had finally made it across and collapsed into the snow, Lao had the bridge dragged across and pulled away from the crevasse so that it could not be used by their pursuers.

They skirted around some huge seracs, mountains of solid ice several stories tall that jutted out of the glacier, and came at last to a crevasse that they did not have the equipment to cross. There was nothing to do but to try to go around it, and as going up slope meant more seracs and bigger crevasses, they followed the crevasse away from the main body of the glacier. It was at this point while they were searching for a way around that they heard the first shots fired. The pursuing soldiers had made it onto the glacier. They had left their jeeps behind at the first crevasse and were now on foot, just as their quarry was.

The bullets came nowhere near them, as they were still out of range, but it underlined the necessity of finding a route quickly. They were exhausted when they came to the point where another crevasse intersected the one they had been following. All Boorman could think about was lying down in the snow and resting, but as he started to crumple, Lao grabbed him by the arm. "Your men are tired," he said. "You have worked them too hard today. Let us go back to the big icebergs and rest there. We may need to make a stand and we will need some cover. If we rest here in the open, we will die without a chance to fight back."

"They walked back the way they had come, the men having to stop periodically to bend over, their hands on their knees, and take deep wheezing breaths. They heard more shots now, but did not have the energy to go any faster than they were going. Lao took his turn with the monk and seemed to be the only one of the soldiers with enough will left to make himself go forward, yet he not only drove himself but the other soldiers as well. The monks did not seem to be as exhausted as the soldiers, perhaps because they had been born to the high altitudes or perhaps because their packs were not as heavy as the soldiers. When Lao finally stumbled under the weight of the Nepalese monk, one of the young Rongbuk monks rushed forward and inquired if he could have his turn carrying the monk before it was too late.

"Too late?" Lao asked, gasping for air. Then he grinned at the monk as he passed his load over to him. "You mean because we are all about to die here, do you not?"

The Rongbuk monk nodded.

"You want your chance to do one last good deed before you die."

The monk nodded again.

"Well, we may die here — probably will — I do not see a way out of it," he rasped. "Too late?" he mused. "It is never too late, yet it is always too late for the things we did not do." He straightened up, helped the young monk lift the injured one to his back, and trudged toward the seracs, now shining bright as immense blue diamonds in the sun.

*

I heard the door open and I involuntarily cringed. I knew that Tong's limousine had finally made its way through the protestors and that he had turned his attention back to me at last.

"Ah, my fine guard, Zhao Tou," I heard Tong say, "I have made arrangements for you to come and work for me as a civilian attaché if you are still interested."

"Of course General Tong sir. And what would my duties be?"

"Oh, this and that and other duties as required," Tong replied, a little laugh in his voice. "I need a smart man such as you to be my eyes and ears in our military prisons. There would be travel and a substantial increase in your pay. Also, Zhao Tou, are you married? Not that it matters, but there are women in prison as well. It is one of the perquisites of the job. Does this sound like a job for you?"

"Of course, General Tong. I will only need to give notice here."

"That is not necessary. I have arranged for you to leave with me today. I would like for you to go to the Tibetan Region with me. It really is the bung hole of the world, but there will be better assignments later."

"I will only need to tell my aunt, General Tong, sir."

"You can call her from my car. I will be taking this woman with me as well. She may become your first bonus. Would you like that?"

I heard his voice louder as he turned and began speaking to me. "I see you still have the ring. That is good. I also have the one who gave you the ring. I just spoke with him before flying here, and today I will take you to him so that we can all be together at last."

"I don't see that happening," I said.

"I find your insolence very aggravating. I expected you to be a little friendlier by now. At any rate, I have you both now — you and Chang."

"No you don't."

"Please, let's not start off on the wrong foot. We will be traveling together; we should at least be civil."

"I would rather die than to do anything that would further your goals. I would rather eat the most loathsome poison."

"Perhaps that can be arranged."

"Give it to me now." I thrust out my hand into the darkness. "May I never have the mark on my soul of having helped you commit your evil deeds."

I heard him heave a sigh. "Zhao Tou, there are two men in the hallway. They are wearing PLA uniforms. Would you ask them to come in please?"

I heard their heavy footsteps as they entered and then I heard Tong order them to soften me up so that I would not be such a nuisance on the trip.

"My dear Director," he said to me, as someone unlocked the door to my cell, "these men are not as civilized as you and I. They can be quite rough. They work with heavy weights to stay in shape, and really do not know their own strength. However, you can save yourself a lot of trouble, as well as a trip to Tibet, and I will even let you keep your precious ring, if you will only come clean with me and tell me the truth about what has been plotted against me and what this new weapon is that we have seen. You have something that I want, and I have something that you want. This is my best offer. I will make you a lesser one in a few minutes, and you may thank me for that one when you could have had this one and a lot less pain."

"There is nothing that you could give me that I would take from you. I would not take the world from you if you could offer that to me as well. To take anything from you would put a stain on my soul that eons could not wash out."

"I am afraid there is no soul," he replied. "There is only your body, and for your body, only pain."

Someone grabbed my arm and jerked me to my feet. The first blow to my stomach knocked my breath away, and I thought I might black out, but unfortunately, I did not. I took more blows to the body and to the head. They contorted my limbs until I felt the ligaments snap, and bent my back until I thought that it would break.

As the beating continued, seemingly without end, I was suddenly aware of Tsering's presence, enveloping me and taking away the pain, and others, like Kenichi and the protestors, praying for me—giving me strength. But the waves of pain piled up against me faster than I could let them through. I was a dam holding back the flood of pain and the flood was rising faster than the gates would let it pass.

They had some kind of stick or club that they struck against my arms and legs until I could feel the bones beginning to break under the repeated blows. I may have screamed; I don't know. I became incapable of rational thought as I blindly and futilely tried to pull away and escape from their attacks. I tried to leave my body, but I could not focus even enough for that as they swung me this way and that, throwing me into walls and bars and fixtures. When I found myself on the floor, all I could think to do was to feel my way to my bunk and try to crawl under it like a terrified animal. But they kicked me, and stomped on my hands until their bones were broken, and banged my head on the floor until one of these blows released me from my body at last.

*

I could not bring myself to look at the dying wretched thing lying on the floor between the two hulking monsters, and so I fled.

*

Clouds were beginning to roll in and the sunny morning was quickly turning gray as the *Eckener* turned and flew up the valley as strong and purposeful as a great fish swimming up a cold mountain river. Many of the *Eckener*'s passengers were beginning to show signs of altitude sickness despite what I had been able to do for them. I primarily concentrated on keeping the captain and crew strong and alert. The others had to depend on the emergency stores of bottled oxygen.

Every soldier in the Rongbuk valley was intently moving toward the glacier, and not one soldier saw the *Eckener*'s approach from their rear.

As Wendy silently drew near the trailing soldiers, she began to sing. It was her battle song, and not one that she had just then made up, but one that she had worked on in the hours since leaving

Kathmandu — decades of time to a being of her mental power. It was her battle song, and it was a song to lift up the hearts of friends and dash the hopes of enemies. It was a song of bravery and of desperation. It was a song that told the enemy to lay down their banners and flee in despair, for the unstoppable was upon them. It had the sound of strings to freeze the blood, and horns to set the blood on fire. It had pipes to raise the hackles of fear, and drums to rock the very stone hearts of the mountains. It was a chorus of the angels of heaven and the angels of hell come together at last for a common purpose. This was the battle song that all other battle songs would have wanted to be if they had just had the courage.

Wendy knew that she had a good song and played it full volume for the Chinese soldiers just as she began to pass over them. It had the desired effect. Many soldiers immediately threw themselves down on the ground, holding their hands over their ears; others threw down their weapons and scattered in terror, also covering their ears; still others ran around in confusion before looking up at the fantastically great machine that was passing over their heads, blotting out the sky and freezing them with fear. It was a good half a minute before the first soldier got his wits together enough to raise his rifle to his shoulder.

That was when Wendy hit them with the swimming pool water. She flushed the pool as she flew over them and the soldiers were drenched in freezing water. The passengers began throwing things out the windows as well. Anything that was not bolted down, they threw down on the soldiers, who found themselves pelted with everything from grapes to mattresses, shoes to bottles of lotion. Luggage, hair spray, electric toothbrushes, travel clocks — every imaginable thing that travelers carry with them rained down on the soldiers — even dishes and skillets and mixing bowls from the kitchen.

As Wendy glided rapidly up the valley, she continued her assault on the soldiers that she passed over. She hit one group with ballast pellets, and another with more freezing water from the ballast tanks and grey water, but it was obvious what her primary target was when she dropped her grappling hook from her main hatch. This three pronged hook was at least four feet in diameter and was attached to a thick steel cable, intended to be able to support as much weight as the *Eckener* was able to lift, or to be used as an anchor in an emergency.

The PLA tank was beginning to swivel its turret around so that it could fire at the *Eckener*. The machine gunner had already begun firing, but he was aiming directly at the large empty nose of the ship, and the bullets were either passing through harmlessly, or were losing enough momentum that they simply rattled around innocuously inside.

It was Wendy's intent just to tip the tank over so that it could not aim or fire its cannon, but when the big grappling hook connected, it tangled in something under the tank or else simply penetrated its underbelly and snagged it. The soldiers bailed out and Wendy found herself dragging almost forty tons of steel up the valley. Wendy could have lifted the tank at sea level, but here in this thin air, she could only continue to pull it behind her. It did provide another advantage, however, in that it rolled and swung from side to side as it was towed, and any soldiers in advance of it had to scramble to get clear of it or be crushed. This kept the soldiers occupied.

Wendy had yet to receive any significant injury, and her mighty battle song reverberated off of some of the highest mountains in the world as she drug her enemy's best weapon like a trophy of war up onto the glacier and out of their reach.

Wendy knew that she was in big trouble with the tank. She could not lift it and she could not get rid of it. Her only hope was to drag it far enough out of reach of the Chinese soldiers that someone could go down there with a torch and cut the tank off of it. However, as she pulled it across the glacier, it fell partway into a crevasse and wedged there. She could not pull it free. To make matters worse, the wind was picking up and blowing her against the pull of the cable, which tended to force her down to the ground. To her additional dismay, the heavy cloud cover was blocking her source of energy and she was beginning to draw supplemental power from her batteries. She countered the downward push of the wind by turning her tail ailerons upward, which brought her tail down and her nose up. This caused the wind to buoy her upward, but it meant that everyone inside was now walking on a bit of a slope.

I realized the trouble that she was in and tried to focus energy into the cable, the hook, and even into the steel of the tank itself, but could not generate enough heat to melt anything. My power was sufficient to heat ground water, or to make a weapon too hot to hold, but the mass of metal present, combined with the giant heat sink of the glacier and the frigid wind, absorbed all the energy that I could conduct into it with barely a rise in temperature.

Out of the corner of her eye, so to speak, Wendy caught a glimpse of movement. In reality, she received an interrupt request from her infrared subsystem. There were several warm objects moving on her port side. She scanned the objects using visible spectrum and applied her pattern recognition algorithms — all of which took place a thousand times faster than can be described in words. She recognized Boorman and Chang immediately. They were with a group of men standing on top of a tower of ice and waving their arms wildly. Judging by the fact that Boorman was armed and there were no weapons pointed at either him or Chang, and the number of men present was the same as she had seen in the satellite photographs, Wendy concluded that the men in the PLA uniforms were friendly soldiers.

She began to reel out more cable so that she could maneuver over to the serac. The wind was gusting more now — sometimes pushing her up, sometimes down. She felt like a kite on a string, but at least she still had power to move on her own to some degree.

She gradually moved over the serac and lowered her main cargo platform, which swung wildly in the wind and crashed repeatedly into the side of the ice tower, bending and breaking the alloy rails and sending big chunks of ice crashing down to the glacier and into the crevasse. The men had to take turns leaping onto the platform whenever it swung close. Two soldiers had to swing and toss the Nepalese monk into the waiting arms of other soldiers, but when they themselves leaped for the platform, they were so exhausted that they fell short and their tired hands could not grasp the ends of the broken rails. Although everyone scrambled to grab their arms they could only watch their friends fall without a cry into the depths of the crevasse, their arms still reaching up to the safety of the suspended platform.

One of the soldiers on the platform was wounded by gunfire from the PLA soldiers who had been approaching the serac from the western edge of the glacier, but when Wendy had rescued all that she could, she swung back toward the east, moving the *Eckener* temporarily out of range again and partly into the wind shadow of the mountain that sheltered her from the gales now coming from the northeast.

The wounded soldier was taken to the infirmary, and the others were taken to the ballroom where they were given hot tea, blankets, and bottled oxygen. Captain Macon asked Boorman to stay in the hold area if he felt strong enough. Chang stayed behind also as the captain explained what the problem was and pointed out the cable, no bigger than Boorman's wrist, that came out of the superstructure above them and fell in a long graceful arc to the tank far below and forward.

"The emergency cable release is not working," the captain said. "I have had my crew trying to repair it, and Wendy has been running diagnostics, but the simple explanation is that the jolt the machinery took when we hooked that tank probably bent the release pin so that it won't slide out and let the cable go. We can reel in and we can reel out, but that's it."

"Can we cut it?" Boorman asked

"It wasn't designed to be cut. It is a special light-weight alloy that is resistant to heat and abrasion. It would take days to cut through it, and then, with the tension it is under, it might snap back and put a hole in one of the vacuum spheres. At the very least, it would probably kill whoever cut through it."

"So what can we do?"

"We have only come up with one solution, but it will probably be suicide for the person who does it. Someone will have to take tools down to the tank and unbolt the hook from the cable. We can also send a cutting torch down. Maybe metal from the tank can be cut away to release the hook."

"Why is it a suicide mission?" Boorman asked.

"The Chinese soldiers are closing fast. We will not be able to get close enough to pick you up. We have been lucky so far that nothing vital on the *Eckener* has been hit, but this ship was not built for warfare. A single bullet might send it crashing to the ground. Also there is the question of what the cable will do when it pulls free."

"Well, I'm your man," Boorman said. "Where are the tools?"

"John, I wasn't suggesting that you go. We can ask the soldiers for volunteers, or draw straws, or something."

"I am volunteering right now. There is no need to waste any more time."

"John," Chang said, "you will most assuredly die, or worse, be captured again."

"Didn't you tell me that everyone on board this ship had come to see me die? Well, they are going to get their money's worth. This is my job and nobody else's. Don't worry; I won't be captured again."

Chang nodded. "I believe you are right," he said.

One of the crew members stepped forward. "Captain Boorman, this cable uses a special spider designed just for it. You can see where the crew is attaching it to the cable. Because of its size and construction and the way the cable is hanging, it has to be attached first and then you have to get into the harness with your back to it instead of facing it. There is a control box on a cable if you need to use it. It is a little bit trickier to get into and out of, but because of the two-stage harness design, you could conceivably detach the hook while you are still in harness. In which case, we could reel you safely in—that is if you didn't hit something, like the side of the mountain; the cable may give you a wild ride when it is detached. Like the other spiders, this one can go down a lot faster than it can come up. We only have one spider for this cable; we never thought we would even need it."

Boorman thanked the man for holding out at least some hope for him, and went to get into the harness. The cargo platform had been raised up higher than the deck so that Boorman could reach his arms into the harness and pull himself up. By the time he got his legs strapped in, he was exhausted again.

Wendy tried to get as directly over the tank as the wind would allow so that Boorman's descent would be more rapid and he would have more time to work on the problem and, potentially, get back into the ship safely. So that Boorman would not hit it on the way down, the cargo platform was moved out of the way by lowering it past the deck and then lowering the leading edge even further until the deck hung almost vertical below the ship. Boorman was now only waiting for the tools to be brought by the crewmen. The tools were going to be heavy and the crew had decided that, to make sure the tools did not injure Boorman when he landed, they should arrange for the tools to arrive first. To do this they had tied a heavy rope to the spider, which hung below it. They would attach the tool kit and the acetylene tanks to the rope and push them out of the hatch just before Boorman began his descent.

The captain had turned away from him and had her hand over her eyes. Sandal was looking at him in horror as if she could not believe that she was really a witness to this event. Most of the crew avoided looking at him at all, going about their own business as he dangled under the cable, his arms and legs swaying with each jolting gust of wind.

Chang was smiling at him enigmatically. He waved a hand at Boorman, the fingertips of his gloves flopping ridiculously. "'Bye John," he said. "See you soon."

So, either busy looking, or busy not looking, no one saw the Ibrahims come into the hold.

"Captain, look out!" Boorman yelled as he saw Nuri Ibrahim enter the hold and pull a small pistol out of his coat pocket, Adara right behind him.

The same thought must have flashed into everyone's mind as they spun around and saw the Ibrahims: they were here for Chang!

The captain grabbed Chang and stepped in front of him, and Sandal joined her. Nuri waved his weapon to signal the rest of the crew to go over and stand with the captain.

"Captain," Boorman said, "I am familiar with his weapon. It's small caliber and only holds one round. He can't take all of you."

"I do not need to shoot everyone," Nuri grinned. "It only takes a tiny spark to ignite the fires of Allah." He pointed his gun at the giant vacuum sphere near where he stood.

"No — don't do that — stop," everyone began yelling.

"Mr. Ibrahim," the captain pleaded. "These spheres are not what you think. You will die horribly if you fire that weapon."

"You are all liars and consorts of Satan," Nuri replied. "I have no reason to believe you. *You* will die horribly, but as for me and Adara, it is not to die horribly, but to live forever in bliss when one dies killing infidels. And there is the greatest infidel of them all, hiding behind you. He is Satan himself, with his lies and corruption of the innocent children. He turns them away from Allah with his deceit. But now I send him back to the flames of hell and you with him." He fired his pistol directly into the wall of the vacuum sphere.

The bang of the pistol was immediately followed by a shriek unlike anything any of them had ever heard. It went into the upper reaches of human hearing and beyond, yet with the sonic volume of a jet engine. Everyone clapped their hands to their ears, their faces contorted in pain from the awful squealing — everyone except for Nuri. The wind rushing into that small hole to fill the tremendous vacuum within picked Nuri up and took him with it. It lifted him and slammed him against the sphere, overlaying the hole made by the bullet. Nuri looked down in surprise to see another hole magically appear in his abdomen. The hole grew larger as the air molecules, rushing through the hole at supersonic speeds, eroded his flesh and took it into the sphere, where it made a pink fog that billowed out into its vast emptiness.

Adara screamed and ran to help Nuri. She grabbed his legs and tried to pull him down, but as he slid down across the bullet hole in the sphere, the hole in his abdomen traveled across his chest, the air cutting through everything in its path. The ear-splitting shriek of the air never diminished as it sliced into him, leaving a great bloodless gash across his heavy coat. He opened his mouth as if to scream, but the air tore backwards down his throat, taking his tongue with it. His face did not collapse as one might expect. Instead it was rapidly erased by the wind rushing through it, the air slicing through his flesh like billions of tiny knives. The teeth and skull lasted longer than the soft tissue, but just as air has eroded the hardest mountains, so this wind eroded every part of him away as it howled through him and into the sphere.

Two brave crew members had crawled up beneath the sphere, and now grabbed Adara's ankles, jerking her feet out from under her before she could move into the direct stream of air and suffer the same inevitable fate as her husband. They dragged her, stunned, out of the way, and left her propped in a sitting position against a bulkhead. Then, communicating by hand signals though the shrieking of the air, they began the drill that they had practiced so many times, but which no one had ever had to do for real. They did not know if it would work, but it was all that they knew to do.

They were losing altitude because of the sphere's loss of buoyancy, and Wendy was desperately trying to maintain vacuum by running the pumps at full volume in order to try to pump the inrushing air back out of the sphere. This had the intended effect of keeping the sphere stable for a little while longer, and of gradually clearing out the billowing pink cloud that now filled the sphere. This cloud of vaporized blood and flesh was being blown out through Wendy's directional louvers, so that from the outside, she gave the effect of a harpooned whale spewing bloody vapor from its blow-hole. Wendy had stopped singing when the tank had fallen into the crevasse, but now that her systems were failing and she was losing altitude, she let out an undulating cry of despair that was carried off by the wind.

Several crew members rushed back down the belly of the *Eckener* and soon came back carrying a sheet of plastic about five feet square, several inches thick and slightly curved. Boorman realized it was a patch.

Crouching low under the sphere to stay out of the main stream of air, they rapidly opened a can and brushed a clear liquid over the inside of the patch. They then quickly thrust the patch out and directly across the main stream of rushing air. The wind immediately snatched it from their hands and pressed it over the bullet hole, which had now been cleared of all debris by the suction of the vacuum, and was beginning to be eroded itself. "Don't look at the light," someone shouted, and there was a brief blinding flash of ultra-violet light in front of the patch. The screeching stopped, and the men heaved a sigh of relief and turned to congratulate themselves. But now an eerie silence had descended upon them; they had all been deafened by that noise that the human ear had not been designed to hear.

While some crew members were nervously watching the patch, others were using hand signals to continue getting the tools ready for Boorman to take down to the glacier. Wendy was slowly beginning to regain her altitude, and the crew was about to snap the tools onto the spider when they all turned at a sudden movement.

Adara was running across the hold, silently screaming. She ran right at Chang, tackled him around the middle and let her momentum carry them both across the short space of deck and out through the open hatch.

Quick as thought, quicker than could ever be said in words, Boorman asked me for help. "Xiao Chen, put me in communication with Wendy," he said as he started the spider down the cable.

The visualization of Boorman's plan went directly into Wendy's great mind and brain, and as Boorman's spider raced down the cable, the passengers and crew felt the *Eckener*'s decks drop out from under and they grabbed something to hang on to. They were quickly in freefall as Wendy continued to increase her downward speed in an attempt to carry out Boorman's plan.

Wendy had pushed herself to be as nearly vertical over the tank as possible to allow easy travel down the spider. She had lost altitude when her vacuum sphere had been punctured, but had been slowly gaining altitude again when Chang had been pushed out. Boorman's idea was that if Wendy could decrease her altitude rapidly enough, and could maneuver quickly enough, using not only her own imaging capabilities, but Boorman's eyes as well, the trajectory of the descending cable could be made to intersect the trajectory of Chang's fall in such a way as to put Chang and Boorman in the same place at the same time.

As the *Eckener* fell toward the glacier, Boorman could see Chang coming closer and closer as he tumbled. Boorman maneuvered the spider into position, relying entirely, he thought, on instinct, not realizing that Wendy was doing the calculations for him and that I was feeding them to his brain. He reached out and grabbed Chang by his thick coat and pulled him to his chest, wrapping his legs and arms around him. He felt the *Eckener*'s descent slowing as he and Chang continued sliding down the cable. He had thought he might be able to save Adara as well, but her trajectory had veered off from Chang's and there was no way to reach her. The *Eckener* was less than a hundred feet above the glacier when Wendy finally stopped the descent. Boorman and Chang were so close that Chang could have dropped the few feet to the glacier.

As Wendy began her ascent, Boorman continued along the cable to the tank, where he let Chang down to the ice. As he began unfastening himself from the harness, he told Chang to start looking through the tank's interior.

"What are we looking for?" Chang asked.

"Tools," Boorman replied. "We didn't bring any."

*

I was being called back to my body. Someone was trying to rouse me, but without much success, for although I felt the pull to go back, I was not snapping back into my body as I had usually done. I focused my attention on my jail cell to see what was happening there.

The doctor had been called and was bending over me where I lay on my bunk. He was giving me an injection in my arm and ignoring the scene behind him.

Tong was furious with the two thugs that he had set on me. "I told you to soften her up, not kill her, you fools! And I specifically told you to leave the hands alone. What if you had crushed the ring, you stupid oaf? I would have made another one from your spine — that is what. If she dies, I do not know what I will do with you. Get away from me. Go back to your barracks. I do not want to see you again, and you should consider yourself lucky if I do not."

"But, General Tong, sir," one of them began.

Tong pulled a pistol from under his arm. "You do not speak to me without permission!" he screamed at them, trembling with rage. "I will shoot you right now! It is taking all of my restraint not to do so. Do not test it."

The two men fell over each other trying to get out of the cell and put a wall between them and Tong.

Tong went over to the doctor who was taking an instrument out of the inside of his coat. I saw that the doctor was no longer carrying a black bag, but had sewn pockets and loops and straps inside of the long black coat that he now wore. These devices kept his instruments and medicines concealed against his body, and now, from the outside, he no longer resembled a Chinese doctor so much as an old-west cowboy.

"Is she going to live?" Tong asked him."

"She has a slight chance," he replied. "We will see if the drug revives her. I obviously cannot check her pupil dilation, but she still has a strong pulse and good blood pressure. She may live but not be alive, if you know what I mean — like a vegetable."

I could tell that the drug was working as the pull on me grew stronger. My body was trying to wake up but could not really do so without me in it. Fantastically, my eyes flew open and I looked down into my own empty sockets. The lips pulled back into a distorted monkey-like grimace, and the arms and hands began to move slowly and randomly on their own, like those of a fetus in the womb.

"Dawn Bang," the doctor spoke, "can you hear me?"

There was no response, other than my continued random expressions and movements.

"Dawn Bang, if you can hear me, hold up one finger."

Nothing.

"I am afraid that she is no longer of any use to you," the doctor said. "We may as well take the hand now."

"Is there any chance that she will make further recovery?"

"It sometimes happens," the doctor answered him, "but it is something that only time can tell us."

"Then I will take her with me. She can still be useful to me. Even if she cannot talk, she has a friend who can. We will leave the hand on for now."

"Zhao Tou," he said to the guard, "go and see if there is a wheelchair in this building to which we can tie her."

"What about the crowds outside?" the doctor asked.

Tong shook his head. "Sometimes I detest being Chinese. They are such stupid people. They do not know what is good for them. How can they be making such a protest over this pitiful rag of a woman? How could she mean anything to them? What fools!" he exclaimed. "Well, I am taking her to a place where she will never be heard from again. Soon, everyone will assume she is dead, and the protests will die as well — here and in the other countries. That is the way it is with protesters: once they know they have lost, they get quiet again. In the meantime we will let the guns of the police make our arguments to the people."

While they talked and waited for Zhao Tou, I made a decision to re-enter my body. Tong was going to take me out of this cell, and I wanted that, but I did not want to be strapped in a wheelchair. Once I was outside, he would no longer be able to hold me. Like Boorman, I had decided that I could choose death, but I did not want to be powerless at the hands of such monsters again. Neither did I want my helpless body to be a pawn for them.

I did not know what form of consciousness could exist in an uninhabited body, but my body moved, animated by some form of life — it opened its eyelids in response to something. Perhaps it felt pain. The nerves were still there to feel pain, and the brain was still there to interpret the pain. If I could, I would rescue it from the hands of the pain mongers.

Before I could settle into my body, the eyes closed, the arms relaxed, and it let out a deep sigh. Had my body died before I could get back in it? Then it took a deep breath. Something is in my body, I thought. The drug had called something or someone — some bodiless spirit — into this spiritless body. I felt disenfranchised. No spirit was going to inhabit my body but me, I decided. I was going in there to evict the squatter.

I tried to settle back into my body, but could not. I wiggled and pushed and squirmed, but it was like trying to get into clothes that were several sizes too small. That was when I remembered! Up from the depths of memory came a recollection almost as if it were someone else's. I had known this sensation before. What if the body were already being inhabited by me? This might not even be my body, but the body of another me from another potentiality, or vice versa, the spirit inside could be from another potentiality, a potentiality where my body did not survive the brutal attack.

Instead of trying to evict the spirit inside the body, I decided to open myself to it. Suddenly, with this decision, we merged and the world took on new dimensions. This other spirit was another expression of the indefinable something that called itself me. Its experiences in its world had been very, very similar to mine, but not one hundred percent. I could see things now in ways that I never could before, not only in all directions at once, but from multiple viewpoints at once. Once upon a time I think I saw in two dimensions, then, when this happened the first time, I began to see in three, and now I saw in four. There was this merging of our not-quite-the-same memories and consciousness that made us one, but a one that was able to see the infinite depth and beauty of the universe. I saw the flow of time. I saw the permutations of choice. I saw how every action of mine would play out and what the potential results would be. I saw past, present and future simultaneously. I became fully and totally aware that not only was I one of the fingers of a greater hand, but that I was the hand as well. My new problem became how to focus on the here and the now. Time and space became one for this new "me". My memory of recent death was not only of being beaten to death but also of having been shot in the head, a potentiality that I realized had not yet occurred in this time-line.

But also, an additional problem was that having become one with myself, I discovered that I still did not fit into my body. I could force it now, I realized, as I had done before, but I realized that this sensation of not quite clicking into place was the sensation that I had been trying to remember in my struggle to see again. I knew that there was a way to see while in my body, and this was it. I could see all around me, just as if I were out of my body. But more than that, I could see from many different points of view at the same time. I could see Zhao Tou roaming the halls of the building, asking people if they knew where there was a wheelchair; I could see the crowds of protestors out in the streets of Beijing, as well as in the streets of Honolulu, San Francisco, and London. I could see John Boorman frantically searching through the shambles of the Chinese tank, looking for tools. I could see the *Eckener*, struggling like a fish on a line, as Wendy tried to keep it from crashing into the glacier. And not only did I see all these things, but I saw the echoes, the reverberations, the ripples of all of the potentialities radiating out through infinite dimensions of the universe. I could see how every action that we perform, every decision that we make, affects not just ourselves, and not only those around us, and was not even limited to everyone in the world, but sends waves across the face of the universe and through the very mind of God.

By not being fully in my body, I could see better than my body—my physical eyes—ever had. Yes, I could see, but could I move? I lifted my arm and I saw it rise! I sat up and I saw myself sit up! Tong and the doctor turned and looked at me. I could not let them know that I could see, and so I made no indication that I knew they were there. "Is somebody here?" I asked. They did not answer, but watched me in amusement. I stood up and felt my way around the room, keeping my face straight with a great deal of effort, for inside, I was laughing with joy because I could see while in my body! They stayed out of my way as I stumbled around the room. I kicked my sunglasses with my foot and stooped to put them on. I then felt my way back to my bunk with my good hand, where I sat down, leaning my back against the cell wall, and wrapping my arms around my bent knees.

After a minute or so, Tong spoke, and I jumped as if I did not know they were there. "How are you feeling Director?" he asked. "We were worried about you."

"If you worry about me so much, you should not send your thugs to beat me up."

"You sound as if you are back to your old self," he laughed. "My associates did much more than I intended. I did not want you to be so badly beaten. The doctor is going to give you a little shot for the pain to show that I do have feelings after all." He looked at the doctor and folded his hands together, laying his head over on them as if they were pillows. The doctor nodded. This was not to be a drug for pain, but a drug to knock me out so that I would be easier to travel with.

The doctor gave me the drug, which I instantly nullified so that it had no effect on me whatsoever. I slumped over on my bunk and pretended to sleep.

The doctor and Tong talked and laughed about other tortures that they had enjoyed together in the past, and new techniques that they had thought of to use in the future.

After awhile, Zhao Tou came back empty handed. "I am sorry, General Tong, sir. There are no wheelchairs in this building. I thought I should report back to you before I searched further afield."

"You are a good man, Zhao Tou. It will be a pleasure working with an intelligent man such as yourself, rather than the apes in uniform that I usually have to deal with. I predict that you will advance rapidly under me. We can carry her between us, no further than we have to go."

They stood me up, and I let my head slump.

"May I help, General?" the doctor offered.

"No thank you, Doctor. You have been very helpful as usual. I do wish I hadn't sent those two men away, though. They can be very useful with dead weights," he laughed.

They half walked and half dragged me out the front door into the sunlight. Of course I could see perfectly, even with my eyes closed.

Outside, Tong was appalled at what he saw. The windows of his limousine had been knocked out, black smoke was coming from the tires, and the crowd was wrestling with the guards at the front door, trying to pull their rifles from their hands. It was total pandemonium, but everything stopped when the crowd saw me. They turned and looked at me and began to whisper. "It is the Director. It is her, and look — she wears the ring. It is the ring that Chang Da Wai gave her. It is the ring of life and death, blessed by Kwan Yin herself."

"This woman is sick," Tong said loudly to the crowd. "I am taking her to a doctor. Clear a way for me." He and Zhao Tou walked me toward the crowd, and it parted uncertainly.

They made a path for us that extended all the way down the street, and they looked at me reverently as Tong and Zhao Tou dragged my feet through the street. I was pitiable to be sure. My hair hung in black tangles down the side of my face. My once pretty smock was torn and filthy. My arms, legs and face were various shades of red, purple, and green. I am sure I stank like something dead, yet, as we passed, some people reached out to touch me as if I were a sacred object. Tong brushed the people aside; just as he did those that offered to help carry me.

I was totally aware of what was going on around me as we moved slowly down the street, yet I was not totally there in that street. I was also in Tibet, where things that seemingly could not have gotten worse, had.

*

"That's a MIG17," Boorman said looking out the tank turret to see what he had just heard fly over. "I think the Chinese call them J5s."

"Is it armed?" Chang asked calmly.

"Most likely. If I remember correctly, it has three 23mm cannons on it and it is probably carrying a couple of heat-seeking missiles as well."

"John," Chang said. "Our efforts here have failed. There is no tool on this tank that can be used to release the *Eckener*. The soldiers are approaching. We must do something else."

"We can fight them and buy some time. You keep looking for tools. I'll hold them off with the machine gun."

"You may fight them if you wish," Chang said, "but it would be better for you if you left them to the gods. Climb up on top of this tank with me. I have something to show you."

As Boorman climbed up, hoping that Chang was going to show him a solution — a way to save the *Eckener* — the J5 came back around and opened fire on the ship. The cannon sliced through the kitchen and the deck that supported it, and ovens, tables, and stoves fell out and tumbled down to the glacier. This was actually a boon to Wendy, as she needed to jettison some weight but had already used her ballast on the soldiers. The J5 had originally come in from the north, but it had circled and its attack had been from the south.

"OK," Boorman said when he had climbed up on the tank. "What is your idea? Make it quick; that MIG is going to cut the *Eckener* to pieces."

"John, You and I are going to die here."

"I knew that when I took the job. What else you got?"

"It is your choice whether the people in the *Eckener* die."

"Then I choose life for them. What is your plan?"

"My plan is for us to sit quietly here on this machine and open our minds to the universe."

"I do not see how that is going to help those people on the *Eckener*," John exclaimed, agitatedly.

"You have come a long way, John. Remember how you could not even walk across the *Eckener*'s floor because of your fear of heights? Where was your fear of heights when you came sliding down that cable at a hundred miles an hour to rescue me. What are you afraid of now?"

"I don't know," John replied thoughtfully. "You are right; I'm no longer afraid of heights. I'm no longer afraid of death. At this point in my life I don't really fear anything except that I am afraid we are going to let those people die."

"Are you afraid of not being John Boorman?"

Boorman paused a moment. "I guess that thought bothers me some."

"Are you afraid that you cannot stand except on solid ground?"

"Sometimes I am afraid that nothing is real, if that is what you mean."

"These are all the same fear as the fear of heights. All fear is the same fear."

John thought silently to himself about that.

"You are not John Boorman, and the things that you think are real, aren't."

"How can I not be John Boorman?"

"The same way that Charlton Heston is not Moses. He is an actor who played Moses. You are an actor who is playing John Boorman. John Boorman is not real, but the actor who is playing him is."

"Moses was real," John replied as if in argument.

"If he was, then there was an actor who played that part thousands of years before Charlton Heston. And that actor still exists."

"If I am not John Boorman, then who am I?"

"I can tell you who you are not. You are not a Tibetan villager; you are not a German Jew in a concentration camp; you are not a roman soldier, and you are not a savage, fleeing from tigers in the jungle, or any of the thousands of other men and women that you have played."

"So those were just dreams?"

"Only in the sense that the world is a dream. You were just as much those people as you are John Boorman, and you are just as much not John Boorman, as you are not those other people."

"I have seen lots of things in my life—some strange and wonderful things," Boorman replied "Who saw those things? Tell me who saw those things, if it was not John Boorman. All those things that I have seen—all those memories will die when I die."

"No. Nothing is ever lost. But nothing that you can see with your eyes is real. John Boorman will continue to live in you. You can even be John Boorman again if that is what you want. The people on the *Eckener* did not come just to see John Boorman die, but to see the real you come alive—to be reborn. They came to forgive you, and for you to forgive them. Now is the time to wake up to what you truly are if you want to save those people."

"How?"

"You are almost there, John, but you need a little help to get past the barrier of disbelief. You have been in contact with Xiao Chen, have you not?"

"Yes, but I don't know what Xiao Chen is?"

"You have seen her."

"When?"

"She was the woman in the prison cell in Beijing."

"That woman was Xiao Chen? How can that be?"

"Xiao Chen is a human being, yet, like John Boorman, she is not real. Like you she does not know her true nature, although she is a little closer to it than you. She has many things to show you if you will open yourself to her completely."

"What should I do?"

"She heard your prayers before she was human. When you prayed as Dorje over the precipice near the Nangpa-la, she heard you. She will hear your prayers now. Close your eyes and open your mind. Try to find the core of your being, and say to Xiao Chen: 'Xiao Chen, Kwan Yin, Chenresig, Metatron, by whatever names you are known, I ask you to hear me. I open myself to you. Fill me with the knowledge that I need to awake from my dream.'"

Boorman did as he was told, and as he found the peaceful unshakable core of himself, he saw a woman being dragged down the streets of Beijing, and suddenly he was that woman, and it was he who was being dragged down the streets of Beijing. He saw with the same omniscience with which she saw, and he was filled with the same laughter with which she was filled, for he saw what a child's playground the world was, and how much greater and more wonderful the universe was than he had ever been able to imagine before.

While mirth bubbled up from the deep cellar of himself where he had kept it locked away for years, the J5 fighter made another pass, flying directly over John's head as it aimed its cannons at the cockpit. The cannons tore into the cockpit spilling men and equipment down onto the glacier.

John saw all of this with his eyes shut and as if from a great height. He watched with compassion and a certain detachment as the Dakini came to escort the dead crewmen across the borderland to the distant yet very near land that was their home.

He saw Wendy as a magnificent, ancient, and indefinable spirit that had come into the world to take part in this drama, as they all had, as had Xiao Chen, as had Holly and Sandal, and Chang and Lao and even Tong, as had every person onboard the *Eckener*. All had wanted a part in this play, and what a fun ride it had been.

But it was not for the people on the *Eckener* to die this way. They would not understand. If they died, they would die in fear and pain. They had not come to this glacier and these mountains to die, and they had not come here to see John die. They had come to participate in his awakening.

Boorman stood up and stretched, and Chang stood up with him. They looked down at their bodies lying on the cold steel of the turret and then back at the J5, just a speck in the distant sky, still making its swing over Nepal.

Boorman laughed to see that the world really was a stage, and the mountains studied him with fascination. "Xiao Chen, Kwan Yin, Chenresig, Metatron, I am ready," Boorman said to the sky and to the mountains, and they seemed to listen.

*

Boorman was awake. I smiled at the thought as I was dragged through the streets of Beijing. But was it I who smiled or he. Our channel was wide open now and I was him standing on the tank in laughing defiance of the J5 fighter, and he was me, being pulled between the rows of silent wondering people. If I was Chenresig, then so was he, and if he was Chenresig, then so was I!

Tong stumbled and dropped me and I went sprawling down on the street, dragging Zhao Tou with me and sending my glasses clattering in front of me. Someone reached down to me, and without thinking I looked up. "She has no eyes," they whispered, "It is just as we have heard." and the whisper went up and down the rows of people.

Someone retrieved my glasses and instinctively held them out to me. I reached out and took them.

"She has no eyes, yet she sees!" they whispered. "She took the glasses from his hand! The Director has no eyes, yet she sees! The Director sees without eyes!" The words washed back and forth across the people like an echo of whispers.

Zhao Tou picked me up, and I thanked him. Then, I began to walk unassisted down the middle of the street, leaving Tong and Zhao Tou behind. The people parted ahead of me in awe and began to close behind me in devotion."

"Shoot her!" Tong yelled at Zhao Tou.

Zhao Tou hesitated and then said, "No, General Tong, I will not shoot her, not even if you made me Prime Minister of China."

"Then I will shoot her, you fool." He drew out his automatic pistol and sighted down the barrel at my back.

Zhao Tou clubbed the weapon out of Tong's hands with his own. "No, General Tong, you will not shoot her either."

The crowd closed behind me. Ahead of me in the intersection I knew there were tanks and soldiers that had been sent to break up the protest. The crowd parted and I walked up to the line of soldiers that blocked the street.

"Where are you going?" The commanding officer asked me, stepping up in front of me.

"I do not know," I replied. "Perhaps I will go to the Great Hall of the People."

He threw back his head and laughed loudly at my announcement. "I do not think so," he said. "I think you will be returning to jail, if you are lucky."

"Why would you prevent me from speaking to your leaders?" I asked

"Why would my leaders want to talk to you?" he asked in return. "You are a speck of dung. Get away from me before I shoot you myself."

I stood there, staring at him for a moment, curiously unable to fathom him, perhaps because he had no depth to fathom, when I heard shots behind me and the crowd began to press forward in a panic. I could see from my higher perspective that the police were pouring out of the station to pinch that segment of the crowd between themselves and the armed PLA forces that blocked the streets.

The commanding officer gave an order and the soldiers in the line assumed fighting stances, rifles and bayonets toward the crowd. The firing behind us increased and the crowd surged in the direction of the soldiers.

"Fire!" the officer commanded, and the soldiers began firing directly into the crowd, dropping dozens of people to the ground. Standing somewhat in advance of the crowd and directly in front of the officer, I was not struck by any bullets, but was momentarily paralyzed by what I was witnessing.

"Stop!" I yelled at the soldiers through the din of weapons fire and screaming."Do you know what you are doing? "These are your own people. They are your family — your aunts, your uncles, your brothers, and your sisters. Your parents and your children are in this crowd. Are you mad? You are spilling your very own blood, and killing your own country."

I was surprised to see many of them hesitate. They stopped firing long enough to see how the officer would react to my words. The gun fire continued behind me, and I heard the screaming of the wounded and dying, but the crowd was desperately trying not to run onto the bayonets of the soldiers and so were pushing back, and trying to pick up their dead and wounded so they would not be trampled.

The officer pulled out his automatic pistol and aimed it at me. I rapidly sent a surge of energy into the weapon so that the heat of it instantly became intolerable, and as he dropped it, I held out my hand to catch it and dissipated the heat just as rapidly. I threw the pistol into the street behind me, where it skidded along the gutter.

The officer looked at me in surprise. Then he ordered his men to shoot me. Not one pointed a rifle at me. He spun around to face them and ordered them again."

"Sir, this is the Director," one of them said, "and she wears the ring of Chang Da Wai."

"Idiots!" He yelled at them. "Give me a rifle!" He snatched the rifle from the nearest soldier and raised it up to his shoulder, immediately throwing it down in pain.

"Let these people through," I said to the soldiers. "They are your families being shot down in the street. They are you; let them pass."

The soldiers looked at each other and then, one by one, they stood at attention and saluted me. Even the soldiers in the tanks saluted me as if to say that they recognized me as the one they now chose to follow. The officer tried to grab a rifle from another soldier, but the soldier raised his rifle to his shoulder and shot the officer in the heart.

I turned toward the crowd. "Take your wounded and go," I said, and they ran past the soldiers to safety.

Down the street, I could see dozens of dead lying in heaps where they had fallen on top of each other as they had tried to get away from the advancing police. Now the police marched quickly up to my position, and in their lead was General Tong. Zhao Tou was with him, but he looked barely conscious as his head lolled about his shoulders. Blood was coming from a scalp wound and his hands were tied behind him. He was being held up by two policemen.

Tong ordered the soldiers ahead of us to shoot me. They did not move. He then ordered the police to shoot me, but the police hesitated.

General Tong was a PLA officer, but he was not directly in the chain of command for the police. The police had thought that the PLA was helping them clean up a protest action, but now they wondered if this truly was the case. They did not want to get crossways with the army, either politically or physically. If the soldiers were not obeying General Tong, then perhaps the army knew something that the police had not yet heard. Perhaps Tong was no longer a general; perhaps he was no longer anybody of any importance. Things like this had happened before in China, and often.

A police officer signaled for the men to stand down and then said to Tong, "General Tong, sir, we must wait for further instructions from headquarters."

Tong began to rave madly. "You do not know how dangerous she is," Tong screamed at the police officer, waving his automatic pistol in the man's face. "She will destroy China." The police officer grabbed Tong's pistol as it swung by his face a second time and disarmed the general. Tong looked at the police officer as if it were the officer who had gone mad.

"Then you should have shot her yourself while you still had a weapon," the police officer replied. "We do not have orders to shoot her, and it appears that the army does not either."

Tong then saw the weapon of the PLA officer lying in the gutter and ran and picked it up. "I *am* the army, you fool," he yelled at the police officer. "Someday I will be China!" He quickly raised the pistol with both hands and pulled the trigger at the same instant that energy from the cosmos flooded through me and into the weapon.

The pistol exploded, tearing Tong's hands apart and spraying blood over his face. He instinctively put his shattered hands to his face to clear the blood from his vision and thrust the jagged shards of his bones into his eyes. He screamed and staggered blindly into the wall of a nearby building, trying to see from his ruined eyes and, as he smeared great streaks of blood along the bricks, gradually began to understand the devastation that had been wrought upon him.

Some of the policemen ran to help the general, whose nerves, numbed by the shock of the explosion, were beginning to awaken, as evidenced by his screams of pain as he waved his arms about, spraying the policemen with blood.

The police officer who had addressed Tong, managed to pull his horrified eyes away from the scene on the sidewalk and spoke to me now.

"You will need to accompany us back to the police station," he said to me shakily.

"I will never go back into that building, and never will anyone else," I said. And there, while the Dakini escorted the dead to paradise, I stood in the middle of the narrow police alley between the People's Liberation Army and the Beijing police, and rose up and reached out my hands.

*

Boorman also reached out his hands as the J5 made its turn over Nepal and headed back towards the *Eckener*. The J5 had killed innocent civilians, but other than that it had not done any significant damage to Wendy or the *Eckener*. The instrumentation in the *Eckener*'s cockpit was there for human convenience, not for Wendy's; her brain was behind the captain's quarters, and everything that was Wendy was still intact and functioning. Therefore, she was acutely aware that the J5 had just released two heat seeking missiles, and that there was no way for her to dodge them, especially being tethered as she was. She struggled desperately to maneuver out of their way, her will to live and to save her passengers, making her frantic as she searched through her data banks for any information that would help her. This was one contingency for which she had never made plans.

The PLA soldiers on the glacier were about to reach the tank. It looked to them as if there were two men lying in a faint on the turret — passed out from anoxia, most likely. If they could reach the tank, there was a possibility that the cannon could be trained on the airship to help shoot it down.

While I held out my hands in Beijing, I was also Boorman, holding out my hands over the Rongbuk glacier as the J5 released its missiles. I was a giant, of blue skin and brilliant white eyes, and with lightening flashing through me from head to foot. The soldiers on the glacier fell back as they gradually began to see me. We looked at my friend, my son, my teacher, Chang Da Wai, who stood beside us on the tank, equally as tall as we were, but projecting an aura of peace and understanding. He nodded, and the energy from the infinite wellspring of energy poured through us.

The channel that we created together was a thousand times greater than what I had been able to open previously by myself — perhaps a million times. The tank instantly began to glow with a dull red color. The color quickly changed to cherry red and then to orange, then yellow, then white with heat. The two bodies lying on the turret vaporized in two green and yellow flashes, like bits of fat thrown onto hot coals. The tank, now a superheated mass of nearly molten steel began to sink rapidly into the ice of the glacier. The missiles, which had seen the heat from Wendy's turbines in the middle of the vast coldness of mountains and glaciers, now saw a new and intensely brighter source of heat. The missiles veered off from their original course and followed the glowing tank down into the crevasse.

The cable, which had already begun to soften and stretch from the heat, parted instantly when the missiles hit the tank. Wendy was set free at last.

The explosion of the two missiles, combined with the cannon shells still on the tank, shook the mountain, and the echoes of it rolled back and forth between the peaks like continuous peals of thunder.

Chomolungma, Goddess Mother of the World, shuddered and seemed to rouse from her slumber. There was a rumbling sound that gradually grew louder—louder than a thousand drums—louder than bombs falling like rain—louder than any sound ever made by man, and the Rongbuk glacier began to quake and heave. The standing seracs tumbled over and new seracs rose in their place; crevasses began to open and to close, and the crevasse where the tank had been gaped wider and wider, becoming immensely huge. That crevasse grew larger than any crevasse that had ever been seen on the glacier, and it quickly spread across the glacier from one side to the other. The glacier began to slip down the valley, a gigantic river of churning ice that ground up and devoured anything on it or below it. Huge blocks of ice, as big as ten story buildings began to tumble over one another down the slope. The noise of it was deafening and went on and on like an explosion without an end. Chomolungma swallowed up the soldiers on the glacier, and they disappeared so totally from the face of the earth that not even a smear of blood was left on the ice as evidence that they had passed this way. The soldiers below the glacier, the ones still alive, turned and ran for their lives.

The air displaced by untold millions of tons of ice blew the running soldiers over before the glacier ate them, and that same enormous wind picked up the *Eckener* like a toy and pushed it toward the rock and ice that made the wall of the Lho-la.

Wendy tried with every maneuvering technique that she knew to fight this sudden wind, and to get the *Eckener* over the top of the Lho-la, but every calculation showed that they would not make the altitude in time, but would crash into the giant wall of rock and ice. Her batteries were weak, the air was too thin, and the damaged sphere was not back to full vacuum. Her nightmares of lying broken here on this mountain were coming true, and her dreams of soaring through the sunlit heavens were ending.

*

We stood high and lifted up our hands in the alley, and the police and the soldiers fell back in fear. We reached out and the mortar that held together the bricks and stones of the jail lost their strength, and the walls crumbled and fell into the streets, empty now except for the Dakini and the spirits of the dead. We stood higher yet and looked out over the city of Beijing. We looked down over the few rooftops that separated us from Tiananmen Square and we saw that it was packed with thousands of people who now looked back up at us in silent awe. We reached out and the walls of government buildings everywhere crumbled, leaving open frames of offices where officials and bureaucrats gibbered and danced in terror. Prison walls all across China fell and prisoners staggered out into the sunlight, blinking in amazement. We saw this as if we had thousands of eyes in thousands of places — as if we saw through the eyes of every prisoner that stared in awe at the open sky. And when we reached out it was as if we could reach out in thousands of directions at once. We reached out to wake the mountain spirit known as Chomolungma.

Then, with a crack that sounded as if a giant had struck her with a mallet, Chomolungma shook herself fully awake. Chomolungma, for whom human beings were like a pestilence of fleas, gave a tremendous shudder. The upper part of the glacier, now hanging unsupported on the mountain's side, gave way and slid down the smooth bare rock that had not seen the light of day for thousands of years until now. It collided with such force into the lower part of the glacier that our human ears heard the sound of it in Beijing.

The thunder of the impact awoke earth spirits for thousands of miles. Mountain spirits that had lain sleeping for ten thousand years shook themselves in turn and sent clouds of snow and ice flying into the air all along the Himalayas.

The impact sent the lower glacier moving even faster into the valley. And as it tumbled and ground its way through the valley, it scoured its walls of any sign that any army had ever been there. The impact of the two glaciers also created a tsunami of air that picked the *Eckener* up, wafted her over the Lho-la like a feather, and dropped her down over the Khumbu glacier and into the valley that led to the long gradual slopes of Nepal and its fragrant jungles.

*

"John," Wendy said, as she glided down the mountain valleys toward the jungles far below, "can you hear me? I have written a new song."

"Yes, Wendy, I can hear you," we said. "Your song is beautiful."

"I thought I saw you die."

"Wendy," we said, "nothing ever dies."

Chapter 16 – Of Hearing the Cries of the World.

Time is no longer a momentous thing for me, so I can only say that all of these things did happen, or will happen, or are happening now. Else how do I see myself sitting on this throne in the Forbidden City where you have carried me, Empress of The Middle Kingdom—Chung Kuo—China. Or am I here? Am I anywhere? I am everywhere.

Chang Da Wai and John Boorman are both here with me—part of me now, yet they are also someplace distant—close, yet far away and high. And though I am here with you, I am also with them in that high place, and I see myself—and all my selves—all my lives, present, past and future—as if from that great height. And I am strangely aware that although I am awake to being all of them, not all of them are awake to being me.

Being more dead now than death itself, I am more alive than life. I am the fish in the sea and in the little pools, the worm beneath the leaf mold and the cricket in the deepest cave, the birds that flock together in intricate folds across the twilit sky, the tiger in the forest and the goats that feed in the high meadow and leap up the mountain peaks.

I see as if with a thousand eyes—no, a thousand times a thousand times a thousand eyes. I see the sun rising and setting in the same instant—and I see the birth of new suns in galaxies so distant that the light will never reach the earth. And I see all the things that we do, each to each other, and I know that others watch as well. And I see the world below me, spinning out its days, drowning forever in the sea of time—yet I see also every day that ever lay across the face of the world, spread out like ripe strawberries, waiting to be plucked.

The very earth must be the tympani of my ears. There is no ripple of water, no wriggle of insect, no desert breeze that I do not hear. I hear the whales singing deep in the blood of the world; I hear birds singing with the very breath of God, and I hear the chanting of pines, waiting for me on a distant hill, where the cadence of their mantra is kept by water dripping into a bowl of hollowed bone. I hear the drums and horns and pipes and strings of every musician, every soul giving thanks, whether in the largest enclave of man or on the loneliest mountain—and I rejoice in every note. I hear the world's complaints like the quarreling of birds in the trees, and I think how big our world is and how close and little we have made it, and I wonder if we will ever throw back the shutters of this sacred mansion and let the winds of paradise blow through. The skull in the cave belongs to me; I am the water dripping in it; I am the whispering pines, the cliffs, the sky, the stars. I have a billion, billion names. Yet I hear the dripping of the water, the whispering of the pines, the wind blowing through the valley, and the hot thrumming of the stars. And I also hear every laugh, every song, every prayer, and every cry for help. And though you do not know all that you are, you are the same as me, and if you call to me by any name whatsoever, I cannot fail to hear you, and I will come.

Xiao Chen

Epilogue – Of a Meeting in Kathmandu.

[Translators Notes: My engineering duties having come to a temporary lull, my company gave me a few weeks off, and with the strange story of Xiao Chen Bang swirling in my head, I decided I would try to find further proof of her existence by visiting some of the places that she had mentioned in her account.

After spending weeks translating it, I had become captivated by the tale, even to the point of saying that I believed it, if I were pressed. However, I knew that there was the possibility that it was a fabrication, and even a possibility that, for some unknown reason, I had been duped by the "aunt" and her supposed nephew, the prime minister, whom I had never seen in an official government setting.

I had not yet heard the news about Tibet, and so I caught a flight to Kathmandu and then a taxi to the hotel where I had booked a room. Along the hair-raising ride through the winding streets, I found my breath often enough to ask the taxi driver about The Eckener – whether he had seen it when it had come to town, and so forth.

"Oh yes!" he replied. "Big giant airplane with no wings. Everyone saw that one. It come in slow and quiet like a glacier almost. Never seen anything like it before. Everyday, people come from all around just to stand at the airport fence and look at it. Some say the Buddha was inside it. Maybe so. Who knows? Look what happened."

"What do you mean?" I asked.

He pointed out the window. "See those people with all that luggage on their backs?"

"Yes. Where are they going?"

"Home."

"Home? They are not from here?"

"They live here awhile, but now they go home. Maybe Buddha let them go home."

"Where is their home?"

"Tibet. Over the mountains."

"But I thought that they could not go home without being arrested."

"After earthquake in mountains, China says 'let everyone come home – no more soldiers; no more prisons.' 'Course, no more prisons anyway," he laughed. *"We heard all prison walls fell down in earthquake."*

"That must have been quite an earthquake," I offered, hoping to keep him talking.

"Very big." He pulled out an old newspaper from a pile in the front passenger seat and held up the front page for me to see it. I could not read it, but it was enough to see the big full-color photograph under the headlines. It was of an immense mountain with sides of smooth bare rock. *"That mountain had ice – you know - glaciers - before earthquake,"* he explained. *"Earthquake rang bells in towns everywhere. People ran out in streets. Birds flew up into sky."*

"Is this picture of Chomolungma?" I asked him.

"That is what Tibetans call it. You know it?"

"I have read about it some. I heard there were soldiers there."

"Maybe so. I do not know. I bet no soldiers there now."

He stopped the taxi in front of a hotel. *"You here,"* he said, getting out to open the trunk.

An elderly bell-hop limped out to help with the bags. I gave the taxi driver a large tip, and once checked in and having followed the bell-hop to my room, gave him another one.

"Thank you sir," he said, dipping his head. *"Chopel welcomes you to Nepal. Maybe soon, I welcome you to my country."*

"Are you Tibetan?" I asked.

"Yes, very much Tibetan. Soon I go home. I am very, very happy." He smiled broadly, showing gaps in his teeth.

"Then why have you not already left?"

"Home is a long walk. I need good boots and a yak first. My son, his wife, and my grandson are going also. They too need boots. We save money, buy boots and yak, then go."

"What has happened in China so that you can now return to your country?" I asked him.

"A very wonderful thing. The Dalai Lama – The Ocean of Wisdom – prayed for China and his prayers have been answered."

"Don't you mean that he prayed for Tibet?"

"He prayed for both, but China needed his prayers more. China was like sick member of family who rants and throws things. The rest of family does not pray for themselves; they pray for one who is sick. Now the prayers have been answered; the fever is over. China is at peace with itself and wants to give back what it took from us in its illness. The Dalai Lama did this. He prayed and taught us how to pray with him. Is it not wonderful?"

"Yes, it is very wonderful, but some people have said that Chenresig was the one who made China well."

"Chenresig and the Dalai Lama are the same."

"How can that be?" I asked, pretending that I did not already know what he would say.

"It is known that the Dalai Lama is an incarnation of Chenresig. A precious one freely comes many times into the world. Who is to say that some incarnations may not be at the same time?"

"I would not," I answered sincerely. *"To what part of Tibet will you be traveling?"* I asked him.

He told me, and it was a long walk indeed.

"And how much are yaks selling for these days?"

He gave me a figure.

"I have always liked yaks," I said. *"I have been thinking of investing in a yak herd. Are you going to have a yak herd?"*

"I very much hope to have a herd someday. But it will be difficult with just one yak."

"Would you like a partner, then?"

"I am not understanding you," he said, puzzled.

I took my belt out of the loops of my pants and showed him the zipper on the inside surface. *"Inside this belt is money. I would like for you to buy at least four healthy yaks – two bulls and two cows."* I handed him the belt. *"I want you to build a big herd in Tibet and tend it for me until I come to visit you. Then I will take half of the herd. Is that fair?"*

"It is more than fair. But you do not know me," he stammered. *"You cannot give this money to a stranger."*

"What more honest person could there be than one who prays for his enemies?"

He looked at me silently with tears beginning to well over his eyelids. "You are a most wise man," he said. "I would be the proudest of men to be your partner in business. I will do as you say, but I cannot take your belt."

"I have another. Besides you will need something to hide the money in. There may be bandits along the trail."

"Yes. Thank you."

"There is also enough money for everyone to buy boots. You should not wait to leave or you may be trapped in the mountains. Also, there is money for food. I want everyone to be in good health when they arrive, so that my yaks can be tended."

He looked at the belt draped across his hands. "They will be well tended. I promise you before the Buddha. But how can such good fortune have come my way? Who are you that you would do this for me and my family? Did Chenresig send you here?"

"You might say that. Please take the money and go; you have yaks to purchase. But there is one thing that you can do for me, if you do not mind."

"Yes, please tell me anything that I can do for you."

"Will you be entering Tibet at the Nangpa la?"

"Yes. Are you familiar with the mountains?"

"I have only read about them. After you cross the la, there is a long valley with a steep cliff on the east side. As you walk past this cliff, look to see if there is a smashed jeep lying on a large pile of sharp rocks. If you see this jeep, look, if it is possible, for human remains – skeletons – scattered about the area. Can you write in English?"

"No, I am sorry."

"What about Chinese?"

"I can write my name – that is all."

"Never mind." I found a sheet of paper and a pen. I drew three crude pictures on the paper: a jeep, a skull, and a pile of rocks. "After you get to someplace in Tibet where you can mail a letter, mail this paper back to me at this address." I pulled an envelope out of the desk drawer in the room and put my U.S. address on it. "But before you mail it, circle what you found in the valley. If you found all three, then circle all three, but if you found nothing like this at all, then just draw a small empty circle. Will you do this for me?"

"Do not doubt that I will do everything that you ask," he replied. "Are these friends of yours?" he asked, pointing at the skull on the paper.

"They are very important friends. I believe that they are there, but they may not be. I would like to know the truth."

"I pray that I may be your light in this present darkness."

"Thank you Chopel. And I pray that you and your family will have long and prosperous lives."

"You have given us everything to make that possible. I have nothing to give you in return at this time, but I would like to give you a Tibetan name."

"What would that be?" I asked, smiling in pleasure at the idea.

"Your name is 'Jinpa,'" he replied solemnly. "It means generosity – one of the six perfections."

*

Chopel left me to my own affairs and I began to unpack. The locked briefcase that contained the Xiao Chen manuscript, I slid under the bed before unpacking anything else.

A glint of reflected sunlight caught my eye, and looking out my window, I could see, as I unpacked, the Swayambhunath Stupa, high on a hill across the way. On an impulse, I decided that I would go there first and see the giant dorje, or vajra, at the top of the three hundred steps.

Concerned that the manuscript would not be safe enough under the bed, I took the briefcase with me down to the lobby to be placed in the hotel's safe before setting out. I took, as much as possible, the same route that Boorman, Sandal and Chang had taken. In Pie Alley, there were exactly two pie shops still in business, just as the manuscript had said. I stopped at the more prosperous appearing one and, unable to decide between two varieties of fried fruit pies, bought one of each to eat as I walked. I peeled the paper wrapping off of one and began to nibble on it. The other, I put in my jacket pocket.

I had finished the one pie by the time I reached the bottom of the stairs that led up the hill to the stupa, and saved the other for after the long climb ahead. As I ascended the stairs, I saw the Rhesus monkeys everywhere, lolling under the trees on the hillside, and only grudgingly making way for me on the steps and handrails of the staircase. I estimated some of the males to be twenty-five pounds or even a little heavier. They showed little interest in me, but were obviously not afraid of me either.

Out of breath, I finally reached the top of the staircase and saw the huge dorje lying horizontal on an ornate pedestal. I studied it for a few minutes while I caught my breath, and then I did something very foolish. Without thinking, I reached into my pocket for the other fried pie. I had just unwrapped it, and had taken one bite, when I felt a heavy blow to my back that whip-sawed my neck and staggered me off balance. I saw a hairy arm reach around my neck, and then I was pitched forward again as the thieving monkey launched off my back. As I fell, I put out my hands to catch myself, but my head struck the end of the dorje with a hard glancing blow. I slid down the pedestal to the stone floor and looked around just in time to see the muscular back of a large monkey as he bounded off with my fried pie in his paw.

Several people rushed to my side to help me up and to make sure that I was alright. I said that I was fine, and that obviously the monkey needed the pie more than I did. They laughed, relieved that I did not appear injured, and walked away. However, I was not entirely un-injured; the injury was just not visible. I began to develop an intense headache and the beginnings of a sense of disorientation. I decided that I was in no condition to appreciate a tour of the stupa and began to descend the steps with the plan of catching a taxi at the bottom to take me back to the hotel. That is the last thing that I remember other than brief snatches of sound and images as if recalled from a dream.

I must have been out of my head for days from the concussion. However, Kathmandu is full of many strange sights, and I am sure that for the next few days I was just one of them. I vaguely recollect leaving the staircase to go and sit under one of the trees with the monkeys. During the night, someone traded me an old threadbare and patched jacket for my relatively new one. They also took my shoes and socks and left me a pair of worn sandals in their place. In the morning, I awoke shivering and not having a clue what had happened or where I was or even who I was, I still had enough presence of mind to put on my new clothes. Sometime later, I remember watching the sun shining through the tree limbs and then the moon, and then the sun again, and then following the monkeys up the hillside to where *some fruit offerings were being laid out in front of an altar. I ran up and snatched my share of the food with the other primates and found myself running down the hill with angry monkeys tearing at my hair and clothes while I stuffed the food into my mouth.*

Sometimes I thought I was a half-Japanese man working for the FBI in Honolulu and that I was on a stake-out under these trees. Some of the monkeys waggled their fists at me with their thumbs and little fingers extended and said, "Hang loose, brudah." Other monkeys would point at me and laugh derisively, calling me such names as "Buddha-head", "Poi-belly", and "Mango".

Later (hours, days, weeks?), I began to have a sense of who and where I was, and tried again to formulate the idea of finding my hotel, and left the hillside to wander through the town. I could not seem to get my bearings, but whenever I asked someone for help, they gave me their loose change instead of directions. I also remember someone giving me a partially filled bottle of water and a half eaten sandwich, which I wolfed down.

The next thing that I remember is being awakened by a man standing over me with a banana in one hand and a paper cup of hot tea in the other. "I have brought you some breakfast," he said. "But please, I will have customers coming soon. You cannot stay in my doorway."

"What's happening?" I asked. "Where am I?"

"You are sleeping in my doorway. You will scare off my customers and then I too will be begging for a living. Here, I have brought you some food. This was to be my breakfast, but now it is yours." He pushed the banana and tea closer to my face and I squirmed away backwards.

"Do not be afraid," he said soothingly. "I am not going to hurt you. Are you ill? You can stay in the back of the shop if you are not well, but you cannot stay here."

"Who are you?"

"I am the owner of this poor shop, which will be even poorer yet if you keep my customers away."

"How did I get here?"

"That, I cannot say. I came here to open my shop, and here you are. I think that you should come in and sit down in the back. Your thoughts do not seem to be clear. Perhaps you have had an accident."

"That is what happened," I exclaimed. "I remember now. I hit my head. How long have I been out?"

"I have no way of knowing that," he shrugged. "But I would say that you have not bathed for a very long time. Please come in."

He set the banana and tea down on something inside the door and helped me to my feet. As I stood up, my head began to throb and my legs became weak. He helped me into the dark shop as I held my hands to my temples. He sat me down on a rickety chair and went back for the tea.

"Drink this," he said. "It will make you feel better."

I sipped the tea and began to look around the shop, my eyes slowly becoming accustomed to the gloom. I saw the various Tibetan style handmade items around the shop. *"Are you Tibetan?"* I asked him.

"No, I am not. I sell these items for my Tibetan friends. They are very lovingly made. I wish I had a better shop to display them in."

"What will you do when your friends all go back to Tibet?"

"Oh, I think it will be many years before that happens."

"But China has thrown its borders wide open and asked all Tibetans to come home."

"Is that so? That is news indeed," he replied as if humoring a child. "Perhaps my friends will send me their handiwork across the mountains."

"You haven't heard about this already?"

"No. I am sorry. Perhaps we should try to find out who you are and what has happened to you."

"I know who I am," I answered him. "I just don't know what I have been doing." I looked down at myself. "I don't even know where I got some of these clothes. Even the ones that are my own are torn and filthy. And I am smelling myself now. How can you stand to have me in here?"

"You seem to be in need."

"Yes. Yes, I do, don't I? I am very grateful for your kindness. I must get out of here so that you can run your business."

"Where will you go?"

"I have a room in a hotel. I think I can find my way back now."

"You are not well enough to walk."

"Well, I don't seem to have money for a taxi."

"My daughter, Lhamo, will drive you."

I agreed to accept his hospitality once more, and in a few minutes, I found myself sitting in a very tiny car next to the most beautiful woman that I perhaps had ever seen. She didn't comment on my aroma, but wrinkled her nose, and despite that the morning was still chilly, rolled down her window. I rolled mine down as well.

She didn't speak as she drove, concentrating on not hitting the children and animals that made the side streets their daytime home.

"Your father is a very kind man," I said.

"Yes, he is," she nodded. "He is always feeding some stray animal or hobo."

"Is that a good thing or a bad thing?"

"It is good, of course, but too many people take advantage of him."

"But isn't it better to be taken advantage of sometimes than to turn away someone who really needs your help?"

She looked at me quickly as if trying to make a swift assessment of me. "That is true, and is exactly what he says. I guess I just expect more from the human race."

"Were you born in Nepal?" I asked.

"Yes. My father is from here, but my mother is an ex-hippie from California," she grinned. "Somehow they got married and had me."

"Does she still live here?"

"Yes, she loves it here. And so do I, despite the Maoists and all that trouble."

"That is my hotel up there on the left," I said pointing. "You don't need to wait. I'll be fine from here. Thank you for the ride, and thank your father for breakfast."

She waved as she drove off, and I walked toward the front door of the hotel.

"Please," Chopel said, blocking my entrance "this hotel is for guests only."

"Chopel!" I exclaimed. "It is me, Jinpa!"

"'Jinpa' is a Tibetan name," he replied suspiciously. "You do not look like a Tibetan person."

"I'm not. You gave me the name after I gave you the money."

"I do not know what money you are referring to," he said with a little edge to his voice. "You should not try your tricks around here."

"Chopel, I am a guest in this hotel. I have been gone for a while, but before I left, I gave you a money-belt full of cash to buy yaks to take back to your farm in Tibet. Why are you still here?" I was surprised at Chopel's denial. I never had any intention of collecting on my loan; I had only dreamed up the partnership so that Chopel would take the money. But now, I was feeling as if I had been conned.

"In the number one place," Chopel replied, "Tibet is closed and I cannot go back there, especially with a herd of yaks. In the number two place, why would I take money from you to buy yaks to take to someplace where we both know I cannot go? And in the number three place, you are wearing a belt. Is that the belt that you claimed to have given to me?"

I looked down at my waist and was shocked to see that it was indeed the same belt. I not only had cab fare all along, but had enough cash on me to buy my own cab. "I do not know what is going on. But I am going to find out. Please ask the manager to step out here."

Chopel went inside and came back in a few minutes with the hotel manager. I explained who I was and what room I was staying in.

"Yes, yes," he replied. "I remember you. Come in. Have you been on a trek? You should have let us know. We were beginning to wonder what had happened to you. In a few more days, we would have called the police."

I explained what had happened – that I had evidently had a concussion and had been living on the streets of Kathmandu for several days, but that all I wanted now was the key to my room, a hot shower, something to eat, and a nap. "Oh, and one other thing, I left a briefcase with you to keep in your safe. I would like it back now."

"But sir, we have no briefcase in our safe."

My heart skipped a beat and I felt panicky. "Are you sure about that? I left it with you. Look again. Maybe you forgot to put it in your safe. Maybe it is in your office somewhere."

"I am sorry, but we do not have a briefcase," he said with concern in his eyes.

I went to my room feeling as if I were about to cry for something irretrievably lost. But then I thought that perhaps I could re-write the story from memory. Or, better, yet, I would just go back to Beijing, explain what had happened and start from scratch with the old *woman and her emperor nephew. I called down to the lobby. "Can you connect me with Royal Nepal Airlines?" I asked. "I need to catch the next flight to Beijing."*

"But sir," it was the manager, "there are no flights to anywhere in China. All the borders are closed very tight. There are many rumors, and we are all quite worried. I will still connect you if you wish."

I thanked him anyway, and turned back into the room, my head spinning. What is going on in China, I wondered. I decided I should call my home office and find out. I got the hotel manager to connect me with the international telephone operator, who connected me back to the States. The secretary in our office seemed surprised to hear from me. I asked her if my boss was still in China, and she seemed even more surprised. "How could he be in China?" she asked. "Nobody gets into or out of China these days."

"But what happened?" I asked. "Everything seemed to be going so well when I was there."

"Is that where you have been?!" She was shocked.

I said that maybe I had better just talk to my boss; this was a long distance call.

She put me through and when my boss picked up the phone, he said, "Man, where have you been?! Mary says you've been in China. Are you crazy?"

"I think maybe I am," I said. "Have you not been to China recently?"

"No way! There may be trouble ahead with them. Did you know that China was in cahoots with some Islamic countries? It just hit the news the other day. Some people are saying that there is going to be a war and China doesn't want to run out of oil like Japan and Germany did in the last one. Did you hear anything like that while you were there?"

"Sort of, but I'll talk to you about it when I get home. I am ready for this vacation to be over."

"What vacation, man? You've been fired for job abandonment."

"You fired me?" I couldn't believe it.

"Not me, man. My hands were tied. Nobody knew where you were or how to get a hold of you. There was nothing I could do."

"What am I going to do now?"

"I don't know man. You can come on back and see if we can get you hired on again. I'll put in a good word – you know that. Or maybe you can get a job with the CIA since you seem to be able to go in and out of China at will." He laughed.

"Thanks a lot. I'll keep in touch."

I hung up the phone and took a shower, putting my clothes in a plastic bag so I wouldn't have to smell them. In the shower, my brain was racing. I was beginning to formulate a theory about what had happened to my world, and it was scaring me. After drying off, I placed one more call to the states – to Honolulu.

"Mr. Bang?" I inquired.

"This he."

"Could I speak to Dawn please?"

"How you know that name?" he asked angrily.

"We have mutual friends," I replied.

"You liar! Who this calling?"

I told him my name was Tomas and explained again that I was a friend of a friend of Dawn's.

"She not have any friend that worth waste of breath. Goodbye."

"Wait! Is she there?"

"If you friend of friend, then I think maybe you know where is she. She dead!"

"Oh, no!" I cried out involuntarily, "When did she die?" Once again, I couldn't believe what I was hearing.

"When she only fifteen years old, just a child. Someone shoot her for drugs. Probably you. You sound like crazy man. You stay on line now while I call police on cell phone."

I hung up the phone and sat down to think.

So nothing in the manuscript had been real. But wait, what about my own memories? They seemed real enough to me, they just weren't consistent with anyone else's. I had been to Beijing. I had seen the destruction. I had talked to Chopel about Tibet and had given him money. I had even translated a complete manuscript. I couldn't have dreamed all that. But where was the manuscript now? There was no manuscript. Yet, suddenly, without a doubt, I believed, against all reason, that everything in that manuscript was real. Somewhere, there was another potentiality – a different reality – a parallel world, in which a blind woman had helped to rescue a lost soul and had stopped a world war. In that other reality, I must have died of my concussion, while in this reality, I had survived but Xiao Chen had died while still a child. I only hoped that where ever Xiao Chen was now, she could hear me from there.

I had my supper and went to bed, and in the morning, I set out to visit the Nepalese man who sold Tibetan handcrafts from his little dark shop.

On the way out the door, Chopel stopped me. "Sir, I hope you are feeling better this morning. I apologize for not recognizing you yesterday. But if you were to ask me, I would say that your own mother would not have recognized you." He smiled.

"Chopel, I am not sure I even recognized myself."

He laughed.

"Do you not have a son who is married and also has a son?" I asked him.

"Yes, sir, that is so. How did you know that?"

"I think someone must have told me. What do they do for a living?"

"They make rugs for the shops to sell to the tourists. But they are not just tourist rugs; they are very good rugs made in the real Tibetan style," He added proudly.

"That is good," I said, waving as I walked away.

The Nepalese man was not at the store; his beautiful dark-haired daughter was behind the counter today.

"May I help you with something?" she asked, obviously not recognizing me.

"Yes, I would like to buy this store."

"I am sorry, but this store is not for sale. It belongs to my father."

"I really only want to buy half of it. Your father can keep half."

"We are not looking for investors either," she replied, a little perturbed.

"Hm, well in that case, would you mind giving me another ride back to my hotel?"

Her jaw dropped. "Are you that American that was in here yesterday?"

"That's me."

"Well you sure clean up nice."

"Thanks. I really do have a business proposition for your father."

"I don't think he'll be interested."

"He said that he would like a nicer shop where he could display the merchandise better."

She looked a little affronted at that. "There is nothing wrong with this shop. You probably think that you can buy it cheap because it looks so poor. My parents work hard to keep this shop. The only reason they don't have any money is because they give it all away, and spend it on things that they think are more important than paint and varnish, like my education, for example, and helping refugees."

"I am sorry if I offended you. Your father helped me yesterday, and I want to help him in return."

"Thank you but we don't need any help. We are doing just fine. We don't need your charity."

"Perhaps not, but I still need yours."

"What do you mean?"

"I have no place to go—no one to go back to. No reason to be anywhere else but here. All I have is money that will soon be gone. Your father could try out a limited partnership, and if it doesn't work, I'll go do something else. I only work from a handshake, so the financial risk is really all mine."

She hesitated, studying me. "Let me talk to him," she said.

*

Lhamo's parents decided that I would stay with them until I got my own place to live, and Lhamo drove me to the hotel to pick up my things and check out, and, as some people do when they leave a hotel room for the last time, she looked under the bed.

"Is this briefcase yours?" she asked.

With my hands trembling, I reached for the briefcase. When I touched it, I felt something like a shock and then a strange warmth spreading up my arms. I laid it on the bed and unlocked it. With my heart pounding in my throat and the room beginning to swim around me, I opened it up to see only some magazines, my passport and a paperback book of Nepalese phrases for tourists. There was no manuscript. That manuscript, I suddenly knew for certain, was lost forever. I sat down on the floor in a heap and stared at nothing.

"What is the matter?" Lhamo asked me, touching me gently on the shoulder. "What did you expect to find in that briefcase?"

"Something from another world," I said.

They found me an apartment close to the new shop location. In my spare moments, I have re-written the tale of Xiao Chen Bang from memory. Once I began to set it down on paper, the words flew from my fingers as if they were being dictated to me. Lhamo found the story, as well as the process of writing it down, fascinating. She stubbornly refused to provide any details of Kathmandu or the mountains, and even managed to keep me out of local areas mentioned in the book.

"Once it is finished," she said, "then you can go and see for yourself if it is true or not."

Later, we walked through some of those places and I told Lhamo about my memories. "Why me?" I wondered aloud. "Why did I bring memories of another life into this one when others don't?"

"You do not know that they don't," she answered me. "Perhaps they do remember, but think that they are remembering dreams. Perhaps you brought those memories back so that you could tell the world about Xiao Chen."

*

The shop is in a much nicer part of Kathmandu where there is plenty of foot traffic from the tourists. The new lighting shows off the authentic Tibetan craftsmanship to its best and we have hired Chopel to be our buyer so that we can guarantee that the best is all that we carry. In return, Chopel can guarantee to the producers – the Tibetans – that they are getting the best possible price.

The shop is on the first floor of a three-story building. Lhamo and I live on the second floor, and our children laugh and play with the children of the refugees who live on the third floor. The refugees are there because our residence has become a well-known stopping place for Tibetans fleeing their country.

The Tibetans have brought us rumors that the Chinese army has marched on its own capital, Beijing, and that the general of the army now pulls all the strings in the government. They say this general is a terrible, cruel, and power hungry man. His name is Tong.

Lhamo is planning a raiding party to sneak into Tibet to bring even more refugees out of their occupied country, and I have reluctantly agreed that this is a worthwhile venture. I do not want my children to grow up in a world ruled by men like Tong, but I am frightened, and worried about what would happen to our children if we were never to come back. I know, though, that someone has to try to save the little fishes from their shrinking pools.

Although I say I have never met Xiao Chen Bang, I <u>did</u> see the aftermath of her presence in Beijing, and I <u>did</u> see the stains of blood in the police hutong. Because of this, I know that she existed, and perhaps still exists in some way impossible to explain.

As I lie in bed, the sun is just beginning to reflect off the peaks of the Himalayas and in through our bedroom window. As that light washes golden across the beautiful face of my still sleeping wife—my wife who insists that someday we will cross the forbidden borders of Tibet—I wonder if it is true that I have never met Xiao Chen Bang.

~~Tomas~

--End of translator's notes]

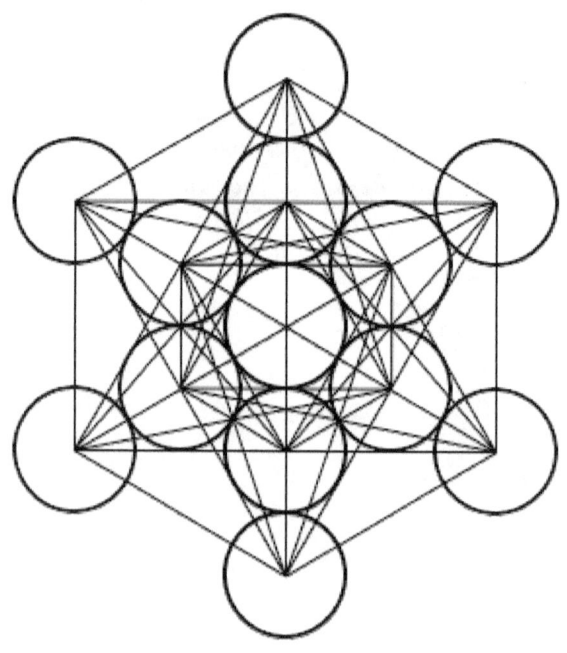

www.ingramcontent.com/pod-product-compliance
Lightning Source LLC
Chambersburg PA
CBHW020242030726
47499CB00001B/30